BLOOD BOUND

"THERE WILL BE BLOOD."

Please note: This series will contain explicit content and dark themes that may be triggering to some. It will include mature language, graphic violence, and abuse. Themes of depression, anxiety, and grief are also portrayed and may be upsetting to some readers. It is not meant for anyone under 16 years old. This is book two of a series.

Cover created by Get Covers

Map created by Teresa Grace

Dragon Knights of Aboria Series:

Soul Bound

Blood Bound

Oath Bound (Coming in late 2027)

To my husband: you are worth every sleepless night, every breath, every ounce of love I give.

To all the Graysons: you deserve love, life—and happiness.

To anyone afraid of their own potential: may you find the courage to shine, and leave light in your wake.

Aboria

Astrida

Estrus

Desert Lands

PART I

PROLOGUE

3 years ago, Dragon Canyon

Corporal Annaliese Hargin had just returned to Dragon Canyon from her year long trip in the High Mountains. Not even a minute after she set her bags down from her arduous journey back, a knock came at her door.

One of her mother's messengers stood before her, swathed in their unique black uniform. Her name was Neena, one of Kira Hargin's longest and most trusted allies. As her caretaker, Neena taught her how to throw her first punch.

Without a shred of warmth in her eyes, she regarded the weary Corporal in front of her, as if she were any other soldier. "Commander Hargin wishes to speak with you."

Anna fixed her with a deadpan glare. Was she not allowed to rest? It had been a grueling flight back, dodging the migrating birds north to avoid the upcoming winter in Aboria. You'd think they would avoid the massive lizard flying toward them. They didn't. "Can I at least bathe first?"

Her gaze narrowed, sharp and unforgiving, dark eyes unsympathetic. "She wishes to speak with you *immediately*."

Anna exhaled roughly. "Fine, but I'm changing clothes first."

Inclining her head in acknowledgment, Neena turned, disappearing down the hallway into darkness.

Feeling as though her boots were full of lead, she crossed the room and swapped the High Mountain uniform out for the Aborian one. The differences between the two were subtle, mostly in colour than in style. Where the High Mountain gear bore greens and golds with blue undertones, the Aborian leaned towards the warmer earthy tones of the canyon and their dragons: deep reds, burnt orange, and umber brown tones. The colours not only paired with the dragons in the region, but they also helped Knights blend in with their environment when they weren't on their dragons. The High Mountain version also had a layer of fur lining, designed to ward off the constant winds that howled through the high altitudes.

She hurled the filthy armor into a hamper and marched toward her mother's office. Her joints ached, her knees grated with every step, but she ignored it. Instead, her mind turned over possible reasons for being summoned at this hour. This urgently. They ranged from something petty—a power play to remind Anna who ran this base, who her mother was—to something world-altering, like the threat of war. That was the extent of Kira's reach.

And every possibility irritated her.

The audacity of that woman—to treat her like just another soldier. To pretend Anna hadn't come from her womb, hadn't been abandoned the day she opened her eyes for the first time. To snatch her dream away after she'd fought so hard to escape this life. To escape *her*.

Taking a deep breath, reminding herself where she was, *who* she was, Anna knocked on the door. A long minute passed, silence ringing through the hallway this early in the morning. A muscle feathered along her jaw.

Then she heard the Commander's stern voice, "Enter."

Enter. No warmth. No love for her daughter returned.

Anna didn't know why she expected differently. She was always left disappointed.

She opened the door, shutting it quietly behind her so she could lean back on it. She wouldn't sit like a good obedient soldier. She didn't want to breathe the same air as her if she could help it. She wanted to get this exchange over with then sleep in the comfort of her own bed.

They hadn't spoken for three years before Anna became Soul Bound. When she came to the Commander with her Dragon Bound, hurting, afraid, and betrayed by the gods she worshipped, instead of letting Anna stay in the base to heal in a familiar setting, she shipped her off to the High Mountains to train. No letters. No presents as birthdays and holidays passed. The pretentious asshole, Captain Faas, was the closest thing she had to a father, which was truly a sad, miserable insight.

And now here Anna stood, back after being Bound for over a year, standing across a room from her mother, and all she got for a welcoming was a curt nod and an order to sit.

It hurt more than she ever wanted to admit. But mostly she hated that she kept hoping for more.

Anna crossed one leg in front of the other, making herself very comfortable against the door. The Commander's sharp gaze cut into her, but Anna ignored it, peering around her office instead. See how she liked the cold shoulder.

It hadn't changed at all, save that the plant she had in the corner that was now shrivelled and brown. The bookshelf hung on the right wall, adjacent to the tall window sitting behind her mother. On the opposite wall, a tapestry of Aboria hung, displaying the continent in an artistic yet cold manner. Leave it to Kira Hargin to find the driest piece of art in the entire kingdom.

The sun was bright, partly blinding Annaliese where she stood, as if it was trying to convince her to sit in the presence of the most powerful woman in Aboria. Still, she held her resolve when she finally locked eyes with the weary commander.

Not that anyone else could tell she was tired; Annaliese had seen sides of her that no one else had, and could see the new wrinkles under her eyes and her pale complexion from being in her office all day. Her skin used to be as tanned as Anna's from all her missions, but ever since she was promoted to Commander, she'd been stuck inside all day. Her poor dragon rarely left the canyon.

Anna wouldn't wish it on anyone. The gods may have forced her to become a Dragon Knight, but she had to admit there was a certain thrill to flying that not even singing in front of a large audience could reach.

The Dragon Knight crossed her arms. "What do you want, Kira? Sorry, *Commander*." She bit her lip from the slip up. The High Mountain base was much more lax, no one was formal. She wished her mother would learn something from their commander. Then again, she was the first female Commander in Aboria and a lot of men had tried to take her seat, claiming she wasn't up for the task. Keeping her people in order and having one of the highest success rates on missions out of all the bases had established herself as a ruthless, capable Commander. Or, as Anna liked to call her: a raging bitch.

"One of our ground patrols has found someone snooping around in the canyon," the Commander informed her coolly. Not a hint of emotion for her daughter's return.

"And?" Many people walked through the canyon to see the dragons. Whether or not they actually saw them was up to the dragons.

Hargin shook her head, a grim line on her lips. "He's heavily armed and is asking for me by name. I want to know what he knows, why he's here, where he's from."

"Aren't there more qualified people you could ask to do this?" She yawned to make the point she'd been flying all night.

"Prince Deximus Fortys was killed a week ago." She paused, awaiting a reaction from her daughter. All Anna did was shrug. Estrus and Aboria were never on good terms. Whoopee, one of their wicked princes was dead. "You disappoint me, Anna. He was murdered and now there is a spy wandering around my base."

Anna struggled to care. "You think King Sylus thinks we killed him and wants to retaliate. Why not attack Kain Castle?"

A prince for a prince.

The Commander drummed her fingers on the desk, a lethal edge taking over her harsh features. "I don't know what he thinks, but I know he's been looking for any excuse to start a war. The dragons took their magic away when they left; their lands are sapped of resources; and, the people are a husk of what they used to be. Why not accuse us of killing his son, the heir to his throne?"

Annaliese read between the lines. "And you want me to question this potential spy to remind him that we have magic on our side?"

She nodded. "Leave him with his tail between his legs. I want him to send word to King Sylus that if he wants to fuck with us, we won't hold back."

Annaliese liked permission to do what she did best, what her mother had trained her to do since birth. "I'll get your information and I'll send your message."

The ground patrol was a group of soldiers who weren't picked by a dragon at the end of their training, but they had proven they were gritty enough to be a Knight. They protected Dragon Canyon and the surrounding area, and occasionally were hired by nearby villages to escort travellers or aid with monster culling.

Anna made the journey down the narrow, zig-zaggy staircase carved into the cliffside, while Aster followed from above. Anna had wanted her to go to her den and rest; the dragon had done most of the leg work to get them home, but Aster had insisted on keeping watch.

The ground base was small and only a few buildings were clumped together on the scrubby canyon floor. Their existence was meant to save the regular rotation of twenty or so soldiers from trekking up and down the narrow, but well-maintained cliff path for food and other supplies three times a day. Anna quickly followed the gravel path running parallel along a trickling creek to a lonely storage hut normally crammed with wooden crates. Today, the building in question had also acquired one young man, who was tied to a chair.

Sergeant Stark loomed over their captive; being half-giant and weighing far too much to ride any dragon, he was one of two officers in charge of overseeing the operation of the ground base. He cracked his blood-stained knuckles, eyeing the newcomer with a gritty sneer. Judging from the new bruises on the young man's face, Anna could hazard a guess at how they spent their time waiting for her.

"*Ahem.*"

The Sergeant turned to her, eyes going wide. "You're back?"

She offered him a slip of a smile while in front of the supposed spy. Stark had fought alongside her mother during the Goblin Wars and was one of the only Knights who didn't fear the Hargin name. "I am. The Commander called me back."

Until Annaliese heard about Prince Deximus's death, she hadn't known the reason for the abrupt order to return home. Only trouble could be spelled out in the wake of the prince's death, and the man in the chair was proof of it.

Stark inclined his head to her respectfully. "It's good to have you back, Corporal. I'll let you have your fun."

He shut the door on his way out and slammed the lock home.

Annaliese grabbed a spare chair and set it in front of the young man. Their gazes locked in a battle of wills, with only silence used as their weapons.

He had short black hair, unwashed and lank, with twigs and leaves embedded into the ebony strands. His sharp jaw was home to a couple days' worth of dark stubble that looked just as unkempt as the rest of him.

But it was his eyes that caught her attention, though; they were dark grey, almost black in the weak light coming from the small lightstone that was meant to illuminate a shed half the size of their current building. His eyes said he'd seen a lot of shit as he matched her glare head on, unafraid. These were eyes that said there was nothing she—or the men around her—could do that would phase him. They were the eyes of someone who had met Zyphril and returned to their world unscathed.

It didn't surprise her. She'd heard that the enrollment age to join the army in Estrus was twelve. She had to be the same age as the man in front of her, and, while the legal age in Aboria was twenty, she had wielded a sword just as long as this man...

"*Relating to a target is not wise,*" Aster advised, keeping a close eye on her Soul Bound from above.

"*I know.*" Gods, she knew. But she was tired and couldn't help it.

"*Thankfully, for your sake, I do not believe he is a spy.*"

Anna ignored the sarcasm. "*You don't?*"

"*He feels different.*"

"*How so?*" She kept her steady gaze on the man as she discussed his motives with her dragon, who was hanging on the walls of the canyon above them, ready to pounce if he posed any threat. He didn't appear to be a threat, however; the Commander had informed her that he hadn't fought the ground Knights. He allowed his capture. Which meant he didn't want to cause harm, or he had something planned and needed to gain their trust.

"*He feels... familiar*," Aster finally said, trying to find the best way to describe this feeling of hers. "*I don't believe him to be a threat.*"

"*But I should still be wary*?" Anna guessed from her cautious tone.

"*Always.*"

Anna crossed a leg over her knee and tapped it pensively, thinking of where she wanted to start with her questioning. "Who are you?" seemed like as good a start as any.

He snorted, striking her with a disapproving glower. "Me? I should ask you the same thing. I asked for Commander Hargin. You look far too young to be a commander of anything. Why did the coward send a woman to do a man's job?"

Ah. Yes. She had also heard that Estrus was full of chauvinists.

Anna moved like lightning. One second, she'd been sitting. The next? She'd struck him—hard—across the face. He wouldn't stay pretty for long if he kept antagonizing her.

He didn't flinch, merely spat a glob of blood off to the side and offered her a crimson smile in return.

Okay. That was new.

"You hit like a man." There was a hint of surprise in his tone.

Anna took her seat again, positioning herself in the same way as before. "I'm surprised you didn't cry like one."

He cocked an eyebrow, intrigued. If he was truly from Estrus, then he was about to be *shocked* by the women in Aboria. "Do you fight as well as a man?"

"Better," she replied instantly, giving him a look that suggested if he tried anything funny, he'd be the first to know how much better she was. There was a reason why Sergeant Stark felt comfortable leaving her alone with him.

The man remained unthreatened, seeming to take her in a new, possibly impressed, light.

"Who are you?" she asked him again.

"Grayson Smith," he answered smoothly.

"Okay," she snorted, "what's your *real* name?"

Grayson Smith? What kind of name was that? She knew one of the patrolmen's name was Grayson, so he could have overheard his name. Smith was the most common last name in Aboria; he could claim to be from any family, and some of them were so large, one of them was bound to accept he was a long lost cousin or something.

He blinked, surprised yet again. But only for a moment before a mask slid over his face. "Grayson Smith."

Sighing, she stood up in front of him and flexed her hand to ready herself for another punch. This time she struck his stomach, making him cough. The interrogation wouldn't last very long if she beat his face repeatedly, there was only so much her knuckles could take. But her knuckles against soft flesh? Well, they had all the time in the world.

"I don't like being lied to. We can do this the easy way... or the hard way. The choice is yours."

His gaze was cold when he looked at her, face still an unrelenting mask. "I can take pain, but I'm on a time constraint, so how about we settle for another question, hmm?"

By Gods, it was like he did this for a living... Maybe he did.

"Are you sure he isn't a spy, Aster?"

"Positive."

Watching him carefully, she eased back into her chair, crossing her leg at the knee. There was just something deliciously satisfying about having all of the control while he was at her mercy. This was just what she needed after having her control stripped from her since she became Bound. "Where are you from?"

"Next question."

"What are you doing here?"

His mask fell into an expression of sombre earnestness. "I want to join the Dragon Knights."

She laughed; it was a genuine one, of surprise and mirth. All of this show just to become a Dragon Knight? There were much better ways to be recruited... if he had good intentions. "We have recruitment centres for that."

He bit his lip, quickly glancing up to the top right of his vision then back down. Annaliese did that when she first became Bound to Aster whenever she talked to her. She'd soon learned to stop that habit, it was a dead give away. But he wasn't talking to a dragon, was he? Aster would have sensed it.

"I'll have a look around," Aster responded to her thoughts instantly, knowing the importance of finding that dragon. He'd get his wish if he was Bound, but something told Anna that he didn't know that, or he would have revealed it from the start.

Approaching him carefully, she inspected what little exposed skin he offered. His clothes were tattered, reeking of sweat and salt, but they were intact, making her job difficult. His dragon could have marked him anywhere. Deciding it didn't really matter if his clothes were torn or not, she gripped either side of the neckline and ripped open his shirt.

He gaped. So did Anna. She was *not* expecting the chiselled chest and six pack—okay, maybe she was a *little*—and definitely not the myriad of thin scars decorating his body. Most looked like stab wounds, while some were clear cuts across his chest. Fingers knotted into his hair, she yanked him forward and peeled the rest of the fabric away from his torso.

She circled him, inspecting every inch of his exposed skin for scales. Thick, nasty scars raked down and across his back. Lashings. He had endured hundreds of them. Not all at once. They layered on top of each other, each one as brutal as the next. The freshest one hardly looked more than a month old as she stared at the pink scar tissue.

He'd lost all feeling on his back, because she grazed a finger along one of the horrid scars and he didn't react in the slightest.

"By Lorelus..." She wasn't sure if the god of vitality had blessed or cursed this man for making him capable of enduring these wounds.

He glanced over his shoulder at her. "Don't tell me a few scars are enough to deter you. Here I thought Aborian women were supposed to be hardy."

She snapped out of her shock. "*Hardy*? We're not *plants*. We're human too—and it'll take a lot more than a few scars to discourage me."

Simmering at his audacity, she continued her search.

There. Amongst the legion of scars on his front, nestled between his ribs and the ridge of his abs, she found what she was looking for. The scar was the exact same as the one she wore on her shoulder. He was soul bound. Whoever this guy was, his dragon bound was out there somewhere...

"*Aster, did you find a drag—*"

A curdling cry came from outside. Men shouted orders seconds later, one of them barging through the hut entrance, eyes wide. He was young and, by the looks of his face and hands, he'd never seen someone bleed before—not as much as the person outside.

Completely forgetting the interrogation, Anna whipped around, sword drawn. Men and women ran in a frenzied panic to get the situation under control. Screams rose above the roar of splintering rock, commands shouted and instantly drowned out by the thunder shaking the canyon floor. Bodies flew across the canyon, seemingly weightless in the ease they flew.

There were too many moving parts to see the cause of the disturbance.

She found Stark among the chaos. "What's going on?"

"Golem." His eyes were fixed on the massive boulder shuddering as it heaved its stone limbs forward. Its arm swung, catching a Knight in the chest, and sent him hurtling into the canyon wall.

Shit.

Swords didn't work on golems. They were going to have to get creative.

The golem knocked aside another set of Knights, crushing their bones with its monumental force.

Stark brandished his battle hammer and charged for the golem. The monster was easily twice his size—which said something when anything was compared to the size of the half-giant. He came up behind it and smashed the back of its leg, shattering into a pile of rubble. The golem tumbled to the side, swinging its arms out to catch its balance, hitting a few other Knights who hadn't moved out of the way fast enough.

The victory was short-lived.

The canyon walls shook, the very air vibrating with magic, deep and seething within the canyon's roots. The golem reached out to the earth, calling on its strength. Rocks broke from the walls, shuddering as they flew towards the golem, latching onto its broken hide. Piece by piece, the stone Stark had pulverised was replaced by more stone—and then some. By the time the ground stopped shaking, the golem was bigger than before and had a bone to pick with the half-giant.

"Aster, can you do something?"

"Not *with that many Knights surrounding it*," she growled, frustrated. She also wasn't close enough to help in a timely manner. "Use *your magic, Anna. This is what you've been training for.*"

Anna peered down at her hands. Her dragon had to be joking after the last time she'd dared to call herself fire's master. There were too many people around, and Faas wasn't around this time to save them if she fucked up again.

"*Use it or these men will die. I did not Bond with a coward.*" Aster's harsh words seared into Anna's mind and seized her muscles. She moved before she knew what she was doing.

She struck her sword against a stone. A spark ignited—it was all she needed to grow it into a fearsome flame. With a war cry, she charged for the golem and pressed the fireball into its side. The stone went hot, but it didn't crack.

"*Hotter, Anna*," Aster hissed in her mind. "*Don't crack the golem's armour—melt its heart. Show these Knights our power.*"

Lorelus, give me strength. Protect these people.

Anna opened up her mind and body to Aster. Magic flooded through her system, fast and unforgiving. It ripped and tore its way through her limbs, snarring her soul in its voracious claws. The heat—the pressure—demanded that she cave in to its will. To let it break her and remould her.

She fought against it, shut out the images of what happened last time she'd called on this magic—at her mentor's insistence. These men needed her, even if the very idea of wielding this much flame terrified her.

"*You are strong*," Aster pressed, impatient but encouraging. "*My Soul Bound does not cave to fear.*"

The flames in Anna's palms flickered violently—then doubled in size and went white. Bigger and hotter than any flame she'd made thus far.

The stone melted under her fingertips—for all of two seconds. The golem spun and knocked her down. She hit the ground hard and gasped for breath, clutching her chest as the world spun.

Anna shook her head, fighting for control over her body. The golem raised its foot and hovered over her. She rolled away, barely—to only have to dodge another attack. In between swings, she tried to close the gap—to reach that heart. It threw its boulderous fists down for her, one after another. Over and over. Every leap to save herself, was a leap further away from her target.

The golem knew exactly what kind of threat she posed and it wasn't going to let her get away with it.

Sweat trickled down her spine. The heat of her flames weren't the cause, it was the sheer fear flooding through her. She'd never encountered anything like this before. Smart, fast—impervious to any attack thrown at it. Her usual tricks wouldn't work here. Only magic would save them.

"I have to get closer!" she called out to anyone brave enough to distract it.

A shadow darted out from behind her and struck the side of the golem. It ignored him. It shouldn't have. While the golem was still focused on her, Grayson wedged his sword—how the fuck did he get that? How the fuck did he get *free*?—in its joints. When it stepped for her, its leg locked up, halting its advance. Realising Grayson was the bigger threat, it turned for him. Other Knights leapt forwards to shove their swords into its joints.

Its back now exposed, Anna scrambled up the heaping boulder, rammed a sword between two segments and used it as a foot hold. She heated up her hands once more and laid them over the golem's back. She put everything she had into it, melting the stone beneath her until it reached the heart. Magic wracked her body, tearing a scream from her throat. The heart dazzled like a ruby under the white hot flames.

Almost there...

Her body shook fiercely. She didn't know how much longer she could hang on—

The heart crumbled under the heat.

Unceremoniously, the golem dropped to the ground. Anna leapt off the pile of rubble and stood in front of it triumphantly, gasping for breath. Her whole body trembled from the strain. None of the Knights seemed to notice as they cheered her on, patting her on the back and welcoming her home.

"Okay! Okay!" Stark broke up the party with an enormous hand. "That's enough. Back to work. We have dead to collect and rubble to clean up."

A ring of solemn silence followed his orders. Knights glanced at each other then scanned the battlefield, the bodies crumbled, distorted, limbs severed—all because of a single golem. They'd put a stop to its destructive path, but the cost was a handful of brave men and women.

Anna let them do their job and approached Grayson on the sidelines. "That was good thinking back there."

He tentatively watched the Knights pray over the fallen and ceremoniously fold their comrades' arms over their chest. They would host a pyre at sunset to honour their name.

"You honour your dead," he answered, befuddled by the idea.

"They fought bravely and died doing what they love." There was no greater death for a Knight than to die in battle.

He frowned, slightly arched eyebrows knitting together. "Where I'm from, death is failure."

Anna eyed him warily, wondering what kind of place he came from to have that kind of ideology. "Death is only the next step in our journey. Zyphril will guide them to the next chapter in their life."

He nodded, seeming to understand now. "I forgot Aborians worshipped the gods."

A strange thing to say. Everyone in Astrida worshipped the gods.

Her gaze drifted down to the sword Grayson had acquired—he appeared to have a knack for that—then she extended her hand to him. "Give me that."

He peered down at the sword then up to her. Thinking better of whatever he was planning, he handed it to her, hilt first. Good. She needed to trust him if he was going to be a Dragon Knight. "I'll see what I can do about you becoming a Dragon Knight."

His body went rigid, eyes widening for a split second before he schooled his features and nodded bluntly. "Thank you."

"You have to tell me your real name, though. Not everyone has to know, but Commander Hargin won't bother with you if she doesn't know your name."

A dark shadow took over his body, muscles coiling tightly around every inch of him; his knuckles went white at his sides. "I can't tell you."

"Then I can't help you. If you want to be a Dragon Knight, you have to trust me. I'm not flying with a stranger."

He winced. "You won't want to help me if I tell you."

"Try me."

He glanced up at her through his lashes, studying her stern expression. She put hands on her hips to show him she wasn't messing around. Without her, he could kiss whatever dream he had goodbye. "How did you make that fireball?"

He asked it like he didn't expect her to answer, so it surprised him when she replied instantly, "I'm soul bound. My dragon gave me her magic; she's a fire dragon. You'll share magic with your dragon once you learn how to wield it."

As if he knew what tipped her off, he looked down at his chest where his telling scar was on full display now that she'd ruined his shirt. "I have magic?"

"Yes. Still want to be a Dragon Knight?" If he could face off with a golem with nothing but the skin on his back and a stolen sword, there was no telling what he could do with magic at his fingertips.

"*His dragon bound, Eran, has an affinity to water,*" Aster informed her, her voice strangely cold and dark. Anna felt her scales bristle like the hairs rising on her arms. "*Make that human tell you who he is. If he doesn't, kill him. He's too dangerous with magic.*"

The certainty in her voice sent a chill down Anna's spine.

Her instincts took over. In a flash, she brandished her knife from the sheath at her thigh and held it steady to the man's throat. He didn't move, didn't flinch, didn't even fucking blink. Those dark eyes held hers, empty, almost soulless, as if he was begging her to end his life.

"Who are you?" she demanded with more urgency this time. If his identity was enough to rattle Aster, he was a threat to be reckoned with.

Those unwavering eyes held hers hostage, a flash of something earnest crossing them for an instant. Acceptance. He was prepared to die, right here, right now. "It's better if you don't know who I am."

"Tell me who you are or I'll slit your throat open right here." Just to make a point, she increases the pressure, a bead of blood running down the length of the blade.

She felt his Adam's apple bob against the knife, but she didn't let up, her wrist primed to move at a moment's notice.

"You'd be doing the world a favour if you did."

Those words gnawed at Anna's insides, stoking the rage simmering beneath the surface. Too many times had she had similar thoughts. Too many times had she come so close to letting them win...

She didn't care *who* he was, if she wasn't allowed to give up that easily—neither was he. "Then why come here at all?" she challenged, fighting the slight tremor in her hand. Not out of fear or strain, but out of anger. "Why go through all of this effort if you're just going to give up when things get too tough?"

What made him think he was cut out to be a Dragon Knight if he couldn't fight for what he believed in?

Something cracked in his features. The stone mask slid free, revealing a man beneath. A man who knew pain like an old friend, who had seen terrors beyond her imagination, who had suffered so much that when a complete stranger offered him a helping hand—he looked like he didn't know what to do with it.

Yet, amongst the pain and hopelessness, there was bravery and determination. They gave him enough strength to decide his own fate.

"My name is Deximus Fortys."

Cold, hard terror sludged through her system, filling her veins and pores with a fight or flight instinct she'd never felt before. Not when she faced the golem. Not when she went against a band of goblins by herself. Not when she performed her first trust fall with Aster.

I just fought with Prince Deximus. A ruthless killer. A man who feared nothing and was feared by all. It was rumoured that if his name was even spoken, death followed in its wake.

And a dragon was *Bonded* to him.

Instinct screamed at her to lean in and slit his throat. But intuition nagged at the back of her mind and told her to *think*.

"*What do you think of Eran?*" she asked her dragon. Was he as evil as the man beside her or did he see something in the prince that no one had ever seen in him?

"*Eran is a kind soul at heart, though he has had his fair share of pain. We all have.*" Her thoughts went to the rider she'd lost when Anna had saved her. She'd been close to her Knight before; they'd spent many good years together before he was murdered. "*If Eran sees something in the human, then maybe we should try to see it as well.*"

To be fair to him, he could have escaped at any given moment. He could have killed every single one of the Knights in this camp. He could have let the golem kill everyone. He could have turned back home with his new power and used it to help his father begin a new reign of tyranny.

But he didn't do any of those things. He stayed and saved these men. He hadn't hurt a single person in his capture. He had nowhere else to turn to and now he was trusting Anna with a secret that would have him killed in a heartbeat if anyone found out.

If a dragon had faith in this man, maybe it was time someone else did, too.

However, instead of relieving the defective prince by telling him his secret was safe with her, she screwed her face up. "You're supposed to be dead."

He shrugged casually, but his eyes were critically sharp as he watched for any sign he needed to defend himself. "I'm hard to kill. People say I'm invincible."

Those words were chosen very carefully, Anna noticed.

"Nobody's invincible."

"I'm still alive." His gaze was unrelenting on her, trying to figure out what she intended to do with him. "I told you my name, the least you could do is tell me yours."

She studied him closely, the flicker in his jaw, the raw intensity in his eyes, the sharp set of his shoulders. He was a soldier through and through, even more skilled in interrogations. He was experienced, despite his young age.

He could be playing her, using the mercies he'd granted the Knights as a reason to let her guard down. If his goal was to infiltrate their base and tear it apart from the inside out—there would be no better man than the Slayer of Souls to do it.

But there was something—*something*—that gnawed at the back of her mind. It didn't add up. His "death" last week and now his sudden appearance at her doorstep. If he truly wanted to infiltrate the base, he wouldn't have told her his name. If he was as evil as the stories portrayed him, a dragon wouldn't have Bonded with him.

She'd play his game for now—but she'd be keeping a close eye on him. One slip up and she had no qualms cutting him down.

She removed her knife, returning it to its sheath. "I'm Annaliese Hargin—the best chance you have to convince anyone that *you* should be a Dragon Knight." She extended her hand to him. "Welcome aboard, Grayson Smith—if that's the name you want to keep."

Last chance to ditch the terrible name.

He didn't hesitate. "I'll keep it."

His hand was solid and firm in her grasp. She couldn't believe she was shaking hands with Prince Deximus Fortys, the Slayer of Souls.

CHAPTER I
A BITTER SURRENDER

Eva closed her eyes and allowed the current to flow through her naturally. She absorbed the static in the air, every sliver of magic the storm could offer her. It was all the power she had to draw on—and she needed every bit of it this morning.

She and Arkon were standing on the shore of Lake Reynor, a massive body of water hidden behind the walls of Dragon Canyon. It was rumoured that water dragons stored treasures of the world at the center of the bottomless pit, but Eva doubted it. Under the overcast sky, the water looked more like a raggedy old boot.

It should be easy—second nature—to control the current, to bend it to her will. Basic technique, that was all it was. Something she could have done with her eyes closed in the Desert Lands. But here? She was tense. Distracted. She had others to worry about. While Aster normally hid in her cave in the Desert Lands to put Eva's mind at ease in case of any accidents, the Dragon Knights here didn't have that luxury. They had places to go, people to protect. Which left her no choice but to practice on the desolate rock beach—away from the lightning-susceptible residents of Dragon Canyon in case something went wrong with her training.

The air crackled around her, telling her there was enough charge for her to use magic. Remembering to control her breathing, she directed the current to her fingertips. They tingled, sparks dancing between each digit. With a deep breath, she reached her hand out, commanding the sparks to fly across the field towards a boulder Arkon had placed as a target. Lightning struck the ground violently—nowhere near her target. Thunder quickly rolled through the dark clouds above.

Arkon's tail coiled around her feet protectively. "Patience, Little One," he crooned, sensing the pressure rising inside of her. "Take your time."

"I don't have *time*," she snapped, breathing heavily. Commanding lightning was taking a toll on her, but she needed to do better. *Be* better.

She took the position Sasha showed her, feet shoulder width apart, fists at her hips. With every breath she took, she moved her feet and hands, controlling the current running through her body. It spiralled from one end of her hands, down to her feet, back up the other leg, ending at the tip of her other hand. It used to be difficult to do this, but she'd practised it so many times that even under the circumstances of today she could do it with ease—

The lightning jolted out of her hands, hitting a nearby tree.

"Damn it!"

"Eva—"

"I'm *fine*."

His tail coiled around her feet so tightly that she lost her balance and fell into the cradle of his embrace. He craned his neck, pinning her with a fierce, crystal blue eye.

"You cannot lie to me, Little One. I feel your distress as deeply as my own." He exhaled, the scent of raw meat and smoke wrapping around her. "It is natural to be upset."

"I'm not upset. Jacob is safe. We ended the war before there could be more casualties. Darius is locked up in the Kain dungeons and will never see the light of day again. All because of us."

King Sylus had accepted King Renkon's terms of surrender this morning. The war was *over*. People didn't have to watch the East in fear anymore. The kingdom could heal and finally know peace.

Eva was proud to be a part of it, to be the one who brought Darius to his knees. Yet worry still lingered and gnawed at her gut.

Arkon loosed a long, grating sigh, knowing what truly laid in her heart, even if she didn't want to admit it. Didn't want to think about the assassins Darius had promised were on their way to kill her.

A bet. King Sylus and Darius had made a *bet* on who could reach her first: if Darius won, he could do as he willed with her, turn her into a weapon for his own use; if Sylus's assassins found her, they were ordered to kill her on sight.

With Darius locked up, Eva highly doubted the assassins would give up and return home. No, Sylus had sent them here to do a job—and they weren't leaving until her head was on spike and Arkon's body was a crumbling corpse.

Thunder growled in the clouds—then a sheet of rain fell over the lake, trampling over the surface at a rapid speed towards them until she was blasted by the wall of water. A shiver chased down her spine.

Every week the temperature dropped and she added yet another layer to her wardrobe. Today, it didn't matter how many layers she wore, a chill had clutched her bones and showed no signs of letting her go.

She climbed out of Arkon's embrace and settled back into her power stance. When she raised her hands, they trembled and so did her connection with the storm. Sparks sputtered and disappeared in her grasp.

"Take a break, Eva," Arkon demanded, his voice low and booming like the thunder in the sky.

"No," she gritted out. "I have to be ready."

She refused to live in fear of an enemy she couldn't see—and the only way to do that was to train her body to react before she could see them.

A growl rumbled in his chest. He stepped away from her, wings twitching in agitation, and glanced pointedly at the boulder he had placed for her. "Then, by all means, use what I've taught you and hit that boulder."

He knew just as well as her that she hadn't been able to hit her mark on a good day under his or Sasha's guidance. But she wouldn't be Eva Greene if she backed away from a challenge.

Connecting with the current in her veins once more, she held her hand out and called out to the lightning in the sky. It struck down instantly, forming an ambiguous bolt in her palm. The hardest part was keeping it calm in her hand. It fought against her as hard as she fought to keep it under control. It wholly resisted her.

Her power and every damn thing in this world fought against her—

As soon as she let her anger take hold, the bolt exploded in her grasp. It shot up into the sky, forking into the clouds.

Eva cried out, cradling her hand to her chest. It had left a black, gaping hole in her palm. Blood ran freely down her wrist, dripping onto the pebbles at her feet, to only be washed away by the obnoxious rain pelting the side of her face.

"Will you listen to me now?" the dragon goaded.

Frustrated, Eva kicked a pebble into the lake. "I feel like a sitting duck. I hate it."

"I know." He shuffled back to her side and raised his wing above her, sheltering her from the rain. The heat of his body made the rain steam against his scales and kept her shivers at bay. She snuggled into his leg, finding comfort in his scaly embrace.

Her hand throbbed, sending a fire up her arm that made it hard to think about anything but the pain. With a grunt, she tore at her cloak and wrapped the wound. A pathetic bandage until she could see a healer. Just the thought of having to sit with one of their rank poultices made her grimace...

Movement flickered in the corner of her eye from the treeline. In a flash, she had her bow drawn and an arrow notched, aim locked onto the heart of the rider astride a horse. The rider didn't need to know that she couldn't fully pull back the arrow with her injury. The threat was enough to halt them at the edge.

Arkon growled, moving in front of her and flaring his wings wide. His roar shook her bones.

"Who's there?" she demanded. Who in their right mind would approach them during a storm?

He dismounted then raised his hands, coming out of the woods. There wasn't an inch of him that wasn't armed; his weapons glinted in the overcast lighting, on his chest, ribs, hips, thighs, and calves. He wore black on black, blending into the shadows of the forest behind him. When she didn't lower her bow, he removed the hood of his cloak.

Scowling, she put her bow away. "Grayson? What are you doing here?"

He closed the distance between them, only stopping when Arkon snarled at him.

"Not a step closer, Slayer."

The indomitable Knight cut a glare his way. Rather than rain pelting Grayson's face, as it ought to, the water ran off the sides of an invisible shield he had over his head. "I'm not going to hurt Eva." He turned his attention back to her, features hard and resolute yet his eyes managed to soften when they landed on her. "You left the meeting quickly this morning... Do you want to talk about it?"

"That's rich, coming from you."

Talk? He wanted her to open up—tell him what was going on in her head? To admit she was hanging on by a thread, barely keeping it together, when she couldn't tell the difference between a truth and a lie with him. When she'd laid her heart bare to him—and he hid his past, the very core of who he was, from her.

How could he expect her to give him what he wanted when he wouldn't offer her the same in return?

He winced. "I'm trying to make things right, Eva."

She crossed her arms, uncertain. Half of her wanted nothing more than to run up to him and hold him, to forgive his sins and for lying to her. It was the part of her that missed that feeling of invincibility he gave her and the part that craved to have his body pressed up against hers.

The other half of her saw the black hair and dark grey eyes trademark of the Fortys family and remembered that he wasn't the man she thought he was. Would she ever see the real him, or would he only show her the parts he thought she wanted to see?

She could trust him as a Dragon Knight, but as a friend? Something more? She didn't know.

His fists bunched up at his sides again, determination sparking in his eyes. "We can talk about whatever you want. Darius, Sylus, my old life. Us." The emphasis on the word gave Eva a hint as to what *he* wanted to talk about. "Where do we stand, Eva?"

She meant to put her hands in her pockets, but her wound stung, and she winced. Grayson closed the gap between them, ignoring Arkon's growls and scooping up her hand. She wasn't given the chance to back away from him.

He'd asked her where they stood, but she didn't know the answer and she hadn't wanted him to touch her and confuse her further until she figured it out. As soon as his hands came around her, all of her apprehension went out the window. All she could think about was how gentle his grasp was. This close, she smelled his distinct scent of leather and steel. He might not be any better at magic than her, but he extruded power and resolve. It was easy to get caught up in it and just stand there and let him heal her.

He held her palm up in the rain. The droplets that fell onto her hand pooled together then seeped into her wound, filling the gap until there was nothing left to fill. The buzz of his magic ran rampant through her veins, spreading up her arm and wrapping around her heart, as if it could heal the scars beneath the surface.

As the rain washed the blood away, Grayson rubbed his thumb against her palm, making sure it was fully healed.

"Um, thanks," she said, awkwardly pulling her hand to her side.

He frowned at her movements, but didn't make any attempts to close the gap she'd made between them again. A shallow breath passed through his lips. "I see... I suppose I shouldn't have expected you to instantly trust me again... Jacob trusts me, you know. So do Anna and Hargin."

She crossed her arms. "Did you kiss them, too? Did you hide a major part of your life from them then have them second-guess every moment you shared with them?"

He hesitated, biting down on his bottom lip. "No."

Eva sighed, her eyes drifting to Arkon, who was still tearing into the earth with slow, deliberate strikes of his talons. She looked down at her healed hand, flexing it gently, before raising her gaze back to Grayson.

Her mind went back to the kiss they'd shared before they infiltrated Darius's fort to save Jacob—the way his mouth had found hers in heated desperation. Wild and ravenous, as if he'd been starved of her all of his life. She hadn't had time to be angry then, only to feel that insatiable, aching pull. The way he'd looked at her, eyes burning like she was the only one who could undo him.

She'd wanted more. She still did.

She wanted to believe it had all been real. Every shared glance. Every touch. The power he made her feel just by being near.

"I want to trust you, Grayson," she confessed softly. "But I... I don't know who you are anymore. I don't know what's real and what's part of the story you tell everyone else."

His gaze didn't waver. It held her like something sacred, searching her face as if the right look could bridge the chasm between them. "I've never been more myself than I am with you," he said, voice low. "That's the truth. You don't have to believe it—not yet. Please. Just let me show you. I'll do whatever it takes to earn back what I lost."

It was the "please" that did it for her. Grayson Smith—Deximus Fortys—was not the kind of man to ask, let alone *beg*, for anything. But here he was—pleading to let him stay in her life.

The truth was, she didn't want to cut him out of her life. Before she knew who he was, he had become an anchor in the insanity that was her life.

Even if their entire relationship had been spun on a web of lies.

Even if she wasn't sure who the man standing before her truly was.

Even if she had to risk her heart to find out the truth.

She couldn't bear to lose him.

She offered him a hesitant smile, not ready to let her guard down just yet. "I can do that... I've never had someone prove themselves to me." The thought stirred something deep within her, leaving her insides warm and aching.

Grayson exhaled, a slow, steady breath. The tension in his shoulders eased, just slightly, like he'd been holding his breath the entire time. But his eyes never left hers, burning with determination. "Leave it up to me. I won't let you down."

He started for her—then halted.

Arkon snarled, stomping the ground hard enough to make the beach tremble beneath them. A tree she'd weakened earlier with lightning groaned and crashed to the ground.

"It is time to leave, Eva," Arkon announced, slipping his tail between them like a drawn line.

She opened her mouth—to protest, to apologise to Grayson for her dragon's behavior—but didn't get the chance. In one swift motion, Arkon scooped her up in his claws and launched into the sky.

"Arkon!" she snapped, adjusting herself in his claws so the wind wasn't so harsh in her face. "*Arkon!*" she added mentally, since he seemed to have suddenly gone deaf. "*We weren't done talking.*"

"*Clearly. You stood there like a helpless fawn, while you let the wolf poison you with his words. You cannot trust him.*"

"*Arkon...*" Eva felt his hurt like her own, the memories and grief of his brothers and sisters weighing heavy on her shoulders as much as his wings. Grayson could be Soul Bound, a Dragon Knight, the man who had sworn to regain her trust—but he would always be the Slayer of Souls to her dragon. The slayer of his kin.

"*Once a Fortys, always a Fortys,*" Arkon snarled. "*He can pretend to be a Dragon Knight all he wants, he'll never change.*"

Eva didn't know what to say or do. Arkon's pain echoed inside her, raw and unforgiving, tangling with her own confusion until she couldn't separate his fury from her need for the truth.

The wind whipped against her face, pulling at her hair, stinging her eyes. Arkon's talons were curled tight around her, but it was the storm inside her chest that truly left her breathless—tight, aching, and uncertain. Her heart pulled in one direction, her bond in another.

Did she listen to her dragon and avoid Grayson, or did she follow her heart and risk the consequences?

CHAPTER 2
REGRETS AND REDEMPTION

"*Did you kiss them, too? Did you hide a major part of your life from them then have them second-guess every moment you shared with them?*"

Eva's words consumed Grayson. The emotion in her words, in her eyes—the anger, the passion, the *doubt*—sliced through him, leaving a big, gaping wound.

She wasn't mad at him for being Deximus Fortys, or even for being named the Slayer of Souls, once upon a time. She was mad that he had lied to her. Upset that every moment they had shared was tainted by the lie and had led her to doubt it all.

None of it had been fake. He had tried his damnedest to fight it, to stay away from her, but he couldn't. He was a moth and she was a beacon of light in a world of darkness. He couldn't fight the perpetual pull of her soul, dragging, coaxing, lulling. He was powerless against her undying warmth.

Grayson clenched his fists at his sides then counted to ten in his mind. He shouldn't have expected anything else from Eva and, especially, Arkon. He wouldn't have been attracted to her if she caved in to him at the first chance they had to talk. He wanted her to make him fight, make him struggle and flounder.

He deserved far worse. He certainly didn't deserve Eva.

The storm cleared quickly after Arkon left. The clouds were still heavy with rain, but they weren't as dark and the uneasy sense of calm chaos faded in the wind.

"*I will pick you up,*" Eran offered, having kept a healthy distance from Arkon and his storm.

"*No. I'll meet you at the ground base.*" Grayson wanted to use the time it would take his horse ride back to ruminate.

For once, the dragon didn't argue with him.

Grayson had told Eva he would prove himself worthy of her. He had to show her that he had never been—*felt*—more himself than when he was with her. The only problem with that? He had no idea how to do it. Matters of the heart were not his thing. If all he had to do was slay a cyclops to prove his worth to her, he'd do it in a heartbeat. Hells, he'd kill anything she asked of him if it meant regaining her trust.

But, he couldn't kill for her this time.

By gods, was it frustrating! His hands weren't made to create, they were designed to destroy. It was all he had ever known. This predicament required a gentle hand and a tender heart.

Neither of which he possessed.

When he was a prince, he didn't have to beguile women. They were drawn to him. Drawn to the danger, his looks, his power. He didn't have to be gentle with them, didn't have to use smooth words—or make any vows—to lure them to his bed.

But he hadn't cared about them, either. He had used them purely to satisfy a physical need. Eva was different. He hurt when she hurt. Heat bloomed in his chest and spread to the tips of his fingers when she laughed. When she looked at him with that uninhibited passion of hers, his body yearned for hers like no other. It was beyond carnal desire. It was a need to be as close to her as possible. To weave his essence into hers and to become a part of that light she shines so brightly.

He would do anything for her, even conquer the darkness within him. She said she would give him a chance, and he didn't intend on wasting it.

Grayson sat with his thoughts the rest of the way back to the ground base, trying not to get caught up in the whirlwind wreaking havoc on his mind. He needed to remain centered, grounded, if he was going to navigate his way out of this.

Jacob was outside of the stables with a mount of his own. When he caught sight of Grayson, he swung out of the saddle, boots sinking into the mud saturating the ground. With heavy footsteps, he closed the gap between them, eyes searching Grayson's features curiously but not entirely surprised to see him.

Grayson handed his horse to the stable master and studied his friend.

Jacob wasn't fully dressed in armour, only in riding pants and a dragon scale jacket to ward off the elements; underneath he wore a green cotton shirt, his family's greatsword strapped to his back. The wind had been unkind to his mop of blonde hair and left it in a dishevelled state Anna would have definitely fussed over.

Especially of late. Since they returned from the twisted fort Darius had turned Brar into last week, Anna had been mother-henning him, ensuring not a single spec was out of place on his blonde head. Which there wasn't. The moment he returned to Dragon Canyon, he sought out Jacob and took him to the healing pools to mend the marks Darius had left on his skin. All that remained of his captivity was a shadow in his gaze and bags under his eyes.

"What are you doing here?" Grayson asked. Though, should he really be shocked to find him about to mount up when his sister had blasted out of the meeting room faster than one could say "May the winds be in your favour"?

Jacob glanced at the reins in his hand, the horse attached to it, then to the stable master who had taken Grayson's away. "I'm guessing for the same reason you are—except you beat me to it. How's Eva doing?"

A jolt raced down Grayson's spine, as vivid as a flogging from Sylus.

How was she doing? He hadn't asked. Not about the surrender. Not about what she thought of Darius still being in Aboria.

Albeit, Darius was locked away—thousands of miles from her—and Eva was safe in a canyon full of dragons, a canyon that Grayson regularly patrolled to ensure it stayed that way. But that didn't matter. He knew better than anyone how easily Darius could worm his way under someone's skin.

And still, he hadn't asked how she was doing.

His visit had been entirely selfish.

Hargin had pulled their squad and the high ranking officers into a meeting this morning and broke the news: Sylus accepted the terms of the surrender. Including leaving Darius here to be tried for his crimes. Renkon—the slowest king to make a decision that shouldn't require much thought—and his court had been in a meeting since to decide Darius's fate.

Eva had fled the room as soon as the news was out and flew off to Lake Reynor. Hargin had half a mind to drag her back to Dragon Canyon, until Grayson pointedly asked her how she intended to do that with a protective storm dragon watching over her. No dragon would go near Arkon. There were only a handful of Knights who would dare approach them, and Grayson wanted to be the one to do it.

"As well as anyone can expect," Grayson answered vaguely.

It had been a week since they brought Jacob home. A week since Eva had captured Darius. A week since Grayson had felt her lips on his. A week, and Grayson hadn't told his friend he'd kissed his sister. It appeared Eva hadn't told him either, because he wrongfully assumed Grayson had gone after her to talk about the meeting. Which was what he *should* have done.

Jacob raked a hand through his hair, a worried line digging into his forehead. "I don't know why she's upset. I thought she would be happy. She won."

Because Eva knew what Grayson knew: Sylus didn't surrender. He would never admit defeat, especially defeat from a woman.

He was planning something.

"Because it's not over."

Jacob peered up at the steep pathway that led to the main base and dragon dens then looked back at Grayson, a sheen of fear swimming to the surface of those russet eyes. "What do you mean?"

Grayson started up the trail for the main base; Jacob walked alongside him. The path was narrow, barely wide enough for two armoured Knights; it was maintained frequently to keep canyon debris off the trail and giving the Knights one less hazard they had to look out for, but not much could be done for the harsh winds blasting through the canyon.

"Sylus doesn't want Eva," Grayson informed him grimly, the words tasting sour on his tongue. "Not alive, anyway. We found out that he and Darius had placed a bet: if Darius reached Eva first, he could turn her into a puppet; if Sylus got to her first, he would kill her."

Jacob swung around to him, grabbing his arm and yanking him to a complete stop. His eyes were wild with horror, but the grip, fueled by anger, was as strong as Grayson's resolve to keep Eva safe. "When were you guys planning on sharing this with the rest of us??"

Grayson fixed him with a droll stare, to hide the fact that his mind had been too preoccupied to think about informing anyone but Hargin of this new development. "I just told you, didn't I? Anyway, Sylus's assassins will know I'm alive by now. They won't cross me in unfamiliar territory unless they have to, which will give us some time."

Jacob remained unmoving, grip unrelenting. An edge sharpened in his eyes, one Grayson had never seen in his friend before. "No. You don't get to decide *when* I find out about these things—especially when it concerns Eva. She's my sister, Gray. The last of my family. You don't get a say in her life, I do, and if there are assassins after her, I want to *fucking* know about it. Got it?"

Grayson blinked, taken off guard. Then blinked again. He didn't know Jacob had it in him to use that tone with him.

Perhaps he'd only ever use it to protect his sister.

Perhaps... he had crossed a line.

He raked a hand through his hair and looked across the way to the wall opposite them. Vines dangled from crags, clinging desperately to the last fragments of Autumn. "I'm sorry. You're right. I should have told you. I'm still getting used to this whole 'work as a team' thing and there's something about Eva that makes me forget that I don't have to do everything by myself."

Jacob's hand moved to his shoulder, squeezing it tight before releasing him altogether. "You can trust me, Gray. You can trust Anna. Everyone on this base. You're not alone anymore."

Grayson cleared his throat, feeling as though a peach's pit was caught in it, then continued up the narrow path, sticking close to the cliff wall. Jacob followed silently, not pressuring him. He always liked that about Jacob. He knew when to push and when not to.

"So," Jacob said, after a few beats of silence, "you said the assassins knowing you're here has bought us time. Time for what?"

"To train," he answered simply, confidently. "Eva still has a lot to learn. I'll train her, show her how the assassins will fight. When I'm done with her, they won't be able to touch her."

Jacob peered up at him under his fluffy bangs worriedly. "You told Hargin you weren't going to turn her into one of you."

"I'm not," Grayson vowed. He'd spent the better part of three years trying to erase who he was. He wouldn't wish anyone to be like him. Especially not Eva. "I'm preparing her for a fight, what she does with it is entirely up to her. She *will* survive this, Jake."

He wouldn't let anyone take Eva away from him. Not Darius. Not Sylus or his assassins. He had shoved the monster deep down within him, but he wasn't afraid to bring him back out if it meant keeping Eva alive. The world would know the name Slayer of Souls once again, except it'd be his enemies who feared him instead of innocent people.

Jacob kept pace behind him, a harsh breeze whipping past and tossing his hair to the side. He let it be, knowing there was no point in adjusting his hair in this canyon. "So I'm assuming you guys have made up then?"

Caught off guard, Grayson's boot caught on a pebble. His hand had to shoot out and clutch the cliff wall to catch himself from that embarrassing stumble. He glanced back at his friend. "Not exactly."

Jacob's eyebrows knitted together. "How are you supposed to teach her if she's still mad at you?" His face scrunched further when silence ensued. "You *have* told her about this plan, right?"

Rolling his eyes at the slightly judgemental tone, Grayson turned back up the path. "No."

"*Grayson.*" Jacob loosed an exasperated groan. "Talk to her. She has to know that you did the best you could given the circumstances and got out."

"She's not mad about that." He wasn't sure if it was better or worse that she wasn't mad about his past.

"She's not?"

"It's more complicated. She thinks I haven't been myself with her. She wants the real me or nothing to do with me."

Jacob blinked, head tilting slightly, as if trying to get a better angle on their conversation in case he'd missed something. His eyes shimmered with amusement in the overcast light. "Oh. That's it?"

Grayson wanted to throttle him for making fun of him and this new experience he was suffering from. "Jake."

"I wouldn't worry too much, Gray," his friend assured him, patting his shoulder. "If Eva was hung up on your past, there would be little we could do to help her work through it, but if she thinks she doesn't *know* you? That's easy."

Grayson rolled his eyes, peering off the edge. They had climbed high enough to cause substantial harm if one of them went tumbling off the side. Tempting. He'd catch him, of course. He just needed a little shove to remember what fear felt like. Clearly.

"It's that easy, huh?" Grayson sneered. "*Enlighten* me."

A grin split Jacob's face. Gods, he was loving this, wasn't he? He had given Grayson plenty of advice over the years, some of it was better received than others, but he seemed to find something particularly satisfying about helping Grayson knit his relationship with Eva back together. Not that he knew Grayson's intention was beyond friendship.

"Spend time with her," he offered freely. "Don't pressure her. Buy her chocolate fudge cupcakes. Be the man you've been fighting to be for the past three years, and you guys will be friends again in no time. Trust me."

Grayson scowled thoroughly and deeply. Eva wasn't a heedless woman to be easily won over by cupcakes. Surely, there had to be more to it than simply spending time with her? "That can't be all."

Jacob halted then turned to him; the wind blasted them from the sides and knocked his tufts of hair aside. "Trust is important to Eva. It was all we had growing up. When we left the village boundaries to hunt, we had to trust in each other to watch our backs. Now that Brar is gone and our lives are far more complicated, Eva needs to know *who* her allies are."

"She knows who I am. She knows I have her back."

"Yeah. She knows what you can do and how you can help her, but does she know your favourite colour?"

Grayson screwed his face up then kept on hiking up the trail. It wasn't short and if they wanted to return to the base before nightfall, they needed to pick up the pace. "Don't mock me, Jake."

"I'm not mocking you." Jacob caught up to him easily. "I'm serious. I don't even know your favourite colour. I tell everyone it's black. You have regrets and fears, aspirations and desires—things that make you *human*. If you want to be friends with Eva again, you have to open yourself up to her."

Grayson grimaced at the idea. Killing a leviathan with his bare hands sounded less risky than telling her about his *feelings*. "I'm not telling her my fears, Jake."

It had been ingrained in him from a very young age that exposing any weakness, whether it be his deepest fears or showing his pain, would get him killed. Too many people relied on him for him to go and get himself killed, even if it was for Eva. There had to be another way.

Jacob shook his head at him then raked a hand through his dense hair. "I'm not saying you have to tell her all of your dirty secrets, Gray. Just give her *something*. You have the biggest collection of weapons I've ever seen and Eva likes hunting—find something in that." Jacob marched past him, haunching his shoulders against the harsh Autumn wind. "I'm not going to spend all day giving you advice on how to make amends with my sister. You're both adults. Figure it out."

Grayson's step faltered, eyes fixed on the back of Jacob's head as he continued up the path without looking back. His chest wound mercilessly tight, threatening to squeeze the air out of his lungs.

Gods, he was a mess. He hated it—the lack of control, the unnerving degrees his body reacted without his permission. The way Eva filled his thoughts. He should be focusing on how he was going to keep her alive. On Sylus's next move. On ensuring Darius never saw the light of day again.

But instead, his mind was running rampant trying to figure out how to make things up to Eva.

"*Infatuation will do that to a man*," Eran remarked smugly, being uncharacteristically quiet until now. He didn't have to say anything. Grayson was torturing himself enough for the both of them. "*I never thought I'd see it happen to you, though. I thoroughly enjoy watching you squirm.*"

"*Come fly down here and tell that to my face, dragon.*"

"*But the view is so much better from up here.*" To make a point, Eran flew past him, maintaining enough distance between them so Grayson couldn't jump on his back and make good on his promise.

He exhaled sharply through his nose and forced his hands to relax.

"Get yourself together," he muttered to himself. "You're better than this."

Grayson glanced toward the corner where Jacob had disappeared, then up at Eran circling like a shadow against the clouds. Something was coming—he could feel it, pressing in behind his ribs. And if he didn't get his head straight, Eva wasn't the only one who'd pay the price.

His fingers dusted over the knives at his thighs, grazing the hilt of the short sword at his hip, then started walking again, this time with purpose.

If he was going to win back her trust, he'd need more than a life full of regrets.

He'd need a plan.

CHAPTER 3
FLOWERS, CINNAMON BUNS, AND CONFESSIONS

Eva rubbed the back of her neck on her way to her room, feeling a tension headache rising to the surface. She thought her troubles stopped at Sylus's suspiciously sudden surrender and Grayson's promise to make things right with her, but now she had to worry about Arkon, too. He was still furious with her and had completely shut her out of his mind once he dropped her off in the stables. Skin-to-scale contact would be the only way to enter his mind until he deemed her worthy to share his thoughts again.

The cool wind slipped through the hallways, and she shuddered in her damp cloak. Man, what she could really use was a nice hot bath and dry clothes. However, before she could enter her room, she stopped dead, befuddled by all the flowers pinned to the door. Roses, peonies, lilies—there were so many blooms it looked like her door had been swallowed by Spring.

After peeking around and confirming this was indeed her room, she went for the handle.

What the...?

Her breath caught for half a second as she opened the door to find many, *many* more flowers all over the apartment. Annaliese was in the middle of it all, plucking one bloom after the other and inhaling their floral scents with a whimsical smile on her face. Scratching her head, Eva waded through the flowers on the floor to the couch. As beautiful as this display was, it was going to suck to clean it up. They'd have pollen in the fabrics for days.

"A new secret admirer?" Eva guessed. Anna had her fair share of admirers in the hallways, but she only had eyes for one man—and he was as clueless as a hare grazing in an open field.

Chuckling, Anna tossed her crimson tresses over her shoulder. After the meeting this morning, she shed out of her uniform, opting for dark, standard issue riding pants and a cream skin-tight under armour shirt. It was as relaxed as anyone around the base got these days. Her steel grey eyes danced excitedly as she handed Eva a gold-tipped envelope. "Not a secret at all."

Brows bunching together, Eva read the letter:

Eva Greene, Hero of Aboria,

You are cordially invited to your own party, celebrating your monumental success. The dress code has no limitations—except no Dragon Knight armour—so please wear the most scandalous dress you can find. My father will hate it, and I will most definitely appreciate it.

Yours truly,

Prince Leonidas Nathanial Kain

The letter almost slipped from her fingers, she was so surprised. Then she read it again—slower this time—just to make sure she hadn't imagined it. "This is all for *me*?"

No one had ever bought her flowers before. And now that she looked around properly, she realised most of them were her favourites. Some only native to her valley. The flush on her cheeks must have been obvious, because Anna was grinning like one of the children in Lensonten who'd just walked out of the sweet shop with a full bag of treats.

"Leave it to a prince to court in style."

Eva rolled her eyes, tossing the envelope onto the table. "He's not *courting*. He wants to get into my pants. There's a difference. Don't tell me I'm the first Dragon Knight he has sent flowers to."

Anna crossed her arms, a stern scowl taking root on her face that made her look remarkably like the Commander. Not that Eva was brave enough to say that aloud. "You *are* the first Dragon Knight he's sent flowers to. He doesn't do these kinds of things for anyone, you know. He likes you, Eva."

She and Leo went way back, like diaper-changing back. Commander Hargin went to Kain Castle frequently during her career and, being a single mother, she often brought Annaliese with her. Anna and Leo used to play with building blocks while their parents went over war plans. If anyone knew Leonidas Kain, it was her partner.

Eva's face flamed. If someone had told her a year ago that she would hold a prince's affection, she wouldn't have believed it. Princes were supposed to fall in love with princesses and rule kingdoms—not court stinky Dragon Knights.

Butterflies fluttered in her stomach. This display was the sweetest thing anyone had ever done for her. She'd have to remember to thank him.

Anna came over and gave her a sharp pinch at the waist.

Eva jumped. "Ow! What was that for?"

"Don't overthink it," Anna said, grinning as she nudged her with a shoulder. "Just enjoy the perks—like having massive parties thrown in your name. We *are* going, right?"

Eva's lips pressed into a thin line. She crossed her arms, then uncrossed them, her gaze drifting back to the envelope on the table like it might bite her. "I don't see the point. What are we celebrating?"

Anna didn't answer right away. Instead, she stepped forward and gripped Eva's shoulders, firm but not harsh. "You *ended a war*, Eva. That is definitely worth celebrating."

Eva's throat tightened. Her eyes dropped to the floor, where crushed petals peeked out from under her boots. Then why did she feel like it had only just begun?

Anna's voice softened. She slid her hands down to Eva's and clasped them tightly. "Eva, victories come far and in between in our line of work. You take them while you can. Celebrate these moments to remind us why we're fighting. Who we're fighting for."

Eva looked down at their joined hands, her throat thick.

Celebrate. That word felt foreign—like it belonged to another life. A simpler one. Before she was Bound. Before Brar was reduced to ash. Before tyrannical kings and evil princes. So much loss. So much pain. Aboria forever scarred by greed. Was *that* worth celebrating?

She didn't feel like it was.

Her gaze drifted to the crushed petals again, then to the faint fingerprint smudge on the envelope. Her name written in royal ink.

This wasn't just about a party. This was about her letting go—of letting that spark of hope flare inside her, daring her to believe that she was a force to be reckoned with.

I ended a war. I stopped there from being more pain and loss. No one else has to hurt like I hurt.

She exhaled roughly, forcing out a shaky breath as her chest loosened. Barely. "Okay," she said at last, her voice softer than she meant it to be. "You're right." She rubbed the back of her neck and added, more wryly, "If nothing else, it's a distraction." A beat passed between them. "But there's one small problem..."

Anna perked up, ready to solve whatever problem Eva was about to throw at her.

“I have no idea how to dance.” Eva pursed her lips, feeling woefully unprepared and timid for her lack of skill. “And I’ve been promised a lot of dancing.”

Anna waved it off. “Pfft. It’s a lot like fighting, just with a little more flair... and a lot less death. You’ll pick it up easily. What you should most be concerned about is what you’re going to wear. Everyone’s eyes will be on you. You won’t be able to get away with something mediocre,” Anna added when Eva pulled out the peach chiffon dress she wore at dinner at Kain Castle.

Eva’s fingers tightened on the hanger. Grayson had been very specific in the look and had paid handsomely for it. It felt like a waste to only wear it once. “What’s wrong with this?”

Sighing, Anna ran her fingers over the chiffon, following the seamwork on the sleeve. “Nothing. It’s a beautiful dress with high quality stitchwork—a fantastic choice for dinner with the Kain family. But this is a gala, Eva. With nobles. Royals. Political allies. You’re not just showing up—you’re making a statement.”

Eva’s excitement for the party dwindled by the second. She sighed, giving the dress one last look before slipping it back into the closet. Her choices were limited—accept the invitation or don’t—and neither option felt particularly appealing. She chewed on her lower lip, then muttered, “Fine. But only because I was promised cake.”

“I’ll personally make sure it’s lathered in chocolate and fudge.” Anna squealed in delight, clapping her hands. “Come on. Let’s go to Lensenton for the afternoon.”

Eva managed a half-smile. A girls’ trip sounded like the kind of distraction she could actually stomach after this morning’s chaos—until she halted at the door, wincing as a very specific memory surfaced. “Um. Can I get a ride with you and Aster?”

Anna paused mid-step, her excitement faltering. “Of course, but why?”

Heat crept up Eva’s neck. It wasn’t the fight that bothered her most—it was the reason behind it. “Arkon and I aren’t exactly talking at the moment.”

Anna’s brows lifted. “What happened?”

Eva blew out an irritated breath and shoved her hands into her pockets. “Grayson happened.”

There was a beat, and then understanding dawned on Anna’s face. The kind that came from years of knowing exactly how tangled feelings could get. She reached for the door. “Why don’t you tell me over some tea?”

When Eva finished filling her in on the events of this morning, Anna fanned herself. Eva peered around the cafe, hoping Anna wasn't drawing too much attention to them. But who was she kidding? It was pouring rain outside and half of the city had come to this cafe to dry off and warm up. And here was a gorgeous redhead, getting all hot and bothered by Grayson's vow.

Of course she was drawing attention.

"Isn't that just the hottest thing you've ever heard? I never knew he had it in him."

Eva sank in her seat in the far corner of the cafe and tore apart the cinnamon bun on her plate. "That's my problem, Anna. How do I know this is the real him? He could be showing me what he thinks I want to see."

Anna brought her mug to her lips and hummed at the delightful smell of coffee. It was a new drink in the cafe and all the rage in town. Soon, all of Aboria would be talking about *coffee*. Eva preferred to stick to her mint tea.

"I think he doesn't know who he truly is," Anna said thoughtfully. "Transitioning between Estrus and Aboria has been difficult for him. Things are done differently on the other side of the water. He's been figuring things out as they go. He's changed so much in the three years I've known him, it's like watching a kid grow up. In the few months he's known you, a light has grown in his eyes. You give him hope that he can atone for all of his sins."

"Me?"

Huffing, Anna tossed her hair over her shoulder. "Eva, you lost everything, save the clothes on your back six months ago. Now look at you. You've made something of yourself. You've shown him that you can be powerful without instilling fear into everyone around you. You bring everyone you meet hope."

Eva felt her cheeks go red. "Oh, I, um, don't know about—"

"Look at you. You're so cute." She wagged her finger at her. "You're good for him. Jacob and I have accepted him as he is, but he needs someone who pushes him to explore a side of him he's been refusing to explore. All that I ask is that you're patient with him. What you're asking of him isn't easy for him."

Eva finished off her cinnamon bun while she considered Anna's request. She already knew what she wanted from Grayson would be difficult for him, and she was willing to put the time and effort into learning more about him—but he needed to do the same. She wouldn't accept half-hearted answers from him.

But was it right of her to *want* this?

She felt Arkon's absence in her mind like a... Well, like a piece of her soul was missing. Where she would normally go to him for comfort and guidance over a decision like this, he was the very reason she was having these doubts.

Following her heart in this instance felt like a betrayal to Arkon. His kin were gone because of Grayson. He might not have been there to witness their demise like Eva had been forced to watch Darius murder her family, but that pain ran deep all the same. The loss—and blame—tore through his soul as fervently as it tore through hers. She would never forgive Darius for taking her parents away, from snatching Erika's life before she even had the chance to live.

And now here she was, allowing the man who had a hand in wiping storm dragons from existence to have a second chance on her heart.

It wasn't fair to Arkon.

But it was it fair of him to deny her heart?

She didn't know.

She didn't *fucking* know.

And it killed her.

Anna reached across the table for her, laying her hand on top of hers. "What else is holding you back?"

"Arkon," she confessed quietly, guilt gnawing at her gut, cruelly, mercilessly. "I don't know if he'll forgive me if I pursue things with Grayson." Eva leaned forward, elbows on the table as she dumped her head into her hands. "It's even worse, because I get it. If I was Arkon, I'd hate Grayson too. Killing the other storm dragons was a horrible crime, a wound that will forever haunt Arkon. I *understand* that kind of loss more than anyone..." She pressed her palms into her eyes, feeling the sting of tears line her lids. "But Grayson is trying to make up for his mistakes. Doesn't he deserve a chance to prove he's a different man now?"

Anna was silent for a long moment, eyes clouded by turmoil and indecision. She chewed on her bottom lip. When her eyes fell on Eva, they were no less conflicted. No shade of assurance. Just the eyes of a friend who was about to deliver a hard truth. "If I've learned one thing in life, Eva, it's that you can't make everyone happy. The one thing you can do is work on your own happiness."

"But how do I do that? Grayson pulls me one way and Arkon pulls me the other way. There's this spark between Grayson and I, and I feel like if I could really get to know him, we could make something great... But how can I brush Arkon's feelings—a part of *me*—aside? Does that make me a bad person?"

Anna's face marred with empathy, a sadness stinging in her eyes. "No. No matter what you decide, Eva, it does not make you a bad person. But this... this is something you and Arkon need to work through. You two have to find a balance. Yes, you two are irrevocably intertwined, Bound in soul and this life you've chosen—but you are still separate beings with rights to your own life. He cannot dictate what your heart desires more than you can deny his draconic instincts. Aster and I have gone through this struggle and I'm sure Grayson and Eran have too. Give it time and the answer will come to you."

Eva sat back in her chair, pointing her gaze upward to fight the tears threatening to spill over her cheeks. She'd never felt so torn in her life, not even when Grayson had initially offered her to become a Dragon Knight. Then, she had a duty to her family—even if it hurt to put them above her dream. But this? This was so much more than a dream and duty. Her soul and heart were at war.

"You'll figure it out," Anna assured her. "I can't tell you what to do here."

"I know." Expelling a harsh breath, Eva returned her gaze to her friend. "I know... Thank you for listening."

She might not be closer to an answer, but she at least knew that this wasn't meant to be an easy decision, which made her heart ache a little less.

Anna waved it off, leaning back in her seat with a casual shrug. "Girl, I'm always here if you want to talk. Speaking of... how are you? Boy and dragon troubles aside. You left in a hurry after the meeting this morning."

Eva shut her eyes, her stomach twisting as the memory returned—walking into that board room packed with officers, the air thick with anticipation. She'd sat beside Jacob, their knees brushing under the table. He'd grabbed her hand and held it tight, clinging to some fragile thread of hope. Then came the announcement.

Sylus was surrendering.

She should've felt relieved.

But instead, her pulse had spiked. The relief shattered the moment Commander Hargin added that Darius—the heir, the monster in her nightmares—would remain in King Renkon's custody.

Why?

Why wouldn't Sylus take back his heir?

The lack of explanation unsettled her more than any threat could. Something didn't add up.

She hadn't stayed for the rest. Couldn't. The walls had closed in, too many stares, too many eyes waiting for a reaction. She'd bolted straight to the Stables, climbing onto Arkon's back and flying hard and fast, as if wind could scour the unease from her bones.

But it didn't.

Even now, the memory lingered—Darius's twisted grin, sharp as shattered glass. Mocking. Promising that she'd never be free of him. Not really.

With a sigh, Eva pushed her hair back from her face and glanced at Anna through the strands. "I don't know," she admitted, her voice thin. "I blew off some steam, but I still feel... useless." Scared. Vulnerable. She laced her fingers together tightly, knuckles paling. "Despite all the training, all the fighting—I'm still here, waiting. Watching. Sitting on my hands while they remain one step ahead of us." Her voice dropped to a whisper. "When will I be able to do something, Anna? Will I ever be strong enough to face Sylus?"

Anna's smile softened into something quieter—full of understanding. She gave her hand a gentle squeeze.

"You are not useless," she said firmly. "You've only just begun your training. Don't forget—Grayson and I have been preparing for this since we were old enough to hold a sword. The officers? They've been doing this twice as long. You'll get there, Eva. I'll make sure of it." She leaned in slightly, her voice low but steady. "As long as you keep going, I promise—one day, you'll become the powerful Dragon Knight everyone already sees in you. But you have to start believing it too. Have faith in yourself."

Tears welled in Eva's eyes for a different reason, blurring the world to soft shapes and light. She blinked hard and whispered, "I'm scared, Anna."

"As you should be," Anna said, not missing a beat. She offered a napkin, her tone warm but honest. "But despite that, you're still here. Still fighting. That's who you are. And I'll be right beside you every step of the way."

Her thumb brushed lightly across Eva's knuckles. "No matter what Sylus throws at us—we'll face it. We'll survive it. And we'll come out stronger."

Eva dabbed the corners of her eyes, letting out a slow breath. Her chest felt a little lighter, even if the fear still lingered. "You make it sound so easy."

"It's not," Anna said with a wry smile. "But it's easier with friends."

Eva gave a shaky laugh and nodded, sitting a little straighter. "Thank you, Anna. I don't know what I'd do without you."

Anna stood with a grin, her tone suddenly all business. "You'd probably go to a royal gala in a dinner dress and cry into a fruit tray. Lucky for you, I've got your back."

Eva gave a half-laugh, half-sniffle, and stood too. "Right. Let's go find something scandalous."

The dress was gorgeous and entirely uncharacteristic of Eva. They'd spent the entire afternoon looking for something that would stun the court yet be fitting of her role. There was even a flirtatious slit that Leo would absolutely love.

The sweetheart neckline left Eva's shoulders bare, the delicate curve of the design drawing attention to her collarbones and the strength in her posture. The fitted bodice cinched at her waist, lifting and shaping her chest with the help of a well-structured corset. But it was the skirt she loved most—sleek and silky, it skimmed over her hips and trailed behind in a modest train. A slit climbed high up one thigh, giving her room to move—and just enough danger to keep things interesting. The fabric faded from a deep, midnight black at the bust to a brilliant sky blue at the hem, the colors flowing like smoke and lightning. Like Arkon's eyes when the storm inside him stirred.

It would definitely be the talk of the court. Murmurs followed them down the hallways as they made their way up to the training rooms. At Anna's insistence, she was going to teach Eva how to dance in her dress. Eva agreed, not realising the stir it would cause until they reached the training level. One by one, heads poked out of the doors as they passed by.

Whistles rang through the hallway. Eva bit her lip, fighting the blush rising on her cheeks, while Anna flipped the bird their way before slipping into a room in her show-stopping red dress. Once Eva was inside, Anna closed the door behind her and rolled her eyes at the drooling Dragon Knights outside.

"*Men.* You'd think they've never seen a woman in a dress before." She twirled towards Eva with every intention of showing off her flowy skirt. When she stopped, the chiffon lace wrapped around her legs like flower petals in a breeze.

They were opposites in every way, and yet, somehow, they made the perfect pair. Eva's dress was sleek and silky, Anna's was puffy and lacy. Eva's was dark like the moonlit ocean, Anna's was bright like a comet in the sky. Eva's followed the natural curve of her body, Anna's enhanced every feature with strategic seams and sparkling embellishments. Where Eva moved like a blade—sharp and deliberate—Anna glided like a flame, radiant and untouchable.

With a graceful flourish, Anna spun into Eva's arms, her laced up back pressing against Eva's front. She tipped her head back on her shoulder, letting her hair flutter down the space between them. "You have the dress, the accessories, and a lineup of partners," she said as she slid a sly grin at the closed door. "Now let's get you the moves."

Giggling, she twirled away from Eva, spinning until she was in the middle of the room. She shut her eyes and began to hum a pleasant tune, swaying to the beat. Lost in the melody, her feet sweeping across the floor in an elegant Waltz.

Eva watched, mesmerised by the ease in which she moved. Anna always had this way about her, of unfettered, eloquent grace, like a melody in motion.

Still humming, Anna held her hands out to her. "Feel the music in your soul, Eva, let it guide you."

Eva waited until the next beat then fell into step with her, following her feet as they went forward then right, back then left. Simple. Just what she needed.

"Your partner will put his hands here." Anna placed a hand on Eva's waist, hand splayed on her shoulder blade, then clasped her right hand, holding it out to the side at chest height. "You will put your hand on him." She took Eva's free hand then placed it on the crook of her left shoulder.

Humming again, Anna led them into the Waltz. Eva shut her eyes with her and lost herself to the rhythm. Forward, right, back, left, twirl—

Eva's foot caught on the long train of her skirt. She stumbled out of Anna's grasp, barely stopping herself from face-planting. Straightening with a sharp breath, she glanced toward the door—only to find a small cluster of Knights watching.

She couldn't fight the flush creeping up her cheeks for being caught in a vulnerable state, despite the jolt of alarm zapping down her spine. Facing them, she planted her feet and waited for it. For them to mock her. Call her a fake Knight again just because she dared to put on a dress in their halls.

Lieutenant Dwight shook his head, reprimanding the younger ones and stepped forward. He couldn't be much older than her father. Laugh lines framed his mouth, and crow's feet fanned from the corners of his eyes. His brown hair gave way to grey, especially in his beard.

Eva's gut tightened, coiling in anticipation.

"Remember to lift your skirt before you step out," he advised, voice warm, not unkind. To her surprise, he moved into a flawless twirl, lifting an invisible skirt from his thigh just high enough to show the proper footwork. "Use your whole body. Your skirt is like a weapon—an extension of yourself. You can make even the smallest movements dramatic with the right flick."

Eva blinked, too stunned for words. Was a lieutenant really giving her dancing advice? Did she hit her head on that last manoeuvre?

Anna lit up beside her, clasping her hands. "You're so right, Dwight! Would you care to join us? We could use your expertise."

He gave a sheepish shrug, his weathered face softening. "My daughter's the expert. No one can spin like my Lulu."

"And *who* taught her how to dance?" She bumped Eva's shoulder, which she knew was meant to ease the tension in her shoulders, but only made her more tense. She was still waiting for them to tell her to get out of their canyon. "Lulu is on tour with the best show on wheels, the Moonfire Mirage. Next time they're in town, I'll take you to the show. You'll love it."

Eva looked at Dwight again, really looked at him. The weight of his years as a Dragon Knight showed in the hardened set of his gaze, but when he spoke of his daughter, there was nothing but warmth. There was no mocking edge, no superior glint. He well and truly just wanted to help.

Her chest ached as an image of her own father flashed through her mind. "You must be very proud of her."

"She's my pride and joy," he said, smiling, unintentionally twisting that knife just a little further. "You look about her age. When you go, tell the ticket master you know me. He'll give you the family discount."

Eva blinked, glancing over at Anna, momentarily speechless. She wasn't used to this—to kindness offered without a test or a reason. No trial to survive. No reputation to claw back. Just a man, a father, treating her like she belonged.

All this time, she'd been so busy proving herself to the Knights—proving she was more than a girl in a pretty dress, more than the pitied survivor of Brar—that she didn't know how to accept simple generosity. It unsettled her. And moved her.

Anna waggled her finger at him. "We'll definitely take you up on that offer. The Mirage is getting expensive as their fame rises." She pulled Eva towards him and placed her hands in the proper positions on his shoulder and in his hand. "Show the boys how a man dances."

Dwight offered Eva a youthful smile before Anna began to hum, louder now that there were more than the two of them. The Sergeant was a flawless and patient lead. While Eva danced with him, other Knights snuck in, drawn to Anna's melody. One had a guitar and strummed along to the tune.

Pairs formed awkwardly at first—young Knights stumbling through the steps—but Anna offered gentle corrections between notes. The tension Eva had carried all day slowly melted from her shoulders. When Dwight spun her, she remembered to lift her skirt and turned with practiced grace.

A light laugh escaped her lips. For once, she wasn't proving anything. She was just... dancing.

Soon, the room brimmed with Dragon Knights—waltzing, dipping, twirling to Anna's melody. Eva danced with so many partners her head spun, each one kind, respectful. Not a single sneer or jeer, not from the veterans nor the newest recruits.

She wasn't the pampered, superficial Knight they once whispered about behind her back. She had bled beside them. Risked everything for one of their own. Walked into the lion's den when no one else dared—and returned with Darius in chains.

She was now one of them.

She was home.

CHAPTER 4
SWEET LITTLE LIES

D*rip... Drip... Drip...*

Darius tipped his head back against the cold stone wall and smiled.

Not one of delight or satisfaction. No, he hadn't found that quite yet. It was the kind you wore when you were at the edge of discovery. The height of intrigue. It stretched across his face and gleamed in the dark confines of his dwelling.

The cold, biting restraints, the wind whispering between cracks in the stone, the flicker of torchlight dancing over old bloodstains. They claimed this place to be a prison, his last station. He called it his salvation. For, it was in this haven of misery and decay and hopelessness, where they allowed him to sit and ponder, to think—to *plan.*

Drip... Drip... Drip...

He'd positioned his tin cup beneath the ceiling leak, not for hydration, but for the sound. Each droplet struck like a metronome—constant, precise, inescapable. A rhythm of decay. It echoed against the stone, a reminder of those who'd lost control. But he hadn't. Not even close.

Pain was a dull teacher. Familiar. Predictable. They'd tried to impress him—bruised ribs, broken fingers, the slow pop of a fingernail lifted from the bed. He didn't scream. He *watched.* Disappointed.

If you wanted to break a man, you didn't beat his body.

You took what he could never grow back.

You took his mind.

You took what he loved. And you crushed it until there was nothing left.

The Aborians were pathetic.

Well. Not all of them.

His cunning little rider was an exception.

He wasn't angry that she'd outsmarted him. No, that would imply she'd won. It was his fault, really—he'd underestimated her. Assumed she was like the rest. Fragile. Predictable. A pretty thing that bled easily.

But she didn't break.

He had seen her fight. Watched the wheels turn behind those eyes. Watched how far she'd go to protect the things she loved.

Not far enough to kill him, though. She would regret that choice.

Because now that she chose to spare him, he was closer to her than any man in his or his father's army ever managed.

And when he escaped—and he *would* escape—she would belong to him.

Not in chains. Not in name.

In mind. In soul.

He would unmake her, one slow moment at a time.

As long as he got past *Dex*, the fucking traitor.

Dex was the one standing between them. Watching her. Grooming her. Shaping her into something dangerous—something that could be turned against their own godsdamn family. And she trusted him. *Believed* in him.

If it were any other woman, he might've thought Dex had gone soft.

But no—Dex was always the smarter one. He didn't waste time with weak things. He saw talent when it bared its teeth. And now she was his—loyal, willing, eager to impress.

All Dex had to do was give the command, and she'd obey.

Darius *envied* that.

She wouldn't follow *him* like that. Not yet. Not without breaking first. But that was the fun part.

Father believed she was too dangerous to be kept alive.

But Darius? He only needed one day.

People were easier to break than dragons. And if their souls were as tightly bound as he suspected... destroying one would unravel the other.

Let Sylus think this cell had slowed him down.

Let Dex think he was winning.

They'd all see soon enough.

Drip... Drip... Drip...

But wait... The drip was different. Footsteps fell in the same beat, growing steadily louder.

Well, well. Come to play again?

He thought they'd given up after the last session. No imagination, the lot of them. Still, he rose from the cot—a laughable excuse of mercy—and sauntered toward the bars. His body ached in familiar places, but pain was just background noise now.

Only this time, it wasn't a pair of guards. Wasn't a procession of threats or a priest with a candle and false hope.

It was a prince.

Alone.

Leon, was it? Darius could never keep the less interesting faces straight. Another polished puppet, doing what Daddy told him. Another soft-blood in velvet gloves pretending to wield a sword.

He had to give him this, though: the man didn't show a shred of fear. Not a flicker in those ocean-dark eyes. No tremble in the jaw. No sweat. No stammer.

Darius hadn't decided yet if that came from naivety or stupidity.

"Hello, little prince." His voice dripped with amusement. "Come to see the show? I'm afraid you'd be sorely disappointed. It appears your men lack the drive to break me."

The prince didn't flinch. He regarded him coolly, head lifted just a little too high. Arrogantly high.

Hands clasped behind his back. Shoulders squared. The big, ornamental sword at his hip gleamed in the torchlight—a polished accessory, only for show.

Naivety, then. It was a rookie mistake to expose the hilt like that. Darius's father would have beaten him then left him to freeze in the wicked tundra winds for leaving an opening like that.

Weakness wasn't an option when Fortys blood ran through your veins.

A gentle breeze swept through the corridor. It carried the rot and mildew of the dungeon—wet stone, old blood, piss—drifting past the prince and slipping through the tiny barred window in Darius's cell.

Leon's nose wrinkled.

Ha! The little princeling couldn't stomach the scent of his own kingdom's underbelly. If he thought this was foul, he should try standing knee-deep in a field of decay, lungs full of burning flesh and metal.

"I bet you haven't seen battle," Darius mused, voice soft like a blade sliding from its sheath. He tilted his head, watching—waiting.

There.

The prince's jaw flexed, just once. A scowl pulled at the corners of his otherwise composed expression, subtle but unmistakable. A crack in the porcelain.

Darius leaned forward slightly, eyes narrowing in delight. That was all he needed to see. It wasn't the scowl itself that intrigued him—it was what lay beneath it. Shame. Frustration. And a spark. A flame flickering feebly at risk of being smothered. A fire he suppressed.

Interesting.

The princeling had led a pampered life. Raised on duty and reputation, not dirt and pain. He wore polished boots that had never touched a muddy trench. Held a sword that had never tasted blood. But he wanted to prove himself. Darius could see it now—etched into that fleeting scowl.

The difference between them was carved in blood and experience. Darius had survived war, dismembered it, savoured it. Leon had only read about it in books, dreamt about it behind his castle walls.

A grin pulled at the edges of Darius's mouth. "Look at you. Manicured nails. Not a hair out of place. No scars. Not a single mark to prove your worth. Do your soldiers respect you? I wouldn't. Who follows a man who won't bleed beside them?"

"When the time comes, I will march with my men," the prince growled, his voice tight with insult. He planted his feet—smart boy. Any closer, and Darius might have found the opening he'd been waiting for.

"I'd be more concerned about what your people think of you," Leon continued, spine straightening with royal pride. "Your own father has abandoned you. Nobody is coming for you."

Darius waited for the other shoe to drop. Two beats passed. No blow. No twist. That was it?

A bubble of laughter escaped him—low at first, then rising like a howl. Despite the sharp ache in his ribs, he laughed hard and loud. The sound bounced off the damp stone like a taunt in itself.

"Gods!" he wheezed, clutching his side. "You're pathetic. You think you can come down here and intimidate me, boy? Renkon better have more sons he can pass the crown down to, or Aboria's future is fucked." He took a few steps closer to the bars, shoulders loose, smile tight with venom. "Where are your balls? If you want to lead your kingdom, you're going to have to dig real deep for them."

The prince shifted his weight, arms folding across his chest. The stance was practiced—measured. He didn't bristle. Didn't blink.

Darius hated that. It meant he couldn't read him.

Men who raged were easy. They cracked.

Men who cowered were easier still. They broke.

But men like this? Who stood firm with cold silence and eyes that gave away nothing? They were either too stupid to see the danger... Or too dangerous to provoke.

"You think Sylus left me here to rot?" Darius snarled, heat rising under his skin. "No. I don't need my daddy to fight my battles. He knows I can take care of myself."

The prince didn't flinch.

But his gaze flicked—just once—off to the side, a minute crack in the veneer. Then it was back, sharper than before. He stood straighter, prouder, the ghost of a smirk dancing behind his eyes like a threat wrapped in silk.

"I didn't come down here to exchange blows," the prince said coolly.

Darius cocked his head, lips curling into a grin that didn't reach his eyes.

"Then what *did* you come down here for?" he purred, batting his lashes, his voice smooth and coaxing, like a viper poised to strike. "Lonely, are we? Trying to make a new friend?"

"We've set an execution date," the prince said bluntly.

No flicker of triumph in his tone. No rage. No remorse. Just that same unreadable, noble-bred mask. No cracks to wedge a knife into.

Darius didn't blink.

Huh.

They were actually going to go through with it.

No trial. No smug announcement. Just a quiet little death scheduled like a dinner meeting.

"What? No trial?" he asked, mockingly aghast. "And here I thought you Aborians were all pure of heart and bound by justice. Your ancestors must be rolling in their graves."

"You're an extenuating circumstance," the prince said. "Everyone in court agrees that your crimes alone justify your execution."

Darius stepped forward slowly, curling his fingers around the bars. Cool iron met callused skin. He leaned in, letting the shadows stretch across his face—less man, more monster. Let the boy see what waited on the other side of order and law.

The prince didn't flinch. But he stepped back.

Not stupid, then. Not brave, either. Just... trained.

"So? What will it be?" Darius prodded, voice silky with malice. "Hanging? Decapitation? Or maybe something a little more *fitting*—like burning me at the stake? Would you consider boiling me alive?" He chuckled, low and fond, thinking back to all the times he sat and listened to the screams, the *begging*, as his toys melted in the pot. That would be ironic, wouldn't it? Given that was his favourite method of execution.

Finally, the mask cracked.

The prince stared at him, aghast, horror bleeding through the cracks in his polished composure. "Do you not value your own life? I just told you you're going to die... and you're eager for the details?"

Darius tilted his head, as if considering the question. His grin stayed sharp, but his mind turned, fast and deliberate beneath the surface.

He *did* value his life. He valued it enough not to waste time pretending fear would save it.

"We'll see if the execution really happens," he said, with a smile that didn't quite touch his eyes. "There are still a few things I have left to do in Aboria."

Disgust painted on the prince's features, twisting his perfectly sculpted face into a mirage of hate. "No one is coming to save you, Darius," he said tightly. "The only time you'll leave this cell is when you're escorted to the chopping block."

Darius leaned his weight into the bars, lowering his voice to something dark and reverent. "I told you," he murmured, "I don't need saving." Then, with a slow, poisonous grin: "The storm dragon rider will be mine."

That fire flared in the prince's eyes. He advanced, gripping the hilt of his sword.

Ah, there it is. Finally. He'd plucked the right string—grinded back the polish to glimpse the man beneath the crown. The fury behind the calm. Darius drank it in like wine.

"You'll never have Eva. After what you did to her family, I only regret that the laws of war are too kind."

Darius laughed, grinning ear to ear. "There's only one way to ensure I suffer, princeling. You have to be the one to deliver the final blow—if you're man enough to get blood on your hands."

The prince ground his jaw. He stood in silence, chest heaving, desperately searching for a response. Darius waited, savoring the quiet fury. Watching how close the boy came to stepping over the line. But he didn't.

When Leon found no words, he turned on his heel and walked away.

Darius laughed at his receding figure. "That's right, boy. Run straight back to your daddy!"

Silence rang through the dungeon. He was alone once again.

The echoes of their scuffle still lingered—bruised into his ribs, scraped into his pride. He sat back in the cot, letting the ache settle like a second skin. Cold stone pressed against his spine as he leaned his head against the wall.

Drip... drip... drip...

The rhythmic sound gnawed at him. Reminding him that the clock was ticking. His time was running out.

He hadn't thought they'd actually go through with it. Execution without trial. No pomp, no declaration. Just silence and the blade. The Aborians—spineless fools—had suddenly decided to grow teeth.

A miscalculation on his behalf.

He closed his eyes for a moment and let the pain pulse in the dark. It sharpened his focus. He'd waited, believing an opportunity would present itself. A weakness. A crack in their defenses. But if they were truly ready to kill him, that window was closing fast.

It looks like I need to move up my timeline.

The thought wasn't laced with panic—no, Darius didn't panic. He adapted. That's why he would be king.

But this... this confinement grated against something primal in him. Not the walls. Not the pain. The *inactivity*. The longer he stayed here, the more time his father's assassins had to find the rider. *His* rider. Snatch his birthright from his hands.

Estrus was slipping.

And that... that he could not allow.

Some time later, a guard came by with a tray of food. He knelt before the bars, head bowed, fist planted on the stone. How one would bow to his king in Estrus. A soldier's vow of loyalty.

Darius remained still, but something flickered in his chest.

The man's voice was taut. "My lord, do I have your word that my family will be unharmed?" His accent was Aborian, heavier with a bit of country twang he'd grown accustomed to hearing out here, yet he spoke to Darius with the familiarity of one of his people.

Darius tilted his head and smiled, slow and predatory.

"Not my word," he said easily. "I'm locked up in this cage, remember? I hold no power beyond these walls." His smile stretched. "But if Keyon made you a promise, then you have *his* word."

And Keyon does not fail me.

Even now, his second was moving pieces. That was why Darius had chosen him—not for loyalty, but for loyalty paired with *competence*. Keyon was ruthless, reliable, and completely unconcerned with morality. A man like that didn't hesitate. He acted.

The guard lifted his eyes, still trembling. "Then I will do as you ask, my lord. As long as my family is safe, I will lay down my life for you."

Darius's grin lingered as the man stood and walked away.

Well done, Keyon.

The seed had been planted. Soon, it would bloom.

He leaned back again and closed his eyes, letting the darkness press in.

They thought they could kill him like a dog in the dark. But they didn't understand. He wasn't a beast caught in a trap—*he* was the trap.

He just needed them to step closer.

"Look out, little rider," he murmured in the sweet, velvety darkness. "I'm coming for you. And this time..." His lips curled. "You'll bow to me."

CHAPTER 5
THEY WILL BE REMEMBERED

Eva stood in front of the bathroom mirror, fingers tangled in her hair as she tried to coerce the long ashen tresses into a new style other women on the base had suggested.

Most of them cut their hair short, in cute bobs or pixie cuts, to avoid the hassle of standing in front of a mirror for twenty minutes with a brush, cramping fingers, and ribbon waiting to tie it all together. But Eva refused to cut hers.

After spending most of her life in her brother's hand-me-downs, more worried about feeding her family than how to wear her hair, she'd learned to appreciate the art of a simple braid. Of tugging a few strands loose to frame her face.

Here, she had the luxury of exploring her femininity—while also learning how to be a badass, dragon-riding, storm-wielding Soul Bound with the power to protect the ones she loved.

She was in the middle of pinning the braid to her scalp when a knock came at the door.

Anna took one look at her and her unfinished hair from the couch, set her book down on the table, then skipped to the door.

"Jacob!" An easy smile pulled on her cheeks as she leaned on the doorframe, arms folding across her chest. Silver eyes trailed over his form, clad in riding pants, an under armour shirt, and a standard dragon scale jacket. "You look good today."

He scratched the back of his head, bashful. "Um, thanks. You look..." He took in her light cotton pants and crop top, then flushed a bright red. Being Bound to Aster, Anna never got cold and could wear summer clothes in the winter while everyone else had to bundle up. "...comfortable."

Anna's shoulders slumped, but Jacob didn't notice. His gaze was already moving to Eva. "I have been given a specific list of instructions and collecting you is one of them."

"Me?" Intrigued, Eva gave up with her hair and left it to fall down her back in a messy braid when she approached him. "Where did these instructions come from?"

Jacob brandished a letter. “Leo. He wants to meet us in Riverwood.”
Anna stepped aside to let Eva through, winking as she did. “Better not keep the prince waiting. We'll spar when you come back.”
Eva grabbed her scale jacket and followed Jacob into the hallway. She snatched the letter out of his hands and read Leo’s specific instructions:

Private Jacob Greene,

These instructions are to be carried out immediately upon reading them:

Drop everything you have planned today. I have a surprise for you

Find your lovely sister

Meet me in the Roaring River Inn in Riverwood

Dress for the weather. We're going on a trek

If you do not comply, I have no qualms bribing Dragon Knights to bring you both here by force.

Your dear friend,

Leonidas Kain

Giggling, she gave the letter back to her brother. She was glad she wasn't the only one who received demanding letters from their prince. "Do you have any idea what this surprise is?"

"None." Jacob scowled.

Eva was overly familiar with that scowl. "You don't approve?"

"It's the last part I don't like. I'm not sure going for a 'trek' is a good idea right now. I hope he cleared this with Commander Hargin."

"I'm sure he did. Besides, we'll have Arkon and Glade with us."

Assuming Arkon would be willing to fly her to Riverwood. He had been silent the last few days and she hoped she hadn't crossed a line with him by accepting Grayson's promise. It had kept her up at night and left her stomach churning over and over. As requested, she kept her distance from Grayson, but she couldn't keep it up for long. At some point, they were going to have to come to some happy medium.

"*I am here, Little One,*" he murmured in her thoughts. His voice sounded distant, as if their time apart had weakened their Bond. "*I will fly you to Riverwood. I long to share the skies with you again.*"

"*Me too... I'm sorry about Grayson.*" She wasn't sorry for caring about him, but she was sorry that the one man she cared about ended up being the one who killed his kin.

"*I know. I also know it is wrong for me to deny your feelings for him. Later we can discuss boundaries, but for now, I merely wish to fly.*"

She could work with that.

When they arrived at the Stables, Arkon and Glade were already waiting near the tack room. Arkon's impressive form filled most of the designated loading spot, leaving Glade only a small section to stretch out her wings. His crackling aura seeped into every corner of the space, filling both the smallest crevices and the largest openings; the other dragons and Knights watched him from afar. They weren't as wary as before, no longer waiting for him to smite them with lightning, but tension still hung in the air, like pressure in the sky before a storm.

Glade lowered her head to them in greeting. "Good morning, Reckless One—Little One."

Eva sniggered at the name Glade had given Jacob. So fitting yet given in a place of love, not resentment. She brushed her fingers over the bronze scales around her snout then turned to Arkon, apprehension tugging at her heart.

Sensing her hesitation, he lowered his head, pressing the tip of his snout into her chest. His warmth billowed around her, cocooning her in his love and protection. "*I have informed Glade of our orders. Are you ready to fly, Little One?*"

"*With you? Always.*"

Once the dragons were saddled, they leapt out of the stables and headed east for Riverwood. Eva eased back in the saddle and let her legs do all the work while she relished the wind in her hair. She had shared the saddle with Anna, but it was nowhere near the same as being one with her dragon bound in the sky. She was *meant* to be here, settled right between his wings.

His mind melded with hers, letting her feel the relief of being with her once again.

Once they were out of the canyon, Arkon sped past Glade and stretched his wings out to their fullest. He flew circles around Glade, pushing his and Eva's muscles in ways nothing else could as the wind threatened to tear her from his back. Eva encouraged him, flattening herself against him and leaning into each turn. This was the true advantage of being soul bound; regular dragon-Knight pairings couldn't perform manoeuvres like this. It required coordination that only those whose minds and souls were bound together could pull off.

By the time they landed on the shores of Riverwood, a thin sheen of sweat clung to her skin, and, despite the fall chill, she slipped off her jacket and tied it around her waist.

Tents were scattered across the river's opposite bank—so many white domes, so many lives uprooted by one man's greed. Yet even amid the hardship, children darted between tents, their laughter carrying over the roar of the river. Smoke curled from a few lit fires, warming the makeshift homes within.

She'd heard whispers in the hallways that the refugees were slowly being resettled in Riverwood, and in other villages less ravaged by the war. The once small town had grown thrice in size, the heart of it made of stone while its body swelled into tents and makeshift structures.

Her heart ached for them. She'd lost everything, everyone she loved—but she'd also found something new: a place to call home, a family that was just as messy as her old one, and just as strong. She hoped the refugees found peace among the chaos of their uprooted lives.

She turned to Arkon and rested a hand on his snout, just between his nostrils. "I'll be back in a little bit. I'm not sure what Leo has planned for us."

"We will be here."

Glade made herself comfortable on the grassy, saturated shores, curling her tail around her entire body. Arkon took off into the sky to keep watch over the city.

Eva followed Jacob down the path, the crunch of gravel beneath their boots gradually giving way to the sharper clack of stone. Dusty tents flanked the road at first, faded canvas fluttering in the morning breeze. Then came squat stone cottages, their windows propped open with crooked shutters and smoke wending from chimneys. As they pressed deeper into the city, the buildings grew taller, the streets narrower. Wooden signs creaked above bustling shopfronts—bakeries, apothecaries, tailors—while the scent of fresh bread and spiced soap mingled in the air. Above each storefront, laundry lines stretched between windows, the homes above alive with laughter, arguments, and the clatter of daily life.

A sense of dread filled her stomach. The last time she had been here, Leo told her Grayson was in fact Deximus Arkayn Fortys, the Slayer of Souls. Her life—and heart—had been flipped upside down. What did he have planned for her this time?

Sensing her nerves, Jacob threw a mischievous grin her way and bumped her with his hip. "You know, it's been forever since we've had some sibling time. Depending on what Leo wants, what do you say we grab dinner here afterwards?"

She leaned into his side, gripping his arm. "I would love that."

Gods, it really had been too long since they'd had the chance to sit down and just talk.

They used to do it all the time before he became a Dragon Knight—lounging in the meadows behind the old barn, sitting by the riverbank with their feet in the water, or watching stars flicker above Brar's hills. They'd spill their hearts out, share the petty details of their day, or dream up lives far bigger than the borders of their hometown.

It had been a simpler time in Brar.

A pang of homesickness pressed against her ribs.

Needing a distraction, Eva bumped her shoulder gently against his. "For future reference, it does not count as a compliment when you tell a woman she looks *comfortable*."

Jacob stumbled on a loose cobblestone, then went a deep, deep red. "I, uh... Are you giving me advice on women?"

"You're in dire need of it."

He rolled his shoulders back and lifted his chin with a wounded sort of dignity. "I am not. I know what I'm doing."

She snorted as they passed a bakery window filled with braided loaves and powdered tarts. "You told Anna she looked comfortable."

"She did! There's nothing sexier than a woman comfortable in her own skin—or the clothes she wears."

Eva paused mid-laugh and looked at her big brother. "Huh. That's actually... not bad."

Jacob rolled his eyes. "See? Your big brother knows what he's doing... What Anna and I have is delicate. I don't want to ruin what we have by being too forward. She gets hit on all the time and I don't want to be 'just another guy' to her. I want to be *the* guy, you know? She's strong and doesn't need a man to tell her she's beautiful and smart and talented, but I want to be there for her if she ever does need anybody."

Eva squeezed his arm. Maybe he wasn't as hopeless as she thought he was. He just needed to find the courage to say these things to the woman he had a crush on. "That's really sweet."

"You think so? Do you think Anna would like it if I told her that?"

"Definitely."

He grinned. "Good." He kissed the top of her head. "I love you, Eva."

"I love you too, Jake."

They walked in silence through the city. Riverwood was bigger than Lensenton, but not nearly as tidy. The once-pristine white stone walls were now smudged with dirt and moss, the roads chipped in places where cart wheels or careless boots had struck. Splintered crates leaned against alleyways, and torn linen hung like tired flags from shuttered windows. The cobbled roads were worn smooth by the constant shuffle of boots and hooves, the stones uneven and muddied by the afternoon rain. Puddles mirrored the cloudy sky above, rippling as people passed through them without care.

Eva wrinkled her nose as a sharp, earthy scent hit her nose—manure, mold, and the sour tang of spoiled fruit from a nearby cart. She didn't remember it looking like this when she visited as a child. Back then, the roads had seemed wider, cleaner. The houses had gleamed under the sun. Now, the city bore the weight of too many people and not enough space.

Still, despite the clutter and the crowding, the city *breathed*. Merchants called out over the din, voices thick with a familiar Eastern Aborian accent and charm. Children dashed barefoot through the puddles, laughing as if the world wasn't teetering on the edge. Someone strummed a lute near a corner tavern, and the smell of roasted meat drifted on the wind.

Riverwood was doing the best it could with what it had—and somehow, the people seemed content with its efforts.

Jacob directed her toward the Roaring River Inn. The moment it came into view, her chest tightened. Her steps faltered, breath hitching, like she'd hit a wall.

The crooked sign creaked in the wind—just like the last time she had come here. The same warped doorway, the same chipped windows staring back at her. Butterflies invaded her stomach.

It was right under that very sign where she'd kissed Grayson for the first time. She hadn't known who he was then, that it was *his* family who thirsted for her power. She hadn't known just how complicated things would get between them. Then, she'd just been a girl drawn to his raw strength, swept up in the gravity of his presence, seduced by the certainty in those storm-cloud eyes. In his arms, she'd felt untouchable.

Now... she wasn't sure what they were. What *he* was, beneath the layers of secrets and silence. If there was anything more between them than lies and distrust.

She blinked hard, forcing air through her nose. In, out. Just a building. Just a door. Leo was just beyond the threshold. All she had to do was *cross* it.

Jacob noted her hesitation, pouted, then returned to her side, looping his arm through hers. “I don't know about you, but I've worked up an appetite flying here. What are the chances that Leo will have plates of food ready for us?”

Just like that, Eva smiled up at him forever grateful for her big brother. He knew what she needed when she needed it. Never let her dwelled on her thoughts too long and knew just what to say to snap her out of it. The air still sat heavy in her lungs, but Jacob's warmth was real, his arm steady and familiar. “Knowing Leo, he's ordered everything on the menu.”

Offering a small encouraging smile, Jacob opened the inn door.

Leo was easy to spot in the rowdy tavern. From the fine embroidery on his cloak to the polished leather of his shoes, it could only be him. There weren't too many wealthy—*not his kind of wealthy*—people in this town who would wear those kinds of shoes this far from the capital. Most wore boots, better suited for Riverwood's muddy streets.

And then there was the tea. He had to be the only one drinking it. People didn't drink *tea* here.

He was chatting with the barkeep, completely enthralled by the tale he was weaving. Eva and Jacob exchanged a glance—noticing something very important was missing.

Leo turned at the sound of new arrivals and beamed when he saw the Greenes. He abandoned his tea and crossed the room with open arms, clapping Jacob firmly on the back before moving to Eva and giving her a gentle kiss on the cheek.

“Welcome. I'm impressed, you arrived sooner than I expected. You must miss my charming company. Would you like some tea before departing? It's chilly out today.” He cast a pointed look at Eva, who hadn't bothered to put her jacket back on. She was still hot from the ride here.

Jacob's arms folded across his chest, not falling for the princely charm in the slightest. “Where are your guards, Leo?”

“Hmm?" Leo turned back to the bar, lifting his teacup for a casual sip. Eva didn't miss that he cleverly averted his gaze from them.

Jacob crossed his arms, foot tapping on the hardwood floor. For once, Eva wasn't on the receiving end of the Big Brother look.

Rolling his eyes, Leo turned to them, leaning an elbow back on the bar. "I don't *need* them, Jacob. Riverwood is surrounded by soldiers. I'm perfectly safe here—especially now that I have two Dragon Knights watching over me." He winked at Eva, which, try as he might, didn't help his case. At all. He could be as charming as a fox, but she wouldn't let him get away with being a complete and utter numbskull.

Eva stepped closer, scanning the room for anyone who could come across as a guard. She'd settle for an undercover one if it meant he'd taken the proper precautions. "What about your escort here? It's a three-day ride. Don't tell me you came all this way *alone*."

Leo shrugged, far too casual for her liking. "I decided not to use one. I'm perfectly capable of defending myself."

Eva said nothing, her eyes narrowing as she studied the casually reckless prince in front of her. The weight of the situation pressed heavily on her chest.

What did he think he was doing, tossing caution aside like it was some inconvenient trinket? He was the Crowned Prince, for gods' sake! If anything happened to him, Aboria's future could crumble.

Jacob's hands tangled in his hair, his eyes squeezing shut in frustration. "Are you out of your *mind*? Did King Renkon approve this?"

"My father knows where I am," Leo said breezily, his tone betraying pride, but there was something stubborn simmering beneath it.

Then, Jacob did something Eva didn't expect: he *slapped* the back of Leo's head. "You're an idiot, Leo. I'm taking you back to Lexxis."

Leo set his teacup down and fixed Jacob with a stubborn glare. "I didn't bring you here to argue. I have a surprise for both of you—if you're willing to take me there."

Jacob put his hands on his hips. "Take you where?"

"To Brar. Or, where it used to be."

A jolt ran down Eva's spine, memories flashing through her mind: hunting, Erika dancing around a bonfire, the scent of freshly made bread. And then the screams. The smoke. Buildings reduced to ash.

"Why do you want to go there?" she asked, trying to keep her voice steady.

"That's where my surprise is."

She wasn't sure she was ready to return. There were too many memories—good ones, tainted by the bad. "Leo... I appreciate—"

He took her hands, holding them firmly. His sympathetic yet resolute gaze met hers, and the tightness in her chest abated. She didn't know what it was about him—she should be furious that he'd come here *alone* or anxious about returning to Brar—but that look, the strength in his hands, let it all slip away. "I know this may be difficult for you, but I promise it's worth it. Do you trust me?"

"Yes." The word came out before she could second-guess herself. It wasn't something she had to think about. She trusted him. He had made it easy from the start and never gave her a reason to doubt him.

A small smile tugged at the corner of his mouth. He dropped one of her hands and laced the remaining one with his. "If you take me to Brar, you won't regret it."

Eva and Jacob exchanged a look, that old sibling telepathy sparking to life despite years of disuse. Leo was on a mission, that much was clear, and it would be better to stay close than try to rein him in.

Jacob sighed, resigned but not entirely displeased. "Fine. We'll take you. But you're flying with *me*." He stepped between them and gently nudged Eva toward the door. "Eva is an inexperienced rider and shouldn't be burdened by passengers."

Eva rolled her eyes. That was an excuse if she'd ever heard one.

She flicked a piece of lint off her shoulder. "I don't have a problem giving Leo a ride."

Leo slid her a sultry look, unabashedly raking in the form-fitting riding pants and long sleeved under armour shirt, and winked. "I have no qualms against it either."

Eva realised what she had said too late and flushed, her skin burning with embarrassment. She hurried out onto the street before she could dig herself a deeper hole. Jacob was *never* going to leave them unattended.

Arkon and Glade were waiting for them right where they had left them. Leo halted in front of the dragons, tipping his head all the way back to take in their majesty. A twinge of nostalgia wrapped around her, reminding her of a time not too long ago when she marvelled at the sight of a dragon.

Eva sidled up to Leo and gestured grandly toward her beautiful, mighty dragon. "Leo, this is my Dragon Bound, Arkon."

Arkon lowered his colossal head to Leo's level, his bright blue eyes gleaming with an intimidating calm. Leo didn't move an inch, though a flicker of uncertainty crossed his face, as if unsure whether to reach out or stand his ground. "It is a pleasure to officially meet you, Prince Leonidas. Eva thinks very highly of you."

"*Arkon!*" Eva screamed down the Bond, her voice laced with mortification. She didn't think it was possible to be more embarrassed than she already was—but here she was.

Leo's gaze slid to Eva, a heated curiosity simmering in his eyes. His lips curled into a slow, knowing smile, the kind that made her insides flutter. He looked back at Arkon with a playful glint in his eyes. "I think very highly of your rider as well."

Eva's heart skipped, but she was too mortified to think about anything other than focusing on the awkward beat of silence that followed. Jacob noticed, his eyes narrowing with that familiar, protective glimmer as he clapped a hand firmly on Leo's shoulder, pulling him toward Glade. "That's enough introductions. You've already met Glade. Let's get moving."

Jacob climbed easily into Glade's saddle, settling in with the ease of someone who'd done it a thousand times. He looked down at Leo expectantly, one brow raised.

Leo turned his attention to Glade and studied the dragon's size with mild skepticism, his arms crossed. "Right," he muttered. "Just... jump, grab the elbow joint, and swing up. Can't be that hard."

He took a few confident steps back, squared his shoulders like a man preparing for a duel, then ran, leaping—

His boot met slick scales, and instead of gripping, it skidded.

With a loud *thud*, followed by a soft *oof*, Leo landed squarely on his back on the gravel, arms sprawled like a starfish.

Eva bit back a laugh, not very successfully, and bent to help him up. "Smooth."

Leo took her hand, brushing off his coat and dignity in one go. "Glade moved," he said solemnly. "I was sabotaged."

Smoke curled from Glade's snout, but she chose to take the higher route and only toss her head back indignantly in answer.

Jacob brushed his fingers over her bristling scales. "She didn't move. You just have the upper body strength of a bard."

"Bards are incredibly fit," Leo muttered, cheeks glowing pink. "All that lute-carrying, dancing, and singing."

Eva shook her head and took pity on him, brushing off the stray gravel clinging to his shoulder. "It's okay. Everyone fumbles on their first try."

"*You hadn't*," Arkon reminded her proudly.

She winced. "*But he doesn't need to know that—or how highly I think of him.*"

Leo dusted himself off, a timid smile on his lips when he looked at her, having no idea they were secretly talking about him.

"*But it's the truth. If you are going to mate with a male, I would rather it be the prince than the slayer.*"

Eva swung his way and threw a fully fledged glare at him. "*We are* not *talking about this right now.*"

"*Agreed.*" Arkon pumped his wings once, blasting the clearing with a gust of wind that sent leaves flying and ruffled everyone's hair. He turned his gaze toward Leo. "*Quick, watch, before you miss your prince mounting a dragon for the first time.*"

Eva turned just in time to catch Leo making his second attempt at the saddle. This time, he made it. Barely. It was a clumsy, ungraceful scramble involving knees, elbows, and an unprincely grunt she wouldn't share with anyone.

He looked like a right fool.

And yet, he wore it well.

There was something endearing in how he brushed it off with a crooked smile, as if daring anyone to call him out. She found herself smiling before she could stop it. She liked this side of him—unpolished, unfazed, unafraid to be ridiculous.

Leo caught her watching and winked.

She rolled her eyes, then swung up onto Arkon in one clean, fluid motion—a perfect, practiced mount. The kind that made the rest of them look like they were climbing furniture in a tavern brawl.

Leo scowled up at her with mock offense. "You don't have to make it look *so* easy. Would it kill you to pretend to struggle just a little?"

She smirked. "Just wait until you see my dismount."

Jacob grumbled under his breath, then gave Leo a firm shove forward. "Hold tight, Prince. The ascent's the hardest part."

Leo obeyed, gripping the handles Jacob pointed out with a touch more seriousness than usual. Glade spread her wings wide, gave two powerful beats, and launched them into the sky. Arkon followed a heartbeat later, riding the air currents high.

A sound escaped Leo—half squeal, half war cry. A *very* manly one, of course. She'd let him believe that if he ever brought it up. Jacob's unfiltered laughter echoed through the open air behind them.

Arkon's gaze stayed fixed on Glade, his eyes sharp and calculating as he studied the rhythm of her wingbeats. "*Wouldn't it have made more sense for me to carry the prince? I am larger and can bear the extra weight.*"

Eva sighed, fully aware. "*Jacob's big brotherly instincts refuse to let any man near me.*"

Arkon growled, the sensation running down the entire length of his body and reverberating through her legs. "*Glade should not have to suffer because he doesn't like that the prince fancies you. Leonidas will ride back with us.*"

Eva grinned. Not just because ruffling Jacob's feathers was always worth the trouble, but because she wanted to ride with Leo and bask in the world below with him.

A familiar nook in the valley came into view just as Leo gave the order to land. They descended toward a small clearing near the main road that threaded through the valley floor, linking the scattered villages to the open plains beyond.

Arkon lifted off the moment Eva's boots hit the earth, his shadow sweeping over the canopy as he soared above the treetops, ever watchful. Her stomach twisted as she scanned the trees, the scent of pine and damp earth tugging at old memories.

King Sylus's army had been pushed back to Estrus after Darius's fort fell—but not all had made it out. For all King Renkon's efforts to flush them out, it would be naïve to believe none had slipped through the cracks.

In a few small steps, they were on the main road, heading North East towards Brar. The road was more accessible since Eva had last used it. Before, it had been more of a trail, flattened only by heavy carts. Now, gravel carved the path and levelled out the roots and holes.

Where it was once empty—barren for miles—there was now a wagon trundling along just ahead, and several travelers far in the distance, mere blurs only her dragon vision could pick out. So many people. She hadn't seen this kind of traffic here before.

Leo walked between the Greenes, failing spectacularly to mask his excitement. His grin tugged at his cheeks, and a spring lightened his step. He did most of the talking—light banter, passing observations, the occasional jest—while Eva and Jacob remained quieter, eyes scanning the forest around them. Partly for nostalgia's sake, and partly to compensate for their prince, who was being far too casual for someone strolling through what had recently been enemy territory.

The forest felt different now.

When she and Grayson had passed through here before, it had been quiet. Breathing in its last remnants of life. But now, there was movement again. Birds flitted between trees. Squirrels darted across the path, cheeks bulging with whatever they could scavenge before winter set in. The air smelled of damp bark and cold earth. Not as vibrant as she remembered from childhood, but it was something.

It was healing.

They reached a bend in the road. Just around the curve, she knew, was a straight shot to Brar.

Or rather, what remained of it.

A wave of dreading anticipation rolled in her stomach, sharp and sudden. She wasn't sure she was ready to face it again—to look directly at what Darius had done to her home again. Her fingers curled into fists at her sides, breath catching just slightly.

Leo stopped walking.

He clapped his hands together once, then held them between his palms as he turned to face them. The Greenes paused, surprised by the sudden shift in his tone. The playful ease had vanished, replaced by a rare seriousness. The furrow in his brow deepened. His lapis lazuli eyes were clear and focused, brimming with something that felt achingly sincere.

"I need to say this before we go any further," he began. "I respect you both. Wholly. You're more than just allies to the crown—you're friends. Friends I trust implicitly. This gift I'm giving you... it isn't a reward or some hollow gesture from the throne. It's an act of friendship. Of loyalty. Nothing more, nothing less."

Jacob tossed him a perplexed scowl. "Okay?"

What else was one supposed to say when a prince declared his friendship like that?

Eva didn't know what to make of it either. Her mind raced with all the things he could have possibly done—because when a prince wanted to leave an impression, his power was near limitless.

Leo just grinned, then turned and led them around the corner.

Eva's breath caught in her throat.

Brar... had transformed. Again. For the third time in mere months.

The remnants of Darius's sorry excuse for a fort—reduced to rubble by their powerful dragons—had been cleared away entirely. In its place stood proud, newly built walls of stone, mined from the very mountains that surrounded them, smooth and strong, crafted with care and precision. They stretched wider than before, encompassing the full breadth of what had once been Brar—and more. The pond, the meadow, all of it now sat safely within the fortified perimeter.

The gates stood open, having just admitted the wagon ahead of them.

Eva caught a glimpse inside—and gasped.

"What is this, Leo?" Jacob asked, his voice quieter now.

Leo only smiled and gestured them forward. "Come inside."

The guards at the gate snapped to attention. "Your Highness! We weren't expecting an inspection so soon—"

Leo waved a hand, easy and calm. "This isn't an inspection. Let these good men continue their work uninterrupted."

The guard nodded, then stepped aside. "Welcome to the fort, Prince Leonidas."

They passed through.

It wasn't finished. Not even close.

Tents dotted the landscape, acting as temporary quarters for the builders. Markers and stakes outlined the framework of what would soon become roads, barracks, a mess hall, even housing. So many buildings—far more than Brar had ever held. It was all neatly arranged, designed with care, not thrown together haphazardly.

It was a colossal undertaking. But the workers moved with purpose, undeterred by the magnitude of what they were building. They were building something new. Something better.

Eva's boots slowed on the gravel. Her gaze swept across the open grounds, past the tent rows and partially constructed walls. She had braced herself for another memory—a flash of pain, a hint of smoke, the weight of the world pressing down on her—but what she found here was something entirely different.

Hope.

Leo said nothing, only led them farther in, toward the heart of the site. There, standing proud at the centre of the growing fort, was a marble monolith. It rose tall like a tree that had stood there for centuries—only it was perfectly squared, polished, and pale.

Eva's breath caught.

It didn't belong in the middle of a forest, and yet... it blended in. Off-white, flecked with soft grey. Quietly noble.

She stepped closer. Her fingers lifted, almost hesitant, then found the smooth, cool stone. The carved letters beneath her touch stole her breath.

Names.

Dozens. Hundreds.

A lump formed in her throat. She read them in silence.

Every name carved into the stone belonged to someone she had known. Someone from Brar. People she had laughed with, fought beside, grown up around. People she had grieved.

Her hand trembled.

It was a memorial. A promise that they wouldn't be forgotten.

The war had taken their lives, but this place was being built on the foundation of their memory. Not erased. Not paved over. Honoured.

Tears pricked her eyes, and she didn't try to blink them away.

For the first time since Brar burned, she let herself breathe.

"Eva..." Jacob's voice cracked like dry bark on the other side of the pillar.

She hadn't realised he had moved to read the names too.

Rounding the corner, she found him standing motionless, his face streaked with tears. He reached for her, catching her arm, and pulled her into a fierce hug.

Confused, she twisted in his hold to see what had shaken him.

Emily Andrea Greene

Hayden Jonathan Greene

Erika Greene

Her breath hitched. Old wounds split open anew, raw and bleeding. She clutched at her chest, as if her hand alone could soften the searing pain in her heart.

Jacob wordlessly pulled her back, anchoring her in his arms. She tried to be brave—for him, for herself—but the composure slipped through her fingers like water. The tears came anyway, hot and silent, soaking his shirt.

A warm presence pressed gently into her thoughts, wrapping around her like a cloak. "*They will be remembered*," Arkon murmured somberly in her mind. "*Always. In your heart, in Jacob's, in mine—and now, forever, in this fort.*"

A shuddering breath left her lungs. Somehow, it didn't feel quite so heavy anymore. They weren't carrying this alone. Not anymore. Even long after they were gone, the names would remain, etched in stone. A reminder to the world who used to sow this soil.

Leo stepped up beside them and gently laid a hand on each of their shoulders. "I personally went through the archives and found the names of every man, woman, and child who lived in Brar at the time of its fall..." His voice was quiet, cautious. "I hope I didn't overstep—"

Eva stepped out of Jacob's arms and wrapped her own around Leo, cutting him off.

"Thank you," she whispered. The words felt too small for what she meant. This wasn't just a gesture. It was a sanctuary for their memories. A place of peace and healing rather than fear and pain. "You didn't overstep."

He returned the embrace, dipping his head into the crook of her neck. "I can't undo what happened," he said softly, "and I can't bring your people back. But I *can* build something that protects others—something that turns this place into a shield instead of a scar."

He stepped back, cupping her face with careful hands. There was no flirtation in his eyes. No posturing. Only compassion. Just the unwavering respect of a man who might not have felt the ache of loss before, but *understood* it.

"I handpicked the soldiers who'll be stationed here," Leo continued. "They'll help the valley villages rebuild and guard them with their lives." Then he looked between them, a quiet hope rising in his voice. "I was thinking... maybe you two could help me name the fort." A pause. "What do you think of Greene Wood?"

Jacob wiped his face with his sleeve and drew a deep, steadying breath. He looked at Eva, as emotionally drained as she felt, but a faint smile tugged at his lips. "We don't need a fort named after us, Leo. Let it keep to its roots. Our father used to say that *Brar* means *to bear* or *endure* in the old tongue. That's what the people of Brar have always done. What this fort will do in their name. What Eva and I will always do."

Leo clasped his shoulder with quiet affection, then turned to her. "Eva?"

She nodded, reaching for both of their hands. "I couldn't have said it better myself."

Leo inclined his head. "Then it's settled." He turned to the monolith, voice solemn yet proud. "Let Fort Brar stand, a place of strength, a haven for all who seek shelter—and a testament to those who endured."

CHAPTER 6

PATIENCE IS A VIRTUE, JEALOUSY IS A SIN

Clenching and unclenching his fists, Grayson lurked in the hallway, staring at the door in front of him, like an idiot. Jacob had told him to be patient, to not worry about Eva. She'd come around eventually. All he had to do was spend time with her and buy her cupcakes. Patience wasn't exactly one of his strengths, but if that was what Eva needed, he would wait. In the meantime, if buying her cupcakes would help assuage the turbulent tides of their relationship, he'd buy out an entire bakery for her.

He had more than a Dragon Knight's salary to fill his coin pouch; he had Sylus's gold. A lot of it. He stole as much as could carry when he raided one of his stash houses along the coast of Estrus. Gold, jewelry, raw mithril, gems—whatever he could fit into his pockets—then sold it in Aboria at non-descript locations. He'd gladly spend it all if it would help regain Eva's trust.

He couldn't think of a better time to make amends than while Jacob was away on whatever errand Leo had called him to do.

"*If you stand there any longer, you'll turn to stone,*" Eran remarked, amusement marring his tone.

Growling, Grayson shoved him out of his mind and knocked on the door before he could delay things further. The sooner he and Eva made up, the better. For him, for his soul.

He waited two solid minutes...

No answer.

He tapped his knuckles on the door again.

Silence.

With his dragon vision, he peered through the door. No silhouettes. Neither of the girls were home. He'd been loitering in the hallway like an awkward, indecisive pubescent for nothing.

A funny feeling played with Grayson's stomach. One he recognised as relief, but the other... it was unpleasant and left him uneasy, hollow.

"*That, I believe, is what humans call 'disappointment', my dear rider.*"

Apparently, he hadn't been thorough in shutting out his dragon.

Grayson immediately removed himself from the hallway and headed for the training rooms. It was the most logical place for the girls to be.

"I've been disappointed. This is not it."

"You haven't been disappointed with something that truly matters to your heart."

Reflexively, Grayson reached for his heart, protected by under armour, dragon scale, and his mithril cloak. He guarded it with everything he had, including the various knives and daggers strapped to his body.

But Eva had bypassed it all.

She had the potential to wreak havoc on his heart—and she wasn't even here to do it. It was frustrating, annoying, even terrifying. He should have been used to it by now, but every time she was near, every time she looked at him, he felt like he was standing on the edge of a cliff, a single breath away from being blown off the ledge. He didn't *want* this. Didn't want to feel so damn vulnerable. He had faced death and destruction; why did she hold the power to shatter his very foundation?

Yet, despite this free fall he'd been thrust into, he yearned to be near her. The wild temper of his heart whenever she looked at him was addicting. The anticipation singing in his veins when her fingers grazed him. There was a hunger, a raw need that he couldn't deny or even look away from anymore. He was drawn to her.

He couldn't explain it.

He shook his head once as he approached the training rooms, attempting to clear his mind.

One by one, he peeked into the rooms, some were vacant, some had Knights sparring, the weight room was full. But no Eva. The deeper he moved through the halls, the more oppressive the silence felt.

He swallowed the tightness in his throat and pushed forward. He needed to see her, never mind wanting to make things right with her. Now it was about calming the raging tides in his heart. Every moment he was away from her was another moment someone else had to snatch her away—Darius, an assassin, Arkon.

He continued down the corridor, his boots echoing the pounding tempo of his heart. Another empty training room.

Another long breath.

"*Eran, have you seen Arkon or* Aster?"

The only other place they would be was above the White Woods practising aerials.

"Aster *is enjoying a sunbeam north of the canyon."*

"And Arkon?"

"I have not seen him since early this morning."

He skidded to a stop, glaring at the nearest window. Eran was flying around the canyon, leisurely stretching his wings while Grayson wandered aimlessly around the base—for seemingly no reason. "*Why didn't you say something earlier??*"

"*Because I did not find it concerning,*" Eran replied, sounding entirely too calm, too composed. An undercurrent of amusement rode his tone that gnawed at Grayson's insides. "*He often secludes himself and goes missing for hours at a time, and I let him be. He's very angry that I Bonded with you.*"

Grayson's throat tightened at the mention of Arkon. "*I did kill his brothers and sisters.*"

Twelve of them to be exact. And while they had been dangerous, no one could deny how rare they were. Grayson had hunted them down thinking he was protecting his kingdom, his people. But the cost of that belief... it was too high.

"*He thinks I betrayed him,*" Eran huffed. "*I did no such thing. I saw the good in you and vowed to drag it out of the cold, dark recesses of your soul. You didn't* want *to kill his kin.*"

That was a lie Eran told himself, even when he knew the depths of Grayson's consciousness better than anyone and could see the truth in his memories.

Sylus had told him that killing them would protect Estrus, that every death was justified for the greater good. And so Grayson hunted them without mercy or remorse. He wanted to prove to his father that he would be a powerful king. Not only would the people of Estrus fear his name, but everyone in Astrida would as well. No one would dare to touch his land, steal from his mithril veins, as long as he sat on the throne.

He didn't realise until it was too late that Sylus hadn't ordered the extermination of the storm dragons to protect Estrus. He had them killed out of fear. Though, what had caused the fear and why he would be afraid of creatures that hadn't set foot on Estrus in over a century was still a mystery to Grayson to this day.

If only he had known. If only he'd seen it sooner, could have saved some of them. Faked their deaths, just as Sasha had, and helped them hide...

Grayson pressed his hands against his face, fighting the dizzying rush of regret threatening to drown him. No. He couldn't think that way. If he started thinking about all of his regrets in life, he would never be able to dig himself back out. He had spent three long years convincing himself that wallowing in self-pity, questioning his every action, wouldn't change the past. He'd done awful things, things he would never be able to undo. But the future... the future could be different. He *could* fight for that—

A hand landed on his shoulder. Instincts had him reaching for a knife as he spun out of the assailant's hold. He thrust his blade up between the ribs, but the assailant—Anna—caught his wrist and swiftly disarmed him, twisting the knife out of his grasp.

She laughed when all he could do was thank Asturias that it had been *Anna* to interrupt his thoughts. If it had been anyone else, they would be dead by now.

Easing out his battle stance, he raked a hand through his hair, calming his mind for both their sakes. "Shit, Anna, don't sneak up on a guy like that."

She shrugged it off with a cocky grin. Without an ounce of hesitation, she tucked it back into the sheath on his chest. "The boys weren't kidding. You *are* on a warpath. Who pissed you off?"

He scratched his jaw, felt the prickle of hairs against his fingertips, and realised he'd forgotten to shave this morning.

Gods. He was a mess.

"Eran. He's wasting my time," he grumbled, shoving his hands in his pockets. While he preferred to keep to himself, it wasn't his intention to make the other Knights wary of him. Sometimes he forgot that changing his name and being Bound to a dragon wasn't enough; the Slayer of Souls was ingrained deep in his very marrow and it took an enormous amount of effort to tamper the monster down and appear like an ordinary man.

He cleared his throat. "Have you seen Eva?"

Understanding flickered across Anna's face. Her posture shifted subtly—shoulders easing, tone softening, a glint of knowing behind her steel grey eyes. "Leo summoned both of the Greenes for a mandatory outing. They won't be back until dinnertime."

A ripple of rage shuddered through his body. His fingers flexed in his pockets. His jaw tensed so tight it hurt. What the fuck was Leo doing summoning Eva like she was some kind of readily available servant awaiting his commands? She wasn't some court doll to be carted around at his whim.

"Where did they go?"

Anna's gaze narrowed. She crossed her arms slowly, weight shifting to one hip as she studied him long and hard, taking note of the tic on his jaw and the slight twitch of his left eyebrow. "Why does it matter?"

He didn't flinch. He held her stare, steady and unyielding. "You know why, Anna."

"Do I?" Her gaze lingered on him, innocence riding her tone despite the mischievous glint in her eyes. Then she glanced down both ends of the hallway, catching sight of two Knights approaching from the far end. Without a word, she jutted her chin in the opposite direction and turned into an unoccupied training room. Grayson followed, his boots quiet against the stone as he shut the door behind him.

Most people sparred with the doors open; the rooms heated up quickly when closed. But he'd been taught never to expose his techniques. Every motion others observed, every habit they noticed, could be exploited and used against him. Only his squad had the privilege of fighting alongside him and seeing his true strengths, so that they could learn and survive with him.

Anna strode to the center of the mats, tying her hair back into a tight braid. Her stance was casual, but calculated. Ready. Watching.

"Eva shouldn't be leaving the base by herself," he said, his voice low and rough. "In case you've forgotten, Darius is still alive, and Sylus's assassins are still hunting her."

Anna rolled her neck side to side, the sound of cracking joints echoing off the walls. She stretched one arm across her chest, then switched, her eyes never leaving his. "Eva isn't alone. She's with Jacob, Leo, and their dragons. Darius is locked up in Kain Castle awaiting execution next week. As for the assassins..." She gave a slow shrug, a cruel grin lighting up her face. "I wish them luck. Eva knows how to give them a warm welcome."

Grayson gritted his teeth. It was all he could do to stop himself from losing his mind. Anna was being far too casual as Eva's teacher, friend, and protector. She was *there* when he explained the threat to Hargin, and yet she didn't appear to care at all. If something happened to Eva...

Anna tilted her head, studying him curiously at a different angle. He hated that look. He'd never tell her that was how Darius used to look at him when he was trying to find a way to get under his younger brother's skin.

Her eyes went wide with recognition. "Hold on. Are you *jealous*?"

Grayson curled his lip, resenting the word. "What do I have to be jealous of?"

"Eva's out with Leo and not here with you."

His body locked up, every muscle coiled tight. A sharp breath wedged in his throat. Was that why anger had been gnawing at him all day? He wasn't angry at Eva for being reckless. Not really. Or even at Anna for being nonchalant. It was Leo. The ease she had around him. The trust.

She had every reason to trust Leo, while with Grayson... she couldn't even stand to look at him.

"I'm not jealous." Jealousy was a heinous emotion. Exploitable. Weak. Grayson Smith was not *weak*.

He couldn't afford to be.

Anna stepped back and slid into a fighting stance, her grin sharp and knowing. "If I can best you in a round, will you give me an honest answer?"

He snorted, planting his feet and taking note of her positioning. Anna was anything but sloppy. She'd earned his respect from day one, when he watched her take down a stone golem with nothing but grit and determination. Still, no one had bested him in the three years he'd been in Aboria.

"Sure."

He moved without hesitation, snapping his leg out toward her ribs. She blocked it with her forearms—tight, practiced. Before she could regain balance, he threw a high jab toward her face. She deflected, but his left fist drove hard into her side. Her breath caught; she staggered, just as he followed up with a low kick.

She blocked with her shin, gritting her teeth. Then—her leg shot outward and slammed into his chest. The impact knocked a cough out of him, staggered his footing, and before he could reorient, she rushed the opening. Her leg swept wide—fast, brutal.

He hit the mat hard, the breath knocked clean out of his lungs.

For a moment, he just lay there, blinking up at the ceiling.

He'd lost his footing. He *shouldn't* have lost his footing.

Anna's hand hovered over him. Her grin was as smug as it was deserved. "Getting a little complacent being the base's best fighter, are we?"

Complacent? No. Never. Distracted, on the other hand... He needed to be at his best now more than ever, but his focus was scattered, especially where Eva was involved. His mind and instincts were constantly battling for control—which put him at risk.

He needed to get his shit together.

Grayson shrugged out of his cloak and tossed it onto a nearby bench. He rolled his shoulder back, pressing his fists together with a sharp crack of his knuckles. If she wasn't going to hold back, neither was he.

"Is that the question you want me to answer honestly?" he challenged, voice steady but tight.

Anna's grey eyes narrowed, their sharpness cutting through him like a blade. He hated that look. It reminded him of being pinned down, vulnerable. He hated feeling like a mouse caught by a cat. "Are you jealous that Leo is out with Eva right now?"

His fists clenched, the muscles in his forearms straining as he fought to control his reaction. Damn it. She wasn't going to let him off the hook. The accusation stung. He wasn't even sure how to answer that—*jealous*? It was too simple, too raw.

"Would you accept it if I said, I don't know?" he muttered, his voice more brittle than he wanted it to be.

Anna didn't flinch. She studied him, her expression not at all moved by his uncertainty. "Yes. Tell me what's got you all wound up."

The words tumbled out before he could stop them, "I don't like that she's out with him."

"Why?"

He shook his head, frustration roiling like a dangerous tide. He had been generous enough. He wasn't about to spill all of this now. Not yet. Not without a fight. "I'll answer if you best me again," he said, his voice hardening. "If I win, you tell me why you're pestering me about this."

Her brow quirked, and for a second, he saw the faintest flash of surprise. She hadn't expected him to turn the tables. Grayson let a smile curl on his lips.

"Fine," Anna said, her voice low, but the challenge in it was unmistakable.

Riding the high of her win, Anna was the first to make her move. A quick right hook came toward him, but Grayson slapped it aside, narrowly ducking under her second swing. In one fluid motion, he caught her wrist and jabbed a fist into her ribs.

Anna reacted swiftly, slamming her foot into his chest then darting back to make space. Grayson staggered but held his ground, his feet rooted this time. He'd be damned if he let her knock him off his feet again.

As she advanced, he readied himself. Before she could lay a finger on him, he kicked out for her ribs—exactly where he'd struck earlier. The grunt she let out was all the confirmation he needed to know he still had his edge. To her credit, she didn't let the pain slow her down, retaliating with a sharp blow to the side of his head. His ears rang, but he didn't lose focus.

Grayson snapped back with a palm to her sternum, then locked his elbow over her exposed arm, pinning it to his ribs. With the right amount of pressure, he could snap the joint in two. He added just enough for her to feel the ache—and to let her know he had her.

With a small breath of acknowledgment, he released her, stepping back. Anna collapsed to her hands and knees, breathing heavily.

"Fuck me. I take back what I said about getting complacent," she panted. "You win that round."

Grayson refrained from smirking. No need to get smug—especially after the ass-whooping she'd handed him in the first round. He extended a hand to help her up, which she took, rising and rolling out her shoulder with a slight wince.

"All right. Fair's fair." She dusted her palms on her legs, her voice sharp but tinged with respect. "What's your question?"

"Why did it sound like you wanted me to be jealous of Leo?"

Anna flipped her braid over her shoulder, letting out a steadying breath to regain her composure. "Because I didn't think I'd ever see the day when you'd care enough about someone to be jealous over them. Don't get me wrong, I'm happy you've found someone to care about—I'm just... stunned."

Grayson flexed his knuckles and wrists, considering her words. He'd grown enough since becoming Jacob's partner to accept that caring for others wasn't a weakness or a flaw. In fact, he liked having people to confide in. But with Eva... this feeling was something else. Terrifying. Chaotic. Dangerous. Uncontrollable. Yet, he couldn't stop it.

"Are you in love with Eva?" Anna pressed.

He recoiled at the very thought. Being in love implied he had a soul capable of *feeling* love, which he most definitely did not. Sylus had ensured that in their upbringing. He'd beaten any sense of compassion out of his bones and punished any ideas of warmth and love that crossed their minds. Jacob had been helping him find that piece of humanity he lost, but to *love*... No. This thing with Eva was not love. He didn't know *what* it was, but it wasn't love.

His lips twisted into a sneer. "You're going to have to fight me if you want that answer," he growled.

He shouldn't even be indulging this, but the urge to hit something, to release the pressure building in his chest, was roaring through his veins.

Anna squared up, fists raised. She was giving him the first move. Fine by him.

He lunged for her, shoulder checking into her stomach and knocking her hard into the mats. Anna gasped as the air was knocked out of her, but she was quick to recover, swinging her legs up to trap his head between her thighs. She yanked her legs down, pushing him off with a force that sent him stumbling back. He hit the ground with a heavy thud, the wind knocked out of him.

Anna was on him in a flash, grabbing his arm as she slid her foot beneath his back and flipped him onto his stomach. She locked his arm behind him and dug her knee into his lower back, ensuring he couldn't escape.

Grayson tapped the mat, yielding.

Anna backed off, blowing a strand of hair that had escaped her braid out of her face. "Are you in love with Eva?" she asked, barely giving herself a chance to catch her breath to get the question out.

"No." The word was final, the answer absolute. It couldn't be possible. A heartless monster like him could never know love.

He climbed to his feet and ran a hand through his hair, catching a palmful of sweat in the process. Anna crossed her arms, scowling at him, but didn't say anything further. She'd asked; he'd answered.

But she wasn't done. Without a word, she closed the gap between them, throwing a swift kick followed by a punch. Grayson ducked underneath, catching her stomach with his shoulder and tackling her onto the mats.

Anna locked her legs around his waist, flipping them over until he was on his back, and she was straddling him. Grayson grabbed her shirt—so thin, too damn thin for sparring—but let it go when he realized the danger of tearing it. Anna used his hesitation, baring her forearm across his throat, pressing down with a firm, unrelenting grip.

"Are you against the idea of being in love, or are you really not in love with Eva?" She eased up on the pressure just enough for him to speak.

"What kind of question is that?"

She didn't look away. "One that needs an honest answer."

"Love is for the weak."

She paused, sitting back on her heels as her eyes softened, but her gaze never wavered. "You don't really believe that, do you?"

He leveled with her, the weight of his words heavy. "Anna, love is a weakness we can't afford. A distraction. Love gets you killed. Sylus made sure of that when we were boys—he beat any trace of love out of us. I don't know what it feels like, and I'm not sorry for it. It keeps me alive, and that's what matters. Darius knows I'm alive, which means Sylus will know soon. He'll send men after me. And when he does, I plan on surviving."

Anna's expression faltered for a moment, a twinge of disappointment flashing across her face. She reached out, her hand gripping his arm firmly. "Love gives you strength, Grayson. I look forward to seeing you experience it."

He scoffed, rolling his eyes. "You sound like Eran."

"Really? Maybe he and I should compare notes," she said with a playful chuckle, rising to her feet. She dusted her cotton pants off and offered him a hand. "Come on. Let's go to Lensenton. I'll buy you a drink."

CHAPTER 7
HONEST CONVERSATIONS

Eva grinned and looped her arms through Jacob's as they strolled through the misty streets of Lensenton. The damp air clung to their clothes, making her hair frizz. She rarely wore it down, but Jacob had insisted on a proper sibling day, and that seemed reason enough to dress differently—leather riding pants, a long-sleeved under-armour scoop neck, and her coziest wool jacket. She couldn't bring herself to leave every weapon behind, though. A hunting knife stayed strapped to her thigh.

Jacob smiled, just as content to be alone with her. They'd spent all day yesterday with Leo, who very kindly bought them lunch *and* dinner in Riverwood. They'd had fun, just sitting and laughing, trading stories. Eva particularly enjoyed the challenge Leo set of exchanging covert glances when Jacob wasn't looking. They'd sent him on his way back to Lexxis later that evening, guarded, despite his many protests. He seemed to have this idea of proving himself—independent and capable of defending his own life—but she wasn't having it. He was far too important to be taking unnecessary risks.

After all of the laughs and drinks yesterday, Jacob had yearned for the days he and Eva would just sit and talk about whatever was on their mind, so he'd suggested today be a sibling day. It might've been the smartest thing he'd said in weeks.

Jacob steered her into the T Lover's cafe. They ordered their respective teas—a creamy Earl Grey for him, a sharp peppermint for her. When they hit the streets again, Jacob cast her a long side glance. "I didn't want to say anything yesterday in front of Leo, but you and Anna have been quite the talk on the base lately with your dancing lessons."

She watched the steam roll out of her cup, ever-so tempted to take a sip to fight off the chill in the air. "And why didn't you want to say anything in front of Leo?"

A wrinkle formed on his nose. "I didn't want him to get any ideas."

She snorted, peering up at him. "Of what, dancing with me at a gala? Gods forbid I have a dance partner."

He glared at her, but it didn't reach his eyes. "I'm just looking out for you, Eva."

She huffed a quiet laugh and shook her head, though her chest tightened a little. Jacob always meant well—even when he drove her mad with his protectiveness. If he kept it up, she wouldn't have *any* dance partners at the gala. Hopefully the two men she had in mind wouldn't be so easily deterred from her brother's overbearing need to protect her purity. It'd be a shame to never know what it felt like to dance with a certain dashing prince... or a brooding Dragon Knight,

"Have you talked to Grayson at all?" Jacob asked suddenly, voice tight.

Eva flinched, taken aback. It was like he could read her mind!

She cleared her throat, calming her racing heart.

Had she talked to him since he vowed to prove himself worthy of her? "Nope."

His shoulders stiffened. "So he hasn't mentioned the training then?"

She peered up at him. He was being oddly tense and vague. "What training?"

He blew out a breath, raking a hand through his fluffy hair. The mist didn't do him any favours and held it up the thick tresses in all kinds of angles. "Grayson wants to train you to fight against Sylus's assassins."

"I already know how to fight," she gritted out. Anna had taught her enough to keep her alive in the Desert Lands—and to defeat Darius. She could handle a few assassins.

He sighed, seeming to expect this response. *Asshole.*

"His assassins are different, Eva. They trained Dex—and I've never seen anyone fight like him. Please, when Grayson brings it up, will you at least be open to the idea? I know you guys aren't on the best of terms right now, but he cares about you. In his own emotionally-unavailable, 'don't look at me or I'll turn you to stone' way. He wants you to live through this."

She turned her head away from him, choosing instead to stare through the fogged-up windows of the shops they passed. Grayson Smith—*Deximus Fortys*—brought on a whole boatload of conflicting emotions she wasn't ready to unpack. Not now. Maybe not ever.

I can put my emotions aside for a few lessons. How hard could it be?

A flicker of heat curled low in her belly, traitorous and unwelcome. She could already picture it—Grayson standing behind her, correcting her stance, his hand on her arm or her waist, that deep voice in her ear. His storm-cloud eyes locked on hers, unreadable. Steady. Steeling her spine while unraveling something inside her.

She swallowed hard. Gods, who was she kidding?

Training with him wouldn't be a simple matter of swords and footwork. Not when her pulse skipped just thinking about it. Not when she still remembered the feel of his mouth against hers.

Still.

She wanted to be strong. To survive. To avenge her family. To defeat Sylus.

And to live long enough to get to him.

"I'll think about it," she muttered, too stubborn to admit she'd already made up her mind.

Jacob slung an arm over her shoulders and pressed a kiss to the top of her head. "Thank you. Now, no more work talk. I'm going to give you a proper tour of Lensenton—Jacob Greene style."

Eva leaned into his side with a soft smile. For the first time in days, she was looking forward to something.

Jacob's tour was infinitely better than Anna's. As much as Eva adored her partner and friend, their ideas of fun couldn't be more different. Anna's tour had taken her through every clothing shop in Lensenton, with a few accessory stands and random knick-knack stalls thrown in. Jacob's, on the other hand, felt like a love letter to the city.

He took her through quiet parks and charming bakeries, a decadent chocolatier, two lively bookstores, a pair of not-so-quiet bars, and a tucked-away alleyway painted in a fantastical collage of colors—dragons twisting through clouds, some with riders, some wild and glorious, all mid-flight.

Their final stop before dinner was a blacksmith's shop. The storefront was a work of art, every piece displayed like it belonged in a museum: polished swords, leather-bound gauntlets, silver-inlaid helms. But it was the glass case of daggers that rooted Eva in place.

Elegant. Balanced. Sharp.

Better than anything the base had ever handed her.

And far too expensive.

She crouched slightly, studying the way the metal caught the dying light, heart tugging with the ache of want. Her pay as a Dragon Knight wasn't bad, and she rarely spent it on anything beyond tea and armor oil—but even so, those blades were still a few months of saving away.

With a sigh, she leaned back just as the shopkeep stepped forward and carefully draped a red velvet cloth over the case. He did the same for the rest of the displays, one by one, as closing time descended.

Jacob nudged her arm. "Shops are closing and I'm starving," he said, already steering her out the door.

Eva cast one last look over her shoulder at the daggers beneath the velvet. *I'll come back for you.*

But when she turned forward again, her steps stalled. An unexpected figure emerged from the bakery just a few shops down, catching both her and Jacob mid-step.

Grayson.

He carried a white box in one hand, a surprising contrast against the stark black of his usual gear. His head was slightly bowed, gaze on the street ahead—until he paused, as if he felt their eyes on him. Slowly, he turned.

His gaze found hers.

A bolt lanced down her spine, rooting her to the spot. The last time they'd locked eyes, his face had been open, vulnerable. But now... now he wore a closed-off expression, the edges of a smile tugging at his mouth without ever touching his eyes.

Jacob stepped forward with an easy grin, unknowingly cutting through the tension. "Hey, Gray. What are you doing here?"

Grayson nodded in greeting but didn't approach further, keeping a deliberate distance between them. "Thought I'd take your advice," he said simply, holding up the white box. His voice was calm, measured. Then his gaze shifted—inevitably—to her.

She still hadn't moved.

Jacob glanced back at her and shot a subtle glare. *Be friendly*, that look said.

Eva sucked in a breath, letting the crisp evening air cool the nerves prickling at her skin. Grayson wasn't going to bite her—she just didn't know which version of him would show up. The one who'd vowed to earn her trust? Or the one who lied so well she didn't even see it coming?

Still, she stepped forward.

When he smiled at her, it changed everything. It wasn't the grim, polite one he'd offered Jacob. It was warmer, freer—his eyes catching the light from the streetlamps like storm clouds parting just enough for starlight.

Which smile came from the real Grayson?

She hated that she didn't know.

"What's in the box?" she asked thickly, her voice not quite as steady as she'd intended. Anything to stop herself from watching the way he stood, the way he looked at her, the way her heart betrayed her common sense.

He held it out to her. "This isn't how I wanted to give them to you, but... you caught me. They're for you."

Curiosity overrode caution. Eva accepted the box then lifted the lid. Her mouth watered, stomach growling its approval. Double chocolate cupcakes with fudge icing. She'd been tempted to buy one earlier when Jacob brought her to the bakery, but they'd just had lunch and she didn't feel like carrying it around with her all day.

A peace offering. Did he know that it was her absolute favourite kind of peace offering?

"Thank you." She glanced at Jacob, who nodded subtly to her, then looked back at Grayson.

Arkon growled deep in her mind. *"Hmph. Does he think that is all it takes to atone for his sins?"*

She refrained from rolling her eyes. *"You know deep down he doesn't. He's trying to make amends, Arkon. I promised him I'd give him a chance."*

"If he's in a giving mood, why not see if he will buy you those daggers you were drooling over earlier?"

"I don't want gifts. I want—"

Him. The real him. She wanted to know it hadn't all been a lie, that she wasn't wrong for feeling this way.

Her grip on the box tightened.

"Look, if you can't say anything nice, get out of my head and go hunt a cow or something. I made a promise, and I intend to keep it."

"If that's how you feel, you can fly back with Jacob and Glade."

And then he was gone. Just like before, the tether between them wasn't cut, but gone slack. Their souls bound by a thin, fraying thread.

Pretending not to be affected by the abrupt hollowness in her chest, Eva turned to Grayson, "We're going to grab some dinner before we head back to the base... Do you want to join us?"

His eyes widened, lips parting in his surprise. He glanced at Jacob then to Eva, a cool mask falling over his features. "Thank you for the offer, but I don't want to intrude on your sibling time."

Her shoulders tensed, just barely, before she forced them to relax. She didn't know if she was more disappointed or relieved, but the relief was easier to accept.

Jacob clapped a hand on his shoulder. "You wouldn't be intruding. Actu ally..." He gave Eva a pained smile. "I just realised I have a meeting tonight, so I have to run."

What? Eva didn't mind having dinner with Grayson if Jacob was around, but it was entirely different if he was going to disappear on her.

"You told me you had nothing going on today."

He scratched the back of his head sheepishly, eyes wandering upward. "I, uh, forgot about this meeting."

Hmm-hm. He was a *terrible* liar.

He backed away slowly, as if she was an ornery bear. "Have fun at dinner! See you tomorrow."

"Jacob."

But he was already gone, rushing down the street. She might as well be a bear chasing him down the cobblestone road.

A sigh slipped through her lips.

"If you're not ready, Eva," Grayson said softly, "we don't have to."

He was giving her an out, a choice. He always gave her a choice, she realised. He held his hand out to her when she first arrived in Dragon Canyon, letting her decide if she wanted to be entrusted in his care. He hadn't let her down then. He gave her the option to back out before facing Darius, in what used to be her home. Whatever choice she made, he fully respected it and supported her.

Lies might have left his lips, but his actions never once betrayed her or gave her reason to doubt him.

She closed the lid on the cupcakes and lifted her chin, striding towards the Atrium. "It's just dinner. It's not like you're going to throw me into a pit of Sandhounds."

He met her pace and cocked a curious eyebrow at her. "Why does it sound like that has happened to you?"

"Because Bruce actually threw me into a pit of Sandhounds. Steel can't penetrate their thick hide. The only way to kill them is with magic unless you can get underneath them."

He grimaced, scanning his memory of his brief time in the Desert Lands. "I don't recall Bruce."

"He was the scruffy-looking Wanderer."

She didn't expect him to remember Bruce. He had only been there for a night, which was hardly long enough to get to know Sasha's band of Wanderers. Astrida called them criminals, but in Storm Cove, they were a band of selfless warriors—by a criminal's standard, anyway—who protected the vulnerable and helped those trapped by the desert. Sasha could try as hard as she wanted to uphold a cold, badass appearance, but she was a Dragon Knight through and through, always trying to give anyone who wanted it a shot at redemption. In return for their honest work—though, "honest" was a bit of a stretch—they still lied and cheated, but they did it for the greater good now instead for their own selfish gain. Sasha and Syran provided them with a safe place to live.

"They all looked scruffy," Grayson ground out. But when his gaze slid back to her, the hard edge softened. "You seemed to have come away unscathed."

Her hand drifted to her thigh, fingers brushing over the jagged scar hidden beneath her pants. A reminder. One of the Sandhounds had gotten too close, and not even the Under City's healing lake could erase it completely. "It was fight or die," she said, jaw tightening. "So I made damn sure I fought."

His eyes followed the movement, darkening like storm clouds before midnight. He looked away, but the tension remained. "Good. But I still want a better description of this Bruce."

She gave a soft, teasing snort, flipping her hair over her shoulder. "Why? You gonna beat him up?"

His head tilted, but he kept walking, the air around them shifting. Cool wisps of power curled around her flesh, making her hair stand on end and a shiver run down her spine. No smile. No softness. Just a simmering heat behind his eyes, the kind that could burn or worship.

"No," he said, low and even. "Beating him up is something children do." He didn't stop walking, didn't raise his voice. "If someone threatens you, Eva, they don't get bruises..." His voice was a whisper of dark promises and destruction. "They get *ruined*."

A beat.

Long enough for the words to land.

Long enough for her to forget how to breathe.

The air around them crackled with the heat of something dangerous, something possessive and dark—and gods, she felt it. The thrill slithered down her spine, coiled in her gut, delicious and terrifying. She wasn't sure what unsettled her more: the promise in his voice, or the way her body responded to it.

He meant it. Every single word.

She leaned into his side, offering a smile to ease his mind. "Leave Bruce alone. He did it to make me feel better."

His eyes narrowed, as sharp as the knives strapped to his chest.

Despite the tension simmering beneath his deathly gaze, she laughed. "He did! Honest."

She pulled out the gloves Sasha had given her, fingers curling around the fabric. Without them, she couldn't use her magic. It wasn't much—just enough to stun, not to kill—but it was all she needed. All she needed to bring Darius to justice.

Her voice softened, but there was a quiet strength beneath the words. "I struggled with my magic in the Desert Lands. I still do, honestly. Sasha would show me these amazing, powerful techniques and expect me to get it instantly. When I didn't... I felt like a failure. I thought that I would never become strong enough to kill Sylus." She paused, her fingers tracing the edge of the gloves, the fabric by no means soft or dainty. Purely functional, they were thick and scratchy, with enough fibres to bring static to life in her hands.

"Bruce wanted to cheer me up, in the only way he knew how. I was furious at him for pushing me into the pit at the time, but afterward, I realised he was showing me that I didn't need big, flashy moves to win a fight. Sometimes the smallest things can change the fate of a fight."

Grayson walked beside her in silence, hands tucked into his pockets, his expression unreadable. But Eva had come to know the difference between his face and his eyes. The former remained still, solid as carved stone. The latter... churned.

Not just anger—though that was there, barely leashed—but something else too. Maybe it was fury at Bruce for endangering her. Or maybe it was directed at her, for believing that she wouldn't be enough.

Anna had slapped her upside the head when she admitted her doubts. Grayson didn't raise a hand. But the storm in his eyes said plenty.

Then, gradually, she watched it fade. The tension in his jaw eased. His shoulders lost their rigid edge. The storm, for now, had passed.

When they reached the Atrium, he opened the door for her without a word and followed her inside.

The warmth hit her instantly.

It was humid, thick like the jungle air north of the Desert Lands. The cold that had clung to her bones melted away, her joints loosening with every step. The scent of greenery, of earth and water, filled her lungs and wrapped around her ribs.

A sense of familiarity. A breath of home.

When Grayson finally spoke, his voice was low—private, but certain. "Do you know what the national animal of Estrus is?"

She blinked, thinking back to the black armour that haunted her dreams. "A serpent?"

He shook his head subtly. "No. That's the Fortys clan's crest."

The Fortys's crest. Not his family's. He never referred to Sylus or Darius that way.

"The national animal of Estrus is a starling."

Her eyes widened in surprise.

A faint, lopsided smile tugged at the corner of his mouth. "They represent freedom. The ability to overcome. The strength in family. They're small—not worth hunting for food or feathers—but the people of Estrus revere them. If you're lucky enough to see one in your travels, it's considered a sign of good fortune. A symbol of hope, passed down for generations." He looked down at her, something quiet and unreadable flickering behind his eyes. "There aren't any starlings in Aboria, but whenever I look at you... I think of them. Of what they stand for."

As soon as the words left his mouth, his expression shifted—like he'd tasted something sour.

The laugh that burst from her lips saved her from turning into a puddle on the path. "What's that face for?"

"I can't believe I just said that." He groaned under his breath, dragging a hand over his face. "Jacob told me to be candid with you, but I don't think comparing you to a bird was what he had in mind." He paused, and she caught the flicker of embarrassment beneath his dry tone. "He said I should tell you what my favourite colour is."

She laughed again, warmth blooming in her chest. The idea of him asking Jacob for advice made something in her soften. It meant he was trying—that he *wanted* to make things right. "Your favourite colour is black, isn't it?"

A smirk broke across his face, his eyes glinting with mischief. "Everyone guesses that, but would you be surprised if I told you it's actually blue?"

She tilted her head. "Are we talking azure blue or sky blue?"

"Azure. Obviously."

"*Obviously*."

She leaned into his side, wrapping her arm around his. Gods, she'd missed this. Missed *him*. The ease, the quiet mischief, the way he made the world feel a little less heavy.

He tensed, caught off guard by her touch. Just as Eva began to retreat, thinking it might be too much, he leaned into her instead, the tension in his frame softening. His eyes met hers, luminous beneath the twinkling canopy lights.

At the end of the path, a host waited behind a podium and greeted them with a bow before leading them to a table tucked beneath a curtain of wisteria vines. A gentle stream trickled nearby, and fireflies drifted lazily around the tree above them. A single candle flickered on the wrought iron table, casting soft gold across Grayson's sharp features.

Once the waiter disappeared with their drink orders, Eva leaned her elbows on the table and gave him a sly look, daring him to correct her.

The last time they'd been here, he'd tried to teach her etiquette—how to speak, how to sit, how to be a *lady*.

Now, in hindsight, it all made sense. Anna had asked *him* to teach her. Who better to instruct her than a prince?

Her fingers brushed the rim of her glass, her gaze distant. "Would you ever go back?" She asked it lightly, casually, instead of voicing the question that gnawed at her: *How much of it was real?*

The secret glances. Stolen touches. The way he'd stood so close. She'd liked the thought that some small piece of him had been *hers*. Something unspoken, something just between them. But what if it had all been part of the lie? A performance to keep her tame, obedient, trusting?

Grayson flinched. Not physically, but it was there, in the way his shoulders stiffened and his breath caught. He looked as if she'd slapped him.

"No. Never," he said, his voice low and final. "There's nothing left for me there."

"Nothing at all? No friends? Not even your favourite fishing spot?"

He blinked, caught off guard. "*Fishing*?"

She shrugged, trying to play off the weight behind the question. "You know what I mean."

A muscle jumped in his jaw as he looked away, eyes focused on something far in the distance. "No. No fishing spot. No friends. No lovers, either."

The admission felt intentional, and though she hadn't meant that—hadn't even *considered* it—relief spread through her, warm and uninvited.

Her eyes searched his face, softening as it naturally did when she took in his handsome features. She wanted to ask about his little brother—about Dravyn. When they spoke about him briefly in the cave, before they stormed Darius's fort, she'd gotten the sense that he felt guilty. He'd left Estrus, the abuse, Sylus—but he'd left Dravyn behind. She didn't know what kind of relationship they had before, but if it was anything like hers and Jacob's, she knew the guilt would have torn through her and she'd do anything to get him out.

But his expression had shifted again. The lines around his mouth had hardened, and a shadow passed over his eyes.

She hesitated. The last thing she wanted was to make him retreat. He'd already given her more than she expected.

She wouldn't push her luck.

Not tonight.

They fell silent, though she wasn't anywhere near done talking. She could see it in his eyes, too, that he had things of his own to say, but he remained silent, either out of stubbornness or uncertainty.

"They have an execution date," she blurted right as the waiter came by to take their order. She flinched when the man gave her a sharp look. Executions weren't exactly a proper conversation piece for the public.

She hadn't once looked at the menu, too fascinated by the Knight in front of her, so she ordered the same dish she got last time. Grayson watched the waiter walk away, a critical look in his eyes. Once he was long gone, he dragged his gaze back to her, solemn. "Hargin told me yesterday morning. You?"

"Leo told me yesterday, as part of his gift to us." The date was set the day after Leo's gala. It had come to her as a relief that the court had decided to execute him—and decided to do it swiftly. She had this nagging feeling in the back of her head that he was going to escape, and it wouldn't go away until he was six feet underground. "Are you going?"

He brought a mug of mead to his lips, studying her over the rim before taking back a healthy swig. When he set the mug down, he remained cool, almost dispassionate in the way he regarded her. "Yes. Why wouldn't I?"

She shifted in her seat, poking her cutlery and watching the glint reflect on the veil of wisteria around them. "Well, he is... your brother."

"Our relationship is vastly different from yours and Jacob's," he said darkly. "I'm going to make sure he stays dead, not to say farewell."

She winced, though she didn't expect anything else from him.

When the silence stretched on, he shifted in his seat, leaning his elbows on the table. His tone was gentler, when he said, "Are you going?"

She ran her tongue over her upper lip, eyes drifting to the white box beside her. Talking about Darius—*hearing* that voice, low and gravelly, wrapping around her like smoke—made it hard to meet his eyes. His voice confused her. It made her want to draw closer, even when part of her told her to walk away.

"Yes. I have to *watch* him die, to be hundred percent certain that he's never coming back..." She forced herself to look at him, to see if he judged her. "Does that make me a bad person?"

His eyes were hard, unrelenting orbs of calm fury. It wasn't directed at her, she knew, but at Darius, of all the awful things he had done, and maybe at himself for being a part of it. "I don't think so. You have every right to watch that fucker's head roll for what he did to you." The protective edge in his tone made her heart flutter.

She nodded, appreciating his validation of her anger. Jacob told her she should let it go, but she wasn't ready to do that yet. Maybe when he was dead, she would.

Grayson cleared his throat, shifting awkwardly. He flicked a petal off the table, eyes fixed on the wrought-iron pattern beneath his hands. "So, you were out with Leo yesterday..."

He didn't finish the thought. Didn't need to.

Another petal drifted from the vine above. She caught it gently, rolling the soft edge between her fingers. "Yeah. He asked Jacob and I to meet him in Riverwood. He..." Her voice caught, emotion swelling too quickly to contain. "He turned Brar into a fort. A real one, where people can take shelter. And he made a monument—for everyone who died. My family's names are on it." She turned the petal in her palm, stroking its center. "I don't know how to thank him. I was so afraid they'd be forgotten, that what happened to them would fade. But now... they'll always be there." She looked up at him, her voice softer. "I feel bad for thinking so little of him before. He is kind and brave, in his own way. There's still good in the world."

For all the gods had taken, Leonidas Kain was one of the few blessings they'd given back.

Grayson moistened his lips, searching for the right words. When he spoke, his voice had changed, lower, warmer. "Leo and I have our differences, but he *is* a good man." He paused, eyes steady on hers. "I don't blame him for hating me. We were raised in opposite worlds. Until I came here, I went against everything he stood for." He gave a dry laugh. "And when

I arrived... I didn't exactly make it easy. I mocked him for being soft. For caring. But now I see it—that strength doesn't always come from a sword." He glanced down, brows drawn. "He listens. Fights the Council when no one else will. He'll make a good king. A better one than I ever could've been for Estrus." He grimaced and added under his breath, "Don't tell him I said that."

A smile flitted across her lips. "I won't say a word."

Arriving with their food, the waiter seemed to sense the shift in atmosphere. He inclined his head respectfully before leaving them to the privacy of their alcove.

Eva's eyes fell on the rack of lamb in front of her, taking in the glistening juices dripping onto the plate. Her mouth watered. The scent alone was enough to stir memories—rich, savoury, mouth-melting. She doubted she'd ever get used to having good food again.

Across from her, Grayson's salmon sat untouched. He prodded the roasted potatoes absently, lost in thought.

Eva would give just about anything to know what he was thinking, if he was struggling to adjust to this new them as much as she was.

It used to be so easy to talk to him, but now it felt like she had to walk on eggshells to get answers out of him. The thought of asking made her tense, of wondering how far would be too far before he pulled away from her.

It wouldn't last forever; he needed to learn how to give pieces of himself to her and she needed to learn to believe him when he shared.

If patience was the price to pay to solve the enigma that was Grayson Smith, it was one she'd pay in a heartbeat. He deserved to be heard and seen for who he really was, not for what he wanted others to see.

Right then, his brow creased, something unreadable flickering in his eyes. Did he know that she could spot the micro expressions in his features that no one seemed to?

She wiped the last bit of sauce with the last potato then set her cutlery down and noticed he still hadn't touched his food. "What is it?" she finally asked, keeping her tone light and casual. "You haven't eaten a single bite."

He blinked, shaking himself out of whatever place his mind had gone. His eyes warmed when they met hers, but a muscle in his jaw tightened.

"Would it be too much to ask..." He trailed off, clearly wrestling with the words.

She didn't press—just waited.

"Will you take me to Brar sometime?" he said at last. "I'd like to pay my respects to your family."

She blinked, surprised by the rawness in his voice.

"I didn't know them well," he went on, "but when we stayed in the cave during the storm, they treated me with more kindness than I deserved.

Your mother made sure I had food and a place to sleep—even though I had no intention of sleeping. She even tried to feed Eran and Glade. Not nearly enough to fill a dragon's stomach, of course, but... it was the gesture that stayed with me."

He set his fork down, clearly abandoning the meal. "I never experienced a mother's love growing up. Sylus took her away from us when Dravyn was still young."

Eva leaned forward slightly. "When you say 'took her away'...?"

Grayson exhaled slowly, the breath catching halfway out.

"He had her killed." His voice was flat, too hollow for anger. "When she was strong enough to walk after giving birth to Dravyn, she tried to run away with him. She didn't get far. No one outruns Sylus's assassins." A bitter breath escaped him. "They brought him her head. Darius used to tell me—back when we were little—that Sylus kept it as a trophy, hidden somewhere in his office. He didn't, of course, there's no magic in Estrus to preserve a corpse."

Eva's stomach twisted. She swallowed down her last bite and set her fork aside.

Grayson noticed. His jaw tightened. "Sorry. I've ruined your dinner."

"No, it's all right." Her voice was soft, but steady.

It wasn't the gruesome image of a mother's severed head that turned her stomach—it was the loss. Sylus had stolen something irreplaceable from them.

She couldn't imagine growing up without her mother's presence—without Emily's laughter echoing in the hall, her warm hands holding hers after a nightmare, her voice guiding her through the mess of becoming who she was. Emily had been her warmth on cold winter nights. Her light during the darkest storms. Her best friend when the world felt like too much.

She looked at Grayson, really looked at him. And for the first time, she didn't just see the slayer, or the soldier, or even the man at her side.

She saw the boy who had grown up without light.

If her mother had been able to give him even a fraction of what she had, the warmth and care she'd always known, Eva knew she couldn't deny him the right to say goodbye. "I'll take you to Fort Brar. You'll get the full Greene tour."

Their eyes met, and for a heartbeat, the world around them faded to nothing but the soft glow of the firefly lights. The smile that tugged at the corner of his mouth was slight, but it reached his eyes in a way that made something stir inside her. It was the same look he'd given her months ago—the one only she could decipher.

She was *finally* getting to know the man beneath the mask.

CHAPTER 8
WALKING A FINE LINE

The waiter came back with the bill some time later. Eva offered to pay for the meal since it was her brother who conspired against them, but Grayson was already placing coins in the man's awaiting palm.

They walked out of the Atrium in silence, her arm looped through his while her other hand balanced the white box he'd given her.

The stars twinkled high above them like diamonds in the sky as they passed by stalls boarded up for the night; shutters were closed to keep the early winter chill out of their homes. A hum reverberated through the city, cool yet inviting despite the darkness creeping at the edges of the lamplight. Daytime gave her purpose—its bustle, its brightness, the sound of children chasing dreams down cobbled lanes. But the night... the night gave her peace. Under the soft glow of lamps and the hush of wind, the city felt like a living thing at rest. And in that stillness, she felt safe.

Eva's eyes drifted to the stars again, admiring their simple, cosmic beauty. She hadn't planned to be out this late, yet the time had gone by unchecked. They had a few awkward moments, silence stretching on too long or unbreaking gazes filled with words unsaid between them. But it was a start. A hopeful start.

It made staying out this late—and the very long walk back—worth it. Arkon's displeasure with Eva's choice to eat with Grayson was evident, the silence filling her mind like a void. Even when she opened her mind up to him, he ignored her.

Her stomach twisted, and she decided it was a hunger pang—definitely not one of guilt.

Slipping out of Grayson's gentle hold, her fingers lingered against his arm a heartbeat longer than necessary before she reached for the box. She plucked a cupcake from the delicious assortment, pretending not to notice the way his gaze followed the motion.

Feeling rude for divulging in front of him, she offered the box to him.

He held his hand up, shaking his head—but his lips twitched, just slightly. "I got them for you."

She pushed the box closer. "But you didn't eat. I don't know about you, but I'm a barely functional human if I skip a meal. Have one, I insist."

He met her gaze, uncertain. But as soon as she sank her teeth into the cupcake, a soft moan slipped from her lips—half involuntary, half reverent. The richness melted across her tongue like silk, coating her mouth in warmth. The notes of cocoa reminded her of a time when she and Jacob would make a day trip to visit the bakery in Riverwood. The desserts on the base were sweet and indisputably delicious, but these cupcakes hit that sweet decadent spot like nothing else.

It was absolute bliss.

She closed her eyes and let the taste flood her senses, lashes fluttering like she might come undone right there.

By the time Grayson hesitantly took a bite from his, she had already devoured hers, licking a smear of frosting from the pad of her thumb like a sacred gift from Asturias. She could have purred. A low hum settled in her chest. It had been too long since something so simple had made her feel this alive.

A laugh bubbled up in her throat as she turned her gaze to Grayson; he'd somehow managed to get the fudge icing on his nose.

Running entirely on instinct, from the days Jacob would make a mess of himself, she reached up to wipe the smudge—but he caught her wrist with reflexes faster than one of her lightning bolts.

They stood frozen on the empty street, with only the soft gleam of the lamplights and the stars for company. A breath was locked in her throat, his eyes as hard as steel.

Shocked by the sudden motion, she tried to free her arm, but his grip was tight, unrelenting. She hadn't been expecting that, and the box of cupcakes tumbled out of her grasp in her effort to be free.

Her eyes dropped to the crumpled box and smushed cupcakes at their feet, heart beating faster. Not out of fear... Possibly. She didn't know *what* she felt. It was potent. It was hot. It was uncomfortable—but not necessarily in a bad way.

She cleared her throat. "Um. You can let go now."

He released her, as if her skin burned. "Shit. I'm sorry. Did I hurt you?"

Eva stepped back, cradling her hand against her chest; the spot he had gripped throbbed with the promise of a small bruise later. "I was just trying to wipe the icing from your nose, why did you grab me like that?"

His eyes fell to the box at their feet then snapped to her wrist and how she held it. He pinched the bridge of his nose. "I'm sorry," he repeated fervently. "I didn't mean to hurt you."

"But you would have hurt someone else?"

"Yes," he answered immediately without remorse. "If someone attacks me, I'm making damned sure I'm the one walking away. If someone comes after *you*, I'll make the last moments of their measly existence the most painful moments of their life. I won't apologise for that. But you... you're not supposed to get hurt."

She stood there in the middle of the street, a gentle breeze slipping between them, as his words sank in. He'd already made it clear that her safety mattered, that he'd kill anyone who tried to hurt her... But it hadn't really sunk in what that truly meant until she experienced his reflexes first hand.

Her heart beat harder against her ribs. He was fast and strong and promised to ruin people for her. She didn't want him to change. The only thing she ever wanted was for him to be *himself* with her. But she had to wonder how well she really knew him if his reaction surprised her.

"Did I hurt you?" he pressed, brow furrowed, the muscles on his throat tight, as if she was the only thing that mattered.

She looked down at the mess at their feet and sighed. "I think the cupcakes are in worse shape than I am."

She moved to pick them up, but he was already kneeling and collecting the crushed box. A growl heaved out of his chest as he stared at it, mouth pressed into a white line. "My training has saved my life more times than I can count, but some days it feels more like a curse. I'll buy you some more cupcakes."

"You don't have to," she said, almost automatically. But he really didn't have to get her more. The gesture alone was the first truss in the bridge of trust he was trying to build.

Silence hung between them. He watched her just as she watched him, her mind still reeling from an instinct so deeply ingrained in him that he reacted to a simple touch. He'd meant to protect himself, not harm her, but what if that instinct couldn't be turned off? Was she to expect that every time she tried to touch him?

"So... this supposedly cursed training," she asked slowly, hoping to break the uncomfortable silence, "is it the same training you want to teach me?"

His shoulders stiffened, eyes squinting into sharp slits. "Jacob spoke with you?"

She nodded. "He said you wanted to show me how to fight against Sylus's assassins. Will I... move like that?" Apprehension rode her tone whether she wanted it to or not. She wanted to fight, but she wasn't sure she wanted to flinch at every turn.

With the shake of his head, he continued down the path. "Not quite."

She followed after him, curious what he meant.

"Hargin asked me to train you months ago," he confessed. "I turned her down. I didn't want to turn you into me." He scoffed under his breath, tipping his head back to the stars. "The gods have a funny way of twisting fate." His gaze found hers again, steady and burning. "If you want me to teach you, I will. What you do with what I teach you... that's up to you."

There was fire in his eyes, the kind that made her heart stutter. It clenched her stomach, as apprehensive as she was eager. He would give her the power and strength she needed to protect herself as well as the people she loved... but she also feared hurting those very same people. If he could barely control it, what hope did she have?

The look he gave her wasn't desire, but it still made her feel bare beneath it. He wanted her to fight. To survive. This was how he knew to help.

She wanted to survive too.

"But," he added, his voice clear and grounded, "I need you to understand something before we begin."

"And what's that?"

"I'm not training you because I think you're incapable. You're a talented rider and a terrifying opponent."

She had to fight to suppress her surprise from both his words and the ferocity in them. The utter respect in his praise was flattering and shocking. Nevermind what she or other people thought of him, this man was once the Slayer of Souls, a Prince of Estrus; he commanded armies, ruled a kingdom by his father's side. Perhaps, what they fought for and how they ruled wasn't honourable or just, but that was why he was here now, walking down a quiet street with her.

"I want to give you an edge," he went on, voice firm, adamant. "This will be one extra weapon in your arsenal."

"Because you can never have too many weapons." Though her tone was teasing, her eyes flickered to the silver glinting under his cloak.

"Never," he agreed, entirely bypassing her joke.

She smiled anyway. "Thank you."

"What for?"

"For not making it about who's better."

It would have been easy for him to gloat, rub it in her face that he had superior training than her. But he didn't. He respected her skills and autonomy, which was so different from everything she'd learned from Estrus's culture, from the Fortys clan specifically.

"What made you leave?" she asked, suddenly curious. She peered up at him in time to catch him flinching.

His jaw rocked back and forth, eyes intent on the street ahead. He was silent for so long, she didn't think he was going to answer her, that this was the question that pushed him too far.

He heaved a heavy breath, "I watched a woman burn alive to protect her son." His voice was flat—devoid of any emotion, be it sorrow, anger, or warmth.

The confession made the hairs on her arms stand on end. Her heart beat just a bit faster as memories of her own swam to the surface. An image of her mother cradling Erika close to her chest hit her first. The flames closing in on them, the fear shining in their eyes, Erika's screams, begging for someone to save them.

She shut her eyes, breathing in the cool, crisp air into her lungs. Forcing herself to remember the good times with her family, Erika dancing, Mom serving them hot meals with a warm smile on her face, Dad showing her how to hold a sword. The sounds of their voices were fading, the feel of her mother's arms wrapped around her was getting harder to remember, the scent of her father's coat was a mere whisper of a memory.

But their names would be remembered, engraved on a monolith that vowed to carry their memories until the end of time. They would live forever in Brar where they were loved and happy.

She opened her eyes to find Grayson watching her. Where his voice had held no emotion, his eyes were roiling with it—pain, regret, fear, anger. Guilt weighed heavily on him above all else.

"As I watched her burn," he said, tone gentler this time, "I remembered my mother. It all suddenly came to me—what she looked like, the sound of her voice, the words she used to tell me when I was a boy. The absence I felt when she suddenly disappeared. I realised in that single moment that Sylus would never burn for us. He'd sooner watch us burn than take our place. But not my mother. She would take our place in a heartbeat. She *did* burn for us."

Her mind went to what he'd said earlier about Sylus killing his mother as punishment for trying to take Dravyn away.

"It was in that single moment I realised that what I was doing was *wrong*. That Sylus's reign was built on fear and control, not because it was the best way for the kingdom to thrive—but because greed and wealth were more important than his family or people. So I left and never looked back."

She was at a loss for words. What could she possibly say after that?

"You wanted honesty, Starling."

"I did—do," she corrected herself. "I do. I just... didn't expect it... or *that*."

She knew the events leading up to his departure would be monumental. An event brutal enough to change his entire way of thinking. But she hadn't known just how bad things were in Estrus. How bad things had been for him.

He grunted. "It's all right. It was too soon."

"No, Grayson. It wasn't too soon. I want to understand. I want to know what makes you *you*. It's just a lot to take in."

He was shutting down too quickly. Before she could utter another word, he'd completely closed himself off, a muscle feathering in his jaw, shoulders rigid, a looming shadow hanging over them.

Loosing an irritable sigh, she let her hands fall loosely at her sides. *You just had to open your big mouth...*

She cursed herself for not taking the time to find the right words instead of fumbling through them. Maybe then he'd see that she was willing to listen, eager to learn—even if the truth hurt. Even if the horrors of his past scared her a little. She'd rather experience it all then to have never known these things.

Too soon, they arrived at the landing pad. Eran was there, emerald eyes tentative as they swung between Grayson and Eva, as if he could see the tension between them like a tightly wound rope. As they neared, he lowered his head, azure scale shimmering under the full moon.

"Good evening, Eva."

"Good evening, Eran."

She reached up, stroking his snout, a longing taking hold of her heart as she did. What she'd give to feel Arkon's scales right now, to have him beneath her as they soared through the skies...

But he was frustrated with her, and she didn't know who she was more angry with—him for making her life more difficult, or herself for letting a man get between them. Even if that man was Grayson Smith.

Grayson peered up at the twinkling sky then frowned at her. "Where's Arkon?"

"Running late," she lied with a casual shrug, hoping it would hurt a little less. It didn't.

He narrowed his eyes on her. "Late? That dragon loves you too damn much to not be within bolt range."

He doesn't love me when the man in front of me killed his kin. But instead of saying that, she said, "He'll be here in a minute."

"Then we'll wait with you," he decided stubbornly, tucking his hands into his pockets.

"No." Panic seized her. "You don't have to do that. Go on ahead."

He couldn't wait. Couldn't know. Not just because they were fighting over him, but because *no one* fought with their dragon. And she was ashamed... so deeply ashamed of it, but, at the same time, she was right to fight for them, for Grayson... right?

Grayson's eyes narrowed suspiciously. "I'm not leaving you alone in the middle of the night in a city with *one* night patrol."

Of course he knew how many patrols Lensenton had. He was meticulous.

Annoyingly so, in this case.

"I'll be fine. Just go."

He crossed his arms and leveled a glare on her. "Where's Arkon, Eva?"

A protective surge rose up in her. Maybe it was because he cut their conversation short earlier when she'd fumbled. Maybe it was a stab at her own pride. Or maybe it was a part of her Bond with Arkon, the tether she couldn't deny, even when they both loosed the connection.

"The whereabouts of my dragon is *my* business, not yours," she bit out.

His fists clenched at his sides, lip curling up in frustration. The air around him seemed to crackle with energy. "It is my business if it's the middle of the fucking night and he's not here to pick you up. Why isn't he here? Is it because of me?"

She crossed her arms. "Not *everything* is about you, Grayson. Just go."

He snarled.

"Grayson," Eran barked. "This is the part where we respect Eva's decision. If she needs help or a ride back to the base, she'll ask for it." He looked at her pointedly, as if the weight of his ancient gaze could force a confession out of her.

"What he said," she shot back.

Grayson's lips pressed together into a tight line, on the edge of speaking further—but then he blew out a violent breath and backed away. "Fine." Annoyance coiling around him like veracious vipers, he spun on his heel and marched to Eran's side. He swung into the saddle with ease. "I'll see you on the mats tomorrow?" His tone came out clipped, clearly speaking out of necessity than want.

She nodded tersely, too wound up for anything else.

"Good."

Then Eran leapt into the air. Gravel stirred around her feet, one piece pelting her knee. She stood still, legs braced to combat the strong gusts, and watched as their forms disappeared into the night, blinking out of existence—for at least a few hours before she saw Grayson again.

The relief she felt was brief, overridden by guilt and frustration. It hung heavy on her shoulders and pressed on her lungs.

"Why did I agree to training?"

Why did she agree to any of this? If she hadn't, her dragon would still be talking to her, she wouldn't have to walk home, and she wouldn't feel so godsdamned wretched about wanting to love someone.

Helpless in the tumultuous clutches of life, she turned for the path leading to Dragon Canyon, and began her long trek home.

CHAPTER 9
HAUNTED

With Eva and Jacob out for the evening, Anna had the night to herself and planned on curling up with a good smutty book, letting the world around her and the incessant gnawing in her chest disappear.

However, she only got through one page before a note slipped under her door. Leo was in desperate need of help for organising the gala. Typical. He always seemed to wait until she was wrapped in blankets with a fresh cup of tea to ask for a visit.

Of course she'd go for him. Unlike him, she had the autonomy to come and go from the base as she pleased—for the most part. It was Eva who made travel difficult, but she could survive a day without her. Jacob and Grayson would keep an eye on her. This was the *one* thing she was allowing herself—a day off. She'd helped Eva and Grayson, but in doing so she'd been ignoring her own problems—which had been working out well until she found herself alone with her thoughts and no one to pull her out. She was always telling Eva to embrace self care, maybe it was time she took her own advice. Even if it was easier to look after other people than herself.

So, here she was, packing and getting ready to head out for a much needed day trip to see her best friend.

She'd just folded a neat note and placed it on Eva's pillow when a knock came at the door.

Praying to Astrida that it wasn't her mother or one of her messengers, Anna pried it open. She was pleasantly surprised to find Jacob on the other side. He looked exceedingly handsome this late afternoon, in a casual, long sleeved shirt and dark riding pants. The deep green worked well with his tan and highlighted the gold in his endearingly unruly hair.

His smile brightened her evening—but her stomach twisted. His timing couldn't be worse.

"Jacob? You're back so soon. Did everything go okay?" With the way Eva was talking about her sibling day this morning, she had expected them to be out well into the night.

He scratched the back of his head, a crack fracturing his smile. "Yeah. We had a great time. It was good to see Eva smile again. But we ran into

Grayson in town and I can't stand watching them fight. So I *conveniently* remembered I had a meeting to attend."

Anna's hands went to her mouth to muffle a laugh. She'd pay handsomely to be the fly on the wall for that conversation.

"You didn't."

He looked at his pocket watch, looking rather smug. "They should be having dinner right about now... which means we have the evening to ourselves." He beamed, proud of his adorable scheming.

Anna winced, adjusting the strap of her pack to accommodate the suddenly oppressive weight bearing down on her. His timing couldn't be worse. They haven't had the chance to talk since they rescued him. She *missed* him. His quiet strength. His unrelenting support. Gods, even his laugh. When was the last time she heard him laugh like they were the only ones in the room?

His eyes jumped to the strap—then her overnight bag. "Oh. You're busy. Sorry. I shouldn't have assumed—"

She didn't let him finish that thought. She pressed her fingers to his lips, momentarily wondering if they would feel just as soft against hers as they did under the pads of her fingers.

I should have kissed him. Give him something to think about until I return.

"Don't apologise," she said, her voice low and gentle. Earnest. "I'm glad I'm the first person you thought of to spend the evening with..." Her fingers fell from his lips, slapping to her side, Her tone shifted, hardening. Bracing. "Any other time, I would drop these plans and spend it with you—but it's Leo."

He blinked, tongue darting over his bottom lip. A red hue climbed up his face so fast Anna wasn't sure he'd heard her speak. But after a moment of processing, the surprise cleared from his face, leaving him solemn with understanding.

Only *this* man understood her bond with Leo. Never questioned it. Never asked her to change. He knew that Leo took precedence above all else. Not because he would be their king one day, but because Leo had no one else in his life he could call on. Jacob, she knew, would be there for him in a heartbeat if he needed him to be—but not even he knew Leo like she did. There were some things that only *she* would understand.

"Is he all right?" he asked, entirely sincere. That's just the kind of man he was. Selfless. Understanding. Was it any wonder that she was in love with him?

She held up the short, vague note Leo had sent her. "Hard to tell. He asked me to help plan the gala." Which could range from "Help me, I'm drowning" to "there are too many bloody options. Help me pick something." She wouldn't know which one it was until she got there.

Brazenly, he lifted a hand to her face, brushing the length of her cheek with his thumb. Her breath caught in her throat. He *never* instigated contact.

"You're a good friend, Anna." The words came out thickly, coarse.

Her heart squeezed, because while she may be a good friend, *he* was a true angel, sent by Astrida to give her the strength to be there for the people who needed her.

She leaned into his touch, the heat, the flutter warming in her belly, wishing this moment didn't have to end. "I'll be back before you notice I'm gone."

"You're impossible not to miss, Anna." His hand stiffened before he dropped it and stepped back, leaving just enough space for her to pass. "May the winds be in your favour."

"Yours as well."

With one last glance, being sure to trace every stunning line on his face, remember every freckle on his cheeks, she slipped past him and hurried to the Stables. If the winds were truly in their favour tonight, they would arrive in Lexxis just before dawn.

Aster was already in the Stables when she arrived. Putting the saddle on didn't take long, required barely a thought, and then they were airborne.

Despite the chilly air slipping through her dragon scale jacket, attempting to sink its claws into her, she barely felt it. Aster's magic thrummed through her body, staving off the cool night and unforgiving winds. That didn't stop her fingers from going numb beneath her fur-lined gloves, though. The strain of clutching the saddle's handles for such a long flight always left her sore and aching, no matter how many times she'd made this trip.

By the time Lexxis came into view, a faint tickle of pink dusted the horizon. Most of the city was still asleep, with only a few lights dotting the streets. Plumes of steam and smoke alike drifted into the sky, from bakeries and forges and everything in between.

A dull nostalgic ache tugged on her heart as her eyes trailed over the beautiful city and the district that had been her home once upon a time. The Emberwalk District. A home to any artist who set foot within its borders.

"*We are not here to reminisce,*" Aster growled low in her mind. Any reminder of Anna's old life—the life she so desperately longed for—grated against Aster's scales.

Anna's grip tightened on the handles, despite this being the easiest stretch of their flight. "*Come on, Aster, you know I'm not leaving you... I could never.*"

For, as much as she loved the thrill of a crowd and watching everyone smile—because of *her* voice, her smile—she could never part with Aster. The dragon had become so irrevocably intertwined in everything that made Annaliese Hargin, parting with her would be an impossible feat. Never mind what the physical consequences of departing with her Dragon Bound would do to her, she cared too deeply for her to abandon her.

But it didn't matter how often she assured Aster or how deeply she let her in her mind, the dragon would always be jealous of the life Anna had once led. Because she couldn't give her the kind of happiness Anna had briefly felt during her times on tour.

She pried her gloves off, tucking them into her breast pocket, and brushed her fingers over her sharp scales. Aster's body came alive under her touch, a series of small vibrations reverberating through each individual scale. The sound rumbling in her chest was softer than a growl but just as loud.

Dragons could be powerful, true forces of nature to be reckoned with—but at the end of the day they could be just as docile as a kitten.

Aster angled for Kain Castle, spreading her wings wide to slow their descent. She alighted softly on the gravel, like a butterfly on a petal. Her wings fluttered just as delicately as she shook out the cold tips. Her head scanned the small, manicured field in search of somewhere to take shelter from the morning chill—but she wouldn't find anything. The castle was hardly designed with dragons' comfort in mind.

"I wish Glade was here," she grumbled, while Anna slid off her back. Once her rider was clear, she curled her tail in on herself and folded her wings over her back. "She would have made a nice hut for me."

Anna patted her foreleg. "I do too." If only to spend more time with her rider.

Sunrise was Jacob's favourite time of day. The moment before the sun crested over the horizon, where the world was silent, seemingly holding its breath, before waking up. He and Eva used to watch it all the time during their hunts. He said it was during those precious quiet moments when they dreamed the biggest. He loved the colours. The silence. A promise of what the day might be.

To Anna, it was just another sunrise. A reminder that she was up far too early—or had pulled an all-nighter—for a fate she had no control over.

"*So pessimistic this early in the morning,*" Aster chided, her mind already half lost to the realm of sleep.

"*There's no one around to be optimistic for.*"

"*Then go find someone. I want to sleep peacefully.*"

Rolling her eyes, Anna patted her dragon one final time before going inside. It wasn't like she was being negative on purpose. She typically took great pride in looking on the positive side of things—but it was easier when there was someone around who needed her to brighten their day. Alone... her thoughts were left to stir and fester.

And fester, they did. When she was alone like this, whenever she closed her eyes, she was taken back to the battle at Darius's fort.

She rode the currents of her fury when they stormed the fort. Her friends had abandoned her—left her alone *in a desert with a bunch of rowdy Wanderers. Her best friend chose* Grayson *over her.*

There would be hell to pay.

But first, she had to get through an army.

There were thousands of soldiers in the field outside of the fort. Every individual highlighted in the clouds with her dragon vision. Too many to discern friend from foe.

"They're in the fort," Aster *informed her, sending her a brief image of two individuals hiding in the stables and a third tied to a post in the centre.* "They appear to be in need of a distraction."

They'd watched Eran fly past the fort—and the ensuing group of soldiers chasing after him. But there were still too many for Eva and Grayson to make a move.

"Then let's give them one they'll never forget."

"Indeed."

A battle cry tore out of Aster's throat before unleashing the first fireball. It sailed through the clouds, piercing the midnight air. The clouds parted, giving Anna a first hand view of the impact. Bodies disintegrated. Men screamed and ran. They scattered like frenzied ants, some running for the trees, others for the ballistas.

"Take out the ballistas!" *Anna demanded down their* Bond.

One arrow was all it would take to bring down a dragon. Maybe not kill, but that part would come later once they were grounded.

"I know. This isn't my first siege."

Aster angled for the closet one, diving low to drench it in her ravenous flames. Their screams were much closer and sliced through Anna's ears. Screams so similar to Niall's when her fire had touched him...

"Focus!" Aster *snapped, grounding her.*

Gritting her teeth, she clenched the handles of her saddle. They ascended into the clouds again, banking hard to line themselves up for the next ballista. The swept down—

Anna caught movement in the corner of her eye—an arrow for another ballista hurdling their way. "Bank!"

Aster twisted without hesitation, wrenching to the side with so much force Anna was nearly tossed out of the saddle. Her stomach lurched up into her ribs, churning her pitiful dinner into her throat.

The arrow hissed passed Aster's wing, soaring into the forest.

Aster only just managed to right herself when another arrow cut through the air, aiming straight for her heart—

A lightning bolt snapped from the heavens and obliterated it into a thousand splinters. Anna ripped her gaze upward to see Arkon flying overhead.

Aster called out to him in thanks, a different kind of heat welling in her chest.

"Focus," *Anna tossed the word back at her.* "Take me down. I'll handle the ballistas."

There were too many of them for Aster to destroy efficiently—not without the risk of getting hit by one of them.

"It's too dangerous. There are too many of them."

"There won't be if you keep to your part of the plan. Besides, I wouldn't be your Soul Bound if I wasn't born for battle."

Aster growled, low and threatening—but she dove for the nearest ballista. "You are not allowed to die."

"I don't plan on it."

"Show them the meaning of true strength."

Aster didn't slow down as she approached the ballista. Men cried out, shouting orders, frantically cranking the wheel to turn the giant arrow.

Anna sucked in a single deep breath, summoning every dark part of her she could muster. Clamping down on the fear, both new and old, she swung her foot over the saddle and braced herself in the crook of Aster's foreleg. Just as they were feet from the ground, Anna leapt off her dragon, feet hitting the oversaturated battleground. The impact shot up her legs, into her hips—she rolled forward absorbing the rest of the impact then skidded onto her feet in front of the ballista.

For a beat, she met the gaze of six—no, eight—soldiers in charge of the ballista. A mixture of shock and confusion marred their faces. The dragon hadn't burned them to a crisp. Instead, she'd deposited a girl in front of them.

Anna didn't give them the chance to process her arrival beyond that. She cut into the first man then the second without a thought. She dug deep into the anger simmering beneath her skin and let her rage fuel every step and every swipe of her blade. No man was allowed to escape her wrath.

In a blink, all eight men were dead at her feet. She climbed the ballista and called onto the fires surrounding her and burned it to ash.

One down. Nine to go.

One after the other, she cut down the men standing in her way then burned the ballista they protected. She had gotten through five when they started catching on to her presence. Before they had been so focused on the dragons in the sky, they hadn't once looked to see who among them was destroying their weapons.

But now they had doubled their efforts to protect the remaining four ballistas. Too many for Anna, who was already getting worn from battle, to take down on her own.

"Use your fire," Aster *commanded.* "They are no match for your flames."

"No." *She'd promised herself to never use her magic on someone again—not after what she did to* Niall.

"Use your flames, or we will both perish!"

Anna's eyes darted from one man to the other, their anger rising with each passing face. Their weapons glinted in the fires surrounding them, taking on their rage with flickering menace.

Her muscles were straining, begging for a reprieve, bones aching. Her lungs felt as if she'd inhaled acid from the wicked smoke. She might not feel the lick of the flames, but the smoke still clamped on her lungs and made fighting that much more difficult.

And then she wasn't given a choice. Three of them leapt for her. She blocked one, raising her sword, and pushed the other back, kicking him in the gut. But the third was behind her, blade aiming to run her through.

Instinct took over. The fire came to life on its own, jumping from an inferno nearby and engulfing the man behind. His screams were silenced in a second, the sizzling stench of melted flesh and hair filling her nose. Screams so much like Niall's*—but before she could stop herself, she was directing the flames to the other two assailants. Then to the others, drowning them all and the ballista in her fire.*

Once she had control over the flames, it was easy to let them take over. They followed her like fiery vipers, sinking their fangs into anything that moved. She took out the last of the ballistas with ease.

When she turned to take on the next soldier, she found no one left to fight. They had either fled or were reduced to ash. The dragons flew above, working in tandem to keep the fires under control, to stop them from spreading to the forest.

So much death. Most of it by her dragon—but she had played a large part in it too. Blood soaked her hands, stained her hair. Ash clung to her armour and smeared her face.

Never again, she'd promised herself. And yet... here she was...

Her fingers curled into her palm as she fought back the memory of that moment—the crackle of the flames, the screams. His scream. The smell of flesh and burning clothes.

She had promised herself, swore to anyone who would listen, that she would never, *never* use her fire to hurt anyone again. And yet, in the heat of battle, when the chaos of the fort had consumed her, she had let it slip. She had let it rip through her. She had burned and torn and destroyed. There had been no other choice, not really.

They wouldn't have made it out if she hadn't.

But at what cost?

She'd lost a piece of herself that night. A piece that she wasn't sure she could ever reclaim—

"Anna!" Leo's voice broke the silence in the hallway. She jumped like a skittish doe, laying a hand on her racing heart. He noted the movement, closing the gap between them rapidly until he was a foot away. "Are you all right?"

"I'm fine," she dismissed, waving off his concern. She'd come here for *him*, not to dredge up her problems.

He crossed his arms, watched her, eyes sharp, discerning. "You're not all right. What's the matter? Aside from having flown through the night to help me plan this gala."

She took in his casual attire, the tailored tunic, the khaki slacks. Even first thing in the morning, there wasn't a single piece out of place. No stray hairs, no snags in his clothes, nails groomed to perfection. It was all he had ever known.

She exhaled, long and strained. "I came here to help—"

He held up a hand, stopping her. His hard gaze formed a pit in her stomach. "Don't. Remember our promise?"

She rolled her eyes with a scoff. "The promise we made when we were kids?" When they were too young to know what they were truly asking of each other. To know how hard life would get for either of them. "Yeah. I remember."

She let her heavy gaze drop. Lately, she felt like she held the weight of the world on her shoulders—if only because if she crumbled, Eva and Grayson would quickly follow. They couldn't afford that kind of distraction. Aboria couldn't afford it.

"Right," Leo said curtly, slapping his hand into hers. "I intend on upholding my end. Do you? Good," he decided before she could even respond. "You can tell me over breakfast. I doubt you ate on Aster's back."

He tugged her down the hallway to one of the many boardrooms. He dragged her inside, slamming the door shut and sat her in a plush chair; a blanket was lain over the armrest and an extra, lap-sized pillow was leaning against the side. Tea was already steeped and waiting for her, along with an assortment of breakfast treats they didn't make in Dragon Canyon.

Anna's heart swelled at the sight of all of her small comforts. It made the overnight flight worth it, even when she didn't expect anything in return. She never did with Leo, yet he always gave. Always listened.

Beyond their breakfast, there were piles of books, colour swatches, fabric swatches, and cutlery, plate settings, and napkins. So much more. So many things for Anna to get lost in and forget about her pestering thoughts.

A weary yet grateful sigh slipped form her lips as she sank into the cushions, pulling the blanket over her lap. The soft, fluffy fabric was soothing, a balm to the aches in her joints—and the lesions on her soul.

She plucked a mini quiche off the plate. "How much have you planned so far?"

Leo sat beside her, elbow on the table so he could face her fully. "You're not talking your way out of this, Anna. We made a promise to always tell each other what's going on. To always listen. I'm here to listen—tell me what's going on."

She plopped the quiche in her mouth and slouched in the chair. Egg, ham, and cheese filled her mouth, warming her bones and soul. Moaning, she shut her eyes and savoured the flavours. The food on base wasn't terrible—certainly not the worst she'd ever had—but the chefs in the Kain kitchen were elite. The best of the best. And their food delivered every. Single. Time.

This little slice of heaven gave her enough strength to say the words she hadn't dared to share with anyone. Out of duty, out of stubbornness, and of sheer survival in the base. "I didn't come away from Jacob's rescue unscathed."

Leo tilted his head slightly, his brow furrowing as he realised this went far deeper than anything they'd ever shared. He knew she didn't have the healthiest relationship with her mother. He knew she had loathed Aster for a time for Bonding with her. He even knew about Niall and her fear of using her magic. But this... This was different. This was admitting weakness. That it didn't matter how hard her mother had drilled a killer into her daughter—she still would never be the Dragon Knight she wanted her to be.

"What do you mean?" His voice was low, steady. Tentative.

"I've killed before," she began, her voice strained, as if speaking the words would bring it all back. "But never with my fire. I swore I wouldn't use it on anyone again after..." Her words faltered, and she shut her eyes, blinking away the emotion that threatened to overtake her.

Leo said nothing, but his silence encouraged her to keep going. The distraction she had desperately craved was slipping away, but the urge to confess it all, to speak the truth, overpowered everything else.

"The accident with Niall," she whispered. "I thought I could get past it, but I can't. When I burned those men, when they screamed, all I heard was Niall's screams—and felt the gut-wrenching guilt that came with it." A tear slipped down her cheek, and she wiped it away furiously, as if it could stop the guilt and shame from suffocating her.

She'd run like a coward after hurting him. It was that very same day Hargin's orders for her return came in. So she ran back to Aboria with her tail tucked between her legs. Didn't look back. Didn't even say goodbye to him. After *everything* he had done for her—she couldn't find the courage to look at what she'd done to him.

Later she had gotten word that he was released from the infirmary—but the water dragons couldn't revert the damage done. She'd marked him forever.

Leo's expression softened, and his hand rested on her shoulder, steadying her. "Anna... my dear Anna. I'm sorry you were forced to use your magic, but if you hadn't..."

"I know," she breathed, squeezing the pillow around her tighter than she could squeeze any human. "They would have died. Darius would have gotten exactly what he wanted. Aboria would be in an even worse position. That army deserved every ounce of flame Aster and I dealt them—but it still hurts."

His hand slid down her arm, slipping into her tight grasp. He squeezed her hand just as hard. "You don't have to bear this burden alone. I'm here. Eva, I'm sure, will listen if you choose to tell her. I know Jacob will. Use us to take the load off. It's what we're here for."

With a trembling breath, she wiped the last tear away, grateful for his calm presence. She had no answers, no easy solutions, but for the first time in a long time, she didn't feel so alone in carrying the burden.

"Thank you."

He pried her hand from the pillow and kissed her white knuckles. "You're the closest family I have, Anna. Never think twice that I won't drop everything to be there for you."

She breathed in through her nose and out through her mouth, steadying her heart and mind. "It's hard to remember sometimes. We're both so busy. You have a kingdom to run—and I'm training Eva, and quite possibly the most valuable asset in all of Aboria." She hated to think of Eva as an asset, or a weapon, but Hargin never let her forget it during their weekly progress meetings.

A frown pulled on his brow. He sat back in his seat, fingers grazing over table cloth swatches. Green and gold were his family's colours, which were expected to be a part of the decor, but people were also expecting fashionable, trendy colours.

"She is valuable, isn't she?" he murmured quietly, almost to himself.

"What do you mean?" It wasn't like him to think of people with values.

His fingers tapped against the swatch book. "It's been bothering me. Sylus's surrender. I know it was Darius's idea to capture her, and Sylus would much rather see her dead—but I find his immediate surrender unsettling."

"You think he's planning something." Anna's words hung in the air, heavy with the uncertainty gnawing at her. She let out a frustrated breath and snatched a napkin swatch, her fingers brushing over the rich winter tones.

Leo swallowed hard. The weight of the gala preparations suddenly felt trivial, a distraction from the larger storm brewing just beyond their reach. "I don't trust Sylus. I don't trust that he's really surrendered. Not for one second. Has the Runaway mentioned anything?"

She rolled her eyes. "I think the name you're looking for is *Grayson*. And no, aside from informing us that Sylus has sent assassins after Eva, he hasn't said anything on his surrender."

A tic feathered at his jaw. "*Will* he say something if he suspects his plans?"

Anna threw him a dark glare. "Of course he will. What kind of question is that? He's going to train Eva how to fight Sylus's assassins."

He scoffed. "No one can train her better than you can."

"Thank you, but not this time. I've never seen them fight. Grayson has. He can show her what to expect. And you know that. You just don't like the idea of them spending time together."

"Of course I don't." He raked a hand through his auburn hair indignantly. "He's a bad influence on Eva—and he doesn't deserve her. She should be with someone who will shower her with gifts and love her so deeply and irrevocably that she will never know what it feels like to be unloved."

Despite the indignant nature of his tone and the huff of his chest, Anna smiled. "And you would be that man?"

He puffed out his chest like a posturing gorilla. "I could be."

She couldn't help it. Her grin grew wider. *So this is what it feels like to be an observer.*

Usually, Anna was the one caught in between two suitors, forced to pick one—or neither—while Leo sat back and watched it all unfold with a smug grin. Bet he was regretting that now.

"You could be. But I don't know, Grayson has really stepped up his game." She was so cruel... but she didn't feel the slightest bit guilty. Karma was a bitch.

Leo's eyes narrowed into slits. He grabbed a booklet just barely within reach and dropped in front of her. "I didn't only bring you here for your amazing sense of style. I asked you to come because you know Eva better than anyone—and I need you to help me make it perfect for her."

Anna opened the book and chuckled when she found a long list of menu items. He was certainly on his way to Eva's heart... and she did promise to make sure there was a chocolate cake at the event.

As they continued preparing for the gala, Anna's stomach churned with uncertainty. They had stopped Darius and he was a week away from being punished for his heinous crimes. Sylus had pulled his men out of Aboria and had left Darius to face his punishment alone. But there was still tension in the air. Leo was right to be suspicious of Sylus. She was too. If she'd learned anything from King Renkon over the years, it was that a king didn't give up without a fight. If Sylus was backing down now, it only meant he had another plan. The war might be over, but he wasn't done with Eva.

Let his men come, let him fear Eva's power. Because Anna would be by her side every step of the way, and together, they could handle anything.

CHAPTER 10
SCARS

Eva rolled her shoulders back, standing in front of the door to the training room. With a deep breath, she tried to shove the nerves out of her mind. Her hand was inches from the handle, yet she couldn't bear to close her fingers around it and push it open. Her dragon vision showed her his red silhouette moving with the grace she had learned to expect from Grayson. His feet and hands flowed in tandem with one another, while he guided them into the next position seamlessly. Each punch was as quick as a lightning strike, his legs just as deadly as they swung in a powerful, sweeping arch. His balance never faltered. There was no hesitation between move sets.

Watching him only reminded her of why she was drawn to him in the first place. His confidence carried him on a different level from everyone else. He wasn't cocky. Far from it. He knew his strengths and weaknesses, had absolute control over his body—and knew he could decimate anyone who stood in his way. He held himself like a seasoned warrior, an undefeated general. An unconquerable king.

It was as hot as the Five Hells.

It's just training, she reminded herself sternly, then shook the nerves out. The training room wasn't the place to be turned on. Especially after the epic fail after their dinner. They went from teasing and amicable to being at each other's throats by the end of the night. Not her proudest moment.

It wasn't even twelve hours ago they were sitting in a veil of wisteria at the Atrium—and now here she was, outside the training room.

She glanced at her left then to her right, where Anna and Jacob *should* have been. Her brother sent word this morning that he would not be joining them because Glade was feeling cooped up and needed a vigorous flight. He hadn't wanted to stall her training on his account, so he *insisted* she still attended Grayson's lesson.

Anna was called away by Leo for help with planning the gala next week. Eva couldn't hold it against her. She'd been told that Anna used to make frequent trips to the castle—before Eva became her partner. Now she never got to see Leo. Because of her. This was their chance to reignite their friendship, and Eva wouldn't take that away from them.

However, that now meant she was alone with Grayson. Dinner at the Atrium last night was a promising start to his making amends. Dinner was very different from sparring. Dinner kept them a healthy distance from each other. There were people around to keep them in check. When they didn't have people to keep them in check, they started to bicker and fall apart.

What was going to happen when they were *supposed* to throw punches?

"*Give him a black eye*," Arkon growled in her mind. "*It is no less than what he deserves.*"

Eva winced from his sudden intrusion. He had left her to walk home last night, forcing her to feed Grayson an awkward lie as to why her dragon wasn't waiting for her at the landing pad.

Did she feel bad for snapping at them when they were only trying to look out for her? Yes. But she also knew that Arkon would have been furious if she had involved Grayson in their fight. He wanted absolutely nothing to do with Grayson, and for her to tell him about their affairs... it would only make things worse between them.

Besides, the walk back had been surprisingly pleasant. A gentle cool breeze through her hair, moonlight filtering through the White Woods canopy. The leaves were changing colour, shifting to a fiery red and ochre yellow. She didn't need her dragon to give her a ride. She lived for years without his wings and could survive a night in the woods.

Even if he was keeping an eye on her from afar. Even if he didn't want her to know he was watching her.

"*I am angry with you*," he grumbled in her thoughts, "*but I do not wish you death—from assassins or ogres.*"

Ripping her gaze away from Grayson's impressive form, she clenched her teeth and thought of cold water rippling over her flesh like a river over stones. The sharp imagery kept her grounded, but it didn't do much to temper her frustration.

"*I would have been perfectly fine without you*," she muttered back. "*You don't have to babysit me if you can't stand the choices I make.*"

His growl reverberated through her mind then he was gone again.

Her heart clenched, gut twisting at his absence. She hated fighting with him, but she felt she had no choice if he was going to judge her for her decisions. It wasn't fair of him to make her feel wretched every moment she spent with Grayson.

Before her thoughts began to swirl too fast, she pushed the door open and marched inside—

Despite spying on him through the door for the past ten minutes, she wasn't prepared for the sight before her.

She'd expected him to be wearing under armour, like she was, for a start.

All that was standing between her and her bundle of nerves was a pair of straight black cargos. His pale skin was an arrant contrast to the darkness in his eyes and his ebony hair; it wrapped tightly around hard muscle honed and carved to mould him into deadly perfection.

It wasn't the rippling, corded muscle, or the defined ridges and valleys of his torso that caught her breath, though, nor the myriad of scars glinting in the early morning sun. No, it was his back and the brutal scars raking from one corner of his marvelously sculpted body to the other. Unlike the thin lines crossing his torso, arms, and abdomen, injuries that spoke of the battles he had fought in and won, the ones there told a different story. They spoke of pain and suffering, torment she couldn't begin to fathom. A warning. To him and those around him.

Her blood filled with ice. Much like the reflexes she'd witnessed last night, those scars were a vicious reminder of his past. A reminder of the things he had done and what had been done to him.

Talking about it—even in small bursts—was one thing, but to *see* what had been done to him. What he had to endure before he came to Aboria... it hit deep in her soul.

It wasn't pity she felt towards him, not even sorrow—but anger, a low quiet simmering fury towards the people who had done this to him.

Grayson spun around to face her, cutting her view from a part of himself he'd never shown her. A bead of sweat slithered between his pectorals, running over the hard azure scales just beneath his ribcage, before slipping between the waistband of his trousers. The scar wasn't any wider than her thumb and was five inches long. A killing blow if Eran hadn't interfered.

Fully aware of her gaze, Grayson cleared his throat and shifted on his feet. "I can put a shirt on if you don't like looking at them."

Them. His scars. His past.

She shook her head to clear her thoughts. "No. It's all right. I..." She moistened her lips, unsure how to say what she wanted to say. "I don't mind them. They're a part of you." Her feet moved before she knew what she was doing, crossing the room until she was right in front of him. She reached out for the scar that marked him as Eran's Soul Bound, pausing a breath away to search his gaze for any sign of protest. He stood stock-still, a stone statue. Except his eyes were ablaze with intense emotion, old and raw, yet new and thrilling. An enigma, he was. She'd give up her salary to know what he was thinking. "May I?"

He met her gaze, studying her curiously, as if he couldn't believe she was standing this close to him.

If he was waiting for her to jump away from him, he'd be waiting a long time. When he realised that, he laid his hand on top of hers and guided her fingers to his scales.

They were warm to the touch, warmer than his hand, and smoother than the scales Arkon had given her. She traced each bump, doing her best to ignore the hitch in his breath. It hadn't crossed her mind until it was too late that his scales would be just as sensitive as hers. The concentrated magic within the scales made her hyper aware of everything that touched them. It was why she wore only the fine scaled under armour shirts; the soft material didn't catch on the scales like other fabrics did.

She moved on to explore other scars. Some were rough and raised, while others were a mere white line blending with the rest of his smooth skin. Cuts, jabs, deep lacerations—he had endured it all one time or another. They all formed him into the man he was today in some capacity, led him to leave his awful life behind and start a newer, better one.

But she didn't recognise the patterns on his back. She couldn't stop herself from tracing a particularly long one from his shoulder down to his hip. These were all raised, layered one on top of the other, inflicted after the one beneath had healed. The one she followed cut across them all and was the last one he received.

"What caused these ones?" Her voice betrayed her, wavering when she didn't want him to hear how deeply affected she was by them.

His fists clenched at his sides, the muscles of his back flexing beneath her fingertips. "Do you really want to know, Starling?"

Starling. The nickname he'd given her made her heart melt. A symbol of hope. Touched beyond words, she laid her hand flat on his back. When she told him she wanted to know the real him, she meant *every* part of him. She wanted to understand him and know him better than anyone else in Astrida.

"Tell me." Last night she'd stumbled, but she wouldn't today.

The tension in his back unfolded beneath her palm. He released a shallow breath, a subtle sigh of relief. Just as she was scared he'd run from her for pushing too hard, he was afraid he'd scare her off with his horrid past. "They're whip lashings."

His back was *covered* in them. There wasn't an inch on his back that wasn't untouched by these vicious scars.

Her hand trembled on his shoulder blade. If he noticed, he didn't show it. "Why?"

Why would someone do this to him? Why did he let them? Why did he endure this agony when he was the most powerful man she knew and could easily make it stop?

He peered over his shoulder. His gaze found hers, eyes as hard as obsidian. "He didn't always need a reason." He, as in his father, Sylus. "Sometimes he was angry. Sometimes he was bored. Sometimes he was too drunk to tell the difference between his family and his enemies. Sometimes he needed to be reminded *he* was in control." His voice was laced with venom, of hatred forged in the very depths of his soul. "It was his way of conditioning us. We learned from a young age how to handle pain, how to take care of our wounds. I got my first lashing when I was five years old."

She halted in tracing another scar across the middle of his back. He received his first lashing at five years old. Gods. When she was five, her father taught her how to ride Hiron. She helped her mother collect eggs from the chicken coop. Her obnoxious ten year old brother pulled on her pigtails. The most painful experience in her life at that point was when she tripped and got sticks and stones in her knees and palms.

And him? He was beaten, tortured. No wonder he became the Slayer of Souls. He had to if he was going to survive his life as a Prince of Estrus. That was no life for a child—for *anyone*. And for him to still be standing here, to have chosen this life over the life he had been given... he was far stronger than she thought he was.

"Your hand?" he said thickly, meeting her gaze again, eyes unreadable, as if he could shield her from his torment. "I can't feel it, but I know it's more gentle than any other hand that's touched me."

He couldn't feel the tremor in her fingers because his back had taken so much damage that the nerve endings had frayed.

Suddenly, the reflexes made sense. He *had* to be fast. *Had* to be brutal.

The hate she felt for Sylus before felt inconsequential to the absolute loathing she felt toward him now. How could he treat his own children like this? She hadn't known such cruelty was possible in this world until she knew the Fortys name, but now she realised she had only just scratched the surface of what kind cruelty lived in this world.

"Why didn't you leave sooner?" Her voice came out a breathless rasp.

He turned to face her and reached up, cupping her cheek. His touch was so soft, so gentle, as his thumb brushed away the tear she'd shed for him, it was hard to believe he was once called the Slayer of Souls. "We didn't know any better. It was the only life I ever knew. I knew nothing of compassion and warmth, or loyalty and companionship. I grew up with death and pain. I spread it like a plague to my people, because I thought I was doing them a service by rooting out the weak."

His hand shook. The invincible, infallible Slayer of Souls, was *shaking*. Hand sliding to the back of her neck, he pressed his forehead against hers, as if she could ground him to this turbulent world. His breath spilled over her cheeks, raw and ragged.

“I called it strength, what I did to them,” he confessed, the words scraping out of his throat. “But with you, I’ve learned what it means to fight for something that matters. I won’t lose you, Eva. I won’t let Sylus or Darius destroy you. I hate everything they stand for and for what they’ve done to Estrus, but I’ll teach you their tricks.” He pulled back, those dark storm cloud eyes locking onto hers with an intense fervour that made her bones tingle.

The intensity in which he loathed his family should have scared her. Seeing him so raw—so hurt by his past that he trembled—should have made her pity him. His adamant oath to never lose her should have made her run. Even when she had made it clear she wasn’t ready to forgive him, he was determined to protect her, train her, give her everything she needed to survive.

But she didn't run.

Why would she when he was giving her everything she wanted? *This* was the Grayson Smith she wanted to see, to get to know better. Grayson Smith free, uninhibited by judgement others cast on him. She wanted everything or nothing.

And as he gazed at her with that thunderous intensity, she realised he was waiting for her to retreat. For this moment of vulnerability and emotion to be too much for her.

“I’m not going anywhere.”

His gaze ran over her form, those eyes, hard and unrelenting, once threatening to shut her out, melted into smouldering orbs filled with longing and desire.

“No, you’re not.” He fell silent, as if he needed a moment to accept that she wasn’t running away from him or judging him for *feeling*. His eyes darted to her mouth, and her heart quickened. Before he gave in to the rising tension between them, he looked away and rolled his shoulders back. His composure sealed him in a mask of resilience and steel. It didn’t take over him entirely, though; the mask allowed a lopsided smile to tug at the right corner of his mouth. “What I’m about to teach you is a Fortys family secret. It has been handed down for generations, perfected by the sharpest of kings and honed by the cruelest assassins.”

Eva allowed the subject to change. This was what she had come here for, anyway. “The Fortys clan isn’t entirely royal?” Kings *and* assassins created this technique.

“While, technically, yes, they’re not all treated as such. Typically, two sons are bred. One is meant to be King—not necessarily the older one—and the other is destined to be his Shadow, a grunt, assassin, enforcer, whatever his brother needs him to be to keep order.”

There was a lot to unpack. The idea of the Fortys clan *breeding* offspring for specific purposes didn't sit well with her. Neither did the idea of Grayson being picked to be the king, because that meant Darius was very likely going to be his Shadow if he had stuck around.

"What about daughters? What was their role?"

The slip of a smile faded, leaving behind a well-practiced stoic look. He stepped back, putting more space between them, and let his hands hang loosely at his sides. "Most of them were killed at birth. For the rare few who were spared, they were often used to strengthen alliances."

Bile rose in her throat. There was more to it, but he didn't have to say more. She could fill in the gaps: they were sold to the highest bidder, whoever had the most land to offer, or the most influence. They were mere objects, creatures of value, rather than human beings who deserved respect and to marry someone they loved.

Grayson jutted his chin towards the mats, moving the conversation along. "If you feel uncomfortable at all, just say the word and we'll stop for the day."

Uncomfortable? He was using the wrong word. Distracted was more like it.

But today, they weren't Eva and Grayson with a complicated history and even more complicated feelings. Today, they were Dragon Knights, training and sparring, bettering themselves so that they could fulfill their duty to the best of their abilities.

"I'm good," she promised, both him and herself. "Throw your worst at me."

A dark grin twitched in the corner of his mouth. "Careful what you wish for."

"I know what I'm asking."

CHAPTER 11

DEATH'S DANCE

Grayson studied Eva closely. *Did* she know what she was asking? She might stand before him, cracking her knuckles and planting her feet, ready for her lesson, but was she ready to see the side of him he dreaded showing her? It was hard enough to talk about the Fortys clan without unleashing the full force of his rage. He'd barely contained it when he started thinking about an assassin landing a killing blow on her—or Darius whipping her, beating her, fucking her until there was nothing left in her soul.

He'd gotten so damn close to losing control. He'd shamefully shown her *how much* the Fortys clan affected him. It was easy. Too damn easy to give in to her. She wanted to know Grayson Smith, but did she want to know the monster beneath the surface, too? Did she want to know every dark thought that crossed his mind? How would she look at him after showing her Death's Dance, knowing who had taught him, what they used to do? When would it be too much for her?

"*Maybe it'll never be too much for her,*" Eran butted in. "*Maybe, just this once, you found someone who is more stubborn than you are. Maybe she'll accept you for who you are, all of your flaws and failures.*"

"*I told you not to snoop, Eran. Out.*" With a simple thought, he tossed the dragon out of his mind and built walls up to prevent him from further intruding. Eran only fueled his hope, but he didn't need hope right now. He needed to keep his wits about him. This was a delicate—and *private*—matter.

"All right, Starling, show me what you can do."

The first time he used her nickname, it had been a slip of the tongue, an instinct he couldn't resist. But she didn't protest, despite its origins and the name coming from him. He hoped she liked it, because she was a starling to him. A beacon of hope in a perilous, unpredictable world. As long as he had her, he'd find his way to the light.

He gestured broadly to the training mats—to the reason they were here. "Pretend you're walking down the street in Lensenton. You're talking to Anna with shopping bags or whatever it is that you do in town."

He wanted to see what kind of instincts she had, if she was ready for the Fortys clan's techniques. Given that Anna had trained her, he expected her to have a basic understanding of awareness and preparedness.

Rolling her eyes, Eva turned on her heel and strutted along the mat away from him. His eyes dropped to her hips, and he couldn't help noting her form had gotten even firmer while she was in the Desert Lands.

She was already a force to be reckoned with. By the time he was done with her, no one was going to lay a hand on her.

Watching their enemies crumble at her feet might become his favourite pastime.

Eva halted in front of the weapon wall, a hand on her hip, regarding the wall as if it held the world's finest jewels rather than an assortment of training weapons. Her right knee was locked, her balance entirely relying on that side to hold her up. She didn't take in her surroundings. There were *far* too many openings for him to take advantage of.

This wouldn't do at all.

His boots were soundless on the mats as he crept up behind her. He crouched, being mindful to stay out of her periphery—then lunged. One arm went around her waist, yanking her firmly against his front, while he brought a training dagger up to her throat. He pressed it hard against the vital exposed flesh as he dragged it across the carotid artery. There was no cut, but it left a deep red mark and would have hurt.

If they had been training in Estrus, they would be using real weapons.

"Dead," he ground out against her ear before stepping away.

She spun to face him, a hand on her throat. Her eyes were wide with surprise. "I—I wasn't ready."

"That's the point," he snapped, perhaps a little harsher than he should have. If she was to survive, she needed to take this seriously. He wouldn't apologise for protecting her the only way he knew how. "Sylus's assassins aren't going to wait for you to be ready. You have to anticipate their attack at every moment." He gestured to the mat where he had slit her throat open. "Show me what you were like in the Desert Lands—and it better be different from what I just saw."

For his sanity, it needed to be better than what he just saw.

She pinned him with a dry look. "When I asked you to do your worst, I didn't mean you could be a prick about it."

That fire in her eyes seared the blood pumping in his veins. Only Eva Greene dared to use a tone like that with him, and he loved it. There was no fear of retaliation, regardless of what he could do or if she could handle it. He felt *seen* when she did that. "I'll be a prick until you start taking this seriously."

Huffing, she blew a strand of hair that had come loose from her ponytail out of her face. "I *am* taking this seriously, Gray."

Gray. There was that name again. Jacob and Anna had used the name countless times, but it sounded—*felt*—different on her lips. Intimate, endearing. It caressed his soul and eased the forever-present weight of the demons on his shoulders.

"You asked me to show you what I'm like with Anna," she scolded him. "I showed you. I don't see a need to watch my back with her, because I know she has my back. I'm not like that *everywhere*."

As glad as he was that she felt safe with Anna, it wasn't good enough. Relying on others would get her killed. "You should have your guard up at all times. Sylus's assassins will go for the kill and they'll take any advantage over you they can get. You have to expect them to attack you or your loved ones at any moment."

Her shoulders dropped, a glimmer of sadness filling her eyes. "That sounds horribly exhausting."

"You get used to it." He'd been doing it every waking moment of his life—since his first whip lashing—and she would learn to do the same if she wanted to live through this.

Her eyes swept over him, growing sadder and sadder by the minute. "You live like this, don't you?" She moistened her lips, tears brimming in her eyes. "Your weapons, the mithril cloak, every move you make—it's because you don't ever let your guard down."

He couldn't bear to see the pain in her eyes—pain she felt for *him*—and drew his attention to the mats.

One day, she wouldn't have to live in fear. He'd track down every assassin, every fucker that wanted to use and abuse her for their own personal gain, and see to it they never got their hands on her. But that day wasn't close enough. Hargin wouldn't let him go on a seek and destroy mission with the tension so high between Aboria and Estrus. He would have to wait until things cooled down before he could start his hunt.

"Again. Show me what you were like in the Desert Lands."

She stared at him, a challenge for him to get the best of her this time, then she turned and walked down the mats again. He already noticed an improvement. Her hand hovered by her hip, where her training dagger was lying in wait. As she strolled away from him, her gaze casually took in the corners of the room, taking note of the benches lining the wall opposite the window. This was a more practised routine, wary yet casual.

It was better than what she'd shown him earlier, but she gave too much away. He knew exactly where she was looking and where she wasn't, which still made her easily exploitable.

He was silent when he came up behind her, using her blind spot to his advantage. Before she knew what hit her, he was wrenching her hand away from her training weapon, pinning it to her back. Muscles primed with anticipation, she spun out of the hold, but his grip remained locked on her wrist. She used the tight quarters, closing the gap even further and thrusting her elbow upward for his chin. His grip slipped from her wrist, but she wasn't watching his feet. As she freed herself, his foot kicked hers apart, breaking her balance, then he threw his weight into her. She fell onto her back and he held his training knife to her throat again.

"Dead." His face was a mere inch away from hers, breath fanning over his cheeks. Those eyes, usually a rich chocolatey brown that warmed his bones, were utterly black as they ran over the length of his body. They took note of every place their bodies met. "But better."

Her breath hitched in her throat. "Was it?"

"Yes." He peeled off of her, giving her space to breathe, then extended a hand out to her. He pulled her up in one smooth motion. "The speed and instinct is there. Once we work on your awareness and reflexes, you won't have to think about your next move, you'll react naturally."

He stepped back and planted his feet, fists braced at his hips. "Watch me closely. I want you to practice these battle stances every morning when you wake up and every night before you go to sleep. You are going to engrain this into your very being."

Eva crossed her arms, watching him slowly shift from one stance to the next with keen interest. She studied the placement of his hands and feet, the way his limbs moved in one fluid movement, never leaving an opening. Individually, each stance was just that, a stance, but combined it became a deadly series of punches, kicks, jabs, locks, and blocks. A dance.

Doing this twice a day would help her form the reflexes necessary to pull off this technique successfully.

"How is this going to help me with Sylus's assassins?" she asked. "They're similar to the breathing routine I do with Anna."

Breathing was just as important as mastering these stances. Inhaling and exhaling at the right moment, increased the impact of each movement. She'd be able to hit harder, faster, all the while maintaining her composure. A warrior was useless in a fight if they got winded two seconds in.

"The assassins practice this dance every morning and every night," he answered patiently. He'd doubted the technique when he was younger too. "By making these stances become a part of your everyday routine, you'll become familiar with their techniques. Blocking their attacks will be instinctual, countering them will be second nature. They won't expect you to know their techniques and won't be prepared to counter your attacks.

While they're caught off guard, you use Anna's techniques to finish them off."

Eva's mouth fell open, eyes alight with wonder. "That's genius."

He shrugged one shoulder, avoiding her gaze. Despite knowing who he was, what he'd done, she still regarded him with undeserved reverence. One day, he hoped he could live up to the hero she saw in him, but that day was far from today. "It's just basic combat theory."

She scoffed, eliciting a smirk from his lips. *Of course* she'd scoff at him. "Give yourself a little more credit, Gray. I don't see anyone else coming up with genius plans."

He looked down at his scarred knuckles, the very same knuckles that had broken countless bones, then flipped his palms upward; they were laced in just as many scars, but they were thinner, made from a blade rather than bone. "These techniques aren't something to be awed by. You are the only person I will ever show them to."

"Why?"

"Because it's a part of me that I can never kill," he confessed quietly. "No matter what else I change about myself, I will always get up every morning to practice my stances and I won't sleep until I've done them again. Every time I do them, I'm reminded of the man I used to be, and I—" He cut himself off then blew out an exasperated breath, eyes shuttering. Did he dare tell her? What would she think of him if he told her his biggest fear? "I feel like I'm slipping into old habits. I don't want to turn into *him* again."

A slight frown pulled on her brow, lips pinching together. Her mouth opened then closed it, the frown pulling tighter.

"What is it?" he pressed. He could tell she had something on her mind, something she wanted to share. Whatever opinion she had, he wanted to hear it. Always.

She chewed her bottom lip, unintentionally drawing his attention to the scar in the bottom right corner. Her eyes dropped to the floor. "Nothing. It's nothing."

"It's not nothing. If something's bothering you, I want to know."

With a shrug, she waved vaguely in his direction, eyes finally meeting his again. "You say you practice this every morning and night... but I never see you doing it."

That was a deflection if he ever heard one. Just as she'd deflected his question last night after dinner when he asked where Arkon was. He'd expected the dragon to meet them at the landing pad like Eran, but he hadn't. And, while Eva brushed it off as him running late, he knew there was more to it. She hadn't quite been able to meet his eyes then and she hadn't met his eyes now.

She was holding back on him. He should be angry, furious, that she wasn't sharing everything with him when that was exactly what she wanted from him—but he couldn't blame her either. It was *her* trust he had to earn, not the other way around. Until he'd given her enough of himself to ease the doubt in her mind, her heart was locked tight and out of sight from him.

That was a bitter pill to swallow, but he did nethertheless, because he vowed to make this work and he'd be damned if he gave up now.

"I have a secret spot," he admitted, his throat tight, though he did well to hide the fact he knew she was deflecting him. "It's private and out of the way so no one can watch the dance."

Her lips pursed, eyes staring past his shoulder as if her mind was somewhere far away. He'd kill to know what she was thinking.

Instead, he said, "I can show you the spot, if you'd like. I won't be much for company," he warned, "I use it as a chance to reflect—to remind myself who I am today, not who I used to be. But we can practice together... if it would help you."

An olive branch—a trembling one with wilted leaves and one gust away from falling apart—but an olive branch all the same. More time together meant more trust, and more trust meant he was one step closer to earning her forgiveness.

She'd already agreed to dinner and training. He'd told her about his family, a secret he thought he'd take to the grave. Seeing the anger and pain—anger and pain she felt for *him*—in her eyes was gut-wrenching enough. He couldn't possibly hope she'd agree to more. It was too much too soon—but he couldn't stop himself from offering. From hoping.

She was his Starling, after all.

"I..." She tongue darted her upper lip, gaze warily pensive. "Anna likes to talk when we train. It helps keep my mind quiet, away from memories I'd rather forget, but sometimes... sometimes I want to feel the pain and fear. I've been too afraid to face it to try meditating or anything, but this will give me the push I need. I think it's important to remember it, so I know how hard I have to work to never feel it again. You know?"

It was a struggle to keep his expression neutral. She didn't want his pity or sympathy. She wanted understanding. Validation. Their pain was different, but they hurt all the same. They were on the path to healing. He was deeply honoured she chose to heal with him. Not Jacob or Anna or Arkon. Him.

"Eran said something very similar to me recently," he confessed, surprising even himself. He'd never admit how afraid he was to face his demons. He'd rather ignore them, but if Eva was willing to try, so would he. "We can work on it together."

The determination in her features was palpable. He pretended he didn't see it, allowing her that privacy, and jutted his chin to her feet.

"Show me the first stance," he commanded.

She started with planting her feet and holding her fists to her hips. He inspected her form, circling around her with his hands clasped behind his back. "Bend your knees more. More," he demanded when she only tweaked them a little. "This stance is the most important one. Without a good foundation, the rest of your technique will crumble." He came up behind her, hand hovering at the small of her back. "May I?"

They'd gotten closer, closer than he had ever been with someone, but he remembered the uncertainty in her eyes when he'd touched her last without asking her permission. He wouldn't make that mistake again.

She nodded.

His palm went flat against her back, pushing forward while his other hand pulled her shoulders back. Once she was in position, he moved a hand down to her stomach, splaying it firmly over her abdomen. She resisted the pressure, maintaining her balance, which was exactly what he wanted. "Keep your centre of gravity here, always. The moment it shifts, you'll lose your balance."

"Balance is key." The words sounded like something Anna would say.

He strode to her front, unable to fight the smile tugging at the corner of his mouth. Perfection. If this was any indication, she was going to pick up the technique quickly. He expected no less from Eva. She was brilliant, a shining star in a world of darkness. His starling. "Very good. Next stance."

She moved into her next stance, trying to mimic his smooth motion, but he stopped her immediately with a raised hand. Her eagerness to learn and master the technique was critical, but if she tried to do too many things at once, she'd get sloppy. He'd rather she'd learn slowly and develop good habits rather than learn it all too quickly and miss vital elements that would keep her alive.

"Don't bother with filler. Just move from one stance to the next. Get comfortable with each position first then we'll work on flow." He studied the second stance, searching for any flaws. He found none. "Perfect. Next."

It took hours to show Eva all of the stances. Some were more difficult for her than others to master. She had the hardest time remembering the last few when he asked her to start from the top. All of it would come with practice, of which he would ensure she got a lot of.

He hated the Death's Dance, its origins, how they had been used to hurt hundreds of people, and that they were the only thing that could bring him solace when the nightmares became too much. But he was learning to appreciate them in a different way. Before he used this time to remember the horrible things he had done and to choose never to do them again. Now, instead, he used it as a way of looking forward. Yes, he'd hurt countless people with the very techniques he taught Eva, but in teaching her, she wouldn't have to fear for her future. She could confidently walk into a fight knowing she would come out on top. If it weren't for these techniques, they wouldn't have come to an understanding. Their pain was out in the open and there was no judgement, no pity, no obligation.

Grayson had never experienced anything more liberating. For the first time in his life, he felt like he might find peace within himself.

CHAPTER 12
MONSTERS IN THE DARK

"Please! No! No, mercy!"

Jacob watched yet another victim being yanked from their family, in a long line up of many families facing the same fate. He sat, helplessly tied to a post, forced to look at their faces, see the fear in their eyes, hear their pleas over and over again.

The pleas fell on deaf ears. Darius seemed to revel in their pain, a disgustingly satisfied smile splayed on his face. Keyon was just as delighted to hear them suffer, standing to his right. The soldiers who followed Darius's cruel commands bore masks of indifference.

Children and women were separated from their fathers, husbands, and brothers, dragged to the dungeons to be butchered and fed to the wyvern. The screams—the fucking screams—tore Jacob apart. His job was to protect the people of Aboria, to stop atrocities like this from happening. But it didn't matter how hard he fought against his restraints or how hoarse his throat grew from shouting at Darius—it wasn't enough. He wasn't enough.

Families were torn apart. Innocent lives taken too soon. The men left behind were given a choice: join them or serve. His stomach roiled violently as he watched men sink to their knees and pledge to serve. Cowards. All of them. Their loved ones were given a death sentence and rather than fighting for them or joining them in the afterlife, they chose to serve the very bastard who condemned them.

Those who resisted, were taken to the dungeon with the others, while those who pledged allegiance were led to the barracks.

The screams that night curdled his blood, slowly, painfully, pushing through his body until it was all he could think about. The only vivid detail he would truly remember.

He didn't sleep a wink, not when the screams became a deafening silence, not when the voided darkness of night laid a veil over him. Darius approached him in the morning, freshly rested. He visited Jacob every morning. Crouching before him, cocking his head to the side like a morbidly curious bird of prey. Those dark onyx eyes studied him with a hint of enjoyment gleaming in the abyssal darkness. That look alone told him that he still drew breath because he was more useful alive than dead. If it weren't for Eva, he would have long since been dead—but not before Darius had his fun with him.

He didn't speak a word to him—didn't have to. He had said all he needed to say already. Those words had haunted Jacob ever since: "You won't know the monster you've harboured until it's too late."

Jolting upright in the blackness of his apartment, Jacob gulped lungfuls of air to abate the ache in his chest. Sweat trickled down the side of his face, dripping onto his bare chest. A shudder wracked through him when his heart finally slowed.

What time is it?

Body feeling heavy and haggard, he turned his head towards Grayson's bed. Empty. It typically was. Likely in the canyon with Eran, practising his stances.

Jacob didn't know how he managed to function on so little sleep. He was rarely in bed, especially of late. There was once a time not too long ago where Jacob didn't understand why he avoided sleeping unless his body absolutely demanded it. These days, he understood.

Gods, he understood.

He buried his head in his hands and sobbed. He let it all out—the guilt, the shame, the fear, the dreaded sense of helplessness, the agonising grief. Everything and anything that clawed its way to the surface, he felt it all and more. It cut through him like a savage blade, leaving gaping, raw wounds in its wake.

He let it consume him until the sun peeked through the canyon, casting its warming ochre glow onto the base. Grayson would be returning soon, and he didn't want his partner to see what a wreck Darius had left him in.

"He's not a monster. He'll never be that man again." A daily mantra he repeated every morning. If he said it enough times, he'd eventually have no choice but to accept it as fact.

Feeling as though his body had been tossed off a cliffside, Jacob rolled out of bed and went through the motions of getting ready for the day. His limbs ached from yesterday's training, each movement stiff and uncooperative. He splashed water over his face, more to shock himself into alertness than to clean off the sweat that clung to his skin. The bath helped some—warm enough to unknot his muscles, quiet enough to let his thoughts drift—but it did little to ease the weight pressing behind his eyes.

By the time he stepped out and dressed, Grayson still hadn't returned. Jacob dried his hands on a worn towel and moved to the desk shoved into the corner, where shadows spilled across scattered maps and scraps of parchment. He reached for a quill, hesitated, then scribbled a short message to Grayson. Another for Eva. No rambling, no excuses, just the essentials: *Gone flying with Glade. Be back before sundown. Don't wait up.*

It wasn't a direct lie. He would be out with Glade all day, but not in Dragon Canyon.

This was something Grayson couldn't help him with. If Grayson went along with him, he wouldn't get the same kind of access. Despite the words that rattled through Jacob's brain, he trusted his partner—but that was as far as the trust went. Not one soldier in Kain Castle trusted him. Very few Dragon Knights did. And they didn't even know the truth. If they knew who Grayson used to be, what he was *truly* capable of, they wouldn't let him live a second longer.

Jacob met up with Karson and his dragon, Bruxon. in the Stables, where Glade was also patiently waiting.

Karson's smile lit up when his bright blue eyes settled on Jacob. If Grayson was carved out of a boulder, Karson was carved out of a mountain. The Knight stood an easy foot over him and had twice the shoulder width. Unlike his cousin, Captain Stark, he was one quarter giant, and only *just* fit in the height and weight requirements to ride a dragon. Even then, Bruxon was one of the largest dragons in the canyon and the only one capable of taking his weight.

"Long time no see, buddy!" His mountain of a friend held his large, corded arms out wide, then pulled him in for a big, warm hug. Jacob clapped him on the back, giving him a good squeeze, before stepping away and smiling up at him.

It had truly been a long time. Too long. It seemed cruel: after going through the trials together, spending months building lifelong bonds, once a dragon selected their recruit, they were sent to different stations. Some had died since joining, while others, like Jacob, had gotten busy with work. Once a month, they gathered in Lensenton and drank their hearts out, but Jacob had missed the last few.

"It's good to see you, Karson. Thanks for letting me tag along today."

He grinned broadly. "No worries, bud. It's the least I can do for you..." A solemn look took hold of his features. "I'm sorry I haven't been around. We all are. What happened to your family is fucked up."

Jacob's throat tightened. He couldn't speak, could barely nod. He'd missed his friends greatly during his time of need. But work came first. It always did. He understood why they hadn't been around.

"We'll make sure that fucker's head rolls. I'll personally make sure you have a front row seat."

"I don't need a front row seat. I just need to make sure nothing stops him from being executed."

He nodded firmly, a rigid line on his mouth. "That, I can do."

Captain of the Royal Guard, Captain Nestor Quade, had asked for Karson to be the Dragon Knight liaison to coordinate security for Darius's execution day. Both King Renkon's personal guard and Knights hand selected by Hargin would be running security. The best of the best.

Usually, Jacob and Grayson would be given the task, but this was too personal. Hargin didn't want them near the security detail or anything to do with Darius. Even when they attended the execution, they were to be under watch by a higher ranking officer.

What Jacob was about to do could strip him of his Knighthood. But he couldn't just sit idly. He *needed* to see the execution block, the surrounding area, the security detail, who was on shift and the schedule. *Everything*.

Darius was dying next week, or his name wasn't Jacob Greene.

He and Karson saddled up the dragons then took to the skies. Glade was especially pleased to have him in the saddle again. They hadn't flown since he returned from Darius's fort. Partly, because she was mad at him for being reckless and getting himself captured in the first place. Mostly, he had been busy with the squad, filing reports, attending meetings, and promising healers and Captain Ahrua that he was all right and that Darius hadn't messed with his head. Not in the ways that would affect his work, anyway. It took *Grayson* vouching for him for them to clear him for duty again.

He ran his hand over his dragon's dusty gold scales, feeling her molten heat beneath his fingertips.

The first time he beheld her was still fresh on his mind. He'd just completed the last trial, exhausted, sore, and homesick. But amongst all of it, he had been awash with a sense of accomplishment. He'd done it. Survived the trials and now faced the dragons in their dens.

His comrades sought out the bigger, stronger dragons, the ones designed to kill and put fear into their enemies. Fire dragons, especially, were popular. But Jacob saw Glade, her sleek body, the scars she bore beneath her bronze scales, the subdued intelligence in her eyes, and knew she would be a better partner for him than any other dragon.

He'd approached her, held his hand out to her, just as he was taught to do. She'd hissed and clawed at him.

Since she had lost her mate a century ago, she believed she was cursed. Every Knight after his death perished shortly after they became partners. She had sworn off Dragon Knights and wished to be left alone.

Until she saw Jacob.

Looking at his inelegant gait, the way he clumsily climbed the cliffs to her den, she knew Hargin wouldn't put him near the front lines. He would be safe.

Then Deximus Fortys became his partner.

One morning, Hargin called Jacob into her office—a quiet room with a single window, facing a wall garden growing in the canyon, two chairs set on the other side of her desk. He remembered how stiff the air had felt, how her gaze cut into him when she told him the news. She was assigning him a partner. But not just any partner. A prince. The Slayer of Souls. And Jacob's orders were explicit: protect his identity, keep tabs on him, and report everything he did. Every word, every movement. He was to teach the prince how to be a Dragon Knight, what it meant to be an Aborian, and keep him in line—if such a thing was even possible.

It was an unfair responsibility for a newly promoted Private. But Hargin had chosen him because, she said, her daughter trusted him and believed he had what it took to change the Slayer of Souls. Another secret Jacob was expected to carry to the grave.

So, he became Grayson Smith's partner—whether or not he wanted to be paired with a killer, whether or not Glade approved.

He was terrified. For weeks, he barely slept, knowing who lay just feet away from him at night. Every twitch of the blankets, every shift of the mattress made his heart lurch. He hated sparring with Grayson, especially after witnessing him obliterate a reinforced punching bag without breaking a sweat. Missions were worse. Jacob didn't fully trust Grayson to cover his back—and Glade certainly didn't trust Eran. The dragons clashed constantly. Glade questioned Grayson's every move. One argument in the field escalated so badly, it nearly got the entire team killed.

Jacob and Glade fought more than they ever had. He tried to follow orders and bridge the gap between their pairs, but Glade did everything in her power to tear the group apart—to protect her rider, no matter the cost.

Six months in, it wasn't Jacob who changed her mind. It was Grayson.

On one particularly dangerous mission, Grayson risked his life to save Jacob's. He'd stepped in front of a fatal blow without hesitation and afterward, he swore he would always protect him. And he had. Every monster they faced, every battle they entered, Grayson absorbed the worst of it so Jacob wouldn't have to. He trained the clumsiness out of him, made him stronger, faster—a real Knight. In turn, Jacob reminded Grayson what it meant to enjoy the simple things, what it was like to be *human*.

Glade noticed. She saw the change, saw the way Grayson shielded her rider, and over time, she let her walls down. Accepted him.

From then on, the four of them became an unstoppable force.

Only Darius had ever come close to breaking them.

When they landed at Fort Ironveil, Glade was eager to add on to Jacob's list of places to check for. "Don't forget to test the ground beneath the chopping block," she insisted as soon as his feet touched the packed dirt outside of the fort. "There might be a tunnel that will swallow him whole before we take his head."

Chuckling, he patted her snout in comfort. "I don't think there'll be any tunnels. Estrus doesn't have any magic, remember?"

"They might have acquired a druid while in Aboria," she argued determinedly.

Karson shook with laughter. "A druid? They live far in the west and want nothing to do with the rest of us. Good luck finding one for hire."

"I'm aware," Glade grumbled, "but the Fortys clan are cunning and hungry. They chased magic out of their lands and now they're after Eva. They will do what it takes to claim their prize—even do the impossible."

"I will scour every corner of the fort for any inconsistencies, Glade," Jacob assured her, running his fingers over the scales of her foreleg. "Trust me. No one wants this bastard more dead than I do."

Settling down with a low huff, Glade lowered her snout to the ground and pressed her claws into the damp soil. The earth responded to her presence like an old friend—softening, shifting, bending to her will. Stones rumbled beneath the surface, rising in jagged clusters that smoothed into curved walls beneath her touch. A roof formed last, flat and slightly slanted, reinforced with packed clay and veined with moss that soaked up the moisture from the fog.

The structure wasn't large, but it was solid. Practical. A single breath of warm air from her nostrils dried the inside just enough to make it comfortable. With a satisfied grunt, she tucked herself inside, tail curling around her body as her eyes half-lidded in contentment.

Bruxon sat just outside, the mist clinging to his scales. He stared at the cozy shelter with a miserable expression, his wings hunched and dripping, but Glade pretended not to notice.

Jacob and Karson faced the fort, the stone palisade that had stood strong all through the Goblin Wars and many wars before it. After Lexxis, this fort was the last line of defence south of the capital. It had served and protected its people for longer than Glade had been alive. Next week, it would be the last thing Darius Fortys ever saw. A privilege he didn't deserve.

The fort was massive, twice the size of Fort Brar. Its impressive walls were home to the biggest barracks in Aboria. His grandfather trained here when he joined the army and had lived in the area most of his life before moving to Brar to be with his grandmother. Perhaps another time, he would bring Eva here to explore Jacobi's old stomping grounds.

Soldiers in the courtyard saluted as the Knights passed them for the main building, where Jacob was promised a warm office where they could sit and go over blueprints and schedules. Later, once the rain had pulled back, Karson would give him the grand tour. None of the soldiers, thankfully, knew who Jacob was—or word would get back to Hargin faster than he could finish training on Big Bertha—they only saw his dragon scale armour and knew he was a skilled, decorated warrior. A warrior of legend.

None of them needed to know that *he* wasn't legendary. Anna and Grayson? They'd have textbooks studying their techniques for decades after they're gone.

They spent the entire day thoroughly going over every lain out plan. Jacob tried to find holes in their schedule, in the patrols, but he found none. Everyone overlapped with each other and the more heavily crowded areas would have double or triple the amount of typical guards. Karson and Quade had been relentless in their scrutiny.

The same could be said for the blueprints. They laid out *everything*. Not a single rock was left unturned during the making of the map. The measurements were accurate—he checked—and the secret passages followed the map to the finest line.

The rain never let up. In fact, it assaulted the fort with a new found vigor as if Jacob had upset Asturias for questioning his friend's thoroughness. Karson took it all in stride. He knew what this meant for Jacob and knew that if he was ever in the same position, Jacob would do the exact same thing for him.

That was what it meant to be brothers in arms. The trials had been brutal, relentless, some would even say cruel, but it was necessary. Without it, Dragon Knights wouldn't have a bond that ran deeper than blood. "We fight together. We die together." That was the Dragon Knight motto. Or, in some cases, "You fuck with one of us, you fuck with all of us."

Darius Fortys crossed a line he didn't even know he crossed. He was going to die one week from today and the world would be a better place for it.

CHAPTER 13
NO SACRIFICES

Eva inhaled through her nose as she brought her hands and feet together, then exhaled through her mouth, sliding into the next position with practiced control. Her right foot lifted in a sharp upward kick, hands tucked tightly against her chest. As her leg came down, she adjusted her stance, grounding her weight and centering her balance in her core. The moment her foot touched earth, she snapped her fist forward, flowing seamlessly into the next pose.

Inhale, shift. Exhale, pivot.

Every stance challenged her balance, tested her awareness, and demanded subtle control over her limbs. It was combat in slow motion, a dance meant to sharpen her reflexes and strengthen the connection between thought and instinct. Though the motions were graceful, there was an undercurrent of tension in her core, a readiness coiled beneath the surface like a spring waiting to snap.

"Good," Grayson called, standing off to the side, arms crossed, feet shoulder width apart. The wind cutting across the plateau they stood on knocked his sable hair aside, exposing a slither of a scar on his temple his hair normally hid. "Now faster."

She slid out of a deep squat, hands falling at her sides.

The White Woods unfolded below them like a living tapestry, stretched wide beneath the endless morning sky. Autumn had set the forest ablaze with color—leaves blushed in gold, crimson, and bourbon. They swayed in the wind like a flickering fire too vast to contain, licking at the edges of the world. The faint rustle of the leaves was peaceful, reminding her of the good times in Brar, settling over her heart and calming her mind.

Beyond the forest, where the colors dulled and distance softened the edges, the tiled roofs of Lensonten peeked through the canopy. Smoke curled lazily from chimneys. Eva could feel the warmth of the Tea Lovers cafe enveloping her, the scents of mint tea and cinnamon filling her nose, as if she was walking through the cafe's door.

The view was breathtaking. Nothing like on the back of a dragon. The world blurred together from the sky. But here? They could take their time to capture every detail.

But, while the famed Autumn-kissed treetops of the White Woods was a stunning view she had dreamed of seeing since she was a child, she had to pull her eyes away to toss an incredulous look Grayson's way. "Faster?"

He nodded, a single sharp motion. Adamant. Just as he'd been all week. There was no room for error when he was watching her. No chance of slacking off as long as he led the reins of her training. Excuses weren't an option. Complaints were punished with a hundred push ups.

He was brutal. Merciless. A demon from the Five Hells sent to make her life absolutely miserable.

Eva wouldn't have it any other way.

They had only been practicing together for a few days, and already she felt a difference, both during training and when she was on the mats with Anna. She was faster, more fluid, barely needing to think before moving. Her awareness had sharpened. She felt more attuned to her body, to her surroundings. All because of his meticulous attention.

But to ask her to go *faster*? It just wasn't possible.

When he realised she wasn't going to attempt the impossible, he rolled his eyes, letting his hands fall to his sides. "Trust the process, Eva."

"I trust the process," she said, no truer words leaving her mouth. She'd been trusting it for days now, and not only felt a difference physically but mentally as well. When she danced, her mind eased. She could sift through memories, nightmares, without the tightness building in her chest, without the ever-present weight of the world pressing down on her. It was... freeing. "But if I go any faster my arms are going to detach from my body and my legs are going to fly into the White Woods and get eaten by a pack of wolves."

A smirk, partly mischievous, partly laced in dark humour. "You and Dravyn would get along together. He complains, despite the consequences too."

There it was. A little window into his past, into the man he was before she met him.

Eva didn't react, only smiled on the inside—until the rest of his words sunk in.

Her arms spasmed at the threat. They were still burning from their session last night, when she'd ended up doing two hundred push-ups.

"It—it wasn't a complaint!"

He shrugged, the casually sadistic bastard. "It certainly sounded like one. Give me a hundred push-ups, Starling."

"Asshole."

How dare he use his nickname for her in the same sentence as his heinous command?

"Sometimes I think you make me do things just so you can watch me flail."

His smirked turned devilish. "I'll admit, I do like watching you, but not here—not while we're training."

A flush worked its way up her face, raising her body temperature several degrees in this chilly morning air.

Usually, their conversations were strictly professional, and when he made contact it was purely clinical. Today, it seemed, he was loosening up. She allowed it. Loosening up meant opening up, and while he hadn't dumped a load of past trauma onto her like he did during their night in Lensonten, he did show her little bits and pieces of himself that only she was allowed to see.

Like this mildly flirty and absolutely diabolical side of him.

"If you like watching, at least make me do a hundred squats instead," she shot back, keeping her tone light and teasing. "And while I'm at it, you can show me exactly *how* I'm supposed to go through the Dance faster."

His gaze swept over her form quickly, head to toe—so subtle she might've missed it if she hadn't been paying attention. But when he chose to wear the tight black under armour shirt, putting his bulging biceps and forearms on display, how could she *not* be paying close attention?

"All right, Starling. Give me one hundred squats, and I'll show you how it's done while you're at it."

Mentally preparing herself for the soon-to-be fire in her muscles, she widened her stance, feet shoulder width apart, then dipped into her first squat, low and slow—just as he demanded of her push-ups.

While she rose and dipped into her squats, Grayson began Death's Dance, arms and legs moving in unison. He moved like water, limbs fluid, muscles bunching like vicious whirlpools then lashing out like the tides in a storm. He didn't look at her once. He wasn't whipping through the Dance at alarming speeds to show off. It was a demonstration of his strength and power—of the relentless training drilled into him from a young age.

And yet, even as admiration curled through her, tightening something low in her belly, a different kind of chill traced her spine. Because if he could move like that... so could the assassins that wanted to kill her. It was a reminder of why she was training and just who she was up against.

He finished before she did, sweat dripping down the side of his face, chest rising and falling with ease. Slowly, he turned, each step measured, just as controlled as his Dance. When his eyes landed on her, watching her bob up and down, there was a hard edge in them, carved by a past of guilt and regret. Once she finished and straightened up, the darkness within them parted, the demons looming over him dispersing.

"Clear your mind when you dance," he instructed. "It's instinct, not pensive. Only then will you move that fast so effortlessly."

"You've been doing it for years, of course you can do it quickly."

"You don't have years, Starling," he said, tone cold and unforgiving. "The assassins are coming. They could already be here—and you need to be ready."

Unease settled in her gut like a stone dropped into a pond, sinking until it hit rock bottom.

She was still getting used to the whiplash—the sudden reminders of the life he'd led before he came to Aboira. She was used to the brooding, to the darkness roiling in his eyes, but this was something different. He was unapologetically ruthless. This was a man who had lived and survived through Hell—and wanted to make damned sure she survived it too.

Swallowing, she nodded. "I will be." Despite the burning in her legs, she moved into the first stance. "From the top?"

"From the top, as quick as you can."

And so she began again, moving as fast as she could. When she fumbled, he stopped her, made her go through the transition slowly so he could see where she went wrong. He corrected her then she went through it again.

As the sun climbed over the horizon, the base woke below them. A gentle hum vibrated through the air. Dragons called to one another from their dens, wings rustling in the canyon breeze. Soon the morning patrol would be coming up as part of their routine. Grayson and Eva finished their session before they arrived.

As they walked down the narrow path hugging the cliff wall, her body quivered, stomach clenching in feverish demand. Grayson took the outside, in case her muscles gave out on her... again. The wind was harsh against the canyon walls, and until her body got used to working out three times a day, she was as brittle as a leaf in the last stretch of Autumn. She hated feeling frail and helpless, but at the same time she didn't mind having him close.

It was different when they weren't training. The brush of his arm against hers was entirely intentional, but instead of guiding her, it was keeping her safe, keeping her warm. And she liked the warm-fuzzy feeling that wrapped around her insides when he did that. They were small things—walking on the outside of the path so she didn't fall, waiting for her to sit at the table first before taking his seat, entering a room and scanning it quickly before she entered—but they added up. She felt cared for without her independence being stripped.

But, despite the way her body eased around him, leaning into the steadiness, the warmth, the strength, she resisted leaning too far, from going too near that edge of no return. Because the fall would be irrevocable and electric. Because when she fell... she didn't want to look back.

So she wanted to be damned sure she wanted to fall. Which meant erasing all doubt, silencing the voice in the back of her mind that told her it was all a lie. And the only way she could do that was with time, of letting Grayson keep showing her pieces of himself, doing the little things for her. Let him prove to her that *he* was here, not the Dragon Knight he was around the base, not the stoic friend Anna and Jacob had come to know and love. But the man haunted by his past, who knew death and destruction like a lover, who chose to use his power to help people instead of cutting them down.

Or maybe it wasn't actually *her* who had the doubts, but Arkon's. Their Bond had gotten more strained over the past few days. She rarely felt him during the day. It was only in the early hours of the morning, when the sun's warmth spilled over the canyon's walls, when Arkon slowly awoke and hadn't had the chance to build his walls yet, when she felt him. Felt his discontent, his festering resentment—but not towards her. Never towards her. Towards Grayson. And it was in those early moments of the day when her doubt hit her the hardest. When her own guilt for ignoring her dearest friend sloshed around in her stomach like acid.

This morning was no different.

She paused on the narrow path, fingers digging into the orange wall, as the acid crawled up her throat. A bitter, cold wind slapped the side of her face, tearing strands free of her ponytail.

Grayson pivoted, bracing his hands on either side of her head, pinning her to the wall, as the gust tore past them. His body was a shield, buffeting the worst of the wind, fending off the cold, too. Hips lined up with hers, heart beating rapidly against her own tempo. Steel and leather wrapped around her, both eliciting a thrill down her spine and dread in her stomach.

Because if she was fully aware of each hard piece of his body lining up with hers—then so was Arkon.

His fury rippled down their Bond.

"You would be a loyal friend if you pushed him off the cliff."

Arkon's intrusion jarred Eva's senses, jolting her body as if she'd been struck by lightning. Her head jerked back into the wall, vision blurring, drowning out the world around her.

His words sliced through her like venom-tipped claws, burning, unyielding. Visceral. He had always been wary of Grayson, his scorn never subtle—but this... this was different. He'd *meant* to hurt her. And that cut deeper than any blade.

"Ow!" Grumbling, Eva grazed the back of her head. Blood came away on her fingertips.

The wind died down, now a soft howl in the distance, and Grayson stepped back, eyes snapping to the blood. They narrowed into vicious slits, as if the crimson liquid had offended him. "Shit. Sorry. I didn't mean to push you that hard. I'll heal it, if you want me to."

"It wasn't you," she muttered, turning her head slightly so he could have better access. "It was Arkon. He... surprised me."

He popped the cork of his hollowed out dragon horn and commanded the water to glove his hand. It shimmered in the morning light, appearing to be a deeper shade of blue. Slowly, carefully, he raised his hand to her head and gently wove his fingers into her hair, tips grazing her scalp in delicious circles.

"He should know to be more careful when you're on the cliffs," he murmured. She hadn't realised how close he was until she felt his breath curl over the shell of her ear.

She looked over the edge, watching the river far below them carve a turbulent path through the canyon, to take her mind off the sensual thrill of his fingers working her scalp. Pair that with his magic seeping into her skull, dulling the pain, and stitching her back together with every pulse of his power... she was in dire need of a distraction.

"He knew what he was doing." Her voice was barely above a whisper, quiet when competing with the wind.

Yet, he still heard it.

"What are you talking about?"

She flinched, not from his tone. No, his tone was kind and open, but the question... it *burned*. He didn't know. She'd gone through great lengths so that he wouldn't find out.

"It's nothing," she managed, voice hoarse and not at all convincing.

He shifted closer, quiet and deliberate, until the toes of his boots tapped hers. His aura coalesced around her, as if it could sense what she wasn't saying and wanted to protect her.

"Talk to me, Eva. Something is going on with you and Arkon, I can see it in your eyes. It's been affecting your training with Anna."

Her head whipped in his direction. "What do you know about my training with Anna?"

"I..." He cleared his throat, hand slipping from the back of her head. "I've been checking in on your training with Anna. She's noticed a difference with you on the mats, says you're more aware of the placement of your hands and feet. But your aerials..."

She didn't know how she felt about him prying into her training when she wasn't with him. But that wasn't why she turned away from him.

Normally, she wouldn't hesitate to share with him. They'd grown accustomed to speaking their minds, in taking solace in each other's company when the world felt too heavy. Normally, he didn't ask about matters that involved Arkon.

"I don't want to talk about it," she said, her throat tight. Talking about it made it too real. It would hurt Grayson, ignite Arkon's fury, and force her to confront a truth she wasn't ready to face: her Bond with Arkon was fractured. Splintering apart at the edges.

Because of Grayson.

When they were alone like this, he was someone else entirely—unguarded, sincere. A man who let her see past the surface. A man who felt deeply but bore the weight of it in silence. Hells, she was starting to believe he felt more than most people ever dared to, and still, he managed to lock it away, never to be seen or heard.

What would he do if he found out they were falling apart because of him?

He took her arm, not roughly but firmly, and pulled her back to face him. "Don't shut me out, Starling. This is a two-way street. If you want more from me—then I want more from you. Tell me what's going on."

She stared up at him, watching the darkness within him churn like angry tides. It wasn't fair of her to keep secrets from him, while she asked him to give her everything. She *knew* that. But what if the truth hurt too much? What if it hurt him?

She'd seen so much of him this past week, been so grateful that he was putting the time and effort into letting her see the real him. It wasn't fair of her to hold back.

"Arkon..." Her voice faltered. She closed her eyes for a beat, head bowing in defeat. "He's... not happy with me."

The dragon's snarl ripped through her mind. "*Do not involve him with our affairs.*"

"*I'm sorry, but he has the right to know.*"

Eager to move on—to pretend she hadn't uttered a word—she continued down the path.

Grayson was ready. He grabbed the back of her shirt and yanked her back. On instinct, she spun, knocking his hand aside, then shoved him into the wall.

He stood there, unmoving, eyes slightly wide—before a grin broke out on his face. "*Very* fast, Starling. I'm impressed."

Not in the mood for flattery, she jerked away from him with a grunt and marched down the path.

"Eva!" Grayson called, catching up to her in three long strides. Damn his long legs. "Stop. *Talk* to me. Please."

The word gutted her. *Please.*

Knowing him more now than the last time she heard that word leave his lips, she *knew* that he'd never beg with anyone else. It was only her.

Only ever her.

She stopped so suddenly, he almost bumped into her. When she looked up into his storm-cloud eyes, her heart splintered in two.

Pain and regret swirled in those eyes—but threaded within was something softer. Hope. Trust. A silent plea to stay close, even if it hurt.

Her throat tightened. She swallowed hard. "I... We... We're not on the best of terms right now."

"You're fighting?"

"Maybe."

The flicker of hurt in his eyes was deep, fleeting—barely there—but she felt it all the same. "Why didn't you say anything?"

She turned her face away, guilt creeping up her spine. She couldn't bring herself to say it—not after everything he'd done to earn back her trust. Not when she finally had him opening up to her. If he knew the truth, he might shut her out again.

"He's angry with you because of me, isn't he?"

Her lips pressed into a thin line. Saying it would only make it worse—for all of them. She owed Arkon loyalty. But Grayson... he had carved out a space in her heart, and it was getting harder to ignore.

With a growl, he stepped back, shoulders tense. "Right. This was a bad idea. From now on, we train separately."

"Grayson—"

"No." He whirled on her, eyes flashing with raw, unchecked fury—and hurt. The kind that wrenched at her heart, knowing she had been the cause of it. She might as well have betrayed him. Maybe she had. "I will *not* come between you and Arkon."

His hands buried in his hair as he turned away, shaking his head like he could shove the thought from his mind. "How long has this been going on?"

Eva fidgeted, guilt twisting in her stomach. "A week and a half."

His jaw clenched. A grim mask slid over his face. "Since we spoke on the beach."

She nodded, unable to meet his eyes. Not out of fear—never with him—but out of shame. Shame for being the true reason there was a rift between her and Arkon. For assuming this was what Grayson wanted.

He sighed—sharp, irritable—then dragged his hands down his face. When he stepped toward her, it startled her. His hands came up to cradle her cheeks, and he pressed his forehead against hers, his breath warm and steady.

"Thank you, Starling. Thank you for having so much faith in me you'd put your Bond on the line." His voice cracked, rough with sincerity. "But Arkon is a part of you. The Bond—it's sacred. It means more than any other relationship in your life." His hands trembled. "Don't you dare make that sacrifice for me. *Especially* not for me. Do you hear me?"

She blinked, stunned by the intensity in his voice. "Yeah," she breathed, before she knew what she was saying. She was unsure if she should be angry at him for lecturing her about relationships—when he clearly had no experience—or grateful that he cared enough to put her dragon before his own feelings.

His fingers curled into her hair, nails scraping along her scalp in the most sensational way. "I need to hear you say it, Starling. No sacrifices for me."

He wasn't letting her go until he knew she would obey him.

"Yes," she said again, firmer this time. "No sacrifices."

It warmed her heart that he refused to come between her and Arkon. He understood more than most what the Bond meant—and respected it more than she did.

"Good." He exhaled sharply, the tension bleeding from his shoulders as he stepped back. After a beat, he gestured to the wall she had shoved him into. "Your reflexes are getting better."

Just like that, he was composed once again. Her words alone were enough to ease his mind.

"We can meet up again this evening." He turned down the pathway, took a step, then halted, pivoting to face her with one final thought. The look he pinned on her rooted her in place. It was the look of a commander—a prince—who would not be ignored. "You'll talk to Arkon, won't you?"

She nodded, throat tight. "I will."

A promise—to both him and her dragon.

CHAPTER 14

MAGIC, CLAWS, AND STEEL

Eva sought Arkon out in his dwelling, buried deep within the cavernous system that wove like ancient veins through the heart of the canyon. Where the other end of their tether called to her.

The air grew colder the further into the dens she walked, stagnant and timid. The soft drip of mineral water echoed in the distance, matching the gentle tempo of her footfalls.

She'd long since past the other dragons, their baying, rustling, and thrumming of wings faded far behind her. They kept their nests close to the heart of the den, where not even Knights were allowed to enter. But Arkon found a spot on the outskirts. A hollow, swallowed in shadow, secluded and still, carved into the stone like an afterthought.

Eva paused at the threshold. The boundary was clear, scorch marks laced the ground in jagged streaks, branching out like lightning frozen mid-strike.

Bet the colony loved it when he marked his territory, she thought wryly, brushing her fingers over a charred groove, the stone still warm despite the near-winter air.

Her gaze caught a glint of crimson in the corner, a shimmer of scales scattered across a boulder.

Aster's.

How often did she visit him? The thought unfurled in her chest, bitter-sweet. She might not have been a good friend, or Soul Bound, but at least he wasn't entirely alone. She'd always be grateful for Aster's steadfastness. Even when the other dragons wanted nothing to do with him, Aster was there, unafraid, always encouraging.

"You do not have to wait for permission to enter my dwelling, Little One," Arkon's voice rumbled in the darkness. He shifted, scales scraping against stone, his form stirring the shadows. Then crystal eyes, as crisp and vivid as the cerulean ocean, illuminated the darkness with an ethereal glow. His aura prickled along her skin, glittered along the walls, swathing this corner of the den with his prolific magic. The intensity never bothered her, though. Where others cowered from it, she took comfort in it.

Eva remained where she stood, hands tucked behind her back, as if she was on parade. "I feel like I do," she admitted, fighting to keep her voice steady. "I feel like we're drifting apart." It hurt to speak the truth aloud, but it needed to be said. They'd let this fester long enough.

She swallowed a lump in her throat.

"You hurt me, Arkon." She still felt the words like a brand on her heart. It was one thing to take a jab at Grayson—it was an entirely different matter to ask her to kill him. End him. Wipe his existence from this world. Because he knew, as much as she feared, that Grayson would let her push him off the cliff without hesitation.

A terrifying thought, but also empowering in a way she never thought she'd enjoy. Having power over a man, one of the most feared in Astrida, made a part of her she didn't know existed preen with dark satisfaction.

"But I also know that I haven't been the most loyal rider..." The truth tasted sour on her tongue. Not for finally acknowledging she was at fault, but for the fact it happened in the first place. "And for that, I'm sorry."

His tail slithered out from under him and curled around her feet, urging her towards him. Her chest constricted, breath catching in her throat. She accepted the invitation, nearly stumbling into him with her eagerness to be near him.

He lowered his head to her, nostrils flaring as her fingers brushed over the scales of his snout—rough, grating, yet soothing.

"He killed my kin, Eva," he said, voice low but not without resentment. "You cannot expect me to forgive him for that."

"I..." Her brow pinched, chest tightening. "I don't know what to do, Arkon. I could stand here all day and defend him. I could tell you about his scars, his past. I could tell you that he is full of regret and guilt for every wrongdoing he has ever done, and that if he could take it back, he would... But he can't. All he can do now is try to make things right. And he's trying so *damn* hard."

Huffing, his tail lashed out behind him like a whip; it sliced right through a stalactite and sent rubble flying into the wall with a vicious *crack*. "I see. All it takes is a few sweet words and empty promises for you to fall for the wolf's trap."

"I have not fallen," she snapped. "Not yet. I won't, not until I get your blessing."

His colossal head turned, a single luminous eye almost as big as she was glaring at her with the vehemence that matched the heat of the merciless sun in the Desert Lands. "Then you will be waiting a very long time."

"Don't." She shook her head, eyes burning. "Don't do this to me, Arkon. I feel like my heart is being torn in two."

"That is your fault for choosing your mate poorly. You have another male chasing your affection that I approve of—yet you cast him aside in favour of a Fortys."

"Stop it!"

Something inside her splintered. She took a step forward before she could stop herself. Her hands slammed his snout, as if she could snap him out of it and force him to look at her. To make him *feel* her, *see* her.

Her body was tiny compared to his, and her strength did nothing against him. But the act alone was enough.

She cared for Grayson. But in that moment, she realised it was more than enjoying his company or feeding off his power and strength. More than physical attraction and desire. It was far more than anything she'd ever experienced, something she wasn't even sure she was ready for—but it was hers all the same.

But she could not—would not—let Arkon tear him down. Not when Grayson was already at war with himself. Not when he bore the weight of his past in silence, refusing to defend himself because he believed he didn't deserve it. She didn't know if Grayson would ever believe he was worth loving. But in that moment, she needed Arkon to believe it, because she already did.

Snarling, his head reared back. Smoke unfurled from his nostrils and maw, scales shuddering down the entire length of his body. He towered over her, claws digging into the clay beneath them as his wings flared out behind him. "You want to fight, human? Then we shall fight."

Before she could blink, his claw lurched outward, catching her around the waist. They curled around her tightly, but not so tight she couldn't breathe.

Wings pumping, he lifted off the ground. Dust and pebbles swirled around them like a vortex—then he lunged into the tunnel, wings scraping the walls as shadows swallowed them whole.

Screaming, Eva clutched his claw—because that was all she could do as they hurled down the gaping maw of darkness. Wind tore at her clothes, ripped her hair out of her ponytail. Sulphur and steel and earth filled her nose—

Sunlight breached the darkness, guiding them out of the tunnel. Arkon didn't slow down as they approached the mouth. He exploded out into the canyon with lightning shuddering in their wake; it snapped at the cliff walls and roared louder than Arkon's furious bellow.

Dark clouds closed in on them, lightning forking across the sky above. Static needled at her flesh, digging deep into her marrow. The pain was so intense, if she was riding in the saddle, she would have fallen off his back. The only thing to stop her from crying out and losing consciousness was the humiliation of being plucked off the ground like an inconsequential pebble. Riding on the heels of that humiliation, rage burned like an incessant fever, raking and purging until it was all she could feel.

At break-neck speeds, they darted through the canyon, weaving through narrow passages and ducking under overhanging vines. His wings beat to the rhythm of her erratic heart, carrying her further, faster, until they broke free from the confines of the canyon.

The White Woods burned voraciously below them, a hungry fire that rustled beneath the power of Arkon's wings. He angled them for a clearing then tossed her at its centre. She rolled several rotations, landing on her feet in the grass, then whirled on Arkon.

There was little a human could do against a creature as ancient and powerful as a dragon, but she was bursting at the seams with emotion she could no longer contain—and if taking it out on Arkon was the only way to relieve the pressure, she'd do it.

He alighted in front of her, wings beating air into her face like a fist. Eva watched in shock as the world tipped, her feet flying above her head as the force of the gust knocked her back and slammed her into the cold, hard earth, the air punched from her lungs.

As she gasped for air, his claw came down, pinning her in place as his talons burrowed into the soil around her. The back of her mind noted that he wasn't crushing her, only holding her still.

He lowered his massive head down to her level and roared in her face. Charred meat and smoke invaded her nose. Saliva dropped from his teeth and landed on her shoulder, seeping through the under armour and clinging to her skin.

Her heart pounded in her ears, fear lurching in her throat. Never once had she seen this side of him. Never once had she thought of him as a primal beast, untamable. Dangerous.

But right here, she was reminded that he was a beast. A creature that killed and feasted on raw flesh. An animal that had thoroughly different instincts than her.

His power pressed into her, jagged and all consuming.

But it wasn't his power alone. Not anymore.

She grabbed onto the tendrils of magic around them. The lightning in the sky responded to her immediately, rumbling its approval in the clouds. It forked violently—then she bent the arch, aiming it for Arkon.

The strike was sudden and sharp. But it didn't pierce. It would never pierce his scales. Instead, it scattered along his coat like spiderwebs, curling and warping *into* him. His wings lit up in a brilliant white flash, revealing a layer of veins beneath the leather.

His roar shook the ground and the trees quaked with fear. The sheer amount of energy wracking through him pulled the pressure of his claws off her just enough for Eva to roll out of his grasp.

She hopped back several feet away, gasping for breath. That one strike alone was enough to wind her. But it had *listened.* She commanded and it obeyed. She was its master as much as Arkon was.

She'd never been so powerful.

A snarl ripped out of Arkon's throat, eyes as vibrant as a lightning flash. "You'll land a strike for *him*—but not for yourself?" Vitriol dripped from his maw, venomous and toxic.

She held her ground, despite the tremor in her knees. "Just give him a chance!"

"I cannot!"

He lashed out, tail swinging her way. She jumped, narrowly dodging the attack. She landed on her feet with the grace of a jungle cat.

"Why!?"

The clouds cracked open. Rain poured from the heavens, drenching them in an instant.

Eva didn't drop eye contact, even as a shiver ran through her body. She would hold her ground, even against her own dragon.

Instead of answering her, a growl rumbled in his chest, and he swiped at her. Eva dashed backwards—then slipped in the saturated field. She regained her footing in the nick of time, bracing her legs shoulder-width apart.

His wings reared back—then he sent a powerful gust slamming into her. Despite the slippery ground, she held fast, leaning into it, just as Anna had taught her. But it did nothing to save her from the wave of mud that slapped into her front.

Grimacing, she spat mud out. "Real mature."

If he wanted to play that way, she called onto the magic in the air, the static yearning for her touch, and swung it at him. An ugly blob of lightning slammed into him from the side, knocking him off balance. Mud coated his right wing, but that didn't stop his tail from coiling around her ankle and tossing her across the field. She skidded several feet, sliding through the mud like a stone slipping across a pond. When she finally slid to a stop, her face ate the ground.

Her body ached as she lifted herself onto her hands and knees. Once-blonde strands were now stained with mud, twinged by grass, hanging around her shoulders. Panting, she climbed to her feet, pivoting towards him as he shook out his filthy wing.

Eva's strength was sapped, muscles bunching painfully around her bones, air a battle to hold onto—but still the storm called to her, enticed her to use more. So she reached out, willing it to gather above them. She wouldn't stop until she was heard. Until he could see what he was doing to her by making her choose.

Sparks flew across the clearing, gathering to an epicenter above them. As much as it called to her, it also fought against her, writhing beneath her command, fighting to be unleashed.

Just as she was about to release it, it exploded and rained over Arkon's scales. He watched the sparkling display with smug amusement then dropped his gaze to her. A chuckle bounced out of his chest. "Is that the best you can do, Little One?"

"Right now? Yes." She collapsed to her knees. Sasha would have been thoroughly disappointed in her lack of control and stamina. "Why?" she rasped. "Why won't you just give him a chance, Arkon?"

"He is a *murderer*, Eva! You are upset because you think I'm not listening to you—but *you* are not listening to *me*! He killed my kin, took their horns and scales as trophies for his father—the man who has sent assassins after you, who ordered the death of your family. He hunted them, elders and hatchlings alike, made them fear every minute of their lives before they met their end. And you're asking me to forgive him, to allow him to mate with you. I will *not* forgive him."

"I know!" she screamed back. She screamed at the top of her lungs, until her voice cracked. "You think I don't know what he's done? What do you think I've been doing with him for these past few days? He's killed, he's razed, he's tortured—he wiped your species from existence..." She paused for breath, lungs sucking in air desperately to keep up. "But it doesn't change how I feel about him," she confessed quietly, voice ragged. Amongst the storm swirling around them, he'd be hard pressed to hear her, but it was all she could manage as emotions welled up inside her. "It doesn't change how I feel about you."

A single tear spilled over and slid down her cheek. She couldn't keep going on like this. He needed to hear her. He needed to listen, because if he didn't, then she had to choose. And she didn't want to choose. Arkon would come first. Always.

But Grayson deserved more than eternal damnation.

She hated that he was forcing her to give him up.

Determination pulsing through her veins, she stepped towards him. Static crackled between her fingertips, licking at the air around her, awaiting her next command. Despite how much she was pleading inside, her voice came out strong, adamant, "Don't make me pick, Arkon. I know you hate that I feel anything for him. I hate that it hurts you so much. But I do. I care about him..." Her shoulders sagged, the weight of their fight dragging her down. "He's family."

And that one truth cracked something inside of her.

She laughed at the bitter irony of it all—that he had somehow become a part of her new found family when it was his brother who had murdered her old one. "I know it hurts. I *know*. My family is gone too, but we've found a new one here in Dragon Canyon." She laid a hand on her chest, where the ache of loss still throbbed and threatened to pull her under some days. "Nothing—*no one*—can ever replace who we lost. But I'm trying to find ways to make the ache hurt a little less. And Grayson? He helps. He fucking *helps*, Arkon."

His luminous eyes shimmered with hurt and betrayal. Its claws raked her stomach as thoroughly as it shredded him from the inside. Jowls pulled back in a vicious, low snarl. His tail lashed out behind him, slamming into trees and knocking them over in a tumbling cascade of several other trees.

He couldn't go on like this for much longer either.

All of this pain—it was her fault. She had found someone who saw past her armour, who held her gently when the weight was too much, who understood her in the space between one breath and the next.

If she'd known from the beginning who Grayson was, what he had done to Arkon, she never would have let herself get close to him. But she hadn't known. And she had trusted him. And now every moment, every quiet glance they shared, was ingrained into her very marrow. She couldn't take them back. No matter how much she wished she could, for Arkon's sake.

So here they were. And that look Arkon gave her—so raw it nearly broke her—dragged her back to the beginning when their Bond was still new, fresh and jagged. When there were no barriers between them, she was drowning in grief.

What would I feel, if I dove beneath the surface and never came up? A memory, a recurring idea, she'd overheard within the depths of his mind. Back then, he'd been drowning in the misery of loss, in the slow decay of heartache. He'd thought about letting go, about slipping under for good before she had come along, but something had made him hold on. He'd been waiting for her, even if neither of them knew it at the time.

Grayson may be the air she breathed, but Arkon was the ground she walked on, the air under her wings. He was her base, her foundation, the very reason she rolled out of bed every morning. His being was so deeply interwoven into hers that his pain was her pain, his hate hers, and his *life* was hers. Without him... she would have been lost long ago.

And without her... he was lost too.

She should have seen it sooner. Respected his pain sooner.

"But..." Eva swallowed, hesitating. Her stomach knotted as the words took shape in her throat. Before she could stop herself, she forced them out: "I'll stop training with him. No more dinners. I won't talk to him anymore."

It was like tearing out a piece of herself and handing it over. After everything Grayson had done for her—standing by her when she was at her lowest, listening when no one else had the patience, reminding her that she was more than just the storm dragon rider—it had come to this. She could already feel the absence like a phantom wound, raw and stinging. He would understand. She knew he would. But knowing didn't soften the burn searing through her chest, or the hollow ache opening in its wake.

You'll find a new way. She told herself the lie because the truth was unbearable. She still had Jacob and Anna—and Arkon, of course. They were always there when she needed to talk, always ready to distract her when the grief became too much. But they didn't understand her the way Grayson did. They didn't let her breathe without expecting instant relief. With them, there was always some version of her she had to be. With Grayson, she could be messy, flawed, angry... *human.*

Now she would have to lock that part of herself away.

They would be enough.

They had to be.

"Little One..." Arkon crooned, curling his tail around her waist and pulling him against his side. His wing hovered over her, casting her in shadow, but, more importantly, keeping the rain off her head. His soul wrapped around her, warming her blood, while his power vibrated through her veins.

Tears stinging her eyes, she breathed him in, his scent of smoked meat, molten metal, and the air after a fresh storm. She stroked his scales tenderly with a bone-deep familiarity.

She needed this. Needed *him.* "I'm sorry," she murmured into his scales. "I'm so sorry I ever tried to push you. It was unfair and selfish. I'm sorry."

It was all she could say, over and over again. Never again would she let someone come between them. People may come and go in her life, but he would always be there. Her rock, her anchor, her *home.*

An immeasurable amount of time passed while she cried into his scales. The rumbling clouds echoed each sob that tore from her throat. But even as the ground sank beneath her, as water pooled around them, as the brittle, cold wind sliced at her face, the knot in her chest loosened.

She knew enough of Death's Dance to perform it alone. It might not be perfect, she might be sloppy and stumble, but she could make it work. She'd spend more time with Jacob and talk to him like they used to, when it was just the two of them, walking through the forest and dreaming of the world beyond their valley. She'd make it work. For them. Their Bond.

"Eva..." Arkon's voice was rough, like stone grating against steel. It jostled her out of his embrace and drew her eyes up to his brilliant blue eyes. "Perhaps we can come to some arrangement, where we both make bearable sacrifices and our pain is shared rather than placed."

Her heart thudded in her chest, each beat hard and distinct, like horse hooves on a plain. She couldn't believe her ears, didn't dare to hope what she'd heard. "You mean it?"

"I have been sifting through your thoughts and memories," he admitted, not all ashamed to have invaded her privacy. She didn't care, though; their souls were one, and she knew that he'd allow her into his mind if she wanted. "I have seen the effect he has on you—beyond infatuation. He is... a little bit of peace for you. I loathe that he is the one who assuages the troubles on your heart, but I cannot deny you the peace or protection he offers you."

The air whooshed out of her lungs in relief. Her heart felt like it might implode with the relief he had gifted her.

He heaved out a long breath; the air reverberated through his entire body, shuddering to the tip of his tail and the very edges of his wings. "Perhaps, when you are with him, you could do me the courtesy of putting your walls up. In return, I will stop speaking ill of him, and when I must be in his presence, I will settle with being cordial."

"I can't ask that of you. It's not fair to you."

"You are not asking, I am offering."

"Truly?"

His ancient eyes held hers, steady and certain. "Is this an amicable solution?"

"Yes," she said instantly, her heart thudding with gratitude. "You may have to teach me how to make better walls, but I'll do what I have to. Thank you, Arkon."

"I have not forgiven him," he clarified. "I do not trust him and he *will* break your heart. But I am respecting that you need your own space to make your own choices and I will not interfere."

That was all she could ask for. She didn't want to carry guilt every time she looked at Grayson. Didn't want her stomach to twist whenever a smile slipped out because of something he said. These feelings—whatever they were—were blooming faster than she could contain them, wild and terrifying in their intensity. She felt like she was standing on the edge of a cliff, the wind already tugging at her. And when she finally tipped forward, she didn't want to fall afraid.

"Thank you."

Like tension springing loose from a tightly wound coil, their Bond snapped back into place—sudden but strong. The impact of it made her chest ache, not from pain, but from the sheer relief of feeling him again. His soul pressed against hers like a heartbeat she'd been missing, a quiet rhythm that made her feel whole again. Her heart swelled with it—with him—because for the first time in what felt like forever, they weren't fractured. They were one.

She leaned into his side, rubbing her cheek into his rough scales. "I missed you."

"And I, you."

Light spilled over the clearing as the clouds parted, giving way to the sun beneath. Arkon tucked his wing to his side, allowing the sun's warmth to seep into her bones.

"You are a mess, Eva," he said with an amused lilt.

A laugh burst from her lips as she took in the mud slowly caking to her skin. Her eyes drew upward to his wings. "So are you."

He rose to his four claws then snapped his wings out. The sudden motion sent the mud flinging into the trees around them; Eva had to cover her face to avoid being sprayed.

"That's just not fair. I can't do that."

He chuffed proudly, scales shuddering down his spine.

"Eva!"

Eva and Arkon's heads tipped back to find several dragons barreling toward them. Aster took the charge, whipping through the air faster than the others. Her crimson scales shone like fresh steel under the mid-afternoon sun.

As they closed in, her wings spread wide to catch the air in them like sails. She landed roughly, claws raking through the earth. Her foreleg extended, giving Anna a path to slide out of the saddle with the grace and finesse of a warrior goddess. The fierce Dragon Knight's hair flung back behind her, wild and free from the gust of Aster's wings.

Before the other dragons could land, her sword was out, eyes vigilantly taking in the utter wreckage of the field. Deep grooves scarred the soil, their edges crumbling into loose dirt where claws had torn through. Charred craters pocked the field, still rimmed with faint smoke and laden with rainwater. Eva stood amid it all, mud clinging to her clothes and streaking her skin, every line of her posture heavy with exhaustion. Beyond her, trees lay toppled in chaotic angles, bark shredded and branches snapped where Arkon's tail had struck, the damage sprawling outward in jagged paths.

"We saw the storm," Anna said, eyes wide as she scanned the chaos. "What in Five Hells happened here? Are you guys okay?"

Commander Hargin's dragon alighted beside Aster, quickly followed by Lieutenant Ahura's dragon. The Commander and Lieutenant dismounted, armed and ready, despite being dressed for all-day meetings rather than battle.

While Anna wore under armour and her scale jacket, Hargin and Ahura donned their dress uniform, with only a sword as protection. They looked like they had just come out of a meeting.

Eva scratched the back of her head, feeling sheepish for alarming them. "We're okay."

Hargin passed Anna and Ahura, standing in front of Eva as if Arkon wasn't crouching beside her, teeth dripping with the silent promise to end anyone who upset his rider. Brows bridging into a firm line and lips pressed so tightly together they were almost white, her expression was a mixture of indignation and sheer disbelief that anyone under her command could be this monumentally reckless and still be breathing.

Eva swallowed, a sinking feeling shoveling out her stomach. Too caught up with her own emotions, she hadn't once thought about what *exactly* they were doing.

Which was wielding lightning in the middle of Dragon Canyon.

Oops.

"Explain what was going through your head when you decided to wield your storm magic on my base, Private Greene."

Eva winced at her tone. Not because it was brutal and laced with savage claws—but because it was entirely the opposite. Nothing but calm, cold fury.

Where Anna brought the fire, Kira Hargin brought the ice, and it *burned.*

"I'm... sorry." It was pathetic, she knew. Unknowingly, she had endangered dragons and Knights alike—all because she couldn't keep her emotions in check. "Was anyone hurt?"

The ire in the Commander's eyes dimmed. Fractionally. Her jaw ticked with the effort to remain composed. "No."

Thank Ebis—or Lorelus or Asturias or *all* of the gods—for that. Eva would have never forgiven herself if someone had gotten hurt because of her lack of control.

"We were working on practicing control," Arkon interjected, tail curling around her feet protectively. "It appears we still have some work to do."

"*What are the chances I get to keep my Knighthood, Arkon?*" she asked him secretly.

"*You are my Soul Bound. I would say the chances are very high. Now, hold your chin up and apologise no more. If they want you to be their weapon, then they must allow you to practice.*"

Lieutenant Ahura levelled her with a glower that would make a goblin shrink back into its hovel. "You were told to train only on the beaches of Lake Raynor for a reason, Private. You may be impervious to lightning, but every one else in the canyon is not so lucky. Remember that the next time you feel the *urge* to train."

Eva inclined her head respectfully. "Yes, sir."

"To avoid another lapse in judgement," Commander Hargin said, voice tight yet still managing to restrain her anger, "you will be spending your entire day tomorrow cleaning the dragons' dens."

Anna sucked in a sharp breath. "Commander, that's a little harsh, don't you think?"

"Quiet, Sergeant," the Commander snapped so viciously Eva winced. Their relationship was far from warm and affectionate, but it still hurt to witness it when all Eva had only known love from her family. "You're here to retrieve your student, not defend her."

Anna crossed her arms, eyes narrowing into sharp points that rivaled her mother's. "As my student, Eva is my responsibility, so if she has to clean out the dragons' dens, so do I."

Eva opened her mouth to protest, but the Commander beat her to it. "This is a punishment, not a squad exercise. Greene will do it alone—and if I find out you helped, you will not go to the gala this weekend."

Anna's face fell flat, anger roiling in her eyes like untempered steel.

Eva touched her arm, shifting slightly in front before she said something to her mother that would get her into trouble. "It's all right. I'll do it alone. Take the boys to Lensenton for me."

Anna looked at her, torn, but then she sighed with reluctant agreement and nodded. "I'll throw them around on the mats for you, too."

Something sparked in the Commander's eyes, but before Eva could mistake it for pride in her daughter, she turned on her heel and marched to her dragon, Lieutenant Ahura steadily in tow.

Once their dragons were mere specs in the sky, Anna turned to Eva with sad eyes. "I'm sorry you got in trouble."

Eva heaved a sigh. "I'm sorry I used magic in the canyon. I suppose that'll give you something to talk about in your meeting next week."

Just this morning, Anna had griped that she and Hargin spent their weekly meetings going over the same points about Eva's progress. At least this time, there'd be something new.

Anna rolled her eyes. "Oh, I'm sure Kira will have *plenty* to say about it..." Her silver eyes trailed over the mud and the tangled mess Eva's hair had become. "Are you okay? Was it really just training... or something else?"

Eva peered up at Arkon, a smile tugging at the edges of her mouth, despite the punishment she'd been dealt. "We had a few things to settle, but we're good now."

Anna looked up at Arkon then dropped her gaze to Eva again and grinned. "Good. I'm glad. How about we get you cleaned up then grab some food? You look like you've worked up an appetite."

"I'm famished."

Arkon lowered his belly to the ground, as low as he could go, allowing her access to his withers. She climbed up his leg and swung hers over the dip in his scales where his saddle normally sat. After a brush of his scales, he took off into the air.

Their bond pulsed—slow and steady—mending at the edges, weaving new threads through the cracks. Stronger. Wiser. Still imperfect, but alive.

CHAPTER 15
UNWAVERING RESOLVE

Grayson crouched at the edge of the plateau, looking over Dragon Canyon on one side and the White Woods on the other. A perfect vantage point for a Soul Bound whose sight was far superior to a regular human's and could see heat signatures through the thick canopy of the forest.

He discovered this place during his first week in Dragon Canyon. It was quiet, private. Just the way he liked it. When he was frustrated and just wanted to scream at the world, he would come up here and scream until his voice was hoarse. When his blood burned through his veins, commanding him to rip and tear through every person that crossed his path, he'd come up here and perform Death's Dance until his body was too sore to hurt the Knights down below.

And sometimes... he just came up here, legs dangling off the ledge, and bathed in the silence. Sometimes Eran joined him. Sometimes Grayson let his guilt and shame rage through him. Other times he forced all the thoughts out of his head and enjoyed *true* silence.

He hadn't brought anyone up here. Not Anna. Not Jacob. The only people who knew about this spot were a handful of Knights who patrolled the plateau twice a day—and Eva. He and the Knights had come to an understanding: they did their patrol, quickly, quietly, leaving him alone; in return, he let them—as long as they did it quickly and quietly.

Eva, though? She could spend as much time as she liked up here. Not just because he liked how the morning sun glowed on her skin or how her hair shimmered in the breeze. No. Because her shoulders lifted a little higher. Her spine a bit straighter. Her eyes lighter when she took in the view. If he could give her that, if nothing else, then he was content.

The sun was just beginning to crest over the White Woods, its rays streaking over the red canopy, setting it afire with life and warmth. The wind up here was gentle this morning, weaving its tentative fingers through his hair with the same care Eva touched the scales on his chest. Such a buttery soft touch from a fierce warrior.

It was a touch that once would have surprised him. Sylus had taught him that a woman's worth lay in her softness—supple, malleable, easy to shape to a man's will. But Anna had shown him the lie in that. A woman who bit back was sharper for it, her mind keener, her will unyielding. She wasn't a burden to be tamed, but a partner to be reckoned with, one who could challenge him, match him, make him better.

His chest tightened with the thought of Eva, the wind seeming to carry her presence toward him. She always came shortly after the sun appeared, and his body thrummed in quiet anticipation.

She'd skipped their session last night, in favour of spending time with Arkon. If she had any other excuse, Grayson would have hunted her down and insisted training was more important—but, in this case, Arkon was more important. He always would be. As he should be.

The ache in Grayson's chest eased at the thought. If she was spending time with Arkon, it meant their Bond was on the mend. Maybe not whole. He wasn't sure it would ever be whole as long as Grayson was in the picture—but he hoped with time he could prove to Arkon that he was worthy of his rider. Prove that he was a different man now, a man who put Eva's needs above all else, including his own selfish desires.

Rising to his feet, Grayson brushed the dirt from his black cargo pants, then shrugged out of his cloak and folded it with care, setting it atop a nearby boulder. He drew in a slow breath, stretching his arms high before rolling his shoulders and bending from side to side, loosening muscles that bunched in anticipation.

Whenever Eva was near, his whole body coiled—like a bowstring pulled taut. A flicker stirred in his stomach, focus narrowing until she was the only presence in the world. It took deliberate effort to remember the rest—the Knights moving about the base, dragons flying overhead, and the assassins still hunting her.

His shadow stretched long across the plateau, spilling toward the narrow pathway that hugged the cliff's edge. The sun sat low, painting the stone in molten gold, but the light did nothing to warm the tightening knot in his stomach.

Grayson's frown deepened. Eva should have been here by now. She was never late.

He shifted his weight, boots grinding against the gritty rock, eyes tracking the winding trail that cut up from the valley below. The air hung still, heavy, broken only by the distant beat of dragon wings between the canyon walls. Every creak of the stone as it thawed from the chilling night, every faint scrape of wind against the plateau's rim set his senses on edge.

She should have appeared by now—her sure stride, that familiar silhouette framed against the sky. Starlight hair shining like a beacon in the shadowed abyss. Instead, the path remained empty, a yawning gap where she should be. Suspicion trickled down his spine. His mind ticked through possibilities—delayed, intercepted, attacked—each one shovelling out his stomach more than the last.

A sharp snap of air behind him caught his attention. He pivoted, bracing—

But he wasn't ready to see Arkon's hulking form. With unnecessary force, the dragon alighted in front of him, pelting him with dust and pebbles. Grayson covered his face, legs braced against the harsh gusts.

Once the dust settled and there was nothing but the howling wind in the canyon, Arkon stared down at him with bold, luminous eyes. A current crackled in the air between them, prickling at Grayson's skin, sharp and intrusive.

He clenched his jaw, purging the pain from his body. He would hold his ground against the black dragon, just as he did many times before with his kin. Though, he rarely came face-to-face with them. Dragons—storm dragons in particular—being the behemoths of power that they were, one didn't just simply walk up to a dragon and kill it. No, it took cunning, and planning. A lot of planning.

"Arkon," he acknowledged, stomach solidifying with unease when he spotted the empty space between his wings. "To what do I owe the pleasure?"

"To *whom* you mean," the dragon snided, drawing out his words in deep contempt. "Eva asked me to inform you that she will not be joining you this morning or evening. She is too busy for the likes of you."

An eyebrow quirked as Grayson studied the irate dragon. His wings flared out behind him, tail whipping through the air behind him, poised for take off at a moment's notice. As if Grayson might suddenly decide to make good on his promise to Sylus to eradicate all storm dragons.

He was going to be waiting a while.

What Grayson was more focused on was the message. It was unlikely Eva used that exact tone or phrase, but he believed that if she was able, she would have talked to him personally.

Trepidation knotted in his stomach. First she didn't show up last night, now she was skipping today. Was she avoiding him? Had he pushed her too far when he demanded she make amends with Arkon? Or was this a part of what she needed to do to make up with him?

He grinded his molars. He needed to talk to her. "What is Eva busy with?"

Arkon turned his snout up at him. "That is none of your business."

"Eva is my business."

In a sudden rush, the air whipped around them, charged with the sharp crackle of raw magic. Arkon's snarl sliced through the stillness like a blade, his colossal head dipping low until his hot, smoky breath spilled over Grayson's face, tingling his skin with both heat and menace. The dragon's eyes burned bright—fiery orbs blazing with fierce possessiveness and an unspoken challenge.

Grayson tasted the sulphur-tinged air, smelt the ancient power rolling off the dragon in waves, and felt the subtle vibration in the earth beneath his boots as Arkon's massive claws scraped against the stone. Grayson didn't move a muscle. Not out of fear, but out of respect to his kin. He would not cower, not even if Arkon were to be his demise. If he was going to die, let it be from the creature who sought revenge the most.

"My rider is *not* your business, Slayer," the dragon growled, spit flinging in Grayson's face. "She has graciously allowed you to be in her presence—but make no mistake: you do not own her."

Slowly, Grayson raised a hand to his face and wiped the saliva off his cheek with this thumb. His gaze was unwavering, burrowing into the dragon's soul, so deep maybe even Eva could feel him looking upon her other half.

"Make no mistake," Grayson reiterated, slowly, purposefully, "I don't claim to own her or wish to. But the Fortys clan is after her, and as long as they still draw breath, I will protect her with every fibre of my being, whether it means teaching her my techniques, killing my clan, or knowing her whereabouts every hour of the day—I will do it and no one will stop me. Understood?"

Arkon's teeth gleamed in a deadly snarl, his scales rippling like thunder rolling across a storm-darkened sky. The sheer force of his presence vibrated through the air, through Grayson's marrow. A warning—but also an admission. If he was going to kill Grayson, he would have done so, but he hadn't, which was answer enough for him.

"Tell me what she's doing instead of training," Grayson pressed, voice low but firm, aware he was pushing Arkon dangerously close to the edge. Still, not knowing where Eva was would gnaw at him like a ravenous beast on a picked bone.

"No."

The wind ripped across the plateau, slicing the space between them like a hot knife through butter. It did nothing to gutter out the rage burning in his veins, fueled by frustration and his ever-growing need to know Eva's whereabouts. He had no idea if she had adequate protection, if she was in trouble, if Anna or Jacob were aware that she was indisposed.

A growl worked its way up in his throat, but he swallowed it down, fighting for composure. Arkon was being purposely vague to get a rise out of him, which was working, but he wouldn't give him the satisfaction of watching him come undone.

A tic feathering against his jaw, Grayson faced him, rolling his shoulders back, holding himself as if he was about to face Sylus. "Will you at least tell me this: did you two talk?"

Silence stretched out before them, carving a deep chasm of distrust and contempt that twisted at Grayson's innards. He had to swallow down a bout of nausea that threatened to bring him to his knees. He didn't know what he feared more: Eva making sacrifices on his behalf or her lying to him about it.

"We did," Arkon finally said, his tone low, reluctant. An offering, of sorts. Not quite forgiveness—or even permission to pursue Eva—but an understanding, laced with respect.

The roiling tides in his stomach eased. At least for the moment.

"And?"

Arkon raised his head loftily, wings fluttering behind him like a posturing male. "We have come to an arrangement."

Grayson had to breathe in a lungful of patience before pressing on. "Which is?"

The dragon's jowls pulled back into an awkward attempt of a smile, eyes glowing with vitriol and hate. "None of your business."

Having said all that he wanted to say, his wings spread wide, catching the next current whipping through the plateau. The wind lifted him off the ground and sent him over the edge towards the White Woods. With the snap of his wings, he threw a powerful gust Grayson's way, knocking him back onto his ass. By the time the dust was settled, Arkon was gone and Grayson loosed a curse.

"Fucking arrogant dragons."

Eva deserved no less than Arkon's soul and his power—but did she *have* to be Bound to a storm dragon? Asturias certainly had a twisted way of weaving fate.

Grayson had never believed in something as frivolous as fate—let alone the gods—but how else was he supposed to explain it all? Eran just happened to arrive in time to save his life. He just happened to end up in Aboria, of all places—where not one, but two others were Bound. And of all the villages to burn, it had to be Jacob's. Of all the people to Bond with a storm dragon, it had to be his partner's sister. And of all the people to occupy his thoughts, it had to be her.

Was it all just to punish him for his sins or something else?

"*The gods work in mysterious ways,*" Eran's thoughtful voice rumbled down the Bond. "*They have their own plans, but we have our own. Do not let the machinations of a god sway you from what your heart truly desires.*"

"*I don't even know what I truly desire*," Grayson admitted wryly, eyes fixed on the clouds. They drifted overhead like the lazy stroke of a paintbrush, each one dissolving into the next.

"*Not yet. Give it time. My instincts tell me Eva will be the key to figuring it out. But if that's true, you'll need to give her all of you—every part you've kept hidden.*"

Grayson shook his head, despite Eran being nowhere near to see it. It was an instinctual reaction to the fear leeching into his heart. "*Not every part.*"

Not the darkest part of him. Not even her light reached that far. She'd laughed when he asked for Bruce's description—but he wasn't joking. If he ever saw the bastard again, he was going to shove coals down his throat for being careless with her safety. To start.

"*She hasn't shied away yet*," Eran persisted. "*Do not pretend to know her limits.*"

Grayson gritted his teeth then rose to his feet. "*Enough. I don't want to talk about it—I want to find her.*"

He just needed to see her.

The dragon huffed, his exasperation trickling down the Bond, as it did often when Grayson veered the conversation away from himself. "*You will find her in the dragons' dens, scrubbing our faeces off the ground. I've been watching her from around the corner.*"

Grayson winced as he projected an image of Eva on her hands and knees, hair falling out of her high bun, while she scrubbed the floor with a brush far too small for the task.

This was what she was missing her training for?

"*Who put her up to this?*" He was going to pulverise every bone in their body.

Everyone knew cleaning the dens was a futile effort. The dragons maintained their dwellings the way they liked it—and the Knights didn't mess with it.

"*I haven't asked. I sensed her presence and chose to watch her from the shadows instead of offering her advice. I thought I might save that part for you.*"

Rolling his eyes, Grayson swiped his cloak from the boulder and marched down the pathway. Not even the treacherous wind blasting past him could slow him down. Not when Eva's time was being wasted on humiliating, mundane tasks. His body pumped ire through his veins, hot and unyielding. She should be training, learning, preparing—not scrubbing floors like some servant. She was the storm dragon rider, an elite amongst Knights—but, more importantly, she was his Starling, and he'd be damned if he'd let her be reduced to servitude.

He was going to beat the living shit out of whoever put her up to this.

He slipped into the tunnel and entered a hallway. At this time of day, there weren't many people out, only those on patrols. Just as well. If there'd been more, he wasn't sure he could stop himself from shoving his way through them.

He passed the officers' floor and took the stairs three at a time, down, down, down into the base's depths, letting the current of his Bond with Eran pull him toward him. Toward her.

Pockets of light lit his way from the holes leading out into the canyon, but as he veered off the path, slinking deeper into the dens, shadows crept in, snagging at his boots. He pulled out his lightstone, casting pale, white light in a wide cone around him. Flashes of colour danced at the edges of the cone as dragons watched him stride through their territory uncontested.

Humans didn't often venture this deep—not without good reason. The dragons preferred to keep it that way. If Eva was already down here, his presence would have unsettled them further. But they wouldn't stop him. Not a Soul Bound. His connection with Eran made him different from other humans, more draconic; though, Grayson didn't feel more or less draconic than anyone else. It didn't matter. It was enough to make the dragons give him a wide berth—and enough to let him reach Eva without delay.

As the current of his Bond grew stronger, telling him he was getting closer to Eran—closer to Eva—Grayson slowed his steps and made them fall a little heavier, so she could hear him coming.

He turned past a large column—and halted, breath hitched.

There.

His Starling.

Haunched over on her hands and knees, back facing him, scrubbing the ground with vigor, as if the fate of the world rested in the results of her hard work. Hair tied back in a messy bun at the top of her head. Knee pads, as well as the durable leather pants, protected her from the harsh stone floor. A thin tank top framed the muscles of her back, leaving him little to imagine, especially as sweat made the material transparent, revealing her breast band beneath.

He swallowed. The ire that had been driving him here flooded out of his system in a dizzying rush, leaving him breathless... and a little lost. Lost because he didn't know what to do with himself now that he was caught in her ray of sunshine. Because his mind had gone utterly blank.

There was something enchanting about watching her dip the brush in a soapy bucket, shake it out, then shuffle over to clean a new spot. It was so... ordinary. *Human.* It disarmed him entirely.

She wasn't a Dragon Knight, not a storm dragon rider, not even his Starling. Just Eva Greene.

And she was beautiful.

The scrubbing stopped. She tilted her head, eyes catching his over her shoulder. “Enjoying the view?”

Feeling a grin curl at the edges of his mouth, he crossed the space, being mindful of the spot Eva had been cleaning and the... excrement surrounding her. He rounded to her front and crossed his arms to stop himself from plugging his nose. If Eva could deal with it, so would he... But the smell was horrendous. While not the worst he had ever experienced, it certainly wasn't the most pleasant. It reminded him of the sulphur fields in Estrus—right next to a decimated, vulture-ripe corpse.

Eva sat back on her heels, the brush resting lightly against her thighs. Smudges of dirt and sweat stained her cheek and forehead, proof of the hard work she didn’t bother to wipe away—because she was too busy getting the job done. He could almost see the faint flush on her skin, the way she must’ve wiped sweat with her rough, filthy hands. His gaze lingered a fraction too long on the parting of her lips as she breathed through her mouth.

“How did you know it was me?” he asked, masking the distraction with a smirk. “I could have been an assassin.”

She rolled her eyes and tossed the brush into the bucket of bubbles. Water sloshed over the rim, splattering across the stone floor. She didn’t so much as glance at the mess—an easy, careless rebellion that made his chest tighten. The only reason she should be down here was to be with her dragon.

“If you were an assassin, Eran—along with half the dragons down here—would’ve said something. Besides, it was only a matter of time before he told you what I was up to.”

That last beat heated his blood for an entirely different reason. She'd been expecting him. Normally, he wouldn't like being so predictable, but something dark and wicked coiled inside of him at the thought of her waiting for him.

Grayson’s gaze slid toward the shadows, catching the faint outline of Eran tucked around the corner. The dragon was practically invisible; without his own enhanced sight, Grayson would’ve missed the telltale gleam of an emerald eye watching.

“You can leave any time. There's nothing for you to see here, nosy dragon.”

Eran huffed in the shadow, indiscernible from the many other noises the dragons were making in the distance. *“I was rather enjoying watching you fawn over your female.”*

“Leave. Now.”

Eyes narrowing, the dragon turned, keeping his tail tight against him so Eva couldn't see, and left in silence.

"Very perceptive, Starling," Grayson murmured, turning his attention back to her. He shouldn't have expected anything less from a hunter.

Her eyes lit at the praise. "Anna taught me a thing or two about taking in my surroundings," she said, gaze sweeping over him in a way that sent his muscles coiling with anticipation.

Heated silence stretched between them.

Most of their time together was spent on the mats or the plateau, where they remained professional and wary of each other—a boundary they'd set without a word. But this was neither, and the heat between them licked at his skin. It was heady. Wanting.

Eva must have seen it in his face, because she suddenly dropped her gaze, eyes fixed on her knees while her cheeks flushed a deep red beneath the dirt.

For all the swagger she carried on the mats, when the rest of the world fell away, leaving only the two of them, her shyness bloomed.

It was fucking adorable.

To save her the embarrassment, Grayson strode toward the water bucket and plucked the brush from its soapy contents. "What are you doing cleaning the dens?"

Sighing, a long, resigned sound, she came up alongside him, so close, her arm brushed against his. With a mildly scolding look, she swiped the brush from his hands. "Hargin's orders. I, uh... I used lightning on the base. Well, *technically*, Arkon did, but since I'm an extension of him, I did too."

She was blathering and nervous and he loved it. She wasn't nervous because she was afraid of him, but because he couldn't stop looking at her like he wanted to absolutely devour her.

Which made him wonder... Had any other man ever looked at her like that?

"What happened?" His tone was sharp, despite himself. He hadn't heard about an attack on the base—and if there had been, he would have fucking been there. But she appeared unscathed, unbothered, so he forced himself to stay calm. For now.

She shook the excess water off the brush then went back to her spot, which didn't look any better than when she first started cleaning it.

Hargin could be a real bitch sometimes.

"I talked to Arkon," Eva said quietly, focusing on her work, despite its futility. She'd been given an order and she'd be damned if she was going to half-ass it.

Grayson spotted another brush in the bucket; it was smaller and softer—a twig compared to a sword—but he grabbed it from the bucket anyway and got on his knees beside her and started scrubbing. "And?"

She blinked at him for a beat, bewildered. It wasn't every day he got on his knees for someone, but Eva would learn quickly that he'd do it any day for her.

After another beat, she turned back to her work. The red on her face bloomed along her neck, barely hidden by wisps of starlight. "We fought. I threw a few bolts at him, and he tossed me around like a rag doll. But we came out okay. We figured it out."

He studied her closely, her jaw, her brow, the way her shoulders eased, even as she scrubbed the ground. She wasn't looking at him because she was focused on her work, not to avoid him.

A productive talk, then. Arkon had alluded to as such, but he wouldn't believe it until he heard it from Eva.

"Good."

They fell silent, only the sound of bristles scraping against rock to fill in the silence. But it wasn't awkward or tense, a sense of contentment settled on his shoulders. The work itself was mundane and pointless, considering how caked-on the shit was, but he didn't hate it—because of the company he kept.

It was shockingly pleasant.

"Thank you," Eva said, her voice soft, despite how rigorously she worked the brush. She didn't make eye contact, but she didn't need to.

He sat back on his heels, eyebrow quirking in inquiry. "For what?"

With one final scrub, she set the brush down and looked at him. Her gaze was rich with emotion—too much for him to understand. He saw the warmth, though, and the light shining within. "For pushing me to talk to Arkon. I..." Her eyes narrowed, brow pinching together as she found the right words. "I hated that I was ignoring him so I could spend time with you, but I also hated how guilty I felt for talking to you. You both were tearing me in two."

His body tensed at her confession. He hadn't expected this—for her to *give*, just as he'd been giving—or for her to be so deeply affected by his and Arkon's conflict. If he had known how much it had hurt her, he wouldn't have even suggested they try.

Selfish bastard. So fucking selfish.

"And now?" he pressed. They appeared to at least be on speaking terms—but that wasn't enough for him. If they were still struggling, he was prepared to call things off. Even if the thought seared his soul.

Her smile lit up the entirety of the dens. When her eyes darted down to his mouth, his stomach tightened. "No guilt. We're still a little rough at the edges, but we've come to an understanding and he's respecting my choices while I'm respecting his space."

"I'm glad." Glad wasn't the half of it, but it was all he was willing to share in that moment. He didn't know if he would ever be ready to tell her how irrevocably she'd ensnarred him.

Even that single glance to his mouth completely unwound him. His blood pumped hot through his veins, heating his core, fueling his desire.

She wanted him. He saw it in her eyes, drifting down to his flexing forearms as he gripped the brush. She was so close—so unbearably close—that he could feel her heat, smell the subtle hint of lilac and pine.

She dropped her gaze again, turning slightly to grab the brush, and began on a spot a little further away.

She wasn't ready. Not yet.

So he would wait.

He scrubbed the ground. Hard. He needed an outlet. The shit-caked ground seemed like a great place to start.

"I appreciate the enthusiasm," Eva laughed softly. "But you don't have to help me. This is meant to be a punishment."

He inwardly smirked as wicked thoughts wove through his mind. "I know, but this is going to take you all damn day if you don't have help." He paused as a realisation struck him. Maybe she *did* know what he was thinking. "Unless you're trying to get rid of me."

Her eyes widened, as innocent as ever. "No! No. I just don't want you to get into trouble for helping me."

Snorting, he sat up and waved the brush in the air around them. "I think you severely underestimate how terrified people on this base are of me. No one is going to punish me for helping you."

She chewed on her bottom lip, eyes twinkling with mischief. "I think you severely *over*estimate how terrifying you are."

His brow quirked at that. He sat back, dropping the brush at his side and just *looked* at her. She was teasing, but there was something in her voice... a softness that settled the monster inside of him. "You're not scared of me?"

She gave it some thought then shrugged casually. No one had ever been so casual around him. Even when he was with Jacob or Anna, there was still an edge to them. Minute, so slight they probably didn't notice. But he did. With Eva, though, he looked and looked and looked for that edge—and could never find it.

And then she cracked the walls around his heart with: "You've never given me reason to be scared of you."

Words he thought he would never hear. Words he didn't know he needed until she uttered them.

This was why he couldn't let her go. She saw *him*. Not Dex. Not the Slayer of Souls. Grayson.

He leaned forward, raising a hand to her face. Slowly, gently, he brushed his thumb along her cheek, smudging dirt along the length of her cheekbone. She leaned into his touch, completely melted in his hand.

"That's because you're different, Starling," he said low with intent. "I don't ever want to scare you..." He leaned closer still, mouth grazing the shell of her ear. "But the officers who put you up to this? When push comes to shove, I get my way."

Breath hitching, she pulled back just enough to look at him. Even after a threat, there was no fear in those eyes. Just down right devious mischief. "And your way just happens to be scrubbing the dragons' dens all day?"

"As long as present company accepts the help, yes."

Her eyes scanned the cavern they sat all alone in. "Dragons talk, what if one of them sees us?"

Grayson stared at her. She hadn't noticed—there wasn't a single dragon within hearing distance of them. Eran was the only one who dared to go near her down here, the others had left this section the moment she set foot in it.

"You're the storm dragon rider," he reminded her, keeping his voice low. Any louder in the space between them would feel like a sin. "They'll stay quiet if they know what's good for them."

Her lips parted in surprise. "I would never hurt them."

His head tilted, eyes captivated by her mouth. He was close enough to kiss her. He wouldn't. Not here, amongst dragon shit. Not now, when they were in the middle of something taut and delicate. "No, but they don't know that—and sometimes it's better when people don't know the things you do."

Her brow creased, lips pursing as she frowned at him. It was only half-hearted—the rest of her attention was fixed on the very minimal space between them. "That sounds..."

"Sounds like what?" he purred. He couldn't help himself, even if it was just a tease.

"Sounds immoral." The words weighed heavily in the air between them.

He'd wanted to hear her say it, to admit it out loud and feel the words leave her lips. He could leave Estrus and change his name, obey Hargin's rules and live by Jacob's code, but at the core of his being, a monster lurked, just waiting to be unleashed. And Eva needed to understand that.

"I never claimed to be moral," he reminded her.

Her lashes fluttered as she peered up at him. He looked at her, and she looked back.

"No, I suppose you didn't."

"Do you still want my help?"

There wasn't even a beat of hesitation.

A vicious little smile curled on her lips then she pulled back entirely and pointed at a small mound of dried shit a couple inches away. “You missed a spot.”

CHAPTER 16
PROMISES IN BLACK

Eva regarded her figure in the floor length mirror some servants very kindly brought to the Dragon Knight room. She didn't know which room from Kain Castle they stole it from, but she was grateful for it, lest she wanted to prepare for this gala with the small mirror in their bathing chamber.

Her hair and makeup were done exactly how she liked it: hair half up in a waterfall braid and the colour of her eyes enhanced by kohl; her lips were painted with a rosy red to compliment her tan. Anna had truly outdone herself this time.

She breathed in through her nose and out through her mouth, rolling her shoulders back and steeling her spine.

You can do this. Never mind the butterflies in her stomach. She looked every bit the elegant courtier Anna had promised she'd make her look, as well as the fierce, storm riding warrior her reputation had promised the people waiting for her she was.

While Anna did her own makeup in the bathroom, Eva brushed her skirt aside, easily thanks to the long slit that went up to her hip, and strapped a dagger to each of her thighs. When she let the skirt hang freely and saw the slight bulge where her daggers stood out, she realised she hadn't thought about where her daggers would go when she bought the dress.

Maybe they weren't that noticeable...

"Don't tell me you're going to a gala *armed*," Anna scolded as she stepped out of the bathroom. If Eva was stunning, Anna was drop dead gorgeous. While her crimson hair was usually as straight as an arrow, tonight it hung down her back in big rivulets. Her eyes, like Eva's, were accentuated with kohl, making them look like true silver under the moonlit night. Her cheeks were dusted with a gentle touch of rogue, softening the hard edges of the glare she set on Eva.

Shit. They are noticeable.

Grumbling, Eva unstrapped her daggers and tossed them casually onto her bed. "I don't like not being armed."

Anna offered her a sympathetic smile. "I know. It's only for a couple of hours, though. The castle is heavily guarded and half of the people on the guest list are Dragon Knights. You'll live."

That didn't change the fact she didn't like it. She might as well be walking into a room full of nobles and coworkers butt ass naked.

Eva crossed the room for her overnight bag and pulled out the gloves Sasha had given her. They were non-lethal, but they sure were an effective stun—

Anna swiped the gloves out of Eva's hands, grimacing at the accessory as if they had been dipped in a questionable substance. "You are *not* wearing these to the gala."

"Come *on*, Anna."

"They're hideous! Do you want people to be talking about that scandalous slit on your skirt or the ugly gloves? *One* of them is sexy."

"If it means I have a weapon of sorts, I'll take the hit on my reputation."

Anna gasped, taken aghast. "You will not! Reputation is *everything*. You will survive a night without a weapon, Eva Greene. I'm not armed," she added as if that would make the uneasy knot in her stomach loosen.

"Yes you are, you *are* a weapon."

Anna smirked.

A gentle knock came at the door, then: "Are you ladies ready?"

"Yes!" Anna called before Eva could get a word out.

Jacob opened the door, Grayson entering behind him. The former wore the same suit he wore to dinner with King Renkon and Queen Althea all those months ago. It still fit him well, but Eva would never get used to seeing her brother in anything but a rundown tunic or a uniform. Despite having watched him run a comb through his hair, it was still a dishevelled mess that refused to be tamed.

His eyes settled on the gloves in Anna's hand then a frown bunched his eyebrows together "Tell me those aren't coming to the gala with us."

Anna threw Eva a pointed look then shook her head. "No, they are not. Right, Eva?"

Eva crossed her arms, debating whether it was worth behaving like a petulant child. When she caught Grayson eyeing her, though, she decided it wasn't worth it.

Those dark, stormy eyes of his took her in slow and heady-like, definitely not missing the way her corset favoured her breasts or the long slit exposing the outer half of her right leg. After that mouth-watering look, she reminded herself to thank Anna for pushing her on leg day at the gym.

"You're wearing black," he noted, his tone a hint huskier than usual. His eyes burned as hot as dragon fire that set her inners ablaze.

"Not entirely." She lifted the hem of her skirt with her toes—potentially giving him a better angle of her bare leg in the process—where the black faded into a crystal blue.

"It suits you," he answered thickly, then cleared his throat, remembering that they weren't alone in the room. He gestured to the gloves before taking them off Anna's hands and tucking them into his breast pocket. "I'll hold onto these for you. I don't plan on being far from you, anyway."

That was a promise if she ever heard one.

"You don't?"

She looked at his stained black dragon scale armour and mithril cloak, reminded that he was a part of the security detail tonight. He'd declined Leo's reluctant invitation and had declared that he would be working. To say Eva was disappointed when he broke the news during their morning practice was an understatement. She had been looking forward to seeing him dressed up for once—and to dancing with him. If he moved on the dancefloor anything like he did on the mats, he wouldn't have been a disappointing partner.

"No." A lopsided smile quirked on one half of his mouth. "I'm your personal guard tonight. Seeing as you're the guest of honour, Hargin saw it pertinent that you had extra protection."

She couldn't resist the answering smile. They hadn't spoken much since he helped her in the dens. Their sessions were silent—or strictly professional—and she was too busy with Anna's training or making amends with Arkon to seek him out in between.

But she hadn't forgotten their moment in the dens. The moment where she nearly threw caution to the wind and kissed him right there. But then, she'd still been uncertain, raw from her argument with Arkon and the guilt of putting the base in danger.

Tonight she felt neither.

"Maybe being unarmed isn't so bad after all," she decided.

Jacob shook his head at them, making last minute adjustments to his tie. "I don't get your obsession with weapons—either of you."

Anna swatted his hands aside and made the adjustments for him. "Leave your tie alone, Jacob Greene, or you'll ruin it." She tightened it then tucked it back in his vest. Their eyes met as her hands slid up his chest to his shoulders. A pink hue climbed up his throat, to his cheeks.

"I—I noticed you didn't bring a date tonight," he blurted, suddenly forgetting about everything but her.

Her smile was all kinds of seductive and Eva made a mental note to ask her how she pulled it off so effortlessly. "I didn't. I was hoping you would ask me."

Jacob's face went from pink to red. "Hopefully I'm not too late?"

"Not at all." Her hand slid down to his hand; she guided him out of the room, casting Eva a wink on their way out.

Grayson chuckled as the door shut behind them. "She enjoys tormenting Jacob way too much."

Eva shook her head, trying not to move it too fast and ruin Anna's fine work. "No, I think she does it just enough. You have no idea how much of a pain he was to grow up with. This is acceptable payback."

His lopsided smile turned into a fully fledged grin. A rare sight, one she planned to enjoy as long as she possibly could. He had dimples in the corners of his mouth and his eyes seemed to shine brighter. He was so godsdamn handsome it made her heart ache.

She didn't need him in a suit, or to be swept across the dance floor. This—watching him like this, unguarded and smiling—was more than enough. They didn't speak much during their training sessions, but they didn't need to. Moving through the stances in unison, breathing as one, processing their own fears together, was more intimate than any kiss they'd shared. She felt like she finally knew the man in front of her.

He seemed to know exactly where her thoughts had gone—because his gaze darkened, heat and hunger rising like a tide. He reached up and traced the length of her cheek with his thumb, his touch impossibly soft. "You are beautiful, Starling."

She tugged on her skirt, not quite able to meet the heat of his gaze. "You sound like you're surprised I can clean up nicely."

He let out a quiet, breathless laugh and looked up at the ceiling like he couldn't fathom why she had gone suddenly shy. She'd been called beautiful before, several times before now, thanks to Leo's persistence, but it felt different this time. There was a certain weight to it. A longing and raw desire, but also something more, something deeper, tender. Warmer.

Her cheeks burned, heat coiling deep in her belly.

And she had no idea what to do with it. Had never gone this far with a man before.

After her nerves nearly rattled the flesh off her bones when they were cleaning up dragon shit, she ran straight to Anna for advice. Her way of helping Eva was to drop a stack of smutty books in her palms before walking away with a sly grin.

Eva had no idea what she was getting herself into until she reached *the* chapter. She'd only made it three pages before her cheeks burned so hot she had to fan herself. By page ten, she wasn't sure whether to thank Anna or throw the book at her head.

Grayson's fingers slipped beneath her jaw, tipping her chin back so she had to meet those intense eyes. "No, not surprised. You've always been stunning. But the black?" His eyes drank in the length of her dress, taking in the beading and the delicate curves. "I've lived in black, drowned in it, bled in it. I should hate it on you. But, by gods, I love it. More than I should."

Her breath caught. She hadn't expected the raw honesty, the ache behind his words. This was all she'd ever wanted from him. And now, he was handing it to her without hesitation.

Taking a note out of Anna's book, she slid her hands up his chest, palms flattening against the harsh, unyielding scales of his armor. Her body ached to know what he felt like beneath her fingertips—not just on the mats, where they'd silently agreed to respect the space. He'd let her trace his scars, but she wanted more.

She wanted to know how long she could run idle circles along his azure scales before he snapped. What he'd do if she traced her tongue across the rigid, coiled muscle of his chest.

The thought alone made her dizzy.

She rose onto her toes, as far as her heels allowed, closing the space between them until her lips hovered just shy of his. She didn't know who she was torturing more—him or herself.

"This is all for you, Gray."

His hands caught her waist and drove her back against the wall, pinning her without force, but with unmistakable intent. He leaned in, voice a low rumble against her ear. "Careful, Starling. Say things like that, and a man might forget you haven't forgiven him."

She cupped either side of his face, coaxing him to look at her. "Maybe I have," she said, her voice steady but soft. "You say you don't want to be him again, Dex, but... he is a part of you. A part of your past that made you the man you are today. And that man is incredible." A deep blush rose up her cheeks.

His eyes narrowed, and her heart thumped in her chest. They didn't talk about Dex. If they did, he was usually the one who brought it up. She hoped she wasn't overstepping by bringing him up, but she felt like this was the last puzzle piece. One last step before she could be ready to forgive him.

"Dex died the day I decided to leave Estrus and I don't ever want him back in my life again."

She shook her head. He didn't see what she saw. "I'm just saying that I'm here for all of you. The man you were five years ago, the man you are today, and the man you'll be tomorrow. Maybe you don't even know who you truly are yet, and that's okay. We can figure it out together. What I do know, though..."

He stood frozen, like a bewildered statue, disbelieving of the words spilling out of her mouth. Words she'd been wanting to say but didn't have the courage to say them until now.

"Say it, Starling," he commanded. "Don't leave me in suspense."

"I forgive you, Gray."

His breath caught, and something in his eyes—sharp, dark, and always guarded—melted as he looked at her. Then his forehead dropped to hers, his breath unsteady against her skin.

"You mean it, don't you?" he rasped, doubt scraping against his throat. "You've honestly forgiven me. Even when I don't deserve it. Or you."

It twisted at her heart that he didn't think he deserved her forgiveness. But she understood. After everything he told her, she understood him better than anyone else in this world. And *that* was why she believed in him. Why she'd fallen so damned hard for him.

"You deserve me, Gray. You deserve this. Us."

A tremor passed through him. His hands slid up her back, then into her hair, threading through it like he needed the anchor. He tilted her face up until their lips nearly touched—

A hard, impatient knock rattled the door. "Come on, Eva, you're holding everyone up!"

A breathless laugh burst out of her. Heat still thrummed beneath her skin, her lips tingling from how close she'd come to finally—*finally*—tasting Grayson again.

Of course her brother had to be the one to interrupt. The timing was so perfectly, spectacularly awful that she almost wondered if he'd been lurking outside on purpose, just waiting for the most inopportune moment.

Growling, Grayson stepped away and ran his fingers through his hair, working on gathering his composure. "They can wait a few more minutes."

She sighed, willing her body to cool down and her thoughts to behave. *Focus on the gala. Focus on literally anything but how close you just were to kissing him.*

"We'll talk later?" she hoped.

A ghost of a smile flitted across his face. "Whenever you want. But before you *thoroughly* distracted me," he said, voice low and rough, "I meant to give you this." From his back pocket, he pulled a small velvet box and held it out.

Curious, she took it. "What's this?"

She pried it open—and blinked. Nestled inside was a silver hairpin, elegant in its simplicity. The design was a cascade of interlocking circles, each one slightly different in size, polished to a soft sheen. A long silver pin slid through the back to hold it in place.

"I had a feeling you'd be wearing something scandalous to piss off Renkon," he said, eyes sweeping down her leg with blatant appreciation. "And I figured you wouldn't have room for a weapon."

Her lips twitched. "But I have you as my guard."

He set a half-mocking reprimanding glower on her. "Always be armed, Starling. Always."

Gently, as if the piece might break beneath his fingers, he held the hairpin in one hand then pulled the pin free with the other. When he gripped it like a knife, she noticed that one side looked distinctly like a handle. Curiously, she poked the tip and wasn't surprised when a bead of blood broke out on her finger.

"You got me a knife as an accessory?"

His eyes met hers, something uncertain flickering in their depths. "You don't like it?"

"No." Her voice softened. "I love it." She turned her back to him. "Put it in, will you?"

He stepped in close, the heat of his body brushing hers. With a tenderness that made her chest ache, he slid the pin into the braid Anna had so carefully twisted into place. His fingers lingered—just a moment—before they drifted to her shoulders. Then his mouth dipped to her ear, his breath sending a shiver down her spine. "Now," he murmured, voice like smoke, "you're ready for the gala."

Her lips parted, breath shallow.

She steadied herself, brushing her fingers down her dress as if that could cool her down. "Let's not keep them waiting, then."

CHAPTER 17
THE HERO OF ABORIA

Jacob and Anna were waiting a little ways down the hallway for them, one significantly more patient than the other.

"There you are!" Jacob broke away from his pacing to meet Eva halfway. "What took you so long? I've had *three* servants ask me when you'll be arriving. Three! Leo will show up himself if you make him wait any longer."

At the mention of the eccentric prince, Grayson's expression cooled, his jaw tightening. "He doesn't own Eva. She'll arrive at her party when *she*'s ready."

She offered Jacob an apologetic smile. "There was a last minute adjustment I needed to make." She smoothed her hands down the soft fabric of her dress. "But I'm ready now."

She led the squad down the hallway and a flight of stairs, her heels echoing softly against the polished stone. The corridor outside the ballroom was already crowded, nobles and dignitaries lining up in anticipation for what Leo had promised would be the grandest gala of the year.

She hadn't asked for this. Hadn't asked for a celebration. Yes, Sylus had signed the surrender agreement. Yes, the war was over—thanks to Anna, Grayson, and herself—and that was certainly cause for celebration. But all of this? It felt excessive. Wasteful.

All she could see were the jewels glittering beneath chandeliers, the trays of indulgent food, the fine silks swathing bodies that had never worked the fields. Resources that could have rebuilt villages like Brar. That could have bought grain for starving families or healing salves for the wounded still recovering in makeshift huts. If she'd known Leo was going to go this overboard, she would've asked him to donate the coin instead.

Her stomach tightened. Her nerves prickled at her skin like a thousand nettles. She'd never been surrounded by so many people—never been *looked at* this much. They were all dressed in shimmering finery, eyes drawn to the girl in the show-stopping gown. The girl who still felt like a small-town hunter beneath the chiffon and lace.

She could feel their stares crawling up her back. Could hear the whispers, low and cutting like a vicious blade.

Arkon's presence wrapped around her soul and alleviated the wasps tearing through her stomach. He opened his mind up to her, allowing her to see through his eyes.

He was flying over the castle in a broad circle, Aster and Eran gliding in an opposite direction as he and Glade. The castle's towers twinkled in the moonless night, candles and lightstones alike illuminating the hundreds, if not, thousands of rooms filling the illustrious Kain Castle.

He banked right, angling his head towards the city of Lexxis and its imperious buildings, almost as tall as the shortest tower in the castle. A halo of light hovered over the city, gleaming in the darkness surrounding it. Only the capital would be fully lit so late at night. In Brar, once the sun went down, it was a matter of hours before the last candle was blown out and the town went to sleep. Here, the city hustled and bustled all night long.

A strong wind cut through his flight path. Wings pumping, he redirected his course and leaned into the wind, knowing it would grate over his scales in the most delicious of ways. Eva savoured every caress on his scales, breathing in as if she was outside with him, soaring through the inky night's sky.

"Miss Greene?"

She snapped out of his mind and looked down at the man a foot shorter than her who had been trying to get her attention. He wore a comically frumpy hat she was sure meant to be stylish. "Hm?"

"Are you ready to be presented?"

"*Thank you,*" she said to Arkon before nodding to the servant. "*I needed that.*"

"*Do not let them fluster you. You are Eva Greene, Saviour of Aboria, Rider of Storms, and my Soul Bound. You are strength incarnate.*"

Gods, she couldn't be more grateful to have him in her life. She hated fighting with him, and was glad they had moved past their differences.

The servant inclined his head respectfully then gestured for the guards at the door to open them. As one, they pulled their half aside and the servant stepped through first, clearing his throat loudly to catch people's attention.

"The Hero of Aboria has arrived!"

Eva couldn't stop herself from cringing, both at the title and the surprising volume of his voice. It was one thing to hear people whisper it in the halls or for Leo to call her a hero, but it was an entirely different ordeal to be *announced* into the same room as their king. She may be Bound and possess a rare power—but at heart she was still a small village hunter, who had tragically lost her family.

Nothing special. Nothing extraordinary.

The string quartet in the corner froze, making her arrival far more dramatic than it needed to be. The silence that followed rolled over the crowd like an avalanche. One by one, people turned to the entrance, critical eyes landing on Eva.

Her stomach took a nosedive for the polished marble floor.

For a beat, the room held its breath while everyone studied, judged, and appraised her. She wondered nervously if she was supposed to give some kind of speech Leo hadn't prepared her for.

But then they turned back to their conversations.

Eva released a breath of relief.

Anna squeezed her arm with a delirious grin, not the least bit bothered by the crowd. Her eyes trailed over the green-and-gold drapes hanging on the walls and ceiling. Lightstones glittered precariously above their heads, reflecting off the gold streamers. Candles encased in thin glass tubes offset the white light above with a warm glow on the serving tables. The massive ice sculpture of a dragon—of Arkon, she realised at a closer inspection—caught her attention and she laughed, opening her mind so her Dragon Bound could see his likeness.

His chuckle rumbled through her mind. "*Now I've seen everything... It does look rather fetching, though. Be sure to thank the prince for me.*"

"I *will.*"

Grayson appeared at her side, following her gaze to the sculpture, then scoffed. "He really pulled all of the stops tonight."

"It looks amazing, doesn't it?" Anna gushed then pointed at the floral garnishes framing the large floor to ceiling windows viewing the famous Kain gardens. The garden itself was illuminated with the same twinkling lightstones hanging from the ceiling, embedded within the shrubs and bushes. "Those were my idea. It seemed like a waste to not bring the garden inside."

Eva grinned at her friend. She saw little pieces of Anna all over the place, in the small details that she expected Leo to miss. "It looks lovely, Anna. You both did a great job."

She beamed proudly, eyes twinkling like lightstones. "Thank you. Do you know what my favourite part is?" She jutted her chin towards the string quartet. Their composer spotted her and offered a little wave towards her before turning to his quartet. "I get to see old friends. They're incredibly talented. Normally they're booked months in advance, but they came as a favour for me."

Jacob nodded to the beat they set. "They're pretty good."

She twirled to him, flaming red skirt fanning out around her as she pivoted. "Come dance with me, Jake."

He wasn't given much of a choice when she took his hand and pulled him to the dance floor. He tossed a pleading look at Eva, but she waved at him in response. Dancing wasn't exactly his strong suit—especially in public. The only time he'd truly danced was with Erika around the bonfire. But, as much as it pained both of them, she was gone now and he needed to find another reason to dance. Eva couldn't think of anyone better than Anna.

"Have fun! Don't trip on her skirt!"

His face flattened into a mocking glower before he gave Anna his full attention. All sense of discontent melted away when he looked down at her. He took her hand and wrapped one around her waist then swept her across the dance floor. Eva's jaw hit the floor as she watched him glide effortlessly. Not a single fumble.

"He's been practicing," Grayson answered while she gaped like a fish trying to figure out when he had gotten *good* at dancing. "I may have given him a few pointers."

Stunned yet again, she swivelled towards Grayson, trying to imagine the Slayer of Souls teaching her brother how to dance. What she would have paid to be the fly on that wall...

He recoiled from the look she befell on him. "It's not that big of a deal."

"Of course not," she agreed to make him feel better, despite it, in fact, being a big deal.

She turned her attention back to the crowd to hide her smirk. If he wanted to pretend showing Jacob how to dance so he could impress Anna—which he thoroughly did by the big grin on her face—she wouldn't ruin it for him.

She caught sight of Leo on the other side of the room, mingling with a group of giggling ladies. He seemed to be trying to escape them, inching back ever so slightly after he replied to one of them, but they were utterly engrossed—no, *enchanted*—by him to notice and moved with him, like waves against the shore.

Eva couldn't blame them for being infatuated. He stood out among the sea of black suits in an ivory suit with coattails. His dark brown hair was brushed but not styled, putting an edge to his polished look. The silver crown atop his head was a stark contrast to his dark blue eyes and made him quite the enticing bachelor.

Eva bumped Grayson's shoulder, choosing to focus her attention on the handsome man beside her. "You're sweet for showing Jacob how to dance."

Grunting, he shoved his hands in his pockets and scanned the room with the vehemence of a starved hunter. "He wouldn't stop asking."

"Hm-hmm. I'm sure he really twisted your arm for lessons."

"He's your brother. You should know how persistent he can be."

She also knew how embarrassed Jacob would have been to ask. He told everyone that he hated dancing, but what he truly hated was that he was bad at it. To admit that to Grayson must have taken a considerable amount of pep talks and hours hyping himself up in front of the mirror before mustering up the courage to ask for help.

And now that Grayson was being bashful about it, it made it all the better.

The couple spun, dipped, and twirled across the dancefloor. Anna's dress fanned out around her in a fiery halo and Jacob never looked lighter on his feet. They were breathtaking to watch, and Eva felt a small stab of jealousy. She hadn't realised how much she wanted to dance until she heard the phenomenal quartet and saw others dancing and having fun.

She surreptitiously peered at Grayson, wondering if he'd dance with her if she asked—or if he'd decline, whether it be for duty or because it'd remind him of the life he'd left behind.

Grayson leaned in, mouth brushing over the shell of her ear. "This is the part where you *mingle*."

Mingle? She shuddered at the thought.

"Mingle with who? I don't know anyone here."

He straightened up and gestured towards the parting crowd carving a path for the Crowned Prince stalking towards them. "I'm sure Leo will remedy that for you."

As he drew closer, a charming smile lit his face—one meant only for her. His gaze roamed over her figure slowly, deliberately, taking in every detail with unhurried appreciation. His eyes lingered on the sweetheart cut of her dress, where black silk met sun-kissed skin, and something hungry flickered behind the charm.

Her heart quickened, which she chose to blame on the nerves from being way out of her element.

Beside her, Grayson let out a quiet huff. "He looks like he's going to devour you," he muttered, his voice dry but taut with something else.

She couldn't stop the laugh that burst from her lips—part nerves, part amusement. It was all she had time for before Leo swept in.

"Eva, darling," he said, his voice warm and fluid, like honey, "you look every bit as ravishing as I hoped you'd be." He cast Grayson a sharp, territorial glance before pressing a kiss to her cheek and slipping an arm firmly around her back. "Come," he said, already steering her toward the heart of the room. "My father wishes to speak with you, and there are people who are absolutely dying to meet you."

She glanced at Grayson. He nodded with a look only she knew how to decipher.

Where you go, I go, it said, and she *loved* that they didn't need to exchange a single word.

Embracing Leo's assistance through this jungle of a party, she let him usher her to King Renkon's table. The soft rustle of her skirt followed her every step, the warm press of Leo's hand at the small of her back the only steady thing in a room that suddenly felt too loud, too bright, too polished.

Queen Althea dutifully sat by King Renkon's side, shoulders pulled back stiff. Captain Nestor Quade and a few other high ranking generals and dignitaries watched her with matching scrutiny.

Their eyes burned into her—dissecting, measuring, judging—as they took in the form-fitting dress, the pinned up hair, and smokey kohl. They looked at her and saw a beautiful woman on the arm of her prince. Not a fighter. A survivor. A warrior forged in a storm. They saw the surface, but she was simmering beneath it, a blade wrapped in velvet.

Let them underestimate you. Grayson's advice was the best damn advice anyone had ever given her. She had nothing to prove to them. They could judge her all they wanted, at the end of the day, she was the one who captured Darius, who was chosen to be Arkon's Soul Bound. She knew that, and that was all she needed.

A general, who's rank was obvious with the blatant display of medals and stripes pinned to his formal uniform, glanced over her shoulder at Grayson. He sat absolutely still—so still, Eva half-expected his spine to snap—like someone had shoved a sword up his ass to keep him that way. Gods forbid the man put a single crinkle in his uniform.

As promised, Grayson stood three feet behind her and proved to be an immovable force against the general's scrutiny. The man's eyes narrowed on the Dragon Knight, but he said nothing when he turned his attention back to Eva. She had to wonder if he was a part of the select few who knew *who* stood behind her.

"My lords," Leo addressed them courteously, if not a little smugly, "may I present you, Private Eva Greene, Arkon's chosen Soul Bound and the woman responsible for bringing Prince Darius Fortys into custody."

"It was a team effort," she corrected. It didn't feel right to take all of the credit when she most definitely couldn't have done it without Anna or Grayson. "Sergeant Hargin and Corporal Smith were just as involved as I was in apprehending Darius."

A dignitary, which Eva could only guess by the stuffed shoulder pads and feathered hat, regarded her down the length of his long, pointed nose. "Ah. The truth finally comes out. You did *not* capture Prince Darius. A woman bringing down that vicious beast of a prince? Ha! Corporal, this party should be in your name."

"His face isn't as pretty," another chimed in. The medals on his coat suggested he was the general's second hand. His posture was just as rigid—maybe even more so, as if rank were decided by how big of a sword they could fit in their ass. "We all know our dear prince has a weakness for..." His lewd eyes dropped to the slit of her skirt. "*Gentle* figures."

Grayson stiffened behind her. The air hummed, his magic pressing against her skin like smoke on the battlefield. She didn't need to look at him to know his jaw was locked, his hands balled into fists. The Soul Bound could have ended the man with a flick of his wrist, yet he stayed silent. Waiting. Letting her take this.

Eva rolled her shoulders back and held her head higher. Her eyes locked onto the men who dared to belittle her after everything she'd done for them. "You want the truth?" She leaned in, voice dropping low but unwavering. "Darius drove my family's sword into my father's heart. He burned my mother and baby sister alive—and made me watch."

The dignitary's smirk fell flat. In the corner of her eye, Queen Althea set her fork aside on her half-eaten plate. But courtly manners be damned. They wanted to see the warrior—they were about to see her teeth.

"When I faced him, I didn't falter. I didn't run. I beat him within an inch of his life. I would have slit his throat on the same soil he fertilised with my family's remains," she confessed darkly, that hateful bloodlust still whispering for her to put an end to him, "but instead I marked him with my power. The web-like scars on his skin? That was from *me*." Her gaze swept across the table, calm and merciless. "Let's see any of you get that close to him and live to tell the tale."

The general's second choked on his wine. He sputtered, slamming his fist into his chest. "Such talk is hardly appropriate for present company, Miss Greene. You've ruined our queen's appetite."

"That's Private Greene to you, Karthas," Grayson growled behind her. "Eva is a respected Dragon Knight. You will address her as such."

The blood drained from the officer's face, which told Eva *he* knew who was standing behind her.

"Indeed," Queen Althea agreed softly. "Do not drag me into your rabble, Colonel Karthas. I am grateful for Private Greene's service—and find it rather refreshing to see a young woman rise amongst the ranks. Sergeant Hargin and Private Greene are a promising pair for our future military. I, for one, will be watching them very closely."

Leo preened beside Eva, giving her waist a little squeeze. "I couldn't agree more, Mother. I think it's time we see more women honoured at events. Don't you think, Father?" Leo angled himself—and, incidentally, Eva—towards King Renkon. She stiffened in his gentle grasp, not quite ready to acknowledge her king after the last time they spoke in a formal setting.

The king's knuckles whitened around the armrests. The glare he fired at his son was as deadly as any of Grayson's strikes—and just as deliberate. When he finally shifted it to Eva, her spine straightened on instinct.

"I agree, Leonidas. Women should be celebrated more." The king leaned into the side of his chair, closer to Queen Althea and stroked his knuckles along the length of her cheekbone tenderly. Eva's blood simmered at the open mockery of Leo's ideals and Queen Althea's autonomy. It infuriated her further that the queen just sat there and did nothing to defend herself, and, in fact, looked quite taken by her husband's affection. "After all, none of us would be here without a woman bringing us into this world."

Leo's grip tightened around Eva's waist. "That's not what I—"

"Thank you for your service, Dragon Knight," Renkon went on as if Leo hadn't said anything. "Your contribution to my kingdom has been noted."

And now came the choice: Eva could take the high road, let bygones stay buried and walk away with her head held high—or she could remember his contempt, the insults, the way he'd dismissed her—and let him feel, for just a moment, what it felt like to be underestimated.

She put a little extra flare when she curtsied. "It is my honour to defend Aboria, Your Majesty. Even volatile creatures, it seems, know how to keep their promises."

Despite how hard he tried to hide it behind a light chuckle, a smirk tugged at the corner of Leo's mouth. The air shifted behind her as well, the simmering tension easing back into the shadows, calm and quiet. She could almost feel Grayson's pride swell behind her.

King Renkon's fingers drummed on the armchair, but his expression remained neutral, despite the ire burning in his eyes. "It appears my son has succeeded where I failed in taming that defiance you call spirit. Remember, Private, your leash is short, and the gods are watching."

"I hope so, Your Majesty. I intend to give them a show worth watching. All of Astrida will know my name. They will know that I am the one who brought peace to this world—not a man, not a king, not even a god."

"Well said," Queen Althea praised, raising her glass in a toast. The men rushed to raise their glasses with her. "May Ebis bless you, Private Greene, and carry you to heights beyond the reach of men."

Eva bowed deeply, her movements measured and respectful. She vowed never to underestimate the queen again. Though she appeared docile and reverent, there was a quiet strength beneath the surface. She lacked her husband's authority, yet even so, the room seemed to bend to her presence. "Thank you, Your Majesty."

She inclined her head, a slight nod of acknowledgment. "Now, go have fun, Private. You've earned this night."

Leo sketched a bow for his parents. "Thank you, Mother. I'll make sure Private Greene has a night she'll never forget."

As he led Eva away from the table he leaned into her and whispered, "You just *love* pressing my father's buttons, don't you?"

"Sorry." She meant it. Renkon grinded her gears, which made it conveniently easy to forget he was a king. "Your father is such an asshole. I can't help myself."

He barked a laugh, tipping his head back, which earned several looks from people. Not scornfully, though, like she expected; they looked at him like they wanted to be in on the joke and laugh right alongside him. "There's nothing wrong with a little bite, love. I *thoroughly* enjoyed it. Especially the part about giving the gods a show. I only hope that I can be a part of it." The look he gave her suggested he was thinking of an entirely different show than she was talking about.

She rolled her eyes. "I'm sure you do. I promise I'm trying to get the hang of this whole..." She gestured around the room, and the people within, at a loss for words what to call it all. "This is a part of my life now, even if I think the pomp and circumstance is ridiculous."

He grinned broadly. "It's not so bad when you get the hang of it. Thankfully, you have an excellent—and outrageously handsome—teacher to be here with you every step of the way."

She leaned into his side for just a moment—long enough for him to feel her gratitude, short enough that his heat couldn't quite wrap around her. "Thank you."

He stopped them a few feet from a gathering that hadn't yet noticed them and glanced back at Grayson, dutifully trailing three paces behind.

"Is he going to be here all night?"

"Yes," Grayson answered, his voice like stone, leaving no room for argument.

Leo turned fully then, shoulders stiffening as he puffed his chest out and tilted his chin up defiantly. "You're going to scare my guests away."

"Not my problem. I've been assigned to protect Eva."

The air shifted between them, a palpable tension that made the hairs on her arms stand on end.

"Protect her from *what*? Darius is locked up and will be executed tomorrow. The threat is gone. Unless..." He arched a taunting eyebrow in his direction. "You're here to keep *me* away from her?"

Grayson's jaw tightened. Despite his expression remaining impassive, it still managed to look as deadly as the blades strapped to his chest. "My intentions are none of your business."

Leo stepped closer, his voice low and steady. "Go sharpen a knife by the buffet—away from my guests."

"No."

A muscle feathered in Leo's jaw. "For once in your miserable life, don't be selfish. You are ruining Eva's first impression of some very powerful people. You know as well as I do how important connections are. If they see you, they won't see the Hero of Aboria, they'll see a frail woman who needs protecting."

Grayson's fists clenched at his sides, a tic working away at his jaw. Those dark stormy eyes could slice right through mithril with the way they looked at Leo. When they shifted to her, they adopted that soft, soulful edge she was so used to seeing. They showed nothing to everyone in the room, but, to her, she saw how he loathed to admit Leo was right. Maybe more so, though, he hated watching her be with Leo.

She offered him a secret smile. *This is all for you, remember?* she wanted to say.

Words didn't need to be spoken between them. He understood—always understood her—and conceded with a nod. "I'll go stand intimidatingly by the cake and make sure there is enough left over for you to take home."

The man knew the key to her heart.

He winked at her before stalking across the room toward the table where a massive chocolate fudge cake waited. Eva watched him go, wishing she could join him on the sidelines. It looked far less tumultuous than the tides she'd been caught in.

You can do this. This was her life now, whether she wanted it or not. Better to embrace it than be dragged into it kicking and screaming.

Besides, she'd already survived a conversation with King Renkon and his closest advisors. Surely there couldn't be anyone more insufferable than that arrogant, misogynistic king.

CHAPTER 18
MURKY WATERS

Eva was wrong.

So very wrong.

There were people *far* worse than King Renkon.

Leo led her around the room with her hand tucked into the crook of his elbow. She felt like a lady, soft and refined—but with a bite if people got too close.

Leo was in his element—effortlessly charming, quick to flatter, the perfect host. He wielded introductions like a weapon, slipping her into conversations with the city's elite: dignitaries with polished medals, high-ranking officers with glinting eyes, philanthropists who praised her while scanning her dress for signs of scandal. Eva smiled, nodded, and offered respectful answers, even when the questions veered too far from comfort—about Arkon, her upbringing, her opinions on courtship and politics.

As pleasant as everyone appeared with their manners and sweet smiles, Eva quickly learned that this was a different kind of battlefield—one where weapons were words and the wounds were invisible. Their praise was barbed, always laced with qualifiers: brave *for a woman*, clever *for a commoner*, refined *for someone without a proper education.*

They dismissed her the moment they were finished mining her for novelty, like she was a temporary marvel—something to gawk at, not to be taken seriously. And yet, they watched her closely.

She saw the way they glanced at her dress, and tried to guess how much it cost. She felt their eyes following the way she moved with Leo, weighing her worth not by what she'd done, but by who stood beside her.

She carried herself with quiet pride and didn't falter, even when she'd rather gouge hers—or their—eyes out. She smiled, exchanged pleasantries, and held her ground with the same determination she'd had facing down monsters.

But beneath the surface, the girl who once dug trenches beside her brother, who'd stitched her own boots and hunted where no one else dared to go, stood on uneasy legs.

She found strength every time her eyes flicked to Grayson across the room, standing stoic and stone-faced near the cake table. Or when Leo's arm tightened slightly around hers to remind her she wasn't alone.

This night was theirs to endure together. But even in the warmth of company, she couldn't help but feel the cold fingers of judgment scraping at her skin.

She couldn't decide which was worse—the women who played at being fragile, porcelain dolls pretending they might shatter at the slightest touch, or the men who ogled her like they thought her worth began and ended with her body.

The women they were talking with currently were no better. A mother and three daughters. Lady Filla, outfitted in an enormous feather hat and a dress that accentuated every curve, owned a brothel in the pleasure district—but Eva wasn't allowed to call it that. The other lords and ladies called it a "gentleman's club," which wasn't fooling anybody. Even her uneducated, small town mind brain could put two and two together.

Eva swore she watched her slip a few people a small pouch of something when they thought no one was looking.

Her daughters flocked around her with their feathered fans. Fans appeared to be the *in* thing these days. Nearly every woman they encountered had one.

Eva had to admit that their use of the fans was impressive; they wielded them like weapons in the ballroom. They hid behind it like a shield when they had something backhanded to say, then let it drop at a flirtatious angle to catch Leo's attention. Watching the feathers flutter in a clearly practiced rhythm was mesmerising. She would have to ask Anna about it for the next event she attended.

"Private Greene, may I ask, who escorted you this evening?" Lady Filla asked, fanning at her breasts—behemoths that heaved with every breath.

Despite having the conversation with Eva, her eyes couldn't stop casting flirtatious glances towards Leo. Except this time she looked at him as if he couldn't *possibly* be Eva's escort.

She was getting tired of people assuming she *needed* an escort. At least with King Renkon, he knew what she was capable of—he just didn't like it. These women, though, hated her because she had Leo's full attention. He was a prize everyone wanted to claim or become, but to her he was a dear friend who only saw *her*, not the weapon everyone wanted her to be.

"No one," she answered, her tone more clipped than it had been the last few times she'd answered the same question from other groups. "I came here with friends."

"How bold," Isabella, one of the Lady's daughters, cooed behind her bright pink fan. "I wish I could be so brave to partake in an event like this unattended." She shot her mother a venomous look, but Lady Filla was too busy staring at Leo to notice.

Bold? Brave? The words twisted inside Eva's stomach. What kind of world did they live in where having free autonomy was considered scandalous?

"There's nothing bold or brave about it," Eva said, barely able to hold back what she really wanted to say to these women. "I just don't need a man's permission to *enter a room.*"

Lady Filla's youngest daughter, whose name Eva forgot, gasped, clasping her pearls. Her mother shot her silencing glare before turning her attention to Eva. "Forgive us, Private, for not being raised in a destitute village. We're not familiar with your backwards way of thinking."

Backwards. *She* was the backwards one?

That did it.

Fists clenched at her sides—because she had no *fan* to hide behind—she stepped forward to show her what happened when you flung insults about said *destitute* village.

Leo caught her waist in the nick of time and yanked her back to his side; to anyone else, it looked like possessive affection, rather than what it truly was—Leo saving their lives. "Eva darling, how about a dance?"

Huffing, she sank into his embrace and let the tension trickle out of her body. It was easy to do with him; he had a certain way about him that made the world around them blur at the edges. It was exactly what she needed tonight—

"I'll dance with you if she doesn't want to, Your Highness," Isabella offered *immediately*.

Eva refrained from tossing a sneer her way. All night people had been vying for Leo's attention—some of them more subtle than others—and it was *exhausting*. And she was just *watching!* She didn't know how Leo did it day in and day out.

Leo didn't cast a single glance the young woman's way; his attention was solely on Eva—as it had been all night. It didn't matter how beautiful or wealthy or eloquent they were, his attention was hers. For that, she was grateful. She would have found herself locked up in the dungeon in the cell right beside Darius by the end of the night if it weren't for him.

"Only if you promise I don't have to talk to any more people," she said, completely aware of the ladies listening in.

His smile was slow and sultry. "No more people. I want you all to myself for the rest of the night."

He held his hand out to her, palm up and waited patiently. She took it and let him guide her to the dance floor. People moved like a parting tide around them, giving them more than enough space to waltz. She tried not to think about how many eyes were on them, and instead focused on where she was supposed to put her hands and feet.

His hand went to her waist, still holding her other, while she gripped his shoulder with possibly more force the necessary.

Leo grinned at her nerves, but there was no trace of judgement. There was only warmth in his gaze. "First time?"

She nodded, locking her gaze on his lapis eyes. "I've been practicing with Anna, but I've never... danced in front of a crowd."

He pulled her just a little bit closer, enough for his warmth to seep into her and calm her racing heart. "Ignore them. It's just you and me, love."

Nodding again, she let him lead, and followed with ease that would make Anna proud. They glided like skaters on ice across the marble floor. Her feet were light, as if she was back in her forest, hunting her prey. She spun like she did every morning and evening during the Death's Dance, but instead of flinging her leg up for a brutal kick, she fanned her skirt outward the way Lieutenant Dwight had taught her.

This was what she had been looking forward to. Dancing, eating and drinking to her heart's desire, forgetting about the world around her. Weaving between partners, she felt as free as she did on Arkon's back in the sky. *This* she could do all night. Nobody could hold her back, weigh her down.

After twirling her outward, Leo pulled her back in, spinning her twice before her back slammed into his chest. Her hands crossed in front of her, holding his as they swayed, following the gentle rhythm of his hips. His mouth dropped to her neck, tracing the curve of her throat with warm lips that left heat in their wake. "You are spectacular, Eva Greene."

She giggled as she turned back to face him, which she chose to believe came from the many glasses of champagne she drank to make it through the scrutiny. Definitely not from the light bubbly feeling in her chest from the look he gave her. A look that made her feel like she was more than just a Dragon Knight or Soul Bound, like a queen or she was Asturias herself.

"There it is." He yanked her close, knocking the breath from her lungs as they twirled around the other dancers. "I've been waiting all night for that."

Her brow pinched together. "For what?"

"That smile. It lights up the whole room. *You* light up the room."

The smile he adored slipped away and the giggles choked in her throat. His words dropped in her stomach like a stone in a lake. He meant it, and said it with such reverence. Reverence she didn't deserve.

"I'm sorry if I've been a pain tonight." She knew that wasn't what he was implying, but she chose to interpret it this way, because it was easier to deny it.

Shaking his head, his hand shifted, knuckles grazing the length of her cheek as if he had to memorize the curve of her face. Like each touch would never be enough, that he had to hold on to her to stop himself from sinking in the sea of chaos around them. "You haven't been a pain. In fact, I rather enjoyed watching you tonight." He tilted his head, admiring her at a different angle, with a slight wrinkle in his brow. "But I fear you're not enjoying yourself as much as I'd hoped you would."

Eva thought about lying to him. After the time and effort he'd put into making this perfect for her, she didn't want to make him think it was all for nothing.

This party was a statement: he *listened.*

The Prince of Aboria sat with her at dinner months ago, asked questions no one else had, listened to her likes and dislikes, and somehow remembered every detail. He made magic happen here. Her favorite foods were served on silver platters, even dishes she'd only mentioned in passing. The centerpieces held pinecones and cedar sprigs—little fragments of her childhood forest, nestled between royal greens and gleaming golds. She wouldn't be surprised if he had handpicked every detail during his visits to Fort Brar, quietly collecting pieces of her past.

The music matched the rhythm she grew up humming, the lighting danced like fireflies from her pond. Even the pattern stitched into the napkins resembled the embroidery her mother used to make.

This was all for her. Every thoughtful, extravagant detail. And for that, she was eternally grateful.

But...

"Leo, I love the food. The music is out of this world. Your charming company is impeccable. As always." She gave him a wry smile. "But your guests are insufferable."

When she expected him to glare at her and call her an ungrateful peasant girl, he beamed like a ray of sunshine and leaned in, brushing his lips over the shell of her ear. "I couldn't agree more."

He tilted his head toward the balcony doors, practically glowing with promise—dazzling lights beyond the glass shimmered like stardust, the scent of fresh air barely slipping through the crack in the frame. "Why don't we get out of here for a bit? There's something I'd like to show you. I think you'll appreciate it."

Her eyes quickly scanned the buffet, but it wasn't the food she was grazing. Lastly, her gaze landed on Grayson, standing stoically by the half-eaten fudge cake, which she hadn't had the chance to divulge in yet. One hand was tucked into the front pocket of his cargos while his other held a pristine white plate with a large fudgey slice balanced in the centre.

He'd saved her some cake. That man was true to his word, through and through.

A twinge of guilt pulled at her stomach. While she was dancing away with Leo and talking to people she didn't care about, the one person she *did* want to spend this night with was standing off on the sidelines, watching her.

Their gazes locked. He must have read something in her eyes, because he straightened up, hand freeing from his pocket and grazing over this sword. His eyes flickered over to Leo, narrowing with a silent threat looming over him.

I can take care of him for you, that look said, which made her want to laugh. Instead, she offered a subtle shake of her head.

She'd see what Leo wanted to show her—then she'd make her way over to him and spend time with her broody Knight.

Eva took Leo's hand and let him lead her around the edge of the dancefloor, ignoring anyone who tried to intercept them. Speculative murmurs followed in their wake, but she kept her gaze forward.

A guard stood outside the door, dutifully keeping watch. He saw Leo as they stepped out onto the balcony and bowed deeply.

"Your Highness, is everything all right?"

"Quite fine, Willem. Do you mind giving us some privacy?"

He peered at Eva, refreshingly seeming to be the only person to not know who she was, then inclined his head respectfully. "Of course. I believe I'm due to patrol the gardens, anyway." He marched down the stone stairs to the gravel path below them.

Eva followed Leo to the edge of the balcony, her breath catching as she took in the view below.

The gardens, veiled in the cool night, should have been swallowed by shadows, but instead, they shimmered like a childhood dream. Lightstones, carefully embedded among the pathways and flower beds, glowed with soft golden hues, outlining winding trails and casting halos around statues of powerful beasts and long-forgotten heroes. Water features caught the light and scattered it like crystals in a cavern, their surfaces rippling with silent enchantments.

It was a mirage of stone and foliage, light and shadow, artfully woven into something otherworldly. Nothing wild or overgrown—as if nature had been gently coaxed into perfection.

And the scent—gods, the scent. Roses in full bloom, lilacs drifting on the breeze, a whisper of cedar, and something sweet and impossible, like honeydew kissed by frost.

All in bloom in the dead of winter.

She'd heard the Kain Gardens were magical, but she hadn't thought they'd meant it *literally*.

"Beautiful," Leo murmured beside her.

"It is. I can't believe you get to see this everyday." She turned her head, only to find him already watching her. That same infuriating, heart-melting smile curved at his lips, like he knew something she didn't. "What?" she asked, a laugh caught in her throat.

The smile didn't falter. His eyes seemed to flicker like the lightstones, alive with warmth and mischief. "While it's true that I can visit the gardens whenever I want..." He leaned in just slightly, the space between them drawn shifting. "I don't get to see you—the real beauty out here—nearly as often as I want."

A gentle breeze brushed past them, rippling through her hair; a strand slipped loose and curled in front of her face. Before she could brush it aside, he caught it between two fingers, slow and deliberate, then tucked it neatly behind her ear, his knuckles grazing the length of her cheekbone as he did. Warmth bloomed where his touch lingered. "How do you do it at the base, I wonder?"

She narrowed her eyes, refraining from rolling them, though her lips twitched. It was clearly a setup for one of his insufferable lines. But she humored him anyway, "Do what?"

"Manage the droves of men that throw themselves at your feet."

Okay. *That*, she was not expecting. Her laughter bounced off the walls of the castle and around the balcony. It was as light and bubbly as her new favourite drink. How much champagne did *he* have? "You'd be surprised how few have thrown themselves at me."

He turned toward her fully then, one elbow resting casually on the stone railing. His eyes narrowed, but not in suspicion—more like he was trying to solve a riddle that didn't add up. "I don't believe it. Not for a second. You're only saying that to assuage my fragile heart." He pressed a hand dramatically over his chest.

As much as she enjoyed the fantastical picture he was painting, she should probably set him straight before he thought Dragon Knights had nothing better to do. "I'm not. Up until a few weeks ago, when we brought Jacob home, many of the Knights hated my guts."

His posture shifted just slightly, the teasing ease giving way to something more attentive. "That's *definitely* not true."

"It is. Comradery is important on the base. Knights usually build that bond during the Trials, but I didn't participate in the Trials."

"That's because you're better than them." He said it without hesitation, like a truth etched into the foundation of who he believed her to be. He looked at her like she was the hero of every story he'd ever admired.

She tossed him a dry look. "I'm no better than any of them. They have a motto, you know: 'We fight together. We bleed together. We die together.' It's more than just words. It's what got them through the Trials. It reminded them who would have their back when everything else fell apart. Who'd still be standing with them when the world turned to ash." She exhaled sharply. "But I skipped all of it. Because Arkon chose me."

"But then you brought Jacob home," he said thoughtfully. "You fought for one of your own. Bled for him."

"Yes." She turned, leaning her elbows back on the railing. Despite the distant hum of chatter and laughter inside, it was quiet out here, save for the soft rustle of leaves in the breeze. She beheld the prince beside her and released the breath she hadn't realised she was holding.

Gods, he was handsome. Everything a prince should be: tall, regal, with just enough playfulness to make her feel at ease, and the right amount of charm to lure her in. He was dangerous—and he knew it. Loved it, even.

She shook her head clear of these wandering thoughts. They led to murky waters, and she already had enough going on without Leo complicating things further.

"So," she said, her tone lighter, "no droves of men throwing themselves at me."

He straightened, puffing out his chest with mock bravado. "Good. I can handle one or two competitors, but droves? That's a bit much. I've already made my father livid with how much I spent on this party."

Her brow lifted. "You didn't..."

"Only the best for you, love." He grinned, eyes dazzling proudly. "We ll... maybe not the guest list. I had little choice in the matter. Next time, the party will be smaller and more exclusive."

A flicker of guilt twisted in her gut. "Thank you, Leo. For tonight. I know I've been prickly. I don't mean to sound ungrateful. I am having fun... with you. You make the insufferable people bearable."

He bowed his head slightly, the grin softening into something more sincere. "I'm honored to serve, my lady."

Ignoring his quip, she gestured toward the food table inside. "I can't believe you picked all of my favorite dishes and desserts. I can't believe you *remembered* them."

He snorted, tapping a finger to his temple. "It's not all air up here, you know." She giggled, and he smiled. "I pay attention to the things that matter."

Suddenly shy beneath the warmth in his voice, she glanced away from those piercing lapis eyes. "That's really sweet of you. Jacob complains about you, but... you're a good man."

He stepped closer, gently laying a hand over hers. His touch was warm, careful. “Of course he complains about me. He doesn’t think I’m good enough for you.”

Her gaze flicked from his hand to his face. He wasn’t joking now—there was real hurt there, quiet and raw, written across the lines of his brow, set deep in his eyes. “He doesn’t believe that,” she said softly. “Jacob is just... Jacob. He’s always been an overbearing, overprotective big brother. After losing our family...” She trailed off. There was no neat way to wrap their grief into a sentence. No ribbon to tie around a past scorched by fire and loss. “I don’t blame him for it,” she continued. “Even when it drives me up the wall some days.”

“I don’t blame him, either,” Leo said, gentle and sure. “He’ll come around. I’m determined to prove him wrong.”

And just like that, the murky waters turned stormy. Especially when he started leaning in, his eyes flicking to her mouth.

She pressed a hand to his chest, stopping him. “Leo, you should know—”

“I know,” he groaned, stepping back with obvious reluctance. “Your affection lies with *Dex*.”

“Grayson,” she corrected, tone sharper now. “If you knew about him, then why did you—”

“Because he doesn’t deserve you,” he cut in, voice low, almost bitter. “And I was hoping I could change your mind.”

She arched an eyebrow. “Oh, and you think *you’re* better?”

His mouth opened like he wanted to answer—but whatever argument he had wilted under the weight of her stare. For a second, the air between them held steady. Taut. Loaded.

She drew in a breath, ready to say more—but Arkon’s voice cracked like thunder through her thoughts.

“*Eva. Stairs. Now!*”

CHAPTER 19
PARTY CRASHERS

Eva had a second to dodge the dagger flying her way.

A second to yank Leo behind her.

The dagger grazed her arm, leaving a burning trail of blood down her bicep—but she was already moving to face the attacker. Heart soaring, she freed the needle-like knife from her hair—

Darkness descended upon them.

All the lightstones inside and out went out.

Screams came from the ballroom. Leo swore under his breath, drawing a ceremonial sword. Eva's dragon vision illuminated a lithe-framed assailant dashing up the stairs to them.

"Don't move, Leo. No matter what you hear—don't fucking move." She didn't know if the assailant was for her or the prince, but she'd make damned sure he didn't get what he wanted.

As fast as a lightning strike, the assailant swiped his short sword free and slashed forward for her throat. Eva ducked underneath, darting behind him, and rammed her knife into his exposed side. Crying out, he thrust his elbow back, catching her sternum. When normally such a hit would be dulled by her armour, she choked on the air exploding out of her lungs in her dress.

"*Behind you, Eva!*" Arkon's cry reverberated in the sky, just before a flash of lightning streak across the sky.

Heart in her throat, Eva whirled out from between the two assailants and gave herself space to assess the new threat.

The newcomer was much bigger, giving an ogre a run for its coin. He didn't have a weapon. He didn't need one. Those mitts he called hands could crush her skull like a bug—

The more lithe one—Twiggy, she would call him—whipped another dagger at her. She sidestepped it but barely had the time to dodge his followup attack. Her body moved on its own to block him, familiar with the angle of attack Grayson had ingrained in her.

Sylus's assassins.

Panic skittered across her chest, claws raking across her ribs.

They'd come for her.

Up until now, there had been a part of her that doubted they were hunting her. A part that had hoped she was free of that bastard of a king.

In her moment of distraction, Ogre Man grabbed her from behind, trunks for arms wrapping around her and pinning her arms to her sides. He squeezed the air out of her lungs.

Twiggy dove, thrusting his sword for her stomach. Her heel swung up, kicking the blade out of his hand. But that didn't stop the dagger in his spare hand—

Grayson's red silhouette came charging out of the ballroom doorway. Without missing a beat, he slammed into Twiggy, tackling him off the balcony. They both toppled over in a heap of snapping twigs and scraping armour.

Knowing he could take care of himself, Eva focused on her own problems, and rammed her heel into the top of Ogre Man's foot, digging the tip into the bone.

A grunt was her only response.

Asshole.

Lungs screaming for air, she threw her head back, bone crunching into cartilage. With a roar fit for a dragon, he dropped her and stumbled back.

Her lungs burned at her first full intake of breath. Her skill throbbed with the vicious determination of a Sandhound on a bone. She ignored the pain and lunged forward, driving her knife into his throat. With a cry of her own, she yanked that fucker right across his trachea and watched him drop to the flagstone—

A red silhouette bounded over the railing, landing in front of her as smooth as a jungle cat. Eva's muscles tensed—until she recognised Grayson's features.

He stalked toward her, barely casting the assassin gurgling on the ground a glance. "Are you hurt?" he demanded, voice low and furious—not at her, but at the people who had attacked her.

"I'm fine." She glanced at the shallow cut on her arm, already crusting over. "It's nothing."

He didn't look convinced. His eyes swept over her like he was counting bruises, tallying breaths.

"Eva?" Leo's voice cut in from behind. To his credit, he hadn't moved from his place.

She turned. "It's all right, Leo."

He approached hesitantly, reaching for her in the darkness. She took his hand and drew him in to scan for injury.

Her fingers skimmed his arms, his shoulders. Dragon vision blurred blood and skin, but his stance, the way he stood—tense but upright—told her he was unharmed.

"What's going on?" Leo asked, a slight tremor in his voice.

The three of them turned toward the ballroom. Screams still echoed from within, guests scrambling in a panic as Dragon Knights and guards fought to contain the chaos. Handheld lightstones lit up the room in flashes—steel clashing, shadows writhing.

Eva's gaze locked onto the invaders. These ones moved differently from the men who had attacked her minutes ago. Less coordinated. Sloppier. But no less dangerous.

Her pulse quickened, not from fear, but adrenaline. It surged through her veins like an electric shock, flooding her with raw energy. Magic ignited her senses, sharpening everything, until her very skin buzzed and her bones thrummed with an intensity she hadn't felt since infiltrating Darius's fort weeks ago.

"It appears someone just crashed your party," Grayson said, his voice edged with steel. "And Sylus's assassins took advantage of the opening." His grip tightened around his sword, knuckles white.

"*Eva*," Arkon's voice was strong and clear in her mind. "*There's a group heading towards the dungeon.*"

Grayson went rigid, eyes narrowing on the dungeon beneath the castle. "They're going after Darius." Uninhibited rage simmered in his eyes when their gazes met. He didn't need to say anything. Neither of them did.

Darius Fortys wasn't leaving this castle alive.

She extended her hand wordlessly, and he slapped her static gloves into her palm.

"Let's move." Like a commanding general blessed by Val, he turned and marched for the ballroom.

"I have men down there," Leo reminded him, following after him regardless. "They won't let Darius escape."

A grunt was Grayson's only response.

Eva peered up at the sky just as another strike forked across the dark clouds looming above them. Arkon's silhouette cast a shadow over them; other dragons' shadows flickered in the distance.

"*Be careful of the others*," she warned him.

"*I will do what I need to do to protect my Soul Bound*," he growled back, still bristly from *her* fight.

"*Fine.*" It wasn't like she could stop him. "*Make sure no one leaves this castle.*"

"*Grayson has already issued the command. Eran is passing the order along to the others. No one will leave the grounds.*"

She blinked up at him, warmth blooming in her chest. *"You're obeying one of his commands?"*

"Stop—it is a reasonable order."

He might not want to talk about it, but she would never forget it. She knew how difficult it was for him to admit Grayson and Eran were right.

"Thank you."

"Focus on your surroundings." He twisted away and out of sight.

Eva drew her attention back to Grayson and Leo as they strode to the ballroom. She stepped after them—then was hit with a bout of dizziness. Shaking her head, she powered through it, breathing in through her nose then out through her mouth as she kept pace with them. Perhaps drinking five glasses of champagne was a bad idea.

"Stay close," Grayson warned her as he opened the door. The screams were even louder inside, true terror and agony ringing through the entire room. Flashes of light caught her attention as swords glinted in the Dragon Knight lightstones.

Knights and guards alike fought to protect the guests, but there were too many people to defend. Despite sticking to the perimeter of the chaos, she stumbled on bodies and slipped on fresh blood. There was no fire, but the scent of ash tickled her nose.

Too similar to the attack on Brar. Her heart thudded viciously, chest tightening—

An assailant spotted them on the edge and charged for them, sword raised—definitely not one of Sylus's assassins. Grayson intercepted him effortlessly, slicing his blade across his stomach, spinning, then thrusting the sword into his throat. Without a beat of remorse, he was leading them out of the ballroom again.

Leo's hand closed around hers. She squeezed him back, grateful for the contact. It kept her grounded and reminded her to focus on the mission: stop Darius from escaping.

As soon as they stepped into the hallway, the screams dulled behind the door, swallowed by the stone. Then—blinding white seared across her vision. It hit so suddenly she reeled, throwing up a hand to shield her face. Spots burned in her eyes, the afterimage of the darkness still clinging like a shadow. Blinking furiously, shapes swam back into focus. The lightstone sconces along the walls blazed with a steady brilliance. Whatever had strangled the light before was gone.

Grayson, seemingly unbothered by the sudden light, was now several paces ahead. Like a plough in a field, he was unstoppable, running over everything in his way.

Leo, still holding her hand, hissed at the abrupt light, but then relaxed as the hallway opened up to him. "Finally—"

The door in front of them burst open. Grayson whirled around just as three men clad in black stumbled out of the room. Laughing, they held up handfuls of jewellery in victory, gold and gems glinting in the light.

"Halt!" Leo barked, sword at the ready. "Those treasures belong to the Crown!"

Their laughter died immediately then their faces fell flat when they noticed Eva and Leo—they didn't see or hear Grayson coming up behind them.

Grayson cut one down before Eva could blink. In the same motion, his blade caught the second across the chest, then drove clean into his gut. The third barely had time to scream before steel kissed his throat.

Panting, Grayson whipped his blade to the side; the blood that had stained it flung off the steel and splattered against the wall. He straightened and faced Eva, darkness swirling in those storm-cloud eyes—for only a beat, then a flicker of hesitation crossed them, as if measuring her reaction to his lethal efficiency.

"You could have at least left one for me," Eva grumbled, stepping around the bodies for the direction they were heading in.

Grayson smirked, falling into step with her. "Next time."

Leo overtook them, turning down an unfamiliar hallway. "This way is faster."

Fire burned in those dark lapis eyes, jaw tight with fury she'd never seen in him before.

She couldn't blame him for it. These people were invading his home, attacking his guests. Knowing what it was like to have people come into her home and desecrate what used to be good and wholesome, she wanted to reach out to him and let him know that the people responsible for raiding his home wouldn't get away with this. She'd make every single one of them regret stepping foot in this castle.

They came across a wrought iron door that had been blasted open, barely hanging on by a hinge. Remnants of sulphur and saltpeter hung in the air, the wall marked with charcoal.

Grimacing at the damage, Leo passed through it and descended the staircase. Torches lit their path, flickering ominous shadows in the dead silence. Despite the flaming sconces, the air was colder, a musky dampness clinging to Eva's skin.

"You said there were guards?" Grayson remarked bitterly to Leo.

Leo slowed his descent near the bottom, eyes landing on the first body. He stared at the pool of blood beneath the guard, face skewed with pain. "There *were*. This is—"

"Keep moving." Grayson overtook him, lifting his lightstone to guide them.

Leo tossed a glare at the back of his head. Eva caught his attention and thrust her chin forward. She'd feel better if she covered the rear, in case anyone came up behind them.

Wordlessly, Leo obeyed and caught up with Grayson further down the corridor.

The stench of piss and sweat wafted through the tight corridor, the first sign of cells appearing within Grayson's cone of light. Most of the cells were empty, but the few that weren't held raggedy criminals. They remained silent, hands clasped on the bars as their beady gazes stared down the direction they headed.

Dread clamped Eva's heart, a vicious cold seeping into her limbs. A tremble took hold of her muscles, loosening the grip on her knife. Her vision doubled, and she stumbled on the stone floor.

Leo glanced over his shoulder at her, concern tugging on his brow. "You okay?"

"I'm fine. Just had too much to drink." She shook her head clear then continued onward.

Murmurs echoed faintly from the corridor ahead. Grayson lifted a hand, signaling for them to stop. He squinted into the shadows, his head tilting slightly as he focused. After a moment, he nodded to himself and turned to Eva. "There are four up ahead—standing guard—and more further in. They're nearly at Darius."

Through Arkon's superior vision, Eva saw what he meant: four figures posted near a heavy iron door further down the corridor. Beyond that door lay the lower levels of the dungeon, the high-security wing where the worst criminals were kept—and where Darius waited.

I won't let that fucker escape.

Grayson's eyes ran over her dress, of which the skirt had fallen victim to many attacks and unforgiving blades. The hem was a tattered mess, the beautiful blue stained crimson. He turned his lightstone off and pocketed it. "Ready?"

She unclasped her heels and placed them on the floor beside them. Forcing the tremble out of her muscles, she rose to her feet, clutching the needle-knife in her hand. "Ready."

Grayson's footfalls were soundless as he glided down the corridor, his sword already drawn, shoulders low and tense like a predator closing in on prey. Eva followed close behind, blade in hand, pulse thundering in her ears. Leo brought up the rear, his stance wary but determined.

They didn't make it halfway before the assailants noticed them.

Grayson was on them before they could blink. He cut the first down with lethal efficiency—efficiency that was *gifted*, not earned. One slipped past him, lunging for Eva, while the last sprinted straight for Leo.

Eva didn't hesitate. She ducked low beneath the first strike, drove her palm into the attacker's gut, and shoved her static glove hard against his chest. Electricity surged through him with a sharp jolt—his body locking up just long enough for her to open his throat with one clean sweep. Blood sprayed the stone as he collapsed.

She spun toward Leo. With surprising grace, he parried his attacker's blow and swiped downward. Eva came up behind him and thrust her dagger between his ribs. The assailant gurgled and dropped without another sound.

Leo offered her a quick nod in thanks. She answered with a faint smile.

Eva turned toward Grayson, prepared to jump in—

But movement in the corner of her eye snagged her attention.

Down the corridor, behind the iron door she'd glimpsed earlier through Arkon's vision, shadows shifted. The door was wide open now. Figures moved inside.

Her breath caught.

The last of the assailants were slipping into Darius's cell.

Oh, no you don't.

Without thinking, she bolted.

"Eva!" Grayson's voice barked after her, sharp and full of alarm.

But she didn't stop.

Bare feet slapping against blood-slick stone, Eva surged forward, adrenaline driving her faster. She wouldn't let them take him—not Darius. That bastard wasn't allowed to get away.

She skidded to a halt at the corridor's end, stomach plummeting as Darius stepped out of his cell.

He was free.

He rubbed his wrists, the shackles gone. Abyssal eyes found her, and a devious smile curled across his scabbed face, half of it raw and mangled, as if dragged across gravel.

Serves the monster right.

"Glad you could finally join us, storm girl."

Terror gripped her heart like a vice. The sight of him—the man who had murdered her family, hunted her, *haunted* her—sent tremors rippling down her arms. Her vision blurred.

No. Not this time.

She clenched her fists, grounding herself in the sting of her own nails. "Get back in your cell," she growled, voice low and trembling with fury. "Or I'll make you."

Darius chuckled. His companion, who she could only assume was Keyon, joined him.

"You caught me off guard last time, girl," Darius said, his tone a razor across skin. "Not tonight. I'm gonna drag you back to Estrus by that pretty hair of yours and make you *mine*."

His words sent a chill down her spine. Fear clawed at the edges of her mind, threatening to root her in place—but she couldn't freeze. Not now. She was alone, the only one standing between Darius and freedom. Until Grayson caught up, she was the last line of defense.

"You have to beat me first," she spat.

He lunged.

She dodged—but he moved with her, faster than she could track. A hand slammed into her sternum and hurled her into the wall. Her head cracked against stone. Hard. White-hot pain exploded behind her eyes. Before she could cry out, he seized the back of her skull and slammed it into the wall again.

Stars burst behind her lids. The world tilted.

Her body slid down the cold, rough surface like water poured over rock. She tried to stand, but her legs buckled beneath her. Balance abandoned her. Three Dariuses spun like phantoms across her blurring vision.

He didn't wait. While she struggled to rise, he grabbed her again and flung her across the floor. Stone tore at her flesh. Her breath left her in a ragged wheeze.

He reared his foot back, aiming for her ribs.

Instinct took over. Eva lashed out, grabbed his ankle, and yanked.

Darius toppled backward with a grunt, landing hard on his ass. But before she could take advantage of it, he snarled and snatched a fistful of her hair, dragging her upright. She screamed, twisting in his grip, then clutched his wrist with her static gloves and unleashed her magic.

A spark zapped beneath his flesh. He convulsed, groaning, but didn't drop as fast as the others had. His resistance was stronger—or maybe she was weaker.

Her stomach churned violently. A wave of dizziness nearly dropped her again.

What's wrong with me? This wasn't from the drinks. She'd felt off earlier, but not like this.

Before she could steady herself, arms clamped around her from behind. Darius pinned her wrists, careful to keep her hands away from skin.

Then Keyon stepped in—and rammed his fist into her gut.

The air rushed out of her lungs. But worse was the way her body curled inward, stomach clenching. The world spun sideways as bile surged up her throat—then she vomited at their feet.

Keyon grimaced at the black ichor mixing with the other contents, taking a step back. "Tck. Looks like she's been poisoned, Boss."

Poisoned? Her hazy thoughts struggled to catch up. *When—*?

The throwing dagger. The shallow cut on her arm.

Desperate to take control of the fight—before the poison dragged her under—she slammed her head back into Darius's face. His nose crunched with a sickening crack, and his grip slackened just enough. She kicked up, knocking the sword from Keyon's hand, then wrenched herself free of Darius's hold.

With a snarl, he charged for her, hands closing around her throat. He slammed her against the cell bars, metal biting into her spine. His eyes blazed—not just with manic hatred, but something far more grotesque. Something that made her stomach turn.

He was getting off on this.

That sick, satisfied glint in his eye—feral and consuming—wasn't just about winning. It was about watching her break. About reminding her that no matter how strong she'd become, she was still his prey. There was a warped reverence there, like he was savoring every twitch of her body beneath his grip, memorizing the way her lips parted in a strangled gasp, how her nails scraped uselessly at his skin.

Revulsion curdled in her stomach, cutting through the haze like a blade.

He wanted to break her. Claim her. Mind. Body. Soul.

Never.

The word pulsed like thunder in her mind, even as her limbs went slack and her vision darkened. She refused to be a trophy. Refused to be a puppet. A plaything.

Fueled by spite and fury, she pressed her palms flat against his forearm. A jolt of static surged through him. Just enough.

He released her.

Eva collapsed against the bars, gasping. Nails dug into rusted iron as she dragged air into her lungs, each breath sharp and burning.

Faster. You need to recover faster. Come on, Eva!

She shook her head, trying to clear the haze. Her fingers fumbled for the knife—never mind the tremor in her grip—and she braced herself for another attack.

But it didn't come.

Darius and Keyon stood side by side, arms crossed like mirrored statues, just watching.

No... not watching.

Waiting.

A dark smile slid across Darius's face.

The world tilted as if the floor had been yanked out from under her. Her stomach lurched. Her limbs gave out.

The knife clattered to the floor as her knees buckled. Pain flared through her legs and spine, but she couldn't stop the fall. She hit the ground hard, eyes unfocused on the ceiling as shadows swirled above.

Fuck. The poison had her now.

"*Eva!*" Arkon's voice was a distant echo in her mind. Desperate. Furious. "*Get up! Fight!*"

I... I can't. Not even her thoughts could reach him now. How was she supposed to fight when her own body was betraying her?

Darius knelt in front of her, filling her vision with his smug satisfaction. She flinched as he grabbed her arm. Tried to pull away—but her limbs barely responded. He lifted her bicep, studying the black, oozing wound that made her skin slick and cold.

"Shit," he muttered. "My father's assassins got to her first."

No. She turned away, a feeble attempt to reclaim something—dignity, strength, *her will.*

She had to move. Had to get up. She pushed against the stone floor, arms trembling like leaves in the wind.

His fingers tangled in her hair, nails scraping against her scalp, and yanked her back. Hard.

Pain burst behind her eyes, and her scream caught in her throat like shattered glass.

"If we can get her to Syd, he'll have an antidote," Keyon said, watching the pathetic spectacle from the doorway. "He's in the city with the others."

"Then what are we waiting for?" Darius hoisted her upright then slung her over his shoulder like she weighed nothing.

She gritted her teeth.

No!

Her arm twitched—then another—and she thrashed, her body a sluggish mess of limbs and instinct. She wasn't going anywhere with him.

They crashed into the doorframe. His shoulder clipped stone, and he cursed.

Then she was falling.

The floor slammed into her ribs, jarring something loose. She barely registered the pain over the ringing in her ears. But she was down. Free.

Move. Crawl. Don't stop.

Her fingers scrambled against stone, dragging her forward an inch at a time. Her legs refused to follow. Her vision swam. The poison was winning.

Behind her—footsteps. Unhurried. Deliberate. Like a predator savoring the final act.

"Oh, how long I've waited for this," Darius purred, his voice low and laced with venomous glee.

He seized her ankle and yanked her back with a brutal tug. Her nails split against stone as she tried to resist, but her strength was failing fast.

He knelt, pressing his knee into her lower back. She clenched her teeth—all she could do to bite back the scream burning in her throat. His mouth dropped to her ear. "You don't get to crawl away. Not from me."

He flipped her onto her back and straddled her, pinning her down with practiced ease. His desire pressed into her stomach, his shadow swallowing the last of the flickering torchlight above.

True terror crawling through her bones, she struck out and caught his eye. Blood welled at the corner of his lid.

He stilled, then smiled. A slow, unhinged smile that didn't reach his eyes.

"There it is," he whispered. "That fire. That defiance. I'm going to enjoy carving it out of you."

He lifted her knife, tilting it to admire the fine blade in the torchlight. "Such a *pretty* dagger." His voice remained low, taunting. "A gift, I wonder?"

He glided the tip along her cheek, leaving a sharp sting burning in its wake. Then slowly, deliberately, he dragged it down to her collarbone. Goosebumps rose on her flesh, sending a tremor through her body.

The blade traced a cruel line across her shoulder, just deep enough to sting. Her body jerked.

His eyes gleamed in delight as blood welled in a thin line where the blade had been. "I'll teach you to obey your master, girl."

Her breath caught in her throat when he paused at the hollow of her shoulder, a wicked sheen in his dark eyes. Ever so slowly, he added pressure to her shoulder, piercing her flesh a little at a time.

A scream tore out of her throat. She thrashed under this weight, kicking out in a futile attempt to throw him off. When the blade touched bone, white-hot agony ripped out of her lungs. Tears sprang in her eyes and she arched against the cold stone floor—

"DARIUS!"

Grayson whipped around the corner, eyes ablaze with something dark and feral. Blood covered every inch of him—his hands, his arms, his jaw—but none of it seemed to slow him. If anything, he was vibrating with unspent rage.

Darius froze mid-motion. His hand still gripped the knife embedded in her shoulder. Slowly, he turned, an unsettling calm overtaking his face.

"Ah, brother," he drawled. "You came. Come to see us off?"

He yanked the knife free with a sickening sound and grabbed a fistful of Eva's hair, forcing her upright. Her knees buckled, the world teetering at the edge of collapse. She couldn't hold herself up, not with the poison and pain ripping through her body.

Grayson took a step forward. Darkness encroached around him, as if the shadows lived and breathed for him. "Let. Her. Go."

Darius tilted his head, mock-considerate. "Hmm. No." He pressed the blade to the open wound on her shoulder, grinning when she choked on a cry. "But you *will* get out of my way."

"Do—don't," she begged of him, hanging on by a thread. "Don't let him leave this dungeon alive."

"Tch. That's right, little rider," Darius murmured, dragging the knife along the curve of her throat, not cutting, just a tease. "Tell him to kill me. Beg for my brother to come back."

Her eyes widened. Much like Grayson, Darius saw him as somebody else, a man anew, not the man he's always been—with different morals. But regardless of what name he bore, he was still the same man she fell in love with.

Grayson didn't move. His breathing had slowed, but his fists clenched with barely restrained violence.

Darius leaned in closer, his voice dropping to something cold and intimate. "I love it when she screams." His teeth nipped at her earlobe. Gagging, Eva jerked her head away, but he yanked her back, holding her still. "Do you scream for my brother, little rider, or only for me?"

Her stomach roiled with nausea. She wanted to toss him over her shoulder and slit his throat open for touching her, for getting the upper hand on her—to avenge her family—but she barely had the strength to hold herself up, let alone speak. "You're a sick bastard."

Grayson's fingers flexed around the hilt of his sword, knuckles ghost-white. "Touch her again," he said, voice low and lethal, "and I will peel the skin from your flesh."

Darius grinned, eyes gleaming. "Don't threaten me with a good time, little brother."

Then he shoved the knife back into her shoulder.

Eva's scream died in her throat, escaping as a cracked whisper. Her vision swam. Pain engulfed her. Tears streamed down her cheeks, each one burning hotter than the last.

"Step aside, Dex," Darius hissed. "Let us pass. Or watch me carve another masterpiece."

"Eva!" Leo's cry came through the haze of her mind. His horror-stricken face paled. "Release her at once!"

Darius laughed in her ear and licked the shell of it with deliberate cruelty. She recoiled in disgust, bile rising in her throat, but his grip only tightened. "Oh, brother dearest, I warned you what I'd do when I saw her again. You didn't listen."

Grayson quaked with fury, blood dripping from his palms; his nails bit into his skin, he was squeezing his fists so tight. The darkness around him thickened, drawn to his rage. "Put her down and fight me, you coward. If it's Dex you want—I'll give you Dex. Just put. Her. Down."

"Not yet, Dex," he said, with a wicked smile. "Your time will come." He heaved her onto his shoulder with a grunt. Good. She hoped the bastard hurt. "Come on, Eva. Our welcome has worn out. These fools won't stop us—not if they value your life."

"N—no..." The words slipped on her tongue. She could barely see the panic in Leo's eyes as Darius started for them. She wanted to scream at them to fight. To tear him apart. To make him regret ever crossing the ocean.

But they didn't. They just stood there. Locked in rage and helplessness.

I am the storm dragon rider, Arkon's Soul Bound. You can do better than this.

With the last scrap of strength she had, she slid a trembling hand beneath his tunic and pressed her palm flat to his skin.

Then she unleashed the power he coveted oh so much.

A violent shock surged from her fingertips, strong enough to make his body seize. Darius let out a strangled sound—a mix of rage and surprise—before his legs gave out and he crumpled to one knee. Eva tumbled from his shoulder, hitting the ground *hard.* The air was punched from her lungs, pain seizing her body.

It was the distraction Grayson needed to charge him, roaring like a dragon when he tackled his brother to the ground. She could only keep her eyes open long enough to see the massive gash in Darius's forehead.

Leo was left to face Keyon, who appeared to be as skilled as Darius. She reached her hand out to him, wishing to help the struggling prince, but she had no strength left in her body. She was fading. Fast.

Movement flickered in the corner of her eye. She turned her head just enough to glimpse someone prowling in the shadows behind Grayson. He was too intent on killing Darius to see him.

The assassin leapt out of the shadows.

"Grayson!" she cried. It was all she had left. Then—darkness.

CHAPTER 20

NEVER UNDERESTIMATE A WOMAN IN A DRESS

Anna leaned her head against Jacob's chest, breathing in that familiar scent of cedar and leather. He rested his chin on the top of her head, his big muscular arms encircling her lean frame. She shut her eyes and let herself melt into the music—and the quick, steady rhythm of his heart.

He'd surprised her tonight with his dance lessons. A far better improvement than the last time they had danced. He'd stepped on her toes so many times last time, she'd ended up *hobbling* to the infirmary. But right now, she just wanted to hold him, be close to him.

"This is nice," he murmured in her hair. "You did a fantastic job, Anna."

She shrugged into him. "It was mostly Leo."

He chuckled, the deep baritone bouncing in his chest and filling her ears. "We both know that's not true. I can see little pieces of you in everything."

She pulled away just enough to peer into those russet brown eyes of his, the affection they held so dearly for her. Flecks of gold stared back at her, catching the lightstones lighting just right.

No one had ever been able to see *her* quite like he did. He saw the soft silks and velvet and found a glimmer of her in them. He knew her love for texture. He knew her eye for colour. Knew just how she liked to highlight the subtle features.

"I suppose I did more than a *little*," she admitted softly. "It's not every day a girl is given an unlimited budget."

Jacob grimaced, scanning the crowd until he spotted Leo with Eva and a group of nobles. His poor sister looked like she was one fake smile away from stabbing herself with a fork. Yet she endured it. For him. "He really did all of this for her, didn't he?"

"You know how Leo gets. When he wants something, he won't stop until he has it."

He ground his teeth. "But Eva's not a *thing*. She's a person—with the potential to make good decisions... or really bad ones."

Anna rolled her eyes at him. She loved him dearly, but the lengths he went to protect his sister was ridiculous. Here they were, at an extravagant gala, surrounded by the wealthiest people in Aboria, served the finest food the renowned chefs had to offer, given a moment to *breathe* away from the stuffy canyon—and he's worried about his little sister.

"I think she and Leo look good together." She said it to prickle him a little, but it wasn't a lie either.

They did look good together

Really good. His auburn hair against her ash blonde. He stood just a few inches taller than her, tall enough to rest his chin on top of her head. He was all refinement and charm, while she was a huntress, reformed by grace.

Anna peered over at Grayson, who was watching them from the sidelines in his black on black armour. Even from the middle of the dance floor, she could see him grinding his molars.

In the three years she'd known him, he cared little for anything or anyone. He had a job to do and he did it well. She'd certainly never seen him get worked up like this before. She was positive that if Leo wasn't Crown Prince, he'd tie him to a post and let the vultures feast—just for touching Eva.

Jacob followed his gaze and frowned at his friend. "I feel bad partying when he has to work."

"It was his choice."

"I'm going to talk to him."

She loved Jacob's empathy.

Squeezing his shoulder, she smiled. "I think he would like that."

His cheeks went pink. "I'll find you later."

"You better."

As he stepped away, the quartet finished their set and lowered their instruments for a short intermission. Conversations rose to fill the lull. Laughter rang from every corner. The scent of honeyed wine and smoked meats lingered in the air, mingling with perfume and the faint metallic scent of the soldiers' armour. Lightstones hovered overhead, casting the ballroom in a brilliant, almost divine, white hue.

Anna threaded through the crowd, finding her friends near the stage. Ostarian, the talented composer, greeted her first, kissing both of her cheeks. "My darling, Annaliese! It's been too long."

"Indeed Ostarian." Her voice naturally lifted and softened, as if she'd never left to become a cold ruthless warrior Dragon Knight. A side of her these dear people would never see.

"Out of the way, Os!" Angela playfully shoved the older man aside and flung her arms around Anna. "Girl, I've missed you! Do you have any idea what it's like being the only woman in the group?" She cast Petro a dirty look, their guitarist and also the closest in age to Angela.

Petro winked at her. "Admit it, Angel, you love the attention."

The young violinist stuck her tongue out at him, and Anna's heart squeezed. Gods, she missed this. Missed *them*. They had everything to smile about and nothing to vex over. They had it all, fame, wealth—a life worth living.

"Your *life is worth living*," Aster growled into her mind. "*You are a fiery warrior, a protector, and a beloved friend. Never forget that.*"

Aster would never understand just how *different* her life was before. She was respected and admired in Dragon Canyon—but she was *loved* and *adored* in Lexxis. Wherever she went.

Mikael touched her arm lightly, drawing her attention back to the group. "Everything all right, Annaliese?"

She painted a sweet smile for them, noticing they were all watching her closely. "Of course. It's been a while since I've been to a gala this big."

Os nodded in thought. "How have you been, dear?"

"*Where* have you been?" Angela pressed. "You disappeared on us."

Anna gripped her skirt, thankful for the volume so they wouldn't notice.

"*My Soul Bound does not cower*," Aster growled. Anna felt her scales ripple through their link, and shuddered in response.

"*I am not cowering*," she snapped back. "*Stop interrupting.*"

"*I don't like how you are with them. You do not need to change who you are for their sake. If they don't like the real you, then they are not true friends.*"

Ignoring the buzzing in her head, Anna waved a casual hand around the room. "Oh, you know, I've been around. My mother has me doing all sorts."

Angela's eyes widened. "Oh! That's right! You left to become a Dragon Knight. You still look..." Her brown eyes quickly scanned the skin Anna blatantly wore on display, "intact."

Anna knew she'd spotted a few scars. They were thin cuts from a blade, nothing horrific like Grayson's scars—but little passed by Angela's attention. Especially one's appearance.

Os waved her off. "Come now, Annaliese looks far better than *intact*." He grinned at Anna, eyes lighting up. He was the closest thing Anna ever had to a father. "You look fabulous, my dear. We'd all love to hear how your training is coming along."

They didn't know she was Soul Bound to a fire dragon. Didn't know that she was no longer a cadet, but a well-respected and feared Sergeant. Didn't know that it was because of *her* that the Slayer of Souls was in this very room with them.

And they would never know.

"I'd hate to bore you on your break," Anna said. "Please, tell me what you've been up to."

For a moment, she wanted to be just Annaliese again—no titles, no armour. Just the girl who used to dream of velvet gowns and standing ovations.

They told her stories of their travels, of vast cities and the thunderous applause of sold-out halls. She laughed with them, rejoiced in the old days.

A sharp pang twisted in her stomach as Mikael leaned in to describe a venue near the southern coast, where walls of glass displayed glowing aquariums filled with creatures from the reefs of the Desert Lands. Magic-infused coral, shimmering eel-fish, sea dragons no bigger than a teacup.

She wanted to be happy for them—truly, she did. And she was. But when they fretted over ruined outfits and bumpy caravan rides, she couldn't empathise. When they griped over long strenuous journeys and poor weather, she could only think about her flights with Aster. The weather had become more predictable with Eran in the skies with them; he, at least, kept the rain off their backs.

But, oddly, despite how hard on the body it was to be a Knight, she couldn't help feeling a warmth blooming in her chest.

If she hadn't become a Knight, she wouldn't have met Grayson or Jacob—

Darkness filled the ballroom.

All of the lightstones went out.

A collective gasp swept through the ballroom, followed by a beat of stunned silence.

Then the screaming began.

Magic shifted to Anna's eyes, filling the ballroom with reds and yellows with her dragon vision. Panic bloomed around her in flashes of heat. Bodies pressed together, stumbling blindly. And among them—figures moving with swift, deliberate strides. Blades glinting.

They weren't Renkon's guards.

"Protect the king!" someone shouted.

"Where's Prince Leonidas?"

Dragon Knights lit up their stones, providing pockets of light, but not enough to illuminate the entire room.

"Anna? What's going on?" Angela reached out for her blindly. Anna took her hand then the others.

"Hold on to each other and follow me. I'll get you out of here safely."

After one final scan of the room in search of Jacob—who she quickly realised would be fine with Grayson watching over him—she led the band to a back door. Even if she didn't have her magic to guide her, she knew the castle so well from her many childhood visits, she could have navigated them through the darkness regardless.

Amongst the commotion in the ballroom, glass shattered around them and two bandits came in from the window. Angela shrieked, clutching

Anna's arm. Anna freed herself from her friend and stood between them and two bandits. Never had she regretted not bringing a weapon to a party in her life.

One of the bandits held a torch in his hand, casting an amber glow over Anna and her friends. They saw her, the beautiful red dress, and the musicians, then laughed. Easy prey.

They were about to learn the hard way to never underestimate a woman in a dress.

Before the bandits could move, Anna surged forward.

Her fist slammed into the bandit's jaw, sending his head snapping back with a sickening crack. As he staggered, she wrenched his sword free with a twist of her wrist and buried it in his chest. He choked on blood, eyes wide, before collapsing to the floor.

Another attacker lunged. His blade tore through the front of her bodice, snagging on the boning of her corset. If the dress hadn't been structured, it would have been her ribs.

A beautiful piece of art—ruined.

Snarling, Anna slashed him across the chest. Blood bloomed against his leathers. He hissed and stumbled back, clutching the wound. "You'll pay for that, bitch."

"Not as much as you'll pay for ruining my dress," she spat.

She reached for the fire in his torch-hand.

And took it.

The flame snaked up his arm, searing through cloth and skin. He shrieked, dropping his weapon to claw at the blaze, but it was too late. She fed it, driving it higher—over his shoulder, across his chest. His armor bubbled, fused to his flesh. He screamed for mercy.

Something twisted in her heart. Then suddenly, it wasn't his screams she heard, but Niall's.

Before she could let the guilt consume her, she stepped forward and drew her blade across his throat, silencing him.

It was too easy to draw on her magic.

Yes, he would've killed them. Yes, he had to be stopped. But the fire—it had obeyed her too well. Answered too quickly. It hadn't felt like defense. It had felt like fury.

Like power.

And that terrified her.

"*You are embracing your magic.*" Aster's approval buzzed through her mind. "*Do not flinch from who you are.*"

Anna exhaled, trembling. The blade in her hand steamed with blood and fire. Her dress, her hands, her soul—scorched.

She turned—and found her friends staring.

Angela had dropped to her knees, hands clamped over her mouth, eyes brimming with tears. Petro's usually warm gaze was blank with disbelief. Even Os, who had known her longest, who had written songs with her and seen her cry over burnt toast, had taken an unconscious step back.

Anna's throat tightened.

They'd only ever seen the singer. The sunshine. The girl in the velvet dress.

Not this.

Not the weapon her mother had forged.

Shame lashed at her heart—sharp, swift, vicious. But she buried it deep. There wasn't time. Screams still echoed down the hall, steel still clashed with steel, and lives were still being taken.

She turned from their horror, hands trembling as she clenched the tatters of her skirt. "We have to keep moving."

Petro dropped beside Angela, rubbing her back gently. "Come on, Angel. Breathe through it. We're still alive."

With Os's help, they got her on her feet. Anna led them quickly, heels slipping on the marble as they passed bloodstains and crumpled bodies.

She opened a broom closet down a quiet corridor, a place tucked away from the screams. It would have to do.

It was a tight fit for four people—cramped, dark, air thick with lavender dust and old linens—but it was safe.

"Don't open the door until the fighting stops," Anna said, locking eyes with Os.

He nodded grimly. Of them all, only he had seen the horrors of the Goblin Wars. He knew what might be waiting on the other side if they weren't careful.

"But… what about the others?" Angela whispered. Her voice cracked, cheeks pale again. "We can't just leave people out there to die."

Petro gently patted her hand, then gave Anna another nod. "Let the Dragon Knights do their job. That's why they're here."

Anna didn't argue. She didn't try to comfort her friend. She just shut the door—firm, final—and turned back toward the chaos.

But then she paused.

A prickling sensation crept along her skin, like icy fingers brushing the back of her neck.

"*I'm detecting something strange in the adjacent corridor*," Aster warned her, confirming her senses. "*It might be the source for the lightstones outage. I've never sensed anything like it.*"

That was a cause for concern on its own, never mind there being something out there that *could* nullify the magic in a lightstone.

Anna looked down at her beautiful, flowing skirt and sighed. If she was to investigate this mysterious source, she should rid herself of any obstacles that would get in her way.

Muttering a curse to Asturias for ruining her lovely night, Anna cut away the skirt at her knees then discarded the fine fabric aside.

With no visual senses to guide her, only this sense of something cold and foreboding, Anna strode through the darkness towards the feeling.

The hallway was completely empty, sounds of battle far away. Her mind wandered to the others and where they had landed themselves amongst the chaos.

Last she saw Jacob, he was with Grayson on the other side of the room, away from the windows the bandits had come in from. She'd lost sight of Eva and Leo, but hoped the guards had found them and were keeping them safe. Until they knew why the bandits had raided the castle, their safety was top priority—

"*Aster, do you see any movement in the dungeon?*" If the bandits weren't after Eva or the royal family, she could only think of one other reason why someone would plan an attack of this scale.

Alarm rang through their Bond. "*There are several bandits heading for the dungeon. The guards are slowing them down, but it's only a matter of time before they reach Darius.*"

Shit.

A beat, then, "*Grayson is going after him.*"

"*Good. He won't let him escape.*" She sensed a prickle of hesitation from her dragon. "*What aren't you telling me?*"

"*Eva and Leo are with him.*"

Fuck. She wasn't going to bother questioning why any of them thought it would be a good idea to let the storm dragon rider and the Crown Prince go after that raving psychopath. They all had their reasons and they were too stubborn to let anyone talk them out of it.

Later, though, she'd remind them how foolish and reckless they were.

"*You're close, Anna,*" Aster warned, confirming what the Knight's senses told her. That cold, hollow feeling was getting stronger, sinking deep into her marrow.

Up ahead, the familiar amber glow of flames flickered against the walls. The fire called to her, three torches around the corner. Her dragon vision showed her five individuals through the wall, standing within the cone of light. Two watching one end of the hallway, the other two watching the opposite end. One stood before a lightstone sconce, offering it an object Anna couldn't discern.

She crouched by the wall, breathing in and out to steady her heart. Five to one weren't ideal odds—but she'd faced worse. After the last two she fought, she knew they were skilled in combat, but not professionally trained. Their moves were sloppy despite their quick reflexes. Something she planned to use to her advantage.

"Use your magic," Aster insisted.

"No. I don't need it."

Shutting out her dragon, Anna stepped away from the wall and strode down the hallway and rounded the corner. The two guards at the end blinked at her sudden appearance, having not heard her approach.

Even in heels, she was as silent as a grave at midnight.

One of them wore a mask, hiding any discernible features on his face, except for the jagged scar bisecting his right eye. The other wore a crude sneer, revealing a gap where teeth should be. His dark eyes ran over her torn up dress, ignoring the sword in her hand entirely.

"You're a little far from the party, princess."

"You're a little cocky for crashing a party full of Dragon Knights."

The other bandits further down the hallway turned her way. They shared a glance with each other then passed their fifth member, who was concentrating on the white stone in his hands giving off a strange glow that made Anna feel uneasy. Four of them stood in front of her, blocking her path.

They stared at each other for what felt like hours, studying, assessing. They knew she wasn't a typical guest of the Kain family. Anyone else would have run away from these odds.

At least they have some sense. Too bad it wouldn't save them.

The masked bandit lunged, dagger flashing. Anna parried, twisting her blade to knock his weapon wide. Before he could recover, she drove her elbow into his jaw. Bone crunched. He staggered back, dazed, and she finished him with a clean slash across his chest.

One down, four to go.

The others hesitated. Not so cocky now.

A second one rushed her, swinging wildly. Anna sidestepped, blade low as she swiped the back of his legs. He collapsed with a strangled cry, his sword clattering to the floor. She drove her sword into back and didn't look back.

Three left.

The last two attacked simultaneously, their blades glinting as they flanked her. Anna didn't retreat. Instead, she stepped forward, forcing them off balance. She swiped at one, pushing him back enough to duck beneath a swing from Toothless. Using the momentum, she brought her sword up in a brutal arc. Steel met flesh.

Two.

The bandit she'd swiped at was determined to join his friends. He lunged, desperation eclipsing pain. His blade came down in a wild arc. Anna blocked it with a grunt, the impact jolting through her arm. He was strong, even wounded. She ducked his next strike and slammed her knee into his injured side.

He screamed—but kept fighting.

She twisted, cut across his thigh, then his chest. He faltered, breath hitching. Still, he swung again.

She plunged her blade into his chest.

He froze, eyes wide, lips parting in shock. No words came—just a soft, rattling breath as he sagged to the floor.

One.

Panting, she scanned the hallway for the last bandit. He stared at her, mouth agape. Anna glared back at the familiar face. She didn't know him by name, but she'd seen him patrol the castle grounds, escorting Leo into the city, and many times in the hallways. Even now, as he held a suspicious stone in his hand, he bore the silver armour the castle guards wore, the Kain crest stamped on his chest like a slap in the face.

"What the fuck do you think you're doing?" she snarled. It was one thing for these men to crash the party—it was another thing entirely to be *betrayed*. An unforgivable crime.

His dagger clattered to the floor. "Th—they threatened my family. They said if I didn't help them free Prince Darius they would kill them. Pl—please!"

He was looking for pity in the wrong person. The moment they had approached him, he should have reported it. They would have protected his family. Instead, he brought them into the royal family's home, allowed them to kill innocent people, and plotted to have the world's most dangerous criminal freed.

Before he could see it coming, she slammed the hilt of her sword into his face. His nose exploded beneath the pommel as he tipped and fell flat on his back, unconscious. Ignoring the state of his nose—perhaps, she'd hit him a little *too* hard—she knelt and inspected the shimmery stone in his hand.

A creamy white, it shone like a diamond but was opaque and iridescent like an opal. She'd never seen anything like it. It was beautiful.

Picking it up, she turned it over in her hands curiously. It was ice cold to the touch, slowly sapping the heat from her fingers.

"*Destroy it*," Aster said, scales bristling as she regarded the stone through her eyes. "*That is most definitely the source of the outage. I can feel it gnawing at our Bond.*"

Anna frowned at the stone. "*I don't feel any different.*"

"*You have far more magic than a lightstone. They are easily depleted, you are not. At the rate it is nullifying your magic, it would take weeks, maybe months, of exposure to rid you of magic. It is a curse upon this land. Destroy it and be done with it."*

A shame, but not worth the risk.

She dropped the stone to the floor then stomped on it, crushing it with her heel. Reduced to dust, the lightstones flickered back on, momentarily blinding her. Blinking, she cast one final glance at the traitor—she'd tell someone to take him in to custody—then hurried towards the dungeon.

She'd just turned a corner when she caught a familiar mop of hair fending off two bandits. Jacob blocked an attack with his sword then rammed his foot into the assailant's chest. He spun in time to duck under a blade that nearly stopped Anna's heart.

Too damn close to getting his head lopped off.

She rushed in, slicing into his side before he could take another swipe at Jacob. Jacob lunged forward, thrusting his sword into his stomach.

Jacob faced her, relief filling his features. "There you are! I've been looking all over for you." His gaze swept over her tattered dress, concern furrowing his brow. "Are you hurt?"

"I'm all right." She turned her attention to the tears in his suit, across his thigh and shoulder. Blood darkened the black material, but they didn't look too serious. "Can you still fight?"

He shrugged his wounded shoulder, proving to her he still had full mobility. "This is nothing I can't handle." He wiped his forehead with his sleeve, peering around the empty hallway nervously. "Have you seen Eva? I haven't seen her since the fight broke out."

"She's with Grayson and Leo in the dungeon. The bandits are here to break Darius out."

A flash of fury peaked in his eyes before it was squelched by something much darker and sinister. "That fucker isn't leaving this castle alive."

Anna wasn't given the time to absorb the darkness in his eyes—Jacob was already gone, sprinting for the dungeon. She ripped off her heels and ran after him, her bare feet slapping the cold stone, each step pounding with dread.

The stairwell swallowed them in shadow. The deeper they went, the more sounds twisted, taking on a darker form—shouts became snarls, the clash of metal grated against the air, the wet crunch of bone and flesh sunk into her bones.

Then a scream tore through the corridor.

Not just any scream.

Eva's.

Anna's stomach clenched like a vice. Jacob surged forward, vanishing through the dungeon door. She followed, and the first thing she saw were the bodies. Guards. Bandits. All crumpled and bloodied in grotesque arrangements only Grayson could leave behind.

"Grayson!" the voice came further down, sharp with panic.

Adrenaline spiked through her systems, pushing her further. Faster.

Then she saw it.

Grayson was mid-duel with Darius, both locked in a brutal dance, when a second figure crept up behind him.

Too far. She wouldn't reach them in time.

Anna didn't think. She ripped the flame from the nearest torch and hurled it straight at the assassin's back.

It fizzled out on impact. The cloak devoured her flame.

Her blood ran cold. She'd only seen that once before. On Grayson's cloak.

Mithril armour. He's an assassin from Estrus.

Shit.

The flames didn't stop him—but they did force him to look away from Grayson.

His head snapped toward her and Jacob. In a blink, he calculated the greater threat. He lunged for Jacob.

Steel clashed as Jacob raised his blade just in time. The assassin moved like liquid shadow—smooth, fast, almost silent. His dagger struck high, then low, forcing Jacob to retreat step by step, defending with sheer reflex. Each attack came closer and closer to its target.

Anna surged in from behind, but he sensed her. With impossible speed, he twisted, catching her sword on his vambrace. Sparks flew. He drove his elbow into her ribs—hard—and she gasped, staggering back.

Jacob took advantage of the opening and slashed, but the assassin ducked beneath it and kicked Jacob's knee, sending him sprawling.

Not just fast. Precise.

She'd never seen anything like it.

After sparring with Grayson, she knew the assassins would be formidable—but they might as well be agents of Zyphril. Death animated in flesh.

The assassin turned for the kill, but Anna was already moving. She screamed, not in fear, but fury, drawing his attention as she swept low. He leapt back, avoiding the blade. Barely. It grazed his thigh.

His eyes narrowed behind the mask, reassessing his threat.

He flicked a throwing knife from his belt—Anna ducked, but not fast enough. The blade snagged in her hair, slicing a lock clean off as it whistled past her ear.

With a roar, Jacob surged upright and slammed into the assassin's side. The man stumbled, caught off-balance by the sheer force of it.

Anna didn't hesitate. She lunged in from the left, driving her sword forward. It slipped through the joint beneath his raised arm, between the plates of mithril and into soft flesh.

The assassin let out a short, broken grunt, then collapsed on the stone floor.

Anna stood over him, chest heaving, sword slick with blood. Her ribs screamed from where he'd struck her, but she didn't feel it yet—not really. Her eyes darted to Jacob.

Still standing. Unharmed.

Relief nearly dropped her to her knees.

Behind them, Grayson looked up—just in time to catch a heavy punch to the jaw. Darius snarled and slammed his brother's face into the wall, fingers twisted in his hair. He reeled back for another blow—

A man rushed up behind Darius, grabbing his shoulder and yanking him away. His eyes were frantic as he took in the growing number of Dragon Knights closing in. "Enough, Darius! Let's go!"

Darius shrugged him off, teeth gritted, eyes flicking between Grayson and Eva. "I'm *not* leaving without her!"

His rescuer seized his arm again, knuckles white. "Yes, you are! We leave now, or we die!"

Darius stared at Eva, eyes burning. His face twisted with rage and frustration. With a vicious snarl, he slammed his fist into the wall—then turned and let the man drag him out.

Jacob turned, eyes wide, and spotted the small, broken form curled in the cell.

"Eva!"

Forgetting Darius, he bolted. Anna followed, heart lurching. Eva was unconscious—sweat clung to her skin, her body trembling with each shallow breath. Thin cuts marred her chest, but it was the wound on her shoulder that stole Anna's breath. It wasn't just deep—it was gaping. Down to the bone.

Jacob shucked out of his blazer, bundling it into a tight ball then pressed it into the wound. "You're going to be okay, Eva."

"Fuck." Anna's eyes landed on Eva's bicep, which had gone black with inky tendrils stretching across her left shoulder and climbing her neck. "She's been poisoned."

"Gray!"

They looked down the corridor—where Grayson stumbled after Darius like a newborn fawn—his gait unsteady, each step laced with raw, unbridled fury. Deep gashes ran from his temple down to his jaw, dark rivulets of blood marring his determined features. Even in his weakened state, his eyes burned with a wild, murderous intensity that sent a shiver down Anna's spine.

Anna leapt to her feet and caught his arm, desperate to snap him out of it—but he jerked free as if drowning in rage.

"Leave him, Gray. Eva needs you to heal her."

Not even the mention of her name slowed him down. He took a staggering step towards Darius. "I won't let him get away," he ground out, voice raw and haggard as he seethed with pent up fury.

Cold hard dread sludged through her veins.

If he went after Darius like this, she wasn't sure they'd ever get Grayson back.

"If you chase after him, *Eva will die*," she snapped. "She's been poisoned."

If that didn't get through to him, she didn't know what would.

The corridor seemed to wait with baited breath, the air taut with tension.

He might not know it yet, but this was the moment he chose which man would rise from the ashes: Grayson... Or Dex.

CHAPTER 21
THE PATH FORWARD

The entire left side of Grayson's face felt like someone had dragged a grater down to the bone. Blood poured into his eye, blinding him on that side—leaving only the right to track his prey. The wounds pulsed with rage, sinking their vicious claws deeper into his flesh with every heartbeat.

Would that stop him? Fuck no.

He was running on fury now—pure, undiluted rage—and the unhinged monster inside him that still heard Eva's screams. It had torn free so fast, Grayson didn't stand a chance of holding it back.

That scream hadn't awakened Dex. It had birthed something worse.

Dex killed for pleasure—for the twisted thrill of watching others writhe, break, beg. But this thing? This thing had purpose. It had someone to live for. To protect. And it would do so without mercy, without hesitation, without a shred of Grayson's humanity left to temper it.

Everything else fell away. The corridor. The voices. His friends.

All that remained was the retreating silhouette ahead—Darius, smug and unpunished, his hands still slick with Eva's blood. Grayson saw those obsidian eyes as clearly as if they were burned into his skull. They had promised more pain. Promised to come back for her.

Because of him.

I won't let him get away. He wouldn't go near Eva ever again when he was done with him.

He stepped forward with every intention of carving into his older brother—but his step faltered. Darkness closed in around him, suffocating him. Darius's retreating form was growing blurry with every step he took into the shadows—

A hand gripped his arm. Snarling, Grayson whirled towards the perpetrator, ripping free of their grasp. Anna flinched, eyes hard and cold when she regarded him. An expression he rarely saw on her face unless the situation was dire.

"Leave him, Gray," she commanded, knowing exactly what she was asking of him by saying it. "Eva needs you to heal her."

He already knew her wounds weren't fatal. Darius wasn't so reckless to kill his greatest prize. It was more important he chased Darius to ensure he didn't hurt her again.

"I won't let him get away." Gritting his teeth, reigning in the part of him that wanted to curse her out for suggesting he forget about Darius. He turned away, set to hunt the bastard down—

"If you chase after him, Eva will *die*." A breath. A beat. "She's been poisoned."

Poisoned.

The word was like a whip lashing to his heart.

All the rage and hate evaporated in the next exhale.

None of it mattered if the light of his life was snuffed out.

He whirled on Anna. "How?"

Eva had told him the assassins hadn't touched her. Only they used poison. Darius's men didn't have the skill—or the nerve—for something like this.

Anna shook her head. "We can figure that out later. Come on."

She darted back to Eva's side.

Grayson stared down the corridor Darius had vanished into. The bastard was long gone, but Grayson could still hear his laughter—echoing in his skull like a scar that refused to heal.

Mocking him.

Reminding him that he'd lost. Again.

A frustrated snarl ripped from his throat as he tore himself away and dropped to Eva's side.

The poison was easy to spot. Seeping from a gash on her bicep, its edges already darkened. A sick, spreading web had crept across her chest. It was close. Too close to her heart. Once it reached there, there would be no pulling her back.

Definitely the work of Sylus's assassins.

"Get me water," he barked, not caring who obeyed. The small supply in his horn wouldn't be enough. He'd need more. A lot more.

Leo raced down the corridor to the water pump and came back shortly, sloshing the bucket around. Grayson was too focused on Eva's paling skin to notice the water he'd spilt onto his cloak. Compared to Jacob's tanned hand clasped tightly around hers, she looked like a wraith with a foot in the grave.

Eyes shut, in a pathetic attempt to push out the dreaded thoughts gnawing at his brain, he reached out to the water with his mind. Clasped it tight in his hold. *Willed* it to obey his command.

One slip. One breath out of place. That was all it would take for him to lose her.

No life had ever mattered more in his hands than this. And there was no monster to slay, no enemy to hunt.

She didn't need his sword.

Or his strength.

She needed his magic.

How could he have let this happen?

He'd volunteered to watch over Eva tonight—specifically because he didn't trust anyone else to protect her the way he could. And yet, it wasn't enough. He wasn't enough.

His magic seeped into her skin, chasing the venom through her blood-stream. The poison recoiled, resisting him, but he forced it out—black sludge oozing from her eyes, her ears, her mouth.

Keep going.

By the grace of Lorelus, it was working. The poison was being expelled. His body trembled with effort, sweat streaming down his temples. The wounds on his face burned. His heartbeat crashed against his ribs. But if it meant saving her, he'd give everything—and more.

Then the magic faltered. Slipped.

Just like Darius.

No, no, no.

The more he reached for it, the more it slipped through his fingers.

For all the years he'd honed his body into a weapon, he'd never once trained it for this. Never thought he'd need his magic more than his sword.

And now—because of that—he might lose her.

Snarling in frustration, he released Eva's hand, in favour of cupping her face. Cold. She was so damned cold in this dank dungeon and that blasted dress.

"Gray?" Jacob called for his attention.

"We have to get her to Eran. I've bought us time, but my magic... I can't." He'd never felt so godsdamn weak. Powerless.

Jacob reached over for him, squeezing his shoulder. Sympathy put warmth in his eyes, when all Grayson could feel was an impending coldness that wanted to snuff out any hope he had of saving her. "It's all right. You did what you could."

Grayson loathed to hear the words on his friend's lips. Words a mother told her upset child when they came in last place in a race.

"*Bring her to the water feature in the garden,*" Eran instructed, the voice in his mind unnervingly calm, despite the havoc Grayson's mind scourged through him. "*Be prepared for resistance. Darius's men are retreating, but some still linger.*"

Good. Grayson had some aggression he needed to work out.

"*Assassins?*"

"*Gone. For now.*"

A shame. He could have gone for a challenge.

Grayson rose, stripping off his cloak and draping it over Eva—to keep her warm, and to shield her. Few things could pierce mithril, and the one person who might was the one who needed it most.

He turned to face the depths of the dungeon, short sword in one hand, dagger in the other. Whatever enemies lurked ahead, they'd have to go through him to reach her.

"Leo, take Eva to the gardens. We'll cover you. Eran's waiting there."

Leo didn't hesitate. He crouched beside her, gently lifting her into his arms. Adjusting her weight, he cradled her head against his shoulder. His once-white suit was stained with grime and blood—but the worry etched into his features said he couldn't care less.

"You're going to be all right, Eva," Leo murmured. "You're in the best hands in Aboria."

Grayson refrained from snorting. Instead, he turned and started down the corridor toward the stairs, Leo close behind.

As soon as they reached the top, the sounds of chaos had dulled—still violent, but no longer overwhelming. The soldiers had fought hard to reclaim the castle, pushing back Darius's forces. Most of their attention had gone to protecting the guests, not hunting down stragglers in the halls.

Fine by him.

The first bastard that crossed his path didn't last two seconds—two knives, one to the heart, the other to the throat. Down. He moved on without pause. Leo led the group, keeping pace with the Knights as they swept corners and cut down anything that moved.

Jacob guarded the prince's rear. Anna held the right, scanning, reacting, moving. Grayson took the front and the left. Every sound sliced through him like one of Eva's bolts—tensing his muscles, sharpening his instincts. A flicker of motion, friend or foe, caught even a glimpse of Zyphril's champion before he reined it in... or ended them.

This he could do.

Kill. Eliminate.

His magic might pale beside the others', but that didn't matter. Not now. He could still end lives. He could still protect her.

No one—*no one*—was laying hands on Eva again.

Outside, Eran stood where he promised, by the fountain—though it was bubbling more violently than it had during Grayson's earlier sweep. The blistering wind bit into his exposed skin now that his cloak was gone, but he welcomed the sting. Let it sharpen him. Nothing honed the senses like pain.

There were far more intruders in the gardens than in the castle. Some were fleeing from guards. Others, too high on the thrill of combat, fought on blindly. A few spotted the squad making a direct path to the fountain—and recognised the prince in their midst.

They gathered fast, forming a cluster far larger than Grayson's team.

Anna moved beside him, sword poised to strike, her face twisted in a grimace that mirrored the rage burning in his chest.

If they wanted a fight, they'd give them one—

A lightning bolt tore down from the night's sky.

The explosion rocked the ground beneath them, the blinding light revealing every shadow in the garden. Electricity arced from the first intruder to the next, and the next, crackling like wildfire through their ranks. Grayson shielded his face from flying debris. Beside him, Anna stumbled with a cry, arms raised.

One by one, the attackers collapsed—hair scorched, skin marked with the same jagged burns Eva had left on Darius.

Above them, Arkon's snarl reverberated through the air. He landed hard at their side, sending trees and shrubs flying with the sweep of his tail. His luminous blue eyes locked onto Eva's pale, shivering body.

"Get Eva to the fountain," he growled, gaze never wavering. Then, whipping his head toward another charging attacker, his voice turned to thunder, "We will take care of this filth."

A blast of fire engulfed the man, reducing him to a smoking heap of cinders. Aster's crimson scales gleamed in the dark sky as she passed overhead, her wings beating hard against the air.

Glade swept in close behind, the flames glinting off her golden scales as she banked low. The ground rumbled, and in her wake, walls of dirt and stone surged up from the earth. The gravel path buckled and cracked as the walls formed a rough circle around the fountain—ten feet high, solid, unyielding. A safe zone. Enough room for Eran to operate, and enough space for the Knights to keep the perimeter secure.

Leo paused, staring up at the black dragon with wide eyes, his mouth ajar. Awe warred with fear on his face as he witnessed the unrestrained power of their dragons—no longer a fairy tale. This was raw force, ancient and deadly.

Arkon lowered his head, fury sparking deep in his eyes—not at the attackers, not at Leo.

But at Grayson.

Grayson met that fierce gaze and felt the weight of it crash over him like a tidal wave. No words were needed. He already knew exactly what Arkon saw when he looked at him.

Failure.

He'd failed to protect his rider. The one sacred rule of Dragon Canyon burned clear in his mind: Never get between a dragon and their rider.

He wouldn't fail her again.

With a hard shove, Grayson pushed the prince forward. "Move it, Leo."

Grimacing, Leo jumped into the glacial water, slipping on his ass while still clutching Eva in his arms. He adjusted her in his lap, settling her between his legs, and wrapped his arms around her waist. His teeth began chattering almost instantly.

Anna and Jacob took guard at the fountain's edge, their weapons glinting in the firelight—sentinels against anything foolish enough to try and reach her now.

"Hold her hand," Eran instructed, approaching with quiet urgency. "Contact is integral."

Considering the way Eran's magic already thrummed in the air—crackling softly, seeping into Eva's pores—Grayson questioned the credibility of that claim. But he didn't argue.

He hopped into the fountain beside them and took her hand, weaving their fingers together without hesitation.

And then—just the faintest twitch. She squeezed. It could have been a reflex A reaction from the cold. But Grayson felt it all the same. Like her soul had brushed against his.

A breath caught in his throat. His vision blurred for a second, heart squeezing tight in his chest.

She was still in there. His Starling. Fighting. Giving him hope.

"This is going to be uncomfortable for her," Eran warned a moment before his magic flared around them. Despite the temperature remaining the same, the water bubbled violently, sloshing against the sides of the fountain. It began to glow and ripple along the walls Glade had erected. Magic seized Eva like a voracious serpent, writhing beneath her skin as it forced the poison out of her.

Crying out, her back arched into Leo's front. Her grip shook Grayson's hand, turning his fingers purple. He embraced the pain, more relieved to feel the *strength* in her grasp. She still had fight in her. She was fighting the poison.

Kick its ass, Eva. The words failed to form on his lips. It felt like a waste of breath to offer encouragement when she couldn't hear him.

Leo dipped his face into the crook of her neck, his mouth grazing where it had no right to be. Grayson's blood boiled at the audacity. If she weren't *dying* right then and there, he would have ripped the prince away from her and let the dark urges win. For now, all he could do was clench his free hand and breathe in through his nose and out through his mouth.

"Shhh. It's all right, Eva," the prince murmured. "I'm here. You're okay." More magic ploughed through her, and the scream that followed tore at Grayson's heart. He held on to her hand as if it was all that was keeping her in this plain. Leo shot a glare towards Eran. "Could you let up a *little*?"

"If I *let up*, the poison will leave permanent damage behind," Eran growled, perhaps a little harsher than necessary, but Grayson appreciated the sentiment. He detested the sight of another male embracing Eva as much as Grayson did. "The poison was close to her heart. Any longer and it would be beyond even my magic."

A truth that rattled Grayson's bones. She would have lived, but the chances of her being allowed to be a Knight afterwards were slim. She could still do what she loved—only because Grayson chose to stay and heal her, rather than hunt down his brother

His eyes shuttered.

Eran's magic was so prolific, so potent, he could see it even behind his lids—icy blue wisps whispering across his senses, glittering like freshly packed snow under a bright, cloudless sky.

It traced the shape of the fountain, flowing through the basin, the pipes, and through Eva herself.

He felt every drop as if it were an extension of himself—just as vivid and familiar as a blade in his hand.

"*What is this?*"

"*Our magic*," Eran answered, a trickle of pride slithering down their Bond.

"*I've never seen it like this before.*"

"*You've never valued your abilities until now. You weren't born to destroy, Gray. This magic we share heals others so that they may keep on fighting for what they believe in.*"

Kind blue eyes flashed behind his closed lids. A woman long forgotten by the world, even by him, for a time. "*You will be the greatest king Estrus has seen, Deximus*," his mother used to tell him as she tucked him in at night. "*You will heal this broken land and return it to its former glory.*"

Back then, he hadn't known how broken his kingdom was. Hadn't known it needed healing.

Even after Dravyn was born and his mother slipped from memory, he'd seen nothing wrong with Estrus.

Not until Pitmedden.

His whole life, he was trained to be a weapon. A curse. Never a cure.

Yet if it weren't for Eran's gift, he wouldn't have been able to save Eva today. Or Jacob—countless times before.

Somehow, his path of destruction had led him to the Greenes—a family that had touched his heart so viscerally it could never be undone.

He didn't *want* it undone.

It was because of them that he finally believed he could be redeemed for the sins of his past.

He would do anything for them.

For Eva.

"*I want to learn more about my magic.*"

He'd stopped honing his skills, believing he knew all there was to know. But now he saw the truth—he'd barely scratched the surface.

Eva trained every day, pushing herself to master her magic so she could use it for good.

He would train to ensure nothing could stop her. Not Sylus. Not poison. Not fate.

"*We will train,*" Eran promised, trying and failing to hide the swelling pride rising in his chest. He shifted his attention to Eva. "*I have purged the poison. I did what I could for her shoulder, but Darius was thorough in his butchery.*" He wouldn't be Darius Fortys, if he wasn't thorough. "*I will need at least two more sessions with her to heal it fully.*"

Grayson opened his eyes, studying the steady rise and fall of Eva's chest. Any semblance of pain she'd been in earlier was gone. She lay limp, at peace, in Leo's lap, her hand heavy in his. Her skin leaked the evil black liquid that tried to end her life, staining the pool and their clothes. The hole in her shoulder no longer looked angry and had stopped bleeding, but it was still deep and would limit her movement until Eran could fully heal her.

"Is she okay?" Leo asked, raising his hand to her neck to check her pulse.

"The poison is gone." Grayson peeled the cloak off her then folded it twice, longways, then worked on wrapping it around her shoulder and securing her arm to her chest to support the tender muscles and tendons there. "She needs rest."

Leo shut his eyes, sagging in relief. "Thank Lorelus for that."

"Leonidas!" The frantic voice came from outside Glade's hut. "Leo!"

Groaning, Leo tipped his head back against the edge of the fountain and muttered a colourful curse his mother would baulk at if she was within earshot.

Grayson slid his arms beneath Eva and lifted her to his chest in one smooth motion. Her soaked dress weighed him down, tripling her weight—but she might as well have been featherlight. He'd carry her through fire if he had to.

"Leo!"

"Here, Mother!" Blue-lipped and dripping, Leo waded out of the fountain. He turned back toward Eran with a respectful nod. "Thank you, Eran. I will not forget what you've done for Eva today."

Eran huffed, steam rippling from his nostrils. "Don't thank me. Thank Grayson. It was his quick thinking that saved her."

Leo barely looked at him. His gaze went straight to Eva, concern etched across his features. "Take her to one of the spare rooms and see that she is comfortable. I'll return as soon as I'm able."

Grayson stared back at him, unblinking. Even after three years, the prince still thought he could give him orders.

He'd make sure Eva was comfortable—but not in one of his rooms.

He'd take her where she belonged.

Without a word, he strode past him for the exit where Anna and Jacob were eagerly awaiting him. "The castle is secure," Anna informed him stoically, despite the worry for her friend in her eyes. "Aster and Glade are doing a final sweep of the grounds."

Jacob's eyes were glued on his sister. "She's going to be okay, right?"

"She's okay, Jake," Grayson promised, holding her closer to his chest as a wave of possessiveness seized him. What'd he kill to have a moment to himself with her, to take a moment to believe the words he spoke.

Shoulders sagging in relief, Jacob brushed a kiss in Eva's hairline. "That was too close, Gray."

Too fucking close. He wanted to be furious with Eva for running off without him and facing Darius alone—but the weight of his relief stopped him. For now. All he wanted to do was get her somewhere comfortable and safe so he could plan how he was going to prevent this from happening again.

"Let's get her inside."

Jacob swallowed, finally meeting his gaze. "Right."

As they stepped out of the enclosure, Queen Althea came into view, marching towards the fountain with a squad of Dragon Knights and her own personal guard. "My son? Where's Leonidas?" she demanded, worry etched into every line on her face.

"Here, Mother." Leo stepped out of the hut. "I'm all right."

She marched in front of his face, fuming. "You didn't follow protocol! You're supposed to head *straight* to the bunker."

He stood tall and held his ground. "And leave my people to fend for themselves? I can fight, Mother. I should be allowed to fight for *my* people."

She cast a white-gloved hand towards Jacob and Anna. "They are not the *heir to the throne*. If anything happens to you, Leo—"

"I am perfectly capable of defending myself! Eva almost died. Those people were here for *her*, not me."

Her spine went rigid. "I don't care. You do not risk your life for *anyone*, not even the storm dragon rider." She raised her hand when he opened his mouth to protest. "I'm not arguing with you in my decimated gardens." She cut a glare to Eran and Arkon before facing her son again. "You are needed in the war room."

Leo looked at Eva's unconscious form, torn. Then, with a deep breath, the fight drained from his posture. His face slipped into a royal mask Grayson recognised far too well—composure layered over frustration and duty.

"Very well," Leo said tightly. "But I'm not done discussing this."

The guards fell in step behind the royals, leaving the rest of them in the garden ruins.

The Dragon Knight squad remained behind. Corporal Blackmoor stepped forward, his eyes flicking to Eva like she was nothing more than a weapon that had misfired.

Heat roiled through Grayson's blood. He saw it in the man's gaze—the disappointment. Like Eva was a failed asset, not a person. But the blame wasn't hers alone. They all bore it.

Corporal Blackmoor turned to Anna. "Debrief in the war room, Hargin. Twenty minutes. Make sure your squad is there."

"Yes, sir."

Fifteen minutes later, Eva was laying in bed with a fresh pair of pajamas and a pile of blankets drawn up to her chin at Jacob's behest. New wrappings held her arm in place to support her shoulder. Grayson had changed out of his wet uniform for a dry one, and his mithril cloak was draped over the tub rim in the bathing chamber. He'd rinsed the blood off his face and hands, and found that while Eran was healing Eva, he also healed the nasty gash along his cheek. Anna and Jacob didn't bother to shed out of their dress clothes.

Grayson ground his jaw, every fibre of his being screaming at him to stay behind, to watch over Eva while the others attended the meeting. In case Darius decided to come back and take her. Worse, if the assassins find out Eva survived the poison and come back to finish the job.

No. *They're dead.* For high target kills, Salik sent three men to do the job. Eva got one, he finished the other, and Anna ended the third. They wouldn't be back tonight—but they would be back. It was only a matter of how long it would take for word to reach Sylus that his assassins had failed.

As for Darius... he would be a fool to return when the castle was on high alert. He'd missed his chance to claim his prize. His focus now was to survive the night. Every minute Grayson wasted in this castle was a mile further Darius was away from him. But he couldn't leave yet. Not until he knew Eva was safe.

"*She is safe,*" Eran assured him. "*Both Arkon and I are here.*"

When he said "here," he meant at the base of their window outside, not giving a flying fuck if they were blocking the barracks or whose precious bushes they were tearing up. Aster and Glade circled the castle, and would continue to do so until the debriefing was over.

No one was entering this room without the dragons knowing.

"Gray?" Anna touched his shoulder lightly. "You ready?"

Loosing a frustrated growl, he turned away from the bed before he could think of more horrible things that could happen to Eva in his absence.

"Yeah. Let's head out."

CHAPTER 22
RUFFIANS AND RENEGADES

The midnight air burned in Darius's lungs like acid, pumping through his veins with every step away from Kain Castle. The Aborians had taken all but his trousers and tunic when they locked him in that dungeon, which—he now realized—they had heated. Against the cold, lifeless stone, he'd fallen asleep shivering most nights. But this? This fresh Aborian air, cutting through the fields and whistling between towers that scraped the sky like Estrus's peaks, was *frigid.*

He cursed the chattering of his teeth as Keyon led him into a shadowed alleyway between two brick-and-brownstone buildings. His feet were half-numb in his boots, and his shoulder still ached from where the storm dragon's magic had grazed him.

Up ahead, the street was lively—mockingly so. Laughter spilled from a nearby tavern window, mingling with the distant pluck of a lute. People wandered the street without a care, utterly unaware of the attack on their beloved castle.

Or the danger sliding past them in the dark.

The clank of metal on stone behind them made Darius's head snap around. A group of knights had followed them into the city.

He clenched his bruised knuckles, heart pounding with a craving he hadn't felt since the night he earned his first kill—the need to hear flesh tear, to hear screaming. To make someone hurt the way he did.

The storm dragon rider had slipped through his fingers. Again.

Up ahead, Keyon had almost reached the mouth of the alley before realizing Darius had stopped. He cursed under his breath. The knights hadn't spotted them yet, but if Darius kept standing there like a damned fool—

Keyon turned on his heel, stomped back, and grabbed Darius by the scruff like an unruly child. "Move," he hissed, hauling him forward and out into the street.

They slammed into a pair of men holding hands. In Estrus, they'd have been executed for such a display, but Keyon barely spared them a glance.

He kept dragging Darius through the crowd like a sack of trash he couldn't let go of.

Gasps and startled glances followed them.

Between the tattered clothes, greasy, matted hair, and unshaven beard, Darius stood out like a curse in a cathedral. These people had probably never seen a speck of dirt in their lives. The streets gleamed. Tailored suits and soft laughter filled the air. Lush silks, polished boots, perfume instead of sweat.

They lived better than most nobles in Estrus.

Disgusting.

Where was the divide between nobles and commoners? Where was the curfew? The guards?

If people were allowed to do as they pleased, to move freely at any hour, they had the power to organize. To riot. To rise.

Letting the commonwealth live without a watchful eye was foolish. Dangerous.

And the women—gods, the women. Glorious curves on full display, soft skin exposed along shoulders and collarbones, chests rising like an invitation he didn't deserve. Yet they didn't act like harlots. None called to men from alleyways. None lifted their skirts or offered the plunder beneath.

They were quiet. Refined. Unafraid.

Some walked alone, without fear or escort, meandering through the lamplit streets with not a single man guarding their steps. No one to protect them from the monsters hiding in plain sight.

Monsters like him.

Keyon glanced over his shoulder and exhaled in relief. "We've lost them. For now."

"There wouldn't be a *'for now'* if you let me kill them," Darius growled, his voice a low rasp beneath the city's hum.

"With what?" Keyon shot back. "You're not armed. No armour."

That was Keyon's fault. He hadn't let Darius scavenge weapons or take the gear off the dead on their way out of the castle grounds.

Darius didn't know why he'd obeyed.

He was a godsdamn prince. The heir to Estrus's throne.

No one told him what to do.

"Keep moving," Keyon warned. "Don't draw attention."

As they passed a vendor's stall, Darius swiped a navy scarf from the rack, wrapping it around the lower half of his face and shoulders. The scratchy wool itched against his skin, but the warmth bleeding into his nose and cheeks was worth the discomfort.

Too many people milled around for the vendor to notice a single piece of fabric missing.

In Estrus, theft like that would've cost him a hand. If he was caught.

He doubted the same rule applied here.

Not until they found out who he was.

Then he'd have a lot more than his hand to worry about.

"Here," Keyon said, veering off into a side street where fewer lightstones—what the Aborians called those glowing orbs that lit up their city—cast their eerie, ever-burning light.

He stopped before a squat building beneath a hanging sign of a sinking ship.

Laughter rumbled behind the thick wooden door, underscored by the scrape of chairs and clink of mugs. Mead, cigar smoke, and sweat curled through the cracks in the wood, sinking into Darius's nostrils.

He hated how familiar it smelled.

How grounding it felt.

He didn't want to feel grounded. He wanted to burn. To seethe. To hunt.

He wasn't done with the storm dragon rider. Not by a long godsdamn stretch.

Keyon skirted past the crowd of drinkers and wenches in the main room and made for the long bar at the back. He pulled a gold coin from his pocket and slid it across the counter.

"A meal for two," Keyon said, "and hot water sent to my room."

"And a bottle of whiskey," Darius added, jutting his chin toward a familiar brand glinting on the shelf behind the bartender.

Keyon rolled his eyes and slid two more silvers across the counter. "Fourth floor. First door on the right."

"Fourth?" Darius arched a brow. Not exactly ideal for a man on the run.

Keyon lifted one shoulder in a shrug and led the way. "Options are limited when the prince of Aboria hosts a gala anyone with coin can attend. It's safe," he added, when the silence stretched too long. "Window drops onto an awning. Hides the alley beneath."

Darius huffed. There was a reason he kept Keyon around—and it wasn't just for busting him out of the castle dungeon.

The room was modest, containing two twin beds, a small table with matching chairs, and a scuffed dresser. He'd seen worse. Far worse. Without comment, he crossed to the basin and began scrubbing away the grime of captivity.

A hot bath and a clean shave later, Darius emerged dressed in fresh clothes—another thoughtful acquisition from Keyon. He kept the navy scarf, tying the ends together and looping it around his neck twice. It covered the lower half of his face and served as a silent keepsake from the kingdom he intended to claim.

Steam curled from the plates on the table. Darius sank into one of the chairs, ignoring the groan of wood beneath his weight. Compared to cold, damp stone, even this rickety seat felt like a throne.

He tore a bun in half, dunked it into the thick stew, and took a bite. A groan rumbled in his chest. After weeks of gruel, he'd have eaten anything hot and filling. But this? His own godsdamn chef could have made this. The meat melted in his mouth, tender and rich, while the spices danced over his tongue, coaxing his senses back to life.

"Do all Aborians eat like this?" he mumbled around his third bite.

Keyon pushed aside his empty bowl, having eaten while Darius bathed. "Not all of them. But the ones in this city seem to."

He leaned forward, elbows braced on the table, watching Darius devour his meal.

"Tell me what I've missed," Darius said. "What are the numbers?"

Keyon scrubbed at the stubble on his jaw, thinking. "We used the last of our mithril during the raid. Of the one hundred fifty-seven who escaped the fort with me, thirty-four made it out of the city. They're spread out in nearby taverns, laying low."

Darius's brow furrowed. The losses were heavy. "What did you use the mithril for?"

A slow, satisfied smile curved Keyon's mouth. "Turns out mithril doesn't just resist magic—it can nullify it. Especially when it's close to the source. The lightstones in the castle? All connected by a conduit system. We used a mithril shard to kill the magic in one. That disruption spread through the entire line."

Darius froze. Then shoved his half-finished bowl aside and leaned in, heart thudding.

Magic had always been Aboria's edge—Estrus had none. But if mithril could negate it... if it could be weaponized...

He could control the storm dragon rider.

"Tell me more."

Keyon explained how he'd discovered it by accident—right here in this room. He'd set a chunk of mithril on the table near a sconce, and five minutes later, the light flickered and died. Their informant inside the castle confirmed the sconces were linked. Enough mithril in the right place could shut down every lightstone on a floor. Maybe more.

Darius drummed his fingers against the table, thoughts spinning. Keyon had always groaned through strategy meetings. Said they were boring, pointless.

Apparently not.

He'd saved Darius's life. The raid cost them over a hundred men. But soldiers were replaceable.

This discovery wasn't.

It was the beginning of something far greater.

"You've done well, Keyon. I'll see to it you're properly rewarded when we return home."

"Home, my lord?" Keyon scratched the side of his head. "Are we giving up on the storm dragon rider?"

"No. Dex won't let her die."

Not if his loss of control meant anything.

In all their years growing up, Darius had never once seen his brother falter. Not when he took his lashings. Not when he was forced to kill his dire wolf. Not even when the generals insulted him to his face for overstepping his command. Dex had always been a storm restrained—quiet, cold, and calculated. He chose his moments. Chose where it would hurt the most.

But tonight?

Tonight, there was no restraint. No control. He acted out of fear—and rage. A very interesting development.

Darius had always known Dex was drawn to power. It lured him like a moth to flame. But this... this was something else. Primal. Raw.

Could it be that he...?

No. He wouldn't be so imprudent.

Love was for the foolhardy. A distraction. A liability.

The Dex he knew would never offer himself up as prey.

And yet—it was the only explanation. Why else would he charge in without thought? Why else leave himself so open for Darius to strike him so hard?

Oh, Dexy. Do you even know what you've gotten yourself into?

This kind of mistake couldn't go unpunished.

He would suffer for his choices.

And what sweeter vengeance than letting the woman he loved—his precious storm dragon rider—be the one to destroy everything he'd built?

Darius would make sure of it.

"We're going home, Keyon. I have plans—but I need resources. We'll return for her when we're ready. No more underestimating her. She's not just a complication." His voice dropped to something colder. "She's a threat. One that's only growing stronger."

Sylus feared her. That much was clear.

But Darius?

He saw her for what she truly was: the ultimate weapon.

And he would stop at nothing to possess her.

CHAPTER 23
CONSEQUENCES

Eva's eyes felt as though they were weighed down by anchors. She tried to open them more than once, but her body ached too much to obey. Everything was heavy, uncooperative, dulled by pain and exhaustion.

The bed beneath her was soft—more forgiving than the one in Dragon Canyon. It smelled of fresh linen with a subtle hint of pine, a quiet scent that brought a strange sort of comfort. Familiar, though she couldn't say why. Her body sank into the feather mattress with a relief that almost felt undeserved.

"*You're awake.*" Arkon's voice drifted through her thoughts, and with it came a gentle swell of relief through their Bond—his relief, felt as her own. It settled in her stomach and coaxed her mind to stir. "*How do you feel?*"

She didn't answer right away. Her body was stiff, every joint protesting movement, but she pushed through the discomfort anyway, mentally cataloging where it hurt the most. Toes. Fingers. Elbows. Knees. Her right arm was bent and secured across her front, tightly bound. That, at least, explained the dull throb in her shoulder.

"*Like I took a tumble down your back and straight into a mountainside,*" she answered wearily. Her mind still sat in a veil of fog, making it hard to reach out to him. "*Why does everything hurt?*"

The question lingered as fragments of memory slowly drifted into reach. The castle. The attack. Assassins on the balcony. Intruders breaching the halls. Darius stepping out of his cell.

She'd stopped him. Hadn't she?

But her shoulder pulsed in response, like her body itself was answering. She searched deeper, and the memory rose with violent clarity—Darius on top of her, hand wrapped around her own weapon as he drove it into her shoulder. That grin, wide and wicked, feeding off her pain like it was his reward.

Her stomach twisted. Nausea crept up her throat, and she had to force the image away before she was sick. She turned her focus elsewhere—anywhere—trying to ground herself in the present, where the bed was soft, the room was still, and Arkon's presence reminded her she was no longer alone.

"Eran had to use a lot of magic to heal you," Arkon said. *"This is an unfortunate side effect, but it shall pass."*

A beat.

"We stopped him. He's still in the dungeon. Right, Arkon?"

Silence followed. Then a slow, reluctant pull in the Bond—like a breath drawn too tightly. *"No, Little One. He fled the castle last night."*

Her body stilled. Horror bloomed low in her chest, hollow and sharp, knitting beneath her ribs and squeezing the air from her lungs.

"How?" she breathed.

How could Grayson or Anna or Jacob let the man of her nightmares go free?

"They had to make a choice. You or him. They picked you, of which I am grateful for." A beat. *"We almost lost you. The Slayer saved your life."*

Her mind recoiled. No.

Darius couldn't be free. Not when her family's death still echoed in her blood. Not when he had driven steel through her flesh and smiled while doing it. He was supposed to pay. He was supposed to bleed.

He couldn't be allowed to keep hunting her.

Fear surged like a wave crashing through her veins. She pushed herself upright, driven by pure instinct.

Pain tore through her shoulder like wildfire.

"Gah!" She gasped, clutching at the joint. The cry that climbed her throat was feral, desperate, but she forced it down, clenching her jaw until the edges of her vision sparked.

"Whoa!" Jacob's voice cracked through the haze. His chair scraped back hard, and in an instant, he was kneeling beside her. "Easy, Eva. You're all right."

She scanned the room, heart pounding, half-expecting to find Darius lurking in the shadows, biding his time. But there was nothing—no silhouette, no danger pressing in from the corners. Just a dimly lit chamber softened by sheer curtains, the overcast light bleeding through in a pale, muted wash. Rain pelted the windows with a voracious rhythm.

"Where is he?"

Jacob's brows drew together. "Who? Gray? He's in a meeting with Anna and a few of the higher ups."

"No." Her voice came out hoarse, more brittle than she wanted it to be. "Darius. Where did he go? You have a rough idea, right? I want to be part of the team."

His eyes flew wide, taken aback. For a moment, he just stared. Then he exhaled hard and sank down beside her, the bed dipping beneath his weight.

"Look," he said, voice low, "I get why you want to go after him. Trust me—I do. Five Hells, I want to be on the damn search myself. I won't sleep until I know he's dead. But you're in no shape to be out there. Eva, you can barely sit up. I don't think you could even fly solo right now, let alone fight."

"I can—"

"*Look* at your shoulder, Eva," he snapped, trying desperately to make her see reason. "Darius knew exactly what he was doing. He slowed the healing. That wound is deep. He cut through a massive section of muscle. It's a miracle you have any mobility at all."

"That's fine," she dismissed. "Grayson can heal me."

Color flushed into Jacob's cheeks. His lips pressed together in a tight line—something he did when he was holding himself back. "You don't get it. He *can't*. Eran will need at least two more sessions before it's even close to normal again."

Her stomach dropped, the words hitting harder than she expected. "What are you saying?"

"I'm saying if you don't take it easy, your arm might not fully recover. Not ever."

No... No, that couldn't be true. He was lying. Protecting her—like always. That had to be it. This was just another tactic to keep her away from danger. Away from Darius.

But she hadn't failed. Not really. It had been the poison. The assassins. That was why she hadn't stopped him.

She wouldn't make the same mistake again.

Before she could stop herself, her legs swung over the edge of the bed. The floor met her feet with a solid, warm thud, and the room tilted slightly. She caught herself before she stumbled, steadying her legs. She refused to collapse. Not in front of Jacob. Not now.

He was already looking at her like she was breakable. Like she'd shatter if he so much as breathed wrong.

She didn't need to give him another reason to fear for her.

Jacob rose to his full height and trailed behind as she made her way to the door. "What are you doing? Where are you going?"

She threw him a withering glare over her shoulder. Would he ever stop babying her? "I'm going to get the truth from the source."

Wincing, he followed her out, snatching a dragon-scale jacket off the back of a chair as he went. "It's cold and raining. If you're not going to have the decency to change, at least wear a coat."

She didn't have much of a choice when he tossed it at her. Reflex took over—she caught it midair, but the sudden motion sent pain flaring through her shoulder like a knife twisting in slow circles. She bit the inside of her cheek to keep from crying out and clumsily shrugged into the coat. Jacob moved in, silently helping her ease it over the injured side. The assist stung more than the wound itself.

She hated needing help. Hated that even something as simple as putting on a coat made her feel like she was crumbling.

Without acknowledging his look of concern, she stepped into the hallway and strode toward the nearest exit. The cold hit her immediately, the rain needling her cheeks like shards of glass. She didn't slow.

The dragons were visible from across the grounds, clustered in the clearing. Glade had formed a massive canopy for shelter, but only Aster had taken advantage of it. Eran stood in the downpour, his wings half-furled like he was basking in sunlight. Arkon waited at the field's edge, still and watchful. When she neared, he lifted a wing over her like an umbrella and dipped his head low, his snout brushing against her chest. His hot breath seeped into her coat and chased away the cold down to the marrow.

"Do not overexert yourself, Little One," he murmured, voice low and rumbling in her mind. "I do not wish to see you in that bed again."

She pressed her fingers to his scales, grounding herself in the sensation of warmth. "I'm all right, Arkon. It's not as bad as it looks." Or at least... she prayed it wasn't. Gods, what would she do if it didn't heal properly? She needed to be out there. She needed to help stop Darius.

His nonexistent brows furrowed. His gaze shifted behind her as another figure approached.

Eran.

The azure dragon moved with slow, fluid steps, lowering his head once he reached her. She stepped away from Arkon and reached up to scratch beneath the rough line of scales running under his jaw. A deep groan rumbled from his chest and vibrated through the ground as he leaned into her hand, almost knocking her off her feet.

"How are you feeling, Eva? I didn't expect to see you this early."

"I'm a little achy," she lied. Truthfully, she felt like she'd been trampled by a bull—and lost. "I hear I have you and Grayson to thank for curing me of the poison."

Her hand dropped loosely to her side. The weight of last night's failure pressed down on her like a stone. If it hadn't been for the poison, she would've had him. Darius would be dead, and the world would be better for it. She would feel better for it.

"Is there any chance you can heal my shoulder today?"

Eran gently nudged her chest with the tip of his horn, urging her to lean into him again. "I cannot heal you yet, Eva. The magic I used last night was dangerous—reckless, even. It would've killed a lesser human. We need to wait a few days before continuing."

She met his emerald gaze, saw the remorse in them, soft and aching. The same pained edge she sometimes caught in Grayson's eyes when he thought no one was watching.

"But he's out there, Eran," she said, voice cracking. "I have to find him and kill him. I can't just sit around and do nothing. If you're worried about hurting me, I can take the pain—"

"No," Jacob cut in, his voice like a whip. "Absolutely not. There's no point in risking your life for something that is not happening. Gray and Anna are already working with Leo and the officers on forming a strike team. They'll find him. You are not a part of it."

"You don't get it, Jake—"

"Don't I?" he snapped, fists clenched at his sides. "That bastard killed *my* parents and little sister, too. He tried to take you. Twice. You think I don't want him dead? I want that fucker in the ground more than anyone—which is exactly why I trust Grayson and Anna to handle it. Let them do their job, and we'll do ours."

"And what is that, *exactly*?" Her voice shook. "I don't know if you've noticed, but I can't use my left arm. I can't train. I can't fight. I can't do a fucking thing like this. I'm weak. I'm useless. I'm a liability to the squad. So if there's a way to heal me faster, even if it kills me—then yes, I'll take it."

Jacob stepped forward, his expression fierce and heartbreaking. "Well, too bad for you, you've got people who love you too much to let you be that stupid."

His words struck like a slap.

"We're going back to Dragon Canyon later today," Jacob said firmly. "And you're going to drop this hunting-Darius nonsense. End of discussion."

"But—"

He jabbed a warning finger in her face, just like he used to when she was small and tried to follow him into the woods. "No."

Tears stung her eyes, an overwhelming wave of emotion catching her off guard. What was the point of all her training—of the endless drills, the scars, the sleepless nights—if she couldn't use it to protect the people she loved? To avenge them? Darius had torn their world apart, and she still couldn't stop him. She was as helpless now as she'd been back then.

"What if he comes back, Jacob?" she asked, her voice barely above a whisper.

The fire in his face softened. His anger unraveled into something tender and aching. He stepped forward and laid a calloused hand on her good shoulder, squeezing like he used to when she'd scraped her knees or woke up crying from a bad dream.

"You'll be safe in Dragon Canyon," he said quietly. "He's running. He's out of men, out of places to hide. He can't get anywhere near you on base." He met her eyes, steady and unshakable. "Eva, you're a talented Knight. An incredible rider. But you're not invincible—and you're not alone. You still have more to learn. And the people who can go after him? The best of them are already out there, doing everything they can. Even if they don't catch him, they'll drive him out of the kingdom, far from you."

She opened her mouth to argue, but he raised a hand, silencing her.

"I know," he said, his voice cracking. "It's not good enough. Not until he's dead. But to me? It's enough that you're alive. That you're still here. I don't care if he lives or dies. I only care about you." His voice faltered. His lip trembled. Tears welled in his eyes, and he blinked rapidly, as if trying to hold them at bay. "Gods, Eva... I thought I was going to lose you."

He stepped closer and rested his forehead against hers, voice dropping to a hoarse whisper.

"When I found you in that dungeon—Grayson had gone completely off the rails, Leo was barely hanging on—and you... you were covered in blood. I thought you were gone. And then I heard this little whimper. Just a sound. But it was you. And I've never heard you sound so... fragile." The tears ran freely now, tracing lines down his face. She felt her own begin to fall, silent and hot. "I can't lose you too," he choked. "Don't make me the last Greene standing. Don't make me bury you, too."

Her heart cracked wide open. All the rage, the frustration, the guilt—it collapsed under the weight of his grief. His love.

Gods. What had she put him through?

They were the last of their blood. The final two threads of a torn legacy. And she hadn't even thought about him—not really—when she'd chased after Darius like a woman possessed. She'd been consumed by vengeance, blind to everything but the fire in her veins.

But what if that fire consumed her? Was dying for her family worth it, if the only thing her parents had ever wanted was for them to live?

To live fully. To live together.

Was any revenge worth leaving Jacob behind?

She dipped her head into his shoulder, body feeling as though it weighed a thousand pounds, and wrapped her good arm around him, clutching his jacket with everything she had—which wasn't nearly as much as she should have. "I'm sorry... I wasn't thinking."

His arms surrounded her in warmth and love. He kissed the top of her head. "You were thinking of them. Don't apologise for that. But live for me, Eva. Please. I don't know what I'd do if I lost you, too."

She nodded against the dragon scales of his jacket. "I'll go back to Dragon Canyon with you. I have a reading list a kilometre long I've been planning on reading, anyway."

Relief filled every pore of his being. "Good. Thank you."

"The rainstorm will clear up shortly after noon," Eran informed them, giving them their personal space; though, Eva noticed his tail had formed a broad circumference around them. "You'll be flying into the night, but the winds will be in your favour."

Jacob nodded to him in thanks. "That gives us a few hours to kill. Plenty of time to get you cleaned up and raid the kitchens."

Her stomach growled, which sounded—and felt—more like an abomination trying to tear its way out of her than a physical reminder of her hunger.

A soft smile flitted across Jacob's face. "Some things never change. Come on, let's get you inside."

Eva cast a final glance at the dragons then let Jacob lead her inside.

They were eating at the breakfast bar in the kitchen when Leo found them. The cooks paid them no mind as they manned their stations—chopping, dicing, and stirring—preparing a lunch that promised to be a slice of heaven, if the aromas in the air were any indication.

One of them had kindly paused his task to make brunch for Eva and Jacob: a delicious plate of crustless sandwiches with a side of raw carrots. The warmth from the ovens had finally chased the rain-chill from her bones.

The kitchen was quickly shaping up to be her favourite place in the entire castle.

Leo went straight to her, his expression taut with concern. A thin cotton tunic clung to his muscular torso, embroidered with green and gold whirls, and a long wool coat hung over his shoulders. His face was unshaven, dark rings beneath his eyes. She wondered if he'd slept at all last night.

Eva hopped down from her seat, facing him fully, bracing herself for whatever disaster had struck while she was out of commission.

He scooped up her free hand and pressed a kiss to her palm before holding it to his stubbled cheek. His eyes fluttered closed, a shadow of relief crossing his face, as if her touch alone could ease the raging tides inside him.

"I can't stay long," he murmured, "but I've been worried about you all day. When I got word you were awake, I had to come."

He met her eyes—lapis blue and bright despite the exhaustion—and her heart skipped. There was more emotion in them than she'd expected. Fear. Worry. And something softer beneath it all, unspoken but potent, threading through the air between them.

She blinked, finally realising there was no disaster to avert. He wasn't here because something had gone wrong—he was here for *her*.

Her insides liquified. He might have a reputation as a ladies' man, but in moments like these, he made her feel like the only woman in the world. It was easy to forget he was a prince who could have anyone he wanted, with a thousand and one responsibilities more pressing than her.

"Whatever you need to be comfortable during your stay here," he said, "just say the word, and it's yours."

Suddenly unsure what to do or say around him, she swallowed the boulder lodged in her throat. "Thank you, Leo, but that's not necessary. We're leaving in an hour. I wouldn't mind stopping by the infirmary before we go, though," she added, glancing toward Jacob—who was glaring at Leo as if he'd insulted her instead of offering her the entire castle. "Hopefully they have a numbing cream for my shoulder. Otherwise, it's going to be a rough ride back."

Leo's charming smile faltered. "Don't go. Stay a few days, at least."

He guided her hand from his cheek to his chest, pressing it over his heart. "I'd worry less if you were here, rather than a three days' ride away."

Eva cast Jacob a subtle look, hoping to ease the growing ire behind his eyes before that glare became permanent. "I made a promise to go back to Dragon Canyon. It's the best place for me to heal."

"Even if it hurts you to get there?"

"Even if it hurts." She turned her hand in his and held it between them, noting how smooth his skin was—nails neatly trimmed, untouched by the kind of work she'd known her whole life. "You can't worry about me all the time, Leo. My job comes with risks. I'm going to get hurt, and there's nothing you can do to stop it."

He scowled. "There is *something* I can do. I could command you to stay here until you're strong enough to fly again."

She quirked a brow in challenge. "Would you?"

He matched her stare, chin lifted with princely resolve. It lasted all of two seconds before he sighed and released her hand. "No, I wouldn't. You're a free spirit. It would be a crime to cage you."

"You'll tell me how the interrogation goes, won't you?" she asked, shifting the subject before he got any other ideas about keeping her locked up in the castle. They'd caught a guard conspiring with Keyon to free Darius. It was doubtful he knew where Darius was hiding, but he might know where the rest of his men were camped—enough to finally bring them to justice.

Leo tilted his head. "And what do you plan to do with that information, if I give it to you?"

"Nothing. I promise." She laid a hand over her heart. "I..." Her voice caught. She moistened her lips, searching for the right words. "I just want to know something is being done. Darius didn't destroy Brar on his own. The men who followed him—they chose to. And they should be punished for it."

It still broke her heart to remember how many had turned on their neighbours—on their own kingdom—when Darius swept through her valley. Many had perished at Fort Brar by Anna's hand, but some were still out there. Loyal. Dangerous. And that knowledge made her stomach turn.

His gaze softened—went molten, even—as he beheld her. "They will be. That is my promise to you."

"Thank you, Leo."

Aboria was lucky to have a prince so loyal to his people.

A knight filled the doorway and cleared her throat to get their attention. "Your Highness, you're needed in the war room."

"Yes, yes." He waved her off, then turned his back to the door as if it could grant them privacy from the cooks, the knight, or her glowering brother. "I suppose this is goodbye—until we see each other again. May the winds be in your favour, love."

"Goodbye, Leo."

He leaned in and brushed a kiss on her cheek. Heat flared under her skin as his lips lingered, the scratch of his stubble warm against her face. Her heart stumbled over itself.

When he pulled back and saw the colour on her cheeks, he winked—swagger returning to his step as he sauntered toward the waiting knight.

Eva absently touched her cheek, still feeling the ghost of his kiss.

Jacob rolled his eyes. "He is terrible at respecting boundaries."

Boundaries. Right.

Last time she and Leo were alone together, she'd nearly yelled at him for trying to kiss her—while she was in the middle of a very delicate, very complicated relationship with Grayson.

Ugh. Men.

She turned to the one stable and reliable man in her life—who was currently shaking his head at her with brotherly reproach. "What?"

"Don't tell me you've gone smitten on him. Do you have any idea how many times I've seen him pull that move on a girl?"

She rolled her good shoulder back, wincing as her back muscles spasmed to compensate for the bad one. "I'm not smitten. I know what kind of game he plays."

Even if it was hard to see it as a *game* when he looked at her like she was the only one in the room.

She shook off the thought before it could root.

"Good," Jacob said. "Because I don't want to see either of you get hurt." He glanced at her empty plate. "Did you eat enough?"

"Yeah."

He jerked his chin toward the door. "Let's get the healers to take a quick look and reapply the numbing cream. The rain should be dying down by now."

Eva thanked the cooks for the meal, then followed Jacob through the corridor. It was a point of pride that she had no idea where the infirmary was—which meant she'd never needed it.

The base infirmary, though? She could find that place with her eyes closed. The healers there knew her by name and joked about her being a regular.

This infirmary stood apart from the barracks—a steepled building that reminded her faintly of a church. A large greenhouse was attached to one side, no doubt filled with all the plants used in their infamous bitter concoctions.

The visit was mercifully quick. A healer changed her dressings and wrapped her arm tightly to minimize movement during the flight. A warm, buttery sensation spread from her shoulder down her arm and across her back as the numbing cream took effect. By the time they reached the dragons, the constant throb had dulled into a distant hum.

Arkon lowered his belly to the earth in a crouch, while Glade, ever considerate, raised a staircase of stone and soil. Her boots slipped once on the muddy steps, but she caught herself before faceplanting like an inept trainee. Still, it was already a blow to her pride having to use stairs just to get into the saddle.

"*You are injured,*" Arkon said. "*There is nothing to be ashamed of.*"

"*I shouldn't have gotten injured in the first place.*"

She should've stopped Darius. She should've watched his head roll this morning.

Jacob settled into the saddle behind her, leaning forward to grab the handles. She cast one final glance back at the castle, wishing it was Grayson behind her instead—his strong arms wrapped around her waist.

With Jacob, she felt like a helpless child needing her big brother's help to ride. But with Grayson? He made her feel untouchable. And she could really use a bit of that magic today.

He'll find him.

If anyone could track Darius down, it was Grayson.

She faced forward, gripping the handle with her good hand and squeezing her thighs around the saddle—especially now that Jacob was using the stirrups.

She shut her eyes, tried to summon the feeling of Grayson's arms, his steady breath at her neck.

But instead, she still felt the ghost of Leo's stubble on her cheek.

Gods. How much trouble have I gotten myself into?

CHAPTER 24
FAMILY TIES

The woods stirred with life beneath the canopy. Sunlight filtered through a lattice of bare branches and budding leaves, casting shifting patterns across the damp forest floor. Patches of frost lingered in shadowed hollows, shrinking beneath the growing warmth, while moss and new shoots pushed up through the thawing earth. The air carried a fresh, earthy scent—loam and bark, with a hint of decomposition.

Birdsong threaded through the trees, while small creatures darted through brambles and undergrowth just beginning to unfurl. Young ferns curled in on themselves, and the first wildflowers—white and yellow—swayed gently in the breeze.

It couldn't be a more perfect day.

For hunting.

And to be named Crowned Prince of Estrus.

Dex halted in the middle of the woods, in a patch of sunlight and tipped his head back to embrace its warmth.

Today Father called him and Darius into his office. Dex is to be King—and Darius his Shadow.

About damn time.

For years, he knew that his father would decide who would take the crown from him one day. For years, he showed Father he could be cruel and ruthless and willing to make sacrifices for the greater good. He honed his mind and body, endured pain and loss.

All for this day.

To be the next King of Estrus.

"Keep your chin up like that any longer and you're going to have your throat slit open," Darius's voice cut through his thoughts.

Dex immediately snapped his head back down, hand automatically diving for his broadsword. He tossed a glare at his older brother. "Is that why you brought me out here, Dari? Not to congratulate your younger brother—but to kill me and take the crown for yourself?"

Something dark and twisted roiled beneath those obsidian eyes, but he only smiled, flashing a set of straight white teeth. "Just offering you some sage advice. That's my job as your big brother, you know."

Dex knew better than to believe anything Darius said when he smiled. Especially after Father chose him to be his heir, not Darius, the oldest, technically the most qualified.

Technically.

Darius might have been in this world longer than Dex, had more time to train and study—but Dex showed results. While being strong and callous were necessary to reign, there wasn't always a place for cruelty. Something Darius failed to understand.

The court required smoother words and a silver tongue. Fear persuaded them to obey, but respect earned loyalty—and more importantly cooperation.

Fear led to revolts, but as long as they kept their nobles fat and happy, they could do whatever the fuck they wanted to the commoners. Fear was necessary in the lower classes. Fear kept them working. Fear kept them in line. Fear kept their kingdom running.

Dex turned away from him and kept walking. Darius had brought him out here to hunt. To celebrate. So they damn well were going to hunt.

Their prey had left easy tracks to follow—not a challenging hunt, unlike some of their prey. Some of them covered up their tracks. Others made new fake tracks.

This one left broken branches, crushed ferns, and trail of blood Dex could have followed blindfolded.

Just by looking at the prey, he knew the hunt wouldn't last long, so they give them a particularly long head start. Perhaps they thought the princes were being merciful and were letting them go.

Darius fell into step beside him, his footfalls as silent as Dex's on the forest floor. "So, what's our plan?"

Dex's eyes narrowed on nothing in particular ahead of them. He wasn't talking about their hunt.

"I have a list of people who need to disappear. As soon as the crown touches my head, I want them gone—and their families and friends. The world will never know they existed."

"Done."

A grin pulled at the corner of Dex's mouth. He'd never been quite able to master the perfect smile like Darius could, as if his soul wouldn't allow him to feel pure contentment. As it was trained to do.

Contentment led to complacency and complacency led to his demise.

Even when Father declared him his heir this morning, Dex accepted it with a nod and a solemn oath. His heart didn't skip. His chest didn't swell... There was nothing.

But this was what he wanted. To be King.

"What of Dravyn?"

Dex's body jerked at Darius's cutting words, but showed no emotion on his face. Better to remain impassive when it came to Dravyn.

"What of him?" Dex asked.

"He's weak. Insufferable. An embarrassment to our name. He needs to go."

"I have plans for him," he answered vaguely. "He has his uses."

Darius snorted. "Like wasting the air we breathe and the food we eat."

Another reason why Dex was chosen to be the heir over Darius. Darius saw everyone at face value. Dex knew there was always more beneath the surface.

Dex's grip tightened around his blade. "Leave him be."

Darius's jaw clenched so tight Dex heard a molar pop, but he said nothing against him.

Their trail was getting warmer. The blood hadn't dried on the leaves they passed. Dex held the delicate budding leaf between his fingers. The blood was cold, but still fresh.

His eyes raked in the woods with well-practiced accuracy.

There. Up ahead. The faintest flicker of movement.

Darius caught on immediately, eyes honing in on their prey.

Silently, they stalked through the woods. They didn't need to speak to know the plan; they had hunted countless times before. They were a unit. One being. As they were trained to be since birth.

They had always known they would rule together, one in the light, the other in shadow, but it wasn't until today when they were told which role they would be given—

Snap!

Dex had been so lost in his thoughts he'd embarrassingly stepped on a twig.

Darius tossed him a reprimanding glare, while their prey ahead gasped, head whipping around like a startled deer.

Dex mentally cursed himself for the slip up and drew a throwing knife from the sheathe on his chest.

Seeming to sense the eminent danger, their prey darted away.

With the flick of his wrist, Dex threw the knife. It embedded itself into the prey's back. Crying out, he toppled over.

Darius moved first, rushing to finish the kill. That was his favourite part of the hunt. Dex preferred the challenge of tracking and catching their prey, while Darius preferred the satisfying end.

Dex knew Darius was on him when the screams started. Dex strolled through the woods, in no rush to catch up to them.

By the time he reached them, blood saturated the ground and a mangled corpse lay at Darius's feet. He'd gone with severing today. Some days it was bone breaking. Others flaying. Once it was cutting, but that had gotten messy and took too long. He saved that particular treasure for the dungeons.

Darius grinned, eyes shining bright under the sun-lit canopy. His hands were drenched up to his forearms in the young man's lifeblood.

Dex looked down at the corpse. He was young. A little older than Dex, fit, eyes once brimming with intellect. A challenge, Dex had thought.

But no.

In the end, they were all the same.

No one matched the Slayer of Souls.

"Let this mark the day," Darius said, raising his knife to Dex. Not threatening, a gesture. "You and me, Dex—together, we're going to rule the world."

Grayson peered up at the sky for what felt like the hundredth time today, catching Eran's azure scales glistening in the sunlight. After days of rain, they were finally given a day of reprieve. Condensation rolled off the tiled roofs of Lexxis, heated by all of the factories in the industrious city. Soot clung to the brownstone walls of the buildings they passed by. Hooves *clipped* and *clopped* along the flagstone streets, sidewalks packed with people. Too many people.

For two days, he and Anna had combed the streets, searching every alleyway, brothel, or tavern—anywhere Darius could hide. But the options were many and the city was vast. Even with sixteen teams of two scouring the streets, they had only covered a sliver of the city.

While his heart was steady and strong, his stomach was a roiling sea of acid. Every minute that passed without any sign of him was another minute he had to slip through their fingers. Hargin only afforded them five days to search for him then wanted them to return to Dragon Canyon and let the Guard continue the search. A fool's errand by then. If they couldn't find Darius in five days, there would be no finding him.

"*No sign of him yet*," Eran informed him. He was flying over the city, keeping watch of the teams. Watching for any change in pattern that might indicate a chase.

Grayson's fists trembled at his sides, the urge to punch something—or someone—rising up alongside the monster slipping through his defenses. It was easier to resort to violence. Pain, his or someone's else, eased the troubles in his mind. Pain was a blissful distraction. Pain brought him results. If he was still Dex, he would have found Darius by now. As soon as word of Prince Deximus's arrival spread through the streets, information was given to him freely—lest they wanted to face the consequences of a woefully dissatisfied prince.

Here, the people had nothing to fear, didn't feel urgency.

"*Which is a good thing*," Eran reminded him. "*These people are free to live their lives without judgement.*"

For the first time since arriving in Aboria almost four years ago, Grayson wasn't sure it *was* a good thing.

Anna pivoted towards the next establishment on their list: a brothel. A sour taste coated his tongue as he entered behind her. His face slid into a firm mask, despite how badly his nose wanted to crinkle at the typical scent of sex and alcohol, mixed with the sweet aroma of Lustre, a euphoric drug popular in brothels.

Anna approached the desk sitting at the base of a grand, winding staircase, ignoring the hungry eyes of a scantily clad man and woman watching her from the railing above. Even in her dragon scale armour, she had an innate talent of drawing everyone's eyes to her. She could wear a paper bag and she'd still be the centre of attention. Fine by Grayson. It meant nobody was looking at him.

He kept his hands loosely at his sides, fingers grazing over the hilts of his blades. These people were too high or horny to think about attacking a pair of Dragon Knights, but that didn't stop the unease trickling down his back. Last time he was in a brothel, he woke up with a knife in his side, a shitty night that ended with a sword being shoved into his chest.

He rubbed his sternum from the phantom pain that had haunted him to this day.

Anna leaned an elbow on the counter where a scraggly young boy, not older than twelve, sat awkwardly a stool taller than him. It wasn't uncommon for orphans to find work in these parts. The Head Lady here at least had the decency to make him work the desk and not the beds. "Have you seen anyone suspicious come through here lately?"

The boy looked at her through his blonde bangs, scowling doubtfully at her with the bluest eyes Grayson had ever seen. "Lady, you do *know* what goes on here, don't you?"

She rolled her eyes, tossing Grayson an impatient look over her shoulder. Everywhere they went, the seedier places seemed to think Anna was ignorant of the less than reputable on-goings in their establishments. Grayson would have laughed if it were any other week, however he did find himself hiding a smirk. "Of course I do." She waved an indignant hand towards Grayson. "Have you seen anyone who looks like him come through those doors?"

Grayson's skin crawled at the heinous reminder that he shared blood with the man they were hunting. It was better for everyone if they didn't go around the city with a wanted flyer with Darius's name plastered all over it, or there would be panic in the streets that one of Aboria's most hated war criminals was out on the loose. Their looks, unfortunately, ran deep in the family. They all shared the same nose and jaw, which made comparing them just as easy. Dravyn was the only one who bore their mother's eyes.

The boy's eyes ran over Grayson with an air of disinterest. "Maybe."

Knowing this was likely a waste of time but not willing to risk losing any leads, Grayson fished a gold coin from his pouch and slid it across the counter to the boy. His blue eyes went round on the coin, jaw slackening. Greedily, he reached for it, but Grayson pulled it out of reach at the last second.

"Ah! Only useful information will earn you a gold."

The boy studied Grayson more closely, particularly his eyes. His lips pursed in thought. "I did see a man with eyes like yours swipe a scarf the day before yesterday. Didn't blame him for wanting to hide the awful gash on his face so I didn't report it..."

Sounded like Darius. He hadn't left the dungeon unscathed. A wound like that was distinguishable and memorable. Exactly something a man on the run would want to hide.

The boy's eyes went wide with fear, gaze bouncing between him and Anna. "I—I'm not in any trouble, am I? Lady Leana will have my head!"

Grayson slid the coin his way again, this time letting him snatch it off the counter and pocket it before the Dragon Knight could change his mind. "No trouble. Where did you see the man go?"

"Up Dowrey Street. Looked like they were heading towards the Sinking Ship."

That tavern was on their list of businesses to investigate.

Grayson rewarded the boy with another gold before walking away. Anna looked down at his pouch, eyebrows popping into her hairline. "Exactly how many gold coins do you have in there and why haven't you been spending that wealth on the squad?"

Shaking his head, Grayson strapped the pouch on the back of his belt and let his mithril cloak drape over his back to conceal it. "I *have* spent it on the squad."

Crossing her arms, Anna shouldered the door open. "*When?*"

"Recently," he answered vaguely. She didn't need to know he'd used it to buy one of their squad members cupcakes. "Let's get moving. The sooner we kill Darius, the sooner we can return to Dragon Canyon."

He'd refused to leave the castle until he knew Eva was on her way back to the base. His biggest fear was that she'd insist on being a part of the hunt, regardless of her injuries. As much as he wanted her at his side, where he could keep an eye on her and keep the fire ants burning through his veins at bay, she was safer in Dragon Canyon. Darius couldn't reach her there—not as long as Grayson was hunting him—and Sylus's assassins would have to go through thousands of Knights and dragons to get to her. One of them being her powerful and protective Dragon Bound.

Anna pulled him to a stop, landing him with a glare that stalled his breath. "Our orders are to bring him in, Gray. Not kill him."

"Darius is dying today." Not a request. He did it the Aborians' way and it got Eva hurt. Now they were doing things his way. If they wanted to punish him for doing them a favour, they could try.

She studied him carefully, a wary edge in her gaze as she took in the composed facade he maintained at all times. If Renkon had seen a glimmer of the bloodlust raging inside of him, he wouldn't have allowed him to roam his streets. He locked down any and all emotions Anna might use against him. Only she knew how to reign him back in, but he didn't want to be reigned in until Darius was dead.

After weighing her options, she nodded, a firm line on her lips. "He dies today. But we keep Keyon alive. We need to bring *someone* back to interrogate."

"Agreed."

His eyes flickered to the narrow street branching off Dowrey Street. The Sinking Ship was only a few feet away. Anticipation welled in his extremities. They were so close, he could almost taste Darius's blood on his blade. He could visualise the light fading from his brother's eyes as he pierced his heart. It had been years since he felt the satisfaction of ending a life. Years since he'd longed to kill someone as violently as he wanted to kill Darius.

Fingers grazing on the hilts of his blades, Grayson marched for the tavern. Anna was right at his side, wearing a mask of steel and resolve. Her usual braid was pinned around her scalp today, preventing anyone from using her long, crimson hair to their advantage. She was one of the few warriors he didn't need to keep an eye on. She could hold her own—and then some—and wouldn't get in his way.

He opened the tavern door, gaze darting from one patron to the next. There weren't many customers at this time of day. A group sitting around a booth and two people at the bar. The barkeep was in the middle of wiping down a round table near the centre. He paused, eyes narrowing on Grayson in confusion. And recognition. It was gone in a blink, but it was all Grayson needed.

When he turned back for the bar, Grayson followed on his heels, fingers itching to unsheathe a knife. He grabbed the man's shoulder and forced him to face him, shoving him back against the bar. "You've seen someone who looks like me."

"Everyone out," Anna commanded in that low authoritative voice eerily similar to her mother's.

Nobody questioned the Dragon Knight uniforms. Chairs scraped against the floorboards and leather creaked as the patrons left without a word.

The barkeep dropped the cleaning rag and held his hands up in surrender, body trembling beneath Grayson's grasp. "L—look, I don't want any trouble! Whatever he did, I had no part in it!"

"Which room?"

"Fourth floor, first one on the right—but they're gone. They left just before sunrise."

He's gone.

Grayson loosened his grip and took a step back. They were too late. The acid in his stomach climbed up his throat. Clenching his teeth, he swallowed it down and began to pace to keep his body busy, to temper the rage churning inside him.

"Where did they go?" Anna continued the interrogation.

The man shook his head wildly. "I—I don't know! They mentioned something about a ship leaving in two weeks time. I didn't hear which port they planned to use or where the ship would take them."

Grayson halted, snapping his head toward the barkeep. Face pudgy and sweaty, eyes too round to be anything but fearful. He was telling the truth.

Estrus. Darius was going back home. Shocking considering what Sylus would do to him for disobeying—then failing—him. The only reason he would go back and suffer the consequences was if he had a plan and was confident he could talk his way out of his punishment.

A sinking feeling filled his gut. It would have to be a fucking good plan.

Ignoring the other rudimentary questions Anna had for the barkeep, Grayson climbed the stairs to the fourth floor and entered the first door on the right.

Spotless. Like no one had lived here for the past few days. The sheets were tucked into the mattresses. Not even a crumb left on the table. Nothing forgotten in the bathroom.

He opened the dresser drawers, looking for *something* that might confirm Darius was here and which port they planned to use of the hundreds lining the Aborian coast. He wasn't stupid enough to use a port in the north east, the most likely ports as they were the closest to Estrus and would cut travel time in half for them. No, he'd take the extended time on the boat in order to avoid risk getting caught at the port. Finding him between Lexxis and the coast would be impossible. Their best shot would be to have Guards watch every single port.

Furious, he wrenched the last drawer open—and blinked, the anger subsiding for the moment. A letter.

Dex,

I've had some time to think while I've been cooped up in this room. I know why you love this kingdom so damned much. It isn't the good food, the easily malleable people, not even the plethora of rich resources easily accessible at your fingertips.

No. You've fallen in love.

The storm dragon rider has a freckle on her left breast. Did you know that?

This pathetic, deluded fantasy of yours won't last long. Love is for the weak. You are not weak. But I'm curious how far you would go to protect her.

I want my brother back. Give him back to me or she'll suffer every day for the rest of her life.

Your brother dearest,

Darius

Grayson's hands shook as he read the letter over and over and over again. Disbelief— *shock*—coursed through his veins, rooting him in place.

Love.

Was that what the bubbly warmth he felt in Eva's presence was? This drive to protect her because living in a world without her was too dark and bleak to be a world worth living in—*that* was love?

"Yes," Eran answered simply.

"Why didn't you tell me?"

"You would have denied yourself one of life's greatest treasures."

"Of course I fucking would have. Only the weak fall in love."

Even if he had been stupid enough to give his enemies a fast track to destroy him, he didn't deserve to love. To be loved. Not after everything he'd done in Estrus.

"Which is it: is it for the weak or do you not deserve it?"

With a roar tearing out of his throat, Grayson grabbed the nearest thing to him—the dresser—and tipped it over. The resounding crash wasn't enough to sate his need to destroy. He whirled for the table and hurled it against the wall, watching the splinters crumble to the floor, as helpless as he felt against the warring emotions within him.

His fury consumed him. Darius was free because of him. The bastard only needed one look to know Grayson's true feelings for Eva, while it took him months to understand what they meant. If he'd pushed himself harder that night, Darius would have never found out about that blasted freckle and Eva wouldn't have almost lost her life. He *hated* Darius for coming back into his life after he had successfully rid himself of his past for three years. Hated him for trying to tear apart the life he had built here, for trying to take Eva away and threatening to use her against him—

But amongst all the rage and hate, there was a glimmer of hope—and something much more tender and whole. Somehow, he'd dug deep within himself without even knowing and found the capacity to *love*. Him. The Slayer of Souls. A man whose name still brought fear to the people of Estrus. In love.

How did this happen to me?

"Gray?"

He snapped his head towards the door where Anna stood, sword at the ready. Her steel eyes landed on the crumpled letter on the floor. He crossed the room, hands still shaking, and swiped it.

"What is it?" She gestured to the paper.

He tucked it in his back pocket. It wasn't important to the mission. "Nothing."

Her eyes narrowed suspiciously then she held her hand out expectantly. "Give it to me, Gray."

"No." The less people who knew about his feelings, the better it would be for everyone. Safer for Eva in particular.

He slipped past her, but she caught his arm. Their gazes locked, steel on steel. "What's in the letter, Gray? It's from Darius, isn't it?"

He ground his jaw, refusing to give away the turmoil within. "It's... personal."

Frowning, she released his arm, opting to study his features more closely. "What does he want?"

"For me to suffer."

CHAPTER 25
BLURRED LINES

The words of the old dusty tome were beginning to blur the longer Eva stared at it.

Squeezing her eyes shut, she sat back in the leather chair in the library, her second home since returning to Dragon Canyon. There wasn't much else she could do with her injury—which was worse after flying for eight hours.

The trip had nearly been the end of her. Or her arm at the very least.

The healers in the infirmary blew a gasket when they saw the angry, throbbing mess her shoulder had become. Every morning she went to them to have her dressings rewrapped and for new ointment applied. The healing process was slow and painful, leaving her lying awake in her very empty room.

With no Annaliese to talk to, she was left to think about how horribly wrong the night at Kain Castle had gone. Whenever she closed her eyes, in the darkness of her room, she saw those evil obsidian eyes looking back at her, mercilessly hungry to claim her body and power. Her skin went cold and clammy whenever she remembered his tongue lapping her ear. Usually Anna's snores lulled her back to sleep when she had a nightmare, the sound reminding her that she was safe, in the heart of Dragon Canyon, surrounded by well trained warriors. With a partner that could kick ass and take names better than any of them.

While Anna was away in Lexxis looking for the very man who kept her up at night, Eva found herself taking refuge in the dragons' den, in the safety of Arkon's claws. When Jacob found her in the morning the first time she'd slept with him, he offered up Grayson's bed while he was in Lexxis. As tempting as it was, it felt wrong to take his bed without his permission, even if the familiar scent of leather and steel was just as comforting as Arkon's presence.

Blowing out a weary breath, Eva glanced at the doorway, where Sergeant Ballos stood guard, keeping an eye on anything that moved within the library. Which wasn't much. Knights rarely came here, preferring to spar, run through the White Woods, or practice aerials. There was a sole librarian and a single helper to put books away, mostly the books Eva borrowed.

Lieutenant Kramer was on the other side of the door, ensuring no one unauthorised entered the library. Both were ordered to be Eva's protection detail after Hargin heard about the assassins' attempt on her life. Normally Eva would have protested, but with her injury... she was basically useless. Against the healers' suggestions, she still practiced Grayson's routine every morning and every night to the best of her ability. There were some positions she just couldn't do with her arm strapped to her side, but she still pushed her body as far as it would go, determined to become a part of the routine. When she finished with the routine, she moved on to Anna's with her daggers (well, *dagger*).

Never again would she be a victim.

After her training in the morning, she came here and took a nose dive into the many tomes collecting dust in the library. Knowing her background, the librarian provided her a stack of books of various topics she might find interesting. She went through two small books yesterday covering mindfulness on the battlefield, and a full encyclopedia of monster taxonomy.

Eva found herself drawn to the books with magic. If she wasn't training with Sasha, she might as well learn something about her Bond with Arkon until she could go back to the Desert Lands.

Magic had quite a fascinating history, revolving around the five ancient elements from which dragons drew their power. Each was a gift from the gods: Val, God of War, bestowed fire to fend off winter's chill; Lorelus, God of Vitality, granted water to nourish the land; Zyphril, Goddess of Death, sent wind to guide their sails; Ebis, God of Chaos and Change, unleashed lightning to bring disorder and ruin; and Asturias, Goddess of Gods, shaped the earth itself, forming the foundation of Astrida.

But there was once a time where the world was void of magic, where humans were free to grow without fear of monsters. They relied on the gods to protect them and nurture them.

Until one day, the gods began to argue with one another, which resulted in a battle that fused the world with magic, referred to as the Shattering. What the gods fought over or how it affected the humans living at the time was glossed over in the text she was reading. This book was more interested in the effects magic had on the world currently.

The amount of magic residing in a creature determined the strength of its abilities. Next to Leviathans, ancient slumbering beasts born during the Shattering, dragons possessed the most magic. The reason why Eva could now use Arkon's magic, and why their souls were intertwined, was because dragons were so magically dense that even their tears possessed magic.

When Eva absorbed his tears, she absorbed his magic. Her powers were limited because her untrained body could only use so much, but given time and dedication, Sasha promised her the magic inside of her would grow and become more powerful. One day she wouldn't need an outside source like a storm or her gloves, her own body would be the source. Then, her power would be unlimited.

That was the power Sylus feared and Darius coveted.

Feeling a migraine coming on from all the reading, Eva put the book down, eyes drifting to the crackling flames in the fireplace dancing in the seating area. The beautiful mantel stretched up to the top of the tower, an intricate carving of a squad in formation mid-flight.

Hearing footsteps approaching, Eva turned in her seat, hoping Jacob had *finally* gotten out of his meeting. It was his turn to report the events at Kain Castle, in a long line of Dragon Knights who had also attended.

"Nice of you to finally—" The rest of her words got caught in her throat when she beheld an entirely different man.

His dark auburn hair was all over the place, blown by the vicious winds on a dragon's back. Somehow, Leo gotten his hands on a dragon scale jacket, which seemed to fit him far better than anything Eva tried on here, but his trousers were a fine cotton, matching the long sleeved shirt he wore underneath. Those lapis eyes dazzled as he took her in, narrowing on the sling.

Heart racing, she closed the gap between them anxiously, taking one of Leo's hands. "Did they get him?"

The charming smile cracked. "No. They're still looking for him." Her stomach churned. If they hadn't caught him after five days, they was no chance of catching him now. "You asked me to tell you how the interrogation went, so here I am."

A frown pulled on her brow. Visiting wasn't exactly what she had in mind when she asked him to keep her in the loop. "You could have sent a letter."

"And miss out on seeing your beautiful face?" He scoffed a laugh, then when she didn't laugh with him, his smile completely fell flat. "You don't seem very happy to see me, love."

She winced, instantly regretful. "Oh. No. It's not that... I was just hoping they might have found him." She shook off her disappointment. It wasn't his fault they hadn't caught Darius. After being cooped up in the base with little to do but read, she was grateful to see a familiar friendly face. "Anyway, how did you get here?"

He tugged on his scale jacket, rolling his shoulders back, and tilting his head up proudly. "I flew."

"You... *flew*?" The man who complained about the two hour ride from Riverwood flew across Aboria to see her? She wasn't sure if she should be impressed or mad that he would make such a trip for her. "How did you manage that?"

"Believe it or not, several Dragon Knights owe me a favour. I called them in, but unfortunately didn't get a choice in what time we left." He rubbed the back of his wind blown hair, the weight of his exhaustion hanging on his shoulders. If he was here at this hour, they must have left at two in the morning. "You guys will work at any hour of the day, won't you?"

"Any hour we're needed," she confirmed proudly.

Smile returning, he slipped past her and studied her books. "I didn't take you for a bookworm." He lifted the book she'd been reading and flipped it back and forth in his hands, a curious look in his eyes. "I have to say, I am wholly disappointed that of the thousands of books you have access to, you pick the dullest."

Giggling, Eva gestured back to Sergeant Ballos, who was dutifully standing by the door. She much preferred the library than Lieutenant Kramer did, but her taste in books didn't align with Eva's. If her table was stacked with romance novels, the Knight would have joined her by the fire. "You'd probably have a lot to talk about with Ballos. She's all about the romance novels."

The Sergeant in question squeaked, a red hue climbing up her cheeks, visible even in the dark room. Eva would have found her reaction strange if she hadn't remembered that the man in front of her was *the* Prince Leonidas Kain. Ladies man to some, a loyal friend to others, and a dedicated prince to all. Being this close to him was considered an honour.

And Eva just offered him up to the Dragon Knight as casually as she'd share her meal.

Leo cast a brief satisfied smirk her way before turning his full attention on Eva. "As much as I'd love to learn more about my noble Dragon Knights, I didn't fly all the way here for them." The heat in his eyes told her exactly who he came here for, and her face went *hot*.

"Would you like a tour?" she blurted. Suddenly, the library was too small to be alone with him.

He flashed her a charming smile. "I'd be delighted."

"Great." She hurried past him for the door. Sergeant Ballos opened it for them, bowing as Leo went by. He ignored the gesture, gaze yet again wondering down to Eva's sling as they strode down the hallway. She intended to take him down to the dragon dens then work their way up from there.

Her escort followed silently behind them.

"How's your shoulder doing? It doesn't look any better than when you left the castle."

She shrugged her good shoulder. "It's a slow recovery. The healers do what they can for me."

"But you have water dragons. Can't they fix you?"

"They can, but Commander Hargin deemed it fitting for me to sit with my wounds for a few days as punishment for putting myself unnecessarily at risk. When Eran and Grayson return later today or tomorrow, they're allowed to heal me." She wasn't sure what she was more excited for: to finally get rid of this sling or to see Grayson and feel his strength again. Eva slid Leo a look when they reached the stairs. More Knights stopped to bow to him before continuing along their way. "Commander Hargin *does* know you're here, right?"

Somehow, Eva doubted the Commander would have cleared a day trip for the Prince of Aboria. Especially with assassins after Eva and Darius still running free.

Leo scratched the back of his head, eyes aloof. "She's probably aware of it *now*." He gestured to the hallway full of Dragon Knights whispering behind them.

Eva internally groaned. Commander Hargin was already furious with her for abandoning Grayson to "chase the man who invaded Aboria to abduct her" when she found out about Eva's unauthorised visitor, she was going to have to clean the dragons' dens spotlessly to make up for it.

"Please tell me your father knows where you are."

Leo took her free hand and tucked into the crook of his elbow as they descended the stairs, patting the top of her palm. "You worry too much about me, love. I can take care of myself."

His evasive answer was enough for her to know she was going to be in *a lot* of trouble later. This also wasn't the first time he'd assured her he could take care of himself.

"Where is this coming from?"

He jolted, nearly missing a step. "I don't know what you mean."

"So, you're going to lie to me?"

"No. I would never lie to you. I respect you far too much to believe I could get away with it." He sighed, shoulders sagging. His eyes seemed to dim as a cloud hung over him. "I may have done something foolish."

Eva's spine stiffened, bracing for the blow. "What did you do?"

He chewed on the inside of his cheek, clearly reluctant to share this supposedly foolish thing.

"I won't judge," she vowed, wondering how many people in his life had actually promised something like that to him. Or how many false promises he'd been given. She was fortunate to have surrounded herself with people who didn't judge her for who she was and what she did—a prince didn't get to choose who he associated himself with.

He turned a soft, tender smile her way, squeezing her hand. "I know you won't. I love that about you. No secrets, ulterior motives, or agendas. Just...

you." He cleared his throat. "Anyway, I went down to visit Darius while we still had him in the dungeon."

Eva's heart froze over. "*Why* would you do that?"

He rolled his eyes at her tone. "The smug bastard was so proud of the destruction he ensued in my kingdom. Of the lives he'd taken, families he had ruined. For what he did to you and Jacob. I wanted to be the one to tell him that he was going to die alone. No one was coming to help him because nobody cared about him..." He dipped his head. "But now I look like the fool. He escaped and I fear they won't be able to find him before he returns to Estrus."

"Do you think he'll go back to Estrus?" The relief that bloomed in her chest knowing he'd be leaving the kingdom left an unsettling feeling in her stomach. She hated that she was afraid of him.

Leo nodded solemnly. "It's his only option. He has nothing here. No resources. No men. You're safe from him for now. It'll give you enough time to train and kick his ass next time."

Next time she wouldn't make the mistake of letting him live.

"So, this visit... What happened?"

His top lip curled up in a very unprincely manner. "I let him get under my skin. I shouldn't have, but I did, and I can't help but envy him. Slightly. His father lets him travel across the sea and invade a kingdom, while mine won't let me step five feet out of the castle without the Royal Guard breathing down my neck. His father didn't come to rescue him, because he had absolute faith that his son could get himself out of being executed. I bet Sylus doesn't care who he'll take as Queen when he claims the throne either."

They reached the bottom of the winding staircase. Their footsteps echoed against the cavernous walls. Even with another hallway to traverse, Eva could hear the dragons baying, their scales and claws scraping against stone. Leather crackled in the steady breeze whistling through the lower half of the base.

She looked up at him, saw the frustration twisting at his face. Suddenly, his visits made sense. "So you thought by coming out here by yourself you would prove to your father, and others, that you don't need to be coddled."

He nodded. "I'm twenty-seven. A prince! I should be allowed to make my own decisions—and mistakes, if it comes to that."

"Then I'll stop bringing it up," she decided. "I'll let you make all the stupid mistakes you want. But if you do need saving, I'll be there." She bumped his side, entirely forgetting about her injury and hissed when pain lanced through her shoulder and down her arm. "Gah!"

Leo hopped away, afraid to hurt her further, then watched her closely while she composed herself. "Are you sure you should be walking around?

Don't put yourself out on my account, love. There will be other times for a tour."

She highly doubted that if Commander Hargin had anything to say about it.

"No. No." She stole a deep breath, pushing the persistent throb to the back of her mind where she could forget all about it and continue the tour. "I'm fine. My shoulder is shot, not my legs."

He looked unconvinced, eyebrows knitted together, teeth gnashing at the bottom right corner of his mouth. "If you promise me we'll stop when it becomes too much, we can keep going."

Rolling her eyes, she marched past him for the whistling tunnel. "I promise. Now, come on. You can't come to Dragon Canyon and not see its inhabitants in their natural habitat."

Eagerly, Leo followed closely behind her, taking in the rough walls, so different from the smooth carved-out ones above, and listening attentively to the dragons ahead. When the walls of the tunnel gave way to the cavern, revealing a seemingly endless cave of dragons, sleeping, sunning, or grooming, his jaw slackened. His head whipped from one dragon to the next as they walked down the vague pathway trailing down the center, just as fascinated by their colours as she was when she first arrived at the base.

They visited Arkon for a bit. The dragon's approval of Leo's presence radiated down their Bond in big, obnoxious waves, making it hard to pay attention to their conversation—or anything, really. Some things were near impossible to shield from each other, but Eva knew for a fact this was not one of them.

Eva left the dens in a sour mood, but did her best to hide it as she took him to the stables, mess hall, and training rooms. Leo would not see the officers' offices this visit. She liked her head where it was, thank you very much.

They explored the plateau above the base, the path winding through the canyon towards the White Woods, then took a quick peek at Big Bertha. While Sergeant Ballos remained silent, suddenly shy, Lieutenant Kramer, the older and more experienced Knight, added a few tid bits to fill in the gaps of Eva's tour.

Leo paled at the sight of the giant training gauntlet all Knights must pass before riding their dragons.

"By Lorelus, I thought Captain Quades's training was brutal." An abrupt laugh burst from his lips. "Poor Jacob must have had a hard time. You and Anna could handle this no problem. Jake? I love him dearly, but the man has two left feet."

She giggled. "He really does. He works harder here than anyone else on the base."

His smile remained, but whimsy filled his eyes. "I believe it. He's a good man, your brother."

"I know. I'm lucky to have him. It's a shame he couldn't join us today." For most of the week, he had kept her company, which she loved every minute of, but today he got pulled into a debrief meeting. The higher ups were interviewing every Knight that was present during the attack on Kain Castle, getting each of their statements and getting to the bottom of what actually happened. Eva was one of the first, having seen the most when Darius was freed in the dungeon.

"Hmm. A shame." Leo didn't sound entirely genuine, but when she saw the heat back in his eyes as he regarded her in the late afternoon sun, she could take a guess as to where his mind had wondered to. "What's next on the tour?"

She went through her mental list of places to take him, checking off every single one except for the last. "I have one more stop in mind. You'll like it, I think."

She led him back inside, curious what he would think of their living conditions. After seeing the rooms in the castle, she imagined he would be horribly surprised.

They stopped outside her room, her hand braced on the handle. "This is it. The last stop then I think we should grab some dinner from the mess hall and find you a place to stay for the night."

She opened the door, but let Leo be the first one inside. Their dutiful escort remained outside, sharing a look Eva didn't see.

Leo's eyes fell on the beds first and the five foot gap in between them. "Anna told me Dragon Knights had to share a room with their partner... but this was not I imagined."

He turned, facing the couch and table in their small seating area, then crossed the room for the bathroom. When he exited, he looked around seemingly for more.

Eva laughed. "What are you looking for?"

"Where's the study? The breakfast parlour? How do you entertain guests??"

She ran her hand over the back of the couch. "We usually sit around the table. I save the chairs for guests and sit on the rug." Horror struck his face. "It's a comfy rug," she assured him. When his expression didn't change, she rolled her eyes. "Leo, it's not that bad."

"Not that bad?" he repeated, appalled. He shook his head indignantly. "I'm talking to Commander Hargin after dinner. You are Aboria's hero, the storm dragon rider—you deserve so much more than a tiny bed and a shelf to your name."

Before he got any more ideas of changing her living conditions, she crossed the room and poked his chest. "Don't meddle with my room. I'm perfectly happy with what I have. If I find out you've talked to Commander Hargin behind my back, you'll find out the shocking power of my gloves."

Smirking, his hands fell around her waist, tugging her closer to him. "I love it when you talk dirty to me." A blush invaded her face. She hadn't thought what she said was dirty, but the husky edge of his voice made it sound like she'd said something absolutely filthy. "And when your face goes that shade of pink? Adorable." Those dark lapis eyes darted to her mouth—then he released her, stepping away and turning to take in the clear two halves of the room. "Don't tell me. Let me guess who's bed is whose."

Needing to calm her racing heart, Eva leaned back on the couch, tucking her free hand into the pocket of her jacket, which she had grabbed before they went outside. She didn't know what was wrong with her. But it wasn't a good sign. Things were just starting to settle between her and Grayson and she wanted to keep it that way.

He wouldn't be able to guess who's side was whose by looking at the beds. As per bunking regulations, they had the same sheets. He'd know by looking at their night stands and adjacent shelves—and drawers if he was brave enough to go through their dressers.

He gravitated towards her night stand, the stack of books, and Teddy sitting on top of them. Carefully, he picked up the raggedy stuffed bear and studied the mismatched eyes and singed fur.

Eva's heart jerked as she remembered the night Darius had invaded Brar. No amount of time would ever help her forget the awful screams she'd heard that night or the scent of burning flesh. She'd forever remember the fear in her little sister's eyes, her terrified screeches when they tore her family apart. Her father's final words still echoed through her mind at night.

A warm drop landed on her hand. She raised it to her face and found a streak on her cheek. Before she could embarrass herself, she wiped the tears away and breathed in through her nose.

"Anna is a sucker for all things cute and fluffy," he said quietly, gaze intent on the bear, "but this isn't her thing." His eyes locked with her. "This is your bed."

She barely managed a nod. "Yes." Suddenly, her mouth was as dry as the Desert Lands. "That was Erika's... my sister."

The solemn look on his face said he'd guessed as much. He set the bear down gently, respectfully, back on the pile of books. "Apologies. I shouldn't be snooping through your things."

"No. It's all right." She picked up Teddy, honestly unsure when the last time she had held him. His fur was coarse, curled at the tips. Despite how many times she'd washed him, the scent of ash still clung to him. "It's getting easier to talk about them... You know, we didn't have much growing up, but we were happy. This bear was Erika's only toy and she treasured it like it was her own baby. She had to leave it behind when we tried to run." Her fingers grazed over the haphazard stitching running the length of his muzzle. Only Anna's mindfulness training stopped her from crumbling into a complete wreck in front of the Prince of Aboria.

She sucked in a deep, steadying breath. "Jacob found it when he returned to the scene—someone had to confirm my story and he wanted to be the one to do it. I cleaned Teddy up the best I could. Taylor gave me a button, and a needle and some thread. He showed me how to clean the ash off..." She swallowed the lump forming in her throat. "It's the only thing I have to remember them by—aside from the monolith you've built. Thank you again for that. It's truly the nicest thing anyone has ever done for us."

A hard to read expression on his face, he sat down beside her, his weight dipping the mattress, and laid his hand over hers. "Eva Greene, you are unlike any woman I have ever met."

She pinned him with a dry stare.

How original.

He shook his head at her. "No. Don't give me that look. Do you have any idea how many women I know who would have let a loss like you experienced destroy them? They would have given up without a second thought. But not you. You're strong, always looking to the future. I love that. You're... incredible." His hand tightened around hers, heat seeping into her skin, which blossomed into something much hotter and voracious as it spread to the rest of her body. His eyes, dark with something unreadable, held hers captive.

She should pull away. A man didn't look at a woman like that without wanting more than just a pleasant conversation. If she didn't move now, she'd be stepping over the boundary she'd fought so hard to maintain.

And yet... she didn't.

When Leo leaned in, brushing the softest kiss over her lips, her breath hitched—but she didn't back away. If anything, her head tilted, granting him better access.

His fingers slid to her cheek, his touch achingly gentle as he deepened the kiss. A quiet sound built in her throat, trapped between protest and surrender. The warmth of his palm sent shivers down her spine, and when his tongue grazed along the seam of her lips, she gave in.

Her fingers fisted in his tunic, pulling him closer as she parted her lips, opening herself to him.

This is wrong. This is wrong. This is wrong. She shouldn't be doing this. Shouldn't be *enjoying* this.

But she was. He tasted of the beef broth from their lunch, rich and familiar, and the faintest hint of wine—undoubtedly from the bottle he'd convinced the chef to hand over before drinking hours. His warmth surrounded her, luring her deeper, further into the point of no return. So utterly intoxicating, he was careful, unhurried, yet encouraging. It would be so *easy* to fall into this, to let herself be carried away by everything that made him Prince Leonidas Kain.

How had she let this happen? Leo was supposed to be her friend. Nothing more. She wasn't supposed to fall for his charm. His endless teasing, those hypnotising lapis eyes—it was all just part of who he was. A flirt. A prince who could have anyone he wanted.

She wasn't supposed to fall in line with all the other women he'd beguiled.

But somehow, he'd slipped past her defenses, crept into her heart before she even realised it.

And now... now she was torn between her unequivocal attraction towards Grayson and *this*—whatever it was—with Leo.

Feeling as though she was being ripped in two, she wrenched her mouth from the prince's, pressing her forehead against his as she fought to gain some form of control over herself. "Leo..."

"Pick me," he implored, panting just as hard as she was. "I can give you the world, Eva. With you at my side, you'll never want for anything. You'll never have to suffer again. Let me shower you with riches and glory. You can have it all."

She pulled away. She didn't want to hear all of the things he could give her if she chose him. Those weren't what she cared about. It was his heart—*Grayson's* heart—that mattered.

One man who would give her the world, and one man who would burn it to ash for her.

"Leo, I..." Catching movement in the corner of her eye, she looked at the door, eyes trailing to the pool of blood sliding underneath. "Go to the bathroom and lock the door—"

With an explosion of shattered splinters, a man swathed in black and steel broke in. Their gazes met for a beat—then he darted for her, blade aimed for a killing blow.

CHAPTER 26

MONSTERS COME IN ALL SHAPES AND SIZES

It happened so fast. There was no time to think.

Eva barely twisted away in time, shoving Leo off the bed and out of her way. The assassin's blade carved through empty space where her throat had been a second ago, missing by a breath.

The assassin didn't hesitate. He came at her again, movements crisp, efficient. *Fast.*

Eva lunged for the knife under her pillow, fingers closing around the hilt just as the assassin grabbed her sling and *yanked.* A strangled scream tore from her throat as white hot agony shot through her injured arm. She swung in desperation with her left, slashing at his ribs, but he twisted, the blade barely grazing his leathers.

This was nothing like the fight on the balcony. She was caught unawares. Panic clawed at her chest like jagged glass—

Then Leo was there. A blur of movement as he slammed into the assassin from behind, sending them both toppling over the couch and crashing into the coffee table. Wood splintered beneath their weight. In a cacophony of limbs, Leo managed to get on top. His eyes searched frantically for a weapon—anything he could use.

"Shelf!" Eva cried, knowing she wouldn't be able to move fast enough to reach him in time.

Leo's eyes snapped to Anna's sword resting on the weapon shelf on the wall. He lunged, fingers closing around the hilt. He whirled back to the assassin—

A sharp *crack* echoed through the room as the assassin's elbow struck Leo's face, sending him staggering back with a shout. Blood gushed from his nose. "Fuck!"

Get your shit together, or you're both dead.

Eva took the opening. She pounced, knife arcing toward the assassin's back—

But he turned *too fast.* He caught her wrist.

She had time for a single breath before his knee slammed into her ribs.

Something *snapped*. Searing agony exploded through her side. A choked scream ripped from her throat as she collapsed onto the bed, vision going dark at the edges.

"*Focus!*" Arkon's shout reverberated through her mind like a whip, jolting her back from the brink of passing out. "*I will take the pain away. Fight!*"

No sooner had he spoken did the roaring agony raking through her body subside. She barely had time to recover before the assassin was on her again, knife gleaming as he drove it toward her gut—

She rolled, knees slamming into the hard floor, then twisted, ramming her knife into his side. Hissing, the assassin struck her with the back of his hand, putting enough space between them to rip the knife out of the unfortunately non-fatal wound.

Now he had a weapon in *both* hands.

For fuck's sake...

Too fast. Too strong.

Her knife was gone. Her breath came in short, sharp bursts. Arkon might have taken the pain away, but that didn't stop her from getting lightheaded from her injuries. Leo was on his knees, holding his face in his hands as he bled all over the living area.

The assassin kicked out, slamming her against the bedside table. Her head smacked into the side table, making her vision swim. He pressed his blade to her throat, his grip like iron.

Eva pressed herself back into the table, nearly molding into the furniture, the edges were digging into her spine so much. The cold blade kissed her skin, warming under the soothing embrace of her blood. Her fingers skittered along the bottom shelf of the nightstand—*her gloves.*

They were just inches away.

Her body screamed in protest as she swung her knee up towards her chest then kicked out, striking his wounded side. He staggered. Her fingers closed around the gloves. The assassin quickly righted himself and dove for her again.

She slammed her left hand into his chest. Power *surged* through her veins, igniting her blood as it crackled through the gloves, into him.

He barely had time to register what was happening before raw current snapped through his body. His limbs spasmed violently. His knife dropped from his fingers, clattering to the floor. The assassin collapsed, his body jerking once before going still.

Eva sucked in a ragged breath, her pulse a frantic drumbeat in her ears. As Arkon's presence slipped from her dazed mind, pain radiated through her sides with every breath. She pressed a shaking hand to her ribs, biting back a groan. *Broken.* Definitely broken.

Somewhere behind the couch, Leo groaned. "I think he broke my damn nose."

Eva exhaled sharply, rolling onto her back, her entire body trembling from pain and adrenaline. "I think he got one of my ribs."

Frantic footsteps sounded in the hallway. "Eva?" Jacob called. "*Eva!*"

She barely had the pain tolerance to hold her hand up high enough to be seen over the bed. "Here."

Her head turned to watch him from under the bed as he treaded carefully over the bodies. His feet slid on the slick pool of blood creeping towards the very nice rug at the foot of Anna's bed.

Leo staggered to his feet, holding his nose in his hands. Blood gushed through his fingers, dripping all over his likely expensive shirt and onto the living room rug Eva knew for a fact was imported from the Southern Isles.

Anna was going to *kill* her.

"*Leo?*" Jacob sucked in a deep breath and was silent for a full ten seconds before speaking again, "Val, give me strength. What the *fuck* is going on here?"

Leo stepped around the couch, passing Jacob, and held a helping hand down to Eva. "It appears I wasn't Eva's only visitor today."

Knowing it was going to hurt and mentally preparing for it, Eva took his hand and let him hoist her up to her feet. A wave of dizziness hit her, pain flaring and making it impossible to breathe. She gripped Leo's shoulder to stop herself from toppling over and focused on breathing.

Jacob's wide eyes landed on the crumpled form in the middle of her room. He studied the black attire and the mithril cloak wrapped around his shoulders. Standard Estrus garb. "An assassin? *Here*? How?"

Leo pinched the top of his nose, tipping his head back. "I'd like to know that, too."

Jacob's head snapped towards Eva. "Tell me again—what's he doing in your room?"

"*Priorities*, Jake," she growled, wincing as her ribs protested the simplest movement. "Sylus knows where to find me now."

Amongst the chaos after the attack, Leo and Eva found themselves seated in Commander Hargin's office. A cleaning team was currently going through her room, wiping any evidence of an attack—aside from the broken furniture and blood-stained rug. Every available Knight was sweeping through the base in search of any more assassins, while dragons searched the canyon. Their magic permeated in the air and set the hairs on her arms standing on end.

If there were any more assassins lurking in the shadows, they would be found soon.

Poor Leo had cotton balls shoved up his nose, nasty bruises hanging under his eyes. Being the cruel, maleficent leader she was, Commander Hargin denied him permission to visit the infirmary. The cotton balls were a courtesy because he wore a crown. Before he could get medical attention, he had to answer some of her questions.

Eva had the unfortunate position of bearing witness to the Commander tearing a strip off the Crowned Prince, lying in agonising suspense for her turn.

"What were you *thinking*, Leonidas?" she continued, sounding surprisingly more like a mother than the Commander of the Aborian Dragon Knights. Though, considering she had known him all of his life and that Anna grew up alongside him, she, of anyone, had the right to berate him. "You cannot go galivanting through the kingdom at your leisure. You have responsibilities—"

"Kira, if you'd let me explain—"

She held up a curt finger to him in warning. "No. I'm not done talking and you do not get to explain yourself. You snuck out of the castle—*again*—and bribed my Dragon Knights. You've been caught canoodling—"

"We didn't do anything."

"—with my storm dragon rider," she went on ruthlessly as if Eva hadn't said anything, "and put your life in danger. Again. You are a grown ass man, not a child—act like one."

"Kira—"

"I don't want to hear any pathetic excuses you've lined up to talk your way out of this. You know you'll walk away from this with only a slap on the wrist. If you were my child, I would have sent you to the barracks to train alongside the men and women who defend your kingdom—make you understand what it's like to live in a world with consequences. But you're not my child, and once your parents have forgotten your serious transgression here, you'll do it all over again in a month's time with another woman."

Ouch. Both Eva and Leo flinched at that. She knew the Commander could be brutal, but this lashing was *savage*.

"Private Greene," she went on, switching targets, "on the other hand, is under my command and will face the consequences of her actions."

Eva braced herself for the onslaught she'd been waiting for. "Will you at least tell me what I did wrong before yelling at me?" She could hardly call making out with a prince a crime. The conflicting emotions that came along with it was punishment enough.

The glare Commander Hargin fixed on her could cut through Grayson's mithril cloak. "One, you encouraged Leonidas's foolish behaviour. As soon as he appeared, you should have sent him back. Oh, and don't worry, the Knights who brought him here will be severely punished as well." She held up two fingers as she ticked off all of Eva's wrongdoings. "Two, you showed an outsider around a highly classified base. Only those I give clearance to are allowed to see it."

"He's our prince," Eva rebuked. Leo was the most trustworthy man she knew. If he, their own prince, couldn't see the base, then *who* was allowed to see?

"And? Do you see me inviting Renkon to the base? No. Because it's *classified*." She slapped a sheet of paper in front of Leo. "You're going to sign this and not tell a single soul about what you've seen today then Private Greene—the other one—is going to take you home."

"Yes, ma'am," he mumbled, sinking into his chair like a scolded child.

"And you, Private Greene—"

The door burst open. With everyone being on high alert, Commander Hargin leapt out of her seat, ripping her sword free of its sheath. Eva tried to get on her feet in a timely manner, but her body greatly protested the hasty movement and sent her back into the chair. Leo almost fell out of his seat in surprise.

Grayson's form filled the doorway, chest heaving as if he had run through the entire base to the Commander's office. Those dark, stormy eyes of his locked onto Eva, studying every strand of hair out of place, the cut on her lip, the bruise forming on her cheek. They missed nothing as they continued their search, noting the hitch in every painful breath. Unbidden fury roiled like a treacherous sea in his eyes.

Growling, Commander Hargin sheathed her weapon then braced her hands on the desk as she seethed. "This is a private meeting, Smith. *Out!*"

His eyes didn't move from Eva, only the muscle flickering along his jaw told her that he'd heard the command. And chose to ignore it. "Glade told me you were attacked. You okay?"

Her ribs ached as she beheld him, his dishevelled hair, the rumpled cloak—the worry etched in the corner of his eyes. Subtle to everyone else, but obvious to her, the only one he had ever let in. "I'm all right."

The hard edge in his eyes faded a fraction.

Accepting her answer for the time being, his gaze snapped to Leo, eyes narrowing furiously. "What the fuck are you doing here?"

Leo sat straighter, trying to maintain some kind of dignity; though, after the tongue lashing Commander Hargin gave him, it was a futile effort. "None of your business, Runaway."

Grayson's jaw rocked, but in the end he decided Leo wasn't worth whatever retaliation he had lined up and turned back to Eva, extending his hand. "Let's get you out of that sling."

"I didn't say Private Greene was dismissed," Commander Hargin spat, she thrust a finger to the door. "Get out of my office, Corporal. That is an *order*."

Grayson threw a withering glare her way that would have made a lesser person sew their mouth shut and back the fuck out of the room. "She's dismissed."

He tugged on Eva's hand lightly, helping her stand. She was hesitant to follow, if only to avoid getting him into more trouble. Taking note of her reluctance, he looked at her with eyes of a whirling tempest. Her breath caught in her throat at the intensity. The air around them grew thick with tension, just as the air did before a storm.

They were eyes that didn't care about repercussions—because nothing else mattered. The look should scare her. A man who didn't fear consequences was a man to fear, especially when that man used to be the Slayer of Souls. But it didn't.

Jacob was in the hallway, pacing in front of the door. He froze when they appeared then rushed to her. "What did she say?"

"She didn't get a chance to finish," Eva answered, casting Grayson a subtle look he didn't notice. "Leo is going to need a ride home, though."

He nodded in understanding. "I'll wait for him." He looked at Grayson. "Take care of her."

Grayson slipped an arm around her waist, supporting her side. For the first time in an hour, she could take a deep breath. She all but sagged into him with relief. "I will."

Dreading the walk down to the healing pools, Eva let Grayson lead her through the base. While one arm was barred around her back, his other hand loosely hovered by his sword. His eyes scanned each corner before they rounded it with his dragon vision. When a pair of red silhouettes appeared in his vision, Grayson tensed, catching her ribs. She flinched, biting back a grunt. The pain eased up instantly once he confirmed they were Knights.

He noticed her wince and frowned. "Sorry. I'm a little on edge."

"We all are."

Someone had invaded their home and killed their own. It would be a while before things returned to normal. *If* they returned to normal.

"Are we moving too fast?" he asked, concern hanging on every word. The downside of being trained by assassins was that they had also trained him to notice *everything*. Including the pain she tried so damn hard to hide from him.

"No. This is fine."

"We go at the speed you can go. Fast or slow, it's all the same to me."

She'd never heard him sound so worried. "It's not as bad as it looks, Gray."

"No? So you don't have a broken rib, possibly two? The wound on your shoulder isn't bleeding through its dressings? If I lift your shirt up, your skin isn't going to be black and blue?"

"Ok...ay." He was *far* more observant than she gave him credit for. "That's fairly accurate. But I'm still standing and he's not."

He smirked at that, eyes shining bright when they landed on her. "Yes, you are. Good job capturing him. Not many could say they've gotten the upper hand on one of Sylus's assassins."

"I learned from the best."

She could have been mistaken, as the lighting in this stretch of the hallway wasn't great in the evening, but she could have sworn she saw a dusting of pink climb up his throat.

Her gaze cast downward as they approached the stairs. They wound round and round in a seemingly eternal spiral, so far she couldn't see the bottom. And the bottom was where they had to go.

Whoopee.

Sensing her reluctance, Grayson swept his arm under her knees then hoisted her into his arms. The motion sent a jarring pain up her side, but it was nothing compared to the constant stabbing she would have endured if he'd made her take every single step. After a deep breath, she relaxed in his arms, savouring the feeling of his strength beneath her.

"It's a shame Lieutenant Kramer and Sergeant Ballos weren't as lucky," she murmured, enjoying the sway of his body as they descended. Guilt gnawed at her for enjoying having a moment with him, while their lives were lost because of her.

"Don't," he ground out, jaw clenching. Steel eyes locked ahead. "You didn't survive because of luck. It's not your fault they died."

She turned her head away from him, opting to watch the steps as they climbed towards them. "They were good Knights."

She couldn't get Sergeant Ballos's vacant face out of her mind. The Knight was two years older than Eva. A talented rider with a promising career. She could have easily made Captain in a few years if Eva hadn't gotten her killed.

Grayson's warm breath grazed over her ear when he sighed, sending a shiver down her spine. "Eva, death is unavoidable in our line of work." His tone was as gentle as his breath.

"I know, but we're not killed in our own home. Usually a monster kills them."

"Monsters come in all shapes and sizes. More often than not, they're wearing the face of a human."

"And he's locked up in the brig..." An unsettling thought that had her head tilting upward to the floor they'd just passed where they held the few prisoners they obtained. If he could slip through all of their defences to get to her, what was to stop him from doing it again? Steel bars wouldn't be enough to stop him.

"He's not going to live long enough to come after you again," Grayson promised.

Her head whipped around to him. The unbidden fury returned with the full force of a tidal wave. But, again, she was unafraid when she cupped his cheek, guiding his gaze toward her. The anger melted into something much softer. A look he only reserved for her, and that just about turned her insides to goo.

"Don't get yourself into more trouble on my behalf, Gray. You've pissed off Commander Hargin enough today."

In a moment of vulnerable tenderness, he brushed a kiss along her hairline. "Let me worry about Hargin. Focus on your recovery. I need you to be strong and able."

"I will be as soon as I can move my right arm again."

He took the hint with a smile. His feet hit the ground, a plume of dust rising above them. The healing pools were down a long hallway, branching off into several large cavernous rooms. Eran was already waiting inside one of them. Water lines rippled over his azure scales and made his emerald eyes luminous as he watched them. The large dragon was truly stunning, a proud display of strength and resilience.

Grayson approached the pool, descending the wide, sweeping stairs until he was waist-deep. He set her down on a bench in the water that went up to her chest. He studied her wet clothes, looking a little lost, and bit his lip. "Would it be all right if I healed you instead of Eran? He's going to talk me through it and if it becomes too much for me, he'll take over, but I want to get better with my magic, so I don't have to rely on Eran all the time to heal serious wounds."

She knew he wasn't a fan of his magic; it warmed her heart that he was trying to embrace this part of him and wanted to be better with it. "Of course. Do what you need to do."

He nodded curtly then cleared throat. "Thank you. Now, unlike Eran, I need to be able to see what I'm doing..."

"So the shirt needs to come off," she guessed with a grin. Witnessing this bashful side of him was something to behold. Who knew the Slayer of Souls could get embarrassed for asking a woman to take her shirt off? "I can take it off, but I'll need some help."

Nodding again, eyes averting from her face, he untied the sling then helped her shimmy out of her top. His gaze hovered respectfully on her wounds, not daring to stray too far. A muscle in his jaw flickered so fast, she thought it was going to pop out.

She reached up, cupping his face with her good hand. "It's all right, Gray. There's nothing here I don't want you to see."

He squeezed his eyes shut, knuckles going white at his sides. "It's not that... You're hurt. I don't trust myself not to hurt you further if I get distracted."

Her fingers traced a slow path down his cheek, the tips catching against several days' worth stubble. They drifted along his jaw, down the curve of his neck, lingering at his shoulder before gliding lower. She followed the length of his bicep, loving the feel of power beneath her palm, until her fingers found his. Gently, she entwined them, lifting his hand and pressing it to her chest—right above her heart. "I trust you. You won't hurt me."

His eyes flashed open, locking onto hers instantly. "Do you have any idea what you do to me?"

"I have a feeling I'll find out soon."

He licked his lips, eyes growing dark with desire. "Hmm. Dangerous territory, Starling. Very dangerous."

She *loved* the name he gave her, especially when his voice was dark and husky like that.

He tore his gaze away from her, drawing it to the wound throbbing on her shoulder. The heat was quickly schooled when he scowled at the angry red mess it had become. "Did you visit the healers while I was away?"

"I did." She glared at his accusatory tone. She wasn't a masochist. Without their treatments, she wouldn't have been able to get a wink of sleep at night. "But I basically undid it all during the fight."

A grunt.

The tingle of magic filled the air. Water climbed up Grayson's torso, wrapping around his arms until it reached his hands where it formed a pair of gloves. Gently, he cupped the back and front of her shoulder then shut his eyes. Warmth radiated from his palms, massaging deep into the tissue. It kneaded into her flesh roughly, feeling as though his magic was digging through her muscles and tendons rather than trying to heal her.

She bit her lip to hide the pain. The longer it went on, the further the pain spread, which she assumed was his magic extending to the rest of her injuries.

Trying not to appear restless while he practiced, she clenched her fists in her lap. By Lorelus, he wasn't anywhere close to being done. If she didn't find a way to distract herself, she was going to pass out.

"What made you want to work on your magic?" she blurted, somehow managing to keep her tone even.

He glanced at her briefly before looking back to her wound. "You did. You've been training hard, both physically and with your magic, doing everything you can to be your own master. After the attack on Kain Ca stle... not being able to heal you... I felt weak. Like I was ten years old again, training with my uncle and getting my ass handed to me. I realised then that there were still things I needed to work on. I'm not done."

She stared at him while he was too focused on her shoulder to notice, yet again amazed by this man healing her. He was truly incredible. It was moments like these when she *knew* she was right to give him a second chance. Arkon understandably had his reservations, but the man Eva saw wasn't the same man who'd killed his kin. Deximus was a killer, a cruel prince who snatched hope out of the hands of his people. Grayson was a good man, who would do anything to protect the people he cared about. He felt far deeper than Deximus ever could. He loved more passionately than people gave him credit for—even if he didn't know it. He was power, resilience, ambition. He used the gifts Val gave him to better the world.

Was it any wonder she had fallen so hard for him? Her feelings for Leo might have snuck up on her, but her feelings for Grayson never shied away from her.

"There," Grayson said, a tremor taking over his body. Sweat beaded on his forehead; he wiped it with the back of his hand. "Arms behind your head."

Without thinking, she obeyed automatically. Her ribs stabbed at her side, but her shoulder—albeit a little tender—had full range of motion. A gasp fled her lips. "I can move my arm!"

A smile quirked in the corner of his mouth, not quite reaching his eyes, which were fixed on the purple bruises on her side—and not her breasts which were on full display.

His palm curled around the bruised side while his other hand held the opposite hip to steady her. Magic swam to the surface, warming her bones—

It sputtered out and fell into the pool, splashing them. Growling, Grayson swiped at his hair then tried again, placing his hands on either side of her.

"That is enough." Eran's tail wrapped around Grayson's waist, lifting him like an insolent child, and plopped him on the bench beside Eva. "You did well to heal Eva as much as you did." The dragon's emerald eye studied Eva's torso clinically, as if he could see the injuries beneath the surface of her flesh. A scaly brow arched curiously. “Quite well. You should be proud, Gray. Rest and let me finish for you.”

He looked like he wanted to argue, but Eva slipped her hand in his and leaned into his side. He went rigid, every muscle in his body tense with years of conditioning telling him this was not okay. Then he eased into the embrace, securing an arm around her back and leaning against the pool’s wall.

Eran's magic surrounded them, kneading and tugging on her wounds much gentler than Grayson's magic. With time and practice he'd heal her just as smoothly. She looked forward to that day, because Eran's magic was pleasant and left her skin buzzing and warm. Bit by bit, it grew a little easier to breathe. Soon, she was able to take a full breath without pain lancing through her.

It had to be almost midnight by the time Eran's magic faded. He dipped his colossal head into her awaiting hands, hot breath spilling over her. “I have done all that I can. The rest is nothing a few daily stretches can't fix.”

“Thank you, Eran.”

“I will leave you in the capable hands of my rider.” With one last nudge into her palms, he exited the pools and leapt out of the massive entrance leading into the canyon. The pump of his wings sent a chilling wind their way. Eva shuddered, suddenly reminded she didn't have a shirt on.

She spun, loving that nothing hurt as she did, in search of her tunic, and spotted it out of reach. Grayson grabbed it then studied the sopping wet article of clothing. “This is going to do absolutely nothing for you.”

She didn't doubt it.

He shedded out of his cloak, which was only wet on the bottom half and much thicker than her shirt, then draped it over her shoulders, tugging it around her front to cover her up.

“Thank you.”

He shrugged half-heartedly. “It'll get you to your room.”

Her room. How much work did the cleaners get done? Was the door functional? Would she find Lieutenant Kramer and Sergeant Ballos’s blood on the floor?

“I'll walk you,” he added, seeming to sense her unease. “If you want to sleep in my room, you can. I'll keep watch all night if that's what you need.”

Her heart melted into a puddle at her feet. Driven by the sole need to be as close to this man as physically possible, she tiptoed and pressed a kiss to his mouth.

What was meant to be a quick kiss in gratitude turned into a heated embrace. His mouth molded around hers, demanding and hungry. He took everything she gave him, hands sliding down her waist and grabbing her rear. He pressed her tight against him, every hard edge against her curves.

Every touch of his fingertips sent shivers of pleasure down her spine. The heat of his body set hers on fire. Her blood burned to have more of him—all of him.

A gasp slipped from her lips. Grayson froze, hands clutching her belt loops. He pulled away just enough to look at her with those heedy eyes. "Did I hurt you?"

"No," she panted, gripping his shirt so she wouldn't fall into a pile of goo at his feet. "I... Um... This is new to me." She hoped she didn't have to say anymore, because this was *clearly* not new to him.

Understanding made his eyes go wide. His grip on her loosened but didn't leave her. "I see."

"That's okay, right?"

His eyes went molten. He pressed a gentle kiss on her forehead. "It is." A shiver chased down her spine. "Come on. Let's get you in some proper clothes and warm you up."

She frowned, disappointment getting the better of her. "But I... I was rather enjoying myself."

He smirked, stepping away from her just enough for her body to feel the void his absence left. "So was I. Tonight, I'm going to hold you close. You're going to sleep better than you have all week, and I'm going to remind myself that you're safe, *alive*, and no longer hurting. And I'll damn well appreciate that you can still kick ass with one arm. Then later, I'll be glad to teach you a few other things that *aren't* on the mats."

Well... when he put it that way, how could she refuse?

CHAPTER 27
EMBERWALK

"Jacob Greene!" Annaliese just rounded the corner and was now charging Jacob's way. His back stiffened at the furious tone. "Do you have any idea how many people stopped me on my way here to tell me my best friend has been attacked!?" She halted in front of him, chest heaving. "Where is she?" Her eyes darted to Commander Hargin's office.

"You just missed her," Jacob answered. "Grayson took her down to the healing pools."

A *whoosh* of air left her lungs. "Good. How bad was it?"

Jacob rubbed the back of his head, fighting off the panic in his chest. When he first walked down the hallway after his meeting, looking forward to spending the evening with Eva—only to find a massive pool of blood in her doorway... He'd never been so scared in his life. "Two Knights confirmed dead so far. Some have been reported missing. Eva's ribs are broken and she has a few other mild injuries. She caught the assassin. He's being held in the brig."

She frowned curiously. "Then what are you doing here? I thought you'd be with Eva."

After the fucking murderous glare he saw on Grayson's face? No, thank you. He and every other Knight on base gave him a wide berth when he was on a warpath—which he definitely was when he heard the news. It was why he got here significantly faster than Anna.

Eva could be stuck with him for a few hours.

Fine by him. He didn't want the responsibility of calming him down. It usually ended with him covered in bruises.

Before Jacob could answer, Commander Hargin's door opened, revealing a wounded prince. The pride looked like it had been kicked out of him—and his nose was the target. Jacob winced. The bruising was darker and had spread to the corners of his eyes.

Anna did a double take then rubbed her eyes, because she couldn't believe who was standing with them. Jacob knew the feeling all too well. He didn't want to think about what the prince was doing in Eva's room before they were attacked.

"What are *you* doing here?"

Leo sighed wearily then flinched, eyes watering. "That seems to be the question of the day. Can I please see a healer now? If I don't get this fixed, I'm perfectly capable of clawing it off my face."

"But then we'd only have your charming personality to appreciate," Anna quipped, feeling absolutely no sympathy for him. Jacob had seen her win a marathon with a broken nose and sprained ankle. Back then, he thought she was the most terrifying creature on the base. Until he met Grayson's bad side.

Jacob clapped him on the back, just to salt the wound a little more. If the prince wanted to play Dragon Knight and walk among them, then he could experience the full package.

"You can see a healer then I'm taking you home."

"Tonight?" Anna and Leo chorused. It was moments like this when Jacob could tell they grew up together. Most days they appeared more like siblings than not.

Jacob nodded in the affirmative. "Yup. Commander Hargin's orders."

"But the sun set an hour ago. I've been up since two this morning."

Anna snorted a laugh. "Have you learned nothing from my mother after all of these years? When have you *ever* seen her offer mercy?"

Leo grimaced, shoulders slumping. "Can I at least say goodbye to Eva before I leave?"

"Nope." That was a big brother order.

Leo scowled, which earned him another wince then a curse under this breath. "I want to make sure she's okay."

"She's doing better than you with Grayson watching out for her. I'd stop making faces if I were you—might cause permanent damage." He wasn't sure how true it was, but it shut Leo's trap.

"I'll come with you," Anna volunteered. "We should fly in pairs."

Jacob took in her windblown hair, the rosy hue on her nose and ears still left over from the chilling winds. "Are you sure? You and Aster just got back."

She shrugged. "We'll be okay."

He certainly wasn't going to refuse her company, but he wouldn't put her in danger because of it. "We'll stop somewhere halfway." Both for her sake and Leo's. The prince didn't look like he could make a full eight hours.

She looked like she wanted to protest, but then she saw what he saw in Leo and gave in with a reluctant nod.

They reached Lexxis in the afternoon the next day. They had flown as far as Hillfar before Leo started falling asleep in the saddle, which worked just fine for Aster because she'd started tailing behind Glade. They rested all through the morning at the fort then returned to their journey back to Lexxis.

While in the fort, they sent word via messenger hawk that they had Leo and would be arriving the next day. When they landed, King Renkon, Queen Althea, and the entire Royal Guard were waiting for them by the gravel pit. Leo slid off Glade's back with the grace of a sack of potatoes, nearly slipping in the gravel and eating shit in front of his parents.

King Renkon didn't move, arms barred across his chest with a schooled but clearly infuriated glare settling in his son. Queen Althea rushed to him, cupping the sides of his face. "Leo! What happened to you?"

While the healers had straightened out his nose and given him a strip with a poultice on it that would ease the pain and swelling, it did little for the bruising.

Leo ducked his head, and Jacob felt a stab of pity for him. The anger he felt for catching him in his little sister's room had faded—but wasn't altogether gone—and all that was left now was sympathy for his friend. Was it stupid for the Crowned Prince to travel across the kingdom with a war criminal on the loose? Abso-fucking-lutly. Did Jacob admire the tenacity and bravery he would have needed to leave the safety of his castle and ride a dragon he didn't know? Yeah, he did. When Leo wanted something, nothing could stop him. It would make him a great king—but a terrible prince. "There was a little... incident at the base."

Queen Althea looked to Jacob for answers, as she normally did when her son was purposely vague. He brandished a sealed letter from Commander Hargin from his breast pocket and handed it to her with a respectful inclination of the head.

"Thank you, Private Greene." She swivelled towards Anna and tutted at her. "Anna, dear, you were just here. You must be exhausted."

While Leo got the cold shoulder from Commander Hargin, Queen Althea very much doted on Annaliese like the daughter she's always wanted. Anna smiled fondly. "It's all a part of the job, Althea. I'll be all right."

"You *must* stay for dinner this time."

"I would love to, but I'm afraid I already have dinner plans with someone in the city."

Dinner plans? With who?? Sure, she knew half of the people in Lexxis, and had a line up a block long of suitors who would love to spend an evening with her, but when did she have the time to set up these plans?

Anna peered at him from beneath her lashes. The look stole his breath.

Oh... Oh! *He* was the dinner plans.

His face went bright red, and he didn't care who saw it. He couldn't remember the last time they had gone anywhere for dinner, just the two of them. Life got busy, work got in the way... there was always an excuse to not take the time for themselves.

But there was no excuse now. Or, at least, Anna was choosing not to let the overbearing weight of exhaustion slow her down. Their dragons needed to rest, anyway, and he couldn't think of a better time to spend waiting for them to recover than going for a night on the town with the lovely Annaliese.

He cleared his throat. "Yes, very important dinner plans, I'm afraid."

Queen Althea pouted, but only half-heartedly. "A shame. You are free to do as you wish, of course." She turned a wicked glare onto her son. "You, however, Leonidas Nathaniel Kain, are not. You are to be confined to your chambers until I feel you have learned what it takes to be a prince—which is not abandoning your duties to whatever it was you were doing all night."

Leo rolled his shoulders back, tipping his chin up. "I said this to Kira and I'll say it to you as well: I will not apologise for my actions. As Prince it is my *duty* to see all of my kingdom and know my people. I want to get to know the brave Dragon Knights who work thanklessly to defend our kingdom so I may better appreciate their work. I want to meet the villages who struggle to farm enough food for the winter so I know how to better support them. I *want* to be a good king—but I can't if you don't let me see what is outside Lexxis's borders. You are doing me a disservice by sheltering me in this safe little bubble you want me to hide in."

His parents exchanged a look. Queen Althea touched Leo's arm, scanning his face and was deeply disturbed by the bruises. "We can talk about this another time."

"You say that *every* time," he snarled then ripped his arm free. Inhaling some composure, he faced Anna and Jacob, inclining his head. "Thank you for bringing me home safely. Wherever you dine, please put it on my tab. It's the least I can do for being an *inconvenience*." He cut his mother a sharp glare then marched down the path towards the castle. A handful of guards followed closely behind.

"He's right, you know," Anna told the royals, respectfully but sternly. "You can't keep him holed up forever. He's more capable than you give him credit for."

King Renkon narrowed his eyes on her. "Last I recalled, I don't give you advice on how to do your job or how to keep your volatile partner in check. You don't know what is best for my son, so keep in your lane and I'll keep in mine." He turned on his heel and strode down the same path Leo had gone down earlier. Queen Althea followed, along with the rest of the Royal Guard.

Jacob shoved his hands into the pockets of his dragon scale jacket. "Asshole."

She laughed breathlessly, not at all perturbed by the king. To this day, Jacob still couldn't figure out how she ended up so easy-going—considering she'd been raised by a mother with ice in her veins, a godfather who had the charm of a griffin, a godmother who oversaw her son's every move more than a dragon did over its brood, and an adoptive brother who'd probably flirt with his own reflection if given the chance. He'd thought his family was quirky until he unraveled the complexities of hers.

"What's so funny?" Jacob ground out. It wasn't like her to let someone talk back to her, even the king.

Smiling, she tapped his chest, fingers curling around his jacket and pulling him closer to her. His heart jolted in his ribcage. This close, he smelt the sweet jasmine soap he'd bought her. A miracle considering she'd been riding for over sixteen hours. "I find it hilarious that the straight and narrow Jacob Greene called our king an asshole. Not to his face, of course, but we'll work on that." Her wink was partly playful, partly seductive. Not that he needed seducing. She had him wholly, irrevocably. "Shall we go?"

Jacob glanced at Glade, who had erected a stone hut for both her and Aster to nestle into. She was now curled up, sleeping soundly with the fire dragon. He turned his gaze back to the castle, chewing the inside of his cheek. "Will he be all right?"

Something was going on with his friend. Usually Leo acted out by spending exorbitant amounts of coin at bars and brothels, or turning up late to galas unapologetically. Not by sneaking out of the castle without a guard and bribing Dragon Knights to cross the kingdom.

Anna looked down at her boots, poking at a loose piece of gravel. Crimson strands slipped from her braid, casting a thin veil around the pensive look on her face. Without thinking, he closed the gap between them and tucked the loose pieces behind her ears. Her skin was hot, as it normally was with Anna, warming his fingers as they grazed along her cheek.

She tipped her chin back, looking into his eyes with those orbs of silver that stole his breath away just like the first time he beheld her. "He'll be okay. This is something we can't help him with. It's between him and his parents." Smiling softly, she took his hand, lacing their fingers together. "It's just you and me this evening."

Selfishly, he wanted her all to himself, but if she was concerned about Leo, he would have dropped everything to support both him and Anna in whatever way he could. He and Leo were close, but Anna and Leo were family. And they looked out for family.

Grinning, he pulled her hand through his elbow, tucking it in the crook. As any gentleman should. She leaned into his side, warming him to his marrow. Slender framed, she could tuck right into his side and disappear, but damn did she pack heat. She was his own personal furnace and he loved it. Eva was always trying to sap the heat out of him.

Once they left the castle's grounds, they caught a carriage to the most popular square nestled in the heart of the city, Emberwalk, a hub of restaurants and entertainment. Businesses formed a perimeter around a square so big he could see it on Glade when they flew over Lexxis. No carriages. No horses. Pedestrians only.

Series of statues made by local artists stood tall on the flagstone for people to appreciate. Singers and dancers were encouraged to perform their art, while people dined on restaurant patios. Music by talented musicians wafted in the air, carrying further down the streets, using its harmonious melody to lure patrons to the square like a siren's song.

Once upon a time, Anna would have been spotted here. A time before Jacob knew her. His mind's eye painted a vivid picture of her standing in front of the unicorn statue, spilling her heart out, letting the whole city know of her love for music. They'd hear of her pain and sorrow, but also her joy and love. She wouldn't be wearing her Dragon Knight uniform, of course. She'd be wearing a deep red gown, the same colour of her hair. Her eyes would shine as bright as the stars at night.

One day, he'd see her shine that bright.

Jacob brought her to Emberwalk with the full expectation that he would stand by her side while she caught up with her friends. Just as he did every time they came to Emberwalk. He didn't mind. The art was interesting and the performers were talented, but his eyes only gravitated towards her smile. It had been a long while—too long—since he'd seen her smile. Not the sweet one she painted on for everyone to see, but the one that made her eyes twinkle with true happiness. Lately, her eyes were clouded by recent events and working tirelessly.

This evening was no exception. Anna veered away from her friends, opting to walk around the edge of the statues, a quiet, brooding look on her face. Content with walking in silence, Jacob let it slide, knowing she would talk to him when she was ready, but after passing his favourite bistro three times, his stomach twisting tighter with every passing, he squeezed her hand. "What's on your mind, Hun?"

She jolted out of her thoughts, peering up at him with an automatic smile, but it faded as quickly as it had appeared. She was never fake with him. "Oh... I was just thinking how funny it is that I was in this city less than twenty-four hours ago scouring the streets for a criminal—and now here I am, with you."

He noted the tightness in her voice, and felt his own dread gnaw at his inners. "There's no sign of him?"

Reports were sent back daily to keep Commander Hargin in the loop and she was merciful enough to keep him in the loop. But every day the reports said the same thing: unsuccessful.

Wrinkles formed on Anna's nose when she scowled. "None. Except for..."

"Except for what?"

Her tongue darted across her rose-red lips, eyes scanning the face of every person they passed by. "He left Grayson a letter, and he wouldn't let me read it. The one thing I asked him when I brought him onboard was that he kept *nothing* from me. Nothing. Not the dark thoughts, his temptations, imperative information regarding his family or Estrus." She tucked her hair behind her ear. "I trust him, but... it scares me that he would hide this from me. *Me.* I'm not going to rat on him or judge him or doubt him. Why would he hide it?"

An uneasy whisper trickled down his spine.

You won't know the monster you've harboured until it's too late. That damn thought crept into his mind again, incessant, merciless. Malicious. He'd been willing to brush it aside, because Grayson had been open and honest with him as well as Anna. But if he was hiding the contents of the letter, what else was he hiding? How many times had they overlooked his actions because they trusted him implicitly?

He chose his words carefully, as to not throw accusations or sow mistrust without evidence, but he didn't want to disregard the very serious problem either. They *had* to remember who they were dealing with, that Grayson used to be the Slayer of Souls and was not a man to let slip into the shadows. "Darius knows Grayson better than any of us. We have gotten to know him as he is now, but Darius has seen a side of him neither of us have seen. He knows what can break him or motivate him. If he hid the letter from you, that means Darius has gotten to him somehow. He knows something we don't and it's enough to get under Grayson's skin."

Her fingers curled tighter around his forearm. "We need to talk to him. I let it slide because it's been a rough week for all of us and I totally understand complicated family dynamics. But I let our friendship get in the way of my duty as his sponsor."

Jacob's heart ached for her. "You want to give him the benefit of the doubt. I do, too. But if he doesn't trust us... how can we fully trust him?"

She squeezed her eyes shut, and he knew she hated that they were talking about him like this. Jacob never thought this day would come. This was so wrong, but they had a job to do above all else.

When Anna opened her eyes, her gaze was resolute. "I'm going to recommend Eva and I return to the Desert Lands." The confession stopped him in his tracks. He knew this day would come, Eva hadn't completed her training when she rushed off to rescue him, but it still felt too soon. He'd just gotten his little sister back. "I know," she went on, holding his arm tight, as if to support his weight. Who knew, maybe she was. "It's hard on you both being apart, but it's the best thing for Eva. She'll be away from Darius—wherever he is—and Sylus's assassins. They won't know where to look for her. Besides, she needs to finish her training."

They were all sound arguments, but the big brother in him didn't want to part with her.

She pressed a kiss to his cheek that he would feel for *days*. His face went flame-hot. "It's for the best, Jake."

He knew that. But bad things happened when they were apart. He feared what would happen this time.

CHAPTER 28
THE PRICE FOR A SOUL

Commander Hargin's office was littered with more papers than a librarian's abode. Dust, both from poor house cleaning and from the sheer volume of parchment, hung in the air and tickled Grayson's nose. Pale morning light filtered through drapes behind the Dragon Knight leader, casting a halo of gold in her otherwise red hair.

Yet, while the office slowly fell into disarray, the Commander didn't fail to uphold her pristine appearance, from the sleek, tight ponytail, to the neatly pressed uniform, even the shine of her boots, she was the embodiment of military perfection.

Grayson's eyes shifted to the askew stack of papers piled up in the corner of her desk, precariously dancing on the edge. All he had to do was blow on the stack and they'd crumble onto the files and books piled up beneath the desk. Reports. Endless reports. Reports from simple, basic missions like monster slaying, others from investigative reports of mysterious phenomena occurring in the kingdom. A large majority of them were from Knights who'd been tasked with finding Darius, Grayson included. Whose every report he sent back was a twist of the knife of his failure.

Darius had likely fled Aboria by now or very nearly was on his way out.

His fingers curled into his palms, hidden beneath the desk, out of Hargin's sight.

"*I want my brother back. Give him back to me or she'll suffer every day for the rest of her life.*" For days, those words had rattled on and on in his mind, taking up unnecessary headspace. No matter what he did, how hard he tried to focus on *anything* else, he couldn't shake the memories that haunted him. Memories of standing by Darius's side in the dungeon in the Keep and watching him flay the skin off his victims. Plucking nails from their fingers. Sinking a blade into flesh, slowly, an inch a day, watching the wound fester and eat them from the inside out.

Any of them could be Eva.

And that fucking *terrified* him. A terror he had never experienced. This one wasn't fueled by adrenaline or bloodlust or even the primal desire to *survive*. This one sank deep into his marrow, clawed its way through his veins to his heart and threatened to pulverise his very being. It kept him up every night.

It wasn't so bad during the nights they shared a bed. The two nights Anna and Jacob were in Lexxis, Eva curled up in his bed, warm and soft, and everything he didn't know he was missing. She snored and it was adorable. Her hair tickled his face yet he found himself burying his face further into the feather-soft tresses.

"*This is new to me*," she'd said moments before he was going to tear her clothes off and take her in the healing pools. Those words gave him pause, rocked him to his core.

This was new to him, too.

He wanted to do this right. As much as his body ached to be closer to her during those two nights they shared his bed, he kept his cock to himself. Not his hands, though. They explored and inquired, learning everything they could about her body. He wanted to know just how to worship his Starling. He wanted her to know that the two nights she spent with him were the first nights he felt completely and utterly free of the demons tormenting his soul.

She was a gift he desperately wanted to be worthy of.

"*You are worthy*," Eran assured him.

"*I'm not*." Because if he was, Hargin wouldn't have called him into her office. He was only summoned when his particular expertise were needed. He had an inkling of what she wanted from him.

Her finger drummed on the desk, reluctance tugging at the wrinkles on the corner of her eyes. To bring him here meant to admit her men had failed, which meant *she* had failed. "I need you to talk to Sylus's assassin," she said, voice tight with frustration. "We've been working him for days. He hasn't uttered a word. Not a single sound."

He leaned back in his seat, casually crossing his ankle over his knee. While this aligned with his plans to pay the assassin a visit, he had an entirely different objective in mind. He didn't need information. He only wanted him to suffer, to send a message to anyone else who wanted to come after Eva. An attack on her was an attack on him—and every fucking monster twisting beneath the surface.

His features were schooled, however, so all Hargin saw was the cocky, swaggering renegade prince she'd allowed within her walls. "I don't do that anymore."

Causing pain and suffering to protect Eva was one thing. Causing pain and suffering to dig information out of someone, to manipulate their mind as much as their body, was a whole other beast. One that was better off left with Dex when Grayson killed him three and a half years ago.

Hargin cocked her head, a predatory sharpness in her grey eyes that made even his skin crawl. "I thought you'd say that."

Silently, she opened the top drawer and pulled out a single piece of paper. She slid it his way. Grayson didn't move to read it. He already knew what it said.

"Still no."

Her eyebrow quirked at that. "Why? Isn't this what you want?"

"I don't want it if it costs me a piece of my soul."

She studied him curiously, lips pursing together. "Hmm. That's new. Fine. Then what is worth a piece of your soul?"

That was a question he anticipated a furlong away.

"Pardon Eva for showing Leo around the base, and I'll do it." Hargin hadn't given her an outright punishment, but that wasn't how the Commander worked. She added to a list of tallies in Eva's file that would affect future promotions and opportunities.

Eva's future was more important than the specific plot of land Renkon had been holding over his head for years. With his particular circumstances, he wasn't allowed to buy land in Aboria, despite having the coin for it, but Renkon promised him property of his choosing if he could prove to be a reliable ally. If he had to let a piece of his old self back in then he didn't deserve to have that land yet.

Hargin's eyes flashed like steel in moonlight. She went back to drumming her fingers on the table. "Interesting."

Grayson didn't like her curious tone, but he didn't show it on his face. Bringing Eva into this negotiation was a risk he was willing to take. Hargin had no vendetta against her. She saw a weapon and wanted to utilize her to her full potential. He could use that to his advantage as much as Hargin could use Eva against him.

"She's a member of my squad," he answered coolly, logically. Dragon Knights looked after their own, but squads were family. Inseparable. Unbreakable.

The corner of her mouth tugged into what could be mistaken as a smile—if it was possible for the heartless creature across the desk from him to smile. Anna didn't think it was. "Your 'squad' is incomplete, and therefore, technically, not a real squad. I pair you four together out of convenience rather than formality."

"So?"

"Find yourself a fifth member if you want to use that excuse with anyone else..." An unfamiliar devious twinkle shone in her eyes. "However, I will pardon Eva. How long do you need?"

"Give me three hours and I'll tell you everything he knows."

Grayson stood before the brig doors, memories of his time here three years ago flashing through his mind. Despite Anna's best attempts to break the news to her mother who he was, Hargin had not taken it lightly and had ordered for him to be taken to the brig immediately. He'd accepted without hesitation, knowing cooperation would be the only way to gain their trust.

At the time, he hadn't expected much from Anna. At the time, he highly underestimated the women in Aboria and didn't think she had as much sway on the base as she had led him to believe. He had expected her to give up once Hargin sent him to this very level. But she hadn't. While he had sat for days in the darkness, Anna fought for him more than anyone ever had. More than he deserved after everything he did.

He'd never forget what Anna did for him. It was only because of her that he was able to stand on the other side of the cell this time. She helped him build this new life, taught him what it meant to be a man without having to instill fear into the hearts of the people around him. If it hadn't been for her aggressively stubborn affection, he wouldn't have learned a new kind of strength that allowed him to be himself with Eva. Wouldn't know what it was to love so wholly he'd do anything to protect her from their enemies.

Breathing in, he summoned walls of ice to encase his heart and mind. He closed off everything Anna and Jacob had taught him. The only emotion he had room for here was hate. Hate fueled bloodlust. It'd remind him that the fucker in the cell tried to kill Eva, that he was only the beginning of a line of assassins, mercenaries, and opportunists who would come after her.

Today's objective was more than getting information. Today he'd send a message to anyone with their sights set on the storm dragon rider that she was not theirs to claim, use, or abuse. She was *his* Starling.

He entered the brig. It wasn't as large as Kain Castle's dungeon, home to only five cells, one of which was occupied. Three Dragon Knights were stationed outside the cell. All of them Majors, each of them with high enough clearance to be aware of Grayson's past. Ahura glanced his way, eyes taking inventory of the weapons glistening in the white lightstone hue filling the rooms, then shifted his attention back to the form suspended by chains in the middle of the room.

“If you're going in there, you have to disarm.”

Wordlessly, Grayson passed the Majors for the table with their own weapons lain out neatly. He unbuckled one strap after the other until all that remained was a single knife, the blade no longer than his middle finger. Gaze locked on the prisoner, too damn familiar to a time he resented. Acid burned the inside of his throat.

Get this over with. Go in, get what you want, get out.

Hardening his body with resolve, he approached the cell door.

Ahura swung his arm out, halting him in his tracks. His eyes snapped down to the unwavering knife in Grayson's hand. "*All* of your weapons."

Grayson pinned him with a withering glare. "Do you want information or not?"

They other Majors exchanged a worried look then turned it to Ahura.

"Are you worried about the safety of the base or what I'll do to him?"

"He killed fifteen Dragon Knights before Private Greene stopped him. If he disarms you..."

"He won't."

Grayson's choice in weapon was intentional. Unlike the Majors and every other Knight that had the unfortunate fate of seeing the assassin's face, Grayson knew exactly what he was getting into.

Grunting, Ahura yanked his arm back to his side then freed the keys from his pocket. The jangle of metal on metal rattled down the hallway. Grayson stepped in then the door scraped shut behind him. He approached the prisoner until he was three feet away.

Naked, they'd restrained him in iron shackles, the chains from his wrists taut with tension as they hung from the ceiling, while his ankles were bolted to the floor. His brown hair was matted down by blood that had dried hours ago. His left eye was swollen shut, bottom lip split.

Grayson listened to the wheezing breaths slipping from his mouth. Fingers were swollen, blackened, or dislocated, the tips still bleeding profusely. Aside from the strategic yet non-lethal cuts, they had not peeled any of his skin away. No burns. Even his manhood was intact. Bruised, but whole.

Amateurs. Did they learn nothing from the handbook he wrote them? Hargin had asked him to make a comprehensive handbook on Sylus's torture methods so that she could better prepare her Knights for interrogations. It seemed to have gone unread after all these years. They hadn't even broken him out of his disassociation. No wonder he didn't make a sound. His mind was somewhere else, far away from the pain and misery. Their words fell on deaf ears.

Grayson recognised the man. He'd led him and the rest of his battalion up north to take land back from a revolutionary group who called themselves the Wayward Starlings.

Absently, he wondered if they were still causing Sylus grief or if he had squashed the uprising by now. They were nearly on their way to being fully exterminated when Grayson left Estrus.

"Vaelrik."

The cloudy haze in his blue eyes snapped into focus on him. Fear sunk deep into his features. "Dex." He swallowed, face contorting as he did. "Salik warned me you were here."

"And yet you still came. Brave."

"I made sure you weren't on the base when I went for my target." His brow pinched together, sweat trickling down the side of his face. "You trained her. She moves like you."

"Good."

Every morning and night they met up to go through the routine. Every morning and night, he watched Eva grow more confident in her movements. She was strong. Fast.

Absolutely breathtaking.

Vaelrik's gaze drifted to the Majors over Grayson's shoulder. "But they don't. You didn't train them."

"I don't waste my time on mediocre grunts." And he didn't give a fuck who heard him.

A slither of a smile touched the edge of the prisoner's mouth. "I've been studying Aborian culture during my time here. I believe the people here would say she is blessed by Val and Ebis."

"I would agree."

A raspy chuckle grated out of his lungs. He tilted his head to the side to get a better angle. "It's not like you to invest in anyone, let alone a woman."

Grayson kept his expression cool, unreadable. Vaelrik would never know of the raging tides tearing through his veins. Never know how his fingers itched to rip his throat out for talking about Eva.

"I've always had an eye for talent."

"You have..." Vaelrik peered at the Majors as they stood on the other side of the cell bars, a wall of muscle watching his every move. Listening to every word. He turned his attention back to Grayson. "It makes me wonder how much you have changed. The Dex I knew wouldn't associate himself with such weaklings. I killed fifteen of them—do know how easy it was? I could have done more if the storm rider hadn't stopped me. I didn't expect her to know Death's Dance."

"And you'll take that knowledge to your grave," Grayson said with more emotion than he intended. Vaelrik picked up on it immediately.

His instincts screamed at him to kill Vaelrik immediately. It wasn't a matter of what he knew about Eva—it was what the Majors would hear about her, and his attachment to her. He didn't trust them not to use whatever they heard against him later.

A grin peeled at the edges of Vaelrik's splintered mouth. "My, how the mighty have fallen."

Faster than he could blink, Grayson rammed his knife between his ribs, puncturing a lung. He yanked it out, and listened to the air whistle out of the hole. It was the only sound Vaelrik made as blood leaked down his side and dripped onto the floor.

"You're going to have to do better than that, Your Highness, if you want information from me," he wheezed.

If he wanted Dex, he'd give him a slice.

Grayson picked his next few words carefully. "I didn't come here for information." He stepped closer, leaning in to whisper in his ear as the tip of his knife grazed over his stomach. He pressed just enough to leave a crimson line in its wake, but not enough to pierce the delicate flesh. "You tried to take away what didn't belong to you." Slowly, he edged the knife deeper, slicing through skin and muscle. He stopped when he felt the stomach lining. Vaelrik's body began to shake, whether he wanted it to or not. "And I'm going to use your corpse as a message to everyone else who thinks they can touch what is *mine*."

He moved back slightly as Vaelrik's body convulsed more violently. But he wasn't shaking in pain, Grayson realised in mild horror.

Despite the blade threatening to spill his stomach open, Vaelrik laughed. A full-bodied, tossing his head back, *laugh*.

"*There's* the Prince Deximus I know." He leaned forward, closing the gap Grayson had put between them, blue eyes wicked—deliriously in pain. "Keep an eye on her, Dex. I won't be the last... Sylus is afraid of her."

Grayson was tempted the plunge the knife in now, end this and get it over with. He no longer took pleasure in torture. He felt filthy, covered in layers of grime.

But he couldn't deny his curiosity. It had always plagued him why Sylus was so keen on killing Eva. It wasn't like him to pour resources into *killing* someone. It was a quick, simple thought, then he moved on. But not this time—and it cost him respect amongst his ranks. Clearly, if Vaelrik was willing to give up information.

"Why?"

Vaelrik cast the Majors a snide glance—as if they weren't worth his time. Which they weren't. Vaelrik was a high ranking assassin in Sylus's army, charged with far more important tasks than being the messenger boy he'd been reduced to. Compared to him, they were mere mindless grunts.

"You want information, Your Highness? They have to go."

Grayson put more space between them and faced Ahura. "Out."

The Major sneered at him, lip curling up in disgust. He couldn't *wait* for Grayson to give him a reason to slit his throat open. Today was not that day, however. "You don't call the shots here, *Your Highness*."

"Hargin asked *me* to interrogate the prisoner when you failed to get the job done. You want to get inside his head? I'm the only one who can make it happen."

Ahura held his gaze, hard as refined mithril ore. A million questions flickered in his eyes, convinced that Grayson would betray them the moment they walked out that door.

All Grayson could afford was a firm nod, and hoped that would be enough

Jaw rocking, Ahura finally relented with a short sigh. Wordlessly, he turned on his heel and marched out the door.

Major Wouters baulked at the back of his fellow Major's head. "Ahura, you're not seriously-"

Ahura stopped at the door, hand on the handle. "They can't go anywhere. If they try to leave, we'll kill them on sight."

You wish.

Seeming to take comfort in his rationality, the other two Majors followed Ahura outside. When the door clicked shut behind them, Grayson faced the assassin, blade steady and unwavering in his hand.

"All right, Vaelrik—talk."

"Did Sylus..." the assassin inhaled a trembling breath, before exhaling roughly, "ever tell you why he ordered you and your brothers to kill the storm dragons?"

His spine went rigid, rooting his feet in place.

The look that settled on him was cold, yet a playful glimmer shone through. Salik trained his men to upheave all emotion and to focus on logic. That glimmer was dangerous. Unpredictable. "Before your grandfather died, a prophecy was foretold: a woman whose hair has been touched by ash, who will mount a black dragon and claim the power of Ebis will be Sylus's undoing. Salik tried to assuage him, but Sylus could not be dissuaded once his mind was made up. He sought out the storm dragons and killed them. When he became King, he trained you to carry on this task."

Grayson stood in shock. A prophecy. Sylus, the most feared king in Estrus's history, was afraid of a prophecy told by an old hag? He would have laughed if the prophecy didn't revolve around the woman he loved.

Sylus wasn't as fearless and powerful as Grayson was led to believe growing up.

"But..." Vaelrik hissed, "now that you've trained her and not even his assassins can reach her, he is going to try other methods."

Grayson's blood chilled.

"Like what?"

"One that will rid magic in all of Astrida."

Grayson barely had the chance to dissolve the boulder forming in his gut before Vaelrik told him *everything*. Most of which was infuriatingly familiar, because it had been Grayson's plan long before he chose to leave Estrus. Sylus had laughed him out of the room at the time, deeming it unnecessary since they assumed all the storm dragons were dead.

But now Arkon was very much alive and his rider was motivated.

He's actually going to do it...

Shit.

Grayson stored as much information as he could while Vaelrik willingly gave it all up. The Majors behind him absorbed everything they understood, but without Grayson explaining the process to them—and admitting that he had a hand in this plan—they would be hard pressed to know what Sylus needed to do in order to wipe magic from the world.

Once Vaelrik was done, Grayson went to work "extracting further information." He knew the prisoner had given everything he was willing to give. Other valuable information would be locked tight in his mind. But the Majors didn't know that. They watched him torment the man, allowed him to do so, because they believed he was doing it for Hargin. Only when he severed the man's head, did they stop him from further mutilating the corpse. Grayson carved the eyes and tongue out of the skull and pocketed them away. A symbol not just for Sylus, but for anyone who witnessed the Slayer's mark.

If they wanted Eva, they had to go through the Slayer first.

CHAPTER 29
HOME SWEET HOME

Against his will, Darius's body shuddered as the cold clamped down on his bones. Winter was just right around the corner in Estrus, frost clinging to the frigid tundra plains. As soon as word of his arrival reached the castle, Sylus sent a wyvern escort to retrieve him and the few men who had returned with him—and sent him straight to the dungeon.

No food for three days, just enough water to keep him alive, and a lashing for every day he chose to go against his father's orders, spread out over the span of a week.

Home sweet home.

He expected no less from his father.

Sylus didn't have to visit his cell for him to know what he would say. He'd heard it countless times. Failure. A mistake. *He* should have been the one to leave. Darius let the words pierce his mind over and over again. Took every beating with gritted teeth. Relinquished the control he had coveted in Aboria back to Sylus. He was still King, after all, still had all the power and men and mithril at his disposal. Darius was a mere pawn to him. He'd let him think he'd broken him down back to the obedient prince he once had. When his time to strike came, he wouldn't see it coming.

On the tenth day after his return, Sylus finally deemed Darius's punishment enough. Water straight from the glacial ocean up north shattered his mental defences, ripping his mind from the numb world he had created and thrusting him into the battered body he'd been left with. His body quaked violently, a pained cry escaping from his lungs before he could clamp down on it.

Fresh clothes were unceremoniously dumped in front of him, narrowly close to the puddle at his feet. His crown landed on top with a sad *thump*.

"Get dressed, you spineless hack."

Darius didn't lift his gaze to meet his father's, those shiny boots were enough encouragement to get his shit together.

Steeling himself, he bent over, ignoring the tearing scabs on his back and the withering ache in his joints, yanking the warm woolen trousers up to his hips. One final shudder wracked through him as the wool shirt settled over this torso. He bit the inside of his cheek *hard* to suppress the relieved moan building up in his throat. He wouldn't show his father how good it felt to be in clothes again, how haggard and aching his body was after travelling and being subjected to his punishment.

"Walk with me." Sylus turned on his heel, dire wolf cape whispering behind him as he strode down the hallway. Darius matched his pace, shoving the sting of his wounds into the deepest, darkest part of his mind. Pain was for the weak, and if Sylus had deemed him worthy to leave the prison, it meant he'd proven that he was still the son he raised.

He followed him silently, without protest. Wherever they were going, it was better than the dungeon. He was getting real tired of seeing the inside of a cell. It was supposed to be the other way. He was supposed to be standing on the other side, gloating, torturing, playing with his latest toy. He'd make it right again. Soon. It was a matter of biding his time.

Sylus took him to the throne room, where Dravyn was already waiting. The delinquent had his legs swung over the arm of the throne, while he played with the reflections of his blade on the rafters above them. Boredom etched lines on his otherwise baby face, making him look ten years older.

His glacial eyes slid to Darius. "You look like a sewer rat, Dari... It suits you." The ends of his mouth quirked into a devious smirk.

"You'll be swimming with sewer rats if you don't watch your mouth."

"Oh, I watch my mouth—what it says, where it goes... and who enjoys it."

Darius was *fully* aware of where he put his mouth. Sylus thought he had beaten it out of him, but he had just gotten significantly better at hiding it. Darius hadn't informed their father, deciding to keep the information to himself for when he was in need of Dravyn's particular talents.

"Off," their father snarled, approaching the throne.

Dravyn leapt out of the seat as if Sylus had set it ablaze then fell to his knees beside Darius, bowing his head low to the king. Subtly, Dravyn peered at Darius through a veil of chin-length hair and crinkled his nose. Darius made a mental note to find him later and break that fucking nose.

"Darius, are you ready to behave yourself?" Sylus demanded of him.

Bile rose up in his throat. "Yes, Father."

"I need you to prove it."

"I'll do anything you ask."

"Good." He raised his voice to be heard outside of these walls, "Bring him in."

Chains clattered on the floor as the door opened, revealing Uncle Salik dragging Keyon, bound and beaten, across the stone. Salik dumped him beside Darius, breaths coming in big, wheezing gulps through the gag. Darius stared at his friend, reminding himself to appear impassive as he accounted for all of his injuries. Face swollen, digits missing, deep gashes leaking through his thin shirt. His whole body trembled, still in the throes of shock. This was done recently, likely as soon as Sylus decided Darius had spent enough time in the dungeon.

Darius's blood boiled. He and he alone was supposed to be punished for his betrayal.

"Prove your loyalty to me, Darius. Prove to me you are still worthy of my crown. Kill him and I'll consider your little venture through Aboria a lapse in judgement."

Keyon's eyes went wide, breathing coming in harder now. They dashed from Sylus, to Salik, then finally to Darius, fear swimming in the depths of those green eyes.

Darius rose to his feet, eyes unmoving from his childhood friend. The only man he ever truly trusted. The man who obeyed his orders without question. Who selflessly risked his life on countless occasions in the name of his Prince. He'd killed, tortured, stole—all for him. Never did he once ask for compensation or reward.

Darius extended his hand to Salik, palm facing up. A quick death. It was all he could offer him.

His uncle reached for his knife, but Sylus held up a hand, halting him. "No weapons. You kill him with your bare hands and don't you once look away from his eyes. You will watch him die until the very end."

It took everything in his weary body to keep his hand steady as he lowered it back to his side.

Bastard. This had absolutely nothing to do with loyalty. It was Darius's punishment. Everything before was typical conditioning, the same conditioning he grew up with. Sylus knew it wouldn't deter him for long. *This* was the consequence of defying his father, for thinking he knew better than him, for daring to break free of his control.

He could deny Sylus now and suffer the same fate as Keyon. Or he could do as he was told and murder his loyal servant. His closest friend.

I will be King one day.

Nothing would get in his way. Not loyalty, not his father, not his fucking brothers. Whatever it took, he would sit on that throne.

With the sole of his boot, he pushed Keyon flat on his back then knelt to straddle his stomach. Fear flashed in his eyes, body tensing beneath him. Darius took no joy in it this time. Cold, prickling dread slithered down his entire being, raking his flesh and leaving him hollow inside.

His fingers closed around Keyon's throat and he squeezed. As commanded by his father, he watched the pain and panic rise in his friend's eyes. Acceptance soon followed, allowing his body to ease against the stone floor. Peace filled them, while Darius forced himself to feel nothing. No regret. No loss. No guilt. He refused to give Sylus the satisfaction of his sorrow. He would be the King of Estrus and he would *not* break today.

Keyon's body went limp beneath him, eyes fixed on Darius, unseeing, falling into eternal darkness.

It's done.

Forcing his body to move, he rose to his feet and faced his father. "Satisfied?"

The king leaned back in his throne, steepling his fingers together. "Immensely. Toss him into the sewers, Salik. The rats need something to eat."

Like an obedient Shadow, he grabbed Keyon by the scruff and dragged him out of the room. Once the door closed shut behind him, Sylus sat up in his chair, catching both of his sons' attention. His fingers drummed over the top of a small wooden box Darius hadn't noticed until the *tap-tap-tap-tap* of his fingers echoed around the room.

It looked like a gift that had been sent to him.

Odd.

Nobody sent him gifts.

"I have an important task for you. The storm dragon rider has grown too powerful." He sliced a glare Darius's way. "She can no longer be killed by ordinary means. We need a weapon our mithril cannot forge."

A cunning smile curled up Dravyn's face. "Ooo. Sounds like a thrilling adventure to me."

Sylus brandished a piece of parchment from his breast pocket and tossed it to Dravyn, who caught it in a flash. "Your brother has done all the work for you. You will visit each of the continents listed and seek out vestiges of the past then return them to me."

Dravyn's head swung Darius's way dubiously. "*You* did research? What kind of beast possessed you?"

"Not Darius," Sylus responded flatly.

All the blood drained from Dravyn's face as he beheld the parchment in a new light, one of awe—and mourning. Darius hadn't told him Dex was still breathing. Hadn't felt inclined to and still didn't.

Dex's betrayal fractured their family in ways none of them expected. They weren't an ordinary family. They didn't love or cherish one another's company. But when one of them was absent—when one of them *chose* to leave them behind—they became something else entirely.

Dravyn, believing the lie that Darius had killed the traitor, hid in his rooms for hours on end, ignoring summons and his Shadow duties regardless of the consequences. Sylus took offense to every failure his men presented to him, filling the dungeons with toys for Darius to play with.

And gods forsaken, did Darius play.

His rage twisted and burned through him, and every soul he touched felt the fury in his veins as he imagined all the things he would do to his brother when he finally found him.

"You leave tomorrow. Do not return until you have succeeded."

The princes dipped their heads. "Yes, Your Grace."

They rose to their feet then marched out the room. It took everything in Darius's body not to turn back and look at the spot his friend once was.

This one's for you, Keyon.

CHAPTER 30
MAY ZYPHRIL FREE YOUR SPIRIT

The pyre stretched higher than any dragon, its ochre glow swaying in the dark clouds above them. Ash drifted through the ranks of every single Dragon Knight in formation; flakes fell onto Eva's shoulders and into her hair.

She wore her formal armour, having spent an hour the night before ironing every wrinkle out of the soft trousers, the long sleeved cream shirt, and rust-red blazer. Her boots were so shiny she could see her reflection on her toes. She'd pulled her hair back in a ceremonial braid that Anna had twisted at the base of her neck into a bun.

The look mirrored Anna's attire, except her friend managed to hold the stoic front better than her. Her expression was unreadable, borderline cold, while Eva struggled to maintain her composure. She'd lost count how many times she'd looked up at the sky, fighting the burn of tears in her eyes. It did nothing to stop the acid churning in her stomach. The scent of burning wood, tainted by the hint of burning flesh, awakened memories she tried to forget. Screams of another time roared in her ears, accelerating her heart.

Jacob's fierce grip in her hand was all she had to her anchor herself when all she wanted to do was curl up in bed and cry for the rest of the day. To pretend the world outside of the walls of her room didn't exist.

They were outside, battling the unrelenting elements, under threat of the brewing storm, because of her. Wind and rain fought to temper the raging fire Varkyss and Nyvara fueled with the pain and loss of their riders. Other dragons fought for the honour of lighting the pyre, but there was only so much space on the field and these two dragons earned their spot beside the thousands of Dragon Knights here to honour their dead.

It's my fault. Their families were crying off to the side away from formation, their wails as deafening as the screams echoing in Eva's mind. *I'm going to be sick.*

Commander Hargin had brought them in for the funeral, to watch their loved ones—mothers, sisters, daughters, fathers, brothers, sons—burn by dragon fire. The dragons' cry through the canyon earlier today was as agonising as Eva's cry when she'd lost her family.

"*It's not your fault,*" Arkon crooned from the skies. He was in the dark clouds, holding back the hungry tempest that wanted to claim this land. She sensed the strain holding the monumental beast back had on him. Knew it would be easier if she was up there with him. But she also wanted to be here to pay her respects. "*They died honourably, in battle, performing their duty. You did not put your blade to their throats.*"

No, just the assassin who came after her. The one who had killed fifteen Knights to get to her. Not one of them stood a chance, men and women who had trained longer than Eva had been alive, yet *she* lived. Why did she have to survive?

"*The Slayer trained you well,*" Arkon was reluctant to admit. "*This is what we must do to get our revenge—keep on fighting and surviving. Every loss is fuel to the fire in our hearts. Not one soul will die in vain.*"

While holding Jacob's hand, she subtly shifted her free one behind her. Grayson's fingers grazed over hers, a feather light touch, but it was all she needed. Knowing he was there was enough to alleviate the anxiety scratching at her chest. The nights she'd spent in his bed were the most peaceful nights she'd had since arriving in Dragon Canyon. As happy as she was to have Anna back, her bed was significantly colder, emptier, without him. She felt his absence like a missing limb. Not for the first time, she wondered if he felt her absence as vividly as she felt his.

Anna had all but locked her in the training room since returning, working her harder to make up for the time she lost while she was injured. The only time they had together was when she met up with him every morning and every night to train with him, and even then it was strictly professional and silent.

Once the pyres settled, the flames no taller than Eva's knee flickering on the mass grave, Commander Hargin marched in front of the formation and saluted the fire. Thumps rolled down the line as they all saluted, pounding their fists over their hearts.

"May Zyphril free your spirits."

With no magic from their dragons, the wind picked up, catching the ashes in its grasp then whisked them away into the setting sun. Goosebumps rose on Eva's flesh. Jacob shuddered beside her.

Commander Hargin turned and addressed the formation, grim lines etched into her features. Her voice, steady yet heavy with grief, carried down the canyon, "These brave men and women gave their lives to defend this base, standing unwavering in the line of duty. They were warriors, riders, and comrades—and though they were taken too soon, they are not lost to us. They live on in the stories we tell, in the battles we fight, in the cause they believed in. Their sacrifice will not be in vain. For them, we fight. For them, we endure. For them, we fly."

"May the winds be in their favour!" Lieutenant Ahura shouted. His cry echoed down the line as every Dragon Knight called after him. Eva's voice was drowned out by the thousands of Knights around her, and she was just fine with that. If anyone heard her, they would have accused her of not following the Dragon Knight spirit. Truth was, she couldn't bring herself to shout as loudly as them when all she saw were the tears of Lieutenant Kramer's children streaking down their red, puffy faces. Seven and ten years old, someone had told her.

Criminal.

So fucking criminal.

After the cheer, Hargin dismissed formation. Eva mindlessly followed Jacob, who hadn't once released her hand. The crowd quickly became chaotic; Anna and Grayson closed in around her, ensuring she didn't get swept away while she struggled to get those families' faces out of her mind. Arkon cocooned her soul in a gentle embrace, warming her bones and heart that so desperately wanted to freeze over and numb out the pain. She held on to their tether with everything she had, afraid of what would happen to her if she let go. He was the only reason the guilt hadn't dragged her down the abyss waiting with its voracious maw open wide to swallow her whole.

"...Did you hear what happened to the prisoner?" a whisper wended its way through the crowd and reached her sensitive ears.

Prisoner. The assassin.

Immediately on the defensive, Eva whipped her head around in search of the talking Knights. She needed more information. Now. If that fucker had escaped, she only had a small window to wet her blade with his blood before someone else beat her to it.

"Eva?" Jacob touched her arm, a tinge of concern riding his voice. "What is it?"

Ignoring him, her gaze zeroed in on two privates with their heads bowed close together as they spoke under their breath. Jacob wouldn't have been able to hear them. Since the attack, she had magic constantly flowing through her senses, heightening her sight, touch—and hearing. Just in case.

The taller one, Private Ramus, if Eva remembered correctly, nodded to his conspirator. "He didn't live through the interrogation."

Private Burns, a stout, burly man, slapped his chest with a dark smirk. "I'll do you one better: I heard the interrogator cut his eyes and tongue out."

Ramus's face twisted in disgust. "Who did the interrogation? The point is to get information—not carve him up like a turkey. They should get written up."

"Who cares?" Burns snorted. "The bastard deserved it. Hargin isn't even going to reprimand them."

Grayson's palm pressed into her lower back, gently urging her to keep moving. Judging by the dark shadow looming over him, she guessed he had heard them too.

"Do you know anything about it?" she whispered, releasing Jacob's hand in favour of falling into step beside Grayson.

He grimaced. "Not here."

Her spine stiffened against his ever-persistent hand. "Did you..." The words clogged her throat, because she feared to say them aloud, to admit he would do something so gruesome in her name.

The look he gave her said it all. He'd promised her the assassin wouldn't come after her again—and he delivered.

She waited for the dread or fear to creep up on her, for the alarm bells to chime in her head that butchering a man who had caused her so much grief was unacceptable. *Wrong*. Leo would have never done something like that. Sure, he'd probably make the assassin disappear and triple the security detail on the base—but mutilation? Never.

Yet... when she should have found comfort in Leo's hypothetical method, she took solace in Grayson's. He really would do *anything* for her. Not order someone else to do it or throw coin at the problem—he'd wet his hands with the blood of her enemies and not think twice about it.

She found Grayson's spare hand and squeezed it. "Later."

No sooner had she made contact, she let it slip and slipped back to Jacob's side, who peered at her, concern rippling across his forehead.

Anna blew out a weary breath, pressing into Eva's other side. "I don't know about you guys, but I could use a drink—or several."

"I second that," Jacob grunted once they escaped the main crowd. Like them, everyone had grouped up into their squads, and were now scattering to the nearest tunnels to take them back to the base.

"I'm buying the first round," Grayson volunteered, the broody look on his face gone, replaced by a partial smile.

"You can buy *every* round," Anna chided him, wagging a reprimanding finger at him. She leaned towards Eva and stage-whispered, "This guy is basically made out of coin—and told no one."

Eva giggled, chest feeling lighter than it had in a few days.

"I filed all of my belongings when I arrived in Dragon Canyon," Grayson shot back, "it's not my fault *you* didn't take inventory."

Anna tossed him a playful sneer.

A flash of red caught Eva's attention. She scanned the thinning crowd, and froze when a surplus of medals glinted in the setting sun. Only one person carried that many medals on her uniform. Jacob followed her gaze and gulped as Commander Hargin approached them with a purpose that only meant trouble.

Anna offered herself up as a sacrifice, sliding past Eva and Jacob to block Hargin's view of them. Standing face-to-face, Anna could have been mistaken as a younger version of the Commander. Same height, hair the same shade of crimson, silver eyes, right down to the curve of their mouths. The only difference between them was Anna's casual stance up against Hargin's, who looked like someone had shoved a rod up her ass.

Her cold grey eyes sliced through every member of the squad then she slapped an envelope in Anna's hand. She moved past her daughter and handed another one to Jacob.

"After the mourning period, you will carry out these orders." Commander Hargin's sharp gaze snapped to Grayson for a beat then she turned and marched back to the base with Lieutenant Ahura on her heels.

Anna read the letter, eyes growing dark with every sentence read, then handed the orders to Eva. Her stomach plummeted once she finished reading.

"We're going back to the Desert Lands."

Anna nodded solemnly. "I recommended it, but I didn't think it would be so soon after the funeral."

Suddenly, her training made sense. Anna wasn't making up for lost time, she was getting Eva ready to leave.

She peered over Jacob's shoulder at his orders. Hers hadn't made any mention of him or Grayson, but she was hoping that it was because her orders focused on her training, while he would be directed to be her protection detail.

Her heart sank when she spotted where Hargin was sending them. "Why is she sending you to Kain Castle's *library*?"

Jacob blinked at it several times. "I have no idea, but I'm *definitely* drinking tonight now." He leaned into her side to read her orders. "How long are you girls going for this time?"

"Three months." Hargin had laid out Eva's training in terms. Three months in Aboria and three months in the Desert Lands until Sasha said she was ready.

"That's..." He scowled thoughtfully. "Actually reasonable."

It was still too long for her, but it beat the five months she'd spent in the Desert Lands before.

She glanced at Grayson, whose gaze was fixed on the canyon wall, eyes far away in a distant land. Light and dark warred for control over those soulful eyes, neither willing to give in. A muscle feathered along his jaw. His expression gave nothing away, but it couldn't be anything good.

While Anna and Jacob discussed the logistics of their missions, Eva inched towards Grayson, brushing her fingers over his knuckles. “A copper for your thoughts?”

Jolting, he turned to her and shook his head clear of his thoughts. His eyes shone brighter when he looked at her, a lopsided smile tugging on the corner of his mouth. “Here isn't the place to talk about it.” Pointedly, his eyes tracked over the last remaining Knights filtering through the tunnels then landed on the charred canyon floor.

“How about over a drink?”

His hand twisted, catching the tips of her fingers with his. “I'd like that.”

Every bar and tavern in Lensenton was packed. Apparently, grabbing a drink wasn't only their squad's idea. They were turned away by three places before they found a spot that could squeeze them in. Jacob and his friends frequented the Dragon’s Horn often enough for the barman to greet her brother with a great big hug. He was a large man, towering over every single Knight in his bar. He had dark, mahogany skin, with the warmest brown eyes to ever smile at her. His beard was sprinkled with white, the only sign of his age.

“Jacob, my man! Good to see you!”

Jacob rapped his back then stepped out of the embrace, grinning up at his friend in earnest. Wherever they went, there was always someone who knew her brother. “Charlie, always a pleasure.”

Charlie surveyed the squad then nodded. “You're in luck. I have one table left.” He waved over a young woman with long raven hair and skin a tone lighter than his. She was uniquely beautiful with her blue-tipped trusses and tall, curvy figure. “This is my daughter Jesmina. You need anything, she's your gal.”

She bobbed into a brief curtsey, strange blue eyes lingering on Grayson longer than the rest of them. A smile curled at the edges of her lips. “Right this way, Dragon Knights.”

Charlie wasn't kidding when he said there was only one table left. Jesmina led them to the far corner—so far out of the way, the only reason it hadn't been taken was because it was forgotten by the staff—to an empty booth shrouded in shadow.

Anna slid onto the bench first, followed by Jacob on one side, while Eva and Grayson filled the other half.

Brandishing a writing pad and charcoal pencil, Jesmina turned her full attention to Grayson. He might as well be the only one at the table.

Eva couldn't blame her. For once, out of respect for the fallen Knights, he wore the standard Dragon Knight uniform. There wasn't a spec of black on him. Seeing him in rust-red for the first time earlier today had thrown her off and she had to pinch herself to make sure she wasn't dreaming.

His regular black garb was handsome in a dark and brooding kind of way. It closed him off from the rest of the world, making him mysterious and alluring. Undeniably sexy. Yet, this uniform was dashing and inviting. He looked like a regular—well, regular was a stretch when he looked like Lorelus had carved him out of the finest slab of marble in existence—Dragon Knight with no demons haunting him. He looked approachable, friendly.

"What can I get for you, handsome?"

"A round of whatever you have on tap, and..." Grayson twisted to face Eva, oblivious to Jesmina's stare. He might have been all the barmaid could see, but Eva was all he could see. "Are you hungry? Get whatever you want."

"Can we get some meat skewers," Jacob started ordering, "and a cheese platter? Ooo! And how about that potato thing with the melted cheese?"

Grayson's gaze didn't move from her, expectant. She shrugged. "I couldn't have ordered better myself."

Nodding, he turned back to the barmaid. "We'll start with his order."

She inclined her head, eyes growing dark and heedy as her eyes roamed over the tailored blazer hugging his broad shoulders and muscular arms. She seemed to be waiting for him to say something further, but when the silence stretched on, she frowned then walked away.

Anna giggled into her hand. "You should go back to wearing black, Gray—or everyone here will be fighting over who gets the right to tear your clothes off."

Eva laughed at the grimace on Grayson's face. Only *he* would cringe from all of the attention fixed on him.

The grimace melted into an easy smile while he watched her. Those storm cloud eyes shined at the sound of her laughter, and when she leaned into him, they lit up like a starry night.

She wished there was a way to capture this moment so she could bring it with her to the Desert Lands. He could change his clothes or strip down to nothing, but it was that smile—the pure peace within it—that made him the most handsome man in this room. So rarely, he allowed himself to be free like this. She hoped this was the first of many times to come.

Jesmina swung by with their drinks and left just as quickly. Both Eva and Jacob dove for their mugs and took the first gulp. She didn't know why

Jacob was so eager to drink, but she definitely needed something to take the edge off the reminder that this was her last night with Grayson and Jacob.

Feeling an uneasy stir in her tummy, she set her mug of ale down and laid a hand on her abdomen. Thinking about returning to the Desert Lands wasn't the best of ideas. She had faced Anna's, Grayson's, and Commander Hargin's wrath for running away to save Jacob and lived through it... Facing Sasha Remoar was an entirely different beast. Literally. She was going to eat Eva alive—

The music ended and cheers roared through the bar. Eva jumped in her seat. Grayson's hand automatically went to her thigh to steady her.

She shook her head clear, ignoring the sly look Anna slid her way, and scanned the rowdy room. They were applauding the band playing in the corner.

No voracious monsters here.

The lead guitarist bowed on behalf of the band, hazel eyes raking over the crowd. They landed on Anna—and stayed on her, growing wide. "My, my, do my eyes deceive me or do I see Annaliese Hargin over there in the dark corner?"

A broad smile graced Anna's face. She stood, inclining her head with a flamboyant air that had Grayson rolling his eyes. Jacob tried to kick him under the table, but ended up hitting Eva's shin instead.

"Your eyes haven't failed you yet, Raffaele," she assured him.

Delighted, he gestured to the band to start playing their next time then he held a hand out to her. "Sing for us, Annaliese dear."

She peered at Jacob, who nodded encouragingly, then beamed like a new morning and hopped to the stage area. She untied her hair and shook out her braid, much to the crowd's satisfaction.

She became an entirely new person. The air around her seemed to glow and buzz with the warmth of her smile. When she sang, the whole room fell silent, listening to her melodious voice harmonise with the instruments.

Their food came around during Anna's performance, and Eva sat back, nibbling on the cheese platter, admiring her friend's talent.

Anna feared her magic because of its potential for destruction, but tonight, unbeknownst to her, her magic played with the candles on tables and sconces on the walls, growing brighter through the crescendo and dimming as she lowered her voice. It was an experience like none other. A thing of beauty, not fear.

Eva peered at her hands, not for the first time wondering if she would ever be able to do something like that with her magic. Hunting, fighting, lightning, storms—all of it destroyed. None of them could put on a beautiful display like Anna.

Food forgotten, Jacob rested his chin on his propped up hand and watched Anna with the wonder of a child before Harvest. The biggest celebration of the year, when people would gift a small portion of their harvest to the gods. Typically, it was more of a big city celebration. Smaller villages like Brar couldn't afford to celebrate, they barely had enough for themselves, let alone to share what little harvest they could bring in with the gods.

"She's amazing, isn't she?" Jacob said dazedly, lost in Anna's trance as she strode through the crowd during a slow and sultry number.

Eva giggled. She'd never seen her brother so hopelessly in love. If only their parents were here to see it. Mom would have made gifts for him to give to Anna, while Dad would have pulled him aside for manly advice.

She pulled a cheesy potato chunk from the platter then pushed it towards Jacob. "You're so cute, Jake."

Jacob's head snapped towards her, eyes bulging, as if her hair had suddenly gone bright pink. "What? Me? *Cute?*" He cleared his throat, deepening his voice. "I'm a man. A Dragon Knight, no less! Not cute. Tell her, Gray."

Snorting, Grayson leaned back, stretching his arm along the back of the bench behind Eva. "I don't know, Jake. As far as Dragon Knights go, you're pretty harmless. Even monsters aren't that deterred by your presence."

Jacob flushed, neck, face, and ears. His cheeks puffed indignantly—which did not help his stance in the slightest. "Come on, man. We're supposed to stick together."

Grayson tapped Eva's shoulder, reminding her just how close he was to her. The entire right side of his body was touching her left, heating her body to the very core. It was a good thing he was more focused on Jacob's flush rather than hers. "I'm more scared of what Eva will do to me if I don't take her side than I am of what *you'll* do to me."

She beamed proudly at the high praise.

Jacob crossed his arms, scowling deeply at his friend. Eva poked the potato platter closer to him, but not before taking another chunk from the plate. They were deliciously addictive. Crunchy skin and fluffy interior, they were baked in the hearth, finished off with a layer of cheese and spices that made Eva's mouth water.

Between Jacob and Eva's obsession with potatoes, if Grayson didn't take one, there wouldn't be any left to try.

The music faded and Anna's voice melded into the crowd as she finished off a final note. Applause filled the tavern. Anna curtsied then skipped back to their table, collapsing into the bench, right into Jacob's side. He had to catch her from falling into his lap, which Eva wasn't convinced was entirely accidental.

"Whoo!" She wiped the sweat from her forehead with the back of her hand. "I do love a drunken, rowdy crowd!" Her gaze bounced to the arm draped behind Eva's back then to Grayson then to Eva with a curiosity burning in her silver eyes. "*He's looking rather cozy with you at his side,*" those eyes said.

Eva answered with a lopsided shrug. "*I'd like to keep it that way, so don't make a big deal about it.*"

As soon as it was brought to his attention, Grayson would most assuredly correct himself, but, for the time being, Eva wanted to enjoy this carefree Grayson a little longer.

Anna's nod was barely discernible. Honouring their silent conversation, she turned her attention to the food laid out on the table.

"Oh! Potato bites!" She snagged the last one, plopping it in her mouth and moaning, which made Jacob's face go even redder. Giggling, forever his tormentor, Anna polished off her ale, somehow laughing and drinking at the same time. She smacked her lips together with a big sigh. Her dreamy eyes trailed over to Eva's half-full mug. Without a word, Eva slid her mug over to her and Anna finished it with a glossy-eyed grin. "Oh no, Eva, it looks like your mug is empty too. Let's go get some more."

Going along with Anna's totally not-so subtle excuse, Eva slid out of the booth and followed her to the bar. They had to elbow their way through another squad then wave for the bartender's attention. Anna placed their order then turned to Eva, leaning her elbow on the bar. She brandished a small vial, dangling it in the space between them.

"Here."

Studying the brown glass vial, Eva accepted it and swirled the dark contents around. "What is it?"

"Contraceptive."

Oh.

Oh!

Heat invaded Eva's face instantly. Slowly, mechanically, her body pivoted towards Grayson in the booth, where he was talking to Jacob, arm still casually resting along the back of the bench where she had been sitting. As if he owned that spot.

Anna followed her gaze, an impish grin on her face. "It's your last night with him, and you two seem... ready. Thought you might want it."

Suddenly, Eva realised why Grayson had stopped them from going further in the healing pools. Neither of them had taken the proper precautions. She hadn't even *thought* about it.

Gods, she really was new to this.

"What about Jacob?"

While he had let Grayson casually keep her within reach, she doubted he would let them sneak off alone together. It didn't matter how much he trusted his partner, he would always be her big overly protective brother first.

Anna grinned. “Let me worry about Jacob. He's going to be too preoccupied to notice what his sister is up to.”

“Thank you.”

From the very bottom of her heart. She'd be a hopelessly lost deer without her amazing partner to watch her back. Her mother had taught her basic self-care, but they'd been too poor to afford something like Anna's brew, so she didn't even know where to find it.

She uncorked the vial, but Anna stopped her, catching her wrist and pulling it away from her mouth. “Don't take it right now or you'll spoil your food and ale. Wait a little closer to the time. It'll last you until your next cycle.”

Nodding and slightly feeling in over her head, Eva closed her fingers around it then tried not to look like a blushing fool when the bartender came by with their drinks. Thankfully, he was so busy, he barely paid them any mind, and was off before they could make the briefest of eye contact.

“Do you have any questions?” Anna asked as soon as the bartender was gone.

Eva shook her head. She'd read the books Anna gave her... but one thought lingered. She peered around at the squad who were none the wiser of their conversation. “No... I read the books you gave me.”

Anna's eyes dazzled with the same excitement she held when she stepped out in front of a crowd. “Good. I want to hear all of the details tomorrow.” She winked then collected their drinks and strutted back to their table.

Eva followed her back to the table, hand slipping to her jacket pocket.

CHAPTER 31
A COPPER FOR YOUR THOUGHTS?

For hours they ate and drank and laughed until they cried. Eva stopped drinking after her third cup. She couldn't remember the last time she had drank this much, and preferred to have a mostly clear mind. In light of the past few days, it felt careless to over indulge.

Would she ever let herself loose again? Let herself drink until her stomach couldn't handle it anymore, or be so relaxed she'd stop looking at the faces of every new patron that entered the building? She didn't know. The instinct was ingrained too deeply now, coiled around her like a second skin. Even in moments of supposed peace, her mind ticked through potential dangers—who was sitting at the nearest table, who had a concealed weapon, who was watching *her*.

There was a time, not too long ago, when she didn't have to worry about these dangers. It'd never crossed her mind, period. But now that time felt like a distant memory, a slither of a simpler life when all she was worried about was how she was going to find her next meal. Letting go meant vulnerability, and vulnerability had gotten her family killed, gotten her hurt. Fifteen Knights had died because she'd gotten careless.

Would she ever be free again?

Perhaps these spiralling thoughts were another reason why she shouldn't drink as much. She used to be able to drink without being plagued by such thoughts, but that, with everything else in her life, was in the past.

"Hey." Grayson bumped her shoulder with his and dipped his head closer, curls at the tip of his locks tickling her temple. "You've gone quiet. A copper for your thoughts?"

It didn't slip past her that he'd used the same phrase she'd used earlier with him. She peered at Jacob, who was looking at Anna with bleary-eyed adoration, then shook her head. "Not here."

Grayson followed her gaze then looked back at her, bringing his hand up to her face and brushing his fingers along her jaw. The simple touch left her skin burning, setting her whole body alight with a yearning only he could satisfy. He had drunk the least of all of them, yet he seemed to be more intoxicated than any of them as he beheld her with eyes so dark she could have mistaken them for the midnight sky. "How about we go for a walk?"

Her heart thundered in her chest, pounding hard in her ribs. *This* was also why she had stopped at three drinks. They had helped loosen her nerves for what might become of their night, but she didn't want to be too drunk to remember it.

"Dance with me, Jake," Anna demanded, already pushing him out of the booth. He compiled without a single glance in their direction. She winked at Eva as she dragged her brother to the small space cleared for anyone who wanted to dance.

Thank you, Anna.

Grayson laced his fingers with hers and led her out of the tavern. The late Fall air was cool and sharp as they hit the street. At this hour, it was empty, save for the crumpled leaves hissing along the cobblestone road; they could have been mistaken for rats under the dim streetlamps.

Grayson secured an arm around her back, holding her close and keeping her warm. She didn't know where they were going—and didn't care. Arkon was in Dragon Canyon, mind closed off from hers. Peace nestled a place in her heart. These were her last few moments in Aboria before she had to leave for the Desert Lands. She wanted to spend every minute—every second—with Grayson, be it a casual stroll down the street or making love under the stars.

He was the first to break the silence, voice as smooth as the breeze against her cheeks, and as soft as the lantern's glow guiding their way. "It was getting too hot and rowdy in there."

"It was," she agreed, finding the cool night air refreshing after sitting in a hot, stuffy booth for hours. "I much prefer the quiet."

"Me too."

They fell silent, with nothing but the pads of their boots on the stone and the rustle of leaves scraping along the road to keep them company. He was giving her space to breathe, to think, to speak when she was ready—just as she'd done for him these past few weeks when getting to know him.

Despite how peaceful the night—the whole city—was, when they passed an alley, her gaze locked onto the shadows, magic lighting up the crates and garbage cans within. No monsters. No assassins to be seen.

She looked up to find Grayson was also scanning the alleyway—and was turning his head to scan the next one on the other side of the street. Always vigilant. Never trusting. Not even at this moment of reprieve.

"Will it always be like this?" she wondered aloud. He halted, gaze locking onto hers. "Will I always be afraid of the shadows?"

She hated that she had to check every crevasse she passed. Hated that she braced herself for a split second before giving it the all clear. But it was a necessity for survival.

His face cracked, raw emotion bleeding through the darkness in his eyes. In the myriad of stars, she could see his pain, his guilt, his fury at everything that had been done to him—and everything the gods had thrown at her.

"I wish I could say no," he said quietly but not weakly. "I wish I could promise the worst is behind us. The world will take. It will take and take until there's nothing left to give. But I will take it for you. So long as I breathe—so long as you'll have me—I will fear the shadows so you don't have to." He took her hand, his skin hot as callouses scraped against her knuckles. There was so much strength in his grasp, as if this was more than a simple need to be touched—he needed her to ground him, tether him. "You're safe with me, Starling. Always."

And she believed him. From the fierce promise in his eyes to the rough grip in her hand and the magic crackling in the air between them—she knew he would do everything in his power to keep her safe. With him, she didn't need to worry about the shadows—or anything outside of the space between them.

It was because of his promise, of the power pulsing out of his very being, that she could finally let herself go tonight.

Never mind the shadows or Darius or Sylus or assassins. Right here, right now, it was just her and Grayson, and she wouldn't let their enemies get between them.

Eva reached up on her tiptoes and brushed a kiss over his lips. It was a soft brush, akin to the very first time she'd kissed him, brewed in uncertainty in both his feelings and her future. But tonight, there was no denying his feelings, and while she still might not know what her future held, she knew she could face it without fear.

A groan pulling out of his throat, Grayson slanted his head, tongue grazing over the seam of her lips. His arms came around her, a hand cupping the back of her neck while the other wrapped around her waist, pulling her tight against him. His mouth worked slowly, leisurely, against hers, taking his time to explore and tease. Every stroke of his tongue stoked the fires clawing inside of her, urging her to knot her fingers into his thick hair in demand.

When his hand slid down to her rear, a moan slipped from her lips. Her body grew hotter, molten under his touch. Fingers dug into his jacket, ready to claw it off him—to feel his skin against hers.

He tasted like mead and steak and peppercorn—and suddenly she was overcome with the desire to know what the rest of him tasted like.

His body responded with a growl rumbling in his chest. Hands seized her legs, lifting her up and tying them around his waist. He walked forward until her back hit a wall, the air flooding from her mouth in a soft gasp.

He froze, gaze snapping up to hers through heady lashes. His breath came in quick pants, fingers digging through the under armour at her sides. Blinking, as if coming out of a spell, he looked up at the wall, then down the street one way then the other. When he turned back to her, he licked his lips, eyes still hazy with lust. "Dangerous, Starling. So very dangerous."

"I remember you telling me you didn't mind a bit of danger."

He smirked at that. "Maybe. But I don't want to fuck you for the first time in a street beside a garbage can."

It wasn't until he voiced it when she remembered where they were. She'd been so intent on *him* that she had quite literally forgotten about the rest of the world. A shameful part of her didn't care and would have him anywhere—

But then she looked down at the garbage can not even three feet away and wrinkled her nose at it.

Chuckling a little breathlessly, he stepped back and set her down on her feet, twining his fingers with hers. "Come with me."

Somehow remembering how her legs worked, she let him lead her down the street, anticipation licking at her heels like lightning chasing a storm.

They paused outside of a double entrance, the wooden doors thick and carved with an elaborate forest etched into the rich oak. One of the higher end inns in Lensenton, where most nobles and merchants rested while on business.

"Uhh..."

Grayson immediately tensed, pivoting to her. He scanned her face for the slightest hint of uncertainty. "If you've changed your mind, just say the word, Starling, and we'll turn back around."

"No!" Gods! No. There were many things she was uncertain about, but choosing to be with Grayson was not one of them. "No, I haven't changed my mind. It's just this place is... nice. *Really* nice." She wasn't used to being in places with marble floors or fancy chandeliers. Aside from Kain Castle. She didn't want to tarnish the place with her muddy boots and the sun-bleached dragon scale jacket she'd swapped out from her formal blazer from the funeral.

He snorted a laugh in disbelief. "I'm not taking you to the shack on the other side of town." That was where most people went when they wanted to be alone. As he described, it did look like a rickety old shack, only held together by its reputation of being *private.*

Suddenly anxious, he licked his lips, examining her face for every detail, like he feared she might be torn away from him at any minute. Or she might run away. "This is..." He paused, considering his words. Finding his resolve, he cleared his throat and started again, "This is new to me, too. As Grayson. Dex was greedy and selfish. He took what he wanted and cared little for his partners." He squeezed their laced hands. "It's different this time. You matter to me, Eva. I want to give you as much of myself as you've given me."

He really knew how to turn her into a puddle of goo. It was a good thing he was holding her or she would have melted right there on the road.

Gods, she loved him. Loved how much he had opened up to her. Loved that he made her feel like she was the only woman in the world for him. Loved the confidence he had in her yet still wanted to take care of her.

This was the man she'd fought with Arkon for countless times. The man she'd fight anyone else for, too. Some people may see the Slayer of Souls or a cold hearted killer, but all she saw was a beautiful man who loved as deeply as she did. He hurt just like anyone else. He beat himself up more than anyone else in this world did. Only he was never allowed to express it.

But for her, he did. He showed her *everything*, and she was eternally grateful to be allowed to see this side of him.

Her tongue darted over her still-swollen lip, bringing his attention down to her mouth. He looked as if he might kiss her again. She hoped he did. But first—she reached up and grazed a kiss on his cheek before tugging him towards the warmth spilling from the doors.

She barely paid attention to the tailored velvet uniforms or the words he exchanged with the receptionist. All she could think about was the heat on her sides where he had held her, the throb on her lips from his rough kiss—the fierce ache blooming in her core.

She was so lost in her euphoria, she hadn't noticed they were going up a wide, arching staircase until her foot caught on a step. His grip tightened on her, keeping her steady as they reached the landing. By the time they reached their room, her heart was running wild in her chest, barely contained by her ribs.

The key freed the lock. Grayson entered first, eyes quickly sweeping over the lavish room that had surely seen far more presentable guests. As he went around tapping lightstone lamps—no overhead lights in here—her feet carried her to the centre of the room. Her boots sank into a plush, shag rug, warm on an otherwise cold, tile floor. A mahogany dresser pressed against one wall, an ornate wardrobe on another. There was a door that led to the bathing chamber. But it was the bed she couldn't look away from. Adorned in rich green silks and white fluffy pillows that took up more of the mattress than she ever could. Silver drapes hung from the bed canopy, elegant and beautiful.

The lock clicked shut, jarring her out of her thoughts. She spun and found Grayson standing by the door, eyes already fixed on her. She didn't think it was possible for her heart to beat harder into her ribcage, but it did—and with it came with so many uncertainties. Not about him. Never him. Of her... and not wanting to disappoint him. She wondered what was going through his mind—if he was as nervous as she was.

"A copper for your thoughts?"

A grin curled at the edges of his mouth. "I've imagined a thousand different ways I could have you, a thousand different times—but I never once thought it would actually happen. Now that you're here, and I only get one night with you... I don't know where to start."

She pressed her palms into her thighs, trying to maintain some level of composure. *It's just like sparring practice... with additional contact.* "I'm not an expert on the matter, but I suppose kissing me would be a good start."

"I suppose it would be." He crossed the room slowly, like a hunter lining up his prey. But instead of hunger simmering in those dark eyes of his, it was appreciation laced with desire. She was a creature to be worshiped, not destroyed.

She waited for her heart to leap out of her chest, but as he neared, it slowed. The nerves ebbed to the recesses of her mind. As his hands slipped around her waist and his unwavering gaze utterly ensnared her, she knew without a doubt that he had never looked at a woman the way he looked at her—with respect, desire, absolute devotion, and all consuming *need.* There was no room for nerves when she tilted her head back to meet his mouth.

There was nothing gentle about this kiss. His mouth crushed against hers, urgent, demanding. Ravenous. Hands claimed her thighs, lifting her, and pressing her core hard against his desire. A moan curled out of her throat as she clawed at his blazer, nails digging deep as he carried her to—she didn't care where.

Her rear hit a desk, eliciting a gasp from her lips. Tilting his head, Grayson's mouth trailed down to her jaw then her throat. Teeth nipped at her sensitive skin, dragging a moan from deep within her chest. His fingers scraped against the fabric of her pants, desperate, hungry, impatient. He tugged her to the very edge of the desk, grinding his hips into hers in the most sensational way. Her own body moved with him, chasing that sweet friction that had noises crawling out of her throat she didn't recognise.

Desperate to feel his skin on hers, she caught the collar of his blazer and yanked it down his back. A smile flitted against her throat as he shucked out of the sleeves, tossing it onto the rug behind him. It still wasn't enough. She was already scraping at his shirt. He broke away a moment to pull it over his head and throw it with the other garment.

She took a moment to admire the corded muscle wrapping around every inch of his torso, every ridge and valley. Her fingers trailed over the rough, azure scar that Bound him to Eran, savouring the growl rumbling in his chest from her soft touch.

Stunning was the only word that came to mind as she beheld him.

“Last chance, Starling,” he murmured, as if it was all he could muster while her hands were on him. “Are you sure this is what you want, now that you know me at my very core?”

Another escape. He’d given her so many opportunities to walk away tonight. Didn’t he know? She’d already made her mind up. He was stuck with her. He’d have to pry her cold, dead hands off him if he wanted to get rid of her.

"I want *you*, Gray," she whispered, her voice breathless, trembling with emotion. "All of you. Grayson. Dex. The man standing before me, your scars, your soul—everything. You're all I've ever wanted."

A sheen glimmered in his eyes, starlight dancing in the lightstone glow around them. His hands moved slowly, gliding up her thighs, arms, throat, until they cupped her face, cradling her as if she was the rarest gem in all of Astrida. Eyes squeezed shut, he leaned forward, not to kiss her, but to press his forehead against hers. His body quaked under her fingertips, heart slamming against her palm. “I don't deserve you, Starling.”

She brought her hands up to his face, brushing her thumbs over the five o’clock shadow dusting his jaw. “Let me be the judge of that.”

When his eyes opened, they were alight with emotion far too deep to unpack with his desire pressed into her thigh. “I promise to spend every day of my life to be worthy of you.”

“You’re already worthy of me, Gray.”

“Let me be the judge of that,” he threw the words right back at her, quirking her favourite lopsided smile.

Her hands fell away from his face as she fumbled her jacket pocket for the vial Anna had given her.

His eyes zeroed in on it, instantly suspiciously. “What’s that?”

Eva pressed her lips shut, fighting the urge to get embarrassed over it. “Anna gave it to me in case we...”

A fully-fledged smile lit up his face, understanding filling those dark storm-cloud eyes. “Of course she did. I’m not going to make you drink it, Starling. I’ll take it.” He swiped it from her grasp before she could protest and chucked the contents down the back of his throat. His face shrivelled in disgust, a shiver chasing down his spine, then he shook it out, managing a wink to alleviate the concern on her face. “It’s highly effective—but it tastes nasty.”

Suddenly it made sense why Anna didn't want her to drink it at the bar, with hours of drinking and eating ahead of them.

He wiped his mouth with the back of his hand then cupped the back of her neck, pulling her flush against him. Teeth clashed, fingers dragged her jacket off her shoulders then knotted into her hair. She tugged her shirt off, pausing the kiss only to slip it past her head. His hands slid down her sides, hot and inviting as they spread their warmth to the rest of her body. A gasp locked in her throat. All she could do was toss her head back and release it in a languid moan.

"You're so fucking soft," he growled against her skin.

His teeth grazed the nape of her neck, driving her need higher. It knotted itself deeper, twisting and turning her inside out. Those fingers, tentative, tantalising, slid to her back, catching the lacing of her breast band and pulling it free. It fell into her lap, but she was more focused on the burning in his eyes as they raked over her with the intensity of a wildfire.

"So fucking beautiful."

With a feather-light touch, he traced the outline of her nipple, ripping a whimper from her lips. Everything he did heightened her pleasure without actually giving in to what her body yearned for.

She'd pocket that information to use against him later.

"Mine."

"Grayson..."

"Hmm. I want you to say my name just like that when I make you come."

Those hungry eyes didn't move from her breasts as his hand trailed down to her stomach, knuckles grazing lightly over her scales. Her breath hitched, body jolting against his as the fire inside of her grew into a roaring inferno with just that simple touch.

"Not so easy to be in control when someone is playing with your scales, is it?"

She clutched his shoulders, gasping for air.

With a smug smirk, he leaned into her, mouth brushing against her ear. "Lie back for me."

She wiggled to the very edge of the desk and laid back, eyes flicking up to the beams in the tall ceiling.

It only just dawned on her that their room was on the top floor.

Then there was no more thinking when his mouth closed on her breast.

She completely lost herself. Her legs clenched around him, fingers knotting into his hair. With every flick of his tongue, she jolted with intense pleasure. There was nothing outside of these walls. Just him and her, free to be their most basic selves, to give in to their desires for just one night.

And just when she thought she couldn't handle it any longer, his tongue rolled over her first scar. She cried out, hips bucking against him.

"Grayson!"

"Just like that," he murmured on her sensitive flesh. Her scales shuddered as his breath spilled over the fine line marking her as Arkon's. "Say my name just like that, Starling."

His teeth nipped then moved to the next one, dragging a long, agonising stroke from one tip to the other. Her hands flew up to her hair; she griped it tight and bit back another cry.

"You're holding back on me," he purred. His lips touched her third scar, and she saw stars.

Fucking stars.

And yet her body was still coiled tighter than a violin string. She was so close to that edge, a single thread away from losing herself entirely.

She'd never wanted to be lost so badly in her life.

"Grayson... Please."

A kiss on her top scar. "Hmm." A nip on the middle scar. "Let me savour you, Starling." A lick along her bottom scar. "We only have one night."

Then, mercifully, his mouth moved away.

His hands moved down to her hips, sliding down to her boots. He unlaced them one at a time, setting them aside gently, as if they were made of glass, rather than leather and steel. When he came back, he tugged on her pants. She tried to hop off the desk, but he held her hips firmly to the solid wood, casting a warning look up to her, before pulling her pants the rest of the way down, freeing her ankles. Just as he did with her boots, he folded her pants neatly and laid them down on the floor beside them. The care he put in with her clothes was oddly sensual and had her insides quivering.

When he was done, he knelt before her and yanked her hips to the edge of the table, hooking her legs over his shoulders. He locked eyes with her, utterly bare before her, despite him having a full view of her. "And it won't fucking be enough."

She didn't have time to sift through Anna's books to figure out what came next. His mouth fell upon her and she fell apart. Sparks flew across her vision. All she could do was hold on to him and let her body take control. It wound tighter. Tighter. An ache bloomed inside of her, she was clenched so tight. She gulped in air desperately in between moans—

Her body erupted and a scream tore free of her throat. She lost all sense of control before she sagged against the desk, releasing Grayson from the iron-tight prison between her thighs.

"Fucking delicious," he ground out, pressing a kiss on the inside of her thigh.

"By Gods. You really are blessed by Lorelus." The god of vitality didn't pull any punches when they created the man who'd just turned her inside out.

Anna's books didn't prepare her for *this*.

Maybe they were mild.

Grayson rose to his full height and gazed upon her with an utterly smug grin born of pure male satisfaction. “Lorelus has nothing to do with it. Come here. I’m nowhere near done with you.” He peeled her off the desk, lifting her into his arms, supporting all of her weight because her bones had dissolved to goo. It was then when she noticed she was completely naked while he still had his pants on.

He laid her down on the feathered bed, silk clinging to the light sheen of sweat on her skin. Soft, gentle kisses traced hot lines down her body, savouring, tentative. Worshipping.

The fire that had fizzled down built up quickly when his lips found her scars. Her hips were rolling in demand, hands clutching the bedsheets, before she knew what she was doing.

Grinning, Grayson slipped off the bed, standing at the end, looking as wicked as the Five Hells and absolutely divine at the same time.

He unbuckled his belt. When his pants hit the floor, Eva’s eyes went wide. He was absolutely stunning. Tailored to perfection by the god he denied having blessed him.

He watched her watch him, eyes blazing with an intensity that made her stomach flutter with anticipation. A cruel grin tugged at one corner of his mouth. “You don’t even know what you do to me, Eva Greene.”

Her whole body burned up when he said her name like that. Like it was a scripture—a blessing from the heavens. She could come again just hearing her name on his lips.

He crawled on the bed towards her, draping the entire length of his body over hers. The weight of him pinned her to the mattress, arms caging her in. It felt so right to have his hips line up with hers, his breath spill over her face. She looped her arms around his neck, curling the hair at the nape of his neck. His eyes shuttered, face going placid from her gentle touch.

“Only you, Starling.”

“Only me, what?”

“Only you can chase away the demons trying to claim my soul.” He brushed a kiss along her forehead. “I don’t want to hurt you. Set the pace. Call the shots. You tell me to stop, and I will.”

“I trust you, Gray.”

Eyes locked onto hers—then she felt the pressure. He started slow, allowing for her to get used to him. But it wasn’t enough. He was so afraid of hurting her, he held himself back, refusing to give in to her body’s yearning to be filled, wholly and completely.

“More.” She arched her back just as he thrust, taking him deeper. Pain lanced through her core for only a moment then he slid out and sank back into her. Instead of pain, a roiling heat took over her body. “*More.*”

Groaning, Grayson gave her exactly what she wanted, taking her straight to the hilt. Her legs wrapped around his hips as she savoured a sense of fullness she'd never experienced.

"Harder."

His hips rolled so slowly, she was worried he wouldn't give in to her request, but then he slammed into her, surging a cry out of her. His mouth covered hers, claiming the noise as his own. Body trembling, he edged her ever closer to that point between bliss and delicious pain. Her nails raked down his back, catching his scars as she fought to hold on to him and meeting him with every stroke.

When she came undone, his roar followed quickly afterward, body quaking above her. Sweat trickling down his back, he laid beside her, wrapping an arm around her waist and pulling her close to him. She curled blissfully into his side, shuddering as his skin brushed over her hypersensitive flesh. He planted kisses on her shoulder and throat, nose grazing the lobe of her ear.

"Are you okay? I didn't hurt you?"

Giggling, she rolled onto her other side to face him. "You didn't hurt me." She cupped his face, savouring the way his stubble scratched against her fingertips. "I'm only sorry that I have to leave in the morning."

Worry furrowed his brow. "You'll be careful while you're gone, won't you?"

"Of course... You'll be careful here, right? I don't know what Commander Hargin has planned for you. Sending you guys to Kain Castle's library is weird."

"We're following a lead I got from Vaelrik. The assassin," he clarified.

There was a lot to unload in that one sentence.

"You knew the assassin?" was her first question.

He nodded solemnly. His fingers absently trailed up and down her arm, leaving goosebumps in their wake. "He served under me. Turns out he's still loyal, after everything I've done. I used it to my advantage."

"And you... carved his eyes and tongue out?"

His eyes hardened. Not a flicker of remorse within them. "I had to send a message."

Eva promised to never judge him. She saw him for who he was, the darkness within and the light he brought into her life, and accepted him wholly for it. The fact he didn't hide the truth from her showed the monumental growth he had undergone for her. Shaming him now for it would be unfair and cruel.

But she couldn't think of the right words to say either. Instead, she tracked a long, jagged scar running from his left clavicle to the right pectoral muscle, just above his nipple.

"You don't approve," he said into the silence.

She blew out a breath, locking her gaze on the scar. "I understand why you'd want to send a message, but... isn't there a better way that doesn't involve maiming and mutilating?"

His fingers hooked her chin and tilted her head gently. Their eyes met. Darkness met by light. "Sylus only understands violence. Now he knows he can't touch you."

She laid a hand over his heart, it still beat rapidly from earlier. "But *you* are not violence anymore." She took his hand and pressed his palm against her own heart. "These hands heal. They protect. They awakened something inside of me I didn't know existed. You were so afraid of hurting me, you held yourself back, even when I told you not to. You let him win by going back to your old ways. You want to send him a message? Show him how different you are now. Show him the man I love."

He stared at her. Blinked. Stared longer. Harder. Disbelief marred his features. "Truly? You... love... *me*?"

She didn't know what hurt more: his doubt in her or the doubt in himself.

She sat upright, facing away from him and crossing her legs. "You don't believe me?"

An arm wrapped around her waist, yanking her back down on the bed. He rolled on top of her, pinning her arms above her head. The weight of his body flush against hers kept her firmly in place. "Doubt you? Never. My ears? Definitely..." He looked at her levelly. "I just never expected to hear someone say they love me."

"I love you, Grayson Smith."

There.

She said it properly, the way her mother used to tell her father—right from the heart. A declaration to the world that *he* was enough for her, that *he* was all she needed to breathe, that it was because of *him* she could bear the hard times they faced.

Warmth filled his features. Smiling, he dipped his face into the nape of her neck, peppering her with kisses that grew hungrier with every stroke of his lips. "I could get used to hearing you say that."

"Good. Because you'll hear it from me everyday when I get back."

She felt his smile grow against her throat before he lifted his face to hers. "You know what I just realised? I haven't shown you the bathing chamber yet."

Laughing, she rested her hands on his shoulders to stop him from pulling away. "What does that have to do with anything?"

His eyes shone with mischief in the dim lighting. "There's something I want to show you."

Too curious, she let him peel her off the bed and show her.

He didn't have to say the words back. She knew deep down in his heart that he loved her. When he was ready, he would tell her. For now, she was going to savour every minute she had left with him. They had rented the *entire* room for the night, so they might as well put it to good use.

CHAPTER 32
FAREWELLS AND DISTANT TRAVELS

Eva felt like a teenager returning from a date when Grayson walked her to the gravel pit just outside of Lensenton in the early hours of the morning. Just a slither of orange stretched across the horizon through the treeline. The ground was laden with a fine mist that clung to her clothes, remnants of the night the sun had yet chased away.

Arkon and Eran were waiting for them, the former's tail flickered behind him like an agitated cat. Eva sheepishly walked up to her dragon, having already said her goodbyes to Grayson before they left the inn. Arkon looked down at her, his mind closed off from her, as promised when she was with Grayson. His colossal head lowered to her level. When her fingers touched his horn, his mind flooded back into hers, seeping deep into her soul and bones.

She exhaled, whole once again.

He recoiled, as if shocked by their own power, when her soul wove its way into him. Crystal eyes locked with hers. "*You are happy.*"

"*I am.*"

His eyes slid in Grayson's direction. He stood apart from Eran, arms crossed and feet planted. A challenge. He'd purposely separated himself from his dragon, his only true protection from another dragon, to dare Arkon to attack him. Judge him. Spit accusations at him. Whatever, he was ready to face it.

For her.

"*He did this to you.*"

She rolled her eyes at the accusation. Could he make it sound any more sinister? "*He did.*"

The dragon swung his gaze back to her. "*I have not felt you this happy since our souls became one.*" Huffing, wings twitching on his back, he approached the Dragon Knight, lifting his head high so he could look down on him. "I do not trust you. I know the darkness you harbour within yourself. Eran shouldn't have Bonded with you. But..." He paused, as if he was searching for one more reason to distrust him. But then he came up empty. "I will accept you as Eva's mate. Her happiness is my happiness. So long as her heart beats for you, I will no longer call you Slayer."

Grayson bowed deeply, respectfully, right fist hovering over his heart. The Dragon Knight who bowed to no one. "Thank you, Arkon."

Arkon's tail coiled around Eva's feet. "It is time to depart."

Her heart clenched. Quickly, she skipped to Eran, reaching up as he dipped his head for her. She ran her fingers over the beautiful azure scales of his snout. "Look after him for me, Eran."

"I will."

"And take care."

"You as well, Precious One."

He exhaled a long, measured breath, fog much thicker than the mist blanketing the forest spilling from his maw and encasing the entire gravel pit. It wrapped around her, cold yet reassuring. Magic tingled along her flesh, coating her skin in a thin layer of frost.

She studied the slight shimmer on the back of her hand. "What's this?"

"Protection from the sun. It won't last you the entire three months, but I hope it will serve you well."

She shouldn't have expected anything less from the compassionate dragon, but her chest warmed at the gesture all the same. "Thank you."

When the fog fell away, Arkon was flat on his belly, awaiting her. She cast one last glance at Grayson, wishing she could crawl back into bed with him a little bit longer. He stood still, as if his feet were rooted to the ground beneath him. He offered an encouraging nod, playing her favourite lopsided smile.

Feeling as though she was swallowing gravel, she swung into Arkon's saddle.

"Eva?" Grayson called. She swiveled in the saddle to meet his gaze. His expression was stoic, but she saw the emotion in his eyes he wouldn't dare show anyone else. "Break Bruce's kneecaps for me."

She couldn't help but grin. "If he throws me into another pit, I'll electrocute him back into the last century."

His smile turned devilish. "You know the way to a man's heart."

Her throat constricted tight. Tears threatened to spill over. "May the winds be in your favour, Grayson."

"And yours, Starling."

With a single powerful thrust of Arkon's wings, they were airborne. Too quickly, Grayson disappeared in the canopy. Too quickly, she wanted to turn around and give him one last hug, to breathe in his scent of leather and steel.

Three months, she promised herself. *I'll be back in three months.* She'd been away longer than that. She could make it three months.

Their flight back to Dragon Canyon was silent. Eva was too busy going through a mental list of everything she needed to pack and where it was hiding in her room. She probably should have packed it before going to Lensenton with the squad, but she'd been too caught up in her grief and guilt to plan ahead.

Arkon was still a few feet off the Stables's floor when Eva leapt out of his saddle and ran for her room. If Commander Hargin found out she had left her mission late...

No, thinking about it was wasting time she didn't have.

She slammed the door open, fully prepared to tear her room apart and deal with cleaning it when they returned—but Anna was leaning on the back of the couch, humming as she braided her hair. Two bags were at her feet, stuffed to the seams.

A feline smile crept up Anna's face at the sight of her partner, in a suspiciously good mood considering the hour. Usually Eva was the chipper one in the morning, far more used to being up this early from her hunting days. "Well, well, well, look who finally decided to come back."

All of the blood in Eva's body rushed up to her head.

Anna finished tying off her braid then tossed it over her shoulder. Rising, she lugged one bag onto her shoulder then tossed the other to Eva. The impact knocked the air out of her lungs, and she had to take a step back to brace herself.

"So?" Anna pressed.

Eva pried the bag open for a quick inspection, and a wave of gratitude hit her harder than the bag itself. Everything she needed for their trip was there. Anna was a gift from the gods. Satisfied, she swung the bag onto her shoulders.

A grin split her face. "So, he *absolutely* knew what he was doing."

Squealing, Anna threw her arms around her. "I'm so happy for you guys. You totally deserve each other."

"Thanks, Anna." Eva squeezed her friend, catching a hint of Jacob's scent in her hair, then headed back into the hallway for the Stables. "So? How did things go with Jacob after we left?"

Her smile lit up the whole hallway. "Oh, you know, we danced, drank some more, made out a little in the booth—then I rocked his socks off. He was still sleeping like a log when I left." She sighed wistfully. "It's going to be a very long three months."

"Tell me about it," Eva grumbled. She still felt the ghost of Grayson's hands on her. With just a memory, her body ached to have him again.

She climbed into Arkon's saddle once again and took to the skies.

Clear skies blessed them as they crossed the continent. Yet, despite the sun's warm rays, the wind's chill dug its vicious claws into Eva's bones, threatening to freeze her blood. Permanently.

When they reached the ocean, she had to pull out extra layers from her bag if she didn't want to catch frostbite. With the colours and terrain—green, yellow, red, sweeping up the sides of mountains—of her old stomping grounds to distract her, she could easily push the cold out of her mind. Gliding over the monotonously blue ocean? She had nothing but her gloves and jacket to keep her warm.

"*How are you handling the cold, Arkon?*" Unlike her, his body would actually lock up if he was too cold. Not exactly an ideal situation when flying over the water in the middle of nowhere.

"*My blood is fine. The wind bounces off my scales. When the land itself is cold, we must be cautious.*"

"*Duly noted.*"

They hit a few pit stops on the small islands speckling along their flight path. When the sun began its descent, they landed on a deserted island sitting on the borders between Aboria, Estrus, and the Desert Lands. Nobody laid claim to it, so it was aptly named No Man's Land.

With a few hours of sleep under their belt, they set course for the Desert Lands again. This flight was by far the most leisurely flight she'd taken to the Desert Lands. Last time, she and Arkon couldn't have gotten away from Aboria fast enough. He had pushed himself to get her to Sasha as quickly as possible. Then on the way back... Well, she didn't know it was possible for him to fly so fast.

This time, there was no rush. Wasting their dragons' energy was pointless and dangerous.

Soon, the water changed colour, shifting from the deep cerulean blue to a pale teal. Fuchsia and ochre glimmered under the clear water. Coral. She looked forward to swimming with the colourful fish again. If Sasha would let her.

The air grew thick with humidity, making Eva's clothes stick to her skin. One layer at a time, she shedded it all off until she was left in her sleeveless under armour and riding pants. True to Eran's promise, the sun merely glided along her skin but didn't penetrate the layer of magic he had enveloped her in.

"*Eran is a powerful dragon,*" Arkon explained her wonder. "*Lorelus granted him magic beyond most water dragons' abilities. You will be protected for many weeks, possibly a couple of months.*"

She sat back in her saddle, having no need to hug his back for the most optimal wind resistance, and considered his words. "*Ebis blessed you, didn't he? You're powerful.*"

"*My magic is strong,*" he explained patiently, "*because lightning can pierce through both scale and mithril. But among my kind, my overall magical power is only average. However, when paired with water magic, my abilities become significantly stronger. Against earth magic, though, my lightning is far less effective.*"

"*Balance,*" she murmured.

"*Exactly. The five elements counter and complement each other. Fire is weak to water but strong against earth. Earth is vulnerable to water yet can resist lightning. Air enhances fire and can amplify my storms, but earth can smother it. I've seen air and water come together to create ice magic.*"

Her mind buzzed with so many questions. The books in the library covered magic, but mostly how the elements related back to the gods. None of them went in depth with the elements coming together to form other kinds of magic.

"*Lightning magic is born from air and fire,*" Arkon added on to her thoughts.

"*So there are other kinds of magic out there? Why can't I find any books on it?*"

"*Knowledge that is passed down from generation to generation gets lost. As the human population grows, creatures of magic are forced to find new places to nest. There are less encounters and thus less people to talk about it and research it.*"

She considered this further.

"*Are there other kinds of dragons?*" If storm dragons originated from air and fire, then surely there were others.

"*Yes, though they are rare breeds. Rarer than I. I've met one nature dragon in my time and have only heard of a corrosion dragon.*"

Nature, Eva could deduce, but corrosion? She couldn't imagine a dragon with that ability.

"*It is said that the dragon produces an acid that could melt almost anything.*"

Eva shuddered at the thought of getting that acid on her skin.

Catching a glint in her peripheral, Eva lifted her gaze to the horizon. A golden hue fell into view, stretching as far as she could see. Just above the horizon, the air rippled with the promise of an unrelenting heat Aboria's summers could never contend with.

They closed in quickly and soon all Eva could see was an endless ocean of sand. Dunes undulated like snakes in the brutal winds, the peaks burnt red from the heat. While Aboria settled to hibernate for the winter, it appeared Summer was on the rise in the Desert Lands.

A powerful gust nearly ripped Eva off her saddle. She had to dig her heels into the stirrups and grip the handles as if Arkon was flying at top speed.

"Sandstorm!" Anna shouted over another strong wind. She pointed north, toward a roiling wall of sand moving towards them. Fast.

Sandstorms were apparently more prevalent in the summertime. Eva didn't experience one during her last visit, but Sasha had warned her enough about them for her to know they needed to find shelter. Yesterday.

Arkon's magic poured over the land with the same urgency clawing at her chest. Flooding her eyes with magic, she searched desperately for a cave big enough for the dragons. Their scales could withstand the assault, but the leather on their wings would be torn to shreds.

"There!" Anna called, thrusting a finger eastward. Eva followed her gaze and spotted a cluster of black stones. It wasn't perfect, but it was better than nothing.

Arkon pumped his wings harder. The wind picked up swiftly, tossing his weight around as if he was no bigger than a pebble. Eva tightened her grip on the saddle, knuckles going white from the tension.

Aster landed first, diving for the biggest gap between the towering formation. The monolith-like structures were taller than Aster, but were no wider than an ancient tree. Anna slid out of her saddle and tucked in tight against her dragon's belly as she curled around her rider.

Sand scratched at Eva's face, slipping through her riding mask. It raked down her arms, tearing at her hair. Eran's magic protected her from the sun's heat, but it did nothing against the sand.

"*Jump!*" Arkon commanded as he hovered above Aster. The winds jostled him, shoving him into one of the stone structures. Eva cried out as pain flared up her leg, where Arkon had hit one of the monoliths. He clamped down on his mind, sheltering her from the pain while she jumped off his back, falling ten feet before rolling into Aster's protective embrace. The dragon swung her wings forward, encasing them in as much leather and scale as possible. Arkon curled around the smaller dragon, using his body to take the brunt of the sandstorm.

Wind whistled between the dragons. Sand scraped against their scales and the rocks surrounding them. Sweat beaded along Eva and Anna's skin, the heat between the dragons' embrace and the desert growing unbearable.

"How long do sandstorms usually last?" Eva whispered in the darkness. Their dragons had sealed them in so tight, only a sliver of light trickled through Aster's wing joint. But even with that small sliver, sand poured in and fell on Eva's shoulder. She wouldn't be surprised if her lap was filled with sand within the hour.

"*Hours*," Anna grumbled, shifting her weight so she sat cross-legged. Might as well get comfy if they were going to be there a while.

Eva copied her and let the tension in her shoulders relax. There was nothing she could do to help Arkon and Aster, only sit and wait.

"Too bad we don't have Glade with us," Eva muttered. This sandstorm wouldn't have been an issue with her around. All she had to do was erect a shelter for all of them to hide in. Arkon wouldn't have to risk his wings.

"Right?" Anna agreed. "Did Grayson ever tell you why *they* had to go to Kain Castle's library? It seems like a scribe's job more than a Dragon Knight's. Especially those two."

Eva rubbed her arm, hissing as it stung where her fingers made contact with several shallow scratches. It was the distraction she needed from thinking about the cold, remorseless eyes she'd gazed into when Grayson confessed he'd been the one to mutilate Vaelrik.

"He said they were following a lead from the assassin," she conveyed, feeling a pit form in her stomach as she spoke.

She'd promised herself not to judge, and she didn't. She knew who Grayson was at his core, whether he knew or not. But she couldn't deny that imagining Grayson carving the eyes out of a skull was an unsettling image--one almost too hard to picture clearly. She just hoped that he'd only use his hands to heal from now on

"Hmm. Must have been a pretty good lead for my mother to order them to look into it further." She glanced at Eva's red-stained fingertips. "Still, his magic could be handy right about now."

Rifling through her bag, she gathered ointment, bandages, and a disinfectant then proceeded to clean Eva's wounds. They'd learned during their last visit that infections were quick to bloom and difficult to eradicate. All wounds, big or small, needed to be dealt with immediately.

They spent most of the hours during the sandstorm in silence, listening to the howl of the wind. Both dragons had closed their minds off from them so they couldn't feel the sting on their wings.

Eva wrung her hands nervously. The last thing she remembered in Arkon's mind was the flash of pain from his collision into the pillar before he shut her out. It had been a nasty gash, which was now being pelted by a relentless wave of sand. She wished he would let her take the pain from him, just as he had done for her. It was bad enough that he was forced to bare the storm alone, without her touch to sooth him.

The storm finally let up just before sunset, leaving them in a cloud of dust and a set of ruins that made the hairs on her neck stand on end.

Arkon and Aster broke away from their embrace, shaking a mountain of sand off their scales as they made space for the Dragon Knights. While Aster and Anna worked on making a fire in the centre of the ruins, Eva inspected Arkon's wounds.

Air hissed through her teeth as she sucked in a sharp breath. His leg was still bleeding, hours later, and his wings were bright red, glistening in the moon's early light.

"Arkon..."

"I will be fine," he grunted, curling his tail around himself and tucking the wings flat against his back to hide his injury. She didn't need to be Bound to him to watch him flinch from the pain.

"Stubborn fool," Aster growled by the roaring fire. "You did not have to shelter me from the storm."

"Then your wings as well as mine would be compromised, Aster."

Huffing, she turned her head away from him, wings fluttering indignantly against her back. "Come join me by the fire. I will keep your blood warm tonight."

A rumble vibrated in Arkon's chest, but he didn't protest as he lumbered over to her, collapsing into her side.

Eva and Anna exchanged a secret glance. They said nothing as they sat on the opposite end of the fire from their dragons. It was too early for them to pry into... whatever was going on between their dragons. For now, they rolled out their bedrolls and slept under the fire's protection.

In the morning, they set out again. Arkon's wounds had mostly healed during the night, but his wings still wavered in the winds. They took as many breaks as he needed, though he was loath to admit he needed them.

At the end of the third day of their journey, Storm Cove fell within their sights.

PART
II

CHAPTER 33
ANOTHER DAY, ANOTHER BLISTER

Fuck this heat.

Fuck his brother for dragging him through the desert.

You know what? Fuck. It. All.

Dravyn Fortys tipped his head back and emptied the remainder of the canteen on his face. The splash of water was a reprieve for a grand total of two blissful seconds before it soaked up the sun's rays like a sponge and seared his forehead and cheeks. He wiped his face with the thin scarf he'd been using to shield his head from the heat. Blisters hissed against his flesh. New ones.

That makes thirty-six. Three more since he last counted, which was last night. Every night. For the past two nights they'd spent on this blasted continent.

Why count?

No fucking clue.

Maybe it was to add to the misery? Or maybe it helped keep his mind off the monotonous land they had found themselves in.

Their father had given them a map—a map Dex had marked with his own hands before he died—and told them to go find a bunch of old forgotten relics. Seemed like a dumb waste of time for a couple of princes, but he insisted that they be the ones to seek them out.

On a whim, Darius picked the Desert Lands. Dravyn secretly thought he picked it because he knew his little brother *hated* being hot. He rarely wore anything more than a short sleeved shirt. Here, he was forced to wear a thin long sleeve to avoid the direct glare of the sun.

Suffocating. The only way to describe the perpetual feeling gnawing at his flesh—

Thawp!

Darius's hand connected with the back of his head. Stars danced in his peripheral vision. For a dazed moment, he couldn't tell which way was up or down. He gripped the pommel of the awkward camel saddle to steady himself—then threw a glare at his bastard of a brother.

It should have been him. Fuck. He *wished* Darius was the one who had defected and had to be put down. He would have prayed to the Aborian gods if he thought it would make a lick of difference.

But Fate was a cruel, cruel mistress.

Darius growled furiously, "You did *not* just use the last of our water to douse yourself."

"Would you rather I die in this insufferable heat? Oh, wait—don't bother answering. I already know." If he was stuck out here with Darius, in this merciless desert, he'd hold on to those two blissful seconds of reprieve. With everything he had.

Darius curled his lip up at him in pure loathing. "Careful, Dray. Father didn't tell me you had to come back with me."

"Don't threaten me with a good time, brother." He was too much of a coward to take his own life, but if he kept pushing Darius's buttons, his brother would do it for him without question. He just hadn't found out which buttons to press.

Grunting, Darius yanked on the reins, pulling the camel to a halt. Dravyn's camel stopped automatically. Muttering under his breath, the Crown Prince rummaged through his packs and fished out the map, which was growing increasingly more wrinkled every time he had to pull it out.

Dravyn missed their wyverns. The wind at least alleviated some of the heat. He could catch a wisp of salt and seaweed in the air if he closed his eyes and inhaled deeply—ignoring the dust and flies. He could distract himself from the monotony, the blisters grating against the constricting fabric—the fact he'd rather be *anywhere* but here. Doing anything but travelling the world with his dickhead of a brother.

Squinting, Darius examined the map closely, glancing at the position of the sun every now and again. His tongue ran over his top layer of teeth, jaw rocking back and forth as he thought through his plans thoroughly.

Dravyn sighed, drumming his fingers against the tough leather pommel, being sure not to direct his dry stare Darius's way. He could sit back and enjoy watching his brother struggle with the map—one of the many things he was utterly terrible at—or he could end their suffering and lend him a hand...

Hmm. What a predicament.

Deciding that getting out of the heat took priority over his own entertainment, Dravyn pointed southward with a grand gesture he knew Darius would hate. He had memorised the map before they arrived in the Desert Lands and knew not only where the X Dex had marked was, but also the location of the nearest settlement. Given their dwindling water supply, Dravyn figured Darius was trying to determine how far they were from the settlement. "South is that way."

Darius shot him a look that made most men quiver. Dravyn had long ago dubbed it his Resting Bitch Face. "I know how to read a fucking map."

"We both know you can barely read a confession note. Do you want to die of dehydration, 'cause if you do, I'll dig our graves right now."

Growling, Darius shoved the map back into a different bag he'd gotten it from. Dravyn didn't bother correcting him. The fearless leader yanked on the camel's reins and guided it southward towards the settlement.

Dravyn kept his head down to avoid the ruthless sun and wiped the sweat from his forehead.

Ah! Thirty-seven. The buggers really snuck up on him if he didn't keep his skin covered. He wouldn't have any blisters if Darius had let them keep their wyverns, but, for once, his logic was sound in leaving them behind: finding an old crumbling ruin was next to impossible in the air. Everything blended together on the back of a wyvern, they moved so quickly. A leaning pillar could be easily mistaken as weirdly shaped rock. So they were forced to search for the ruins on foot. Well. Camelback.

They reached the settlement in good time, which was an upgrade from the last one. Where the other had rags and poles for them to take shelter in, this one had buildings made of packed sand. The design reminded him of the forts he used to make in the snow—to his father's dismay. They built them into the sides of the largest dunes, the ones that not even the strongest of winds could tear down. If they had been on a wyvern, they would have missed the settlement.

They paused at the edge of the boundary line, formed by a hip-high wall made out of the same packed sand as their buildings. A defensive perimeter. Question was: what were they defending from? Estrus had its fair share of nasty beasts for Dravyn to know that they couldn't be the only ones to have the same problem. However, they had seen neither hide nor hair of beasts here. Only desperate, malnourished people, who had tried to kill them for their supplies—and paid for it.

Dravyn eyed the people in this settlement, noting the children being corralled into their homes, while the men gathered in the long street leading directly to the well in the centre.

Defenders or scavengers?

Both princes dismounted, but when Dravyn moved to follow his brother, Darius held his hand out, palm up. "Give me your canteens, I'll fill them. Stay with the camels."

Travelling without camels was a death sentence. Protecting them was almost as important as a healthy water supply.

Wordlessly, Dravyn collected all five canteens from his bags and passed them to Darius. The Crowned Prince accepted them without breaking stride, their collection of canisters in one hand, his broadsword balanced in the other.

He advanced toward the gathering settlers, sword angled down, casual but with an underlying threat. A murmur rippled through the crowd. Men and women glanced at each other, waiting for someone—anyone—to step forward, but no one did. The absence of a leader left them hollow-eyed and hesitant, shifting like cattle unsure of which way the wolf would turn.

When Darius crossed the boundary, the settlers instinctively recoiled. Dust scuffed under their boots as they shuffled back, the crowd parting wide for him. He didn't raise his voice, didn't even slow his pace; authority radiated from the deliberate weight of each step, from the quiet certainty that he belonged on whichever ground he chose to walk.

Resting Bitch Face is triumphant yet again.

Darius filled their canteens and returned to Dravyn's side without hassle. A shame. Dravyn wouldn't have minded fighting his way through some pesky scavengers. At least then the pain he felt would be earned.

With barely a glance in his direction, Darius mounted his camel and set a course for the ruins. Dravyn heaved a sigh as he climbed into his saddle.

Another day in paradise.

CHAPTER 34

HISTORY BOOKS AND APOCALYPTIC ARTIFACTS

"Have you heard anything from them yet?"

Jacob tipped his book down just enough to look at Grayson over the top, then peered at the intimidating stack of books they had yet to read, and then at the pathetically tiny stack they had sifted through. Both being well-read, intelligent men, they should have been halfway through the stack by now. The librarians had given up bringing them new texts after observing their disappointingly slow pace. They were probably wondering why Commander Hargin would send *them* to read a bunch of books. Jacob hadn't doubted her orders. Until now.

The reason they were behind was right across the table from him.

"No," Jacob answered curtly then went back to reading his passage. He'd lost his place in the paragraph and had to restart. Again. He was a patient man, but his partner—*Grayson*, of all people—was testing his limits.

Grayson's heel tapped restlessly against the marble floor, the sharp rap of his boot echoing all around the tower. The librarians had already asked him to stop—twice—and received the same response: a death glare.

"You're sure you didn't receive a hawk this morning?"

Jacob stared at him. Hard. Who in the Five Hells was this man standing in front of him? Because he sure as hell wasn't Grayson Smith.

Grayson Smith was calm. Collected. Unshakable. He didn't fidget, didn't get antsy. And he definitely didn't waste this much energy fretting over other people.

Yet here he was, restless like a caged beast, tension coiled in his shoulders, his jaw set tight. This wasn't the man Jacob knew—this was someone else entirely.

Granted, Eva and Anna weren't *other people*, but still... This behaviour was suspicious.

"You know the hawk cage is the first place I check before breakfast... and lunch... and the last thing I do before bed." He damn well knew because he followed him to the cage before breakfast and lunch and bed. "What's gotten into you?"

Grayson chewed on the side of his cheek, redirecting his gaze to the unread stack of texts. "They should have arrived by now."

Jacob rolled his eyes. Hecouldn't *believe* what he was hearing. Normally, *he* was the anxious one. Being the calm one for once was unnerving. How did Gray do it all of the time?

"It's been three days," Grayson pressed, seemingly trying to convince Jacob to do something about it. "Eran and I made it in a day and a half."

Jacob inhaled a breath of patience then blew it out. "First of all, Eran is one of the bigger dragons in the canyon, he's faster than most. Even if Arkon can keep up with that pace, Aster can't. Secondly, you were on a time crunch. Anna showed me their flight path. If everything goes according to plan, they'll reach Storm Cove by the end of today. Expect a missive in two."

Grayson was entirely unconvinced, the death glare he'd been aiming at the librarians for the past couple of days turning on him now.

"Look," he went on, now understanding how his father felt when he explained to him and Eva that their chickens weren't pets after catching them dote on the new chicks. "I know being away from the girls is difficult. Trust me, I miss them as much as you do, but they have their mission and we have ours. Focus."

After a moment of consideration, Grayson nodded and went back to reading.

It was important that Eva learned how to use her magic, but it was more important that he and Grayson focused on their mission. The assassin had told them King Sylus intended on ridding the world of magic. Their job was to find out more about the vestiges the assassin mentioned, how they were used to destroy magic, and where they could be found. A scribe's job, honestly, but Jacob understood that this information was sensitive—and possibly world-ending—so it made sense why Commander Hargin set them on the case. Still... he couldn't shake the feeling that he was missing something.

Jacob forced his eyes back to the page. He was all for studying battle strategies and combat theory, but these old, dusty books were as dull as bricks. The handwriting was difficult to decipher, often scribbled in haste to get the *riveting* revelation out on paper before the thought slipped from the author's mind. His eyes strained painfully to pick out the important bits.

Most of what he could decipher circled back to the Shattering—a cataclysm that split the world apart thousands of years ago. Astrida had once been a single massive continent; now it lay broken into scattered shards across the seas.

The texts couldn't agree on whether the Shattering itself, or the events leading to it, had unleashed magic. What was clear was that before then,

Astrida had been as barren of magic as Estrus. It was a peaceful time in history, but frustratingly little was written about it. Then came the Shattering, and magic poured through the cracks like floodwater—wild, raw, and merciless. It warped everything. Monsters clawed their way into lands humans once ruled, and new races appeared—dwarves, elves, druids. From then on, survival boiled down to one choice: adapt or die.

Centuries of war divided the land. Whole peoples were driven into exile or wiped out. Somehow, humans endured, though monsters remained a constant threat, which was why the Dragon Knights had been founded. The Goblin Wars had been the last great reckoning, cutting down humans and monsters alike. No one knew when the next would come.

Yet, despite all the death and carnage, there was no mention of a vestige of great power—or even several of them.

Once he finished yet another useless book, he tossed it onto the "read" stack, earning a glare from a passing librarian. He was too busy rubbing his eyes to notice. After a quick temple massage, he peered through the fluffy fringe threatening to poke his eyes at his partner. Grayson's eyes, while looking stoic and pensive, didn't move on the page. Actually, come to think of it, he hadn't flipped a page in a while.

The asshole wasn't reading.

Groaning, Jacob tipped his head back, looking past the rafters nearly impossible to see they were so high up, and stared at the gods watching him.

Asturias, you're testing me, aren't you?

The Queen of the Pantheon would do that—stick him in a room with a renegade prince, who apparently had more important things to think about than the mission at hand, and see how long it would take for him to snap.

It took strenuous effort to pull his head down to look at his partner. "Gray?"

Silence.

"*Grayson*," Jacob pressed. When his partner still refused to look at him, lost in his thoughts, he threatened: "Don't make me use your other name."

Grayson snapped out of his evidently deep thoughts and shook his head clear. Blinking, he regarded Jacob skeptically. "Why aren't you reading? You're the one who insisted we *focus*."

Jacob crossed his arms, feeling the vein in his temple throb. "I finished my book. You haven't turned a page in hours."

His eyes shifted sheepishly as he scratched the back of his head. "I've been thinking."

"Clearly." Jacob inhaled sharply, finding it deep—*deep*—within himself to remain calm. On a more level note, he added, "You're not telling me everything. You said no more secrets, Gray."

You won't know the monster you've harboured until it's too late. Would those words ever stop repeating in his head? When would Grayson stop hiding things from him—from Anna?

Sighing, Grayson set the tome down on the table and looked at him. "I know. You're right, I haven't been entirely forthcoming with you."

Jacob steeled himself. Whatever he had to say couldn't be worse than finding out the partner he had to trust his life with used to be the Slayer of Souls. Right? If Jacob could forgive and live with that, he could forgive Grayson for whatever else he'd been hiding. He just needed to know the faith he had in him wasn't misplaced. He wanted to confidently trust him again.

Grayson's mouth pressed together in a tight line as he collected his thoughts. "Hargin asked me to interrogate the prisoner."

Jacob worked very hard not to show any physical signs of his shock—and horror. "You mean the assassin who was beheaded then whose eyes and tongue went mysteriously missing?"

Grayson rolled his eyes at his tone, which Jacob felt held the right amount of concern considering the subject matter. "Eva's already given me grief about that."

Eva? When did he have time to tell his sister this?

"What I'm about to tell you, I didn't tell Eva," he said, and Jacob didn't miss the slight bitter edge to it. "Sylus's plan to rid the world of magic was initially..." He hesitated, mouth pressed in a tight line. "It was initially *my* plan."

Jacob stared at him for an immeasurable amount of time. He knew Dex had done awful things he wasn't proud of. Had killed people, destroyed families, suppressed entire villages, in his father's name. It had taken Jacob a while to get over it, to see the man Grayson was trying to become, to *want* to help him become that man. But, he hadn't realised how much he had brushed aside, how woefully ignorant he had chosen to be—until this confession. The man across from him had, at some point in his life, devised a plan that would wipe out a large portion of the world's population.

Destroying magic didn't just mean removing it from the air and land. It meant killing every single being that had magic in its blood. Dragons, goblins, druids, Soul Bound. Everything. This plan was *truly* evil.

He swallowed the jagged rock in his throat. "And... you were actually going to do it?"

Grayson's gaze didn't waver. Jacob couldn't decide if it would be more or less terrifying if he looked away. "No. My father said the plan was an unnecessary use of time and resources."

Jacob released a breath of relief. His partner hadn't been *entirely* evil back then.

"I keep thinking that if I hadn't been so eager to please Sylus, that if I hadn't unearthed long-forgotten, forbidden knowledge, he would have never found out about the vestiges. He wouldn't be attempting genocide..." His brow puckered, eyes strained. "This is my fault."

Guilt. That was what had kept him so preoccupied. To hide from it, he had fixated on Eva and Anna's progress. But there were some things he couldn't run from.

Jacob swallowed. "Does Commander Hargin know?"

"No. No one. Only you. I'm..." His throat bobbed. "Sorry."

Jacob flinched at the apology. Quite possibly the first apology he'd ever heard from his friend. "Hey, man, there's no need to—"

Grayson's hand slammed on the table. "The *entire world* is in danger because of *me*, Jake. Don't pity me. Hate me. Curse my name. Tell me what an abhorrent man I am."

"If I did, I'd be lying." Jacob kept his tone level, on the verge of playful, if only to ease Grayson's mind. The news had been shocking, but Jacob knew he wasn't that man anymore. If Grayson was to do it all over again, he'd never bring a plan like this to light. "Look, it's done now. You're here, with me at this table in this stuffy library, researching for a way to stop Sylus. So, instead of moping, use that brain of yours to help me get through all of these godsdamn books."

A smirk tugged at the edge of his mouth. "That sounded like one of my pep talks. I'm rubbing off on you."

Jacob relaxed into the cushions. "Yes, well, you've learned from me over the years, I figured I should try to get *something* out of you." His eyes wandered back to the book he'd just finished. He laid a hand on the rough leather bindings. Gods, it was old, older than he likely thought it was, held together by the magic in the stone beneath his feet and its tentative caretakers. *One* of them had to hold the answers they sought. "Why is Sylus doing this? Why go to such extreme measures all of a sudden?"

"He didn't *need* to wipe out magic before," Grayson agreed thoughtfully. "Something between then and now has changed."

"Eva?" Jacob guessed.

Grayson nodded gravely. "He was content when my brothers and I killed all of the storm dragons, but now that Eva and Arkon exist..."

"She's a threat," Jacob finished when he didn't. "But why? Why did he order you to kill the storm dragons to begin with?"

"There is a prophecy: a woman whose hair has been touched by ash, who will mount a black dragon and claim the power of Ebis, will be Sylus's undoing."

Jacob's eyes went wide. Goosebumps rose along his arms, hair prickling on the back of his neck. That description was eerily familiar. Too familiar to write off as a coincidence. "That's Eva."

He sat back in the plush leather chair, shoving his hair out of his face as it fell over his brow.

Five Hells. This was a lot to process.

His little sister, prophesied before she was born—before his parents had met each other—to bring down a kingdom. If he doubted the gods' existence before, it was hard to argue with their existence now. Sylus knew she was coming and ordered the storm dragons' extinction to prevent her from fulfilling her destiny.

Every death, every tragedy, every moment of agony that Eva—that he and so many other people—had suffered through was entirely by design from beings with power far beyond their understanding. All for what?

They may never know the answer.

Would she ever have the normal life he wanted her to have?

Grayson leaned his forearms onto the table, eyes as hard as tempered steel—and just as sharp. "It's going to be all right, Jake."

"How can you say that?"

As far as he knew, every decision he had made wasn't actually *his* decision—it was a god pulling strings from above. His little sister's life hung in the hands of a god's whim. A whim! Who was to say what they had planned for her? The gods were just as cruel as they were benevolent.

"Because I'm going to be with her every step of the way," Grayson declared, as if his presence alone could compete against a god. "She may be the one described in the prophecy, but that doesn't mean she'll be doing it alone. Whatever she needs from me, I'll give it to her. So will Arkon. So will you. So will Anna. She's going to live through this."

A fact. A truth, even.

His confidence was built off of trust in Eva's abilities, but also in their own to back her up. She would survive this. There was no other option for either of them.

"All right," Jacob relented. "If we're to help her out, we better make some headway on the location of these vestiges. If we can gather them before Sylus does, we have a shot of beating him."

"Agreed." Grayson cast aside his tome, in favour of rolling out a map on the table. "When I first looked into these vestiges, I was able to determine rough locations for each of them."

"I don't suppose you remember where these locations are?"

Grayson shook his head, shoulders slumping as he gazed at the map of Astrida. "It was almost ten years ago. I dropped it as soon as Sylus dismissed it. It'll take too long for us to research it now, but..." A devious smile sprouted on his lips. "There is a device that has the power to track anything your heart desires."

"Great. Where is it?"

A frown pulled on Grayson's brow. "That, I could never figure out."

Any hope Jacob had of finding these weapons of power before Sylus fizzled.

He sat back in his chair, feeling the weight of their mission heavy on his chest. "Great. So, we don't know where the vestiges are, we don't know where the one thing that could track them is—but Sylus has all the information he needs to find them." His fists clenched in his lap, frustration bubbling in his chest like lava. He could have one of them already for all we know."

"He doesn't." Again. Grayson was so confident. Jacob didn't know where he got it from. "Even if he has my marked map, he'll have a hard time obtaining them. Each one is protected."

"By what?"

"Ancient, powerful magic."

How wonderfully vague.

Grayson tossed him a deadpan glare. "Don't give me that look, Jake. This all came from *one* book I found in Sylus's library ten years ago." He gestured broadly around the tower. "There are more answers here somewhere. This is one of the biggest libraries in the world. Knowledge has been passed down from generation to generation to generation, protected and cared for by the Kain family. Everything that ever happened in this world is written down in one of these tomes."

Jacob followed the gesture, taking in the enormous bookcases that seemed to stretch on infinitely, despite the tower only being so big. They were in one of the many sitting areas littered around the place. This one was perched on the second floor balcony, looking over the entrance, a welcoming receiving area for anyone who sought knowledge. A long reception desk cut the space in two, preventing anyone without permission to enter the rest of the library.

The librarians and scribes at work took these books' and artifacts' security seriously, to the point where they were all armed in some manner, trained by the Royal Guard. Some sections were quarantined off to even Jacob and Grayson. They'd been promised by the Head Librarian that if there was something relevant to their research within the closed off areas, it would be brought out for them, under the condition that they were supervised.

Sighing, he pulled a fresh book off the stack and hunkered down. He waited until Grayson flipped a page. Like hells he was reading through all of these books by himself. But it appeared Grayson had worked through whatever he needed to work through. His foot had stopped tapping, leaving them in utter silence, as his eyes flew across the page at an enviable speed.

They made more progress in the past few hours than they did in the last three days combined. Near the bottom of their stack of records, of which the librarians had dispersed to refill, Jacob uncovered a reference to the vestiges—five relics, each a gift from the gods. Bestowed upon the finest warriors of the time as a means to maintain peace during the rapidly growing population. However, their power proved to be too much for the warriors to handle. War broke out, so monumental, the world Shattered.

The next book went into the vestiges themselves in more detail, rather than the war. Together, they formed an entire set of armour, forged not just with divine power, but with the very elements themselves.

The halberd was a gift from Ebis, the god of chaos. Its blade was imbued with untamed energy, so powerful it could split the sky in two with a single strike. Those who wielded it risked losing themselves to the weapon. The yearning for chaos was too great, even for the most disciplined of warriors.

The gauntlet came from Val, the god of war. Forged in the heart of an eternal blaze, it was said to burn as fiercely as the god's own wrath. When clenched, it could ignite with white-hot flames, turning even the weakest strike into a devastating blow. But such power was ravenous, never stable. It demanded strength, discipline, and an unrelenting will. Without them, it would consume its wielder as readily as their enemies.

The shield bore the blessing of Lorelus, the god of vitality. Unlike the others, its power was not one of destruction, but endurance. The surface of the shield shimmered like a still lake, yet it could veer and warp, absorbing impact like the tide against the shore. It granted resilience beyond mortal limits, mending wounds and steadying weary hands—but only to those who carried the will to endure.

The cape belonged to Zyphril, the god of death. Woven from the breath of the dying, it carried the weightless silence of the final moment before a soul departed. When worn, it allowed its bearer to vanish like mist, their movements as fleeting as the wind. But with each use, whispers grew louder—remnants of lives lost, shadows that could not be outrun. Death gave freely, but it never forgot.

And finally, the chest piece—bestowed by Asturias, queen of the pantheon, goddess of earth and judgment. Forged by the very marrow of the world, it was an unyielding force, offering protection only to those worthy of carrying its weight. Asturias had gifted it not as a blessing, but as a test—for only those who could bear the burden of leadership, of sacrifice, would be granted its strength.

Jacob's blood ran cold after finishing the book. A full set of armor, each piece imbued with divine purpose. Each piece carried both terrifying power and consequences.

King Sylus couldn't be allowed to obtain all five—but Jacob wasn't entirely sure *they* should either. The vestiges should stay where they were, hidden from the world, where *no one* could use these weapons—

"*Ahem.*" A slim young woman swathed in pale blue robes stood at the edge of their table, bashful eyes darting from Grayson to Jacob, lingering on what he presumed to be a ratty mess at the top of his head. "I'm sorry to disturb you, Dragon Knights. The library will be closing soon." She wrung her fingers nervously in front of her, bright green eyes furtively on him. "Is there perhaps something I can help you with?"

"This is a highly confidential mission," Grayson shot her down immediately in a tone that induced a quake in her slender bones. "Only a handful of scribes have been given permission to know the subject matter." Because the girl wasn't terrified enough, Grayson glared at her.

"Oh. I'm s—sorry. I only wished to help. I'll just be on my way..."

"Wait," Jacob called, stumbling out of his seat. "You have artifacts here, right?"

She halted, a faint smile on her lips. "Yes. We have artifacts from all over the world as well as different time periods. Is there anything in particular you're curious about?"

"Do you have anything from the Shattering?"

Grayson cast him a silent look of inquiry. Jacob's answering shrug told him he'd explain later.

She blinked. "The Shattering?" Thinking, she tapped her fingers on her chin. "I haven't seen anything in the displays that old, but something like that would require specific care and attention. Far more than what most of us could provide. I can only think of one place where you could find such an artifact: in the Royal Vault. You will need King Renkon's permission to enter it."

"Thank you."

She inclined her head then scurried away.

"What was that about?"

"You said there are generation's worth of knowledge here, right? I've found a few books that cover the Shattering and the vestiges—but nothing on the device. What if there's nothing because it hasn't been around for the public to account for it?"

Grayson's eyes widened. "You think it might be in the Royal Vault?"

"It's a long shot, I know, but it's the best one we have aside from sitting in this library for weeks."

Grayson grimaced. "What are the chances Renkon will see us this week?"

"Low, but he's not our only royal. I know someone else who would gladly help."

Grayson's grimace deepened, but Jacob didn't care. They had set their differences aside plenty of times before. They could do it again. For the sake of Aboria.

No, for the sake of all of Astrida.

CHAPTER 35
SOME THINGS NEVER CHANGE

Eva was given a full five seconds to behold the cerulean beauty glistening on the horizon. When the late buttery light from the sun danced on the lazy waves rolling in—chef's kiss. She couldn't have asked for a better ending to her day after flying through the desert and getting shredded by a sandstorm.

Except for the lightning bolt arching from the beach their way.

She could have done without that.

"*Brace!*" Arkon's voice ricocheted through her mind while he snapped his wings wide open, throwing them into a complete stop. Eva's rear flew out of the saddle from the sudden, aggressive manoeuvre, but her arms and legs held her firmly to his back.

The bolt soared past them—aiming straight for Aster.

"No!"

Eva reached out to the bolt, her mind instantly connecting with the chaotic energy hurtling towards her best friend and dragon. Mental grasp tight, she *yanked* the bolt to the side, narrowly missing Aster's wing, and sent it into a dune. It exploded on impact, sand spewing in all directions.

Aster snarled in the direction of the blackened sand then tucked beneath Arkon's shadow for protection.

Syran emerged from the Storm Cove, rising high above the cliff face, his great black wings eclipsing the sun dipping below the horizon. His amber eyes glowed in the growing darkness, honing in on Aster with predatory glee. "You lived. Well done."

"Fuck you!" Anna screamed from her saddle. Aster growled, flames trickling out of her jowls, mirroring her rider's ire. "We gave you word that we were coming. That was an unprovoked attack!"

Sasha rose from her saddle, standing on the stirrups, unphased by the beat of Syran's wings or the seaside wind that tousled Eva's ponytail. Midnight hair undulated behind her like a war banner, warning them too late of her intent. A visage of the wrathful Desert Queen and a once proud Dragon Knight pushed around too many times.

Her thin cropped top moved in the harsh wind, leaving the flat plains of her stomach—and the myriad of scars, which contrasted against her dark skin—on display for everyone to see. Warrior badges. Testaments to her strength and skills as a fighter.

"Unprovoked? Ha! I offered you a place among my Wanderers, food, shelter, a place to train safely—and how do you repay me?" Her voice, as sharp as a whip crack, was laced with venom and vitriol. "You disappear in the middle of the night. You disrespected me, then have the *nerve* to return and demand more training. Do I look like a whore for you to cast aside when you're not in the mood?"

This was what Eva had been afraid of. Though, the true extent of the damage hadn't been clear to her until now.

Moistening her lips, she rose in her seat, meeting Sasha's vehement gaze head on. "Can we land and talk more civilly?"

Sasha crossed her arms, tilting her head as she considered Eva's request. Her dark eyes narrowed on the impact dent in the dune below them. "Did *you* or Arkon deflect my bolt?"

"I did."

Her lips pursed. "Have you been practicing?" A simple, casual question, but Eva didn't miss the weight it carried.

"I have."

Not as much as Eva liked, but if it put her back in Sasha's good graces, she didn't mind bending the truth a smidge.

Sasha seemed to see through her lie regardless and produced a wolfish grin. "Prove it."

Here we go again.

"It's sandworm season and they're causing travellers trouble. Hunt and kill twenty of them—by yourself—then we'll see about letting you stay with us."

Eva's stomach plummeted to the ground a hundred feet below them.

Killing Sandhounds and giant scorpions, Eva could get behind. Sandworms?? By *herself*? She was almost swallowed whole the last time she ran into one!

"How am I supposed to kill *twenty* sandworms by myself?"

A devious smirk spread across the desert queen's face. "If you trained as much as you should have, it'll be a cake walk for you."

"I was gone for a *month*."

Sasha raised an incredulous eyebrow at her. "A month is plenty of time to hone the skills I gave you."

Forget the fact it took Eva *five* months to get a handle of her magic under her scrupulous supervision.

Arkon growled, scales bristling beneath Eva's legs. "Syran, this is madness!"

"No, brother," Syran rebuked, a lofty lilt to his tone that Eva definitely didn't miss during her time away. She didn't know much about Syran, but she knew he was much older than Arkon—and liked to rub it in his face whenever the opportunity arose. "Madness is letting your rider do as she pleases. You know the extent of our power. Only a disciplined body and mind is worthy of our full strength."

His words cut through her like a jagged blade. A rebuttal bubbled in her throat, but she clamped it down. He was right. She did as she pleased—she left for the Desert Lands without a care of the consequences and rushed in to save Jacob without a plan. If it weren't for Anna, Grayson, or Arkon, she would have wound up dead—or Darius's puppet—ages ago.

Shame clenched at her heart. Her fingers closed around the handles of her saddle, frustration ripping through her. She wanted to master her magic, hone her body to make it strong enough to end Sylus's reign, and kill Darius for murdering her family, more than anyone, but why was it that *she* was always getting in her way?

"I'll kill them," Eva announced, sounding far more confident than she felt. But if Sasha believed it was possible, there must be a way. Despite her reckless and seemingly redundant methods, she'd never led Eva astray. "Whatever it takes to prove my worth to you, Sasha, I'll do it."

The retired Knight sat back in her saddle, hands resting casually on the pommel. A satisfied smirk ignited something vicious in her eyes. "Good. You have until the sun rises. Happy hunting, girl."

The ground stilled beneath Eva's feet, not even sand rolled down the crumbling dune to her right. Moonlight spilled over the desert, a cool wind—but not as chilling as the last time they were here—brushing over the nape of her neck. Sweat clung to her skin, trickling down her spine, despite the refreshing air. Her veins burned, lungs even more so. Muscles spasmed in her legs and arms, fingers twitching. Her gloves were so saturated with sweat, their weight doubled and felt like they could slide off her hands at any minute.

But they were all she had.

Arkon and Aster, along with Anna, flew in circles above her, a gust from their wings occasionally reaching her, helpless as they watched her take down one sandworm at a time.

Sixteen she'd gotten so far. The first few were clumsy attempts. Arkon's anxiety spiked through her, distracting her so much she had to close him off, making it that much harder to use her magic. With his soul guiding her, his advice fueling her confidence, she could hold on to the chaotic energy easier, and find ways to tame it to her will.

Without him?

Well. It turned into a battle of wills—hers against the mighty Ebis.

A rumble vibrated beneath her bare feet. She'd left her boots in the saddle, opting for efficiency rather than comfort. Her feet picked up on the faintest vibrations before the beasts had the chance to zero in on her location. It gave her just enough time to rub her hands together and build up a charge.

Static prickled at the hairs on her arms as power surged through her once again. It seared her blood and bones, tearing a cry from her throat. With every charge she built, the pain intensified, getting closer and closer to ripping her to shreds. Which was why she'd limited herself to one strike. One strike to slay the beast. One shot to hit her target.

The rumble grew stronger, threatening to throw her off balance. She braced her legs, feet sinking into the sand. The dune beside her quaked fiercely. The charred remains of the last sandworm crumbled behind her.

An arch of lightning breathed to life between her hands. Not nearly as powerful as the one Sasha threw at her. Not big enough to take the worm down in one strike.

I need more. Give me more! She wasn't sure who she demanded this power from. Her body had given it her all two strikes ago. The last one was noticeably weaker. This one sputtered, dripping plasma precariously close to her toes.

Closer.

The ground undulated. The dune collapsed entirely.

She needed a bolt *now.*

"Come *on!*"

"*Wield, Eva!*" Arkon cried, his roar thundering above her and shaking her bones.

"*I'm trying!*"

The sandworm burst from the ground, leaping almost high enough to catch her dragon in its maw. It missed and sank back into the sea of sand. Her gaze fell to the point it had disappeared—a mere ten feet away from where she stood.

Her heart pounded against her ribcage, stomach thrashing. She wasn't sure if it was fear or a side effect that churned her stomach, but it didn't matter when she hurled. She fell to her knees, heaving her lunch, which felt like so long ago. Her stomach clenched, in dire need of fuel.

"Get up! Fight!"

She was vaguely aware of the thunderous vibrations coming her way, right below her hands and feet. But she couldn't move. Her joints had locked together. Body giving in to exhaustion.

"I... can't."

She—failed.

The worm was close now. So close she could smell its rank breath amidst all the dust and sand.

Arkon swept down, scooping Eva up in his claws. He twisted out of the way, just as the worm exploded from the ground. Screaming, she gripped his claws with all her might—which wasn't much—as she was jostled around, popping a few of her vertebrae.

The sandworm swung its massive body for them. Arkon pumped his wings, the crackle of leather snapping in her ears. It wasn't enough. The worm's shadow loomed over them—

A bolt of lightning cracked down from above, slicing the worm right down the middle. The two halves broke away from each other and collapsed on opposite sides of them.

Arkon landed, wings fluttering gently to clear the whirling dust clouding their vision. His claw opened up for her, allowing her to stumble a few steps before she fell to her knees, heaving on an empty stomach. Tears and sand stung her eyes, making it impossible to see.

Two thuds sounded on either side then rapid footsteps neared.

"Eva!" Anna slid to her side, automatically pulling her hair back away from her face. "What's wrong?"

When she opened her mouth to speak, her stomach roiled and she heaved again, inhaling dry air. Anna passed her a canteen, of which Eva greedily drained now that they didn't have to ration their water.

"She overworked herself," Sasha informed her dryly. The desert queen crouched in front of her, studying her dispassionately. "Nice work."

"I..." Eva swallowed, her throat feeling like sandpaper. "I failed." Her fingers curled in the sand, coarse and grating. She deserved the pain. She needed to be better. Faster. Stronger.

Snorting, Sasha fell back onto her rump, laying her legs out flat in front of her. The pale moonlight dancing off her dark skin gave her an ethereal glow, like a creature from another time and place. Not a renowned and feared warrior. She'd decimated fields of goblins in her prime, yet Eva could barely kill sixteen sandworms. "I never expected you to kill twenty, not even if you trained every single day."

Eva blinked at the queen basking in moonlight. "What?"

She shrugged nonchalantly. "With those gloves, you shouldn't have killed ten—but you did."

Anger flashed through Eva, but before she could raise her voice, Sasha kept going, "You're ready."

Scowling, Eva sat back on her heels and wiped bile from her mouth with the back of her hand.

"For what?" She meant to sound more snappish—more furious with her teacher's vagueness—but it barely came out as a choked demand.

Sasha's dark eyes glimmered in the midnight air, dancing like the stars above them. "For *real* magic. You've shown you can manipulate lightning and endure its price. Now it's time you learn how to summon your own... if you stick around for the entire term."

Eva peered up at Arkon curiously, her mind slowly catching up with Sasha's words. *Real* magic? Was what she'd been doing for the past six hours not *real* enough for her? It certainly felt real to her body. She could barely hold herself upright. "What are you talking about?"

Sasha shook her head. "I'll tell you tomorrow. Get some rest. We left your beds as you left them. Both of you," she added, gaze sliding in Anna's direction.

"Oh. No. I think it's best we focus on—"

Sasha cut her off with a hard glare. "When are you going to stop being afraid of your power, girl? You fear hurting someone? *Own* that power, control it, be its master, so that you may never hurt anyone again."

Eva laid her hand on top of Anna's clenched one and squeezed it. "Let's get strong together. There's no better place to practice than here."

Anna returned the pressure with a fervour, eyes still hesitant. She glanced back at Aster, who nodded. "It is time, Anna."

She blew out a trembling breath then schooled her features, turning into the fierce warrior Eva knew so well. "All right. I'm in. Don't complain to me if you get burned, though."

CHAPTER 36
SOUL MAGIC

"All right," Sasha said as Eva and Anna hiked up the furthest pillar on a lineup of rocks that protected the cove from the brunt of the temperamental tides. It jutted out from the beach at a precarious angle, only just managing to hang over the waves throttling the other jagged rocks protruding just as precariously around them. This one stood the tallest and widest, giving the three of them enough space to stand shoulder to shoulder. The mid-afternoon sun beat down on them, but Eran's protection still held strong against its sizzling heat.

A familiar pang of homesickness gnawed at her gut. They'd only been gone for a few days, and she already missed Grayson, Jacob, and their dragons. They took away the weight the world seemed determined to thrust on her shoulders.

Anna had sent a hawk back to Dragon Canyon as soon as they settled into camp—which, to Eva's surprise, was exactly as they had left it. She had half-expected the Wanderers to toss their bedrolls aside or repurpose them for their own use, but everything remained untouched. Dust coated the fabric, and a few scorpions had made nests inside, but otherwise it was as if Sasha had been waiting for their return.

The thought warmed Eva's heart—briefly. The next morning she woke to a quiver thumping onto her stomach and Sasha's voice ordering her to "Earn her keep."

Some things never changed.

"We'll start with a warm up," Sasha announced at the tip of the pillar.

She turned away from them, facing the vast cerulean ocean ahead, and held her hand up to the sky. Static crackled in the air around them before a blue hue emanated from her palm. Plasma oozed out from between her fingertips, twining together into a long rope that coiled around her feet and slithered off the side of the rock. Her fingers curled around the rope, Sasha raised her wrist then snapped it. Lightning lashed out, cracking in the space above the ocean, leaving behind a resounding thunderous roar. Smaller shoots splintered off the main bolt, forking further across the ocean.

An incredible display of power and control.

A "warm up," she called it.

Ha!

Though, judging by how easily Sasha called on her magic without breaking a sweat, maybe it really was just a warm up for her.

Anna glanced over her shoulder to the dragon cave where Aster was safely nestled inside. Arkon ensured she wouldn't be struck by stationing himself outside, eyes vigilant on the sky where the lightning had been. If Eva concentrated on the tether between them, she could feel the energy around them crackling on his scales. The power was naturally drawn to him, like a current seeking the ground.

When Sasha turned back around to her pupils, she wore a smug grin Eva wanted to wipe off.

Show off.

"Your turn."

Anna looked at Eva expectantly. Rolling her eyes, Eva took Sasha's place at the peak of the pillar then rubbed her gloves together until a big enough charge prickled at her skin. She took control of the static in the air, gathering it in her palms, condensing the current.

When the heat became too much, she held her hands out in front of her. A bolt shot out from her palms, soaring across the ocean. It grew larger as it picked up remnants from Sasha's ostentatious display of magic, crackling violently. A *boom!* rent the air, shaking the stone they stood on.

When she turned back, Sasha's blank stare met her. "That was wholly underwhelming." She pivoted towards Anna. "Your turn, girl. No dawdling."

Jaw tight with resignation, Eva stepped away to let Anna take her place. Anna shook her hands out at her sides, breathing in through her nose then out through her mouth. She peered back at them, noting the short distance between them. "You might want to take a few steps back."

Eva made movements to adhere to her friend's request, but Sasha caught her arm and yanked her back in place. "No*pe*." She put emphasis on the P, making a popping sound with her lips. The cool, callousness in her eyes made Eva's blood simmer. "We're not moving an inch."

Worry coloured Anna's silver eyes as they darted between them. "But you could get hurt."

"Do you *want* to hurt us?" Sasha drawled out, inspecting the nails Bruce and freshly buffed this morning.

"No."

"Then you won't." She fanned her hand out, examining the back. Her dark skin glowed under the sun's praise, seeming to thrive in the heat rather than sizzle.

"It's not that simple," Anna ground out, jaw rocking back and forth in her agitation. If Sasha wasn't careful, she'd find out why people on the base feared her and not just because of who her mother was.

Rolling her eyes, Sasha met her gaze, not the least bit concerned by the wrath of the fire Bound. "Of course it is. *You* are in control of your magic, not the other way around. Face the ocean and shut us out of your mind, if you must. You *will* wield today, Hargin."

Eva wanted to argue. Anna shouldn't have to wield if she wasn't ready—not yet. But then she caught a glint in Sasha's eyes. Something unfamiliar. Not doubt or disappointment, but something softer, rarer. A flicker of hope... and faith.

Sasha wasn't pressuring her for the sake of bullying her or to prove a point. She wanted to offer what no one else had dared: a nudge forward. Not because Anna was the Commander's daughter, but because Sasha believed in her—even when Anna didn't believe in herself.

Eva realised it then—she'd been showing her faith the wrong way. Silently, she stepped forward and clasped Anna's hand. "You've got this, Anna."

Terror twisted across her friend's features. She drew her hand away, shaking her head. "Niall said the same thing—now he has a scar not even magic can heal."

An image flashed in Eva's mind of what a horrifically awful wound Anna must have inflicted for a water dragon to be unable to completely heal it. Despite the terrifying thought, her expression remained neutral, supportive. "You're a stronger Knight now," she said, voice unwavering, just like her faith in her friend. "I've seen you use your power. It's amazing. Beautiful. Be our light and guide us out of these dark times."

She chewed on her bottom lip, searching Eva's face for the confidence she had in her. After a moment that seemed to stretch on eternally between them, she drew in a deep, steadying breath and faced the ocean. "I can do this," she whispered to herself, repeating it over and over. A mantra that built her confidence with every word.

Anna moved as fast as a lightning strike, flint sparking against the edge of her knife. A spray of ember-dust leapt into the air, flickering like restless stars before knitting themselves together. Flames swelled, coiling and twisting until they melded into the shape of a dragon cradled between her palms. Its wings beat once, scattering sparks, the firelight painting Anna's face in molten hues.

She thrust her hands forward, and the dragon obeyed. With a deafening *whoosh*, it surged outward, stretching and swelling until it rivaled Aster in size. Its body burned white-hot at the core, orange and crimson flames rolling off its form like streams of molten lava. Heat radiated with every wingbeat, searing the air as it spiraled upward.

The dragon let loose a soundless roar, its fiery maw gaping as it twisted toward the heavens. Then, with a final pump of its wings, it exploded high above in a spray of shimmering sparks. Gold and scarlet embers cascaded like falling stars, raining down in a spectacle that stole the breath from Eva's lungs. It reminded her of the firework display she'd watched as a child—only this was wilder, grander, as though the entire horizon had been set ablaze.

Eva's jaw went slack as she beheld her friend's true power for the first time. Until now, Anna had only shown her parlour tricks. *This* was what magic looked like when it was free and uninhibited. She understood Anna's fear—Hells, she felt it herself somedays—but this was a moment to admire. Celebrate.

Eva only hoped she might one day be as skilled.

"Flashy," Sasha remarked noncommittedly, hands on her hips, head tipped back as she watched the remnants of the firework flicker over the ocean. "Very good control. You had an image in your mind and projected it clearly. That'll take you a long way with soul magic."

Anna scratched the back of her head, not quite ready to be praised for her magic. She better get used to it, because Eva intended on celebrating this victory with her tonight over a couple of drinks and a swim through the reef. "Image projection was the first thing Faas taught me. He said there was no point in learning magic, if I couldn't project."

A smile curled at the edges of Sasha's mouth. "Faas knows what he's talking about. Too bad he's a prick."

Eva swivelled towards her teacher at the familiarity in which she spoke of the Soul Bound Captain who lived in the High Mountains. "You know him?"

Sasha's expression slid into one akin to the face one made when they discovered a bug on their shoe. She dusted a grain of sand off her shoulder. "I fought alongside him during the Goblin Wars. We were the only Soul Bound of that generation and trained with each other often. You kids are lucky to have teachers. Everything we learned, we learned from trial and error."

While Sasha never let them forget how powerful and apathetic she was, Eva often forgot that the retired Dragon Knight had lived an entire lifetime before Eva was born. She'd fought bravely in the Goblin Wars, earned the trust of King Renkon, even befriended Grayson's mother before she was slain—all before coming to the Desert Lands to hide from the very man who'd killed her friend and becoming the Wandering Queen. A lifetime of pain and loss and strife.

Was Eva destined for the same fate?

No. She refused to share the same fate. She would master her magic and bring the Fortys clan to justice for their atrocities.

"What's the difference between the magic you're going to teach us and the magic we've been practicing?" Eva asked, her mind racing. Every book she'd read on magic discussed the elemental forces and the powers derived from them, but none had ever mentioned soul or blood magic.

Sasha fixed her with a dry, reproachful glare. "Haven't you been listening?" She shook her head, her expression like a parent scolding a child. "You're Soul Bound. Arkon gifted you with a tear, which binds your soul to his. But this tear also infused with your blood, and through it, your blood gained magic. That's why your blood gives you physical enhancements—better eyesight, hearing, infrared vision, and the ability to manipulate the elements around you."

Eva frowned, trying to wrap her mind around the layers of magic at play.

"Soul magic," Sasha continued, "is a different source entirely. Can you guess where that source comes from?"

"Our dragons' magic?" Anna guessed, fingers tapping against her chin as she considered the lesson.

"Correct," Sasha said with a nod. "You had to master your blood magic first to build up a tolerance for soul magic. Soul magic draws more from your essence and will take a greater toll on you. An inexperienced user could face fatal consequences. But since you've shown me you can handle the strain, from this day forward, we'll focus on using your soul as the primary source, not your blood." Her gaze sharpened like the fine tip of a blade, as if to determine one final time if they were truly ready for this next step. "Soul magic is wild, potent, and virtually limitless. The only real limitation is your imagination and stamina. If you can imagine it, you can create it."

Eva's heart raced as she absorbed the weight of Sasha's words. *This* was where her true power came from—the power she needed to protect those she loved, to save Aboria. Finally, she could be the hero everyone believed she could be.

Her fists clenched at her sides, unable to hold back the surge of anticipation.

"How do we tap into our soul magic?" she asked.

Sasha tapped her temple. "Now, my pupils, it is time to meditate and undergo some self-reflection."

Eva and Anna exchanged a secret glance. Without a doubt, that had to be the most underwhelming instruction they'd ever received from Sasha Remoar.

"Sit."

With the subtle shrug of their shoulders, they obeyed, sitting crisscross, knees touching as they faced the retired Knight before them.

"Close your eyes. Let darkness and nothingness fill your minds."

Eva let her lids flutter shut, breathing in the salty air, catching a whiff of sulphur and molten metal—remnants from their magic. As she breathed out, she pushed the world around her—the seagulls' calls, chatter from the cove, the crashing waves against the shore—out of her mind. She let darkness encase her, wrap around her like a blanket. Nothingness floated on the edge, a caress against the walls of her mind...

A flicker caught her attention in her mind's eye—an obsidian flame dancing in the endless nothing. There was no light, no sound, no breeze across her skin. Only void.

The flame seemed more tempting than ever, if only because it was *something* in this barren place. At least with it, she could feel.

What unsettled her most was that this emptiness was inside her own mind. No warmth, no comfort—nothing. She hadn't expected it to be so utterly hollow.

Drawn to the strange swirl of darkness, she stepped closer, her feet finding purchase on an unseen floor above a sea of colourless void. She still wore the same clothes she had chosen that morning: a sleeveless under armour shirt, the loose, thin pants she'd bought on her last visit here, daggers strapped to her hips, bow and quiver slung across her back.

As she neared the flame, its undulating tongues licked the air like curious vipers. Her skin prickled as though she stood too close to fire, yet no heat warned her away. Sweat beaded on her brow, sliding down her cheek and spine.

The air thickened—heavy, suffocating.

A wave of smoke burst from the flame, coiling around her mind with an inescapable, oppressive grip. True darkness closed in.

She coughed as the smoke filled her lungs, covering her mouth with the crook of her elbow. Her eyes burned, tears blurring her vision.

Then came the screams. They echoed from every direction, carried on a sudden wind that tore through her mind. The closer she drew to the source she had mistaken for her soul, the louder, more deafening they became.

But this wasn't her soul. It couldn't be. This was a nightmare—*the* nightmare. The one that claimed her every night.

Erika's scream rose higher than anyone else's, a shrill that pierced Eva's heart. "Eva! Save me! Help me, Eva!"

Desperately, Eva swatted the smoke aside, calling back to her sister. But the smoke was too thick. A handful twirled out of her grasp to only be replaced by more.

"Erika!!"

The burn in her lungs became too much. She fell to her knees on the dirt ground, the impact jarring her hips and spine.

"No! Please, no!"

Not again, not again, not again, not again, not again.

Dark laughter grazed over the shell of her ear—

"Very good," Sasha's voice cut through the nightmare like a hot blade, severing her from the darkness.

Gasping, Eva clutched her chest, heart beating rapidly beneath her palm. She gulped down breath after breath, air filling her lungs. Clean, crisp air. Not burning smoke.

Bright, blistering sunlight skewered her eyes. She winced as pain lanced her skull.

Sasha stood in front of them, hands braced on her hips as she watched Anna intently. "You see it, don't you, Anna? Now grasp it, will it to take form."

Blinking back tears, Eva turned to Anna and found a small orb of fire hovering between her palms. No sparks or embers made it, just raw magic.

Amazing.

"Now hold on to that for ten minutes," Sasha instructed, an unconvincingly restrained excitement shining in her eyes for her prized pupil. "We'll start with endurance before we go any further." She pivoted towards Eva, noting the hands clenched in her lap. "You have some shit to work through first, it seems."

Eva dipped her head, fingers digging deeper into her gauzy pants. Despite her meditation practices with Grayson, grief and guilt still gnashed at the inner workings of her mind, sneaking up on her at unexpected times. Like when she was trying to unleash soul magic.

"Keep at it until you can clear your mind," Sasha advised flatly, disinterested in the student who couldn't recognise her own soul from the nightmares living within her.

Shoving aside her insecurities, Eva peered up at her teacher, refusing to let a little set back stop her from mastering her magic. "What am I looking for?"

A smug smirk tugged on the corner of her mouth. "Nuh-uh, kiddo. You have to find the answer on your own. First you must clear your mind. Once you have, you'll know what you're looking for."

She gritted her teeth. "That is the most frustratingly vague—"

"*That* is the lesson I am leaving with you," Sasha snarled, a warning whirling in her eyes. "Anna and I will give you space to meditate."

The fire orb in Anna's hand flickered out in the breeze whipping past them. She groaned, head tipping back in defeat. "Shit. So much for ten minutes."

"*You* are the source," Sasha reminded her sternly. "If you feel a wind coming, you must feed the flame—brace yourself, and the flame, for the impact—or it will be snuffed out." Sighing, she spared a glance Eva's way before giving Anna her full attention. "Come. We'll work on it over here. We'll leave Eva to get her shit together."

Anna looked at Eva, concern wrinkling her brow. "Do you want me to stay?"

"Nope," Sasha cut in, throwing her hand up and blocking her path to Eva. "She needs to do this by herself. Eva needs to decide if she is going to let the past hold her back or if she's ready to move on."

"I'm ready," Eva barked. This overbearing guilt she felt wasn't a *choice*. She didn't ask to be afraid whenever smoke permeated the air and dragged her back to the unyielding nightmare. She didn't *want* to fear the mere thought of Darius finding his way to her again, of being defenseless to stop him from taking her from everyone she loved. If she could lock those fears away, she would. But they plagued her like an incessant, hungry beast.

"You're clearly not. Keep meditating. Find me when you've figured it out." Sasha gripped the front of Anna's shirt and yanked her up to her feet. "Leave her, or you fail her as a friend and a mentor."

Shoving Sasha's hand off her, Anna held Eva's gaze. Regardless of what Sasha said, all Eva had to do was give her the word and she'd stay by her side.

It was tempting to give in to her fears, the doubt that told her she couldn't do this alone. But maybe Sasha was right. Maybe this was something she had to do without Anna.

Besides, she was never truly alone. Arkon was with her. Always.

His soul wrapped around hers, holding her in a tight yet loving embrace. "*Always*."

Eva met Anna's gaze, a new determination igniting within her. "I'll be all right. Focus on your training. I'll catch up to you soon."

A light smile flitted on her lips. "You better. If we come back after our term and *I'm* the stronger one, my mother will be pissed."

Her tone was teasing, but beneath that, a sharper truth settled in Eva's chest. Anna had just shown her what they were capable of when they refused to let fear rule them, and it had been magnificent, beautiful, powerful—everything Eva wanted to be. She had thought she'd laid her grief and guilt to rest, but now she saw clearly that she had only swept it under a rug, distracted herself with training, while letting it fester and grow unchecked.

That ended today.

If she had any hope of catching up, she needed to master more than just her body. She needed to master her mind. Every fear. Every hesitation. Every shadow of doubt lurking in the corners of herself.

I can do this.

She *had* to.

Her pulse thrummed through her veins like Arkon's wingbeats as she looked out over the edge of the pillar, the wind tugging at her hair and clothes. She'd come this far, overcome every obstacle Sasha had thrown at her. This was just another test of her will. A challenge against her determination. She wouldn't let her own mind be what stopped her.

No more running.

No more hiding.

She would outshine the darkness threatening to consume her.

CHAPTER 37
RIDDLES IN THE SAND

Biting back a hiss of pain, Dravyn leaned his ass back on a sun-blackened pillar then unlaced his boots, draining them of sand one at a time. Heat seeped through his pants from the stone; if he placed a bare hand on it, it would have seared his flesh. While the desert smelt like dust with an undertone of decay, these ruins left a metallic tang on his tongue, sharp as a blade pressing against his throat.

Their camels wouldn't come near the rubble they'd discovered, which he should consider a good sign since they didn't react this way to the other remains of an ancient civilization they'd found a few days ago. But he couldn't bring himself to be moved by the clear sign of progress when his feet looked like he'd taken a grater to them. The damned sand had gotten in his boots while they explored the ruins for any sign of entry—coming up empty—and he'd left them to steadily fill, thinking he could find an answer quickly. He had not and the sand had made him pay for it.

Growling in frustration, Darius swung his sword for the biggest pillar, both in height and width—the most likely one to allow them entrance to the ruins below. Sparks flew and singed his shirt. Swearing, he patted his shirt down before it set him aflame.

Idiot.

Eyes shuttering, Dravyn tipped his head back against the pillar he leaned against and envisioned being back home, bathing in his chambers, accompanied by his two favourite concubines. Brandy had a way with her tongue that made him see stars, while Graham's cock piercings elevated his pleasure to bone-quivering heights. He missed his bath. His bed. The cool winter breeze on his balcony. He missed being able to summon his concubines at will, to order them to make him forget where he was, who he was, or the role his father had thrust upon him.

He could almost feel Graham servicing him now, taking him away from this dreaded desert...

But Graham wasn't here—so what the fuck was touching him?

His eyes shot open, darting down to his crotch where a fucking locust crawled out of the waistband of his pants. A bolt of terror shot up his spine, jolting him right out of the sweet illusion he'd wrapped around himself. Choking on a scream, he slapped the abomination off and broke away from the pillar before anything else decided to crawl on him.

He shuddered.

Graham would have never let a bug touch him.

To take his mind off the lingering feeling of the locust, he approached the main pillar, stationed in the centre of the ring of monoliths. He studied the immaculate condition this was in compared to the others that had let time and the desert be their master.

One pillar was tipping at a precarious forty-five degree angle, while one of them had chunks missing on the corners. The one closest to him had been horizontally cleaved in two, the other half a few feet behind it, as if something big had swatted it clean off with its tail. Another one looked a breath away from turning to dust, and the one furthest from him had entirely given in to its masters and was nothing more than a pile of rubble. Give that one a few more years, and it'd become just another grain of sand.

The main pillar, while entirely intact, was so weathered, he barely saw the symbols on it. He'd certainly missed them the first few times he'd passed by. Only the delicate brush of red caught his attention.

No... Not symbols. A mural. Intricately painted once upon a time, now reduced to muted, faded colours that nearly blended perfectly in the dark stone. He had to squint his eyes against the razing sun to see the mural fully.

A towering man stood by a forge, a gauntlet held between the tongs in his grasp. It was massive, far bigger than any gauntlet had a right to be—the red that had initially caught his eye. Yet, despite its inefficiency, this man seemed to revere it. It emanated a glow that, even today, exuded power. Five robed figures surrounded him, either fearing the mysterious gauntlet or basking in this new creation. The back of each robe was gilded with a different symbol: a dove, a stack of books, a tightly wound coil, ox horns, and two swords crossed at the centre. The bird, books, and coil cringed away from the gauntlet, while the ox and swords embraced it, seeming to share the glow of this armour piece.

Odd.

Curiously, Dravyn approached the mural, specifically the coincidentally empty space below the forge. The mural faded to black here when the rest of the picture took up the pillar from corner to corner.

Tentatively, his fingers ran over the weathered stone, tips grazing over the rough, aged rock—until they caught on a lip. There! The lip extended further upward and down, forming a vertical slit. He found a corner and followed the line further until the shape of a door fell into his sights.

"Dari." He waved Darius over, mind too entranced by the depiction to pay attention to his brother's wanderings. Nevertheless, Darius came to his side, studying the door but seeing nothing.

"What?"

"There's a door here."

Darius clapped him on the shoulder, a cruel smile on his lips. "Congratulations, Dray, you've proven your usefulness. Open it up."

Dravyn scanned the pillar for some kind of handle or mechanism to open it, but he couldn't find anything.

It has to open somehow...

Stepping back, he regarded the mural again. Despite the faded images, the symbols hadn't lost their shape or colour. They were designed to survive the unforgiving desert.

He had the sinking feeling that they had something to do with opening the door.

Seeing that the mural had nothing else to give him, he looked around the ruins, stretching his mind for the answers.

Five pillars. Five symbols.

Curiously, he strode over to the next most intact pillar and studied every faucet visible. His eyes were immediately drawn to a dash of purple at head height. One of the symbols—the tightly wound coil.

"Darius, look at that pillar over there for me. Is there a symbol on it?"

Darius inspected the one closest to him then scowled. "A dove."

It couldn't be a coincidence. They were a part of the key.

"Look around the pillar for anything that stands out to you. These pillars are somehow linked to the mural."

For once, his brother didn't argue with him. They both studied their own pillar, inspecting every bump, crevice, or splash of colour for any hint. He spent almost an hour on his before his foot caught on something at the base. Sand stared back at him. He dragged his foot along the base again—and collided into something solid beneath the sand. He dropped to his knees and pushed sand behind him, aside—anywhere but at the base.

Sand. Sand. More sand. When would he be free of these accursed grains?

But then—his blistering fingers scraped against stone. He kept digging until a shape began to unfold beneath his fingers. A square platform. A smaller circle was set in the dark stone.

He cleared the sand, blowing it out of crevices. When he laid a hand on the circle plate, it shifted under his weight. Quickly, he swiped his hand back before he could trigger the plate.

His eyes darted from one pillar to the next. He bet each one had a plate beneath it. His gaze landed on Darius, who was already unearthing the plate below the dove pillar. Dravyn moved to another pillar, digging the base out of the stack of books and ox horns, which meant the dissolved one Darius was working on had to be the crossed swords one.

Great. One of these buttons probably unlocked the door. But which one? Could they try all of them until one worked or did they only have one shot?

He was missing something.

His gaze landed on the centre pillar again. It had given him all of the information so far...

He fell to his knees at the pillar and began to dig. Ignoring the blisters forming and the grains getting under his nails, he dug faster, tossing the sand from side to side.

Stone bit into his fingertips. He blew away the remnants, revealing—words. Not a plate or lever, a simple "press and move on" kind of solution. Instead of giving him a physical puzzle, the desert—of all things—slapped him in the face with a poem:

Born in silence, raised in flame,
I thrive where order breaks.
I am the hammer's echo,
The forge of kings and tyrants alike.
I do not choose sides—
I only demand them.

Darius's shadow eclipsed the taunting words as he came up behind him. "What did you find?"

Groaning, wishing he was anywhere but here, Dravyn rocked back onto his butt, not giving a damn if sand found its way into his pants. "It's a fucking riddle, Dari."

Darius dropped a deadpan glower on him. "Then solve it. What does it say?"

Dravyn moved aside so his brother could read it. Darius loosed a sigh that could have been mistaken as a growl from anyone who hadn't heard his growl before. "Great. They can never be easy, can they?"

"That would defeat the purpose of the riddle," Dravyn responded dryly. "These symbols align with the answer. Pick the right one and the door will open."

"Fuck it. I'm not going to stand in the middle of a bloody desert and contemplate the meaning of life. We'll try them all."

Darius marched across the ruins, heading straight for the ox horn pillar. He stomped on the plate like it was the skull of his enemy—

A powerful gust of wind exploded from the narrow hole in the pillar, a cannon blast of air that ripped Darius off his feet and flung him into the main pillar. His skull cracked against the hard stone that echoed around the ruins. He slid down to the base, a crumbled form of the Prince of Estrus.

A beat of silence swept through the ruins.

Fear raked down Dravyn's spine. He ran after him, skidding to a stop beside him and falling to his knees. It didn't matter if Dravyn lived or died, but if Darius died here, their father would punish him severely for failing his Shadow duties—then name him the Crowned Prince.

Dravyn would rather die than wear that cold, obsidian crown.

He shook his shoulders. "Darius?" Blood stained the wall behind him when his head lolled away. Cold, hard dread pulsed through his veins. "Darius!"

A moan rumbled in his chest. Slowly, Darius lifted his head, eyes blearily taking in the ruins, as if he had forgotten where they were. He reached for the back of his head. Crimson stained his fingertips. "Fuck."

Dravyn shoved him to hide the relief filling his chest. "Idiot! Let's *not* throw ourselves at the super old, magical puzzle."

Darius landed him with a withering glare, more of himself. "At least I narrowed down the answer. It's *not* that—"

The ground rumbled beneath them. The air stilled, sand shivering along the surface.

Darius's eyes narrowed, tracking the ripples in the sand. "What was that?"

Dread knotted in Dravyn's stomach. They were about to find out what kind of beasts the Desert Lands had to offer. Whatever it was, it must have heard the blast from Darius's lapse in judgement.

The tremors increased in speed and strength—directed straight for them.

"Climb!" Darius ordered, and Dravyn wasn't about to argue. Whatever could burrow through this much sand this quickly was a creature not worth the fight.

Dravyn leapt for the nearest pillar, nails instantly biting into the many ridges carved into the hard stone. His feet found purchase in deep grooves, pushing him higher and higher. Just as he reached the peak—a flat, crumbling plateau—he spared Darius a glance as he perched on the precariously hanging pillar.

The vibrations became unbearable—then the ground gave out, sand cascading into the gaping maw of the big fucking worm. The enormous beast breached the surface, climbing higher than the pillars they took refuge on. The explosive movement sent sand flying, pelting him with an abrasive slap. A groan reverberated in the air then shuddered right up to the peak of his pillar, jarring his bones. The worm sank beneath the surface once more, leaving behind a plume of dust that shrouded the ruins in an impenetrable haze.

All Dravyn could do was pull his scarf across his face and try not to breathe in the dust. His fingers dug into the plateau for all that he was worth. There was no fucking way he would give that worm an excuse to come back.

They waited with bated breath for the cloud to clear. For the worm to lay siege on another unsuspecting set of ruins. Sand rolled down the surrounding dunes, ground still trembling as the persistent beast circled their location like a frenzied shark. Each time Dravyn thought it was safe to climb down, the worm returned like an incessant blister.

Seeing as it was going to hunt them for a few hours, Dravyn made himself comfortable on the pillar peak, dangling his legs off the edge, and pulled out his sketchbook and a thin stick of charcoal. When packing his things for this trip, he'd hesitated to bring this—what need did he have for a sketchbook when hunting vestiges?—but his itchy, need-to-be-busy fingers won over practicality.

He drew a detailed copy of the mural, ensuring to highlight the symbols so he could think on them later. In the bottom corner, he wrote down the riddle.

Hours passed by, the sun long since dipped beneath the horizon, before they deemed it safe to climb down. Darius caught a glance of the sketchbook before Dravyn tucked it away in his pack.

"You get everything down?"

Dravyn slid him a dry look. "No. I thought it was the perfect time to dabble in erotica."

Darius stared him down, deciding whether or not he was being serious—to be fair, he had a fifty-fifty chance of being right—then turned away. "Great. Let's resupply then come back."

Dravyn had to do a double take to make sure his brother was indeed the one speaking—because there was no way Darius Fortys would let him get away with his usual sarcasm. But it was definitely his brother, because while he'd rather blow up the front door than solve the puzzle, he would also rather die than reveal how much pain he was in. The blast had knocked his head pretty hard, and Dravyn doubted that was the extent of his injuries. Resupplying was ample enough cover to hide the fact Darius needed to lick his wounds, or risk perishing in this unforgiving desert.

While that wouldn't be the worst thing in the world, it also meant that Dravyn would have to wear the crown. After seeing what it had done to his father and brothers, he wanted to keep his distance from it.

CHAPTER 38
LIKE CALLS TO LIKE

Grayson's fingers lingered over the blades strapped to his thighs. The dimly lit hallway did well to conceal them this far down the castle's depths. The dark walls did well to absorb any light they gave off in between lightstone sconces. Shadows embraced his cloak, becoming an extension of himself as if he belonged down here, in the deepest, darkest recesses of Kain Castle. He thought he'd explored everything there was to the castle, but this section had somehow eluded him.

It was no wonder that the guards blocking his path wouldn't step aside. If he came across someone who was the embodiment of this kingdom's best kept secret, he wouldn't let them pass either. He'd gotten past the initial set of knights guarding the entrance by relinquishing only his visible weapons. They'd foolishly thought he couldn't possibly have more than three weapons on him at a time. These knights, however, would not be so easily fooled. Their trained eyes spotted the hilts of his throwing knives from the end of the hallway.

"Hand over your weapons," the senior-most knight ordered, extending his hand expectantly. Pins and stripes decorated his shoulders to demonstrate the heroic and valiant deeds he had done over the course of his service.

It'd be a shame to get blood on them.

Grayson's hands stilled just above the hilts, muscles coiled and primed to throw them. "No."

They could take his main weapons away, but he would not take a step further without a single weapon. An instinct so deeply ingrained in him that he *physically* could not hand over another blade.

The knight crossed his arms, leaning all of his weight onto one foot. Clearly, he was not threatened by Grayson's presence—or he was so confident in the other two knights' abilities he thought they would be enough to stop him. "Then you're not going into the vault. I don't care who you're with." His masked eyes shifted to his Crowned Prince.

Leo groaned under his breath, pinching the bridge of his nose. "By the gods, Runaway, just give him your bloody knives."

"I don't take orders from you."

"Gray," Jacob warned on his other side. His fingers clamped down on his shoulder. He'd already given up his sword and boot knife at the first sign of resistance. Grayson wouldn't be so willing. "Come on. We're going to be the only people in the vault."

"Unless you plan on slitting our throats once we're inside," Leo pressed, "hand your weapons over to Captain Mahone."

Deep down, Grayson knew he was being unnecessarily obstinate, but since Eva had left for the Desert Lands he'd been on edge. He couldn't shake the feeling that he needed to be *ready*. For what, he didn't know.

"*Eva is all right*," Eran assured him. "*Unless you think the message that arrived last night was a forgery?*"

No. He recognised Eva's handwriting from anywhere—a sloppy series of scribbles of an unpracticed hand, woven together by her determination to learn and to better herself. They had arrived in the Desert Lands safely and were with Sasha. Apparently, she'd already learned things from Sasha she was eager to show him. He knew it was this new soul magic she mentioned, but his mind went to the night they'd shared before she left. The night his Starling cried out his name in pure ecstasy and filled his heart with so much warmth he still wasn't sure if he was dying.

"*I love you, Grayson Smith*," she'd said, words spoken from her very soul. Words he couldn't bear to say back in fear of it all being a dream. He was convinced as soon as he confessed what his blood sang whenever he saw her, he would wake up and find himself back in Estrus, committing every heinous crime she would condone him for. Once the words were said aloud, he might as well admit to Darius that he was right and paint a target on Eva's back.

"*What would Eva want you to do?*" Eran asked gently, fully aware of the danger in invoking her name to sway him. It wasn't a tactic he used lightly. He cared for Eva as deeply as Grayson did—and would never dare besmirch her name with casual use.

Grayson ground his teeth. If it was for the sake of the kingdom and countless other lives, she'd ask him to hand over his weapons. She'd remind him that his body was a weapon as much as his swords and knives, and tell him to listen to Jacob and Leo's logic: they would be the only ones in the vault.

Relinquishing a lungful of air, Grayson freed the knives from their homes and slapped them into Captain Mahone's awaiting hands. "You lose them, you die. Got it?"

The captain visibly swallowed beneath his helmet. "Understood."

Jacob squeezed his shoulder in silent thanks then dropped his hand to his side as the knights stepped aside. Leo went first, approaching the large steel door behind the diligent guards. His dark blue eyes traced the golden bolts and locks sealing the round entrance. Magic hummed in the air, grazing over the hairs on Grayson's arms and sending a shiver down his spine. Neither Jacob or Leo reacted to it, only enamoured by the majestic construction of the door. Ignoring the magical protections, even a dragon would have trouble breaking it down.

Leo approached the door, raising his hand to the handprint embedded at the centre. A gruesome spike jutted out of the palm with veins draining into the inner workings of the steel. He pressed his hand into the print and grunted after a mechanical *ka-thunk* hissed through the air. His blood drained into the veins, disappearing into the door. Locks and bolts shifted and grinded within the mechanism, a soft glow emanating from the silver markings etched into the steel.

With a rush of air, the door popped open a crack. Invitation enough for Leo to pry it open the rest of the way and welcome them inside.

He pulled a handkerchief from his breast pocket and wrapped his hand. "Only royal blood can open the vault," he explained to them as the Dragon Knights took in the seemingly eternal room stretching out before them.

Gold glinted in the corners, coins, relics, tools. Gems bigger than Grayson's head shimmered in several display podiums. Old, delicate tomes were preserved within glass cases. Mountains upon mountains of treasures lured them inside.

Once they crossed the threshold, the door closed behind them, sealing them in. Grayson's pulse jumped at the thought of being stuck in here. He didn't need his magic to know there was only one way in or out, and all it would take to be trapped in here forever would be a single whim from Leo.

Instinctively, his fingers searched for a blade—and found nothing.

"So, you mentioned a device," Leo was saying, unbothered by the door locking all three of them in a room together. His gaze swept over the treasures as if they were an everyday occurrence; given the lavish lifestyle his parents bathed him in, Grayson wasn't surprised. These treasures weren't overly shocking for Grayson, either. Jacob, on the other hand, appeared to be entranced by all of the shiny objects, his face aglow with wonderment and pure childlike glee. Grayson envisioned Eva wearing the same face. She'd run straight for the gem studded dagger protruding out of a pile of other nameless treasures. He'd help her steal it, too, if she wanted it. "What kind of device are we looking for?"

"I don't know," Grayson answered with a shake of his head. Focusing was becoming increasingly more difficult as time away from Eva gnawed at him like a cancer. "It could be anything. A dowsing rod, a compass, a stack of tarot cards, dice—whatever else you can think of. Its purpose is to lead us to the vestiges."

Leo, of course, demanded to be debriefed on their mission before allowing them entrance to his family's secret vault, information of which Hargin granted them to give.

The prince pinned him with a dry glower. "How wonderfully vague of you."

Grayson shrugged, choosing not to let Leo get under his skin today. He suddenly cared far less about the prince's opinion—especially now that Eva had made her choice clear. Leo's honour and steadfast loyalty hadn't been enough to sway her from the darkness within Grayson. "Hope you brought snacks. We could be here for a while."

Leo's eyes narrowed, clearly sensing a shift in Grayson and trying to pin down the cause of it. If he dug too deep, the princeling might just find something he didn't like.

Jacob, naturally, wedged himself between them and redirected their focus to the true depths of the Kain family's wealth. "We need to find this as fast as we can. King Sylus could already be searching for the vestiges. Every minute we waste is another minute he gains the advantage."

"Rightly said, my friend," Leo agreed, shifting gears. "Split up. Leave no stone—or gem—unturned or overlooked. If you find anything of interest, bring it back here. We can sift through them together. *One* of these has to be what you're looking for."

Grunting in agreement, Grayson began his search further into the trove, leaving Jacob to look near the entrance, while Leo started with all of the cases on display. He skipped past the mountains, following the narrow path wending from one side of the room to the other. His instincts told him the device wouldn't allow itself to be buried beneath rubble, if it was indeed imbued by ancient magic destined to breathe life into this world as easily as it could take it away. Call it intuition, the gods speaking to him, or the magic in his blood resonating with the device—he just knew it.

"*Like calls to like*," Eran evoked.

"*I'm not an ancient device.*"

"No, *but the magic that flows through your veins is the same as mine. Magic can neither be destroyed or created, just reshaped.*"

Grayson halted his gait for a beat before continuing on; he needed a minute to let his words sink in. Try as he might to keep his gaze vigilant, everything began to blur together, into one long streak of glitter and gold. But he kept going, following the invisible tether gently luring him. "*Are you saying your magic can be dated back to the Shattering?*"

"*I'm saying* all *magic is. Listen to these instincts. They have never failed me.*"

He wasn't sure about letting an unknown force guide him, but Eran's trust in it flowed through him like a river leading him to the sea. As he had discovered through his practice of magic, he learned that releasing the restraints on his mind and body was the best way to tap into its power.

He shut his eyes and let the smallest, nearly indiscernible changes in his body, direct him. With a tug here and a whisper there, he was led to the far reaches of the room, out of sight from the others. Each pull grew stronger, more urgent than the last.

Something was here, calling to him—pulling him away from the others. He had to fight against the voice in the back of his mind warning him not to trust it. Not to be so easily beguiled by an invisible force

But Eran trusted it. If he could fit within the castle walls, he'd follow the tether, too.

At the end of the tether, he found himself in front of a small mound of treasure, no taller than his hip. Jewels sparkled back at him, coins trickled down the sides—an aura more powerful than Eran's emanated from the stack. It coiled around his bones and thrummed through his veins. His heart beat harder against his ribs. Sweat beaded along his forehead.

Every self preserving instinct in his body told him to go back the way he came—every instinct but the one that drew him here. Despite the air being heavy and oppressive, the promise of danger lured him ever closer. Partly out of curiosity, and partly because he felt he had no choice. Whatever had brought him here was in this mound.

Grayson fell to his knees and began sifting through the treasure, fingers grazing over every piece he could find. He had to trust that once he made contact with the source, he'd know he found it. There were too many objects to sift through, otherwise, and he could be here for hours.

He started from the top and worked his way down, brushing pieces aside as he went. He had only gone a quarter of the way through, where the mound's core sat, when a powerful zap singed his fingers. Ignoring the pain, he blindly latched onto the source and yanked it out of the mess he'd made.

In his hand was a small round device, no thicker than his thumb or bigger than his palm. Time had rusted the metal plating. It looked like it would crumble if a breeze swept through the room. Surprisingly underwhelming if this was indeed a device that could seek out ancient artifacts capable of mass destruction.

As if in answer to his unspoken disappointment, a red glow radiated from beneath the layer of rust, the shell growing hotter and hotter, searing his flesh. Hissing, he tried to drop it, tipping his palm vertically, but it clung to him, biting into his skin like a rabid beast.

The rust peeled away, fluttering to the floor, revealing a golden layer underneath. The heat subsided, the red hue giving way to the brilliant, shimmering gold. The lid popped open. A spindle spun like a propeller, making a maddening clicking noise every time it passed the North bearing.

Sigils around the compass edge swirled and twisted violently, knotting into each other.

When they finished moving, it spelt Grayson's true name in an elaborate cursive handwriting: Deximus Arkayn Fortys.

A taunt from the gods.

A sign that he could never repent for his sins.

"*You don't know that*," Eran argued.

What else could it mean? The gods saw him as Dex, not as Grayson.

Growling at the accursed device, he wrenched it free of his palm, expecting to find melted flesh beneath. His palm, however, remained unscathed by the blazing heat burning him only moments ago.

More angry at the gods than curious about the magic within the compass, he shoved it in his back pocket. It was then when he noticed the back of his hand bore a new mark. Tattooed over the scarred flesh was a compass star, with intricate, ancient patterns taking up the entire space of the top of his hand.

Grayson bit back a snarl. Not only were the gods mocking him by putting his old name on the compass, they had now branded him like cattle.

"Grayson!" Jacob's call bounced around the mountains of treasure. They might as well be in a canyon, the acoustics carried his voice so far.

Grayson went back the way he came, more purpose in his stride. Jacob and Leo were near the entrance with curious objects in their hands. The former had a scroll from a forgotten time in one hand, protected by a steel sleeve with markings similar to the ones on the vault door. Leo had a divining rod between his hands that moved with the same languid motion of a cat's tail. Both were intriguing artifacts, laced with magic, that had the potential to lead them to the vestiges they seek.

Jacob looked at his empty hands and frowned. "Did you find anything?"

Reluctantly, Grayson revealed the compass, locking his fingers around the edges so they couldn't see the shame the device forced him to relive. The lid popped open, showing off the spinning dial within.

Jacob's russet eyes lit up beneath the golden embrace. "Whoa. That is the nicest compass I've ever seen." Before Grayson could stop him, Jacob stole it from his grasp for further inspection. The lid snapped closed, the shimmery hue dimming into a dull, weathered piece of metal. Jacob scowled at it, lifting it to his face to study the sides—which now bore no calligraphy to shame Grayson further. "Weird. Why did it do that? It was all smiles for you."

Leo's head tilted as he caught a glimpse of the tattoo on Grayson's hand. "I'm beyond an expert on magic, but I believe it has bonded with our Slayer... This is the device we've been looking for, isn't it?"

"No idea, but it..." Grayson took the compass back, wanting nothing more than to stuff it back in his pocket and forget about it. But once it was in his hand, he suddenly felt compelled to keep it out in the open. After being buried in darkness for so long, it wanted to bask in the light a little longer. "It called to me."

Leo crossed his arms, eyes narrowing on the pocket. "Bound to you or not, I'm not letting you walk out of my vault with anything but the tracking device."

"Fine by me."

"How can we tell if it's the device or not?" Jacob asked, ignoring Grayson's reluctance for the time being. The look he slipped his way suggested they'd talk about it later.

"Does it track only the vestiges, or can it find other things, too?" Leo wondered aloud, scrubbing his cleanly shaven jaw in thought.

"It tracks whatever you command it," Grayson answered, having found at least *that* much information on the device. Technically, it tracked the heart's deepest desire, but if Grayson was its chosen wielder, he could make it seek the vestiges. There was nothing he wanted more than to find them and protect the world Eva coveted.

"All right," Jacob decided. "Let's test it. Make it track something you know the location of."

Having no clue how it worked, Grayson stared at the insufferable, clicking dial and projected one thought: *Where is Jacob Greene?*

The dial snapped to a stop immediately, but not in Jacob's direction, who was right in front of him. The dial pointed a few degrees south of East.

He scowled furiously. What was it pointing at?

"*The Desert Lands are in the East,*" Eran reminded him, a little smugly if Grayson dipped into his soul deep enough. "*And guess where your heart's greatest desire is?*"

He gritted his teeth. He was fully aware of where Eva was, but he wasn't looking for her. He'd commanded the compass and it *would* obey.

"Well?" Jacob pressed.

"I'm working on it," he ground out.

Show me where Jacob Greene is, he demanded the stubborn divine object. He wanted—*needed*—this to work. They had to find the vestiges before Sylus, and without the map he'd made years ago to guide them, this was their only shot. Fuck the fate of the world—Eva's life hung in the balance.

After another beat of stubborn disobedience, the dial slowly shifted in Jacob's direction. It trembled there, as though it understood his true desire—knew that every command he gave circled back to Eva one way or another.

Grayson's grip tightened on the compass to hide the relief wracking through him. "This is it. We've found it."

Jacob tossed the scroll onto a nearby pile and rubbed his hands together with a grin pulling at the edges of his mouth. "Great. Now all that's left is to save the world."

If only it would be so easy.

CHAPTER 39
PEACE WITHIN

It didn't take long for Eva to fall back into the routine she had followed before leaving the Desert Lands. Every morning, just as the first pink streaks of sunrise kissed the horizon, she and Arkon left the cove to hunt. Mostly giant lizards, their blood still chilled from the night. Everything else proved too fast, too large, or too clever to catch.

After dropping her prey in front of Utilda, Storm Cove's resident cook, she crossed the beach and climbed the farthest pillar. Arkon curled at its base, water lapping against his half-submerged scales, grounding her as she sank into the far reaches of her mind. He pulled her back when the weight of her emotions became too much—or when he decided she needed a break.

The sun never touched her skin, thanks to Eran's protection, but its heat still licked at her flesh, leaving a constant sheen of sweat. Her body ached for water; her stomach clenched with hunger if she lingered too long in her inner world. Without Arkon's careful, paternal watch, she might have collapsed from dehydration long ago.

But she was tired of failing.

Day after day, she let her demons drag her under. No matter what she tried—killing her family before their screams began, silencing Darius's cruel laughter, even sacrificing herself to spare them—the result was always the same: screams, death, a voracious ache tearing her from the inside out.

It never stopped. She was cursed to relive that day, over and *over*.

Yet she pressed on. She endured. Because there *had* to be an end. There had to be. She believed in that more than in Fate, more than in gods or otherworldly forces.

She drew in a sharp breath of salty air, bracing herself for another attempt, but Arkon raised his head, level with the pillar, and looked at her. "Perhaps," he said cautiously, as if expecting her to snap, "we should try a different angle."

Exhaling, Eva glanced over her shoulder at Anna, far across the beach, her eyes locked on a maze sculpted from sand. Without her magically enhanced vision, Eva couldn't have seen the intricate paths, but Anna's control was unmistakable. Two dozen fire-mice scurried through the labyrinth, each moving as if with its own mind, yet fully under her command. Power, control, focus—Anna grew stronger every day.

Meanwhile, Eva remained perched on her rock, unable to pass the first step.

She dipped her head in frustration, pinching the bridge of her nose. "I feel like we've tried everything, Arkon."

"Brute force isn't the answer to everything," he replied, his voice firm but patient. "You may have been able to throw yourself at a problem repeatedly until it bent to your will before—but not this time. We must try something different."

He shifted beneath her, water slapping against the pillar and soaking her lap, then rose to sit before her. His tail coiled protectively around the base of the pillar, while his wings fanned outward, shielding her from the harsh sun. She tipped her head back to meet his glowing crystal eyes, and found them steady—gentle, yet resolute.

"This is not a fight to the death," he said, each word deliberate. "You cannot kill what plagues you—but you *can* accept it. Let it shape you. Use it to forge yourself anew."

She crossed her arms, a snort of bitter resentment escaping her. "A fight to the death would be easier," she muttered, the words tasting like failure and defeat.

His scaly lips peeled back into an awkward smile. "Perhaps." He tilted his head, regarding her thoughtfully. "Let go of your guilt, Little One."

She was *trying*, but hearing her little sister's screams broke her will. Every. Single. Time. The simpering fear-driven part of her wouldn't let it go. Wouldn't let her forget the people she'd left behind.

"Think of a time when you could find peace within yourself," he pressed. "When guilt doesn't addle your mind and you are... *free*."

Eva wasn't sure there was such a time, not since Brar was destroyed. All of her memories beforehand were tainted by the horrors of that night. Regardless, she searched her mind for a time when her mind was quiet. When the screams didn't follow her and she could let her thoughts truly wander without fear...

When her lids fell shut, she felt the ghost of warm, strong hands on her, guiding her arms and hips, sometimes her feet, into position. A breath of encouragement in her ear. A sense of invincibility swathing her in a cloak—a cloak as impenetrable as mithril.

A smile pulled at the edges of her mouth when she opened her eyes. "I have an idea, Arkon."

She jumped to her feet and slid into the first stance Grayson ever taught her. She moved into the next with the ease of a familiar memory from one stance to the next. Her body knew what to do before she did, easing into the hot, heavy air. She flowed like a sunflower in the breeze.

She knew the dance as well as the man who had taught her, could do it with her eyes closed even. Her mind cleared as darkness cocooned her in a gentle and familiar embrace. Here, it was just her body and the next stance. She ebbed and flowed to the rhythm of the dance. No screams followed her here. No evil laughter to taunt her.

Just blissful *silence.*

Within the velvety darkness, she found warmth, a static prickling luring her with a gentle hand. Outside, she felt her body flow through the Death's Dance, while in here she floated in an endless void. But this time, she wasn't afraid. This darkness wrapped around her, welcomed her within its folds.

Up ahead, a blue flame flickered in the distance. Even from here, she could feel its power, sharp and prickling—yet not painfully so. Enchanted by the simple beauty of it, she followed its light, feet skating across an invisible plain as if nothing weighed her down. The prickling grew stronger, the air heavier, as she neared, like the air before a storm.

This was what she was supposed to be looking for. She just knew it.

She reached out to it, calling it to her palm. It obeyed easily, as if magic had always been second nature to her. Wisps of lightning danced around her hand, twirling, flickering along her skin. Power zapped at her flesh, demanding she give it shape. Hungry to be set free into the world.

What shape do I give you?

In a blinding flash, the void was replaced by a plateau. The dark expanse replaced by the fiery canopy of the White Woods. The air was light and crisp, filling her heart with joy and *peace.*

She knew then what shape to give her new power.

Opening her eyes, she envisioned a set of twin daggers, just as powerful and prickly as the soul within her. They took form in an instant.

A laugh burst from her lips as she spun into the next position, lightning daggers dazzling under the full light of the sun. No storm to aid her. No gloves.

Just.

Raw.

Magic.

"Arkon! Look!" Though, she didn't need to catch his attention; he was already watching, just as he had been for days. An immovable force for her to fall back on when her resolve faltered.

Those old, crystal eyes, which had held patience and encouragement for her, now held a hint of sadness. "Well done, Little One."

She cut the tether that bound her soul to the magic in her hands. Her hands tingled as the daggers dissipated, making her palms feel empty, hollow, without their magic flowing between her fingers. Her blood sang at a high staccato, singing along with the elation in her heart, even if it appeared Arkon didn't share the same relief she did.

"What's the matter?" After working on this for weeks and listening to her complain every single day, she expected him to be happy for her.

He lowered his colossal head for her, nudging her chest with the tip of his horn. "I am immensely proud of you, Little One. You have done well to come this far. But I only wish that Deximus Fortys hadn't been the one to help you."

She recoiled at the name Grayson loathed. "I thought you accepted him as my mate?"

"I did and still do, as long as he makes you happy, but that does not change what he has done to my kin."

She wrapped her arms around his snout, wishing she could hold all of him in her arms. "You don't hate me for loving him, do you?"

"I could never hate you, Little One. I do not condone your choice in mate, either. Perhaps, there is more to him than being a Slayer. Perhaps he does deserve your heart if he has helped you find peace within your heart."

She brushed a kiss on the small scales around his nostrils then stepped away to look into his crystal eyes. "Thank you. I hope one day he will earn your forgiveness."

He shook his scales out. "Let us not dwell on your mate. You have accessed the magic within your soul, but that is only the beginning of your training. Are you ready to unleash your gift onto the world?"

She grinned. "I am."

CHAPTER 40

RAGE OF A WRATHFUL GOD

Darius waited until the dead of night and for Dravyn's snores to fill their tent before he slipped outside, a satchel of healing supplies in hand. A mildly cool breeze stirred his hair, offering him a reprieve the sun never gave them. Biting down a groan, he sat in front of the tent, tipping his head back to look at the stars.

They were different from home. Clearer. Brighter. The moon was twice the size, illuminating dune peaks while enhancing shadows at the bases.

Tonight, Darius needed to rest his wounds. They would reach the settlement tomorrow morning and he needed his strength, proven by the sloppy kill earlier.

A bandit had tried to ambush them, but despite the massive pounding in his skull and the sharp pain in his shoulders, Darius overpowered him and pilfered the corpse.

A rather convenient corpse that had a satchel of healing supplies. A bag worth its weight in gold in these parts. He hadn't shown a flicker of relief when he found the bag hidden amongst the corpse's clothing. Didn't want to give Dravyn the satisfaction of seeing his older brother in a—mildly—weakened state.

He unfurled the satchel and sifted through the contents. A green, rancid poultice and bandages. So different from the healing herbs used in Estrus. The mere scent of it left a coppery coating on his tongue—a taste he had learned to associate with magic. It took him days to acclimate to it when he first arrived in Aboria. Even longer to figure out the source.

It was Keyon who figured it out...

Clenching his jaw, he dipped his fingers into the jar and scooped out a generous amount. Shutting out images of his friend, he rubbed the poultice on the back of his neck and shoulders. His skin immediately began to tingle, a pleasant numbness sinking into his flesh. He probed around his skull for the gash beneath his hair and rubbed the last of it into his scalp.

A haze took over his mind, like a pleasant buzz disconnecting his mind from his body, but not so much that he wasn't aware of his surroundings. He felt the grains graze over his face as the wind stirred around them. He felt the sand shift beneath his rear as he relaxed into the desert night. His mind, while wrapped in a blissful daze, was still sharp.

It was the weirdest high Darius had ever experienced.

As he gazed up at the stars, allowing the effects of the healing poultice to wash over him, he thought back to the ruins they had to leave behind. That was definitely the location Dex had marked, where the ancient artifact was hiding. He tasted the magic in the air before he experienced it first hand.

Question was: what kind of artifact needed to be protected so thoroughly?

Of all the things, a riddle blocked their path, one Darius didn't doubt Dravyn could solve. The delinquent was many things—annoying and willful and troublesome and unpredictable—but he took after their mother above all else. She had the cunning and resolve to worm her way out of serfdom into a king's bed and bear three sons. If anyone could figure it out, it would be him.

Darius hadn't thought to ask Sylus why these vestiges would be able to help them kill the storm dragon rider. But if this much magic was required to protect it, it must be one of great power.

One powerful enough to overthrow a kingdom, perhaps? No. Sylus wouldn't be foolish enough to send him after items of power he could use against him. No, he hadn't told Darius everything...

He glanced back into the tent, absently noting the motion didn't hurt, and watched Dravyn sleep, as vulnerable as a newborn babe. Sylus hadn't sent just anybody to accompany him. He'd sent his most conniving son. The one who chose to tear families apart from the inside out, rather than Darius's usual method.

Dravyn was his failsafe. If it looked like Darius was going to turn against Sylus, Dravyn would be the one to stab him in the back.

But only if Darius gave him a reason to.

Darius tossed the remnants of the supplies into the endless grains of sand and laid down on his bedroll, a knife tucked at the small of his back. He fell into a half-sleep, allowing his body to get the rest it needed while still keeping alert.

When the sun rose, they ate their breakfast in silence, as they usually did, packed their camp, then headed for the settlement. They reached the dwelling within two hours, sheltered by the sun with a yawning cave entrance welcoming everyone into its embrace. When they entered its shadow, the temperature dropped noticeably, and Dravyn groaned, ripping his scarf off at the first chance he got.

Blisters dotted his fair skin, following his hairline and the arch of his brow. If the brat didn't spend most of his time indoors, his skin wouldn't be so affected by the sweltering heat. Dravyn licked his chapped lips as he scanned the small encampment, pale blue eyes eagerly in search of the woman who had given him a sweet nectar drink the last time they came here to resupply.

Darius spotted her coppery hair from the entrance, despite her stall being so deep in the cave. Without mentioning her to his brother, he strode across the encampment for her. For a woman, she was surprisingly resourceful and knowledgeable of the area. She knew which plants were edible, which ones they could drink from, which ones lured lizards and rodents. As much as Darius was loath to admit it, their time in the desert would have been even more unpleasant without her guidance.

Dravyn noticed the direction he was heading and quickly caught up to him, passing him to reach the woman first. He grinned like a lazy cat who had found its next meal. "Shaikyn, dear."

Her soft, buttery eyes roamed over his lean frame, a chuckle bubbling in her throat. "You're too young to be calling me 'dear', sweetie."

Dravyn scowled furiously, puffing his chest out. "I'm no boy, I can guarantee you that."

She snorted. "You're, what, sixteen?"

"Twenty," he grumbled, shoving his hands in his pockets and slouching. Five years younger than Dex, eight younger than Darius.

Darius pushed the adolescent aside and approached the vendor. Her shoulders stiffened, the soft, endearing look she had for Dravyn hardened into a mask of caution—but not fear, which he found fascinating. "We need more supplies."

"It'll cost you." Her tone had gone flat, opposed to the light, teasing one she'd used on Dravyn.

"Coin isn't an issue."

"Careful how loudly you say that. You might pique someone's interest."

"I've piqued plenty of interest. Do you see me hurting for coin?"

Her eyes raked down the length of him, sizing him up like he was one of the criminals exiled here. She had no idea how different he was from these vermin.

"No." She cleared her throat, breaking eye contact in favour of examining her wares. "What will it be today?"

Darius gave her a list of supplies they needed, when Dravyn annoyingly tacked on his nectar drink at the end. Gritting his teeth, Darius cut him a glare when she turned her back. Fool, for wasting coin on frivolous drinks. Every minute they spent in a settlement was a minute they could be recognised. The last thing they wanted was for the Dragon Knights to get wind of two mysterious figures—who just happened to look like members of the Fortys clan—roaming the desert...

"Hey, did you hear?" a passerby said to another.

"I heard rumours of our fateful black and red dragons flying for Storm Cove."

"They've been back for a couple of weeks," a third one added. "The lucky bastards in the south get thunderstorms all the time while she's training."

Thunderstorms. Black dragon. Training.

Darius's spine went rod-stiff. Before he knew what he was doing, he peeled away from the stall, murmuring for Dravyn to stay with the vendor, and followed the group.

He trailed behind them, keeping enough distance to avoid suspicion, but close enough for him to still hear them clearly.

"Do you think Eva will go in the Pit again? I made a lot of coin off of her last time."

Eva.

Something deep within him stirred.

The woman who had reduced his once-indomitable brother to a spineless lapdog was here. The bane of his existence—a thorn in his side, haunting his every misstep—had come to him at last. And with her, the key to everything he deserved.

He was beginning to think the Aborian gods did exist.

He let the group continue on and turned back to the stall.

Shaikyn was just handing Dravyn a bag of supplies when he returned. His younger brother noticed immediately, raising a pair of curious brows. "What was that all about?"

Darius ignored him. He pulled the map from his cloak and laid it flat on the counter, locking eyes with the woman.

"Where is Storm Cove?"

"What's in Storm Cove?" Dravyn asked.

Shaikyn let out an incredulous snort. "Oh, you *so* do not want to go there."

Insufferable woman, he thought. Always thinking they knew what he wanted. He had half a mind to open her throat right there for talking back. But—he'd learned the hard way not to underestimate a woman.

"Why don't I want to go to Storm Cove?" he asked coldly.

"Again," Dravyn chimed in, "*why* do we need to go to Storm Cove?"

Shaikyn ignored Dravyn completely, her gaze locked on Darius, studying him. Measuring his resolve.

"Sasha Remoar owns those lands," she said at last.

"And?"

She shook her head, incredulous. "All bets are off in the Desert Lands, but there's one thing everyone agrees on—you don't fuck with Sasha Remoar. Some call her a queen. Others call her a curse. I call her Ebis incarnate. She and her dragon rule the southern half. Those who don't like it have moved north."

"What color is her dragon?"

The question made her flinch. She blinked, confused, as if it had come out of nowhere. "Black."

His heart slammed against his ribs. The thrill of the hunt lit his blood on fire.

Two black dragons.

His little rider had a teacher...

He tapped the map. "Show me."

Seeing that he was dead set on this, her eyes rolled then she pointed to a cove on the far south east side. Days' worth of travel with no guarantee of running into more settlements, especially if the continent was divided by this Sasha. They wouldn't survive the trip—or they'd be worse off and then he would be too weak to claim his prize.

Wordlessly, he snatched the map then marched for the mouth of the cave. Dravyn easily matched his pace. He caught his arm just as the sun bathed them in its relentless heat, and yanked him to a stop. "Darius, what are you doing?" He lowered his voice to avoid being overheard, "We know where the vestige is. Why are you asking about Storm Cove?"

Darius jerked his arm free. "She's down there."

Dravyn's face fell flat, all sense of the mischievous younger brother gone. Taken over was the third prince of Estrus. The true Shadow of the family. "Oh, *fuck* no. Don't do this to me, Dari. If I have to hear about that damned storm dragon rider one more time, I'm going to sew my ears shut."

"She's here, Dravyn. Unprotected."

"We don't know that. We're sticking to the mission. Leave her alone."

"No," he snarled. He couldn't—wouldn't—leave her. Not when he was so close he could taste her blood on his lips. She had made a fool of him, and of Dex. He wouldn't let her get away with it.

Rolling his eyes, Dravyn tossed his hands in the air. "Drop the obsession, will you? She'll never be your puppet."

In a fit of rage, Darius grabbed his shirt and shoved him into the cavern wall. His fists trembled against his chest. "This isn't about making her my puppet." The words grated out of him, harsh, burning in his throat. Years of training and control—gone, shattered by the thought of *her*. Only she could make him quake with the rage of a wrathful god. "She took our brother away, Dravyn. I want her to hurt. But I want *him* to hurt more for choosing her over us."

Something flickered behind Dravyn's glacial eyes. Sympathy.

Disgusting.

"Dari..." His voice was rougher now, thick with emotion Darius didn't understand. "Dex is dead. She has nothing to do with him."

"He's alive," Darius growled, slamming his fist into the rock beside Dravyn's head. He flushed out the pain from his body. It was nothing compared to the roiling tides in his blood. "I saw him in Aboria. He's a Dragon Knight now—a *fucking commoner*. And he's been protecting her this whole time."

Dravyn froze. The blood drained from his face. For a second, his expression cracked—eyes wide, lips parted, almost dazed. Not with rage. Not with betrayal.

Relief?

No. Couldn't be.

It vanished almost as quickly. He blinked, swallowed hard, a mask of composure sliding over his face.

Darius narrowed his eyes but said nothing.

"I thought you killed him?"

"I thought I did, too." Darius's fingers curled into a tight fist, the same hand that had dealt the supposedly lethal blow. The memory of standing over his younger brother, watching the light fade from his eyes, was vivid, as if he had done it yesterday. He still remembered looking at his hands, the sword drenched in Dex's blood, and feeling more cold and hollow than ever before. "A dragon Bonded with him. Saved his life."

Dravyn failed to hide his surprise when his jaw went slack. "A *dragon* Bonded with him? How is that possible? Why save one of us?"

"Who gives a fuck?" Darius snarled. "He's out there, living a different life. He *left* us." Left them to rot in a cold, lifeless kingdom under the rule of a father as harsh and unforgiving as winter itself.

"And he's protecting the storm dragon rider..." Dravyn clasped his chin, deep in thought. "Why would he do that?"

Darius didn't fault him for not understanding. Dex was the slayer of the weak, not a protector. But if he saw him now, saw the wild fury in his eyes after Darius had hurt Eva Greene, he wouldn't recognise their brother. The pathetic man he had become.

"Because he's *in love* with her," Darius spat, the words tasting like ash in his mouth. "Don't you see, Dravyn? We have to make them hurt."

Dravyn didn't answer right away. His eyes flicked to the ground, jaw clenched. Then he swatted Darius's hand away, and gave a vague shake of his head. Not in disagreement. It was all he could do to wrap his head around Dex's resurrection.

Darius slapped his cheeks, yanking him back to reality. "Focus, Dray. We need a plan. Storm Cove's too far for our camels."

Dravyn exhaled, nodding stiffly. "Yeah..." He raked a hand through his hair, eyes finally snapping into focus when he looked at him. "We need to lure her out here."

Darius nodded in agreement. A cruel grin spread across his face. “And I know just what will bring her to us.”

He knew his little rider well enough. She'd come for him—and then she would finally be his.

CHAPTER 41
OH, TO BE QUEEN

Anna held her hands out toward the two firehawks twirling in the air before her. When splitting her focus across multiple creatures, she found it easier to guide them with her hands—separating, steering, and coaxing their movements as though they were extensions of her own body.

Her right hand darted to the side, and the larger hawk—Emerath, as she'd named him—banked sharply, wings flaring as he swooped low to snatch a pebble Sasha had placed deliberately along the beach. At the same time, her left hand pressed forward, commanding the hawk with the longer tail feathers—Rhaelen—to tuck her wings in tight and duck cleanly through a narrow loop Bruce had strung together with driftwood and fishing line. Crude, yes, but effective.

Sweat gathered at Anna's brow, stinging her eyes. The telltale signs of magical strain crept in: her fingers trembled, her breath came shorter, and the heat in her veins had gone molten. If she judged right, she had maybe five minutes left before the magic began to revolt against her control. Until then, she pushed the hawks to weave between obstacles, wings flashing as they filled the bucket with pebble after pebble.

When the strain finally broke her hold, her hawks faltering against her commands, Anna gasped, forcing herself to let go. She pictured a valve sealing shut in her mind, and with that thought, the magic sputtered out, leaving her spent but steady.

"Very good," Aster praised at last. She had been silent until now, not out of indifference, but because Anna left her with nothing to say. Her rider was wielding her magic with a confidence and grace Aster had long hoped to see. There was little more she could ask for.

But Anna's magic wasn't without its conditions. She had accepted that this was a part of her as much as Aster was, but she would always be cautious of this power.

She would only use her fire in the shape of animals. That was her condition. Creatures were tangible shapes, something she could picture clearly in her mind and grasp firmly without fear of losing control. Raw, uncut flames were different. Wild. Untamed. Hungry. They obeyed no master and didn't care whether they touched friend or foe—their purpose was to *burn*.

Those were the kinds of flames that hurt Niall. The kind she detested.

Aster, however, cared little for the form Anna chose to wield her flames, so long as Anna was no longer running from it. For nearly four years she had denied this part of herself, burying it under fear and shame. Now, at last, she was beginning to let it breathe.

And Anna had to admit, there was a certain kind of... freedom in embracing herself wholly and completely. Like she'd found the missing piece in her soul.

When Anna lifted her gaze, smiling up at her dragon, it was unguarded and radiant, the kind of smile that reached her eyes, crinkling at the edges.

Aster's wings fluttered against her back as she watched her Soul Bound beam in the sunshine. Her golden eyes seemed to shimmer with pride, shining brighter than the cerulean water under the sun's attention. "Do you see what you've been missing now?"

Anna rolled her eyes and flicked her braid over her shoulder, turning toward the boulder tucked in the narrow sliver of shade near the cliff. Her canteen, still surprisingly cool, sat atop it with the promise of quenching her parched throat. She tipped her head back, gulping the refreshing water down.

She'd discovered during her training that while the desert heat didn't bother her, using too much of her magic threatened to overheat her.

"I do," she admitted at last, lowering the canteen to the rock again. "But I don't regret taking this long. I..." Her words caught as a memory struck—Niall on his knees, screaming, clutching his face while her fire consumed him. Her fists curled tight at her sides. "I needed time to figure things out on my own. I'm not like Faas—and I don't want to be. Power and brute force are his way, but mine is finesse. Precision. Both can be effective, both deadly—but this way, I feel like I have more control."

Aster's huff carried a note of exasperation, but that proud gleam in her eyes didn't dim. "I have to admit, as frustrating as it has been watching you struggle to come into your own, it has also been a privilege. You did what you felt is right for you—and I am proud of you for it."

Anna cut her a sidelong look, dry as desert sand, refusing to let the warmth of the words reach her heart. She could feel it in Aster's soul that she spoke the truth, but a bead of doubt still trickled down her spine. "That's not what you used to say."

How many nights had they clashed over this very thing? How many times had Aster called her a coward, weak, for burying her fire instead of wielding it? The arguments had carved scars of their own—sharp words thrown like daggers, silences that lasted hours, sometimes days.

Aster lowered her colossal head now in submission. The tip of her horn nudged gently against Anna's hand, urging instead of demanding. Against her better judgment, Anna relented, her fingers tracing the length of polished bone—smooth, warm, solid beneath her touch. A deep rumble of contentment stirred in Aster's chest, vibrating through Anna's arm, through the sand, through the air itself. The heat radiating from her dragon was the only true warmth Anna felt.

"I thought it was what you needed," Aster admitted at last, her voice low, raw. "But I see now that I was wrong."

Anna's brows shot upward. A dragon—no, *her* dragon—actually admitting fault? That was rarer than rain in the Desert Lands. A grin tugged at the corner of her mouth before she could stop it. "That's a first. Should I mark the date down somewhere? Maybe carve it into this cliff so you can't take it back later?"

Aster gave a gruff snort, jerking her horn from Anna's hand and turning her head aside with theatrical indignation. "You need not rub it in, Fierce One."

Laughing, Anna lifted her hands, beckoning her dragon to come back. Reluctantly, Aster returned to her, putting extra weight into the embrace this time. "I know," she murmured against her scales. "I know you only want the best for me, Aster."

"This does not look like training."

Anna froze midstroke. Her head turned slowly toward the voice. Sasha was leaning on the cliff wall, arms folded tight, dark eyes trained on them with cool detachment. A strong gust whipped her black hair over her shoulder, carrying with it the briny reek of seaweed rotting along the beach.

Anna didn't move away from her dragon. Just because Sasha and Syran weren't the affectionate type didn't mean she and Aster had to hide their bond. "I'm taking a break."

Sasha didn't blink. "Break's over."

A beat passed between them.

Eva might let Sasha lord her power and seniority over her, but Anna grew up with a cold, hard bitch as a mother—and wouldn't take it as lightly.

Anna shifted her weight onto one hip, palm braced against it, her own glare sharp enough to cut. Since discovering her soul magic, Sasha had been relentless—harping on her daily, driving her to exhaustion, always inventing a new way to push her past the brink. Her attention never wavered, her expectations never eased. And while part of Anna found it flattering that a legendary Dragon Knight whose name would be etched in history saw something in her—she hadn't come to the Desert Lands to be forged into someone else's vision of greatness.

"You have another student," Anna gritted out bitterly. Since Sasha seemed to have forgotten Eva entirely. "Someone who could actually use *your* help."

Sasha snorted, throwing her hand toward the other side of the cove in lazy dismissal. Anna didn't need to look—she already knew Eva was still there, dancing on the pillar with her lightning daggers. She had been grinding through Grayson's stances for days, daggers flashing in rhythm with the glittering waves, her body trembling as she fought to hold her magic until the end of the dance.

She fought well. She fought hard. And *earned* those daggers. Anna loved her for it, heart swelling with pride when she heard her victory cheer from across the way.

For the weeks leading up to her first successful summoning, Anna had kept her distance from Eva. Sasha wanted Eva to wrestle with her magic on her own. It had been *fucking hard* to leave her alone. Every fibre of Anna's being had begged her to stand at Eva's side, to cheer her on, to remind her she wasn't alone.

But Sasha had a point, even if it was cruel.

If they had trained shoulder to shoulder, Eva would have been forced to watch Anna breeze through every challenge while she struggled to even summon. Shame would have eaten her alive. Resentment would have festered. And jealousy—which Anna feared the most—would have driven a wedge between them. Eva's development would have been hindered further.

So Anna obeyed, kept her distance. When they sparred, they were silent, save for a few tips. When they ate, they stared in the bonfire's hypnotic blaze, close enough to take comfort in their presence but not so close to break the silence.

And now that Eva had finally wielded—Sasha rewarded her with more silence.

Heartbreaking. Sadistic.

All too familiar to Anna's upbringing.

"You," Sasha said, voice smooth as a blade, not sparing Eva a glance. "You are far more interesting. Faas taught you well."

The backhanded praise stung, though Anna refused to show it. Her jaw tightened as she snapped back, "Faas actually sat me down and talked me through the process. What have you done for Eva? Thrown her to the wolves and called it training?"

Sasha's lip curled, her finger jabbing toward Anna's face like a dagger. "Don't lecture me on my methods. She needs this."

"No," Anna said firmly, stepping forward, hands clenched tight at her sides. She liked to think she wasn't a violent person, but when she looked at

Sasha, all she saw was her mother—always cold, always disapproving. She *hated* that. For her. For Eva. They deserved better. "She doesn't. Eva thrives on encouragement—not this cold shoulder routine you're pulling."

Sasha's eyes narrowed, her tone almost mocking, "You think friendship is going to save her? Tell me, how will her friends help her when they're all dead or gone—when they turn from her because they fear what she is?"

Anna flinched. Clearly, this was deflection. It wasn't a secret that Sasha's career had been a constant battle for survival, both on the battlefield and amongst her ranks. But that didn't make her words untrue. They were Dragon Knights, and war loomed over their heads like a tightening noose. People would die. That was the nature of their calling.

Anna couldn't deny the way dragons sometimes flinched from Eva and Arkon. Couldn't ignore the whispers that trailed behind her in the halls. The narrative had shifted since Eva's first days in Dragon Canyon. No longer the pitied, chosen Knight, she had become something else: the woman who faced Darius Fortys not once, but twice—and lived. The woman who could end their dragons' lives on a whim.

It hadn't really hit the base until that reckless day in the canyon, when she and Arkon had unleashed in the canyon. No one had gotten hurt, but it was a brutal reminder of the power walking in their midst.

And if they saw her attempt half of what Sasha was capable of... fear would spread like wildfire. Fear of *her*.

"You may be around now," Sasha pressed on ruthlessly, "but you won't always be there for her. The sooner she learns to cope on her own, the better off she'll be. But..." Her mouth twisted, "maybe you're not entirely wrong either."

Anna blinked. Wow. Twice in one day. What were the chances of that?

Sasha's gaze flicked across the cove, toward Eva still repeating those same stances with stubborn determination. "It has been rather sad," she added dryly, "watching her do the same thing over and over again."

Anna's eyes narrowed into a blade-edged glare. "Maybe if she had a teacher, she'd be doing more."

Sasha sighed, a long-suffering sound, reluctant—like Anna was an annoyance she couldn't quite dismiss. "Fine." Then a dangerous glint flickered in her eyes, and one corner of her mouth curved up into a smirk. "If you can summon a likeness of Aster and hold it for ten minutes, I'll consider talking to Eva."

Anna's stomach dropped. Her eyes went wide. A dragon that size she could conjure in a burst—but ten minutes? Ten minutes meant feeding the fire without pause, wrestling to keep it whole when her magic wanted to unravel. "Ten minutes?" she echoed, incredulous.

“Yes.” Sasha’s grin widened, sharp as broken glass. “Why? Don’t think you can do it?”

Bitch.

Grinding her jaw, Anna planted her feet and lifted her hands, gathering her focus. “No. I’ll do it.”

“Excellent.” Sasha turned with a sweep of her hips. “I’ll be watching from my throne. Bruce found figs in the market.” She paused mid-step, pivoting back to point a finger toward Anna. “Oh—by the way. If you hear any rumors about fights breaking out in the north… ignore them.”

Anna’s brows knit. Sasha’s tone was casual, but there was something too deliberate under the surface. Caution, edged in warning. “What’s going on?”

“Nothing you need to concern yourself with. Typical Desert Land politics.” Sasha’s shrug was careless, but her eyes lingered too long. “Focus on your training—and don’t tell Eva. She’ll want to run off on some vigilante crusade, and that’s not why she’s here.”

Cold words. Dismissive. And yet Anna knew they carried truth. If Eva caught wind of people in danger, she’d chase after them without hesitation. And Anna… she’d follow, even if it wasn’t their fight.

It was moments like this that left a sour taste in her mouth—the moments she had to be pragmatic, calculating. The bitch she hated to admit she could be.

“I’ll keep it quiet,” Anna said at last, lips tightening. “But if it escalates—you’ll tell me, won’t you? If it’s too dangerous to stay here…”

Sasha rolled her eyes. “Dangerous? As if any of these plebs could touch either of you. You’ll be safe under my watch—and under your own magic.” She glanced at the sun’s angle, already moving past the conversation. “Now, summon your dragon. Your pupil is waiting for me.”

Teeth clenched, Anna drew a sharp breath and called her magic forth. Flames rose, curling into the shape of her dragon—solid, luminous, burning. She had just locked it into place when Sasha vanished behind the cliff.

For a flicker of a second, Anna considered letting the construct unravel out of spite. But she knew—even without a direct line of sight from her so-called throne—Sasha would know.

Oh, to be queen.

CHAPTER 42
ONE'S OWN MASTER

I haven't truly slept since you left. The bed is too empty, too cold. My soul is restless without you to chase the demons away. I know you're right where you need to be, but you took a part of me when you left—and I want it back. I want <u>you</u> back, Starling.

So train. Wield your power like no one else before you. Break Bruce's kneecaps for me. And come home.

—G

Eva couldn't help but smile when her eyes ran over the words of Grayson's letter. The messenger hawk came in yesterday morning with three letters: one from Commander Hargin, wishing them luck and reminding them they were in the desert to train, not sightsee; a letter from Jacob, which Anna immediately snatched up, holding it close to her chest as she ran away to the quietest corner in the cave to read; and the last one was from Grayson.

She kept his letter tucked against her heart at all times, ready to pull out whenever homesickness clawed at her. She hadn't expected him to respond—her own letter had been intentionally short, carefully vague in case the hawk was intercepted or someone back at base took it upon themselves to peek. The last thing she needed was to endanger her mission, or worse, expose what she and Grayson had.

But his letter had been shockingly intimate.

The distance between them suddenly felt more than just an ocean her dragon could cross—it was an uncrossable chasm carved straight through her chest.

She missed him.

Gods, she missed him.

His strength, that powerful, commanding aura, the scent of leather and steel wrapping around her, the heated way he looked at her. Her bedroll wasn't nearly as comfortable as the bed they'd shared, but she felt his absence all the same. It was just as cold and empty as he said...

And with the reminder of their night together—of how hollow every night after felt without him—in came a trickle of guilt. Not for being with him. No, she'd never regret opening her heart to Grayson and letting herself *be* with him. But she'd left someone else behind, too. Leo had given her everything,—gifts, royal treatment, his *heart*. He begged her to pick him. And how did she repay him? She left without a goodbye, without explaining that she'd chosen Grayson. That she was so, so grateful that he'd given her a place to be herself. Had made her feel cherished and special. No one had ever done that for her, not even Grayson.

And yet, he didn't understand her the way Grayson did. Their pain and grief forged a more powerful bond than anything Leo could have given her. Perhaps, in another life, where she was just a small town hunter, and he was an adventurous prince. Maybe they would have met in that life, and she would have fallen for his charm, his resilience—his relentless pursuit to be his own man, not conform into the mold his parents wanted him to be. She would have seen his grit and determination, and want to match him at every turn.

And he would have fallen for her, whatever part of her drew him in.

But not in this life. She'd experienced too much hurt to accept the soft kind of love he held for her.

Train, Grayson's letter said. *Wield your power. Come home.*

She held onto those words. They got her through the guilt, the harsh desert winds, the relentless training.

She would master her magic. Then she would go home to the man she loved.

Tucking the letter safely into her breast band, Eva rose to her feet and began her post-hunt stretches. She raised her arms over her head, relishing the relief in her spine as it popped in several different places. Her body ached, muscles, bones—even her *soul*. Anywhere imaginable, and it hurt.

If she thought Sasha's training had been brutal before, it was nothing compared to what soul magic demanded of her. Half the time she couldn't even finish Death's Dance before her grip slipped and lightning sputtered from her hands. She was improving—bit by bit, hour by hour—but never fast enough.

Meanwhile, Anna was summoning fire dragons as big as Aster and weaving packs of wolves out of flame. Magic obeyed her every command as though eager to please. Sasha all but worshipped her progress, showering her with attention and guidance.

Eva, on the other hand, stood on her pillar scraping by with pure Greene tenacity. Whenever she tried to ask for help, her reluctant teacher only waved her off with a dry, "Keep doing what you're doing, kid."

Frustrating. Infuriating. She wanted to scream at the sky, the ocean, at the godsdamn desert.

Why was *her* mentor the disinterested one? Anna's might be a prick, but at least he *trained* her—

A whistle shot through the cove, and Eva jolted out of her post-hunt stretches, turning to Sasha as she emerged from the cave. The retired Dragon Knight crooked her finger at her, a smirk that made Eva's blood simmer tugging at the edges of her mouth.

Oh. So *now* she wanted Eva's attention? How gracious.

Glaring, Eva crossed the beach—because she wasn't going to miss an opportunity, no matter how minute, to learn something—toes curling in the soft sand as she closed the gap. "I'm not a dog," she snapped once she was within hearing range.

Sasha's eyes shimmered in the morning sun. "And yet you still came. Good girl."

Eva crossed her arms, every unsavory word in her vocabulary dancing at the forefront of her mind. Spending time with unsavory characters would do that.

Seeing that Eva had no witty comeback, Sasha unhooked a bow from her back. Not any old rickety bow the Wanderers used, either. It was *Eva*'s bow. The one she'd hidden under her bedroll after her hunt this morning so no one with sticky fingers would be tempted to take it.

Sasha tossed it at her as if it was a piece of trash, not one of Eva's most valuable possessions.

With cat-like reflexes ingrained in her from her hunting days, Eva caught the bow, cradling it close to her chest. "Careful! I don't have the materials to mend it here."

"Who's fault is that?" She shook her head. "Never mind that, now. Come on." She turned and walked down the beach, heading for the trail out of the cove.

"Where are we going?" Eva called after her, refusing to move without answers. If this was one of her menial tasks... "Where's Anna?"

Sasha shrugged a single shoulder, not a care in the world as she walked away with a hip sway that told everyone *she* owned this beach. "Working on what I told her to." She peered back at her, waiting expectantly. Impatiently. "You, however, have been slacking off while she's fully embraced her training."

Her anger drove her forward, kicking up sand as she stomped towards the Desert Queen. "Slacking off?" she repeated furiously. "You have the audacity to tell me I'm *slacking off* when you haven't given me a wink of your time! How am I supposed to get better if I don't know what the fuck I'm doing??"

Sasha met her ire with a devious smirk, dark eyes shining like the stars on a moonless night. "There it is. That *fire*. I've been waiting weeks for that fight to come out. Do you know how boring it is to give you an order and all you say is 'yes, ma'am'? What kind of ship do you think I run here?"

Eva's mouth opened then closed when she didn't have a response. It hadn't crossed her mind that she was being mindlessly obedient. During her last visit here, Eva almost constantly fought back, but then... "Commander Hargin said—"

Sasha's eyes rolled to the Heavens and back, stopping Eva in her tracks. "Hargin demands obedience. She needs it or she'll lose respect from the other Dragon Knight Commanders. I am not Hargin."

Anna begs to differ. She didn't need to voice it for Eva to notice that look on her face. The one that said: *I hate how you treat me, but I respect your leadership.*

Eva was getting acquainted with the feeling.

"Out here, you need to learn how to stand up for yourself. With your power especially, you have to understand that *you* own it. Not Hargin, not Renkon—not even Arkon. It's yours now. *You have to learn how to own it.*"

When Eva said nothing, only blinking in response to the shockingly deep lesson, Sasha continued hiking up the narrow path up the cliff. Eva had to follow one step behind her, forced to stare at the back of her flowing midnight hair.

"You've mastered your mind and body. Now it's time you learned how to master your magic."

Eva bit back further arguments because... because it sounded like Sasha had *almost* complimented her—which was more than she had ever gotten out of the bitter woman before. She didn't want to ruin it with a side comment.

When they reached the top of the cliff face, instead of turning down the worn down path leading to the Under City, Sasha took her off the trail, further south.

They went a solid ten minutes without speaking, giving Eva plenty of time to wonder where they were going. There wasn't much at this end of the desert. The winds from the ocean were strong, stirring the sand and shredding anyone or anything that came near it. Not even the dragons came this way; the wind wasn't worth the extra ten minutes saved on travel time.

Eva had to tuck her face into her collar to protect her skin from the harsh winds.

Just when she was beginning to question her teacher's motivations, they entered a rift in the winds, where the air was thick and *still*. The hair on Eva's arms prickled, picking up something about this place her senses couldn't. In the centre of the strange phenomenon, a cluster of cactuses were arranged at various distances from the line in the sand defined by shells.

Eva blinked. She knew a shooting range when she saw one. "What's this?"

Sasha thrust her chin at the bow hanging on Eva's back. "We're expanding your horizons. You're familiar with daggers, but it's wasted on your powers. You can do so much more..." She pressed her lips together, restraining herself. Surprisingly. She sighed. "But, if weapons are all you can do right now, we'll work on building you an arsenal."

Eva eyed her suspiciously. "Why are you being nice?"

Sasha recoiled, face scrunching up in deep distaste. "I'm not being *nice*. Your lack of imagination has thoroughly disappointed me—but that doesn't mean I'm giving up on you. You certainly haven't." A light, disbelieving chuckle bounced out of her chest, either amused or impressed by Eva's tenacity. It was hard to tell. Eva usually only heard her laugh when she was mocking someone.

Sasha pointed at the bow, all serious now. "Use that and summon arrows."

Arrows?

Eva looked down at her bow, the smooth woodwork sitting perfectly in her grasp, worn down after endless hours of use. It hadn't quite clicked with her that Sasha hadn't brought the quiver. An archer was always limited by how many arrows they had... Unless she could make her own.

That is... genius.

Jaw tight with determination, Eva shut her eyes and searched for her source. Finding the power within herself was the easiest part—once she got over the initial hurdle.

Magic built up inside of her, tingling, crackling at her fingertips, waiting to take shape.

Opening her eyes, she readied her bow. Taking a deep breath, she imagined an arrow in her grasp. The carved wood smooth against her fingers, feathers brushing over her skin with the faintest touch. She caught the faintest wisps of maple still lingering on the bow.

Lightning seeped out of her fingertips and wove together into the shape of an arrow, sitting on the notch of her bow. Eva's heart beat faster, harder, the strain already taking its toll. Sweat trickled down the side of her face.

It took all of her concentration to hold the arrow's shape, then even more effort as she loosed it out into the world. Before it could strike home on a cactus, however, it sputtered out and disappeared.

Gasping, Eva dropped the weapon and fell to her knees, fingers sinking into the hot sand. Her breaths came in jagged gulps, the dry heat grating against her lungs.

Forming the arrow hadn't been too difficult, notching it hadn't been too bad either—but releasing it, and maintaining it mid-air, had thoroughly drained her.

"Again," Sasha demanded, surprising her. She stood not too far from her, a calculating look on her face as she regarded Eva's form. Her long fingers tapped against her cheek pensively as she watched her pant on the ground. "You will get stronger the more you practice."

Somehow finding enough energy, Eva glared at her. "What? So I'm interesting enough to train now?"

Eva already knew exposure would make her stronger. Why else did Sasha think she was doing it on the beach with her daggers?

Sasha's eyes rolled so dramatically the Heavens could see it from up there. "Oh, please. Of course you were boring! I can't help you meditate, I'm not a mind reader. And your Death Dance with those daggers? The most mundane thing I've ever seen. You could at least *try* to be more creative." She flicked her hair over her shoulder, batting those narcissistic eyelashes of hers. "Now. Again!" She gestured to the cactus Eva had aimed for. "We're not leaving this spot until you've hit that cactus with a lightning arrow!"

CHAPTER 43

WHISPERS IN THE DESERT

Anna looped her arm through Eva's and released a long, blissful sigh as they descended into the Under City. The air cooled with every step, trading the furnace heat of the desert for the fresh, damp air of this cavern. Down here, shadows stretched wide, swallowing the walls of the cave. From the top of the incline, Anna could make out the glittering reflection of the lake from the faint glow of lanterns and firepits illuminating this otherwise dark city.

The settlement was a testament to humanity's resilience. Despite the harsh, merciless wasteland outside, they had found a home here. A haven to most. Tents patched with faded cloth, fixed time and time again; wooden shacks leaning at odd angles, refusing to crumble; and stalls brimming with goods both fairly traded or stolen, some of it ordinary trinkets—and others less scrupulous.

The air was filled with vendors beckoning customers, children laughing as they chased each other down the street—with an underlying trace of arguments Anna picked up with her acute hearing from the far corners of the cave. Smoke and rotting wood perforated the streets. Roasted meats and sugary treats called to her deprived stomach.

The sun's heat didn't bother Anna the way it affected most of the people here, but after weeks of training, of pushing herself to the brink of overheating too many times to count, Anna had rediscovered her appreciation for the cool, moist air in the Under City. A breath of respite that tamed even the unruliest of hearts.

But, of course, they weren't here to cool down. No, that would be a mercy, of which this desolate wasteland had none of. No. Sasha sent them on an errand.

Neither of them would complain, though.

Eva shut her eyes, breathing in the moist air. "I know we're just supposed to grab more figs for Her Royal Highness, but there's no harm in dawdling, is there?"

A grin unfurled at the edges of Anna's mouth. "Of course not. We just had a hard time finding them..." As they passed by, a vendor called out to them, offering them small baskets of figs. Anna ignored him. "*Fresh* figs," she corrected once they were several paces away. "After all, Sasha deserves only the best. Besides, we've earned this."

They really had. Eva especially. Since Sasha had *finally* started giving her proper guidance, Eva's progress had leapt forward in bounds Anna could hardly believe. Last week, she'd shown Anna the shooting range, a fascinating little vortex of silence and reprieve from the constantly blowing sand. It gave them the space to work safely and to push themselves.

Eva could now summon arrow after arrow, each one striking true with unnerving precision. She was working on unleashing several at once, but the aim was less to be desired. But, being the stubborn, tenacious force of nature she was, Eva wouldn't let that stop her and kept trying until she was on the verge of collapse—or Anna had to drag her from the range to eat.

While Eva practiced, Anna focused on her own magic, taking advantage of the wide open space. She was determined to expand her magic beyond copies of a single animal. Instead, she challenged herself to hold different forms in her mind all at once—feathers and talons, fur and claws, muscle and sinew. She had to picture not only what they were, but how they moved when she commanded them: slithering, running, flying. Her proudest combination so far was her fiery hawks, Emberath and Rhaelen, alongside a wolf she dubbed Mysta.

This morning, they turned their practice into a game of cat and mouse. Anna's task was to dodge Eva's arrows, while Eva tried to pick off her animals. It was challenging—frustrating, even, to go up against a well-trained hunter—but also unexpectedly fun.

And that was exactly what they needed after spending all month training non-stop. A part of Anna suspected that was why Sasha had asked them to get more figs instead of making Bruce or one of her other cronies do it—rewarding their hard work with a moment to breathe.

But she'd never admit to it and Anna couldn't prove it.

They passed by a vendor with trays of jewelry on display. Gemstones and polished rocks stared back at them, dazzling beautifully in the candlelight. If Eva and Anna hadn't visited a nameless mining village up North in the jungle, Anna would have thought these pieces were fake. But they were as real as the pieces Leo bought her from time to time. Gems nearly cost nothing here, just another form of currency to these people, but it was the metal—the gold and silver that wove the pieces together—that made them valuable here.

Anna caught Eva eyeing a simple yet beautiful sapphire ring. It would have cost them a fortune in Aboria, but here it was only a few silver coins.

"If you like it," Anna said, "you should buy it. You'll never find a better price."

Eva slid her a wary glance. "You sound like Leo." As soon as the words left her mouth, she frowned and hurried away from the stall.

A suspiciously curious reaction Anna definitely didn't miss.

She caught up to Eva, folding her hands behind her back with what she hoped was a teasing smile. "What's that frown for?"

Eva shrugged noncommittedly, keeping her eyes ahead, clearly more interested in focusing on their mission than whatever that was. Too bad for her, Anna found this *far* more interesting. Because this didn't only affect Eva—it affected Leo too. She and Eva were close, but she and Leo were family.

"I don't know what you're talking about."

Anna stuck to her side like a prickly cactus. "Come on. You'd have to be blind to not see that frown. Something's happened between you and Leo. Out with it—or we'll take this into the Sandhound pit."

Eva halted in the middle of the street, eyes dropping to the ground, smoothed out my centuries of use. "He asked me to pick him instead of Grayson. Begged, really." She swallowed then cleared her throat. "I, um, obviously didn't, but I..."

Anna took her hand, squeezing it, then pulled her to a less busy street. This city wasn't like Lensenton where there was a bench to sit every other block, but they found a small pocket amongst the bustle to talk more privately.

Anna hadn't anticipated this. She knew Eva was different to Leo, not just a distraction or something pretty to show off to his court. She was real, a rare treasure, a true friend. But Anna hadn't known he had *told* Eva that. And was rejected. Her heart went out to him, and when they got back, she'd make a trip to Kain Castle to visit him—but right now she had a very guilty looking Eva, who was tearing up Anna's heart, because she had absolutely nothing to feel guilty about.

Eva met her gaze, licking her lips nervously. "Do you think he thinks I've been using him? I really appreciate everything he's done for me—and I know he didn't do any of it expecting anything in return—but he—" She stopped herself short, brows smashing together in a concentrated scowl. "Grayson just gets me the way no one else does. He looks at me and sees *me*. With Leo... he's great. Kind. Generous. He *listens* and he looks at me like *I'm* royalty. If things were different... *maybe*... we could have worked..." Her words trailed off, caught between her unnecessary need to explain her choice and this guilt she felt for making the choice.

"Don't feel guilty for choosing what will make you happy," Anna said gently. Both men were incredible in their own ways, and both were lucky to have Eva in their lives. That was the truth about love: you chose it. It didn't choose you. And sometimes you had to sacrifice something for that love. "Leo will understand. He might hurt for a bit, but he can't fault you for finding happiness with someone else. It's your life. You get to pick who you spend it with."

A sheen shimmered in Eva's eyes. Sniffling, she wiped at her eyes before a tear slipped free. "Thank you, Anna."

She shrugged it off, trying to hide her own emotions. Down a dark, dank street was hardly the place to be crying over love and boys. "Of course. It's what best friends are for. How many times do I have to tell you I'm here for you?"

After everything, did Eva still not know how much she loved her? She was the little sister she'd always wanted, the friend she'd yearned for all her life—a kindred spirit who hurt as much as she did but still fought every damned day to put a smile on her face. Their bond ran as deep as the Bonds with their dragons.

Eva cracked a smile. "Maybe just a few more times."

Anna returned the gesture then pointed back to the street they came from. "Now, let's go find some figs before Sasha sends a search party."

They found a vendor near the end of the track who boasted about the fresh figs they'd picked just this morning. After Anna and Eva dug through one basket to ensure the vendor hadn't snuck any rotting fruit beneath all the newer batch on top, they bought two baskets and hauled them back to Storm Cove.

They'd just climbed the long, winding path to the Under City's exit when Anna caught a concerned-looking fellow half-running, half-stumbling into the city. His eyes were wide, soot staining his forehead, crimson leaking down his arm as he tripped into a pair of vendors.

"It's gone!" The words came out in a haggard gasp, barely audible from where Anna and Eva stood. It didn't appear Eva heard him, but Anna directed more magic to her ears to hear the rest of the man's panicked rambling. "The fig orchard. The people. Everyone!"

"Slow down, boy." The burly vendor wrapped a massive arm around his back and heaved him upright, guiding him towards the back of his stall. "Tell us more about what happened..."

Their voices carried too far. Anna wanted to follow them to get more information. She had a sinking suspicion it had something to do with those rumours Sasha had warned her about—only this didn't sound like an ordinary fight. A farm had been destroyed. *Many* people had died.

Something was going on in the Desert Lands—something bigger than Sasha let on.

Anna glanced at Eva as they stepped out into the sunlight, none the wiser of the stirrings in the sand. For now, Anna would leave it that way. She didn't want to cause alarm without gathering all of the information first.

They walked back to Storm Cove in silence, the sun's light oppressive, the thoughts in Anna's mind suffocating. Her body wound tight, magic pooling at her feet and seeping into the land around them, searching for anything untoward. They were alone, of course, on the path to the cove. It wasn't a frequent stop for people, unless they wanted to face Sasha's wrath, but now Anna couldn't help feeling like they were being watched.

"*That is not possible,*" Aster declared, her shadow sweeping over the sand in front of them. Anna tipped her head back just enough to catch a glint of crimson scales as she passed overhead. As soon as she sensed Anna's unease, she left her typical sunbathing spot to check in on them. "*I detect neither hide nor hare.*"

"*Is that supposed to make me feel better?*"

Eva followed Aster's flight path with a curious frown. "Is Aster all right? Did something happen?"

"She just wanted to stretch her wings." The lie tasted acidic and burned on its way down her throat. "I think sitting on her rock all day every day is finally getting to her."

"*I do not 'sit on my rock all day',*" Aster grumbled down the Bond. "*I am rejuvenating my magic after suffering through the excruciatingly cold nights.*"

Anna rolled her eyes at her dramatic dragon. "*Why don't you curl up to Arkon's side? I'm sure he'd be content to keep you warm.*"

"*I already do,*" she snipped, then, before Anna could recover from that small but very *big* tid bit of information, she continued with a more sombre note, "*I see no one within a hundred feet of you. You are safe.*"

"*But remain wary?*" Just because they were safe now, didn't mean they would be safe ten minutes from now. Aster, especially, learned that the hard way with her previous Knight.

"*Always. And speak with Sasha. I agree she is hiding something from you, and I do not like it.*"

"*I'm on my way now.*"

They climbed down the narrow cliffside path, the sharp stone crumbling beneath their boots, and crossed the arched pale beach toward the cave. The air cooled as they stepped inside, trading sun-scorched heat for still, damp air. Each step weighed heavier than the last, as though the endless questions and possibilities circling Anna's mind had settled into her bones, dragging her down.

Inside, torchlight licked across the cavern walls, casting long shadows that swayed over Sasha, Bruce, and a handful of trusted allies. They were gathered tight around a round table, the surface spread with a map of the Desert Lands. Tiny carved figures stood sentinel on various settlements, like soldiers frozen mid-command.

The rest of the cave was deprived of people. Cleared out.

"Another one's gone—the report just came in this morning—"

As Anna and Eva neared, Sasha raised her hand—a sharp gesture that cut Malakai off mid-sentence. In one quick motion, she pulled a cloth over the table, snuffing the map from sight.

Too late.

Anna knew a war map when she saw one. Many times when she was a child, she and Leo had interrupted meetings such as this. They'd told their parents it was by accident, but even then they knew something was wrong. It was in the tension in their shoulders. The creases around their eyes. The delicate attention their parents gave them to hide the truth from them.

Eva was too busy carrying her basket of figs to the food storage to notice. Bruce followed after her, giving her a hard time for taking so long getting the figs. Their banter echoed through the cave, but Anna barely registered it.

Her eyes locked with Sasha's, and in that single glance Anna *knew* they needed to talk. She wasn't a child anymore. People couldn't hide things as easily as they used to from her anymore.

"Are you going to drop those figs off?" Sasha asked finally, her tone casual but tight as a guitar string. "Or are you planning to stand there all day with them?"

The silence strained, sharp and taut. Malakai, ever the opportunist, slid between them with a toothless grin—save for three gleaming gold ones. "I'll take them to storage. Let you ladies... *chat*." His voice trailed off as he reached for the figs and saw the hard look in Anna's eyes.

Anna didn't spare him a glance. She stepped up to the opposite end of the table, laying her palms on the cloth that hid more than paper and ink.

"How bad is it?" she asked, her voice low.

Sasha snorted and leaned back, folding her arms. "It's not bad. Manageable." Her words were firm, but they themselves sounded like a lie. "For now."

The admission unsettled Anna more than a scream in the dark would have. Concern carved lines into Sasha's brow—a look she thought she'd never see on the veteran.

“I’ve never seen anything like this,” Sasha confessed quietly. “Not here, not in the Desert Lands.”

Eva and Bruce reemerged from the storage room, their voices carrying as they headed for the exit. They completely bypassed the table, which Anna was sure was Bruce's intention all along.

“All I’m saying,” Bruce went on, running his hands together greedily, “is if you go in the ring again, I can make it worth your while.”

“Hmm.” Eva’s hum was amused, but there was a hard edge to it that would give anyone pause. “Make a pile of coin I’ll never spend… or make good on a promise to a close friend. What to pick?”

Bruce cocked a brow. “And what promise is that?”

“That I’d shock you clear into the last century if you cause me grief.”

Despite the threat, he laughed. A full-bellied sound that carried far even after they left the cave.

Anna smirked. *He's in for a shock if he thinks she won't follow through.*

Knowing Eva could handle herself out there, Anna turned back to Sasha. The warrior was smiling faintly, as though Eva’s barb had eased the weight of troubles weighing down on her. But Anna wasn’t fooled. Beneath the grin, shadows still stirred in Sasha’s eyes.

“What's going on?”

Sasha cast the exit one last glance, deemed it safe to talk, then yanked the cloth off the table.

The north side looked like a layer of Hell.

Figures that represented troops took up residence in three settlements, but the part that took Anna's breath away was the thirteen settlements that had been crossed out with red ink. Scratched off the map. Out of existence. As if this crude sketch didn't represent real living, breathing people.

“Not *living or breathing any longer*,” Aster remarked, the words void of compassion for these people.

Anna winced. Aster was being harsh to protect herself—and her rider—from getting too invested in the people of the desert. Investment led to compassion, and compassion posed a risk of getting reckless. And recklessness meant death.

Sasha raked a hand through her hair. “What had started as miscellaneous fights has now turned into more organised attacks—and the group is getting bigger.”

“They're recruiting as they go,” Anna guessed, and Sasha nodded in confirmation. “What's their target? Objective?”

“I don't know. Anyone I send in to get information never returns.” Her fists clenched at her sides. “They're a tricky bunch, with no rhyme or reason behind their attacks.”

Anna could attest to that. The destroyed settlements were scattered throughout the North, while neighbouring settlements were left untouched. It wasn't about looting, otherwise they wouldn't leave some settlements alone. It wasn't mindless carnage—people had lived to warn others. It was like...

"It's like they're trying to spread fear."

"That's *exactly* what they're doing," Sasha agreed, her anger scraping out of her throat in a frustrated growl. "But *why*? When the goblins did it, they wanted people to scatter, get lost in the woods, peg them off one by one. But here—" she gestured to the map "—they're letting people go. It doesn't make any gods damn sense."

Anna would have to agree with that. She rubbed the tip on her chin in thought, studying the map.

"What do we do?"

Sasha met her gaze from across the table, dark eyes blazing with relentless determination. "The 'we' you speak of does nothing. *I'm* handling it. It's Desert Land business, not Dragon Knight business. Understood?"

Anna leaned away from the table, crossing her arms. "And I'm assuming you still want me to keep Eva in the dark?"

Sasha didn't blink. "That's a given. The moment she hears—"

"Yeah, yeah," Anna interrupted her, waving her hand dismissively. "She'll want to help them. What a terrible quality to have." Sasha narrowed her eyes sharply on her, but Anna ignored it. "Give Eva more credit. She *can* be impulsive, but she's learned a lot since we were last here. She's not going to run haphazardly into danger."

"Forgive me if I don't believe you," she responded dryly. She thrust a finger toward her. "Do. Not. Tell. Her. That is an order."

Snorting, Anna flipped her hair over her shoulder then turned on her heel. "I didn't know retired Knights were still allowed to give orders." She marched for the exit, with every intention of finding Eva.

"Anna."

She stopped short at her tone, but didn't look back. Her teeth gnashed together, fists balling at her sides.

She hated this part of her job: the secrets. The lies. The fucking politics. Eva was her friend and a damned talented Knight—she deserved to know what was going on. While she stood in the cave talking to Sasha, people were dying, being uprooted from their homes. While they trained and went for leisure walks in search of figs, an army was being built.

But there was Jack shit she could do about it—because it wasn't her problem. Not her kingdom. Not her orders.

And it killed her. Every day, piece by piece, her soul would chip away, knowing she had the power to help these people—but she wasn't allowed to.

That was the difference between her and Eva. Her mother had long since beaten the obedient little soldier into her. Had ingrained the importance of following orders, despite her own personal feelings. But Eva? Orders be damned—if people needed a Dragon Knight, she'd be there. Anna fucking admired that of her, wished she could chisel the shackles her mother had caged her in and be just as free as Eva.

But she wasn't strong enough. Not yet.

One day.

"I won't tell her," Anna promised, the words bitter in her mouth.

Feeling heavy and stiff, she forced herself to move, leaving the Desert Queen alone with her fucking map.

One day.

CHAPTER 44
AN UNEXPECTED VISITOR

Eva woke up first thing in the morning. Just as she did every morning. The sun had only just begun to rise, a mere red sliver lining the horizon. There was just enough light to catch in Eva's hair, filling it with warmth rather than the harsh white the midday sun would drape her in. Dawn was the perfect time to hunt in the Desert Lands—everywhere, honestly—but especially here.

The air had warmed enough to not leave a chill in Eva's bones—thus making aiming difficult—but not so much so the land was baking away under the sun's glare. The ground was cool to the touch, colder still beneath the sand, where most of her prey would be slowly rousing from sleep. The cold would hold them in its frigid clutches a little while longer, slowing their movement, dulling their senses.

Dawn was the only hour *she* was the hunter. The beasts of this land were too strong and fast, otherwise.

Silently, she moved—a smooth, steady gait honed by years of hunting in the forest—for the cliffs. The gulls still slept in their nests, huddling with their young to fend the chill off.

She reached the stables nestled at the edge of the Under City, where stone met sand and the world opened up into a vicious, merciless landscape. The stable hands barely blinked as Eva passed, grabbing the reins of a waiting mare, just as she'd done many times before, and walked alongside it.

Periwinkle shadows dusted the dunes as a glimmer of the sun touched their peaks. The breeze was already heating, swathing Eva in a thin layer of sweat already.

She shut her eyes, allowing the mare to guide her for a time. Magic flowed out of her feet, casting a wide net around her and the mare, touching every grain of sand, root, underground river—or monster—within its circumstance.

Until she found her prey, she relished this moment of silence. This time of *being* where it was just her and the sand giving beneath her boots.

The only time she was truly alone. No dragon. No friends. No mentor. No Wanderers.

Just her and a horse she didn't know the name of. Mostly because the man she rented her from never deigned to tell Eva her name.

It was during this time, she practiced Death's Dance, breaking it up into smaller sections so she could always be moving forward. Grayson would probably cringe at her butchered version, but it was the only time she had to practice it these days, between hunting, soul magic training, and sparring with Anna, as well as making her evening swims in the reef with Arkon. She was too exhausted at night to lift her hands, let alone have enough strength left in her legs to swing her body around in one powerful, sweeping arch.

She could call on her soul magic without going through the dance, just remembering what that peace felt like was enough. But on the more challenging days, she still performed it through its entirety to calm her mind. If he could see what she could do with it now...

She could imagine it now, that lopsided smile, curling just one corner of his mouth, eyes shining with pride he wouldn't dare express any further than his eyes. His eyes were for her and her alone. And they told her so much.

Her heart ached, a dull throbbing different from the aching loss of her family. This one didn't hurt as much, and yet... it was almost as crippling. Because this time he was alive, reachable, waiting for her—but they had their orders. His required him to stay, hers pulled her away.

A *month and a half left*. And she had so much to tell him. Perhaps she could take him to that bar they went to last and buy him a drink—or a few—and he'd let her gush her heart and soul out. Then he could tell her everything he wasn't allowed to in their letters. And then... maybe... They could return to that inn and make love all night again. That night, then the next night, and the night after that. For as many days and nights and stolen moments of peace as he would have with her.

The thought of seeing him again made the withering, hot days bareable. Thinking about touching him helped her push her muscles beyond their limits. Hearing his voice in her head, both in that cold instructional way of his and the deep smoldering tone in her ear, made wielding easier.

Train. Wield like no one else before. Then come home.

She intended to do just that.

A prickle in her fingers snapped her out of her thoughts. Her senses had picked up on some prey ahead. A den of sleeping lizards several paces ahead.

She halted, crouched, breath entering her body slowly then leaving silently.

The morning sun crept higher, casting soft gold across the dune her target slept in. A pair of desert birds darted overhead, their wings flashing pale in the light. They hadn't seen her—wouldn't warn the lizards of her presence. These birds were never far from the giant lizards; they acted as an alarm for the lizards, warning them of predators, while the lizards protected the birds' nests.

Beside her, the mare huffed, attempting to pad the sand impatiently. Her hooves were enchanted, just as Hiron's were, keeping her a couple inches off the ground. Eva ran her fingers through her mane and offered soft cooing words of encouragement to keep her quiet, similar words she'd spoken to her father's horse to keep him docile. This mare had a much better temperament than the gelding, but Eva couldn't help missing having to fight with him.

It had been a part of her routine. Her life before Arkon and Dragon Canyon, before Sylus and Darius. A simpler time.

At least she didn't have to fear assassins in the Desert Lands. Sasha's Wanderers reported anyone suspicious—then dealt with them accordingly. Despite this being a land of criminals, it was the monsters and sand and sun she mostly had to look out for.

Slowly, Eva crept toward the den, leaving the mare behind, the air around her growing still, as if the gods above were watching. Each step was measured, careful not to stir the sand. These lizards had hyper sensitive scales and could pick up on the faintest vibrations in the ground.

She paused a few feet away, drawing her bow and pulling the string taut. No quiver. No arrows. She didn't need them.

The air crackled, raising the hairs on Eva's arms. Magic condensed around her fingers until a quivering, white-blue bolt formed in her grasp and notched on the bow. This part was as easy as breathing—as long as her mind was quiet, at peace.

She inhaled once more. On the exhale, she loosed the arrow. Three more immediately forked out as the main arrow arched over the den. They rained down from the sky, striking the dune above the den. The ground rumbled, sand rolling down the steep hill. The lizards stirred, but they were slow—the cold seized their blood the same way it did their dragons. The only difference between them was that they were much smaller and had to rely on shared heat and the den to keep them warm through the night.

They piled out of the den one at a time, frantic yet sluggish.

Drawing the string back again, Eva unleashed five more arrows. These ones homed in on their prey, striking each one true in the heart.

"Yes!" She allowed a victory fist pump into the air.

Controlling five arrows at once wasn't easy, especially with moving targets, but she couldn't deny she was getting better at it. Not when three weeks ago, she couldn't even hit five cactus at once.

A spring in her step, she hurried to collect her prize, calling the mare over as she went.

Eva stood in front of them, hands on her hips as she regarded the five giant lizards then peering back at the horse. They were as long as the mare was tall, and twice as heavy. She usually came back with one and it was enough to feed everyone for the night.

She scratched the back of her head sheepishly. "I might have gone overboard this morning." She had been so caught up in the hunt, in the fact that she could fire five arrows at once, that she hadn't stopped to think *how* she was going to get them back to Storm Cove. The mare could *maybe* take three of them.

Arkon was still sleeping, so she couldn't ask him to bring them back.

Sighing, grudgingly deciding to leave two behind, she got to work. One by one, she dragged the lizards alongside the horse then heaved it onto the mare's back. She protested, teetering after the second one. The last lizard, she secured rope around its torso then attached the other end to the harness. Not exactly ideal, but they'd make it work.

She was just about to leave when Eva caught movement in the corner of her eye. Her instincts took over. She drew her daggers as she pivoted towards the movement then planted her feet.

A figure crested a dune in the distance, swaying as they reached the top—then collapsed, tumbling down, down, down the hill.

Eva didn't waste a beat. She ran for them, abandoning the horse. When she reached them, she remembered her training—lest she wanted to face Anna's wrath for putting herself in harm's way—and scanned the immediate area for any dangers.

The area clear, she fell to her knees and flipped the man over.

Blisters covered his face and chest where his shirt had been slashed open. A wound bled from his right shoulder down to left abdomen. Sand absorbed most of the blood, clinging to his skin as it clotted. His face was bruised and just as bloody as his chest, but Eva found no wounds responsible. Cracked lips barely parted when his hazy eyes settled on her.

He inhaled a shuddering breath, seeming to take all of his energy just to breathe. "Z—Zyphril?" he rasped. "You are... more beaut...iful than the tales say."

Eva unclipped a canteen from her belt and tipped the flask over his lips gently. "Zyphril has not come to claim your soul today," she promised.

He choked, sputtering, on the first few sips, then he took the canteen from her with a trembling hand and drank greedily.

Eva allowed it. They weren't too far away from the cove to concern herself with water. "Who did this to you?"

He shook his head, sitting up with Eva's help. "My family... Please, my family. They're not too far behind me. Do you have enough water for them?"

She set the man down gently then hiked up the dune, shielding her eyes with her hand to avoid the sharp glare of the sun. The desert was empty for as far as her Bound eyes could see. Not a single soul. Not even a trace.

Her stomach knotted. This man must have come far. Dehydration had made him delirious and made him think his family had been with him every step of the way.

Feeling as though her feet were weighed down by lead blocks, Eva skidded down the slope to the man's side, kneeling into the sand beside him. Moistening her lips, she looked down at the withered man, her chest tight with sympathy. She was all too familiar with the loss of family. She wouldn't wish that on anyone. It didn't make breaking the news to this man any easier. Her voice wavered as she said, "They are with Zyphril now."

His face twisted in agony. Too familiar. Too close. "M—my boys? They're gone?"

Eva took his hand, squeezing it as tight as she dared. His fingers were so thin, she feared breaking them if she used her full strength. "I'm sorry. I'm so fucking sorry."

A tearless sob racked through him. Shaking his head, he turned away from her, curling in on himself like a broken leaf. "Leave me be. Let Zyphril claim my soul, just as she's claimed my family."

Her heart went out to him, fucking tore at the seams for him and his family... but this man didn't get these wounds on his own. That slash down the middle was from a sword, not a claw. *Someone* had done this to him. To his family.

"Where do you come from?" she pried softly, trying to pull the man from his spiralling thoughts. "Tell me who did this to you and your family."

The man didn't move, save from the tremor in his body.

"I know you hurt," Eva pushed, a little harder this time. "Gods, I *know* it—but you must *live*. For your family. Only you can carry their memories. Let them live on through you. Help me avenge them so you may find peace."

He paused his sobbing, releasing a trembling breath. His fingers clenched into the sand with the remaining strength he carried. "The men responsible have no name. They only sweep through our settlements, take what they want, and leave death in their wake."

Eva's body went rigid, a sheen of sweat that had nothing to do with the heat breaking out on her skin. Her mind went to the man she saw the other day, rushing into the Under City with a gash on his arm, looking panicked and stricken. Anna hadn't been concerned by his appearance—after all, it was the Desert Lands and people picked fights all the time—so Eva had brushed it off.

But now... what if he had been another victim? How many people had come to the Under City to find shelter? How many people had she wilfully ignored while their homes were being taken, families slaughtered?

I have to tell Sasha. She wouldn't stand by and let this happen to her people. This had to stop.

"We—we managed to escape, but..." He swallowed, body clenching, as if the memory was too much for him. "We fled... without provisions. Three days we ran... hoping we'd find... *somebody*. Three days in this godsforsaken place."

"Arkon, I need you."

She felt him stir immediately. *"What is it, Little One?"*

"I'll explain later. Just get here."

He sensed her urgency, saw a flash of the man in front of her through her eyes, then he was airborne.

"Help is on the way," Eva relayed. "There is a lake not too far from here with magical properties. It'll heal your wounds, give you strength to keep fighting. Just hang in there."

He had to live. For his family.

They were back at Storm Cove in less than twenty minutes. Arkon carried Eva and the man on his back, while he held a disgruntled mare in his claws. He set the horse and Eva's catch down gently on the shore then took Eva and the man to the entrance of the Under City.

Sasha and Anna were already outside, with Syran and Aster standing guard on either side of the entrance. Several people had gathered around inside to see what the commotion was about, but they didn't dare approach the dragons.

Sasha looked down at the dying man without a hint of sympathy for him. Her hands rested comfortably on her hips, close to her sword, yet not quite threatening. Not that this man was much of a threat.

"Explain why you brought someone into my territory without my permission, girl."

Eva flinched at the callous nature of her tone. "He's dying, Sasha." Like she needed any further explanation. She really couldn't have expected Eva to just *leave* him there. "He needs the lake."

Sasha shook her head, studying the man's hazy eyes. Eva would have mistaken him for dead already if she didn't catch the slight rise and fall of his chest. They were wasting time he didn't have. "The lake can't heal this. He's beyond help." Dismissing him, she looked up at Eva, the dispassionate mask of a warrior falling into place. "What happened?"

"I—I found him during our hunt." Eva cleared her throat, gathering her thoughts, calming her mind. "His family was attacked by a group of bandits. They were forced to flee without provisions."

Sasha and Anna exchanged a look. A look Eva didn't like; it spoke of secrets and lies. They *knew* about the attacks.

"Hmm. I'm sure he did. I want to hear it from his mouth."

Eva bit her lip. Talking back to Sasha had never ended well for her—especially in front of a crowd. Sasha had carved her place among the lawless and orderless. Maintaining that control was vital. If her student started mouthing off, it would look like weakness. It would *smell* like weakness.

And weakness out here was blood in the water.

Eva knew too well what men did when a woman faltered. She'd seen it in the way they circled Commander Hargin, waiting for the first stumble, eager to drag her down like hounds from the Five Hells. They hadn't just wanted to see her fall—they wanted to tear her apart. She'd felt it herself during Leo's gala.

She didn't want to jeopardise everything Sasha had built here, not after she had scraped, clawed, and gouged her way to the top.

Sasha nudged the man with her boot. "Oi! You still alive?"

The man groaned, clutching his chest. Eva wanted to offer him some form of comfort, but she kept her feet planted, heart clenched.

"You don't have much time left," Sasha informed him callously. "Do you want to die a coward or a hero?"

At her words, his eyes came into focus, landing on her in the same awe-struck manner he had when he first saw Eva. "Zyphril?"

"Wrong god. Ebis."

His eyes shuttered, arms trembling as he brought his hands to his chest, clutching them together in silent prayer. "They took my home. My family. My life. Please, Ebis, for all the chaos in this world, unleash your power unto them. Save who you can in the North. Restore peace to the Desert Lands." His final breath left his body and hung heavy in the air around them.

Eva stared at his lifeless eyes, feeling as though Sasha herself had shovelled out her insides. Gone. She was too late to save him.

"*He is with his family now,*" Arkon murmured in her thoughts, holding her soul close to his. "*It is what he wanted.*"

Her eyes burned. "*But... it's too soon. We could have saved him.*"

"*Sasha spoke the truth. The lake would not have helped him. He was too far gone.*"

Her throat tightened.

Anna stepped away from Sasha and laced her fingers with Eva's, standing shoulder to shoulder with her. "How much longer are you going to wait? How many more people have to die before you take action?"

Sasha didn't acknowledge her, just stared at the man, everything and nothing swirling in her dark eyes. She held so much power in her fingertips, stopping this needless bloodshed would be easy for her—but who got to decide if what she used her power for was right or wrong?

"What are you so afraid of?"

Sasha's eyes narrowed into sharp slits, a warning tipped with venom. But when her eyes slid to Eva, something softened in them. "Fuck it. Pack your gear and make the necessary arrangements. We're leaving at first light tomorrow."

Anna moved into action straight away, as if she had been waiting for this very moment. She squeezed Eva's hand. "I'll inform Hargin of our situation," she said quietly. "You good to gather supplies?"

Eva nodded absently. She couldn't remove her gaze from the dead man. She didn't know how long she stood there before she could move. Probably too long.

A storm was brewing in Astrida. First Darius's escape, then Sylus's assassins—and now unrest in the Desert Lands. Trouble seemed to follow them wherever they went. She couldn't help but feel responsible for it. Maybe it was silly for her to think that way—she had no control over the actions of others—and yet, she was the common denominator between all of these events.

She looked up at Arkon, who had been waiting with her silently. "Can you help me?" Her voice came out hoarse, her throat dry after standing out in the open for so long.

Without needing her to say more, he curled his claws around the man's now-stiff body. She climbed into his saddle, and they flew along the cliff's edge, following it to the very tip of the cove. She slid down his body and started to dig. Once the hole was deep enough, Arkon set him down gently then pulled the sand over his body. She placed a pile of stones at the head of his grave then clasped her hands together and murmured a prayer for him and his family.

It wasn't enough. A few simple words was never enough.

But she hoped avenging him and all the other lives lost would be.

CHAPTER 45
FAMILY

Jacob found Grayson on the field beside Kain Castle. It was a cool morning, mist still clinging to the grounds like the last breath of night. Clouds hung above them, pregnant with rain and the promise of another monochromatic day. Jacob settled further into his dragon scale jacket, grateful for the soft, warm lining fending off the day's chill.

Eran sat with his tail curled around his claws, wings tucked tightly against his back, watching his rider move with the speed and fluidity of a raging river.

Between Grayson's hands, a rope of water followed each motion, stretching as his arms spanned the length of his body, then tightening into a ball as they met. The water wove around his torso and limbs, shooting out from his heel with each kick. Before it could travel more than three feet, it snapped back into his hands, seamlessly flowing into the next movement.

Jacob blinked. The rope had grown thicker, longer, and he hadn't seen Grayson pull a single drop from the dew at his feet. Grayson was creating the water himself.

That was new.

Jacob cleared his throat, keeping a respectful distance. Grayson had come out here to be alone, as he often did during their stay at the castle, wrestling with the compass and its cryptic guidance toward the vestiges—a venture that had yielded little success. Jacob usually gave him space.

But this morning was different.

Grayson froze mid-jab, muscles coiled with a control Jacob could only hope to one day master. Slowly, deliberately, he lowered his hands, planted his feet, each movement measured and purposeful. He turned toward Jacob, sweat beading on his forehead, soaking into his rumpled shirt. Strands of hair clung to the side of his face; the stubble along his jaw glistened in the soft light.

Jacob frowned, troubled. "Have you been here all night?"

"Couldn't sleep," was his gruff reply. "What is it?"

His frown deepened, tightening the line of his brow. Jacob was used to retiring before Grayson and rarely noticed when Gray came in after him—but staying out all night was unusual, even for him.

Jacob pulled the still-sealed letter from Anna from his breast pocket. The messenger hawk had arrived this morning, just as Jacob had climbed the tower to check for any new reports. But there was only one letter attached. Every other time, there had been two.

It spelled trouble.

Jacob didn't want to find out what kind of trouble until Grayson was with him. Just in case.

Grayson's eyes narrowed in on the letter. He closed the gap between them rapidly, despite having worked all night. The water hovering around him dropped to the ground, leaving puddles in his wake. "Who's it from? What does it say?"

"Anna," Jacob answered. "I haven't read it yet."

Grayson's shoulders stiffened, eyes flicking between him and the letter. "Well? Are you going to open it?"

If Jacob thought Grayson's temper was on a short string then, it was nothing compared to now. The muscles in his jaw seemed to be permanently flexed, feathering more so at the slightest inconvenience.

Ignoring his sharp tone, he peeled the envelope open and slipped the letter free. Anna's elegant script filled the sheet. Dread sank heavy in his gut with every word. He didn't know what he was expecting to find. Guessing a part of him hoped that Eva's accompanying letters had gotten lost on the flight here this time. Hoping Anna would write about how much she missed him and how much she was looking forward to coming back to him. He certainly wasn't anticipating reading a breakdown of events taking place in the Desert Lands. He didn't want to read that Anna and Eva were getting involved. Didn't want to think about his girlfriend and sister diving into a fight that wasn't theirs to fight.

Wordlessly, he handed the letter to Grayson, still absorbing Anna's clinical debrief.

He swallowed. Hard. This wasn't their first time seeing combat—not by a long shot. It definitely wasn't the first time he was too far away to help. But knowing that didn't ease the pressure squeezing his chest. He usually found out about the harrowing danger *after* the fact, not before.

Grayson took the letter and read it. Once. Twice. Three times. His face darkened with each pass. "I don't like this."

"Neither do I," Jacob agreed. "Why isn't Sasha handling it herself? How bad is it over there?"

Grayson ran a hand through his hair then rubbed the scruff on his jaw. "I don't like this," he repeated, faster now, as if his mind was running faster, calculating. "Something isn't right."

Jacob looked at the letter, now crumpled in Grayson's fist. "You think this is a trap?"

"Not for us. This is definitely a letter from Anna."

Jacob knew that much. He'd recognise her writing from anywhere; it even carried her sweet jasmine perfume.

But if it wasn't a trap for them...

He was almost afraid to ask: "Do you think this is a trap for Eva or Anna?"

Eran approached them, dipping his head to nudge his rider's shoulder. "It is unlikely," he said, mostly speaking to Grayson, who had gone silent, eyes hard. "Who would want to trap them?"

"I can think of at least one bastard," Grayson growled, completely crushing the letter in his hand.

"But Darius doesn't know where Eva is," Jacob reasoned. As much as he feared Darius finding out her location, the chances of him actually finding her in the Desert Lands were low. That was a part of the reason why Commander Hargin had sent her there—to keep her away from Darius and Sylus's assassins.

"He has his ways," Grayson ground out.

"You're being paranoid."

"I would have to agree with Jacob," Eran said gently. "Eva is safe. She can handle herself—even in this time of conflict in the Desert Lands."

Grayson's breathing came in harder. "So, what, I'm just supposed to stay here and stare at a fucking map while she's flying into a warzone?"

The thought didn't sit right with Jacob either, especially when he worded it like *that.* If Commander Hagin knew—which he was sure she would soon, if Anna also sent a letter to Dragon Canyon—she would likely order them not to engage, or send backup. *He* wanted to be that backup. Gods, he'd fight tooth and nail with anyone who tried to take the mission.

But he wouldn't be the backup, because they had their orders.

"We have to find the vestiges," Jacob said weakly, hating that the words even left his mouth.

Grayson sliced him down to the marrow with a glare. "Fuck the vestiges, Jake. I don't care how many people Sasha has under her command, or how powerful Eva has gotten with her magic, or how capable she is. I know she's strong. I know she's powerful. But that doesn't mean I'm going to stand by and do nothing."

He's going, Jacob realised with cold clarity. The moment he'd read the letter, Grayson had already made the decision to leave, and there was nothing Jacob could do to talk him out of it.

He wasn't even sure he *wanted* to. It was cowardly to hide behind his partner's decision, but he was glad Grayson was willing to break the rules when Jacob was so willing to leave his girlfriend and sister in the Desert Lands.

A surge of relief coursed through him. Relief that Grayson didn't hesitate. Relief that someone else had taken the weight of the choice off his shoulders.

"Are you in?" Grayson gritted out.

Jacob hesitated only a second—the pathetic, cowardly part of him afraid of the consequences they would surely face when they returned. He was done sitting and doing nothing. If Eva and Anna were walking into danger, they weren't going to sit this one out. They were a squad. Family. They fly together. They fight together. They bleed together.

"I'm in."

"Then let's fly."

CHAPTER 46

FLY TOGETHER. FIGHT TOGETHER. BLEED TOGETHER

They flew in formation due North. Sasha and Syran took the lead, while Anna and Aster, and Eva and Arkon followed close behind in a tight triangle. They were fast, but conscious of the dragons' stamina.

With every pump of Arkon's wings taking them further away from the cove, Eva's stomach twisted tighter. This wasn't her first time going into combat or willingly flying into battle—but it felt different this time. The stakes were different. It wasn't personal. Jacob wasn't in danger. Her family weren't the ones in trouble. She didn't know these people they were about to help.

But, while her stomach might be a nervous wreck, her mind was calm. Clear. Ready.

They had a plan. A location. Rough numbers. And a three woman army. Sasha herself had lived through the Goblin Wars, fought through hordes of goblins with only Syran to count on. Anna was an accomplished warrior in her own right and had overcome her fear of her magic. And Eva—she was ready to prove herself. She was no longer the scared little girl who ran from armies. She had learned a lot since becoming a Dragon Knight, from Arkon, Anna, and Grayson. Now was the time to let the world know who the new storm dragon rider was—and that she wouldn't cower in the face of danger.

Arkon's body vibrated beneath her as their thoughts slipped together. While the wind was harsh and grating against Eva's skin—even with her dragon scale armour protecting her—it gathered around his wings and carried them further and faster. "*Our power will put fear into our enemies and hope into our allies.*"

She tucked into his back, digging her heels into the stirrups, molding her body against him to give him the least wind resistance possible. The sooner they put a stop to this rogue group, the sooner her heart would be able to settle. She hated that she hadn't known about it sooner, that countless families and innocent people had suffered while she sat safe and snug in Storm Cove. Later, when people's lives weren't on the line, she'd talk to Sasha and Anna—*especially* Anna—about keeping secrets from her. That hurt cut too deep to unpack now. There was no time—and her mind needed to be focused on the mission at hand.

They had set off at first light this morning and set a course for Last Drop, a settlement central west of the Desert Lands. Once they sat down and studied a map of the rogue group's attacks, they saw that the settlement was one of the last ones in that area that hadn't been hit yet. If they were right, Last Drop would be hit tomorrow, which would give them all night to set up for the attack.

"Look ahead," Aster called, bobbing her head towards a glittering pool of water several furlongs away. If Eva didn't have her magic flowing through her eyes constantly, she wouldn't have been able to pick up on it.

Sasha caught Aster's call and lifted a fist then flashed two fingers—two hours. She followed it with a sharp, sweeping motion down and out—fast landing. The signal was clear: they'd reach Last Drop in two hours and needed to make a quick dismount before their dragons drew the sand-worms' attention. Or worse.

Eva inhaled deeply, fighting off the nausea curling in her gut. She forced herself to focus on the land below. Out here, knowing the terrain could mean the difference between life and death. Every detail mattered. The more they observed, the better their chances.

The desert stretched out beneath them, wide and unforgiving. Wind-sculpted dunes rippled like waves, broken only by jagged ridges that cut the horizon. Some too steep to climb, others sloping enough to use for cover. Clusters of vegetation began cropping up more often now, drawn to the hint of moisture that reached even this far from the oasis. Acacia trees twisted out of the sand, their roots buried deep. Under their shade, wildflowers and sage clawed their way up from the dirt—soft purples and dusty greens breaking up the endless yellow.

Stones littered the terrain—boulders cracked from the heat and scattered like bones, smaller rocks smoothed by centuries of wind. Succulents clung to them, their thick leaves hoarding water, while lichen crept across the shaded crevices in muted greens and greys.

And then things began to shift. Slowly. The air changed first—drier than the jungle but heavier than in the heart of the desert, brushing her skin with a kind of sticky warmth that reminded her of the summers back in Aboria. The dunes leveled out, traded for patches of cracked stone and soft, silty ground. Palm trees appeared, their fronds swaying lazily in the breeze like they had all the time in the world. Rocky outcrops gave way to shallow caves—shelter for whatever creatures made it this far out.

It was beautiful, in a way. A slice of paradise carved into the middle of a wasteland. The oasis shimmered ahead like it had been waiting for them. A beacon of hope, safety. Reprieve.

Last Drop finally came into view, tucked along the eastern edge of the lake like a clutch of seashells on the shore. It sprawled out beneath the tallest dune, a hulking mountain of sand whose long, sloping shadow swallowed nearly every structure beneath it. Dome-shaped homes clustered close together, built from sunbaked clay and packed sand, their rounded roofs blending seamlessly into the desert's palette. Chimneys poked up like ant hills, some puffing the last wisps of smoke from afternoon cook fires.

Beyond the domes, narrow irrigation trenches carved the earth into neat rows of farmland. Eva spotted tough desert crops she'd grown accustomed to during her time here—stubby gourds and thick-skinned fruits that looked more like rocks than food. Spiny plants and knotty vines, all hoarding water beneath bitter rinds and thorny skins. Everything here had to fight to survive. Even the crops.

But something felt wrong.

The hairs on the back of Eva's neck rose, eliciting a shiver down her spine.

The streets were empty.

At this time of day, people were typically out preparing for the evening—hauling water, returning from their stalls, gathering in small circles to laugh, argue, cook. There should've been children pointing skyward, wide-eyed at the dragons gliding overhead. Instead, the streets were deserted. No voices. No movement. Just the eerie stillness of a town holding its breath.

Eva narrowed her eyes, calling on her dragon vision. The red glow of body heat lit up the insides of the domes like lanterns. People were there. Dozens of them, maybe more. But they weren't outside. They were tucked away—in their homes, in the hidden caverns nestled deep within the towering dune.

A low rumble vibrated through Arkon's chest as his gaze swept the terrain, fixating on the sprawling cavern system that stretched further than Eva could track. "*I agree. Something feels... off.*"

That did it for her. Paranoia was one thing—hers was constant. But when Arkon felt it too? That meant trouble.

"Sasha!" Eva called ahead.

Sasha glanced back, eyes narrowing as she met Eva's gaze. She didn't hesitate. Raising one hand, she gave a tight, twirling motion—circle around—then jabbed two fingers toward the far side of the largest dune—regroup, east side.

Aster banked first, taking point while Syran followed up along Arkon's side. One by one, they landed, stirring up torrents of sand as they alighted as softly as possible. The Dragon Knights slid out of their saddles and met up in the centre of the circle their dragons had formed.

Anna tossed her braid over her shoulder and crossed her arms. "I'm not the only one weirded out by the eerily silent town, I take it?"

"No," Sasha agreed, chewing on her thumbnail, gaze fixed ahead of her on nothing in particular while she planned. "It's not uncommon for folks to hide when they see Syran's shadow. And with a group of marauders raiding other settlements, I don't blame them for being cautious, but I still want to err on the side of caution."

Dropping to one knee, she began carving a quick map into the sand with a stick. It wasn't rough—it was *precise*. Streets, domes, farms, terrain. All from memory.

Eva barely breathed. This was what working with a high ranking, decorated soldier looked like. Grayson worked similarly before they had raided Darius's fort—sharp, methodical, thoughtful—but with Sasha it felt more clinical and her attention to detail was spot on.

"Our objective is to scout and recon," Sasha started, tone level and clear. The voice of a Commander. "There may be enemies already here—or it may just be fear keeping them quiet. Either way, remember there are friendlies in the settlement. They're scared and will act unpredictably. Do *not* engage until I give the signal. The last thing any of us want is innocent blood on our hands." A shadow clouded her eyes, brief but deep. It told Eva everything she needed to know: it didn't matter how good you were, sometimes you still made mistakes. The kind that didn't just leave scars—but ghosts.

"I'll take point and walk in head-on. If someone wants to show their teeth, they'll show them to me." She drew a line down the main street between buildings. Next, she drew two flanking paths. "Eva, I want you on top of this dune and command the high ground. If anything moves that shouldn't, you'll see it first. Anna, stay close to me but out of sight. Be ready to move if I signal." She turned her gaze upward to the dragons. "Arkon, stay hidden behind the dune and keep Eva covered. If she's compromised, you *level* that hill. Aster, I need you in the air, provide cover fire. Be Eva's reach and Anna's eyes."

"What about Syran?" Eva asked.

Sasha quirked a smile up at her dragon. "He's going for a little swim. If things go sideways, you'll discover the true power of elemental affinity."

A knot tightened in Eva's stomach, fluttering like restless wings. Did it ever get easier? The tense moments before a mission—the breath held, the churning stomach, the pounding in her chest—always felt like standing on the edge of a cliff. She'd felt that same bated unease the night she and Grayson crept through Darius's fort, planning its downfall. Back then, she'd wondered if she was the only one feeling it. Watching Sasha and Anna—calm, steady, untouchable—it was hard to tell if their composure was real or just another mask.

But nerves or not, she'd faced that edge before. She'd pushed through fear and doubt, and she would do it again. There was no room for hesitation—not when so much was at stake.

Sasha rose to her feet, rolling her shoulders back and expelling a sharp breath. "May the winds be in your favour, Dragon Knights."

Silently, the Knights slipped apart, each moving into position like shadows melding with the dunes.

Eva's first attempt to climb the steep dune was clumsy. Her boots dug into loose sand, only to slide backward with every step.

At last, she found a narrow ridge, a knife's edge of sand. From here, the entirety of Last Drop sprawled out beneath her: twisting streets, clustered domes, the lake shimmering in the late afternoon sun as a backdrop. Sasha's route carved a clear line through the centre, flanked by buildings no taller than Eva.

The sun pressed down relentlessly, its heat radiating off the sand and threatening to bite into her skin. She felt Eran's protection begin to waver, allowing a sliver of the heat to nettle her flesh. Sweat beaded at her temples and dripped down her spine, but Eva remained still, balanced on the precipice. Her bow was ready, fingers tingling with magic barely contained—alert, but waiting.

Sasha came into view, striding down the main street with the swagger of the Wanderer Queen. To the untrained eye, she looked like she was casually strolling through the settlement, but Eva caught the flicker of movement by her hip—her fingers danced near the hilt of her broadsword. Magic hovered around her, a dense aura of power that undulated in the air like a heat wave. Whatever she might face down there, she was ready.

Eva watched Anna move into position, slipping between alleys, matching Sasha's pace as she approached the centre. She was sleek like a cat, silent as a shadow—the embodiment of Zyphril coming to claim your soul.

People shifted within their dwellings, some leaning in to each other, murmuring, speculating, while others moved closer to the windows to see who dared to walk their streets as if she owned this oasis. Their attention was so fixed on Sasha, they didn't bother to look up and watch Aster circling above them in a slow, arching perimeter. They didn't notice the large black dragon slip into the water on the far side of the oasis either.

Eva's heart pounded so hard against her ribs, it felt like it was trying to break out of her chest.

"Calm yourself," Arkon warned her. *"Breathe in through your nose and out through your mouth. You are a hunter and the people below are your prey."*

She breathed in then pushed the air out through her lips, steadying her heart and slowing her mind. *You can do this.*

Sasha reached the lake's shore, eyes raking over the silent settlement vigilantly. "My name is Sasha Remoar," she called, her voice carrying far through the hard-packed walls of their homes. "I mean you no harm."

After a quick stirring within one of the homes, a man stepped out and approached her, his hands held up above his head. His back was to Eva, but she could see the tremor in his shoulders as he approached her. His salt-and-pepper hair swayed in the gentle breeze sweeping through the settlement.

Sasha locked eyes on him instantly, body tense, but hands resting casually at her sides, appearing as non-threatening as possible.

"Where are the others?" the man asked, a light tremble in his voice that even Eva could pick up from the top of the dune. "Three dragons flew overhead."

With magic flowing into her eyes to catch the smallest movement down below, Eva watched as Sasha's eyes narrowed into sharp slits. "They won't harm you."

"Where. Are. They?" His head snapped left and right, looking for them. When his gaze dashed to the dune, Eva ducked, lying flat on the sand. "Bring them here. They need to be here."

Sasha's hand moved like lightning—drawing her sword. "What do you mean they *need* to be here?"

"The girl—the storm dragon rider—please—bring her here—"

A knife darted out of a window, lodging itself into his back. Crying out, he stumbled forward toward Sasha. She didn't move a muscle as he tripped and fell at her feet—

Then Eva's blood froze. Her breath left her lungs. The world threatened to give out beneath her.

Darius Fortys stepped out of the same home the knife had come from. A younger man, bearing the same black hair and sharp jaw as Darius and Grayson, trailed behind him, twiddling with the twin knife to the one in the man's back.

Arkon growled in her mind, low and vicious. Fury pulsed down the Bond needle-sharp, flooding her veins with the need to rip and tear into Darius. His wingbeats sounded behind her, sand stirring as he ascended the dune.

"*Don't*," she warned him, too afraid to take her eyes off of Sasha as she faced Darius and who Eva assumed was Dravyn, Grayson's younger brother. *"There are families down there. If you jump in, you'll put them in danger."*

His snarl ripped through her mind.

"*We have our job and Sasha has hers.*" Eva never thought she'd be the one to have the level head of the two of them, but as her eyes scanned the settlement and watched more people shift into view, funneling out of the cave below her, she realised just how important her job was. She couldn't move from her perch and help Sasha, no matter how badly she wanted to.

"Where are you hiding my little rider?" Darius demanded, unbidden cruelty lacing every word as his voice ricocheted off the stone buildings and rang painfully in Eva's magically enhanced ears.

Sasha curled her lip up at him. "You know nothing of the woman you seek if you think you can lay a claim on her."

Chuckling, a dark, twisted sound that grated against Eva's ears, Darius drew his sword. "You clearly don't know who I am."

"I know *exactly* who you are. I was at your mother's side when you clawed out of her womb. I watched you take your first steps. I saw the evil in your eyes before Katherina did." Her gaze snapped to Dravyn, her eyes softening a fraction before she covered it up. "You have her eyes. It seems she left something in this world to remember her by."

The knife he was spinning between his fingers halted. He spat on the ground between them. "I have nothing in common with the woman who abandoned me."

She quirked an eyebrow. "Is that what you think? Your brother told me a different story."

Dravyn's eyes went to Darius.

"Not that one," she corrected sharply. "*Dex* told me she tried to run away with you and was killed for it. She tried to protect you from Sylus, to give you a better life—and she paid the price for it."

Darius stepped forward, aiming his sword for her. "Leave that fucking traitor out of this."

She hissed, entirely unafraid of him. "Ooo. Touched a nerve there. He didn't like talking about you, either."

He took one more step. Sasha didn't move an inch, remaining calm, unbothered by the furious cruel prince in front of her. She truly was as fearless as the Wanderers said.

He smiled; it was cold and dark and sent a shiver down Eva's spine despite the desert's heat. "I'm going to enjoy carving your flesh from your bones. You'll tell me where your student is—and when I find her, the world will bow to *me*."

Eva's blood simmered—hot, furious, unrelenting.

How *dare* he.

The arrogance of this bastard—to stalk her through shadows, to haunt her dreams, to twist his claws around her soul and scar her in ways that still bled. And now, to come back. Again. Smirking. Declaring his intentions for her to the world. As if she was still the same girl he could break.

No.

She was *done* running. Done flinching. Done letting him rule her life.

Every wound he carved had forged something harder beneath her skin. Molded her into fury, into wrath, into *chaos*. The world wanted her to be a weapon, used by their hand. She'd give them a weapon. But she only obeyed one master.

Herself.

Eva rose, slow and steady. Her feet sank into the sand. The humid air clung to her skin, her armour, hot and heavy, plastered to her back. The blinding sun pierced the corner of her eye, forcing her to squint. Her hands, instruments of precision that had never failed her on a hunt, trembled with unequivocal *rage*.

But none of it mattered.

Because after today, she'd be free.

A clean shot. Not what he deserved—but it would be *enough*.

Magic sparked at her fingertips as the arrow formed, slipping into place on the string. A steady breath slipped past her lips, slow, measured, as she drew the bow back. The arrow's crackle pressed against her cheek, a whisper of chaos and power.

Exhaling, she let go.

The arrow sliced through the air—fast, sharp, precise—carving a path toward Darius's back, aiming true for the heart.

But then—*snap!*

The arrow fizzled out. Ten feet shy of its mark, it vanished like smoke curling into the wind.

Her heart seized in her chest. The world ground to a screeching, grating halt.

The shot was perfect.

Too close to miss. Too familiar to fail. She'd made this shot a hundred times. So why...?

What the *fuck* happened?

"*Mithril*," Arkon snarled through her mind, his anger coiling tight in her gut. "*I can smell it in the air. I couldn't sense it before, but now its acrid nature hangs in the air and burns my nostrils.*"

Her breaths came in harder, faster, as fear clawed through her chest. "*How? I thought our power could break it?*"

"*Break it, yes. But he has found a way to weaponise it—and it can stop our magic.*"

Eva wasn't given a chance to think on it further. Darius turned and locked eyes with her in a heartbeat. The dark smirk of her nightmares spread across his face.

"Found you."

And then chaos broke out.

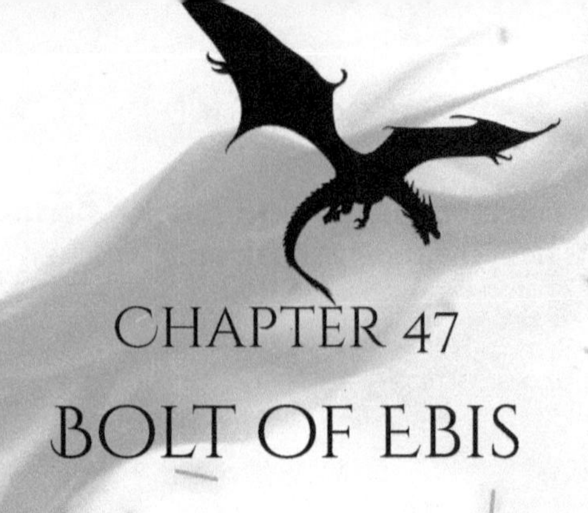

CHAPTER 47
BOLT OF EBIS

Darius broke out into a run for Eva—but not before Sasha dove for him, slamming into his legs and knocking him off-balance.

He hit the ground hard, a grunt torn from his throat as sand sprayed into the air. Sasha rolled, springing to her feet, sword drawn in a flash of steel. No magic. If the mithril had fizzled out Eva's arrow, it would prevent Sasha from using her magic.

Darius recovered just as fast. He twisted, kicked out—Sasha dodged, barely—and their blades clashed with a teeth-jarring clang.

From the top of the dune, Eva froze. The sun blazed above, sand shimmered below. Her lungs ached, her bow forgotten in her grip.

Sasha swung again, fierce and fast, but Darius blocked with ease, pivoting to strike. Metal screeched as he forced her back with every blow. Without her magic, she looked mortal. Slower. Too damn slow.

Behind her, Dravyn leapt into the fray from the side, short sword raised. Sasha spun just in time to deflect the blow with her sword, but the force of it sent her staggering backward. She dropped to one knee, sand grinding into her skin, and barely lifted her blade in time to parry Darius's next strike.

Two against one.

Darius's blade caught her shoulder. Blood welled.

Eva's grip tightened on her bow. It was Brar all over again. Eva standing helpless while people she loved were being cut down in front of her.

I'm not helpless this time.

She moved—

"No," Arkon barked, tail catching her around the waist. "We have our orders." His attention wasn't on Sasha or the Fortys brothers—it was on the bandits emerging from the buildings, converging on her mentor.

Then the lake exploded.

Syran burst from his hiding spot in a torrent of white-blue light, water cascading off his wings and raining down across the settlement in glittering sheets. With a roar, lightning arched across his scales—latching onto every droplet.

The puddles below crackled to life, electrified, forming a glowing circle around Sasha and the others. It was subtle, but Eva saw it—how the air shimmered where the magic met the weaponised mithril. A perimeter. A warning.

Focus.

Coming back to her senses, Eva pulled the string back, magic crackling at her fingertips. The bandits had made a fatal mistake leaving the cover of their buildings.

She released.

The arrow soared—then forked in the sky, splitting into twenty streaks of deadly light. They rained down across the settlement like a barrage of falling stars, striking clean and true.

Panicked, the survivors ran—straight into Syran's puddles. The moment their boots hit the water, the magic caught. Electricity surged up their legs, locking their bodies in place with a snap of muscle and bone.

Long enough for Eva to strike them down.

Aster swooped low, wings grazing the rooftops, hurling fireballs into alleyways and narrow streets. Each blast forced the enemies out of hiding, funnelling them toward the open. Toward Eva.

One by one, they fell.

With every arrow she unleashed into the world, her body weakened. Sweat clung to her skin as she stood tall on her perch. Her limbs trembled as soul magic tore through her. But she didn't stop. Couldn't. She pushed herself—just as she had hundreds of times under Sasha's relentless command.

This was what she'd been training for.

Arkon abruptly severed their connection. The last thing she saw through him was a group of bandits flanking the dune, closing in to shut her down.

His roar shook the air, primal and raw.

Eva didn't hesitate. She let him handle the flankers and refocused, scanning the battlefield until her eyes locked on Anna.

She was in the throes of close combat with Dravyn—sword against sword, fury against fire. The bandits, now wary of the open space around Sasha and Darius, had shifted their attention elsewhere.

And they were closing in around Anna.

Anna drove Dravyn back into the alley, her sword a blur of steel. Emberath dove from above and clawed at his face.

He parried, but his boots slipped in the sand as he stumbled over a crate, splintering it underfoot. He recovered quickly and twisted to dodge Rhaelen's sweeping attack that hissed as it struck the wall behind him. The flames sputtered in the sand-choked air, smothered almost instantly.

Anna snarled and advanced, shoulder-checking him into another crate. It cracked beneath his weight, but he surged forward, catching her off guard. His elbow slammed into her ribs—she grunted but didn't back down.

She retaliated with Mysta, bolting straight for him with a hunting howl, forcing him to duck underneath the wolf. He rolled, came up low, and swept for Anna's legs. She leapt, barely clearing the strike, landing with a grunt as her boots skidded on loose sand.

He lunged.

She caught his blade on her own, sparks flying in the narrow alley as their swords met. Grit kicked up around them, biting at their skin, stinging their eyes. Anna pushed harder, eyes wild with determination, sweat trailing down her temple.

Two bandits broke from cover, racing toward her from behind.

Eva didn't think—she drew her bow taut and loosed two arrows. They arced cleanly through the air and struck both men down mid-stride.

Anna spared a glance at the bodies before driving a boot into Dravyn's gut. He staggered back, winded.

She didn't give him time to recover.

With a flick of her wrist, Emberath and Rhaelen reappeared and darted for him. They burst, smoke and sand filling the alley in a choking plume.

But when the smoke cleared, Dravyn was gone.

Eva scoured the streets for his silhouette from the top of the dune—but she was so focused on Anna and Dravyn, she missed a straggler. One of the bandits had crept up behind her for a flank.

Only the soft shift of sand warned her.

Eva whirled, whipping her dagger from its sheath. She was fast enough to block his blade, but not strong enough to stop the force behind it. The weight of him crashed into her, and she lost her balance.

They tumbled down the hill in a flurry of steel, grunts, and tangled limbs.

They hit a wall. Air exploded from Eva's lungs, a cry tearing from her throat.

No time to think. To feel the pain.

A flash of steel—

She caught his wrist just in time, twisted, and drove her dagger into his ribs. He sagged against her with a strangled cry.

Eva shoved him off and rolled to her feet, chest heaving, eyes sweeping the street for more threats.

Nothing.

Then she heard it.

A cry.

And a dragon's roar.

A death rattle.

Eva froze. The sound split through the chaos like a blade, and her stomach clenched. Her breath caught. Muscles locked. The world narrowed as a familiar terror surged up her spine.

No. Not *again.*

Not *another one.*

Faces flashed through her mind—too many. The ones taken too soon. The ones she couldn't save. The ones who left her behind.

Her heartbeat thundered in her ears, drowning out the battle cries.

She didn't know who it was. Didn't know where it came from. Only that it sounded final.

Please. No more.

Afraid of what she'd find, she tore through the walls Arkon had thrown up and forced herself into his mind. The full weight of his grief slammed into her—crushing, suffocating—squeezing the air from her lungs.

It clouded everything. Thoughts blurred. Emotions bled. She couldn't sift through the Bond to find the agonising truth. Only that something was breaking inside him.

Gasping, she clutched her chest and forced in a breath. "Arkon? Aster—?"

"No," he cut in, halting that thought in its tracks. "*She and Anna are unharmed.*"

Then that meant...

Eva's head snapped towards the lake.

Sasha was on her knees at the shore, a sword running through her stomach and out of her back. Yet, despite the grievous wound, she stared up at Darius with defiance. Unyielding. Unbreaking. A fire in her eyes that not even steel could extinguish.

He stood over her, grinning, a twisted delight shining in his eyes as he basked in her final moments. His chest heaved from the fight, sweat staining his clothes. Blood streamed freely down the side of his face, dripping from his jaw onto his shoulder. His clothes were torn and marked with crimson—skin bared where Sasha had struck him.

Behind her, Syran lay crumpled, his body rigid with pain—of his Soul Bound's pain. His wings shuddered against his back as he heaved to breathe in a single breath.

Sasha coughed, blood sputtering out of her throat. She groaned, hands wrapping around the sword—not to pull it free, but to steady herself. She had already accepted her fate.

But Eva hadn't. If she could just get to her. If she could just kill Darius in time. They could take her to the Under City. Heal her.

"It was a good run, kid," she ground out.

Snorting, Darius freed his spare sword and held it steady with two hands. "No, it wasn't," he spat. "You were a disappointment, Sasha Remoar."

"I wasn't talking to you," she grunted. Her gaze lifted—past the burning streets, past the gathering bandits—and locked onto Eva. "It's your turn."

Darius scoffed. "How touching."

"NO!" The scream tore from Eva's throat, raw and helpless.

Darius raised his blade—and brought it down in a brutal arc. The blade connected with flesh. Sasha's head hit the sandy shore and rolled towards the water, leaving a red trail in its wake.

For a beat, silence smothered the world.

Then Syran's roar shattered it—a primal cry that shook the air and made the ground tremble. A cry that ricocheted through Eva's mind. Another cry to add to her night terrors. Another death she couldn't stop.

It clutched at her heart, jagged and savage, tearing at the pieces left behind.

And it wasn't just hers.

Where Syran's cry faltered and faded into oblivion, Arkon's rose in its place—a deeper, older anguish that filled the sky and bled into the desert, into her bones. His pain became her own—undeniable, oppressive.

Trembling with unbidden rage, Eva charged. Magic surged through her blood, sunk deep into her marrow. It possessed her, gave her impossible strength, inhuman speed. She cut down every bandit in her way with the precision of Val and the efficiency of Zyphril. She *became* a bolt of Ebis.

In mere seconds, she was on the shore—

Then she was cut off.

The magic carrying her was *ripped* away.

She stumbled, breath catching, limbs reeling from the loss. Panicked, she searched her body for an ounce of magic.

Nothing.

"*Arkon?*" A desperate attempt to hold on to her power.

Where his presence had once been, warmth and fury and strength—only a cold, hollow void remained.

The truth struck like a blow: the mithril barrier—she'd charged straight into it.

Nonononono. This can't be happening. Not *like this.*

While she was rooted in terror, Darius came up behind her, grabbing the back of her neck.Furious—at him, at herself for falling into their trap—Eva whirled and slammed her fist into his face. Bone met flesh with a sickening crack. He staggered backward, surprise flickering through his eyes.

She didn't wait. Rage propelled her forward. She hit him again. And again. Her fists were wild, uncontrolled, but they *landed.* One to his jaw, another to his cheekbone. Blood burst from his nose.

He responded with a venomous grin, spitting a blob of red into the sand. "Good. Use that rage and hate. Hit me with everything you have."

So she did.

Her legs trembled, her hands curled into fists, and she charged.

Darius let her. Dodged her first swing, caught her second. Twisted her arm and shoved her to the ground.

She went again.

He caught her arm, and slammed his fist into her ribs. She gasped, stumbling back, breath stolen. Before she could recover, he spun and hit her across the face with the back of his hand. The blow sent her crashing to the sand.

"Come on, little rider," he purred, "you can do better than that."

Holding her ribs, she rose once more. He spun, leg whipping around so fast it was all over within a blink. His foot slammed into her chest, forcing the air out of her lungs and sending her back into the sand.

The world spun as she struggled to catch her breath. Her lungs felt as if they had been crushed beneath a dragon's claw. No matter how hard she tried to get back up, her limbs flailed and slipped in the sand.

Darius stood over her, cocking his head like a predatory bird as he watched her flounder. "Look at you—desperate to avenge your mentor, and you can't even stand. Pathetic." He crouched at her feet, eyes narrowing critically. "Don't worry. We'll work on that."

Anna moved like a thunderbolt—sharp, fast, lethal. A blur of crimson, she aimed her sword with a precise thrust for his head. He rolled back, narrowly missing the blade, and ended on his feet, sword already blocking another blow.

Anna stood between them, her braid falling apart down her back, strands dangling in her face, moving with every steady breath she took. "Touch her again," she growled, fury dripping from her voice, "and I'll kill you."

Darius laughed, bloody and unbothered. "You can try."

Then Dravyn slammed into her from the side.

Anna barely ducked the first hit. The second—an uppercut to her gut—sent her skidding backward. She recovered fast, and went for him next, each strike precise, razor-sharp, and always *just* out of reach.

Until she grazed Dravyn's thigh. Grunting, he fell to his knee, giving Anna the opening to ram her sword into his chest—

But before she could thrust forward, Darius arched his blade downward. Her sword hit the ground.

Dravyn lunged, tackling her to the ground.

She fell hard.

Eva tried to crawl, but her elbows buckled. Her muscles wouldn't obey, no matter how much she screamed at them.

Anna rolled, kicked upward, nailed Dravyn in the chest. He staggered. She turned—but Darius was already there.

He drove a kick into her side, then stomped onto her shoulder. Anna shrieked, but rolled back to her hands and knees—struggling to get to her feet.

Darius's heel connected with her cheek. One more hit to the back of her skull—and she went limp.

"Anna!" Eva's voice cracked in the harsh desert air.

She didn't think. Didn't hesitate.

She *ran.*

She collided with Darius full-force, screaming, fists flying with no rhythm, no technique—just pure, unadulterated need to survive.

He let her hit him. Once. Twice. Then he caught her arm and yanked her close, his face a breath away.

"You're slowing down," he purred, eyes alight with dark satisfaction.

And then he drove his knee into her stomach.

Eva crumpled, mouth open in a soundless cry.

Still, she rose.

Still, she fought.

Until Darius knocked her down again. Hard.

Dravyn seized her, wrenching her arms behind her back. She thrashed, but it was useless—her strength had fled. Darius stepped forward, uncorking a vial of shimmering, opalescent liquid.

No.

She didn't know *what* that was, but she knew—*knew* deep in her marrow—that if she drank that vial, there was no coming back.

He gripped her face with one hand, squeezing until her lips puckered. Then he poured the liquid down her throat.

No!

She jerked her head, tried to spit—but he clamped her jaw shut. Pinched her nose closed.

She struggled, kicked, her lungs screaming.

No!

"*Arkon!*" her desperate call didn't reach him. He was *gone.* And she'd never felt more alone.

Tears pricked in her eyes. It was hopeless. Her lungs were burning, body growing heavy.

He couldn't win. She *couldn't* let him win.

But when black dots swam into her vision, her body made the choice.

She swallowed, the liquid slithering down her throat like molten ice. She choked on it, sputtering as she fought to open her mouth.

Darius released her, stepping back, watching her gasp, sucking in as much air as her lungs could take while Dravyn held her firmly in his grasp.

The liquid settled in her stomach like a lead stone. It heaved, but kept it down.

Then the darkness came to claim her.

CHAPTER 48
THE LAST STORM DRAGON

Arkon's roar split the sky.

Gone.

First Syran.

Then Eva.

It all happened so fast. One minute he was grieving the loss of his brother—then Eva *disappeared*. He felt her fury and grief as his own. They both hurt. They were both furious. And their souls blended together, blurring the lines between human and dragon.

His mighty warrior had charged Darius, blinded by fury and grief. Arkon was too stricken to remember the mithril barrier. Too distracted to *move*.

The moment she crossed it, he lost her. His chest was left cold. Empty. She wasn't dead. No, if she was then he would surely follow Syran. But their Bond had been severed. Broken. Ripped away.

He needed to get her back.

Snapping out of his grief and running on pure rage, Arkon dove for the shore where Darius had slain Sasha. He was met by the vision of his nightmares.

Eva was unconscious, a crumpled version of herself, draped in the arms of their enemy. Not Darius. The youngest Fortys. Dravyn. He looked like barely a man, but he held her effortlessly.

Darius strode over to Anna, who was lying face down in the sand. He grasped her hair. The sharp pain in her scalp woke her up. She screamed, in anger, frustration, not in fear, and thrashed, trying to wrench herself free. Darius brandished a knife and held it level to her throat.

Arkon landed, his weight and power making the ground tremble beneath him. He might not have his magic within this ring, but that made him no less powerful.

He roared at the brothers, flaring his wings behind him. Aster dropped beside him and hissed, baring her teeth at them.

"Release my Soul Bound!" Aster demanded.

Darius didn't flinch, only readjusted his hold on Anna, wrapping an arm around her waist as he hoisted her up. The blade didn't move from her throat.

"Move an inch, and I'll kill her."

Arkon's wings flattened against his back, terror seizing his bones. To kill Anna was to kill Aster. A world without Aster was a dark and perilous place. And he knew Darius wouldn't hesitate to kill her. Anna meant nothing to him. It was Eva's magic he wanted.

Aster hissed again, her claws digging deep into the sand.

"Fuck you!" Anna wrenched in his grasp, elbow slamming into his ribs. Grunting, he stepped back—but when she moved to flip him, his blade sliced into her skin. Not deep enough to be mortal, but the blood running down her neck had Aster's scales bristling.

"Stop," Aster begged. The fierce fire dragon, who commanded respect in the dens of Dragon Canyon, bowed her head to the ground, wings flat against her back. "Don't hurt her."

Arkon didn't see fear for her death in her yellow eyes. It was something much deeper. Fear of being left alone—even for a slither of time. For losing another rider.

Tears welled in Anna's eyes. "Aster—"

"No," she growled. "Live. For me. I will tear the world apart to find you."

It wasn't his call. Eva, while in danger, wasn't at risk of losing her life. Any move Arkon made, would put Anna's life on the line—and Aster's. He would not be her undoing. For her, he rooted himself in place. For her, he withheld every urge to snatch Eva and Dravyn and fly far away from Darius, to throw Dravyn into a mountainside and hold his rider close.

For them, he vowed to find Eva and Anna. They would not be held captive long.

Darius grinned. "Good dragons. Now, stay. Follow us and face the consequences." Just to remind them who held the power, Darius dragged the knife two more inches along Anna's neck. Her face scrunched up, refusing to give him the satisfaction of seeing her in pain.

Aster backed away, riding low on the ground. "Don't hurt her."

"Mark my words, Prince," Arkon said, voice deep and rumbling in his throat, "for every wound you inflict on Eva, I will add a day to your suffering."

Darius's eyes shined bright. "When you see your rider again, dragon, she won't recognise her own Dragon Bound."

Dravyn lugged Eva onto his shoulders. "Let's move, Dari. We're wasting time." He marched for the cave entrance beneath the biggest dune in Last Drop. Where Arkon couldn't follow.

Darius shoved Anna forward, holding the blade against her ribs as he led her to the cave.

Arkon's instincts roared at him to take action. To stop them from disappearing into the darkness. But he couldn't move. His body was consumed by rage and grief and bloodlust.

Once they were gone, he tossed his head back and screamed into the sky. He thrashed his tail to the side, knocking into the buildings. He stomped, carving craters in the ground.

His outrage must have destroyed the ring, because his magic flooded back into him—then exploded out of him in a vicious wave. Lightning arched all around him, striking sand, walls, the very air. Everything it could sink its claws into.

"Arkon!"

Aster full tackled into his side. They rolled in a heap of scales, wings, and claws, crushing buildings and trees as they went. She came out on top and pinned his head to the sand.

"Enough!" she snarled in his ear. "You are a storm dragon—the *last* storm dragon," she added more breathlessly as the weight of her words hit her. "Have some dignity. Compose yourself."

"Dignity?" Arkon echoed incredulously. With a sharp whip of his tail, he knocked her off of him and climbed to his claws. "What dignity? I've lost it all after I failed to save Syran and Eva. I am a pathetic excuse of a dragon."

Still, instinctually, he searched for his Bond, the tether that kept him grounded to the world he had come to loathe. She was the only thing that kept him from turning to stone in his cave. And now all that remained of her was *nothingness*. An endless abyss of cold, smothering nothingness.

Just when he thought he would never be alone again, he felt the pressing weight of it on his scales, as if a mountain had fallen on him.

"We will get them back," Aster promised, confidence blooming in her voice.

"How? We can't track them." Not after Darius had severed their Bonds, not after he took them down the cave.

"Anna sent a letter to Jacob when she sent her sit rep to Hargin."

Jacob. *Dex.*

"Do you think they will come? We didn't know Darius was behind the attacks at the time."

"Do you think Grayson will stand by while Anna and Eva take on a group of bandits by themselves?"

No. Arkon didn't think Dex would take the chance that *something* might happen to Eva. Regardless of her skill. Regardless of their power.

He would come.

And, for the first time in what felt like hours, Arkon felt hope that he might see his rider again.

"Come," Aster commanded in the haughty way that she did, as if she had every right to be making demands. "Let us give Syran and Sasha a proper farewell before scavengers desecrate their bodies."

Hearing rubble turning over, Arkon scanned what was left of Last Drop, catching a few people shifting underneath the crushed homes. None of them were civilians. While Anna was scouting, she found a pile of their corpses stashed away in one of the homes, too far away to smell or notice the gathering of flies.

These survivors were men Darius had left behind. As much as Arkon wished to end their pathetic lives, it would be wise to keep a few of them alive to question them. Perhaps they would know where Darius would take their Knights.

Two survivors were scrambling side by side, frantically trying to escape the burrow they had found themselves in, but the stone encasing them was too heavy. Arkon lifted the stone—then caught the little mice with his tail, coiling it tight around them, giving them no chance to escape. The others, he did not care if they lived or died under the rubble, but these two, he'd make sure they lived. Long enough to get answers out of them.

Aster watched them struggle coldly then scooped up Sasha's body and laid her between Syran's claws.

He sat back, his heart heavy with grief and the burden Syran had now placed upon him.

He was now the last storm dragon.

CHAPTER 49
BROTHERS' QUARREL

"Dari."

Darius ignored Dravyn's call. Again. The delinquent was as relentless and grating as the dead weight on his shoulders. There was no time to slow down. This was the furthest he'd ever gotten.

He had her.

He fucking *had* her!

They had to keep moving. The further the better. The further they went, the higher the chances were that he got to keep her.

There was no sign of Dex at Last Drop. A fascinating little detail—one he'd unpack later. Which meant that Dex wasn't in the Desert Lands at all. Which *meant* that Darius had time to break in his little rider before he came sniffing around.

That much was certain: Dex would come for her.

It was just a matter of how quickly he found them. How much time Darius had to carve out her will and string her up like a marionette.

Dex would rue the day he ever left them.

"*Darius*," Dravyn snapped, breath ragged. "We've been moving all damn night. I don't give a flying fuck about your agenda. I'm starving, exhausted—and my shoulders feel like a wyvern's been sitting on them all day."

He stopped without waiting for permission, heaving Eva off his shoulders. He caught her in his arms before setting her on the ground gently. He let her head down slowly, resting it against his thigh as he sat beside her. As if she were some fragile thing that might shatter if he breathed wrong.

He would learn soon that she was far from delicate.

Once she woke up.

His alchemist had brewed him a potion laced with mithril and poison, mild enough to not kill his little rider, but strong enough to weaken her. Guarantee the nullification of her magic. He would have to keep her subdued until he could properly train her.

But he couldn't do anything with her like *this*. Unconscious. Weak. Feeble.

The poison half was *too* effective. Both Knights had been out for hours. Possibly all night. There was no discernible way to tell what time it was in the dark labyrinth, and his watch was broken during the attack.

Half dose next time, he reminded himself. They would have to experiment with how often to give her the poison before she gained her magic back.

He wasn't too concerned, though. Since the dose, her skin had paled, hair turning nearly white—especially under the lightstones. Her face had hollowed, features drawn. He'd know when to dose her again. The moment color crept back into her skin.

Giving in to his infuriating brother's whining, Darius dropped his burden at his feet and slithered down the wall, shoulders braced against stone.

Dravyn winced as a whimper left the girl's lips. "You could at least pretend you want to keep her alive."

"I don't. She's passed her usefulness."

He'd only made so much Mithbane—had only enough time to make a few vials. He hadn't expected the brew to take so long to make while plotting out the destruction of the North. Or to have two Soul Bounds to deal with.

Wasting it on both of them was short-sighted. The dragons were long gone. There was no way to find them now.

He drew the knife from his thigh and knelt beside the redhead, ignoring the sharp flare of pain radiating from his side. A wound from earlier—minor, but persistent.

The blade caught the light, glinting silver against the lightstones set aside on the ground within their small cavern. It cast a shadow across her pale throat.

He lined up the edge along the sliver of red he'd marked earlier.

One quick slice.

That was all it would take.

She'd bleed out quietly on the floor.

Utterly boring.

He would have loved to hear this one scream. She was just as defiant and fiery as his little rider. She would have given him hours of entertainment.

But they didn't have time for that.

So he tightened his grip on the hilt and—

"Wait," Dravyn stopped him. Specifically, something in his voice stopped him. Urgent. Commanding. For a second, he reminded Darius of their father. A first. He didn't know Dravyn had it in him to be anything but an infuriating twerp. "Are you sure you want to kill her?"

The blade stayed where it was, resting cool against her throat. "Yes. She's a waste of resources."

"So is Eva," Dravyn shot back, dry as sand. "We weren't supposed to raise an army, raze settlements, or kidnap Dragon Knights. But we did. And somehow, we have enough supplies for all four of us because of it."

"We don't have enough Mithbane for both of them."

"Make more."

Darius didn't dignify that with a response. Never mind that he didn't have the time to brew it again. Even if he had the recipe. Dravyn clearly missed the point.

He stared down at the unconscious girl, once a warrior with such rage in her eyes—reduced to a withering flower, a breath away from being torn from this world. "Then tell me," he said tightly, annoyed that they were even having this conversation. That he'd let his brother give him pause. Make him *think*. "Why would I let her live?"

He studied those glacial eyes, searching for even a flicker of compassion buried within them. Dravyn had never liked it when Darius and Dex hunted for sport—or when they experimented on their prey in the dungeons. *Too crude*, he'd said. But Darius had always suspected it was more than that: Dravyn didn't have the stomach for it.

It hadn't escaped his notice, either—how carefully Dravyn had handled Eva. Always adjusting her when she slipped from his shoulders, keeping her comfortable, even unconscious. Setting her down gently. Resting a hand on her shoulder, as if that simple gesture could offer a shred of comfort in this labyrinth of shadows and bitter winds.

And now, he was protecting her friend.

Why?

Dravyn's jaw tightened as he held his unwavering gaze. "Eva's already slipped out of your grasp once, hasn't she? When she wakes... even without her magic, she'll be hard to control. If you have leverage..." His eyes flicked to the girl on the ground. "You could keep her under control."

Darius's fingers twitched, hungry to feel blood spill across his palm. But he didn't move. Not yet.

Dravyn had a point. His little rider was elusive. And he had made a bad habit of letting her slip through his fingers. Keeping this one alive would ensure cooperation. And when the time came to break his little rider in—it might prove useful.

He pulled the blade away and slipped it back into its sheath.

He'd allow her to live. For now.

Then he rummaged through his pack, yanked out some rope, and tossed a length at Dravyn. "Tie her hands. Tight. And make sure you use a proper knot."

Dravyn caught the rope with a lazy smirk, tossing it from one hand to the other. "Believe it or not, brother, I have tied someone up before."

Darius's lips curled up into a sneer. "I don't give a flying fuck. If her knots come undone, it's *your* head on the line. Got it?"

Dravyn's smirk slipped, replaced by a slow, deliberate eye roll. "Got it."

They moved efficiently, binding the girls in silence. Once the knots were secure, they settled down to eat, the cavern filled with the soft scrape of pouches being opened and the scent of dried meat permeating in the tunnels.

This cave had been a fortunate discovery, found during their pilfering of Last Drop. A sprawl of tunnels twisting beneath the sand, linking to other settlements like veins.

The fools who once used it as a hidden passage between settlements and storerooms never saw it coming. He and Dravyn made sure of that.

They went from settlement to settlement, using the tunnels as cover. They burned their homes, slit their throats, scattered their bodies across the sand. No survivors meant no one could accidentally stumble into them and tip off Dex of their location.

He'd give the little bastard one thing—Dravyn's obsession with his sketches finally served a purpose. The map he drew was irritatingly precise, almost obsessive. Without it, they might still be wandering in circles, but thanks to his compulsive itch, they had every turn and exit memorised.

After they'd eaten their fill, Dravyn flicked crumbs off his knee and leveled his gaze on Darius. His voice was low, and carried a sardonic edge. "So, what's the plan now, oh wise and malevolent prince? Back to treasure hunting? Back to Estrus? What do you intend to do with these women now that you have them?"

Darius's eyes fell on Eva's sleeping form. The poison had paled her complexion, but bruises had bloomed along her jaw and cheek. He bore mirroring ones on his knuckles.

The moment he brought her back to Estrus, Sylus would have her killed. No. That wouldn't do. He needed time. Space. A place to break her in properly. Train her. Mold her. Make her his.

Did he want to continue hunting the vestiges? Sylus wouldn't have sent him after them if they weren't powerful. But now, with Eva in his grasp... handing those relics over would be a mistake. He finally had the power he needed to overthrow him. All he had to do was learn how to wield it.

But what if he had his storm rider *and* the artifacts?

With his little rider and the vestiges in hand, he didn't have to stop at taking Estrus. Not when Astrida was full of magic and resources ripe for the taking. Just waiting for the right man to draw out its potential.

Now *that* was power worth pursuing.

"We go back to the ruins," Darius decided. "We find whatever rusted relic Sylus wants."

And then?

He'd gut Dravyn. Cut himself free of the loose ends. Set up a new base in the Desert Lands, somewhere no one would think to look. Take his time with Eva. Strip her of whatever defiance remained and rebuild her from the inside out.

When she was loyal—*truly* loyal—they would begin.

Artifacts. Cities. Kingdoms.

And when the time came...

The world.

CHAPTER 50
THE DESCENT

Darius, Dex, and Dravyn were summoned to the throne room. It was Dravyn's thirteenth birthday, though Dex doubted this was the reason for their summoning. Dravyn was a mere afterthought to Father. Later, Dex would bring his little brother a present—a sketchbook and charcoal set—when the hallways were quiet and the shadows were long.

Darius was the first to kneel before their father, bowing his head low to the man looking upon them coolly from his throne. Dravyn followed, if only so he didn't get beaten again for disobedience. Ironically, his birthday was the only day of the year he was reliably obedient.

Dex remained standing, despite the involuntary weakness in his knees, demanding he bow to this man—a habit ingrained in him until the day Father told him he would be King one day. And Kings bowed to no one.

Father leaned back in his obsidian throne, eyes as dark and emotionless as the stone beneath his ass. He regarded his sons not as sources of pride nor as inconveniences. They were mere pawns. All they would ever be to him until the day he died and Dex took the throne.

"Do you know what day it is, boys?" he asked, his voice as cold as the blood running through Dex's veins.

None dared to answer him. They knew better.

Father's cruel gaze turned to Dravyn's bowed head, and Dex's back stiffened—a minuscule shift in posture. He couldn't show more; even that much risked being mistaken for concern for his brother. "It is your little brother's birthday. I have a gift for each of you."

A breath left Dravyn's lips, head snapping up to meet his gaze. His excitement was quickly schooled, the smile replaced by a turned mouth and steel in his eyes. Father raised his hand—and he flinched, snatching his head back down. Shockingly forgiving, he ignored Dravyn's error and snapped his fingers.

The doors behind them opened, though Dex did not turn around. If anything, his body tensed, preparing. What would it be this time? Would he have to kill or endure?

Gifts so rarely were objects of celebration in this castle...

A sharp, little yip! startled him, but still he refused to look back. This was a test of will. It had to be.

Of which, Dravyn failed wholly. As soon as he heard the puppy's bark, he whirled around, eyes alight with childlike wonder. "Direwolf pups!"

A rare breed. A remnant of the magic that once flowed through these lands centuries ago. Breeds like that had long since faded without magic to nourish them, but dire creatures didn't require magic to live, only to be created. Slowly, the magic in their bloodlines faded, leaving them with one breeding family left.

Father must have spent a fortune on them.

Why? What gain could he get in wasting his coin on them?

Dex didn't remove his gaze from Father, not even when a stiff smile pressed into the king's cheeks.

Dravyn turned back to Father, suddenly hesitant. "These are for us?"

Father rose out of his seat slowly then descended. His charcoal eyes swept over his sons, pausing just a moment on each one. Dex's stomach clenched when their eyes met.

"A gift for each of my boys. Raise them, train them, mold them well."

Darius grimaced as he beheld the puppies. "Can I turn it into an attack dog?"

"They are yours. You can do what you want with them—as long as you keep them alive," Father added, most definitely for Darius's benefit. Dex saw the twisted dark shimmer in his eyes before Father forbade them from killing them.

Dex withheld a scoff at both of his brothers' actions. Where one failed to hide his empathy and excitement—the other revealed just how sickeningly cruel he could be. If this was a test, Dex most assuredly was the only one to pass.

Deeming it safe to pique his curiosity now, Dex turned.

Three servants stood with three puppies leashed at their feet. Though, "puppy" was a stretch, given their proportions. Their paws were as broad as Dex's hands, their heads nearly twice the span of his own. Each body already rivaled a medium hound in bulk. Yet they still carried that unmistakable puppy softness—the floppy ears, the fangs no longer than a fingernail, and the boundless enthusiasm of creatures too new to understand the cruel world they had been born into.

One was grey, dappled with large black clouds. One cloud in particular swallowed its left eye and snout. Those eyes were a bright fair blue that was an uncanny match to Dravyn's.

The other bore crimson fur, as dark as dried blood. Amber eyes stared back at them, shining like freshly molten gold. A white stripe ran down from the top of its throat to its chest, accompanied by a white dusting on its humorously fluffy tail.

Lastly, Dex's gaze fell on the pitch black puppy. The fur was matte, seeming to absorb all light around it. Those eyes, while alight with youthful exuberance, blended into the shadows. They watched him with a keen intellect the other two didn't quite have.

A kindred spirit, *he thought reluctantly. He shouldn't compare himself to a mutt—he was destined for greater things than this dog could ever achieve.* And yet... *he couldn't stop seeing himself in this beast.*

Dravyn abandoned his spot and knelt in front of the dappled puppy. The servant released the direwolf, letting it run into his open arms with the leash dangling freely in its wake. "This one's mine! I'll call you Patches."

He ruffled the dog's ears, giggling as it licked his face.

Dex fought the slight burn in his chest when he looked down at the black puppy. It was a strange, warm feeling, as though a bud was unfurling in his chest. He didn't know what to call it—or even if he liked it.

He held his hand out, beckoning the black beast. The puppy obeyed eagerly, running like a clumsy newborn deer to his feet. He didn't kneel to pet the dog, merely stared at it. "Good dog. I'll call you Shadow."

Darius cut a glare his way. "Don't insult me, brother, by naming your beast after my title."

Dex lifted one shoulder in a careless shrug. "This one will probably do its job better than you."

Darius sneered at him, but before he could respond, Father stepped between them, passing them for the door. He didn't look back at them when he said, "They're your responsibility now. Train them well."

And so they did.

For three years, Dex dedicated four hours in each day training his direwolf. At first, he was wary of the beast, of Father's true reason for gifting them. But as time stretched on, and Father didn't bring up the wolves again, Dex allowed himself to get... attached.

Perhaps he did not play with the wolf the way Dravyn did or feed him bloody prime cuts of meat like Darius did. Acknowledgment *was enough for Shadow. A simple, "Good boy," sent his tail wagging, tongue lolling to the side. It was enough for Dex, too—to know that he had someone to watch his back, to obey his every command without question, to seek only to please him. He was a companion he grew to rely on, both in the privacy of his chambers and out in the streets.*

They were inseparable. No court, assassin, or creature could tear them apart.

Until one day they were called back to the throne room, on Dravyn's sixteenth birthday. On his sixteenth, Dex was told he was going to be King one day. On Dravyn's...

"Kill them," Father ordered.

At first, the brothers were confused. Father had not mentioned anyone who had displeased him lately. Dex himself dealt with a threat just last week. They were alone in the throne room, save for their loyal companions. Even Darius, who had merely named his direwolf Dog, was confused by the command. His head tilted in that creepy, calculating way of his, eyes narrowing in concentration.

It was Dex who broke the chilling silence. "Who do you wish eliminated, Father? I will dispose of them at once."

He said nothing, but his gaze dropped to Shadow at his side. The direwolf was enormous now, even while sitting, his head was level with Dex's.

Father didn't have to say anything further.

Dex's heart stopped beating. For a moment, he wondered if this was what it felt like for one of his victims to watch him enter the room—a hopeless sense of inevitably. A cold clamp on their lungs, iron filling their stomach.

A moment was all he had. Father was watching, and he couldn't afford to reveal any weakness.

"No," Dravyn gasped, head snapping to Patches. She caught his attention and automatically leaned into him, shutting her eyes in anticipation for head scratches. "You said I could keep her."

Father didn't blink. Barely cast Patches a single remorseful glance. "I did. Have you not had three long years with her?" When he did look at her, it was full of contempt. Disgust. "Now kill her."

Dravyn looked to Dex—as if he *might be able to save their direwolves. But not even he had that much power.*

Beside them, Dog yelped then fell to the ground in a heap of fur and limbs. Darius held a knife, blood dripping at his feet. He looked down at the corpse, a frown tugging on his brow. Not one of grief or regret, but disappointment, like he was expecting more of a fight, as his other victims usually did. But why would Dog fight back? The beast had utter faith in his master until the moment Darius's blade pierced his heart.

Dex's hands moved on its own accord, ripping his knife free. His fingers wound tight around the handle, leeching blood from his palms.

"Do it, Dravyn," he snapped at his younger brother. "It's just an animal. Slaughter it like you've slaughtered countless others before."

Cold. Detached. That was what he had to be. That was the son Father had raised him to be.

He turned to Shadow. The direwolf didn't flinch at the blade. Had no reason to. Until now, he had watched Dex draw a knife many times over, and never once did he turn the blade on his faithful hound.

Grip tightening, he forced himself to look straight into his loyal companion's eyes. See the implicit trust he had in him, in his well being and safety.

He wanted to remember that look—not the fear that came after it.

"Let this be a reminder for you," Father's voice rang out behind him. "This is what weakness feels like. To love is to expose your throat to anyone who wants to take your throne from you. Remember this feeling so when the urge rises up again, you purge it before it becomes your undoing."

Forcing his mind to empty, Dex thrust the blade forward.

The fear never came.

Grayson was warned—but he didn't listen. Time and time again, Sylus told him love was weakness. Love would be his undoing. Grayson thought he had escaped his clutches, had thought he could finally be free. He had grown complacent.

And now Eva was heading into danger, and all he felt was *fear.* Fear of losing the light in his life. Fear of never seeing that light in her eyes, hearing her laugh, feeling her gentle touch on his skin.

"*She's going to be pissed,*" Eran warned him. Yet, despite his grievances in defying Hargin's orders and racing across the Aborian Ocean, the azure dragon's wings beat hard against the wind, cutting the air like a blade. Glade kept pace with quiet ferocity. She was older than Aster, larger, stronger. They reached the Desert Lands in a day and a half. The sun was cresting over bone-dry hills as they hit land, and still, they didn't slow.

"*Maybe,*" Grayson mildly agreed. "*I hope so.*"

Let her rage at him. Let her flip him onto his ass if she wanted. So long as she was *alive.* He wanted to find her standing tall on a mound of her enemies, bloodied but laughing. He wanted her to be furious with him for leaving his post. For not trusting that she had it handled.

Better that than dead or hurting.

Just the thought had Grayson pressing tighter against Eran's back, heels digging deep into the stirrups to fight the wind threatening to tear him from his dragon's spine.

The compass sat on the saddle beneath him, fixed to the leather with a thin layer of ice that was melting every second they spent in the air. Under Eran's instruction—and his own absolute refusal to fail—he kept restoring the ice, stealing moisture from clouds, the very air, from the sweat beading on his skin, but once they reached the Desert Lands, it became a near impossible feat and all he had was his sheer will to stop the ice from freezing.

He passed on directions to Eran while the powerful dragon propelled them ever closer to Eva, obeying the compass like a directive from the gods.

Grayson breathed in through his nose, taking in the dry heat into his lungs, then exhaled, feeling the desert grating against his throat. It was better than the nausea roiling in his stomach.

He peered over at Glade and Jacob's rigid form lain over her back. They hadn't once asked them to change the pace.

Grayson wasn't sure whether to take comfort in Jacob's silent solidarity—his partner standing firm beside him without hesitation—or to feel a rising unease that even Jacob, the one who usually grounded him, was now hurtling just as fiercely toward Eva and Anna.

"Gray."

He snapped his head forward—and the breath was stolen from his lungs.

Smoke.

A massive black pillar that climbed higher than the dragons in the sky. North East. Exactly the direction they were travelling in. It smothered out any and all hope Grayson tried to nurture.

"You don't know it's a bad sign. Aster's fire is powerful. In this heat, it might have gotten out of hand."

"Is that supposed to comfort me? Why isn't there a storm to reign it in?"

Was Eva caught in the middle of the fire? Suffocating? Burning?

The smell of melted flesh filled his nose. He still remembered what ash tasted like when it fluttered onto his tongue. Remembered the sound of hair searing to the roots. Remembered what his lungs boiling alive felt like.

"Go, Eran. Fly like you've never flown before."

His dragon obeyed without question.

As if the gods answered every prayer Grayson hurled up their way, a gust of wind swept under his wings and carried him far and fast. They weren't just a dart. They were an arrow. Hurtling straight and true for their mark.

Glade fell behind quickly. It didn't matter. Nothing else mattered until he had Eva in his arms. He needed to breathe the same air as her. Feel her heart beat against his. Hear her say his name.

Smoke swallowed the sky, turning the horizon into a curtain of black. It burned his eyes, choked his lungs. The ice encasing the compass shattered, crumbling like flakes of charred flesh. Grayson shoved it into his pocket and braced.

Eran dove.

Grayson's stomach launched through his throat. He held fast, squeezing his thighs around Eran's torso—until they slammed into a body of water.

A bubble of air formed around his face instantly, a reflexive gift from Eran's magic. Grayson inhaled, the cool breath soothing his scorched throat. The water rushed around him, dousing the heat simmering beneath his armour, sinking into his bones.

They broke the surface. Eran's head whipped towards Arkon and Aster as they stood at the edge of a mountainous pyre.

Relief struck hard and fast, staggering in its ferocity. Arkon was unharmed. Breathing. *Alive.*

Which meant Eva was alive.

Grayson didn't wait. Eran hadn't even reached the shore when he leapt from the saddle, crashing knee-deep into the shallows. He ran.

Fuck the heat from the blaze.

Fuck the ash that coated his tongue.

Fuck the godsdamned sand that dragged at his boots.

Nothing would stop him now.

Not until he had eyes on Eva.

But as he neared the dragons, he noticed that their riders were missing. Instinctively, Grayson's eyes darted across the scattered remains of Last Drop.

Buildings were reduced to mounds of sand and piles of scorched debris. Palms were blackened and skeletal, their charred limbs clawing at the sky like the hands of the dead. Farms lay ruined, either charred black or soaked in stagnant water. The narrow streets were scarred with deep craters and gouges, as if the earth itself had been clawed apart.

Bodies were strewn like forgotten dolls—some crushed beneath rubble, others discarded in the open. Hands grasped futilely at dust, severed legs lay twisted, and a lone head rested grotesquely among a shattered crate.

This was no mere skirmish. It was a massacre—a battle of brutal and unrelenting scale.

Grayson's throat tightened. His heart hammered as he searched desperately for any sign of his Starling.

But there was nothing.

Only silence—and the crushing weight of her absence pressing down on him like the desert sun. Vicious. Relentless.

Remember this feeling, Sylus had once told him when he was young and thought he had learned all that there was to shield himself from his cruelty.

The memory had faded over the years, a dull scar beneath the surface. Now it slammed into him, fresh. Raw. The slow, crushing helplessness that squeezed the air from his lungs. The excruciating dread, drowning his mind in fear and pain and grief.

And that made him fucking *furious*.

That fury swelled in his chest like a maelstrom, gathering momentum, a tsunami barreling toward shore, unstoppable and merciless. Its claws raked through the walls of his control, scratching, tearing, desperate to break free. His blood churned through his veins, thrashing wildly, dissolving his resolve with every beat of his heart. That acidic blood dropped from his palms, hands clenched so tight his nails dug into flesh. He barely felt the sting. Barely heard anything above the pounding in his head.

Control he'd spent years perfecting shattered in an instant.

He remembered every moment with vicious clarity. Every lashing, every beating, every choice he was *forced* to make. He'd buried himself in ice to hide from the truth—that it had all hurt, that it all had a cost. Every waking moment he spent allowing Sylus to control and manipulate him only added to the pyre of his ire.

And now this fucking world wanted to take the one gods damned thing that made it all worth it away from him.

He would sooner burn the world to the ground than let that happen.

Grayson turned toward Arkon, each step a harbinger of his wrath and fury. A silent promise of death and destruction. His eyes locked on the black dragon before him. The one who had sworn to protect Eva. The one who could split the sky in two with his power. The one he had once bowed to—and would never forgive.

His voice came out low and simmering, "Where is she, Arkon?"

Arkon lowered his head to meet his gaze, a guttural snarl unfurling from his throat. "Do *not* use that tone with me, Slayer."

The name made him flinch. Another reminder of what he'd been made into. Another reason for the anger to rise up.

He stepped forward, embracing the blistering heat of Arkon's breath spilling across his skin. Welcoming the threat of those vicious teeth, bared and glistening inches from his face.

"Where. Is. Eva?"

Before either could detonate, Aster shoved her body between them, bumping Arkon back with a sharp shoulder. The storm dragon growled low, but she shot him a warning glare that silenced him before his temper could spark.

Then she turned to Grayson, her gaze cutting and solemn. "There was an ambush. We saw it coming. We were ready for it. We *thought* we were ready for it," she corrected herself grimly. Bitterly. Her crimson scales shuddered down her body, revealing a layer of yellow scales beneath. "We were winning. We had them. But then Darius—"

"Darius?"

The words sent a bolt down his spine, threatening to freeze him in place. Instead, he clenched his fists at his sides, body trembling, forcing himself to *move*, to *feel*, outside of his own body. Because what he felt inside was raw and ugly and voracious.

He turned his ire back to Arkon. "Fucking Darius was here—and you didn't tell me? Didn't bring her home *immediately*?"

Arkon snarled back, static crackled along his scales in warning. "We didn't know he was here—until it was too late."

"So you just let him take her?" That's *exactly* what he did, because Arkon had the power to stop him, to turn him into a pile of cinders. But he didn't.

"I did not *let* him do anything," Arkon barked back, tail thrashing violently behind him. The tip struck a piece of rubble and sent it flying across the ruins.

"Darius set a trap," Aster said, cutting them off. "He found a way to weaponise mithril. Nullify our magic. Sasha fought against him... and lost." She swung her head towards the pyre. A pyre large enough to swallow a dragon.

A pit opened in Grayson's stomach. He had been so focused on Arkon, Eva's absence, that he hadn't realised—Syran and Sasha weren't here either.

He stared at the pyre, feeling as though he was falling—and Eran wasn't there to catch him. The ground was coming up fast as reality sank deeper into his bones.

Sasha Remoar, a warrior he'd studied in great detail as a prince. Eva's mentor and protector. Gone. Bested by his older brother. It didn't seem possible... yet that pyre said it all.

Aster shut her eyes, maw clenching tight. "Eva lost control. She fell right into Darius's hands. He took her magic. Anna tried to save her, but between Darius and Dravyn..." A pause, jagged as broken glass. "Without her magic, she couldn't stop them."

No.

Grayson barely breathed. Couldn't.

No, no, no, no.

"He held a knife to Anna's throat. Said he'd kill her if we tried to intervene. So we... let them go." Aster's eyes met his, sunken in with a familiar hollowness Grayson knew too well. "I couldn't bear to lose another rider."

NO.

His eyes snapped to Arkon, blood boiling like molten ice in his veins. "You could have stopped him. All it would take—"

"And risk Aster and Anna's lives?"

"They know this job has its risks." The words came out before he even thought them through. By the time he realised what he'd said, it was too late to take them back.

Arkon was on him in the next beat. Claws shoved him down into the ground, talons curling into the sand like they wished they were curling into him instead. His fangs came within a hair's width from Grayson's face. For the first time, trepidation trickled down his spine when facing off with the storm dragon. Other times, he hadn't cared—or thought—that Arkon would kill him. But this time he did care, because Eva needed him. This time, it looked like he might actually kill him.

Eran surged forward, teeth snapping in warning near Arkon's throat. Aster butted in, flaring her wings out and putting space between the two dragons.

Arkon ignored them, those vehemently blue eyes fixed solely on Grayson. His voice grated against his skin, each word sinking into his marrow, "You are only alive right now because my Soul Bound wishes it," he ground out. "Do not speak so casually about Aster and Anna's lives again."

There was a certain inflection in the dragon's tone that made Grayson keep his trap shut and let the weight of his words settle in the air around them.

He glanced at Aster then looked back at Arkon—and saw it. *Heard* it. Aster was to him, what Eva was to Grayson, and Arkon felt just as fiercely as the woman he loved. Threatening her was a line he had unintentionally crossed.

In all of his rage, something else shifted inside of him. It ran just as deep as his ire, but it made him feel cold and hollowed out instead.

Shame. That was what this feeling was.

He swallowed, only to feel sand clogging up in his throat. "You're right," he said, tone level, cool. "That was callous and uncalled for. I'm sorry."

Smoked puffed out of Arkon's nostrils, then he backed away to Aster's side. Eran's tail curled around Grayson and pulled him out of the crater and into the safety of his claws.

He leaned back into his dragon, loathed to admit just how much comfort he took in his dragon's presence. He was a grounding force that Grayson hadn't even realised how much he had come to rely on—until his whole world started crumbling around him.

"*You may be able to hold your own*," Eran rumbled in his mind, "*but that does not mean you have to be alone.*"

"Darius took them through there," Arkon informed them, sounding just as weary as Grayson felt. He pointed with his tail towards a collapsed cave entrance buried within a crumbling dune.

Magic surged through Grayson and raked the land, burrowing into the fractured stone. The cavern was vast. It branched into a web of tunnels, lacing the earth with a maze of endless choices. It didn't matter. The compass would guide him.

Climbing to his feet, Grayson marched towards the cave with every intention of digging his way through the ruins.

"Stop."

Eran's tail swept around, catching him mid-stride and forcing him to a halt. "You cannot go in there, Grayson. It's too unstable."

"I don't give a fuck. Eva's in there—I have to find her."

Before Darius could sink his claws into her. Before the woman who had taught him how to live was gone. After everything—after she'd accepted every broken piece of him, his scars, his flaws, his demons—he couldn't let Darius destroy her. He wouldn't let her become another one of his brother's puppets.

Not her. Never her.

It wasn't until Eran's tail coiled tight around his body that Grayson realised he was breathing faster, harder. His entire body was trembling uncontrollably. His chest was tight, feeling as though his lungs were being compressed into thin ribbons.

"He can't... he can't..."

"*She is not lost, Grayson,*" Eran said, pressing his snout gently into his chest. "*We will catch them. We'll get her back.*"

Hope. He'd given him a slither of hope.

Dangerous. So fucking dangerous.

"*She is strong,*" he went on ruthlessly, forcing him to believe in a world where his light still shone brightly. "*She will fight. Resist. She is still yours. And you will stop at nothing to get her back.*"

His. Yes. Until the very end.

Hunting people had been second nature to Dex. If unleashing the monster was what it took to bring her home, he'd let him out in a heartbeat.

He shook off his dragon's ministrations and snapped open the compass. The needle swung firmly southwest—the *opposite* direction from Estrus.

Where is he taking you, Starling?

Does it matter?

No.

It didn't matter where Darius took her. Grayson would find her.

A shadow loomed over him for a moment before Glade landed beside Eran.

Jacob's boots were already on the ground before the dust even settled. He sprinted across the craterous sand, eyes wide and searching—first the ruined settlement, then Arkon and Aster, finally locking onto Grayson.

"Where are Eva and Anna?" His voice cracked, urgent but trembling, like he had a suspicion but was afraid of being right.

Eran's reply came heavy with sorrow. "Darius has abducted them."

Jacob's face lost its colour. He staggered backward, barely able to keep his footing. Glade was there instantly, one claw steadying Jacob's back, bracing him.

"No. No, this can't be real..." His breath hitched, eyes swimming with disbelief and panic. When his hair fell in front of his face, he swiped it back immediately. He looked back up at Grayson, desperation flooding his gaze. "Tell me it's a lie. *Please*."

Only a slight tremor in Grayson's hands betrayed how much of a mess he was on the inside. "We're getting them back, Jake."

It wasn't a matter of *if* they would find the girls, it was a matter of when. Before Darius could hollow Eva out.

Jacob's breath hitched. He turned sharply to Arkon, eyes wide with fear. "Can you feel Eva?"

The dragon lowered his massive head. "I couldn't feel her when she was unconscious. But now that she's waking, there's a pulse. Faint... but steady."

Aster gave a solemn nod. "I can feel Anna, too. Barely. Just a flicker. Like a whisper brushing against my soul."

"Are they all right?" Jacob asked.

Arkon's eyes darkened with uncertainty. "She lives. But I cannot sense her condition beyond that."

Jacob turned to Grayson. "The compass?"

He nodded grimly. "Tracking. But to the southwest."

Which he didn't understand—and it infuriated him that he didn't.

Arkon shifted, his body coiling slightly as he looked toward a makeshift hut of leaning stone slabs. "Perhaps," he rumbled, "they can enlighten you."

With a sweep of his tail, the roof crashed to the ground, revealing two men huddled beneath. They squawked at the sight of the storm dragon and scrambled back against the far wall, faces pale with fear.

Prisoners.

Darius's men.

Men responsible for Eva's disappearance.

That voracious ire rose to the surface again, ravenous for revenge. For blood.

They weren't Darius, but it was a start. He'd find his answers—but first he was going to take his frustration out on them. He needed a clear head if he was going to save Eva and wetting his hands with their blood was the fastest way to get there.

He approached the ruined hut, blood pulsing hot in his veins. Glade's magic thrummed through the air around him, reshaping the shattered stone. Walls sealed in around them—sturdy and whole—until only a single door and window remained, allowing just enough light in for them to see the vitriol in his eyes.

"Gray, wait." Jacob caught his arm, brow furrowed as he glanced nervously at the men huddled in the corner. "You're not going to..." He locked his lips, finding the strength to speak his fears aloud. "You're not going to torture them, are you?"

Grayson pinned him with a dry glare. "They're not going to give us information freely, Jake. Darius isn't taking them to Estrus—I need to know why. Their lives, and ours, depend on it. If you can't stomach it, wait outside."

It wasn't fair of him, Grayson knew that. Jacob had always been the softer of the two, the counterbalance that kept him tethered when he sank too far into his old ways. The voice that reminded him he was still human.

But fairness had no place here. Not now. They didn't have time for mercy, or the luxury of gentleness.

They needed results.

And Dex... Dex knew how to get them.

Jacob seemed to see that on his face, though Grayson tried his damnedest to remain neutral. Resolution settling into his features, he released Grayson and leaned back against the wall. "I don't like it, but I'll stay."

Grayson wouldn't say it aloud, but having Jacob there evoked a sense of relief that he wasn't expecting.

It didn't dull the rage burning through his veins or change what he was about to do. The need to make them bleed was still there, an old habit he couldn't refuse. But it wasn't the same this time.

Maybe because some part of him trusted Jacob to stop him before he went too far.

Or maybe because—for the first time—someone had chosen to stay.

He wasn't just a weapon forged by Hargin and Sylus anymore.

He was a friend to Jacob first.

And somehow, that made the hollow inside him a little less empty.

Grayson followed Jacob out of the hut, hands soaked in blood. Jacob went to Glade silently, eyes glazed over. Grayson went to the oasis and knelt in the wet sand. He didn't feel the moisture soak through his pants, didn't feel the change in the air as day shifted to night.

He rinsed his hands numbly, fully aware of everyone's eyes on him. Waiting.

They could wait.

He'd tortured those two men... and it had been easy. After managing to go these past three years without torturing anyone, he'd expected to flinch after the first scream. He didn't. He was numb to it—their pleas, the screams, watching them try to crawl away from him.

There were some things the body and mind never forgot.

"It had to be done," Eran assured him with a mute kind of sadness. He knew what this did to his rider. Not the act of violence—but that he didn't feel *anything* for having done it.

It fucking terrified him.

Eva had told him his hands were meant for healing. And he did. He healed those men then inflicted more damage over and over again until he got what he wanted.

What would she say to him if she was in that room instead of her brother?

"We now know what Darius intends to do."

"We do." Grayson rose to his feet, leaving his hands to dry in the arid air. *"I'm going to rip him to shreds, Eran."*

For taking Eva. For forcing him to turn into this monster again.

"You and I both."

When he faced the dragons, it was Glade who broke the silence. "And? What did you learn?"

"They're going after one of the vestiges," he answered numbly. "There's one here."

Darius hadn't come to Desert Lands for Eva. She had just been a convenient coincidence while he scoured the desert for his real mission.

No one in Dragon Canyon or in Sasha's rank betrayed her. Eva had been careful, just as she'd promised him. Just the gods and their cruel, cosmic timing. Twisting the threads for fun.

Bastards.

Aster hissed, wings flattening against her back. "He has Eva, now he wants the vestiges. When will it be enough for him?"

Grayson's hands clenched. "That's the thing about Darius. Power, gold, kingdoms—none of them will never be enough."

"He has to be stopped," Jacob declared, moving away from Glade to stand in the middle of their dragons. The wind stirred around his boots, kicking up sand and carrying it over the carnage not even twenty feet away from them. "He has Eva, and he's after a vestige. He likely knows where the others are. If that's the case..." He exhaled sharply, gaze dropping to the ground in shame. "We can't let him leave the Desert Lands alive. I know I'm pointing out the obvious—and I'm partly to blame why he's still alive in the first place." His voice cracked with restrained anger. "I should've let Eva kill him when she had the chance. But now, this is more than revenge for our family—for what he's done to countless other families."

Grayson rubbed the scruff along his jaw, absently wondering when the last time he shaved was while his gaze fixed on the horizon. "It's one thing for Sylus to possess the vestiges; he'd use them to wipe out magic from this world—which is bad." His tone hardened. "But not as bad as being in the hands of a power-hungry maniac." He dropped his hand and straightened, meeting Jacob's eyes. "Darius won't use the vestiges to wipe magic. He'll use them to control the world."

Glade lowered her head to Jacob's level. "We will stop him, Reckless One. We will get our revenge and protect Astrida, as is our mission as Dragon Knights."

Eran nodded in agreement, meeting Arkon and Aster's gaze, likely noting the impatient grooves being carved into the earth beneath their claws. "Well said, Glade." Lastly, his emerald eyes fell on Grayson. "We will find our squad mates and finish this once and for all."

Grayson's jaw clenched, hand moving to his shortsword. Soon it will know the taste of Darius's blood. Soon Darius would get exactly what he wanted—he'd get his younger brother back.

"Then let's move."

CHAPTER 51
A LESSON IN CONTROL

Copper and something bitter coated Eva's tongue. Her lips were cracked. Throat dry. Swallowing was painful. Her muscles ached. Breathing earned her a sharp jab in the ribs. Wounds throbbed in more places she could count.

She was afraid to open her eyes.

The ground beneath her was cold and unforgiving, pressed against the curve of her ribs and hip. No sand. No moss. Just dry, jagged rock. The air was cool but not harsh, brushing over her skin with an out-of-place kindness. Except she knew better than to believe she was somewhere safe. Her hands were bound in front of her. Too tight to move, not enough to cut off circulation.

There was a body beside her. Warm. Solid. Their breaths were slow and shallow, as if they were sleeping. They smelt of sweat and dust with an underlying natural musk that reminded her of home. She couldn't pinpoint what about it was familiar, but it was enough to ease the tension in her shoulders.

Maybe. Just maybe. She wasn't as deep in shit as she thought she was.

Maybe the person beside her wasn't who she thought they were. Maybe they were just a wary traveller, tying her up to be on the safe side until they could figure out if she was friend or foe.

Maybe Sasha and Syran were still alive. Maybe she hadn't watched her mentor's head roll across the sand. Maybe Darius hadn't forced her to drink an awful potion that had cut her off from Arkon.

She ventured a peek into the world around her, being sure to keep her body still, preserving the illusion of sleep.

The cavern swam into focus first. It was massive, shadowed at the edges, stretching wide beyond her eyes could show her. The air was cool and sharp, but dry enough to sting her throat with every breath. The stone beneath her was rough, like it had been shaped by claws, not water.

Stalactites loomed from the ceiling like malicious fangs, jagged and uneven. They hung low in places, hunched like creatures ready to pounce, and her foggy mind imagined them twitching toward her with each flicker of light.

The illumination came from two lightstones at the centre of camp. They bathed everything in a ghostly hue, casting long, unnatural shadows that moved when nothing else did.

Stalagmites jutted from the ground in crooked formations, forming an uneven circle around what passed for their camp—if you could call it that. A ring of broken rock and half-rolled bedding. No fire pit. No comfort. Just stone and the hissing wind.

Further back, past the light's reach, the cave expanded into dark tunnels, their mouths gaping and black, like the cave itself had a throat. The way the sound echoed—a warbly whistling—made it impossible to guess how far those tunnels went.

Her eyes continued adjusting, tracing every detail, until they landed on Anna.

Her breath hitched.

Bruised. Bloodied. Still.

But *alive*.

Tears burned behind her eyes and she bit down on the inside of her cheek to keep them at bay. It was selfish, maybe, to feel this kind of relief in a place like this. Surrounded by shadows and monsters. But she couldn't help it.

Anna was here.

She wasn't alone.

But that sliver of hope shriveled the moment her gaze shifted to the figure lying beside Anna. The man whose turbulent eyes watched her from across the huddled lightstones.

Darius Fortys.

Her breath caught in her throat. A coldness seeped into her bones, spreading faster than the damp air around her. His stare held the kind of horror nightmares were built on—dark, patient, and brimming with unhinged satisfaction. The corners of his mouth lifted, a slow and knowing smile curling like smoke from the fires in the Five Hells.

Dread twisted in her gut. Her stomach clenched, then flipped, forcing bile into her throat. She turned her face away, squeezing her eyes shut.

Nononononononononono.

She didn't have to see him. She could *feel* him. That was the worst part. The way the space around him bent. How her skin prickled just knowing he was near. The memory of his voice—his laughter as he watched her family burn—crawled up her spine like a thousand spiders.

She looked back at Anna—still unconscious, her hands bound like Eva's. Curled inward, defenseless. A few feet away from Darius. Too close.

Could she make it to her in time?

Could she even *move*?

Her body ached in a hundred places. She hadn't tried to shift yet, hadn't tested her limbs. For all she knew, her legs might not work. She might be broken and not know it yet.

But gods, she wanted to run. To throw Anna over her shoulder and run. To scream. To fight. To reduce this cave to rubble and never look back.

But her body refused.

She lay frozen. Trapped in the space between horror and instinct, between fear and fury.

This wasn't just bad. This wasn't just trouble.

This was a living nightmare.

Darius pulled a knife free from the sheath strapped to his thigh, holding it out like an extension of himself. The blade hovered over Anna's exposed neck, its edge glinting under the cold light.

"Try it," he murmured, voice as smooth and deadly as the steel at her throat, "and she dies."

She couldn't breathe. Air caught in her throat, brittle and dry, like breathing through cracked stone.

True terror sank deep into her bones. One wrong move—one wrong *breath*—and Anna's life was forfeit.

Desperate, Eva reached for the only hope she had left. She pushed through her panic and reached out with her heart, fumbling for the invisible thread that had once connected her to him. Her dragon. Her sword. Her shield.

"*Arkon?*"

Please, please, please—

Silence answered her.

Cold, pressing silence.

Not even a flicker of his power. No spark of comfort, no crackle of distant thunder to let her know he felt her. It was like grasping at clouds, like screaming into the void.

But there was *something*. Barely.

A breath on her heart. A ghost of warmth. Gentle, tentative fingers brushing over her soul, *just* out of reach.

Their Bond hadn't shattered. Not completely. But it was fractured. Distant. Like he was behind a door she couldn't open.

Panic tore at her chest like a voracious beast, all claws and teeth, chewing through the thin thread of control she had left. She forced air into her lungs and pushed herself upright, slowly, warily, spine scraping against the cold stone wall behind her. Her armour was gone, leaving her defenseless, weaponless, in her under armour and riding pants.

"Don't hurt her." Her voice was hoarse, grating against her throat.

He only grinned, that sickly dark grin that left his eyes smouldering with infernal evil. The blade at her throat glinted, a reminder more than a warning. He'd gotten his message across loud and clear, and he knew it.

The young man beside her jolted, coming awake with a swift inhale like he'd surfaced from a nightmare. His gaze found Darius first—sharp, startled, wary—then shifted to her. And stayed. He blinked once, slowly, nostrils flaring slightly. His eyes widened as he studied her—taking in every detail of her bloody, swollen face—like it mattered.

Grayson's younger brother didn't look anything like she'd imagined.

Not a monster. Not a shadow of Darius.

He was... almost gentle, in the way he looked at her.

His chin-length hair hung loose around his face, tousled and damp with sweat. Dirt smudged one cheek, and the collar of his tunic was ripped, exposing a bruised collarbone. But even battered and bleeding, he was handsome.

His features were soft, but hardened by the scruff dusting his jaw. He looked a few years younger than Grayson—his body not yet shaped by the same brutal horrors his older brothers had endured. And his eyes...

They were startling. Icy blue, like glacial waters—beautiful, clear, and strangely sincere. Confident, steady, like Leo's, but not guarded and haunted the way Grayson's were.

There was no hate in them. No hunger for power.

It made her breath catch, hope flickering in her chest like a rekindled flame.

"You're Dravyn, right?" Her voice was a rough whisper, harsh in her throat, scraping through the cavern. "I'm Eva."

For a heartbeat, something unguarded flickered across his face. Surprise, mostly, but beneath it, a stunned sort of ache. Like her knowing his name meant more than she could have imagined. "How do you know me?"

"Don't talk to him," Darius snapped from across the camp. His blade caught the light, flashing in warning.

She turned away from Darius, refusing to give him the satisfaction of her attention. Let him spit his commands. She might be tied up in a cave with no sense of where she was—but she wasn't his to command. She'd cooperate, if that's what it took to keep Anna breathing. But submission? That, she would never give him.

Dravyn, on the other hand? Grayson had described him as the kind one. And that look she saw just now confirmed it. The fact that she knew his name had plucked a cord inside of him. Maybe she could reach that part of him. Maybe, if she was careful, she could find a way to convince him to help them.

"Grayson told me about you."

"Grayson?" Dravyn's brow creased, mind churning with too many thoughts to unravel at once. "You mean... Dex? He told you about me?"

Darius was beside them in a flash. The knife was suddenly there, carving heat into Eva's cheek. No time to flinch, let alone breathe. Blood trickled down her face and dripped off her chin. Those abyssal eyes were level with her face, dark and haunting. "When I give you a command, pet, you *obey*."

Her heart battered against her ribs, but she tipped her chin up and met his gaze. Glared at him with everything she had. The tip of the knife was pressed too tight to her flesh to talk, but she hoped he got the message loud and clear: "Fuck you."

A grin curled on his lips. "Ah, there it is. That fire." He pressed harder. Pain lanced up her face. She fought the tears, refusing to give him the satisfaction. "You think you can be bold because I won't kill you. But make no mistake, pet—I have no qualms about expanding that pretty mouth of yours."

The blood drained from her face at the visceral image he painted, leaving her heart pounding in her throat. Fear crawled down her spine like a drip from a faucet. If she could have melded into the wall behind her, she would have, just to get away from his oppressive aura.

He leaned in, nose grazing along hers. Then he tilted, pressing the flat of his tongue on her cheek as he licked the blood from her face. Her blood turned to ice, freezing her body in place as he violated her.

"Get the fuck off me!" She twisted away from him then tucked her boot into his stomach and kicked out, sending across the camp.

Snarling, he rolled onto his knees and grabbed her ankle. With a single yank, he was hovering over her, blade poised over her shoulder—where he had carved into her last.

At the sudden memory, her shoulder began to throb, remembering the agony of the moment—and the days of recovery afterwards.

Fear stilled her breath.

He was going to do it. His eyes said it, the way his fingers tightened around the hilt, preparing to gouge out her shoulder again. He wanted to see her suffer—would enjoy it, too.

"Darius—"

Darius shot Dravyn a sharp look. "Shut up, Dray."

"Fine," Dravyn muttered, crossing his arms as he leaned back against the wall. "If you want your *pet* bleeding into an infection and slipping into a coma, that's on you."

Darius snarled—then turned his attention to Eva, eyes glowing in the shadows. "Keep fighting, little rider, it only makes me want to break you more."

He slid off of her, slithering back to his side of the camp. He sifted through his bag then tossed a small pouch at her feet. "Eat."

She didn't move at first. Couldn't. The place where his tongue had touched her still burned, ice cold and vile. A part of her wanted to spit—another wanted to retch.

But she reached for the pouch. She didn't know how long she had gone without eating. And out here, in the desert, when any meal could be your last, it was a death sentence to turn down any opportunity for food.

Her fingers trembled as she pulled it into her lap. Bread. Dried fruit.

She hesitated, despite the desperate pang in the stomach.

A shift of movement caught her attention. She watched Dravyn rifle through his bags, brandishing a canteen. He handed it to her, his grip lingering a beat before she accepted the offering. "Drink first. It'll help make the food go down easier."

Her gaze flickered to Darius, who watched their exchange with the keen awareness of a predator. His expression was unreadable, a mixture of dark heat and caution, as if he was expecting her to act out. And wanted her to.

Her gaze dropped to the canteen, throat tight. Her body commanded that she uncork it already and chug the contents, but the last time they'd forced her to drink something, she fell unconscious and lost her magic. Worse, her dragon.

"There's no Mithbane in it," Dravyn said, an unexpected soft edge to his voice. "It's just water. Promise."

She had no reason to believe him. To trust him. For all she knew, the small glimpses of compassion she caught were an act. Something this family seemed to exceed at. Grayson hadn't seen him for years. He might not be the same man he left behind. And yet... there was something in his eyes. They were watching her, not with amusement or cruelty, but something harder to place. Something she desperately wanted to hold onto.

She couldn't afford to die. So she uncorked the canteen, didn't bother to sniff it—there was no point, she intended to drink regardless—and tipped her chin back as cool water slid down her throat. Clean. Untainted. A balm against the raw scrape inside of her.

For now, she would obey, but she wouldn't submit. Darius could do whatever he wanted to her, she would not break. Would not cave.

And when the right moment came, she'd remind him why he wanted *her* to be his weapon.

Anna woke shortly after Eva finished eating. She took their current captive state with far more grace than Eva had. Her grey eyes swept the cavern in a cold, calculating scan, cataloging every detail.

Eva wanted to tell her it was pointless. They'd be moving soon.

Darius and Dravyn were packing their supplies, unaware Anna was awake. Eva might've seized the moment to slam Darius's head into the nearest stalagmite—but she had no idea where they were. If this was still the cave system she'd spotted from Last Drop, it was a labyrinth. One wrong turn and they'd die before finding a settlement.

As Eva met Anna's gaze across the camp, a shared understanding passed between them, an unspoken whisper: *Figure out our bearings first. Then make a move.*

Darius must've sensed the attention. He snapped his head toward Anna, a cruel grin peeling across his face. "Look who finally decided to join us."

Anna spat at his feet. "Fuck you."

Unbothered by the venomous words, Darius kicked a pebble over the puddle of saliva. His head cocked to the side, sharp, predatory as he looked at her. "Do you know what we do to defiant women in Estrus?"

Anna stiffened.

His grin widened. "Oh yes, you do. Of course you do. They let women read in Aboria. Fill your heads with ideas. Teach you to talk back." He turned to Eva, voice slick with mockery. "Tell me, peasant girl, do you know what we do to women like that in Estrus?"

Eva swallowed the lump in her throat, feeling the weight of his oppressive aura looming over her like a guillotine.

It was answer enough for him.

"We strip them naked, tie them to a post, and throw stones at them. Not the smooth little pebbles you'd find on a beach..." He strode to a nearby stalagmite, taking the tip in his grasp. In one sharp, brutal movement, he snapped it free—a jagged shard the size of her palm. He crouched in front of her, holding it up. Showcasing the edges. How his fingers curled around them with curated practice.

Her heart pounded in her chest, horror sinking into her gut and leeching into her veins like acid.

"We use rocks like this. Helps *bleed* the defiance out of them," he said, almost sweetly. As if he was doing them a favour.

Then, without warning, he spun and struck. The rock whipped across Anna's face with a sickening crack. Anna hit the ground with an agonised scream. Blood poured from the gash carved in her cheek as Darius loomed over her.

"Anna!" Eva lunged—to strangle the life out of him—but Dravyn caught her around the waist, pinning her back against his chest. "You bastard!"

Darius crouched in front of Anna, who clutched her face between bound hands. Tears streaked down her face, dredging lines through the layer of blood smearing her skin. But even as Eva saw how hard she tried to stop the tears, to hide the pain, a single crack revealed it all to them—the hate, the fear, the agony. Her heart twisted at the sight, because she knew Anna wouldn't have shown any of it if she wasn't in so much pain.

I'm so sorry, Anna. She'd brought this on to her friend.

Darius raised the rock again. Anna's eyes blazed, bracing.

Dravyn's grip pinched at Eva's waist—as reflex, or to hold her steady, she didn't know.

Satisfied, Darius tossed the rock aside with a smirk. "Since you missed orientation," he purred darkly, "I thought you needed a quick lesson: resist, and I'll strip you down, tie you up, and beat you with a rock. And if *she* resists—" he jutted his chin toward Eva "—you die. Am I understood?"

"Yes," Anna hissed, still glaring at him with fire in her eyes.

Eva wrenched herself free of Dravyn's hold and stumbled to Anna's side. Darius stepped back without comment, already turning his focus to packing the camp, erasing every trace, like none of this had ever happened.

Eva tore a strip from her under armour and dabbed gently at the gash. Anna didn't wince. Didn't move. Her eyes were locked on Darius, molten silver forged in rage and hate.

"I'm sorry," Eva whispered. She didn't know when they'd get another moment like this. And there were things she needed to say—just in case. Tears burned at the corners of her eyes. "I'm sorry you got dragged into this. I love you. You know that, right?"

It was one thing to let him cut Eva. Hurt her. But Anna? To watch her friend bleed for the very thing Eva loved most about her—it tore at her very being.

They weren't making it out of this. Not alive. Not whole. And that terrified her. Not her own death—but losing Anna. She'd already lost so much. Her family. Her home. Sasha. Syran... She couldn't lose Anna too. She'd rather die herself than let that happen.

Anna's stare snapped from Darius to Eva—not with sorrow or fear, but with a fierceness that made Eva's throat tighten. She gripped Eva's wrist, steady and strong. Her voice was low, but unshakable, "We live through this. We endure. We survive. You hear me?"

A tear slipped down Eva's cheek. Even when half of Anna's face was shredded and bloody, she still found the strength to hold her chin high and maintain that sharpened steel in her eyes.

Gods. She admired this woman so damned much. The thought of a world without Anna twisted at her heart like a blade.

And she was right. No fear. No regret. Survival—that was all that mattered.

She drew a sharp breath, locking her grief behind steel doors—before Darius found a crack in her armour.

"We endure," Eva whispered back, steeling herself. Things were only going to get harder and she needed to hold tight. Remember who she was. What she fought for. And who she loved.

Darius came up behind her and gripped her arm, yanking her away from Anna. "Break time's over. Let's move." He caught Anna's arm next, dragging her upright mercilessly.

Dravyn cast a wary glance over his shoulder at them, but said nothing. He strode ahead toward the two tunnels at the far end of the cavern, a map in hand—sketched in charcoal, worn at the folds, but surprisingly detailed.

Eva blinked at it. She hadn't known anyone in the Desert Lands bothered with maps. Most navigated by landmarks or trail markers. That was the way of wanderers and outlaws.

But Dravyn barely glanced at the page. His confidence didn't come from paper. It came from memory.

He directed them into the right tunnel with the ease of someone who'd walked these paths a thousand times.

Darius shoved Anna to start moving. Eva hesitated before filing behind her, feeling as though she was about to willingly walk into the maw of a great beast. But the only monster she was truly aware of was the one behind her.

Goosebumps dusted her skin as the walls narrowed around them, stone pressing in tight on either side. Darius kept close behind them, herding Eva and Anna like livestock, always just a step too near.

Her clothes snagged on jagged edges. Loose strands of hair tore free and clung to the stone. Shimmying between crags was difficult with bound hands, but she said nothing. She followed Dravyn's lead in silence. Bit her tongue at Darius's cutting remarks—whether aimed at her, Anna, or even his own brother. She kept her head down and did what she was told. To keep Anna safe.

She savoured the moss that brushed her skin in the tightest places, welcomed the slick trickle of moisture down the walls. Anything that reminded her there was more to this world than stone and menace.

The deeper they went, the more alive the path became, and Eva began to recognise sounds: the scrape of steel sheaths against rock—Darius and Dravyn's weapons. It grated against her ears and sent a shiver through her spine. The rustle of her clothing as it brushed the stone, the tear when she yanked too hard. Boots scuffing along the uneven ground, kicking up dirt. Darius's breath curling down her neck. And beneath it all, the faint, ever-present hum of the cave breathing around them, shifting.

Trickling water echoed through the tunnels. They passed the mouth of a river once, black and slow-moving. She glimpsed wildlife along the edges—pale lizards darting through cracks, bats clinging upside down. And bugs. Gods, the bugs. Ants with pincers. Roaches the size of her thumb. More than one scorpion skittered across their path, its stinger poised. Eva had held her breath once as one skittered in front of her face.

And yet... it was the monotony that truly gnawed at her.

Step after step, time bled together. No sun. No stars. No sense of up or down. The silence left room for her thoughts—dangerous, aching thoughts. The pain of Sasha's death throbbed in her chest, every step a reminder of the things she never said.

She would've given anything for just a few more minutes. To thank Sasha for her guidance, her infuriating patience, her belief in Eva—even when she never said it aloud. She'd even welcome one of Sasha's long lectures, or those "pointless" tasks that always turned out to be training in disguise.

She missed the stories of the Goblin Wars. Her brutal honesty. The fierce pride Sasha carried as Syran's Soul Bound.

The ache of that loss pulsed stronger in the dark.

What would Sasha say to her pupil now, captive, lost beneath the sand? Would she berate her for falling into Darius's hands? Would she demand Eva fight them—even when the odds were stacked against them—and die an honourable death, rather than let Darius pick apart her humanity a chunk at a time?

She shut her eyes, the last words Sasha spoke to her ringing in her ears, "*It's your turn, kid.*"

Eva knew exactly what she meant. Arkon was the last storm dragon—and she the last storm rider. They held the power for change. To destroy kingdoms or to forge new ones.

It was up to her to wield it for good. To protect. To change the world for the better.

Some days (or nights, there was no way to tell) the weight in her chest threatened to burst. Grief. Homesickness. The simple ache of missing what it felt like to be safe. Somehow, she kept it buried, locked beneath the iron she'd wrapped around her heart.

Keeping it safe. Keeping it close.

When they made camp to rest for a few hours, she caught herself staring at Dravyn.

She couldn't help seeing glimpses of Grayson in him—the shape of his nose, the arch of his brow. It made her wonder what Grayson looked like before Sylus's conditioning had stripped him of his innocent youth. Before his body learned violence as instinct.

Had his eyes ever looked as soft as Dravyn's did when he noticed her watching him? Her heart twisted when he spun his charcoal pencil over his knuckles—just like Grayson did with his knife.

Too many days had passed with his face flashing in her mind's eye. Of his lopsided smile. The peaceful look on his face as he slept beside her. The sheer bliss in his features as he came inside her. The absolute menace in his eyes when he promised to ruin anyone who'd hurt her.

If he knew Darius had her captive, he'd stop at nothing to get her back. An irrefutable fact. He would come for her and he'd kill anyone who stood in his way.

But he didn't know Darius had her. Didn't know that her body was weak and aching, that she feared the eternal labyrinth they were trapped in, feared for Anna's life as well as what future Darius had planned for Eva.

They were on their own.

And maybe that was for the best. She didn't want Grayson to worry. Didn't want Darius to use her against him.

She'd find her way home to him.

Always.

No matter what it took.

She'd always find her way to him.

CHAPTER 52
A RELENTLESS PURSUIT

Jacob could feel himself slipping.

He tried so damn long to hold on.

Just one more hour, he'd tell himself. *Power through it. Eva and Anna are depending on you.*

The world was depending on them. Darius was going after one of the vestiges Commander Hargin had entrusted them to find. Every hour lost gave Darius more ground, more time with them.

But he'd promised himself one more hour two days ago. He'd lost feeling in his toes. His thighs were cramping, knees rusted at a forty-five degree angle. His palms were covered in blisters from the friction against the handle, while the tops of his hands were blistered from the heat.

Gods.

The heat.

How had the girls not melted away under the constant oppressive weight of the sun looming over them? They'd spent months in this heat, training, swimming, hunting. Three days in this blasted land, and he was already shriveling like a flower on a volcano.

His head was so heavy, all he could do was peer through his lashes and veil of hair at Eran and Grayson up ahead. Always ahead. Neither of them appeared to be affected by the heat or the lack of rest.

Not once had they stopped to rest. Or shown an inkling that they needed it.

Just a little longer....

Warm, solid arms wrapped around his waist from behind. He felt the brush of lips against his ear. "Rest, my love."

Anna's voice cut through him like a balm. She was always there exactly when he needed her to be. He twisted. "An—"

The words died in his throat. She wasn't there. Her warmth and unwavering strength—gone.

And then suddenly the world was tilting.

Glade's bronze scales slipped past him.

He was no longer in his saddle.

He was falling.

The illusion shattered, replaced by the roar of wind, the rush of air whipping past his ears, tearing at his clothes, his skin. His stomach lurched into his throat as the dunes rushed to meet him.

"Jacob!" Glade's voice sliced through the wind—and then she was diving, wings folded tight against her back.

It took longer than Jacob wanted to admit to snap out of his daze. He forced his limbs out, arms and legs spread to slow his descent, muscles screaming as he fought the air pushing up against him.

Glade moved like a dart, claws outstretched. She caught him mid-air and crushed him to her chest, wrapping her wings around them as they hit the sand with a bone-jarring impact. His brain rattled in his skull, organs slamming against the walls of his body.

Then stillness.

Silence.

Glade shook the sand from her scales and uncurled her claws. Jacob crawled out, limbs trembling.

He barely cleared her before his arms gave out. His face hit the sand and he rolled down the side of the dune, landing in a graceless heap at the bottom.

A flurry of wings kicked up sand as Eran landed beside him. Grayson jumped down, boots thudding into the dune by Jacob's head. He crouched, eyes sharp as they swept over him.

"You okay?" Grayson demanded, voice clipped. Hard. "What happened?"

Jacob shook his head, brushing sand from his hair as he pushed himself upright. His gaze drifted to Glade, who hissed at Eran as he approached.

"I'm fine," she snapped, then rose to her full height. Her wings flared wide, casting a long shadow over them. The brief shade didn't cut the heat, but Jacob savoured the moment out of the sun. It was the first relief he'd felt in hours.

Eran's eyes narrowed at the way her right wing trembled, struggling to hold position. Jacob saw it too. Guilt surged through him as he staggered to his feet.

"Glade, you're hurt." *Because of me. Because I'm not strong like Grayson.* "Let Eran take a look."

Her wings slammed shut against her back, and she bared her teeth, scales rippling with a violent shimmer, gold flashing between the cracks. "Don't you dare. Don't ask him to look at me when *you* won't look after yourself. You think I can't feel it? We may not be Bound, but I *feel* your life force fading, Reckless One."

Grayson stepped between them. His eyes burned with the fury of the merciless sun, his voice cutting like hot steel through flesh. "We don't have time for this. Eran, fix her fucking wing—then we leave."

"No," Glade growled, backing away from Eran as he attempted to approach her again. Her chest heaved, wings twitching in protest. "We can't keep pushing like this. If we don't stop, if we don't rest, *you* will be the one who collapses when we finally find them."

Arkon and Aster alighted on either side of Glade. Arkon turned a cold glare on Jacob, clearly noting he wasn't on his dragon as he should be. He'd been just as ruthless as Grayson—demanding they go further, faster. As if any time apart from Eva, no matter how little, was unbearable.

And they both acted like Jacob was the problem. Like he wasn't hurting just as much as they were.

"What is the hold-up?" Arkon demanded.

"Glade's wing is sprained," Eran said, standing at a respectful distance. Calm and composed—entirely the opposite of his rider. "She can't fly until I've healed it."

Arkon huffed, stirring a cloud of sand around him. "Then heal it and let us be done with this."

Glade bared her teeth, a hiss curling from her throat. "No. No one touches me until we rest."

"Darius has Eva!" Grayson's voice was sharp—clipped and cold. "I won't let her suffer a minute longer than she already has."

Aster threw a withering glare his way. "Anna is also with them, suffering alongside Eva... but Glade is right." Her amber eyes shifted to Jacob, and the harshness in them softened. His throat tightened. *Gods*, it was like looking into Anna's eyes: the same tender gentleness—and brutal fierceness. "If we keep going like this," she said, "you'll both collapse. Even if you won't admit it."

Her gaze landed on Grayson, unimpressed, unapologetic. His skin was raw and red, blisters blooming across his nose and hands. A stark contrast to Jacob, who—though struggling—had at least known the sting of Aboria's summers. Grayson hadn't. Estrus had never prepared him for this kind of heat.

Still, Grayson curled his lip at Aster, stubborn defiance burning beneath sunburned skin. "I can take it. We keep going."

Aster bared her teeth. Smoke pluming between them as she snapped, "Are you willing to kill your partner to spare the girls a few less hours with your brothers?"

Grayson's fists clenched. His jaw ticked. When he looked at Jacob, his expression twisted—torn between Jacob's health and Eva's safety.

But Jacob took the choice from him. He pushed himself upright, shaking sand out of places it had no right being. "It's fine. I can keep going."

For Eva. For Anna. He'd push himself as hard as he needed to.

A muscle fluttered at Grayson's jaw. He looked away, and for a moment, the fire in him faltered. With a heavy sigh, he hung his head. "No. We'll make camp." The words were leaden. "The sun will be down soon anyway."

He didn't look at Jacob again.

"Glade," he said instead, voice clipped, "make us a shelter. Let Eran fix your wing. We leave at first light."

And then he turned on his heel and walked away, skirting the edge of the dune like he couldn't bear to stand in their shadow any longer.

"Where are you going, Gray?" Jacob called after him, too weary to follow.

Grayson didn't look back. "I'm going hunting."

Jacob's heart twisted. He knew when his partner was mad at him. Usually, it was because Grayson was being too harsh, and Jacob had to pull him back. But this time... this time it was different.

This time, it was because *he* wasn't enough.

Not strong enough. Not gritty enough. Not disciplined enough to push his body beyond its limits. To keep moving when his legs refused. To endure, the way Grayson always did.

"I will accompany you," Arkon said, voice like stone.

That put a stumble in Grayson's step.

His head snapped toward the dragon, fury and surprise flaring behind his eyes—then, without a word, he turned away again, marching onward. Arkon followed in silence, his heavy tail etching a deep groove through the sand behind him.

The ground trembled beneath Jacob.

He turned just in time to see Glade gathering the sand with her magic. A wall rose in a seamless arc, forming a dome that stretched high overhead. A chimney rose from the center, and a wide entrance stood open at the base—large enough for a dragon to pass through.

The sand beneath his feet hardened, packing tightly into a smooth floor. In one corner, a mound rose and then dipped into a broad trough. A hole burrowed deep into the earth, and with Eran's help, a geyser of fresh water burst free, filling the basin until it shimmered with cool relief.

Selfishly, Jacob rushed forward and plunged his face into the water. The chill shocked his skin, but it was heaven. When he finally surfaced, a sigh slipped from his lips. He drank until his stomach ached, then stepped aside to let the dragons have their fill.

By the time he turned around, Glade had already formed a firepit in the centre and crafted two cots from sand, just tall enough to keep them off the floor—away from the scorpions and snakes that waited for their next victim in the night.

Glade padded up to him and nudged him toward one of the cots. "Rest, Reckless One."

"But I—"

She shoved her snout into his chest, firm and unrelenting, knocking him off balance. He stumbled backward and collapsed onto the cot with a grunt.

"Ow," he muttered, rubbing his ribs. "Are you sure there's nothing I can do?"

Aster curled up around the firepit, her tail snaking to the edge of his cot, eagerly awaiting to light the fire. Glade settled down beside his cot, giving Eran enough space by the trough to do his work on her wing.

"Rest is what you can do," Glade insisted. "Eva and Anna need you strong—not half-dead."

Jacob winced at that. He did feel like he was hanging on by a thread. A very thin one that was fraying at the edges.

Still not quite able to let it go, Jacob turned to Eran. "How's Gray? Like, how is he *really* doing? Not what he wants me to think. He's... different."

Jacob had seen him angry before. Distant. Even cruel. Especially in those early days of their partnership. But this—this was something else entirely.

He looked down at his blistered hands, then toward the dune Grayson had disappeared behind.

He'd let it go back at Kain Castle, when they read Anna's letter. Even brushed it off when Grayson lost it after learning Darius was involved. But the torture... that had been harder to stomach. Yes, those men had played a hand in Eva's capture and Sasha's death. But their screams—gods—their screams had taken Jacob straight back to the fort. Agonised. Drawn-out. Designed to maximize suffering.

And then there were his eyes.

The light Jacob had watched slowly grow in them over the years was flickering out. Did Grayson even realise how far he'd fallen? Did he *care*?

The hate in those eyes was getting louder. The fury—and something darker—was clawing to the surface, tearing his friend away and replacing him with something else. His throat went raw just thinking about it.

Grayson was out for blood—and nothing else mattered.

Jacob knew, with a certainty that chilled him, that once they found the girls, nothing in this world would stop Grayson from killing Darius. And it wouldn't be quick. Wouldn't be clean. Those eyes didn't speak of justice.

They spoke of torment. Of anguish buried so deep it warped the soul. They weren't the eyes of his best friend. Not even of a wronged Dragon Knight. No... They were the eyes of something much worse.

The eyes of the *Slayer of Souls*.

Eran's magic glittered against the ceiling as he healed Glade. His eyes were fixed on her wing as he spoke, "You will be safe, Jacob."

"That doesn't answer my question."

Aster snorted. "Doesn't it?"

"I want a straight answer, Eran," Jacob demanded, anxiety prickling at the back of his neck.

You won't know the monster you've harboured until it's too late.

Eran's eyes were fixed on Glade. "I cannot give you a straight answer, Jacob, because he has shut me out of his mind."

Jacob's heart pounded. "What are you saying?"

"I'm saying that all I can guarantee you right now is that you will be safe. Eva and Anna will be safe once we find them. And if we don't, or if we're too late... I don't know what my Soul Bound will do."

A pit formed in Jacob's stomach.

Darius was right.

It was too late.

CHAPTER 53
WHATEVER IT TAKES

Arkon could feel her.

His Soul Bound. His other half. His reason for living.

With every mile they closed the gap between them, the tether wove tighter. The pull grew stronger.

Eva was close. Maybe a day away. Maybe less.

Which made it all the more infuriating that they'd chosen *now* to stop. So close... yet still so far.

He had half a mind to take to the skies and fly ahead, to leave the others behind and tear the skies apart until he found her. But their Bond wasn't strong enough for that—not yet. He could sense her when she was awake. He'd felt the sharp void when the mithril poison numbed their connection. Felt the ache in both their hearts to be near one another again.

But it wasn't enough to lead him straight to her. For that, he needed her mate. And the compass only he could wield.

So here he was, grounded in the heart of the desert, trailing the dark knight as he stalked his prey—making sure he didn't charge off after Darius alone.

Ironic, really. After all the hate and distrust Arkon had once harbored toward him, Grayson was now the only one he trusted to bring Eva home alive.

And stranger still... Arkon hadn't realised just how much Eva had changed the Slayer—until she was torn away from him. For that, he let the guilt gnaw at him. Just a little. For not seeing the man Eva loved.

Not truly.

But he'd been there all along—in every hard choice, in every small mercy. Always giving her a say. Always putting her first. Always willing to do the dark, bloody things no one dared speak of to keep her world from falling apart.

And now that she was gone—taken by the very man Grayson had sworn to protect her from—Arkon saw it. The darkness Grayson had kept at bay. For her.

The sun was on its way down, casting purples and oranges over the dunes, and they still had not found prey. Not for the lack of options. There was plenty of wildlife.

Grayson had picked a direction and marched, seemingly not to care where it took him, how ruthless the sun was, or how the sand fought against him. He grunted and seethed and growled. Arkon allowed it, feeling the need to do the same welling up in him like an overfilled dam.

They came across a den of Sandhounds buried in a passing dune. Grayson didn't spare them a glance, though Arkon knew he could see them with his Dragon Vision.

Arkon couldn't hold back anymore. He shut his eyes—and let the dam burst.

A bolt of lightning forked across the sky. It cracked against the earth, spearing a Sandhound through the skull. The rest of the pack scattered, scrambling out of the den and scampering down the dune—away from Arkon.

Grayson cursed under his breath and turned away, shielding his eyes.

Ignoring him, Arkon pawed at the dune until the scorched remains of the hound emerged from the sand. He scooped it up in his claws then dumped it at the Slayer's feet.

He hadn't followed Grayson into the desert to be his pack mule. Let him carry the kill back.

Grayson stared at it, jaw clenched as smoke curled from the corpse. When his gaze lifted to Arkon, his eyes held the hard edge of steel—and the roiling fury of fire barely contained.

"What are you doing here?" he asked, voice low, accusatory. "I didn't ask for your help."

Arkon looked down at the corpse. "No. You didn't." He had followed Grayson for many reasons, but one stood above the rest: they had something in common, even if Arkon loathed to admit it. "You care deeply for Eva."

Grayson stiffened, shoulders tensing in the last light of day. "I do. Of course I do. Do you think I'd fly across the world for just anyone?"

The certainty in Grayson's voice caught Arkon off guard—no hesitation, no mask, just raw truth. Out here, with no one else to deceive, the conviction was unmistakable. His feelings were undeniable. But Arkon was Eva's Dragon Bound—a piece of her soul that Grayson couldn't deny.

"No. I do not." Arkon's eyes narrowed as he watched the shadows coalesce around Grayson, cloaking him like a herald of Val. His voice dropped, heavy with warning. "I also believe you would do anything for her."

"In a heartbeat," he said without hesitation. His jaw clenched, fists tightening at his sides as he studied the dragon. "What are you getting at?"

Arkon's gaze shadowed, the weight of his words hanging between them. "You are a danger to her. Your soul bleeds darkness. And darkness is drawn to darkness."

"Like calls to like," Grayson muttered, his voice low, as if recalling an old memory.

A chill seemed to fall over the desert as Arkon's shadow lengthened, twisting around the Dragon Knight like vicious claws snaring him in a cage of shadows. They still had a few hours before Arkon would begin to feel his blood to coagulate and freeze him in place. Including his heart. "Darius won't be the last."

Grayson's eyes flickered with pain and resignation. "I know."

For a long moment, neither spoke.

Arkon hated what he was about to ask of Grayson—and hated even more what it would do to Eva. But the thought of Darius turning her into one of his puppets terrified him more.

Then he spoke, softly but without mercy. "We bring Eva home. No matter the cost."

Grayson's jaw tightened. He brandished the compass from his pocket. It held West as surely as the North Star guided travellers north. He didn't answer right away. Arkon could feel the war raging inside him. Pain. Love. Duty. Rage. All vying for control.

But when Grayson finally nodded, there was no hesitation. "No matter the cost."

And in that moment, Arkon saw the shift. Not in body. But in his soul.

The light that Eva had kindled in him dimmed behind his eyes.

And the Slayer of Souls stirred beneath the surface.

CHAPTER 54
THE CLIMB

It felt like they were drifting aimlessly through a maze with no end in sight. No sun to warm their bones. No breeze to stir their hearts. Just darkness, forever encroaching. Jagged walls, incessantly snaring at their clothes and hair. Fear was a constant weight pressing between Eva's shoulders, cold and inescapable.

She'd learned the rhythm of the caverns—could pick out the rasp of Dravyn's breath from Darius's shallower huff. Could sense the shift in air just before Darius's hand found her again.

"Good pet."

"There's my little rider."

"Show me that fire."

Eva numbed herself to his taunts. Shut out the vile promises he whispered in her ear when the cave pressed them together. Things he would do to her once he found a suitable place to "break her in." She refused to show him fear.

She would escape. His little promises would never see the light of day.

Her body ached. Wounds stung, healed when she slept then reopened when they were on the move again. Bruises throbbed. Her wrists were raw to the bone, staining the rope red. She'd stopped asking for food and water, and instead got used to the vicious pang in her stomach and the dry scratch in her throat.

Darius had the effects of his Mithbane down to a T. He knew exactly when her powers began to surface, when she began to feel the warmth of Arkon's soul creeping into hers. During the brief moments between sensing him and being forced to drink the poison, she sensed her dragon's worry pulsing through her, his fierce determination wrapping around her like a shield.

He was out there, looking for her. She could feel him getting closer. Somehow, he was able to track her. And somehow, just knowing that was enough. She clung to that hope with everything she had.

She would survive.

Anna would survive.

She just had to hold on a little longer.

Finally, after what felt like years, Eva caught a speck of light in the distance. It grew with each step, until it filled the tunnel like starlight pouring through a cracked ceiling. Dravyn led them on, the light expanding until there was no more shadow to hide in. He'd tucked the map away some time ago, no longer in need of it when their exit was so clear.

Sunlight burned her eyes as they neared the exit, too sudden after being closed off from the world for so long. Heat flooded through the exit, reminding them that while the caves had been cool and moist, above them the ground had been dry and desolate.

Apprehension trickled down her already dripping spine. This was exactly what she and Anna had been waiting for. Once they were outside, they could work on catching their bearings. Form a plan. Escape.

But leaving the caves also meant they were close to whatever Darius was after. Whenever she tried to pry, he'd been vague as to where they were going. All Eva knew was that after he found this artifact, he would begin her *conditioning*.

When she should have found relief when they stepped out into the open desert, Eva only felt dread. It clawed deep into her gut and twisted hard, until bile scorched the back of her throat.

She spat unapologetically into the rough, dry sand. She used the excuse to look around, just as she knew Anna was doing the same.

They hadn't emerged from a dune, like the one they'd entered. It was more like a hole—in a big fucking crater. Getting out without a dragon's help—or any animal's—was going to take all day. And judging by the sun's relentless glare overhead, they had all day to do it.

"Move it."

Darius's knee rammed into the base of her spine. Eva stumbled forward and landed face-first in the sand. She tensed, bracing for him to yank her back up—like he'd done so many times before.

But his eyes weren't on her.

They were on the sky.

Her heart leapt into her throat.

Dragons.

He was looking for dragons.

Eva jerked her gaze upward, scanning the endless blue. For a shadow. A speck. *Anything.*

But there was nothing. Not in the narrow window the crater carved into the sky.

Anna gripped her arm and hauled her to her feet. Their eyes met—steel to resolve. In that breathless moment, no words were needed: they had to reach the top of the crater first.

If they got there first, they'd have more time to survey their surroundings. If they had a rough idea of where they were, they could make a run for it. They'd have a head start.

The slope loomed above them—impossibly steep, a cruel mountain carved from the merciless earth in a bottomless sea of sand. She scraped what strength remained from deep in her bones, shoved the pain down into the hollow places.

Then, without a word, they began to climb.

The sand was a furnace beneath their trembling hands, loose and treacherous, slipping with every desperate grasp. Each step was a battle—feet sinking, sliding, the moisture they'd gathered in the caves, sizzling under the relentless glare of the sun. The air hung thick and suffocating, heavy with dust and heat, squeezing the breath from their lungs like a vice.

Their wrists, bound tight and raw, turned every movement into agony. They clawed at the burning sand with ragged fingers, scraping, dragging, refusing to give in. Behind them, Darius and Dravyn moved slower, weighed down by their packs—and their misplaced confidence that Eva and Anna wouldn't outrun them. They didn't know that this was a race.

The brothers were fools to think they were complacent. The heavy, unbearable weight of everything—the fear, the anger, the raw ache of Sasha's loss twisting inside Eva like barbed wire—only fueled her will to taste freedom again.

They could belittle her, hurt her, steal her autonomy—but they could never take her spirit.

And when she reached the top—gasping, trembling, moments from blacking out—she saw it.

The speck.

Small. Distant. But unmistakable.

Her heart surged. A rush of life ignited in her chest like flint to tinder.

Their Bond might have been fractured. Their souls torn. Her senses half of what they once were. But she knew him. In the powerful sweep of his wings. The sinuous rhythm of his tail. The way the sky seemed to part around him as he led the charge.

Arkon.

"We make a run for it," Anna hissed at her, her voice sharp with urgency, eyes locked on the brothers still scrambling up the slope. They hadn't seen Arkon yet. "Run with everything you have and don't look back."

They had two minutes, maybe less before the brothers reached the peak.

Now was their chance.

Eva cupped her mouth with both hands and screamed—raw, desperate, shattering her throat with abandon: "ARKON!"

He tossed his head back as his answering roar cracked across the desert like lightning striking stone. His wings pumped faster. Harder.

Another followed—deep, possessive, hers.

Eran.

Grayson.

They were here. She didn't know how they were here. How they knew they were in trouble. And she didn't care. He was *here*. For her. And may Zyphril have mercy on the soul who dared to get in his way.

More shadows split the sky—four dragons in all, darting into view.

"Run!" Anna seized her hand and yanked her forward, shoving her to the rim. Together, they skidded along the edge of the crater—toward freedom. Toward their dragons.

Eva's legs screamed in protest with every stride. Muscles bunched, threatening to tear. Her lungs burned, collapsing in on themselves.

But she ran.

She ran until black spots swam in her vision, until her thoughts blurred and her limbs felt like they no longer belonged to her.

And still, she ran harder.

They were so close. She caught the brilliant gleam of Arkon's eyes—fierce, familiar. The shimmer of Eran's azure scales, streaking across the sky. She could almost make out Grayson's form, anchored tight to Eran's back—

Something slammed into her from behind.

Air punched from her lungs. Her knees hit the ground hard. Sand filled her mouth. She gagged, coughing instead of screaming, fury ripping through her as Darius's hands locked around her waist.

And then—he hoisted her like a sack of grain over his shoulders and took off, running the opposite direction.

"No!" Eva thrashed, heaving against him, but his grip was iron, unmoving. Her bound wrists made it impossible to get leverage.

"Eva!" Anna's voice cracked as she skidded to a halt behind them, eyes wide with horror.

Dravyn charged at her.

Anna was ready. She dropped low, ducking beneath his arms as he lunged to grab her. Spinning behind him, she drove her foot into his spine with a vicious snap. He grunted and staggered forward—then swept his foot out, hooking her ankle. She went crashing to the ground.

Before she could scramble back to her feet, he was on her. He flipped her onto her back and slammed his fist into her temple. Her body went limp.

"No!" Eva screamed as Dravyn slung Anna over his shoulder, casting one sharp glance at the dragons thundering toward them. "You bastard!"

She pounded her fists into Darius's back. She kicked, twisted, bit into his shoulder. Anything to slow him down. Anything.

But Darius was a wall. Unflinching. Unstoppable.

She was so caught in the fight, in her own desperate fury, she didn't notice the change in terrain. Didn't see the crumbling ruins until Darius slipped behind a pillar, its massive stone arch tilted at a steep forty-five-degree angle.

"Dravyn!" Darius barked. "You better have a fucking answer to that riddle!"

Dravyn stumbled into the ruins, red-faced and drenched in sweat. His eyes flicked from pillar to pillar, thoughts tearing through his mind like a wildfire.

Under his breath, he muttered: "*Born in silence, raised in flame, I thrive where order breaks...*"

"Hurry!" Darius snapped. The dragons were nearly on them now—so close Eva could feel the crackle of Arkon's magic shivering through the air.

"*I am the hammer's echo, the forge of kings and tyrants alike...*"

Darius's grip tightened around her legs as he drew his sword with the other hand. "Dravyn, if you don't pick a fucking pillar, we're dead!"

"*I do not choose sides—I only demand them.*"

Dravyn's gaze swept over the symbols carved into the pillars. A dove. A stack of books. A coiled snake. Ox horns. Two crossed swords.

Darius's attention was fixed solely on the dragons.

This was her chance. She rammed her elbow into his spine.

He grunted, his back arched, knees buckling from the strain. She slipped from his grasp, hitting the ground rolling, then sprang to her feet and barreled into Dravyn with every ounce of force left in her.

Anna tumbled off his shoulders, landing hard. She groaned, lifting herself to her hands and knees, dazed.

"Run, Anna!" Eva shouted. If she could just hold them back long enough—Arkon's lightning would keep Anna safe until he could get to her.

Eva grabbed Dravyn's sword from the ground. She didn't think, only spun—and slashed Darius across the chest. Not deep. Not lethal. But enough.

He roared.

Anna came up behind him, threw her bound hands over his head, and yanked back hard. He let out a strangled cry and stumbled back. Sword grasped tight in her hands, Eva moved to open up his gut for the vultures to feast on.

But Dravyn recovered swiftly. With a brutal lunge, he twisted her wrist sharply, wrenching the blade free from her grasp. Pain lanced through Eva's hand as the cold steel slipped away.

Before she could react, Dravyn grabbed her bicep with an iron grip, his fingers digging into her flesh like roots burrowing into the earth. He hauled her toward a nearby pillar, his strength unyielding and relentless.

His voice rang out, hoarse and desperate as his foot slammed down on the button at the base of the pillar with crossing swords: "War! The answer's war!"

The ground began to tremble.

A low rumble swelled beneath their feet, then a loud, grinding groan echoed through the ruins. Stone shifted. Dust poured from ancient cracks. And then the monolith split open as a slab of it sunk into the ground. A gaping maw yawned wide in its centre, revealing only a pitch-black descent.

Darius swung himself forward, tossing Anna over his shoulder. She landed hard on her back with a cloud of dust. Then he stomped on her chest.

She cried out as the air wrenched from her lungs.

Dravyn's grip was impossibly tight on Eva's arm as he led her towards the gaping hole in the monolith.

"No!" Eva twisted, digging her heels into the sand, yanking on her arm, fighting with every last shred of strength. But the brothers were rested, well-fed, and uninjured. She was none of those things.

Dravyn hauled her like she was nothing—just dead weight.

The tremor grew stronger. The earth *shivered* with a deeper, hungrier rhythm now.

Eva's stomach flipped. She knew that vibration.

Dravyn faltered mid-step. His voice turned sharp: "Sandworm, Dari!"

Darius froze, fist cocked back as he knelt over Anna. For a second, his gaze lingered—eyes burning, jaw clenched. Then he dropped her and ran.

The entrance door began to rise, stone grinding against stone in a deep, shuddering groan that echoed across the ruins. Dust rained from the seams, the ancient mechanism trembling with effort.

Dravyn yanked her inside, swatting at the wall of sand falling onto them as the door rose up beneath their feet to shut them in.

Darius lunged forward, just clearing the rising slab as it heaved itself up.

Eva's heart stopped.

Anna curled in on herself, gasping for breath. She was out there alone, in the middle of the ruins and the baking sun, with a Sandworm circling like a shark that had caught the scent of blood.

The last thing Eva saw was the sand shifting beneath her, rippling. Caving.

"No!"

Then the stone door sealed shut.

And the darkness swallowed them whole.

CHAPTER 55
ALONE

Silence pressed in on her for a beat—then Eva shoved past the brothers in the dark and slammed into the door, pounding her fists until they were slick and hot.

"*Anna!*"

A grating rumble trembled through the door, like the earth itself was shifting. Sand whispered against the door. The wind whistled down the hallway.

But there wasn't a shred of noise from Anna.

Never mind being sealed inside ancient ruins with Darius. Never mind that her body was moments from breaking. Never mind that she'd been ripped from her dragon again.

Annaliese Hargin. Her best friend.

Gone.

In an instant. Too fast. No chance to save her.

Eva collapsed onto her knees. Pain jolted up her legs, but she barely felt it. The tears came, hot and ugly. Her anguish ripped out of her throat.

She should have tried harder. Fought harder. Run faster. If only she had just pushed herself a little more—Anna might have lived.

The horrifying truth of her situation settled on her shoulders with the weight of this entire godsdamn forsaken desert.

Light burst around her, flooding the hallway in a pale, sterile glow. Shadows shifted against the door—elongating, closing in, growing bigger. Suffocating.

Hands touched her shoulders. Gentle. Tentative. So out of place, they made her skin crawl. She flinched and curled in on herself.

"Come on," Dravyn murmured. There was no edge in his voice. No cruelty. Just sympathy. Remorse even.

"No!" She clawed at the door, even as he pulled her away. Her limbs were too weak to fight him. "Let me go! Anna! We have to—"

"She's gone," he said. It wasn't a taunt. Just a truth.

Gone.

A low snarl tore through the silence as Darius shoved Dravyn aside like a piece of debris. His fingers curled into her hair with merciless intent, yanking her head closer to his face. The pale glow of the lightstone carved shadows across his features, twisting his smirk into something dark. Cruel.

"You disobeyed me, pet." His voice was a growl—low, haunting, soaked in rage and a sick kind of satisfaction. Like he *wanted* her to defy him, had been waiting all along for her to bite back.

A tremor rattled through her, raw and unyielding.

Alone. Alone. Alone. The word pounded in her mind like a hammer against steel.

"I told you what would happen if you disobeyed." His breath was hot, bitter against her skin. "Now your friend is dead—and it's your fault."

Your fault.

Alonealonealonealonealone

"But I think it's time I teach you a lesson—just in case it hasn't sunk in."

"Darius," Dravyn cut him off—sharp, commanding. "Later. We need to find the gauntlet first."

Darius's grip tightened, fingers twisting with cruel precision into her scalp. Pain exploded, white-hot and blinding. She cried out, her knees buckling under the weight of it.

"No," he snarled, eyes burning with dark promise. "She learns *now*."

A brittle sob cracked out of her chest.

She wasn't a fighter anymore. Not a Dragon Knight. Not the Soul Bound Arkon chose to share his power with.

She was just a girl. Broken. Small. Alone.

The worst part?

Some dark part of her agreed with him. Maybe it *was* her fault. Maybe Anna really was gone because she wasn't enough. No matter how hard she tried, she'd never be enough.

The walls pressed in—narrow, uneven, cold. The ceiling above slanted low enough to feel oppressive, like a mouth half-closed over its prey. Jagged shadows carved themselves along the walls, cast by the white glow of the lightstone Dravyn carried. Every pillar looked the same: smooth stone, ancient carvings, endless repetitions down a corridor that seemed to stretch forever into darkness. A maze made to be lost in.

The air was dry and stale. She could taste old dust on her tongue. Her breath rasped too loud in the silence. The stone beneath her withering boots was gritty, worn by time. There was nowhere to run.

Her pulse pounded in her ears as a grin spread across Darius's face, all menace and satisfaction. He leaned in close, licking a tear off her cheek with a slow, deliberate drag of his tongue from her jaw to the corner of her eye.

"Good girl," he purred, voice smooth like honey, but as deadly as a viper's poison. "You're starting to get it now."

Revulsion twisted in her gut. Her knees nearly gave out, but he kept her upright in his vicious grip.

She didn't fight. She couldn't. Not anymore.

He pulled her toward one of the looming pillars, pressing her cheek against the cold stone. The surface scraped her skin. Her shallow breaths rasped against it.

"Rope," Darius snapped, holding out his free hand expectantly.

Dravyn didn't answer immediately. She heard the faint rattle of gear as he dug through his pack—then silence. Hesitation.

Eva didn't move. Didn't breathe.

"Darius," Dravyn said, quiet. "If she gets an infection in here, she'll die."

"Let me worry about that," Darius hissed. "Now. Give. Me. The. Rope."

A beat.

Then the rope slapped into his palm.

Darius wound the rough tweed around her shoulders and legs—once, twice, a third time—pinning her to the pillar like a trophy. He tied her wrists last, cinching them tight behind the column. Her shoulders screamed. Her knees knocked together. She tried to breathe, but the space felt thinner, smaller, choking.

He stepped back, admiring his work like she was some prized catch.

"How many lashes do you think Father would order for her defiance, brother?" Darius asked softly, like they were discussing weather.

Eva's heart plummeted. Lashes. An image of Grayson's scarred back seared through her mind.

Dravyn's voice came stiff and detached, "Three."

Darius smiled, cold and slow. "And for attacking us?"

"Five."

"And for showing weakness?"

A pause.

Her gut tightened.

"Ten."

"That's eighteen lashes," Darius said with a quiet finality.

Eva's blood chilled at the verdict.

"Untie her hair."

"What?" Dravyn's confusion cracked his voice.

"You heard me."

A sigh. A shuffle of boots on stone.

His hands—reluctant, shaking—unraveled what remained of her ponytail. The tangles fell loose in clumps, strands of dried blood and sand sticking to his fingers. Her hair dropped around her back like a curtain, catching in the ropes, heavy with filth.

Then he stepped away—and she felt it. The seeping cold of his absence. The last thread of comfort, gone.

A tremor began in her chest and spread through her limbs. Her vision blurred. The silence thickened again, dense as fog. The pillar pressed into her ribs.

Alone.

Alone to face him. Alone to bear the pain. Alone to grit her teeth through the terror.

Behind her, the whip hissed along the stone like a viper hunting prey.

She flinched. Every nerve in her body coiled tight.

Then silence. A silence so heavy, it felt like it could crush her—

Crack!

At first, she felt nothing. Just a wisp of air. A sharp breath in her lungs. Her brain didn't register the pain.

And then it did.

Heat tore down her back. Fire bloomed across her skin, wild and unforgiving. Her knees buckled. She couldn't even hear her own scream—only the echo of it, reverberating down the hallway, jagged and feral.

Hair whispered as it fell to the floor, its weight slipping from her scalp, as if a piece of her soul had crumbled and dropped with it.

The second lash came before she'd caught her breath.

Her body jerked on instinct, the rope digging deep into her arms. The stone scraped her cheek. She sobbed—not from the pain alone, but from the helplessness. From the violation.

More hair drifted to the floor. More pieces of her dissolved into brittle, shapeless echoes of the woman she used to be.

By the fifth, the screams gave out. Her throat was raw. Her strength bled away. The world narrowed to fire, dust, and stone.

By the eighth, something inside her broke. Snapped clean and quiet. She sagged in the restraints. She felt nothing. Heard nothing. Saw nothing.

Somewhere around ten, her mind fled from the pain, retreating into darkness where nothing could touch her.

When she awoke, she was on the ground, and Dravyn was brushing what was left of her hair out of her face. Behind him, somewhere distant, she heard a huff of a breath.

"She broke easier than I thought," he said bitterly. "I'm going to check out the temple. Clean her up. I want to keep moving."

Darius's heavy footfalls faded.

Alone.

CHAPTER 56
THE ONLY WAY IS FORWARD

Eva couldn't move. Not because pain threatened to consume her if she so much as breathed. Not because her body had no more strength left to fight.

But because she'd lost the will to.

Moving without permission was an act of defiance—and defying Darius meant death.

Not hers. Never hers.

He'd made that clear. He would kill the people she loved. Again. And again. And again. Her family. Sasha. Anna.

If only it *were* meant for her.

But what kind of puppet would she be to him if she was dead?

She wanted nothing more than to shut her eyes and pretend she was back home in Brar, snuggled under the blankets with Erika in her arms. To be in a time where she was safe in her village with her family. To hike up the mountain every morning and bring her catch home.

It was a simpler time.

Maybe she hadn't been happy, but at least she wasn't being hunted and tortured by cruel princes. She still had everyone who cared about her.

Eventually, she would have let her dreams go. She would have assimilated into the village. Married one of her fellow hunters, had children and trained them to be good hunters too...

A life she never wanted. Never once asked for.

If she could do it all over again... would she have crawled inside that cave, knowing where she'd end in almost a year's time? Could she give up the bonds she'd forged? To forget what it felt like to love a man with every ounce of her being?

No...

She couldn't.

The pain, the loss, the irrevocable heartbreak. It hurt, it scarred, it stripped away a piece of her soul she'd never get back.

But with the suffering, something stronger was born. Something worth living for.

Love.

Love for the people still standing. For the men who had stood by her side through thick and thin—the very men who had crossed the world to find her. For the dragon who saved her life and showed her a world outside of her valley's walls. For the prince who loved her more than she deserved. For Anna. For Sasha. Her family. For a world shrouded in darkness that needed a light to guide it.

As if a cord had been struck inside her, she inhaled, feeling like her first breath in days. She became aware of her body and surroundings.

The temple she found herself in seemed to thrum beneath her, as if it was alive and reacting to her presence. Silence rang through the air—but not true silence.

Within the pool of light pushing away the darkness, a strange noise tickled her ears from behind.

Shwing! Like that of a blade cutting through grass.

Except it wasn't grass.

Shwing!

It tugged on her hair, making her head lighter with every slice.

Shwing!

She froze as the blade came close to her ear.

The air stilled—then Dravyn moved into view. He knelt in front of her, pieces of her hair tangled in his bloodied hands.

"You're awake." He offered a half-hearted smile—as if that was all he could give her. "Good."

Her gaze fell to the blood on his hands, then to the blood pooling on the stone beneath her. Instinctively, she tensed, waiting for him to reveal the knife. To mark her back further.

His eyes narrowed, the smile tipping downward. "I'm not going to hurt you."

"Forgive—" she choked on her own words, the sound of her voice startling her. So jagged and raw. Unrecognisable. "Forgive me," she tried again, hating how brittle and broken she sounded, "if I don't believe you."

He tilted his head—not like Darius, with his unnerving calculation, but with something quieter. Thoughtful. "Fair," he said after a beat. "I wouldn't believe me either."

She blinked at him, caught off guard by the honesty.

Her eyes went back to the blood on his hands, the clumps of blonde falling at his feet.

He followed her eyes and gave a small shrug, almost sheepish. "Figured if you're going to survive all this, you might as well not look like a butchered scarecrow."

He slipped behind her, and she tensed. He knelt over her and held the knife in front of her face, flat side facing her. He angled it so she could see her reflection. "Not bad for a Shadow in training, eh?" He smirked, but it didn't quite reach his eyes.

Her breath caught in her throat. She tried to look past the swelling, the bruises and cuts, and look at the hair he clearly wanted her to see, which now hovered just above her shoulders. But she couldn't look away from her eyes. They were so... dull. Lifeless. Devoid of hope.

Was that how she would look from now on?

She couldn't stand the sight of them—of what they'd done to her. What she *let* them do to her.

She tucked in her chin and squeezed her eyes shut, willing the tears to go away before Dravyn could mock her for having a moment of humanity.

The knife returned to its sheath with a hiss.

"Shit," Dravyn muttered behind her. "I just wanted you to see that it isn't entirely ruined, but let's be honest—it's pretty fucked."

His tone caught her off guard. It wasn't flat or mocking. But did she dare believe he felt empathy for her?

Once she was sure the tears wouldn't fall, she opened her eyes again. "Why would you do that?"

His hand closed around her arm gently. "Can you sit upright? It'll be easier to clean your back."

Again: "Why?"

They had shared more silent glances than words before this. And all of this time, she had wondered why he was so gentle with her. Why did remorse flicker his gaze when he watched her? Why step in between her and Darius?

He let out a low huff. "Even broken and bleeding, you're still stubborn."

"I'm not broken," she snapped, feeling her fire rekindle. Darius had come close to shattering her will, but she was still here. Breathing. Fighting. She wouldn't let him get that close again. And if he did... she would remember the people she loved.

His hand tightened just a tad. There was no aggression behind it. It felt more like encouragement. "Good. And before you ask *why* again—Dex needs you to be strong."

Her spine stiffened.

"Darius seems convinced Dex is in love with you—a notion I never thought possible. But if Dex has allowed himself to feel love, maybe there's hope for us yet. Some of us. So, tell me, Eva..." His voice dropped, slow and deliberate, "Do you love my brother?"

Don't answer.

It was a trap. It had to be.

He increased the pressure on his hand then slipped his other one underneath her and lifted. She tried to sit up, but the effort was mostly on him while she bit her lip down and breathed through the pain.

"That's the worst of it, I promise," he said gently. "Oh! It looks like I missed a few stragglers."

Shwing-shwing.

"Better."

Eva stared at the floor, mind sluggish as she dredged through her thoughts, trying to figure out why he was being so kind. Was this part of their game? One kind brother to build up hope—then a cruel one to tear it away.

It had to be.

But she wouldn't fall for it.

She held her heart close, wrapped tight in dragon-scale armour.

He cut away at what was left of her shirt until it slipped from her shoulders and landed in her lap. Not even her breast band had survived the whip. She folded her arms across her chest, clinging to what little dignity she had left.

Fingers brushed her shoulder. She flinched—waited. But he only flicked loose strands of hair off her skin. One floated down, long as her forearm, and landed on her ruined shirt.

It was really gone. Her hair. The tips now tickled her neck and bare shoulders, leaving her back exposed. Raw. Empty.

"I found out recently Dex is still alive," Dravyn murmured.

Her breath locked in her throat. She didn't look at him.

"All these years, I thought Darius killed him when he defected." He reached into his pack, pulling out a few clean rags and a flask that made her nose wrinkle. Alcohol. "But he hadn't." He paused, soaking the cloth. "Do you know what I felt when Darius told me he was alive?"

She stayed silent, fists clenched. He'd said sitting up would be the worst of it, but if those rags were going where she thought, that had been a lie.

"Relief," he said quietly. Then, with no ceremony, held out a bottle of vodka. Of all things. The bottle wasn't even small. "Drink this."

She shook her head, not used to how light it felt with so much of her hair gone. As tempting as it was to chug the whole thing, to numb herself and forget where she was—she didn't love the idea of being blackout drunk with Darius lurking nearby.

"Suit yourself." He tipped the bottle back, took a swig, then smacked his lips and set it down within easy reach.

Gently—so very gently—he pressed the cloth to her back.

A grunt slipped through before she could catch it. She bit down hard, the taste of copper blooming across her tongue.

He worked in silence, laying one rag after another, raking her back with fresh fire each time. Her body trembled, black dots swimming across her vision.

She snatched the bottle, grateful he hadn't put it far, and yanked the cork free. Ignoring the sharp pull of pain in her back, she tipped her head back. The vodka scorched down her throat, her stomach burning as if filled with fire ants.

But the daze that followed?

Worth every fucking drop.

"Whoa!" Dravyn ripped the bottle from her hands. "Let's not kill ourselves. You haven't eaten much." He sighed irritably. "I should have thought of that *before* giving you the booze. You can tell I've done this before," he remarked sarcastically, the derision dripping off each word.

"Done what before?"

"Taking care of someone. And before you ask *why*—I'm doing it for Dex. If he's found happiness away from Estrus, the person who gave it to him is precious."

Precious One, Eran had called her.

The words stabbed straight through her chest.

A horrid pang of homesickness wrapped around her ribs and squeezed. She would've given anything to see Grayson. To feel that aura of invincibility again. To sink into his warm, solid arms and let the world fall away. To hear his voice. To hear him promise to destroy anyone who hurt her.

Dravyn gathered more rags, kept them dry this time, and wrapped them carefully around her torso. His hands were clinical, respectful—never straying, never lingering.

At this point, Eva wouldn't have cared if he touched her. But she appreciated that he didn't.

"So, I'll ask you again, Eva," he said, more insistent this time. "Do you love my brother?"

"Yes," the word came out in a choked sob. Everything she'd bottled up came to the surface, and she felt it all with the force of a tidal wave. She missed him. Gods, she missed him so damned much her heart could burst. "More than anything."

He moved around to her front and lifted a soaked cloth to her face, gently dabbing the scrapes on her cheek. The alcohol burned through the wounds, but she didn't show it. His gaze flicked to her raw wrists then to the shirt bunched in her lap.

He stepped back, rising, then began unbuckling his armour, dumping one piece at a time on the floor as if they were worthless chunks of metal—not rare, impenetrable mithril. When he ran out of armour, he gripped the hem of his tunic and peeled it up and over his head. Scar-marred snow white skin stared back at her, hard muscles sculpting every inch of his torso.

In a blink, the visage of marble and pain was gone, the tunic the only thing she could see as he held it out to her.

She blinked, confused. The shirt stayed in the air between them, soft and worn from use. It stunk of sweat and grime—and that familiar scent she'd mistaken for home. Steel. It reminded her of Grayson.

He gave it a little wave, as if coaxing a skittish animal. "Here. I promise it won't bite."

"Why?" she rasped.

He rolled his eyes. "Again? Do you question Dex this much?"

"Grayson," she corrected him. "His name is Grayson. And yes. If there is a need for it."

"I bet he *loves* that," he said dryly.

"I think he does."

Right then, his eyes softened. He placed the tunic in her lap then sat back on his rear. He dragged his pack toward him and rummaged through it for a dirty tunic that had seen far worse days than the one he gave her. He slipped it over his head then went about buckling his armour back on.

"What's he like now?" he asked, quieter. His gaze couldn't quite meet hers. "How can you love someone like him?"

She blinked, taken aback by the question—and the sincerity in his eyes. His age showed in that moment, as did the quiet love for his brother, even if he didn't know how to name it.

"He's the bravest man I know," she said, quiet but not weakly. "He's strong, not just physically. After everything he's endured..." After enduring countless lashings when she could barely withstand the ones Darius had inflicted on her. "He still wakes up every day and chooses to fight. To do good. Even when it would be easier to fall back into who he used to be. He may be feared and hated by most, but it doesn't stop him from doing his duty. He's the best damned Dragon Knight anyone has ever seen. But that's not why I love him."

"It's not?"

"No. I love him because he's not perfect—and doesn't pretend to be. He just tries to be his best self. And, for me, that's enough. *He's* enough."

Dravyn stared at her, something unreadable flickering behind wide eyes, his lips parted like he might respond—but he said nothing.

"And I know that he'll find me," she went on, letting the truth sink in her core. "He'll burn the whole world to the ground until I'm back in his arms."

Because that was who Grayson Smith was. He could hide from the Slayer all he wanted, but deep down, Dex was as much a part of him as Grayson was. The only difference between then and now was that Grayson was around to balance him out. To stop him from going too far. He'd only hurt those who deserved it. Because she'd learned very recently that justice wasn't enough to stop the bad guys. Sometimes they needed to face the Slayer's wrath.

Dravyn tilted his head curiously. "And that doesn't scare you?"

"No. He may think it does, but I knew what I signed up for."

He blinked again. Stared some more. Then he nodded, slapping his knees as he rose to his feet. "Put that shirt on. It's mithril. It'll keep you safe... Unless you want to walk around this temple with your tits out?" He arched an eyebrow, as if to dare her.

She shuddered at the thought. "Not particularly."

Lamely, she lifted her arms above her head—or tried to. The pain lancing down her back stopped her from lifting them halfway.

"Here—"

"No," she ground out. "I can do it."

He looked like he wanted to protest, but then he shrugged and turned his back to her. "You have one minute, then I'm stepping in. We shouldn't keep Darius waiting."

The mention of Darius sapped whatever warmth Dravyn had given her.

She didn't give herself the chance to hesitate. Biting down on her lip, she tucked her arms in the holes then threw them up and let the tunic shimmy down her body. The fabric scraped over her wounds, but she didn't flinch. Not this time.

The hem fell down to her mid-thigh. Grayson's shirt had fit better, just enough to cover her rear. With Dravyn's? She felt like a toddler trying on his clothes.

Finding the strength within herself, she climbed to her feet and faced down the eternal darkness outside the lightstone's ring. Somewhere in there, Darius was lurking, waiting for them. She could either move on her own volition—or he could hunt her down and drag her into this temple's depths.

She peered back at the door.

No escape. No mechanism. No sound to even indicate Arkon and the others were trying—or could—break it down.

The only way was forward.

She had to endure Darius just a little bit longer, until she could find the right moment to escape.

For Grayson, she'd keep fighting. For Jacob, she'd hold her head high. For Anna, she'd keep living. For Sasha... she'd never give up. Not now. Not ever.

Whatever it took, she'd find her way home again.

"Come on," Dravyn said.

Clenching her fists, she followed him into the temple's depths.

CHAPTER 57
THE UNRAVELING

Anna stared up at the brilliant blue sky. Not a cloud in sight. Just endless colour—vivid and impossibly wide. So open. So unapologetically beautiful.

It looked like a painting. One of the pieces she used to stare at with Leo in the art gallery, back when she believed the world was full of wonder and stories always had happy endings. Back when they only had each other for company, while their parents were busy running a kingdom.

She'd forgotten how *blue* it could be, not quite cerulean, not in the desert. More cornflower. She'd forgotten how the light shimmered in the air, like the sky itself was humming a song only the wind could hear.

Tears pricked at the corners of her eyes.

She hadn't thought she'd see the sky again—feel the sun's warmth on her skin—before she died. Those caves had been so dark, the lightstones pale and ghostly against the walls. Down there, she'd felt like she was already one step in the grave. They'd certainly been deeper than six feet.

She was living on borrowed time. She knew that. As soon as she lost her usefulness to Darius, he would kill her. She'd made peace with that the moment he forced Mithbane down her throat.

She had lived well. She had sung before crowds. Danced in front of lords and ladies. She had made mistakes—gods, so many—but she had also found a love worth fighting for. Built a family when her own had failed her.

No regrets.

Even now, as her lungs rasped for breath, broken ribs stabbing with every inhale, and the sand rumbled beneath her spine, she didn't regret a thing.

The sandworm was right beneath her. The earth trembled, grains shuddering as it opened its maw to swallow her whole. Dust billowed into the air, clogging her throat, making her already struggling lungs scrape for something—*anything*—to hold on to.

What will kill me first? she wondered grimly. *Suffocation or the worm's digestive acid?*

No. That wouldn't be her last thought.

She shut her eyes.

Let it be Jacob. His smile. His laugh. The little things he did to brighten her day—the things he didn't think she noticed. But she always did.

The ground gave out beneath her. Hot breath hit her back—

A roar split the air.

Then claws snapped around her waist, yanking her sideways so fast the world blurred. Wind tore past her ears.

Pain exploded inside her—flashes of white-hot agony as her body twisted midair. A rib punched through her lung. Her ankle snapped like a twig. Her scream shredded her throat but never made it out.

Slam!

Stone cracked. The world came to a jarring halt. For a moment, all she could do was exist inside pain and whiplash. She was alive—but barely holding on.

Arkon's claws eased open, crystal eyes locking on her the moment they stopped moving. His breath shuddered against her body. He was curled around her protectively, cradling her against him as he took the brunt of the impact. Behind him, his back was braced between two fractured pillars. Blood streamed down the webbing of his wings, trickling over dark scales that rose and fell with labored breaths.

Wheezing, she stared up at him. It was all her body would allow her to do while she processed what had happened.

He'd *dived* for her.

Headlong. No chance to pull up. He'd seen the pillars. Known he'd crash. And still—he'd come for her.

To save her.

To save Aster.

She would've found that incredibly heartwarming—*if her body didn't feel like it was shattering apart*. Or if the sandworm wasn't breaching, now only twenty feet away.

The sandworm's roar rattled the air as it reached the peak of its climb, its shadow swallowing them whole as it loomed over them. The ground quaked violently as gravity called it back to the desert. It arched towards them in a final effort to claim its prize.

With a low, pained growl, Arkon pushed onto three claws, cradling her tightly in the fourth. His wings pumped—once, twice—and then they were airborne, twisting out of the worm's path. Once they were clear, he angled himself towards the others. Toward Jacob. Toward her beautifully fierce dragon.

Eran shot past them, a guttural warrior-cry ripping from his throat as he dove straight for the worm. Claws out. Teeth bared. He collided with the creature's thick, segmented hide, the sheer force of impact sending shockwaves through the air and tipping the worm off balance.

The beast shrieked, an ear-splitting screech that shattered the dunes and sent birds scattering in the distance.

Eran clung tight, wings fanning for balance as he sank his teeth into the worm's side, blood spurting in thick ropes across the sand. The worm twisted violently, trying to dislodge him—but Eran held fast, using his back claws to rake down its side, carving deep, searing wounds.

Then Glade struck.

The sand trembled as her magic surged beneath it—ripples racing outward like a current. A dozen stone pillars erupted upward, towering and jagged. They curled like fists around the worm's body, slamming into it with earth-shattering force and pinning it in place.

The worm bucked. Thrashed. *Screamed.* It coiled and writhed, but the more it fought, the more the stone gripped tighter, locking its joints, anchoring it to the desert floor.

Eran launched again—this time for a break in between segments. His jaws closed around soft flesh. With a savage wrench, he ripped free a chunk of meat, spraying blood like a fountain.

The worm's roar faltered into a gurgle.

Glade's scales bristled as more columns rose, driving through the worm's body like spears.

By the time it collapsed, twitching—its massive frame half-buried in its own blood and sand—the dunes had gone still. The sky was clear again. The only sounds were the dragons' victory cries, echoing like thunder over the horizon.

"Anna!" Aster's voice tore through the air, raw and trembling. She banked hard, gliding toward Arkon's flank, closer than she dared in mid-flight. "Speak! I cannot feel you."

Anna's fingers twitched against Arkon's scales. She wanted to answer. Gods, she wanted to wrap her arms around her dragon's neck and bury herself in that familiar warmth, tell her she was back—safe, home, where she belonged.

But her lungs couldn't hold air. Her chest spasmed, sharp and shallow. Each breath grated like sandpaper inside her, ribs grinding with every pulse. Darkness nipped at the edges of her vision, and her heartbeat sounded distant, as if it had already abandoned her.

"Something's wrong," Aster growled, her voice dropping to a dangerous pitch. "Land. Now."

Arkon's wingbeats shifted. With a final pump, he veered clear of the ruins and touched down just outside, giving the sandworm a wide berth. His claw unfolded with tentative care.

Before it fully opened, Aster was already there. She shoved past him, shouldering his massive form aside without hesitation. Her snout pressed into Anna's face, warm breath spilling against her skin.

"I'm here. I've got you. But you must stay with me." Aster's voice was hoarse, cracking under the weight of panic.

More tears welled in Anna's eyes. She was home. In her dragon's embrace.

She could let go now.

"Anna?" Aster snarled. "You will not die. Not now. Not before me. Hold on." She tipped her head back. "Get Eran. Now!"

Then she was back, curling tighter around Anna, as if pressing close could anchor her to this plain.

Glade alighted nearby—and then Jacob was there, skidding to her side. He seized her hand, tears streaking down his cheeks as he pressed a kiss to her knuckles.

"I'm here, baby. Everything's going to be all right."

A fresh wave of tears burned her eyes. Not from pain—she'd long since gone numb to the wreckage of her body. No, this ache ran deeper, slicing clean through her soul.

Because he was here. So rugged, so heartbreakingly handsome.

And she couldn't tell him how much she loved him.

She tried. Gods, she tried. But the words lodged in her throat, sealed behind the weight of broken ribs and collapsed lungs.

Then water sloshed around her without warning, cool and sudden, lifting her slightly from the bloodied sand. While she stared up at her beautiful Knight, Glade had formed a shallow basin beneath her.

Eran stepped forward, eyes glowing like molten emeralds.

The water bubbled and began to glow, casting its blue, shimmering light against Aster's scales and Jacob's sunburnt face.

Pain slammed into Anna like a tidal wave.

The magic didn't trickle. It crashed. Crushed. Pounded into her broken frame with the full force of a tsunami. Every pulse of power struck like a hammer to the bone—snapping her shattered ribs into alignment, flooding her lungs with air.

She arched off the basin, spine bowing under the force of it. Her scream ripped free—half agony, half a desperate cry for air.

Then her lungs filled.

She gasped, dragging in breath after breath like she'd been drowning for days. Her body shook violently. Muscles twitched. Nerves sparked awake.

The pain didn't vanish. But it became bearable. Contained. Her ribs were fixed. Her lungs were hers again. And that—*that* was enough.

Everything else, she could fight through. *Would* fight through.

The water stopped bubbling, the glow fading into the sea of sand.

On the other side of Aster, Eran staggered. A tremor rolled through his scales. Then he collapsed, gasping as the light in his eyes dimmed. His sleek body hit the sand with a heavy thud, scales glistening beneath the desert sun.

Arkon turned sharply, wings rising to cast a protective shadow over the fallen dragon. His voice rumbled with quiet concern. "You pushed yourself too hard, my friend."

Eran huffed a laugh, dust curling from his nostrils. "'*Friend*'. I haven't heard you use that word in an age." He dragged his head toward Aster and Anna, his breath coming in slow, pained gusts. "I've mended what I can, but this desert weakens my magic. Once we reach water, I can finish the healing, Anna."

She swallowed, her throat dry and raw. "You saved my life, Eran. I can bear the pain as long as I have to."

Jacob squeezed her hand. Then, gently, he lifted it to his cheek and pressed her palm there as if to remind himself that Anna was with him. "I love you, Anna," he whispered. "I love you so godsdamned much."

She smiled faintly, brushing her thumb along his jaw. "I love you too, Jake."

A scream shattered the peace that had befallen the ruins.

Her blood froze.

Grayson.

He stood at the base of the monolith, a single strand of water suspended between his hands—condensed, honed, and lethal. The magic slashed at the black stone in furious bursts, sharp enough to carve through steel—yet it barely scratched the surface.

He struck again. And again. Desperation fueled every motion, wild and frenzied.

When his magic gave out, he didn't stop. He threw himself at the wall, fists pounding, over and over, knuckles splitting open until blood smeared across the stone like war paint.

"EVA!!" He spun to face the group, chest heaving. His eyes—no longer just angry, but feral—searched for his next target. "Glade. Open this *fucking* door. Now!"

Glade stiffened at his tone, but stepped forward all the same. Her claws brushed the surface of the monolith, and the earth answered her call—magic rippling through the ground, reaching, searching—

Then fading.

She drew back, wings fluttering against her back in agitation. "Something ancient and powerful protects this temple. This door is sealed with magic beyond mine. I cannot open it."

Grayson let out a growl, low and guttural, like it was clawing its way from deep inside his chest.

Anna grunted as she shifted, trying to sit upright. Jacob caught her immediately, easing an arm around her back for support.

"It's a puzzle," she said, wincing with every breath. "They had to solve it to open it. That's how they got in."

Grayson turned to her like a storm turning toward land. He crossed the space in three strides.

Aster snarled, wings flaring protectively as she pulled Anna tight against her chest.

Grayson didn't flinch. Didn't blink. His eyes burned with something cold. Voracious. A hunger that should never belong to a man trying to save the woman he loved.

Anna froze.

She'd seen that look before. On Darius, when he thought he had Eva cornered. But in Grayson, it was different—more dangerous. Because Darius wanted power. Grayson wanted vengeance. And when love twisted into fury like this... it had the power to raze worlds.

"How did they solve it?" he snapped. His voice was clipped, sharp. The last thread of his self-control was unraveling with every breath.

Anna wet her cracked lips, heart pounding. She never thought she'd see the day when she'd fear her friend.

"I don't know," she said softly. "I was a little preoccupied at the time."

Fighting Darius had demanded everything—her mind, her body, her instincts. She hadn't seen what Dravyn did. Hadn't even thought to look.

A beat of silence.

He simmered beneath the surface.

"Think. Harder," Grayson snapped, his voice tight and sharp. "Eva is on the other side of that door—with Darius."

"I'm aware," she bit back—then immediately winced, pain rippling through her side as punishment for the outburst. "So instead of snarling at everyone like a rabid beast, use that brain and *find a way in*."

Growling, Grayson marched back to the monolith and studied it with trembling shoulders.

Jacob glanced at him worriedly then turned his attention back to Anna.

"How long has he been like this?" she asked him, keeping her voice low. She might not have her magic to amplify her hearing, but Grayson still did.

Exhaling, he raked a hand through his sweaty hair. "Since you guys left for the Desert Lands. He got worse after Arkon told us Darius had you..." His brow furrowed. "I don't know what to do with him, Anna. He's shutting me out—shutting *everyone* out."

They turned and watched Grayson move away from the monolith to study the pillars. His eyes narrowed on a pillar bearing a symbol of bull horns. He stepped closer, scanning its surface relentlessly until his gaze locked on a small plate near its base.

He stepped on it—

A shockwave slammed into his chest. He flew back like a ragdoll and hit the monolith hard enough to rattle its surface.

"Gray!" Jacob swung out of Aster's claw and ran to him, boots slipping slightly in the sand. He dropped to one knee beside Grayson, helping him up with a grunt and brushing grit off his armour. "What was that? What happened?"

Grayson grimaced, testing his shoulder with a wince. "It's a riddle," he said tightly, rotating his neck until it cracked. "One of these pillars is the answer."

Anna leaned heavier into Aster's side, forcing her eyes to focus past the haze of pain. Heat shimmered off the broken sands. Sweat trickled down her temple.

A *riddle*? Of course. This place had been built to keep people out—people exactly like Darius. What better way to keep testosterone fueled meatheads from taking power that didn't belong to them than something that made them use their brain?

Jacob stepped forward, eyes scanning the inscription carved into the monolith's base. His lips moved silently, then stilled. "War," he breathed.

Grayson's head snapped toward him. Then his gaze raked over the nearest pillars until he found what he was looking for. "The swords..." he muttered.

He didn't wait. He charged toward it, sand kicking up around his boots. Anna held her breath as he slammed his foot onto the plate.

A deep *grinding* sound shook the air. Stone against stone. The monolith's door cracked open, dust spilling from its seams like a breath exhaled after centuries of silence.

Anna's stomach twisted. The air shifted—subtly, but unmistakably wrong. The heat wasn't oppressive anymore; it felt hollow, like a void breathing down her neck. Even without her magic, she could sense the ancient force stirring, as if something older than time itself had turned its gaze on them. It sucked the warmth from the air, coiling around her bones like a damp, unshakable cloak.

Her body shuddered despite herself. Pitch blackness stared back at them. It was like a hungry maw of a sandworm, but without teeth. And somewhere in that darkness was Eva.

"How are we going to find her?" she asked, voice hoarse. Tracking someone through desert or forest left trails, clues in sand or leaves—but in that temple? Nothing.

"We?" Aster's sharp echo cut through her thought. "No. You're in no condition to move. You will stay here with me." Her claws tightened gently but firmly around Anna's waist, pulling her close to the warmth of her chest.

Fuck no.

Anna's heart hammered. She wouldn't let Jacob and Grayson storm that temple alone. Not when Eva needed her.

"I'm fine," Anna insisted, twisting against Aster's hold—but a searing pain stabbed her side. She gasped, swallowing down the shock as her body faltered.

Grayson shook his head, voice low but firm. "Stay with the dragons, Anna. You'll only slow us down."

Ouch.

He strode toward the temple entrance, the lightstone glowing steady in his hand. "Let's move, Jake."

Jacob glanced back at her, torn. He hated leaving her behind—especially now, after just being reunited—but Eva was his blood, his family. And Anna would never want him to choose her over Eva.

Most of all, Grayson needed him. She didn't know how far gone Grayson was, but Jacob was the only one who could ground him—whether Grayson showed it or not. Anna felt it in her bones. Grayson was always listening.

"I'll be right here," she promised softly, meeting Jacob's conflicted eyes.

Arkon dipped his massive head toward Aster, who curled protectively around Anna. "She will be safe."

Glade stepped closer, her voice low but sharp as a blade. "There isn't much four dragons can't take on. Focus on your task ahead—that's where the true danger lies. Return to me alive, Reckless One, or I will turn your corpse into a golem."

Jacob blinked up at her, swallowing hard. "You wouldn't actually do that... would you?"

She narrowed her golden eyes, unblinking. "Die and find out."

"Jacob," Grayson snapped, his voice sharp as steel, already stepping into the temple's shadowed maw. His silhouette blurred against the creeping darkness. "Move it or stay. I'm not waiting."

Jacob muttered a curse under his breath, fingers tightening around the hilt of his broadsword as he drew it with a practiced flick. He glanced back—just for a heartbeat—at Anna, eyes flickering with a mix of determination and yearning. "I love you."

The desert wind stirred her hair against her flushed cheeks. "I love you too. Come back to me," she whispered, voice trembling with a fragile hope.

"Always." His grin was brief but full of promise. Then, without another word, he crossed the threshold.

The ground beneath her shifted violently, a low rumble rising through the sand. Pebbles tumbled from the monolith's face. The massive door groaned and slowly rose from the earth, sealing them inside with a final, reverberating thud.

Anna clenched her fists, nails digging into Aster's warm scales as her heart pounded in her chest. Helplessness gnawed at her, the ache of having to wait for their return sharper than any wound.

But they wouldn't fail. Not with Grayson's fierce, burning bloodlust driving him forward. Not with Jacob's unwavering courage standing firm against the darkness. They would bring Eva home.

She swallowed hard, a silent prayer caught in her throat. She just hoped they weren't too late.

CHAPTER 58
NO ESCAPE

Dravyn trailed behind their merry little group. *Someone* had to keep an eye on the woman bleeding all over the dusty labyrinth floor. Darius didn't make it any easier for Eva with his demanding pace. But he didn't push her either. His attention was fixed on their surroundings, feeling for the slightest shift in the air, listening for anything out of place.

Twice, they had run into a trap, one of which had nearly lopped Dravyn's head off.

The hair on his neck prickled. That uneasy weight of being watched had settled on his shoulders the moment they stepped inside—and it hadn't left since. Whether it was the temple itself keeping tabs on them or something darker hiding in the shadows, he couldn't say.

A delightful little thought he kept at the forefront of his mind. This was no place to let his guard down.

And he wasn't crazy. He knew something was fucking with them—because the traps only showed up when they were headed the right way. Take a wrong turn? Nothing. The temple didn't care. But make progress, and it started to fight back.

Good. The sooner they found the gauntlet, the sooner they could get the fuck out of this place—and the godsforsaken heat.

He had to hand it to Eva, though. She was handling being stuck in a dark, oppressive, ancient temple better than he was. Wounded and weary, sure—but steady. She wore a stoic mask and reacted when she needed to, weaving between arrows and ducking under a swinging axe like it was second nature.

He was impressed. Her skill, her mindset, her sheer resolve. Most women he knew wouldn't have made it this far. When Darius had whipped her, he'd thought that was the end of it. That she'd finally cave to the torture, the abuse—the pain that had to be wrapping her like a second skin.

But she hadn't.

She woke up and chose to fight.

She chose to live.

Darius was wrong about her. He seemed to think she'd break down over time, but Dravyn suspected she'd only get stronger. More stubborn. More immune to Darius's special brand of torment.

A *battle of wills*. He was grimly amused by the idea of Darius finally meeting his match. In a woman, no less.

Oh, he did enjoy irony.

It was tempting—to goad her, push her just far enough to challenge Darius until *he* reached his breaking point. But doing that meant Eva would have to endure more whippings. More torment. More pain.

Normally, he wouldn't have cared. He'd have done it without a second thought.

But Eva wasn't normal.

She was Dex's lover.

No. *Lover* was too casual for what she was to Dex. If she loved him half as much as she claimed—which Dravyn wholly believed, after seeing the way her eyes lit up when she spoke about him—then she'd seen more of Dex than anyone else. Dex had *allowed* her to see more. Which meant she was something to him... something beyond Dravyn's comprehension.

He didn't know what it felt like to love. Or to be loved. To know someone so deeply and irrevocably that they consumed your world. But he'd seen it. Been curious about it. Never brave enough to explore it.

Love was a weakness. Love was exploitable. And the proof of that was limping right in front of him.

If he'd learned anything these past few days, it was that he never wanted to love. Maybe Darius wouldn't be the one to hurt him, but someone would. There was always someone else.

You're an idiot, Dex.

Did he really think he could escape their family forever? That he could just run away and start a new one across the sea?

But it was done now.

All Dravyn could do was mitigate the damage.

Which was another reason he stuck to the back—out of sight from Darius's prying eyes.

In his pocket, tucked safely away, was a vial of Eva's blood.

While she was unconscious—bleeding into the temple, saturating the very earth with her essence—Dravyn had filled a vial. He could've filled more, but he didn't want to risk them clanking together or Darius noticing the bulk in his pocket.

Since they'd left the main hallway, Dravyn had been laying a trail—one drop at a time, once a minute. Very precise. Very intentional. Most of all, very subtle.

Not enough to draw a monster. Not enough for Darius or Eva to notice if they happened to double back—which they'd already done more than once.

But enough for Dex to find them.

Assuming his tracking skills hadn't dulled in his time away from the family.

A tremor beneath his boots was the only warning he got—then iron spikes exploded from the ground.

Dravyn leapt back just in time, landing near the edge of the trap as one spike shot up where his chest had been a moment ago. He braced for more—from the ceiling, maybe—but nothing else came. Just that single cluster ahead of him. A dense spread of spikes, varying in height for maximum coverage.

It was a miracle Darius and Eva survived. They were caught in the thick of it—forced into near-impossible contortions to avoid being skewered.

Darius was arched backward, braced against a spike behind him, one leg extended out—hovering above a shorter spike below. His hands were raised overhead, gripping the air for balance. Blood dripped from a gash on his left bicep where he hadn't moved fast enough.

Eva had leapt up at the last second. She now hovered precariously between two spikes—feet planted on one in front of her, back pressed to the one behind. One slip, one twitch, and she'd be impaled by the spike below her.

Blood seeped through the tunic he'd given her, blooming across the fabric like ink on parchment in a beautifully macabre pattern.

Essence of Eva, he'd title the sketch if he had the time to draw it.

The scrunched up vision of agony on her face wasn't nearly as satisfying to look at, however.

With a tentative step, he tested the trap in case any more spikes try to make an appearance.

But while Dravyn cautiously crossed the trap, Darius eased out of his humorous position and wove his way to Eva. She tensed against her spikes, sweat beading down the side of her face. Her legs were already trembling with strain. She watched him as he came astride, eyes wide like that of a doe that realised she'd become the wolf's target.

He reached up for her—she tensed, knuckles going white around the spike. "Wh—what are you doing?"

He didn't answer.

Before Dravyn could reach them, Darius knocked the back of her legs out and heaved her onto his shoulder.

"Put me down!"

She kicked and slammed her fists into his back, but he didn't falter until they reached the other side of the trap. Seeing it was only going to activate only once, Dravyn hurried across the forest of spikes.

Darius flipped her off his shoulder, barely giving her time to steady herself. He caught her forearm in a tight grip and yanked her flush against him, a dark smile grinding across his face. "It looks like you still have some fight left. It's no fun when my toys break so easily."

She spat on his face.

His fingers dug into her jaw, pulling her closer. "You're a glutton for punishment, aren't you, little rider? Want me to whip you again? Do you enjoy it?" He tilted his head, a cruel thought crossing his eyes. "Does Dex hurt you when he fucks you?"

Dravyn's stomach clenched. He quickened his pace and slid between them. "We're close to the gauntlet, Dari. I want out of this fucking desert—then you can have your way with your new toy."

Darius's eyes narrowed on him. "Don't think I don't know what you're doing, little brother." His voice dripped slow, thick as molasses, venomous like a viper's strike.

No way he noticed—

Sweat beaded at the back of Dravyn's neck, heart pounding. Yet he wore a mask of dry indifference, hand resting on his hip, easing into a smile Darius hated. "And what might that be?"

Darius stepped back, but his Resting Bitch face didn't soften. "You're trying to spare my little rider from her fate—but you can't save her. And if you get in my way again, I'll gut you like a fish and leave the wildlife to finish the job."

Dravyn laughed—a deep, genuine laugh. He'd heard that threat before, countless times, and while Darius meant every word and had followed through on many people in the past, Dravyn couldn't help but find it amusing. "Isn't that what you did to Dex? Seemed to work out for him. Maybe you should gut me and find out what happens."

Slow and steady, Darius unsheathed his knife; steel danced in the light-stones' glow. Dravyn didn't blink. Didn't feel a lick of fear.

Maybe he'd finally found the button that pushed Darius too far.

Eva shifted behind him. "You kill him, and we'll be lost in this temple forever."

Dravyn refrained from showing his surprise, from twisting around to look at the woman who'd just defended him. Who had absolutely no reason to do so.

Dex had been the only one who'd ever protected him before—especially after learning of his preferences. He'd sworn to take that secret to the grave with him. And he had.

Darius scoffed. "Tch. Now isn't that just sweet? The decrepit defending the delinquent. When I'm done with you, you'll learn not to waste your time on sewer rats."

He shoved Dravyn aside—then rammed his fist into Eva's gut.

She doubled over with a strangled sound, heaving. The vodka she'd chugged earlier erupted onto the stone floor. She crumpled to her knees, her body trembling under the weight of pain and sheer exhaustion.

If Darius kept pushing her like this, she wasn't going to make it out of this temple alive.

He loomed over her, fist primed to strike again. "Pick yourself up, pet. I will not tolerate weakness."

On shaky legs, using the wall for support, she climbed to her feet and lifted her gaze to meet his.

Never mind the vitriol roiling in her eyes, a satisfied smirk curled on his lips. Wordlessly, he stalked down the hallway.

Dravyn moved to her side and slipped his arm under hers, pulling her from the wall. "You okay?" he asked under his breath to keep Darius from overhearing. He was on a tight string, and the last thing Dravyn wanted was to yank it tighter. Not for his sake. For hers.

Eva squeezed her eyes shut, one arm braced across her stomach. She was trying so hard to hold herself together, to deny Darius even a sliver of satisfaction. So hard, she couldn't even speak.

Dumb question.

No sane person would be okay in her position.

"Don't show weakness. Keep moving." Dravyn tightened his grip under her arm, steadying her; not just for her, but for himself. His thoughts still reeled from the moment she'd stepped between him and Darius. She had defended him. Not out of pity. Not to make a point. Just... because.

No one had ever done that for him. Not like that. People feared the Fortys clan too much to stand up to them. Or loathed them so much they'd rather watch them burn.

That was just who she was.

No wonder Dex had fallen for her. He had no choice. How could he ever resist such warmth and kindness?

Her breath came slow and ragged, but she didn't collapse again.

No words passed between them, but in the silence that followed, something lingered. A quiet, unspoken promise.

They would survive this. Together.

CHAPTER 59
NOT FUCKING TODAY

Not for the first time, Jacob's eyes drifted down to the bloodied lock of ashen hair in his left hand. His grip on his sword faltered, the blade quivering in his hand, just thinking about the blood in the main hallway.

So much blood. Too much. Intentionally brutal yet precisely enough to keep her alive.

His stomach clenched, another dizzy spell hitting him hard, *knowing* that it was Eva's blood all over the floor. That she was the one suffering by Darius's hand.

Her hair was scattered, tangled like angry roots, matted in the dry puddles, slipping between cracks, as if the temple was claiming her soul.

Those bastards had defiled his sister. Nearly killed Anna. And were now on their way to one of the weapons that had the power to wipe magic from Astrida.

Jacob wanted to keep a level head, to be the voice of reason—because Grayson definitely wasn't that person—but the fine line between restraint and release was getting thinner and thinner. He wanted to scream Eva's name until his voice gave out—or she answered back. Until she was back at his side and smiling like she used to when she was a kid.

He wanted to cry. Anna. She was alive. *Safe*. Healing with their dragons. For one terrifying moment, he thought he was going to lose her. Those silver eyes, ones that lit up his world, had been dull, hazy, lost in a fog he couldn't follow after. Her blood had been hot and slick in his hands. He'd been ready to barter with the gods to save her. But then, she came back to him, and he'd never been more grateful in his life.

He wanted to curse the gods for doing this to his family—for pushing them beyond their limits and staining their souls. They were determined to see them break, to watch them crumble under the weight of fate. But he wouldn't let his family fall. He hadn't been there for his parents or Erika, but he was here now, for Anna, for Grayson, for Leo, for Eva. He wouldn't let the gods tear them down.

He didn't know what condition he'd find Eva in—if she was still his sister or some hollowed-out version of her—but he promised himself that no matter how he found her, he'd be there for her. He hadn't been there for her after their family was murdered—not in the way he should have been.

Not when she stopped laughing. Not when he noticed the bags under her eyes grow darker. He told himself she would come to him if she needed him—and when she did, he'd drop everything. But she never came, and he wasn't sure if it was because she didn't need him.

She shouldn't *have* to reach out to him.

Never again.

Please, Eva, hang in there.

They were close, according to Grayson.

The compass had started whirling like a headless chicken the moment the door ground shut behind them—but Grayson had found a trail. It was nearly imperceptible; even Jacob's trained instincts hadn't caught it in the lightstone's glow.

Drops of blood.

When Grayson first pointed them out, Jacob panicked. After the bloodbath in the main hallway, the thought of her still bleeding, leaving a trail—it was too much. But Grayson had reasoned with him: if she were still losing blood uncontrollably, the drops wouldn't fall in such a deliberate pattern. These fell in rhythm. Purposeful. Not a sign of danger—but direction.

So they followed the trail, catching each new droplet just before the pool of light slipped past it.

Beyond the pale ring of light, the world disappeared. Dust hung thick and unmoving, the silence pressing against Jacob's skin like wet cloth—heavy, smothering. The place felt like a haunted house in the ghost stories he used to tell Eva as a kid.

Goosebumps rose on his arms. He couldn't shake the encroaching feeling that they were being watched. Guided. Not by the trail they were tracking—but by something else. Something unknown. Something... beyond.

Regardless, whether it was a trap laid by the gods, or Darius's own making, they ploughed ahead.

The silence between them stretched on. Since they found the trail, Grayson had gone terrifyingly quiet. Not that silence was particularly out of character. On missions, they limited communication when danger arose—and inside an ancient temple, Jacob couldn't think of a better time for them to *be* quiet—but it was the way the silence hung between them. The tension was tighter than a stringed bow, crackling with energy Jacob didn't understand. It felt brittle, moments away from snapping.

Usually, Grayson spared him a glance, to ensure Jacob was keeping up with him, but he hadn't looked back once. Not since Jacob had picked up a piece of Eva's hair. It was like he didn't care if he kept pace or not. If he lived or died in this temple. He was so focused on the hunt, on finding Eva, he'd completely shut out everything around him...

Something shifted above.

A pebble struck Jacob's shoulder and bounced to the ground, the sharp crack of stone on stone shattering the temple's silence like a scream in a tomb.

He looked up—and froze.

A segmented tail hung from the ceiling, twitching, gleaming like oiled iron. It reared back.

Jacob's breath hitched. Then he moved.

He dove to the ground as the barbed tail snapped down, slicing the air where his head had been. Rolling fast, he scrambled to his feet, broadsword raised. The monstrous scorpion scurried down the wall, its legs skittering with unnatural speed, pincers snapping through the heavy air like guillotines.

A lump rose in his throat. Eva had told him once—half laughing—about the time a scorpion like this nearly killed her. He'd been scared for her just hearing it. But this wasn't a story. This was now. And unlike Eva, he had no magic to cleave it in two.

Where the hell was Grayson?

The tail struck again. He barely dodged, the barb brushing past his arm. A pincer lunged—he twisted under it, stumbling. Another snapped toward his face. He slashed in desperation.

Clang!

His sword bounced off the armoured pincer, jarring his arms with the force of the deflection.

"Shit!"

The scorpion swung, hitting him full-force with one massive claw. Jacob slammed into the wall, the impact sapping the air from his lungs. Pain lanced through his back as he collapsed, blinking spots from his vision.

Pincers boxed him in.

Think, Jake. Think—

A roar tore through the temple.

Grayson.

He came charging out of the dark like Val himself, voice raw with fury. The very ground seemed to tremble beneath his feet.

The scorpion spun—but not fast enough.

Grayson's blade came down in a savage arc, slicing through the creature's tail like butter. A wet crunch, then a geyser of blue blood erupted, showering him head to toe. The scorpion shrieked, its body convulsing.

Grayson didn't pause.

He stepped in—slammed his sword into the exposed gap in the scorpion's underbelly, drove it deep, then ripped it sideways. The blade tore through flesh and chitin with a sound like tearing meat and snapping bones. Blood sprayed the walls in fat, steaming gouts.

The creature writhed as its pincers dragged itself away from them, but Grayson followed it. Relentless. He hacked through one leg. Then another. Then another. He was breathing like a beast, every strike fueled by something far more primal than efficiency.

In a last ditch effort to survive, it swung a pincer at him, claws wide open to close around his neck. He caught the base with one hand, snarling, and drove his sword through the joint until it cracked. The scorpion screeched, wrenching its pincer free.

It tried to run.

Grayson didn't let it.

By the time he finished, nothing remained of the scorpion but a twitching, mangled heap. Chunks of its carapace were scattered across the floor like discarded armour. Blood pooled beneath Grayson's feet, a deep royal blue, slick and glistening in the lightstone's glow.

He stood over the corpse, soaked to the bone, chest heaving. His knuckles were white on the hilt, as if the sword wasn't just a weapon—it was the only thing anchoring him in place.

Jacob stared, wide-eyed, pinned to the wall, both by pain and self-preservation.

Grayson didn't even flinch, gaze locked on the corpse. As if waiting for it to come alive so he could start all over again.

A pained sigh shuddered out of Jacob's throat.

Grayson snapped his attention to him, teeth bared like a cornered animal. "What are you doing?"

Jacob winced at the tone, at the cutting edge slicing right through his gut. It wasn't like he *invited* the scorpion to attack them, yet with the look Grayson pinned on him, he might as well have lathered himself in butter and painted a big sign saying "free buffet".

"Stop stalling."

Jacob shoved off the wall, his legs unsteady beneath him. "Stalling? You think I *purposely* lured that monster to us? Why in Five Hells would I do that?"

Grayson didn't flinch. His glower was dry, merciless, carved from ice. "You're scared of Darius. You're drawing this out so you don't have to face him again."

The words hit harder than Jacob wanted to admit. He'd been scared. Still was. For the fight ahead of him. For what condition he'd find Eva. But it wasn't fear that had nearly gotten him killed—it was desperation. Their ceaseless hunt. Not once had they stopped to make a plan. To *think* about what they were really walking into, with Darius, with this temple.

And it wasn't Jacob's fault.

"Excuse me?" His voice came out rough, disbelieving. He'd put up with a lot of shit over the years—from Grayson, from their enemies, from himself—but not this. Not today. Not fucking today. "We've been running around this temple for hours—no plan, no intel, no backup—because *you've* lost all sense of reason. That scorpion? *You* were so lost in your rage you ran right past it. I get that you're stressed and angry, but this—" he gestured to Grayson, to the simmering rage and bone-deep fury barely restrained behind his eyes "—this needs to stop. If Darius or this temple doesn't kill us, you will."

The air shifted. That crackling energy Grayson wore like his mithril cloak snapped tight, colder than before.

Grayson's voice dropped, quiet, lethal. "I'll do whatever the fuck I have to to get Eva back. You can either get out of my way—or you can join the scorpion."

Silence. Just *silence* rang between them.

Jacob stared, breath lodged in his throat.

There it was.

The moment he had been waiting for, but hoping—no, *praying*—would never come.

The day Grayson Smith died.

"Then do it," he rasped. "If that's what it takes."

Because if Grayson was truly gone—if this version, this weapon shaped by grief and rage, was all that remained—then better Jacob die now than watch him lose himself further.

Or maybe... maybe it would be enough to snap him out of it. To draw some line in the sand before it was too late. Before Grayson forgot what it meant to care about something other than vengeance.

Jacob's gaze held steady, even when Grayson's jaw tensed. Even when that furious glare faltered, and he wanted to sag in relief.

"Do it or don't," Jacob said, quieter now, twisting the blade just a little more. Pushing him deeper or pulling him out, he didn't know, but at least then they would stop bickering and get to what really mattered. "We're wasting time Eva doesn't have."

Grayson didn't answer. Just turned away. In a voice barely more than a growl, he said: "Fine. Then keep the fuck up."

He strode ahead into the dark.

And Jacob followed, unsure if he was following his best friend into battle or Deximus Fortys.

CHAPTER 60
FROM ONE MONSTER TO ANOTHER

Eva squeezed her eyes so tight white dots swam behind her lids. She clenched her fists until her palms bled and the pain flashed through her arms. Sometimes, she purposely stubbed her toe on an uneven slab. Just to feel *something*.

Anything but the fire down her back.

It didn't matter what she did, if she hunched over, shifted her weight, straightened her shoulders—nothing alleviated the pain. It clutched her in its ravenous jaws. Possessed her. *Became* her.

Yet amongst the bottomless pit of agony she had fallen into, she bit her tongue and held her chin up. She had no choice. The moment she showed weakness, the slightest hint that she couldn't handle it, Darius was there. As if he had some kind of sixth sense that could detect when she was about the crumble. Then she would find a new welt or bruise, a new reason to limp or wince.

Show no weakness, Dravyn had told her—and she played those words in her mind over and over again like a mantra. They might just be what saved her life.

When she wasn't trying to drive the pain out of her body, she was taking in the vastness of the temple, memorising every turn they took, every misstep they wandered into. The temple had thrown enough traps and wrong turns at them, that she was wondering if it was trying to make an opening for her. Or maybe she was just delirious from starvation and dehydration.

When they took breaks—as few and far between as they were—Dravyn gave her a few pieces of dried fruit and meat, and a couple of gulps of water. Just enough to keep her alive. Enough to keep her weak. Feeble.

She hated how brittle she felt. Hated how Darius's Mithbane had reduced her body to skin and bones. Now, if she tried to fight them, she wouldn't be able to overpower them. She wouldn't be able to run very far. She wasn't even sure she could fend for herself if it came to having to hunt for food or make a shelter.

But she wouldn't let it break her. Not when her dignity was lost. Not when her autonomy had been stripped. Not when she felt as powerless as Darius said she was.

Pain and suffering is only temporary, she'd tell herself when she hit her lowest points, alone and afraid, wedged between Darius and Dravyn. She'd get out of this... Somehow. She just had to bide her time until the moment arose...

Or you can stay with Darius, a voice whispered in the back of her mind. *Let him make you stronger. Let him break you and remold you into a weapon worth fearing.* This voice had been growing louder the closer to the artifact they got. A hum buzzing just behind her ears, taunting, teasing, reminding her how fragile her mind had become.

She was tempted to blame the artifact for allowing true weakness to seep into her thoughts; it made sense, if this item was magical and powerful, it could make her feel and hear things that weren't there...

Or she could own up to her despair, see it for what it really was: Darius was whittling her down. Slowly, piece by piece, he was chipping away at her armour. The lack of food and water was deteriorating her body. The encroaching darkness was heavy, too much for her already weary soul. Slowly, ruthlessly slowly, she was sinking.

There was no way to tell how long time had passed. She'd lost count how many times they'd paused to rest. She wasn't even sure when the last time she truly slept was, aside from when Darius gave her too much Mithbane.

Gods, she was tired. So damned tired. Her feet felt like her boots were filled with lead. Her arms might as well be tied to anchors that she was dragging behind her.

How long can I keep going like this?

Why was she fighting so damned hard? If she gave in, Darius would feed her properly. Let her bathe in the last of their water. He'd stop adding to her long list of reasons to falter.

Yes. Why fight? Darius will look after you, just give in...

Eva shook her head. The movement, even small, threw her off balance. She stumbled. Dravyn's hand seized her arm and righted her. "Steady," he murmured in her ear. He released her just as quickly as he'd caught her.

She didn't look back at him. Didn't dare look at him after Darius had punished her for defending him. The less attention she drew to herself, the better off she would be. The higher chance she had of making it out of this.

But she hoped he knew how grateful she was for his help. It wasn't killing Darius and freeing her of this misery, but it was something. Those little moments reminded her she was still human. Not just a *puppet*. They were the thread she clung to when the tears burned in her eyes, the only thing keeping her from unraveling completely.

She was beginning to realise that he was just as trapped as she was. Not physically and he certainly had enough autonomy to eat as much as he wanted and to bring a bottle of vodka along for the ride. But she watched them when they hit an intersection: Dravyn provided the information, and Darius made the decision. If Dravyn talked back, Darius belittled him. If Dravyn tried to take charge—especially when he was in the right—Darius overrode him. And Dravyn let him. He didn't fight back. Never once raised his hand to defend himself. She didn't know if it was out of fear or lack of options. Because where would he go? Who would take in a Fortys Prince?

In that, she found a weird sense of comradery. She wasn't alone in this. Not entirely.

You really are losing your mind. He's still a Fortys. He helped kill Sasha and Anna. He captured you. He does nothing to stop Darius from beating you.

A bout of nausea hit her. Biting back a groan, she wrapped her arms around her stomach. Her eyes fixed to the back of Darius's head, who hadn't noticed yet. Hopefully, he wouldn't for a while, if she could keep her stomach under control. She was getting better at it, every time the cycle came back to this.

Withdrawal.

It was usually the tremors that gave her away. The sweat she could hide, use exertion as an excuse. But, try as she might, she couldn't stop her hands from shaking, her teeth from clattering. Her body was warning her that the Mithbane was on its way out of her system and she needed another dose. Soon.

She pushed her body as far as it could go, held on as long as she could bare it, and searched desperately for Arkon's soul, for the tether that tied them together. For any magic that could free her from this prison. But she could never pass the tremors. Her lips parted before she could slam down on her resolve, and Darius heard her chattering teeth. Moments later, that evil silver liquid slithered down her throat and her traitorous body went still, complacent once again.

Not this time.

If she prepared her mind and body enough before they came this time, she could find a way to control them—or at least limit them.

That's what you thought last time.

No. She refused to let those dark thoughts slip in. They would not be her master—

The ground rumbled beneath her feet.

Her joints locked up, muscles coiling on instincts. Her gaze bounced down both ends of the hallway, to the ceiling, to the floor, to the walls. Dravyn closed in behind her, his warmth a breath away.

The tremor ceased.

No trap. Not one they could see, anyway.

Dravyn blew out an irritated breath. "That's the third false trap. The temple is fucking gaslighting us."

Darius peered past them, a cruel smile curling on his face. "Or maybe we're not the only ones triggering traps."

A gasp slipped past her lips before Eva could stop it. Grayson and Jaocb found a way into the temple. They were coming.

Before hope could bloom deep into her bones, her stomach churned violently. Acid rose in her throat, and she balled her hands into fists, pressing her lips tight together to keep it down. To hide any sign of her withdrawal from Darius.

"Or," Dravyn said tightly, "the temple is fucking with us. This place isn't normal and it would be foolish to assume it is. Let's move, we can't be far from the gauntlet now."

A gauntlet?

All of this—for a piece of armour?

Darius tossed a sneer at him then continued down the path. Dravyn trailed after him. Neither of them looked back at her, knowing she would follow like the obedient *pet* she was.

Because what other choice did she have? Alone, weak, worn thin—she wouldn't last five minutes in this gods-cursed temple if it decided to throw another trap her way. She'd be dead before she took her second breath.

And yet... her feet dragged. Her head turned. She couldn't stop staring down the hall they'd come from. Somewhere back there, Grayson and Jacob were navigating this labyrinth, maybe even getting closer. Maybe calling her name.

If she ran—if she risked it—could she find them before the temple claimed her? Could she even make it ten steps?

Then the floor trembled beneath her boots.

It started small. A low hum, like wasps trapped in the walls. The sound grew manic, voracious, seizing the temple from the inside out. Stone cracked underneath her. The walls groaned. Dust rained from the ceiling as stone shifted violently. Her legs buckled, forcing her to stagger toward the wall for balance.

A sharp crack split the air above her.

She looked up—and a massive slab broke loose. It crashed to the floor just ahead with a deafening *slam*. Dust exploded in a thick cloud, swallowing everything. She coughed, eyes burning, lungs clawing for air that wouldn't come.

Torches ignited on the walls either side of her.

When the dust settled, she blinked at the jagged pile of rubble in front of her.

A wall.

Darius and Dravyn were gone. Sealed off.

Her chest heaved—not from fear, but from sudden, blinding clarity.

This was her chance.

Freedom. Within her grasp. The idea was so foreign she didn't recognise it at first.

She wouldn't waste it.

Her limbs screamed as she moved. Muscles seized. Bones ached. But she took a step down the hall—away from the wall, away from Darius. Her heart pounded like thunder, loud and relentless, against her ribs. Another step. Another. Each one less certain, more frantic. Until her body remembered the rhythm.

She was running.

Boots slapped against the stone, every impact jolting pain up her calves and through her spine. Her breath burned in her throat—raw, ragged, torn from a body unfit to run. She'd been starved, drugged, dismantled piece by piece—yet still, she ran.

Torches flared to life as she passed, casting ochre hues along the corridor like flares of hope. The temple—no, the gods themselves—seemed to guide her toward freedom. Never mind the dark unfurling behind her. Her body was a husk, brittle as a leaf clinging to autumn's final branch, bones light, muscles trembling. But she didn't stop. Couldn't. Because something—someone—wanted her to reach the end.

Just like one of Anna's runs, she told herself, a knot of grief gripping her heart. Anna had pushed her hard, stretched her endurance until she thought her legs would snap. But she never left her behind. She always believed Eva had one more step in her. One more mile.

I'm going to make it out, Anna.

Endure.

Live.

Survive.

A stitch sliced at her side. Her arms pumped sluggishly. Her boots felt like they were filled with wet sand. Tears sprang to her eyes—hot, aching, bleeding—but she didn't wipe them away. She didn't slow. She didn't falter.

Keepgoingkeepgoingkeepgoing

Don't stop.

Somewhere ahead, something shifted in the air.

A pull. Gentle at first—like a thread snagging on her soul. It swelled in her chest, between her heart and the darkness ahead.

She'd know that feeling anywhere—like the echo of her own heartbeat, like breath in her lungs. Even with her power stripped, her Bond dulled, she knew it in her bones.

Magic.

Her steps faltered. Her head jerked up.

Grayson.

She didn't know *how* she knew. Didn't know how it was possible for him to have so much power she could feel it in her magicless state. She didn't care.

He was *here*.

"Grayson!" Her voice tore from her throat, hoarse and desperate. The name echoed off the stone. She barely heard it over the ragged rasp of her breath. "Jacob!" she called, hope flaring in her chest so bright it hurt.

She waited for an answer. For a footstep. A voice. Anything.

But only silence returned.

The torchlight flickered ahead of her, flames guttering as though the very air recoiled. Shadows twisted on the walls, stretching longer than they should, coiling like fingers ready to snatch her by the throat.

Another breathless second passed.

Then she heard it—footsteps. Dragging along the ground, slow and grating. Stone scraped beneath a heavy weight, too deliberate to be anything good. Something massive stalked the hall.

Her heart plummeted into her stomach.

Not Grayson.

Not Jacob.

She stumbled back a step. Then another. But the shadows followed, lurching toward her with an ancient hunger.

This wasn't freedom.

It was a trap. And she'd foolishly run straight into it like a hope-deprived maniac.

A breath hissed past her ear, cold and primal. Dread knotted deep in her bones.

Eva ran. Again.

Not toward freedom.

But away from a predator.

CHAPTER 61
DUTY

They weren't moving fast enough.

Weren't fighting hard enough.

This godsforsaken temple threw every fucking trap in its arsenal at them, and still Grayson wouldn't slow. He wouldn't falter. He wouldn't stop.

Not until Eva was safe.

The temple reeked of rot and depravity, like the walls had absorbed centuries of blood and betrayal and were still exhaling it through the stone. Every breath scraped his throat, thick with dust and ancient suffering. The walls whispered if you listened too long. It might have once been a sacred place to worship Val—as evident by the many depictions of the god of war in the various rooms they'd found themselves in.

But now it was nothing more than a tomb. Old. Decrepit. Ravenous.

For souls.

And maybe that was fitting. He'd buried enough of himself already.

Jacob's voice still echoed in his ears. Sharp, accusing, but worse—true. That was the part that festered. It clawed at his chest, seared through his ribs, squeezed his lungs tight.

Do it or don't.

Grayson had *wanted* to. Gods, in that moment, with all his fury snarling just beneath his skin, he'd wanted to ram his sword through Jacob's ribs—into his heart. He wanted to tear into him like he'd torn into that scorpion. Not because it would solve anything, but just to *shut him up*. To stop him from trying to drag him back, to save what little humanity Grayson had left.

He didn't want to be saved.

He was beyond it.

Grayson didn't have what it took to save Eva. Dex did.

He couldn't afford to worry about Jacob. Not down here. Not in this place, where the air thickened with every step, where something ancient and cruel watched from the walls. He couldn't think about what Darius might be doing to Eva right now—not without losing what little control he still had.

All he needed was rage.

Rage, and the will to keep moving.

Something Dex excelled at.

The sound of stone grinding against the earth hit them first. Then the temple began to shake—not for the first time, but this time it was violent. Visceral. Jacob stumbled behind him, swearing under his breath.

Grayson planted his feet, sword ready. Always ready, in here.

But then it stopped.

And nothing happened.

They exchanged a glance. Dread crept up Grayson's spine like vines—

He crushed it.

No time for dread. No time for fear.

Kill. Survive. Find Eva.

That was it. That was all that mattered.

The temple had grown more volatile with every step. Each quake hit harder than the last. Magic thickened the air, choking it—flooding the halls until it bled from the stone. It pulsed through him now, feeding his power, winding tighter with every breath. Preparing him.

Kill him. Save her.

The words beat through him. Not in his own voice. Feminine. Cold. His mother's, maybe. A voice he had long since forgotten.

"Grayson!"

His heart stopped.

That voice—raw, cracking, but unmistakably his Starling's.

Something inside him *shattered*, like an ill-tempered blade.

She'd called his name. Not Jacob's. Not Arkon's. *His.*

"Eva!"

"Grayson, wait!" Jacob called. "What if it's a trap?"

Grayson didn't answer. He moved like a wraith through a graveyard, boots silent over stone. Trap or no, it didn't matter. If it got him one step closer to her, he'd take it. He wasn't risking her life on a what if.

An intersection rose ahead.

Footsteps—coming from the left.

His heart lurched before he could stop it. *I'm coming, Starling—*

Slam!

He collided headfirst into a body. Bone against bone. Skulls struck and limbs tangled.

But Grayson was already moving—rolling, flipping the figure beneath him, pinning them to the floor.

"Star—" the word died in his throat.

The eyes staring up at him weren't Eva's. Not even close. They were as black as the temple's depths.

Behind him, Jacob sucked in a breath. "Grayson—"

A grin cut through his jarred brain. Dark. Twisted. Familiar.

"Hello, brother," Darius said.

Grayson's knife was already lunging for his ribs.

Darius twisted, jamming a foot between them, and kicked him off. Grayson hit the ground, rolled, and landed beside Jacob.

"She's not here," Jacob murmured.

Grayson snapped his head toward Darius—and caught sight of Dravyn, staring at him wide-eyed. Standing in an empty hallway. No one else.

Grayson's lip curled up, grip tightening on his blade. "Where is she?"

"We got split up," Dravyn said.

Darius's smile vanished. His head turned slowly, eyes honing on Dravyn. His glare was sharp enough to draw blood—cold, venomous, and full of quiet promise.

Dravyn didn't flinch. His jaw tightened, but his gaze stayed fixed—locked on Grayson. Rigid. Unwavering. Unyielding.

He hadn't slipped up. That had been deliberate. A choice. He was helping them. Why?

Grayson didn't have time to dig for the answer.

"Jacob, go," he hissed. "She can't be far."

"On it." Jacob didn't hesitate. He backed up a few paces, then disappeared into the corridor where they'd heard Eva's voice.

"Dravyn," Darius snapped.

Dravyn cast Grayson one last look. A flicker of something passed between them—warning... or an apology. Then he nodded once and slipped after Jacob, silent as a shadow.

Then it was just the two of them.

Darius's gaze raked over Grayson, a familiar rage roiling just beneath the surface of those obsidian eyes. It had always been there, festering as long as Grayson could remember.

No one hated Sylus more than Darius, and Eva was his way out. His key to freedom.

For years, Sylus dangled wealth and power in front of him like scraps just out of reach. Promised him the crown. Promised him the future of Estrus and all its resources.

But then came Dex's sixteenth birthday.

And Sylus stripped it all away.

He chose Dex's quiet, calculated fury over Darius's loud, volatile rage.

Darius never forgave that.

And when Dex thought Darius would turn against him for taking the crown, his hatred for Sylus only grew stronger.

Because it hadn't been Dex's fault.

Sylus had dangled the throne like a carrot, then yanked it away the second Dex came of age. *He* was the one who robbed Darius of everything.

But it wasn't until Grayson walked away—left the family, the crown—that Darius finally turned on him. And Grayson hadn't blamed him for that. They'd made plans, a future together, and Grayson abandoned him. Both of his brothers.

But now Darius had his sights set on Eva.

That was the line.

Kill him. Kill him. Kill him. The words ricocheted through his mind, beating his skull relentlessly. Smashing every bit of resolve that stopped him from going for the kill.

"Tell me, brother," Darius purred, "did you come here for her... or for me?"

"What difference does it make?" Grayson spat, fists tightening around the hilt of his sword. Just one opening—that's all he needed. One slip, one second. "You're not leaving this temple alive either way."

Darius grinned, sweet but far from deadly—like poisoned molasses. "Are you sure about that, Dex? If you came for her, you would've chased her. Not stay here... with me."

His words sank deep.

Grayson stiffened. He hadn't thought to go after her. Jacob was the tracker. The hunter. He would find her. Protect her. Grayson was the weapon. He was meant to face Darius.

Wasn't he?

But the thought coiled like a barbed wire inside him. Jacob hadn't been enough to stop the scorpion. Or the warg. Or that godsdamned giant cobra.

What if he wouldn't be enough to bring Eva home?

His stomach twisted, a knot of doubt winding tighter.

He gritted his teeth, forcing the panic down.

Jacob had to be enough. Because Grayson couldn't be in two places at once. Because he wasn't the one best equipped to track her.

Because he had to deal with *this*.

Darius's voice slithered in, "Who do you think will find her first?" he mused, as if they weren't standing on the edge of tearing each other's throats out. "Dravyn's fast, but the Knight—he's a hunter, like his sister. He'll get to her first, I think." A pause. A tilt of his head. "In a twisted way, I hope he does. Because then you get to see the gift I left for you."

He froze, blood curdling through his veins.

The main hallway flashed in his mind. Blood—pooling on the floor, splattered across stone, streaked like ribbons on the pillars. And Eva's hair, clumped and matted—discarded like scraps.

His voice came out rough and ragged, held on by only a thin, fraying thread, "What did you do?"

Darius shrugged casually, his grin spreading across his entire face, cutting deep grooves into his cheeks. "Nothing you or I haven't endured before."

He whipped her.

The fucking bastard whipped his Starling.

The words echoed in his skull, each pound shaking something loose inside him. Something he'd kept buried. Something vicious. Unrelenting. Draconic.

He'd seen it when Arkon protected Aster. Felt it countless other times from Eran when Eva slipped into his mind.

Magic flared in his chest—hot, volatile, clawing to be unleashed.

But no.

Magic would be too clean.

He wanted to *bleed* him.

His grip flexed around the hilt of his sword, but even that wasn't enough. He wanted flesh. Bone. To tear the fucker apart. The taste of blood in his mouth—Darius's blood.

His breath came rough, uneven.

He saw the smirk still curling on Darius's face and snapped.

All thought vanished.

Except one: Grayson wouldn't stop until Darius was choking on his own blood—gagging on every last drop.

With a guttural growl, he surged forward, swinging wildly, reckless but fierce. One blow caught Darius off-guard, cutting a shallow line across his cheek. The sight of blood pushed Grayson onward.

Darius's eyes shone with cold hatred as he landed a savage uppercut, snapping Grayson's head back. A brutal knee drove into Grayson's gut, folding him in half. He coughed, choking on the air, but his grip on his sword didn't waver.

"Is that the best you can do now, Dex?" Darius purred, circling him. "You've gotten weak. You don't deserve to get her back."

Snarling, Grayson charged for him.

Darius ducked a wild strike and delivered a crushing blow to Grayson's temple. The world tilted. Dazed, Grayson stumbled, barely catching himself before he fell.

Before he could recover, a brutal combination knocked him off balance—elbows to ribs, fists to face. Pain exploded behind his eyes. The temple seemed to spin, the walls closing in.

The last thing he heard was Darius's voice, cool and slick, in the darkness closing in on him, “Sylus was right. Love does make you weak.”

Then darkness swallowed Grayson whole.

When Grayson woke, he wasn’t in Val’s temple.

Wasn’t even in the desert.

He was lying in a four-poster bed, blue chiffon draping from the canopy above. The gauzy fabric danced with the breeze slipping in from a large, open window. Morning light pooled across the floor—soft, silver-gold, unfamiliar. Just like the room.

It was a bedroom unlike anything he'd had before. Warm colours on the walls and fluffy pillows on the bench under the window. Small comforts, like a chair in the corner and a mirror hanging on the wardrobe—a rug on the hardwood floors. Nothing grand or showy. There was a beauty in its simplicity.

Grayson waited for the panic to creep in. For his heart to slam against his ribs, for the fire in his veins to roar back to life.

He shouldn’t be here. Shouldn’t be warm, or comfortable. Shouldn’t be in a bed he didn’t remember getting into, wrapped in linen that smelled like lavender and sun. He shouldn’t be allowed to breathe this easily when Eva was out there—trapped, alone. In danger.

But he was.

Then it didn’t matter.

He turned his head, and the world slipped away.

Ash blonde hair spilled across the pillow beside him, like sunlight spun into silk. Her skin glowed against the white cotton sheets—flushed from sleep, warm and real. Lips, soft and parted slightly, were curved with the remnants of a dream. He didn’t know what she was dreaming about, but he hoped—*gods*, he hoped—it was him.

Eva.

Untouched. Unharmed. Unburdened by duty and sacrifices.

Disbelief warred with longing. He hesitated, terrified to break the illusion—then reached out anyway, brushing his thumb gently along her cheek.

Warm. Soft. *Real.*

His throat tightened, chest aching, filled with emotions that didn't belong to a man like him. Emotions he didn't know how to name. He only knew that he'd never felt more free, more *whole*, in his life.

How did they get here? *Where* was here? Was it safe to be here?

But the questions slipped away the moment Eva opened her eyes. They were heavy with sleep yet clear and bright—like dawn breaking through storm clouds. And then she smiled—a small, tender curve that softened the weight crushing his chest, a quiet promise that maybe, just maybe, they could have this.

"Mornin'," she mumbled, rubbing the sleep from her eyes.

"Have I ever told you how beautiful you are?"

She laughed, breath light and airy, as if the weight of the world had lifted from her shoulders. "Nearly every single day." She studied the lines etched into his face, her bottom lip poking out just a little, like she was trying to read him. "You had another nightmare, didn't you?"

He could barely nod, afraid that if he spoke again, the fragile spell of this moment would shatter—and she'd disappear.

"What was it this time? Sylus? Darius?"

He couldn't speak. Wouldn't dare.

She read him like an open book anyway. She inched closer, her fingers gentle as they cupped his cheek. "It was me again, wasn't it?"

Her lips brushed his forehead, soft and certain. She wove their fingers together, lifting their left hands. Matching rings glinted—silver bands threaded with black diamonds.

"Do you remember my vow to you on our wedding day? 'Forever and always.' I'm not going anywhere, Gray. No one can take me from you—and if they try..." Her voice dropped, lips barely grazing his. Her other hand slid up his chest, callouses tracing the scars she knew so well. "Let the Slayer come out. Let him ruin anyone who dares to lay a hand on his wife."

Gods be damned if he didn't love hearing those words. If he didn't love seeing her, feeling her here beside him.

But it still didn't feel real. Not yet.

He slid his hand behind her head and pulled her close, sealing their mouths together— desperate to feel her, skin on skin, body to body, soul twining with soul. Then, and only then, would this be real.

He wasn't sweet or gentle or loving. This wasn't about worshiping her body or satisfying the fire crawling through his veins. This was a claim. He intended to mark her in every conceivable way possible. With his teeth, his scent, his essence. The world would know that Eva Greene was *his* and that no one could take her from him.

Giggling, she broke the kiss, laying a firm hand on his chest before he could draw her back in. She brushed her nose against his, warm and playful. "Easy, tiger. We've made the chickens wait long enough. Help me feed them... then I'll let you drag me back to bed."

"Chickens?" he blurted.

He waited for the bubble to pop. For reality to come crashing in.

Waited.

Nothing.

Rolling her eyes, Eva slid out of bed, giving him a full view of the curve of her back and the gentle sway of her hips—a sight he could drink in for days. "Yes, the chickens." She shot him a teasing look, which faltered the moment their eyes met. "That nightmare really shook you, didn't it?" Moistening her lips, she took his hand and pulled him out of bed.

He followed without hesitation—he'd follow her to the end of the world if that was where she wanted to go.

She led him to the bay window and nestled in front of him. His arms slipped around her waist, his chin resting on her head, like muscle memory. As if he'd done this a thousand times before. As if this morning were just another chapter in a life he'd always known.

"Look at this," she said quietly. "We made this. It started with nothing, and now it's our home. Do you remember?"

Outside, sunlight spilled across the fields in long, golden streaks. The grass swayed gently in the breeze. To their right, a squat wooden coop stood fenced in with crooked boards, a few chickens pecking idly near the gate. On the left, a line of trees marked the start of a forest, its shadows cool and quiet. Peaceful.

No other buildings. No smoke rising from chimneys. No city gates or castle walls.

It was only them. Alone. Hidden in a field, between a creek and the woods.

He knew this place. The land Renkon had promised him for his service.

"I remember."

But he hadn't accepted Hargin's offer. He'd rather trade a piece of his soul than a slice of this life.

So how were they here?

He shifted slightly, arms tightening around her. Something tugged at the edge of his thoughts.

"*Grayson...*" A whisper touched the edge of his mind, a deep rumbling. Familiar. So far away.

His gaze lifted to the clear blue sky. Endless. Empty.

"Where's Eran?" he murmured. "Where's Arkon?"

Eva peered up at him, frown deepening. "At the canyon with their brood. They'll be here tomorrow morning to take us back for our rotation." She twisted in his hold, taking his face in both hands. "Are you okay, Gray?"

"Is this real?"

It looked real. Felt real. By gods, he *wanted* it to be real.

But he couldn't remember anything after the temple. Not building this home. Not their wedding. Eran's brood.

It was too beautiful. Too perfect.

"*Grayson!*" Eran's voice was louder now, more demanding. Urgent. If things were really as peaceful as they appeared, Eran wouldn't sound so frantic.

Something was wrong.

And that killed him. Because he wanted nothing more for this to be real. To hold Eva in his arms like this every morning. To help her feed their chickens. To *have a future* with her.

But it wasn't possible. Not for him. Not for what he needed to do.

"*Grayson! Wake up!*"

His eyes snapped open, staring up at the black ceiling. Magic and dread alike coiled around him, gathering to him as if it was his to command.

He was back in the temple.

And Darius was nowhere to be seen.

CHAPTER 62
NOW OR NEVER

Pain raked through Eva's legs, up her ribs, across her back. Every breath was fire. Every step felt like her bones were held together by threads that could snap at any moment.

Keep going.

She didn't know how long she'd been running. The corridor ahead never ended—it just stretched, stone bleeding into more stone, light shifting in strange, unnatural patterns. Her vision blurred at the edges. Sweat clung to her skin. Her back screamed every time her arms moved.

But she couldn't stop. Not while the sound of claws scraping against stone echoed behind her. Not while the stench of blood and something ancient and haunting permeated the air.

Not while *it* was still chasing her.

Her boots caught on the uneven ground and she stumbled, slamming a hand to the wall to keep herself upright. A pained gasp fled her lips—it was all her lungs would allow.

Grayson...

She'd heard him. She was sure of it. Just a whisper behind the roar in her ears. That tiny scrap of hope fluttered inside her like a beacon on a stormy night.

The monster hissed. Close. Too close.

Her legs kept moving before her mind caught up. She wasn't even sure where she was going anymore—just that she had to *move.* Had to survive. The temple could twist reality all it wanted, but it couldn't erase the one truth that kept her breathing: *she had to get back to him.*

The corridor bent again, and she turned with it, blinking away the black spots creeping in from the edges of her vision. Her blood felt thick, heavy. Her skin, too tight. Her lungs, never full enough.

The scraping behind her stopped.

Eva nearly tripped on herself at the abrupt silence that followed. Her heart thrashed against her ribs, pounding in her ears. So loud, she was sure the creature could hear it.

Her breath hitched as she pressed herself flat to the wall, every nerve screaming to run, hide, *scream*. But her throat was dry. Her mouth tasted like copper and dust and dread. She needed this moment to catch her breath.

She dared a glance behind her.

For the first time, she beheld the creature—because that was what it was, not man nor beast—that had been chasing her for only gods know how long. A scream locked in her throat.

Whatever it had once been—beast, human, or *other*—it had long since rotted into something else. Something *worse*.

Its flesh was a sickly grey, limbs long and gangly. The hide was stretched thin against muscle and veins; even from where she stood, she watched in grotesque fascination as its pulse beat through its veins. Feathers jutted out of its elbow joints, once long, beautiful appendages, now mottled, limping tendrils dragging behind it like chains.

Cocking its faceless head, it peered behind it, as if it could sense something in the looming darkness she couldn't see. Where eyes should be, shallow hollows took their place. There was no mouth, just a narrow hole layered with rows upon rows of teeth—a perfect channel for sucking souls straight from the husks of its victims.

Its spine shuddered down the length of its back, an external structure of individual bones, as if its ribs had been shoved out of its back in a brutal fight a millennia ago. They seemed to glisten with a black ichor and dripped from the tips, slithering over the thin, stretched hide, leaving hissing, rank marks in the floor.

Acid.

And the smell—gods, the *smell*—was death, bile, and despair. It seeped into her lungs, into her soul, clinging like a film.

And then it turned its oval head back to her, and Eva's stomach knotted. A warbling whisper escaped its mouth, sounding as though it was hissing and gurgling on its own acid at the same time.

Move. Now.

Sucking in a deep, rattling breath, she turned and hurried down the corridor.

The monster gave chase, foreclaws carving deep gouges into the stone floor. Its long sinuous tail whipped out behind it, thrashing into the walls without a care for the crumbling ceiling. Pebbles broke away, pelting the creature.

It might not care, but when one caught Eva's shoulder, it threw her completely out of balance. She careened into a wall with a pained cry, before shoving away, pushing herself back into a run. There was no time to stop. No time to think about the fire raking down her back.

Just run.

Torches lit her path, guiding her down the endless hallway. On and on she went, pushing herself, begging her body to keep going. It barely obeyed her, but somehow—*somehow*—it functioned enough to keep her just a few paces ahead of the monster.

She felt a flicker of magic in the air. A gentle caress on her soul.

The Mithbane was wearing off.

Now, if only she could live long enough to feel Arkon's soul one more time.

An intersection loomed ahead. Torchlight stretched in all directions. She had to pick a path—and fast.

Going straight had gotten her nowhere. So left or right were her options.

As she came up to the intersection, she banked hard left, boots skidding on the dusty stone as she turned. The monster was too big to turn as quickly as she did, which bought her enough time to race to the door at the end—an actual end!—of the hallway.

Running on pure adrenaline, she slammed into the wooden door. It splintered into a million pieces on impact, and she lost her balance, stumbling into the room until she fell onto her hands and knees. Stone bit into flesh—but she ignored it and leapt forward just fast enough to dodge a long, arched claw swiping for her back.

The monster had caught up and was right behind her.

She spun, weaponless, crawling backwards like a crab as it advanced. Her muscles were spent. Her lungs were sapped dry. Her heart was about to explode.

Her back hit an altar bathed in candlelight.

This was it.

There was nowhere else to run. What she had hoped would be an escape from this hell, was nothing more than a cage—

Her fingers closed around a rock. One the size of her palm.

Her eyes jumped up to the chandelier flickering above the monster. They honed in on the jagged metal and the brittle chain holding it to the ceiling.

One shot. It was all she had.

The foul stench of rot was eminent. That horribly warbling whisper from the creature's mouth was louder. Its shadow crept higher, grew darker, looming and hungry.

Now or never, Eva.

Summoning the last of her strength, she pulled her arm back—then whipped it forward. The rock darted across the room, over the monster, and struck the chain. The impact jolted the chandelier. It swung with an awful screech under the strain. Wax dripped onto the monster's back. Eva's breath caught—

The chain *snapped.*

The chandelier dropped onto the monster's spine, catching on bone and flesh. The monster reared back with an ear-splitting roar.

Eva immediately covered her ears and curled her feet to her chest, pressing herself tight against the altar. Claws swiped through the air, its tail whipped around the room, that awful maw screamed and screamed as it bucked to throw the chandelier off.

Her stomach dropped. The chandelier was supposed to kill it. But it seemed to only send it into a desperate frenzy for survival. She was stuck between an altar and an enraged monster—waiting for it to bleed out or for it to kill her during its struggle.

Stupid. So stupid.

I'm sorry, Arkon.

For a heartbeat, something tugged at the edge of her mind. A ripple through the Bond. Pain. Frustration. Fear.

Then—

Dravyn burst through the doorway. His eyes snapped to the monster immediately, going wide—then they swept through the room, fast yet thorough, until their gazes locked.

"Need help, Precious?"

He didn't wait for an answer—she clearly did—and leapt for the monster.

Steel met rotten flesh with a sickening squelch.

His blade drove deep into the creature's neck, splattering black ichor across the walls. The monster reared back with an ungodly scream, limbs flailing, and *ripped* the sword from its own throat with unnatural strength. Foul blood poured from the wound, thick and bubbling like oil.

It swiped at Dravyn with a grotesque limb. He sidestepped the spindly claws with a breath to spare—

Then Jacob was there, barreling through the doorway with a war cry that spurned hope in her heart. His blade plunged into the creature's hindquarters with brutal force. It shrieked, body buckling, dragging its limbs across the floor in a thrashing attempt to recover.

Dravyn didn't hesitate. He surged forward and thrust upward, driving his sword into its chest. Bone cracked. Rancid flesh split apart in steaming, molten layers. The beast spasmed, its mouth opening wide in a silent, twitching scream.

Jacob charged then *leapt*, both hands gripping his sword. He brought it down, aiming for the neck where Dravyn had torn it open earlier.

Steel cleaved through tendons and vertebrae in a single, powerful stroke.

The creature's head hit the ground with a heavy, wet *thud.*

It rolled once. Twice. And stopped at Eva's feet.

The body spasmed violently, limbs jerking in horrible disarray—blood and ichor spilling onto the floor, soaking into the cracks.

Silence.

And for a moment, all that remained was the sound of Eva's ragged breathing.

Panting, Dravyn heaved his sword onto his shoulder, placing a hand on his hip. He looked down at her, face smudged by blood, hair matted by grease, shirt torn where claws slashed at him. And smiled. *Smiled.*

"You just *had* to make friends, didn't you?"

Tears burned in her eyes. She didn't know if it was from pain, relief, or dread. They all melded together in a big messy conglomerate of emotions.

A sword clattered to the ground on her right. She turned—barely—then let her tears run freely.

Jacob stared at her, lips parted, hand still loose from when he dropped his sword. His gaze traced every bruise, every cut, the way her hair fell around her shoulders. Sorrow filled his eyes. His bottom lip quivered. "Eva..."

"I'm here, Jake," she croaked. She wanted to run to him, but her body wouldn't obey. She was stuck, wedged between a monster's head and an altar. "I'm here."

He staggered forward, barely clearing the limbs in his way, then he dropped to his knees in front of her—and pulled her in for a fierce hug. Pain flared up her back—her entire body, really—but she ignored it, because she was in her brother's arms. She wrapped her arms around him and breathed in pine and sweat and dust. Breathed in *him.*

"I got you," he murmured into her hair, holding her close. "I've got you."

"Well... well... well..." Slow, deliberate footsteps entered the room. Eva's body seized. She'd become overly familiar with that gait. The weight of his boots. The way the buckles clinked together with every step. "This family reunion is more touching than mine was."

Dravyn straightened, shoulders rigid as he slowly turned to face his oldest brother. Sweat trickled down the side of his head, a slight unsteadiness in his stance as he took in the sight of Darius standing there bloodied but otherwise whole. Dravyn's eyes briefly flashed to the entrance, searching—but the hope in them quietly died as it became clear the curse of this temple hadn't claimed Darius.

Jacob jumped to his feet and reached for his—sword, which was on the floor several feet away. He swore under his breath then stood between her and Darius. His eyes narrowed sharply. "Where's Grayson?"

Her breath caught. Grayson was here. He was close. And *missing.*

"Dex is currently..." A slow, sickening smile. "*Indisposed.*"

Jacob stiffened in front of her. "What did you do to him?"

Darius shook his head, creeping closer. “The question shouldn’t be: what did I do to him? It should be: what I’m about to do to *you*.”

Eva caught his sleeve, holding him to her side. He couldn’t face him. Not without a weapon. Not when he was outnumbered. Not against Darius.

She'd already lost Sasha and Anna, to lose him too—her blood, her shield, her one constant in the chaos her life had become... Her heart couldn't bear it.

Show no weakness.

She wouldn't cower behind Jacob while he faced the brothers. She would stand by his side. She would fight until every bone in her body was shattered. Until her lungs couldn't draw breath. Until her will to live was crushed.

Using the altar for support, she pulled herself upright. Her fingers grazed over cold metal. A sharp buzz jolted up her arm, but she didn't remove her gaze from the brothers. Her hand closed around the piece—a weapon, maybe?—and pulled it off the altar.

It was... a gauntlet. Beautiful, a deep red, like dried blood, with gold etchings whorling along the metal. It was heavy, but not impossible to wield. *Massive*, way too big for her fingers to properly slip into.

Not a weapon.

A glove.

And *this* was what Darius was after?

When she looked up, she noticed that the room had gone still. Darius and Dravyn stood frozen in place on the other side of the room, their eyes fixed on the gauntlet in her hands. Even Jacob had gone stiff, eyes wide as he beheld the artifact. She didn't know how Jacob knew its significance, but apparently it was very significant if it stopped Darius Fortys in his tracks.

She traced the elegant metal plating, wrapping around the piece like dragon scales. It thrummed beneath her fingers, a gentle rhythmic pulse, as if it was alive.

A flicker of magic danced on the surface, faint but steady. Though, she had a feeling it was only faint because her magic was suppressed. Her body reacted to it, goosebumps rising on her arms. A warm trickle down her spine.

This piece was powerful. And feared.

“Eva,” Jacob swallowed. “Hand me the gauntlet.”

“Why?” She glanced at Darius, who was slowly creeping forward. Cautious. Wary. Not of her. He'd proven he wasn't afraid of her. But of the gauntlet. And its power.

Her fingers tightened around the metal, pulling it closer to her chest.

“You don't know what you're messing with,” Darius said, his voice low, controlled, as if he was coercing a child. “Do as he says.”

No. Darius wanted Jacob to have the glove so that he could kill him and take it for himself.

No... He want Jacob to have it, because he knew Jacob wouldn't wield it.

No. She wouldn't give up this power. Not when she was so close to being free of him.

If *he* feared it, she *wanted* it.

She balanced the gauntlet on one hand, pressing it close to her body for leverage against its weight, then she slipped her other hand inside.

"No!"

Soft leather curled around her fingers, closing around her hand and forearm. The whole gauntlet shifted and molded around her, adjusting to her size.

"Kill her brother, Dravyn! I'll get the gauntlet."

Power hit her—like a tidal wave. Gasping, she stumbled back into the altar as it flooded through her veins and wove into her muscles. A red hue emanated from the metal plating, climbing up her arm, searing her flesh with ancient magic not even Arkon could fathom. Golden threads climbed up her arm like spiderwebs under her flesh, carrying the immense power with it.

A booming voice entered her mind, violent, angry: *This weapon is not for you!*

So it *was* a weapon.

Not meant for her? *It is today.*

An oppressive weight slammed down on her. She reached out for Jacob for support—but he was gone. He was fighting Dravyn and had drawn him away to keep her out of the fray.

You think you can bend the will of the gods, mortal? Give the gauntlet to my champion.

The words repeated in her head. Bending gods' wills? Champion? She didn't know what it all meant. What she did know, though, was that she wouldn't let Darius hold power over her anymore.

This time she had the power—and she intended to use every ounce of it to *end* him.

Darius was on her in a flash, hands closing around the gauntlet. She snatched it away in time and slammed the heel of her palm into his chest. He went *flying* back, as if a rope had yanked him back, across the room. He hit the wall with a sickening thud.

Startled, Eva looked down at her palm. The magic in her veins gave her strength to face Darius on her own two feet, but she hadn't expected *this* kind of strength.

Rapid footsteps filled the doorway. Eva whirled, ready to face another monster. Another foe. Anyone who wanted to strip her power away.

But the figure who filled the doorway wasn't an enemy. Wasn't a vile creature hungry for her flesh.

It was the man she loved. The face she saw when she closed her eyes and thought of home. The presence of raw, unkempt power she so dearly craved. Eyes she could sink into for eternity if he let her.

The man who never wanted her power or her dragon. Just her.

Grayson.

He halted, chest heaving, as if he'd run across the desert for her. His skin was red, blistered on his forehead and knuckles. Jaw sharp and further defined by the week's worth of beard. His hair was in disarray, matted down by blood and sweat. Royal blue splatter stained his clothes; crimson filled in the tears in his armour.

Yet, despite all he'd endured, he was still heartbreakingly beautiful. Still Grayson. Irrevocably hers.

"Eva," the word barely left his lips. Her heart fractured at the familiar way he said her name, like it was a prayer. The only word worth knowing.

Her vision blurred, heart swelling so much it hurt.

She needed him. His arms around her. His mouth against hers. Body pressing into her, his warmth and strength seeping into her bones, until they became one.

Her body moved before her mind could catch up. She took the first few steps—and then suddenly Darius was in front of her. His hand closed around her throat, the force shoving her onto the altar. Pain exploded up her spine, white light flashing before her eyes.

He ripped the gauntlet from her grasp and slid it over his hand. The power that had fueled her, pulsed through his veins. Gold wove into his flesh. Those abyssal eyes adopted a flicker of red. The hand around her throat tightened with newfound strength.

Gasping, she clawed at his arm, kicked at his hips—but he wouldn't budge. He'd become immovable.

Grayson came up behind him, silent as a wraith, a dagger glinting in the torchlight. Darius caught his wrist with one hand and *crushed* it. Bone crunched beneath his palm like brittle gravel. Grayson's eyes flared with pain, but he didn't make a sound. The dagger fell from his grip and he caught it with the other hand, going for another strike.

Darius released his wrist then backhanded him—which sent him skidding across the floor, still. Eva choked on a scream, fighting for control. For any advantage. But he was too strong. The gauntlet gave him immense strength.

Not again.

She was powerless.

You're weak. You're weak. You're weak.

He laughed darkly, low and gravelly, as if a demon had possessed him. "So *this* is the power my father wanted. Oh, little rider, you will be *mine*. And I will rule the world."

His? She was getting sick and tired of people claiming power that didn't belong to them. It was her body, her magic. Only she got to decide what to do with it.

A coil inside of her snapped free.

Magic tore through her body with the intensity of a maelstrom.

Raw energy crackled down her nerves like fire on frayed wire, lighting up places she hadn't felt in days—weeks. Limbs that had gone dull with pain. Scars that had gone cold. Pieces of herself she thought she'd lost.

Her bones screamed. Her skin burned. Veins pulsed with heat, stretching to contain the flood. It shoved against her ribs, twisted in her gut, clawed behind her eyes. Like it was trying to remake her from the inside out.

And then... she felt it.

Felt *him*.

Arkon.

His relief poured into her, fierce and blazing, replacing the pain with his love—his need for her. It wasn't gentle. It was consuming, like wind over fire, like a storm slamming into dry land.

The world fell away, leaving her with just his soul. Some parts were twisted by fury, marred by grief. Others intertwined with a desperate longing to see her, to feel her weight between his wings, her fingers on his scales.

"*I've finally found you, Little One*," he whispered through their Bond, gentle, as if afraid that if he spoke too loud she'd be torn away from him again.

"*It's good to have you back*," she answered, fresh tears in her eyes. She wouldn't let this moment be taken from them. She'd never let anyone take her dragon away again. "*I need you to take this pain away. I can't fight Darius like this.*"

"*Grind his bones to dust*," he snarled, then the pain slipped away, replaced by the warm embrace of his soul.

Eva focused on all the rage she held in a specific corner in her heart just for Darius.

No one was allowed to take her will away.

She used it as fuel for the ember burning in her chest. Her magic pulsed in her veins violently and fought to be released out into the world. She held her hand to the side, imagining a sharp, crackling dagger. Small but efficient. Deadly and familiar.

She raised her head, pressing her neck further into his palm, just enough to catch Darius's attention—keep it fixed on her and not the blade. He grinned, watching her fight against him, struggling against his strength.

"You have something to say, pet?"

"Fuck..." she whispered, leaning into him. "You."

She drove the lightning blade into his side.

CHAPTER 63
RESIGNATION

Shock twisted Darius's features. His hold on Eva's throat loosened. She pressed the advantage and kicked him backwards. He stumbled, holding his side. He looked down at the blood pulsing between his fingers in disbelief.

But the gauntlet glowed. Fierce. Angry. The room flooded with an ominous red hue. A buzz took over the oppressive silence of the temple, sizzling just beneath her skin.

Dravyn and Jacob froze mid-fight to behold the glove's power. Eva had to shield her eyes from the immense heat radiating from it. Grayson slid to her side, each movement slow, pained. His knuckles brushed her lower back—light, but grounding. A silent vow. She leaned into it, if only for a moment. Just to remember what it felt like to be his.

But that moment was all they had time for.

The blood leaking out of Darius's side slowed. The shock that had splayed on his face now warped into blood-infused rage. His grin was dark and haunting.

"Looks like you're going to have to try harder than that to kill me, little rider."

Dread sank deep into her chest.

That had been a killing blow. Just what kind of power did this artifact possess? If a dagger to his lung didn't kill him, what would it take to be rid of him?

Then he moved.

Steel scraped against stone as he surged forward, faster than a man who'd just been stabbed in the side should move.

Grayson intercepted him—blade flashing, footwork fluid and ruthless. They collided with a roar of pressure, steel clashing against brute force. Sparks burst. Blades screamed. Water coiled around Grayson's limbs like living armour, shimmering as it absorbed each blow, sealing wounds before they bled. The gauntlet's power struck like a battering ram, but Grayson's magic knit him back together, over and over.

Eva circled around, boots skidding over rubble and debris. She let the lightning build, let it burn in her grasp. Her hands trembled. Her chest heaved. Arkon held true to his promise, dulling the pain. She felt him near the surface, tether taut, desperate to help his rider.

She positioned herself behind Darius then launched forward.

The blade she formed crackled with unstable light, vibrating with hunger. She slashed—but Darius caught her wrist mid-swing and slammed her into the floor. The world tipped. Her breath exploded out of her lungs, blade flickering.

Grayson tackled him off her before the second blow could land.

Magic roared through her. Her fingers curled, and the lightning returned, wilder this time. Feral. Desperate.

Grayson ducked a gauntlet punch that shattered the altar behind him. Eva swept low, slicing into the back of Darius's legs. He roared. Blood gushed. But still—he didn't fall. She spun out of his grasp before he could grab her.

Grayson surged again. He cut deep across Darius's chest then stepped back, blade poised to plunge for the heart.

For a heartbeat, they had him—

Then Darius curled the gauntlet into a fist and slammed it into the ground.

The shockwave fractured stone, and hurled them both back. Eva struck the wall. Cracks webbed behind her skull. Copper coated her tongue.

She watched Darius rise through the haze—glowing, healing. The gauntlet fed off it. Off the carnage. The violence.

Grayson stood, chest heaving, arm limp at his side, knuckles torn open. The water that had protected him before was a puddle at his feet, rippling, struggling to reach him. He was running out of magic.

So was she.

For all the pain Arkon took away, he couldn't stop her body from crumbling under the pressure. Couldn't stave off the effect magic had on her—especially in her already weakened state.

Meanwhile, Darius looked like he was just getting started. Power oozed out of him in thick, oppressive waves.

But they couldn't stop. Not because Eva hated him with every fibre of her being. Not because Grayson thirsted for his blood. Because if they didn't—if they failed here—Darius would take this unrelenting power out into the world. And nothing would stand in his way.

Eva dragged herself upright, calling on her magic one more time. Embracing the void whispering her name.

She charged.

He caught her blade, and their magic collided—lightning against brute force. Her knees buckled. Her lungs screamed. But she didn't stop. Behind her, Grayson charged, fast, silent

He struck from behind. Eva struck from the front.

Darius twisted out of their attacks. They crashed into each other—teeth, skulls, and limbs. Grayson rolled so she landed on top, his arm braced instinctively around her back. For a moment, their eyes met—and she saw it. Not fear. Not uncertainty.

Resignation.

He knew what she did: they had to stop him. Or die trying.

"Stop trying to help," he ground out. "You're getting in my way."

The words tore deeper than any lashing could tear through flesh. It wasn't even the words themselves that hurt. It was the fact they were coming from *Grayson*. The man who had only ever built her up.

"What?" she barely managed through the razor blades in her throat.

Already dismissing her, he rolled to his feet and shoved her toward what remained of the altar.

She stumbled back, breath lodged in her throat. Her heart fought to make sense of his sudden callousness, while her mind viciously reminded her that now was not the time to think when the man she loved charged for Darius with a deafening roar.

The gauntlet burned, red-hot and vibrating—

Something cracked. The ceiling. The air. Everything. A deafening, unnatural pulse of pressure shook the very walls. Stone split beneath Eva's boots. Cracks veined across the floor like lightning.

Chunks of stone rained down. Dust blinded her. Crying out, Eva dropped to her knees and threw her arms over her head, bracing against what was left of the altar.

A roar tore through the temple.

Then the world split apart.

Sunlight pierced the gloom like a blade. Heat crashed over her in a wave. Sand cascaded down like waterfalls through the yawning fracture above.

When the dust settled, she uncurled—and found herself encased in a bubble of shimmering blue water. Protected. Safe.

Grayson and Jacob were cocooned by one too, not far off.

But Darius, Dravyn, and the gauntlet were gone. Buried or free, she didn't know.

Glade's bronze scales shimmered in the raw sunlight, proud and bristling. She'd ripped open the temple.

The magic that had been permeating the air since she arrived was gone. Sapped the moment she slid the gauntlet over her skin.

The bubble popped. Eva blinked the remaining dust from her eyes.

"Eva!" Jacob coughed. He stumbled to his feet then rushed to her side. "Are you okay?"

"I'm—"

Pain hit her all at once.

Bone-deep. Muscle-tearing. Sharp and searing and endless.

"I'm sorry, Little One," Arkon crooned in her mind. *"I can't hold it back any longer."*

It was too much. The exhaustion. The magic. The starvation. The fight.

Her body gave out.

Her eyes rolled back, and she collapsed into her brother's arms.

CHAPTER 64
THE COST OF SURVIVAL

When Eva awoke, stars twinkled above her.

Bright, beautiful stars.

Water sloshed beneath her, cool and still. Deep enough to soak her hair and spine, not deep enough to drown her. There was no hum. No warmth of magic. Just water. Just quiet.

Azure scales glittered to her right. Midnight scales to her left. But it was the crimson ones—those catching the firelight ahead—that squeezed the breath from her lungs.

She sat up—too fast. The stars reeled above her, spinning like a broken wheel.

All at once, the camp stirred. The dragons lifted their heads in her direction and figures—*three* figures—turned from the fire.

Jacob was the first to reach her, dropping to his knees at her side. "Hey," he murmured, taking her hand gently. "You're safe, Eva. You don't have to move."

But she did.

Ignoring him, she forced herself upright, one burning limb after another, and stepped out of the basin. Her gaze locked on a slender figure limping toward her. Crimson hair, loose and windblown, a perfect echo of the scales behind her.

Her body screamed with protest, every step a battle. But still, she moved. One foot. Then another. She wouldn't believe it until she felt her. Heard her.

Tears blurred her vision so much she could barely make out her face. But when those arms wrapped around her—she knew.

Anna. *Alive*.

Eva collapsed into her, a choked sob tearing from her throat as she clutched her best friend with everything she had left in her.

"I never thought I'd see you again," Eva murmured into her hair.

Anna's cry echoed her own. "We made it. We. Made. It."

They did.

They'd lived. Survived.

But at what cost?

Darius and the gauntlet were missing. Eva's body, even after Eran's healing, still felt brittle, a breath away from shattering. And her spirit... only time would tell how fractured it truly was.

Arkon's snout brushed gently against her back. She flinched, instinctively bracing for pain. But there was none.

"*Sit by the fire, Little One*," Arkon urged, his voice a balm across her weary mind. "*Eat. Drink.*"

Only then did she realise how hollow she felt. How violently her stomach clenched at the mention of food.

She was starving. Empty.

But for the first time in what felt like years, she wasn't alone.

Anna took her hand—firm and strong—and led her to the fire. Jacob rummaged through the bags, eventually pulling out a small metal container of leftover lizard stew and a canteen. He handed her the canteen first, then set the container beside the fire to heat. Her mouth watered just thinking about warm food.

The sand shifted beneath her as she sank down between them, Anna on one side, Jacob on the other. They filled the silence with quiet, mindless talk, as if they were afraid silence itself might shatter something inside her.

Maybe it would.

Her gaze drifted across the fire. Grayson sat on the far side, still and silent. She tried to catch his eye with a faint smile, but he didn't look up. His eyes were fixed on the flames, unreadable. Darkness swirled in those storm-cloud eyes.

She didn't like it.

You're in my way, he'd said. But had it really been him? Could he have meant it? After everything they'd been through—after everything they'd built—how could he say something so cruel?

She wanted to believe it had been a lie. That he'd only said it to push her back. To protect her. But even now... he barely acknowledged her existence.

You're weak. Too weak to stand by his side.

And she let the thought sit there. Because maybe it was true.

He was strength incarnate. Power and precision. An agent of Val.

And she—she had needed saving.

She hadn't been strong enough to beat Darius.

When she finished her dinner, she stood, dusting the sand off her pants, then rounded the fire to his side. Only then did he look up at her—and the look in his eyes killed her.

Gone was the warmth. The affection he held for her. Only guilt and sorrow and pain filled those eyes. And she couldn't help but think she was to blame for it.

She licked her lips, feeling moisture on her skin for the first time in ages. "Can I sit with you?"

His throat tightened, then he held his hand out to her. She took it, and he helped her ease into the spot beside him. She leaned into his side, taking his warmth, breathing in familiar leather and steel. He stiffened at first, but eventually relaxed, securing an arm around her waist and tilting his head into hers.

"You've been quiet," she murmured, so Anna and Jacob couldn't hear them over the crackle of the fire.

"I have a lot on my mind."

She tipped her chin up to see if the hard edge in his eyes had faded now that she was with him.

It hadn't.

"A copper for your thoughts?"

Fire danced in his eyes. "Not tonight, Starling."

Hollow. The nickname sounded so hollow on his lips.

She should have flinched, but instead she balled her hand into a fist at her side. Out of sight.

"I've never seen you use magic like that before," she tried again, grasping for anything that will stick. "You were incredible."

He winced and withdrew from her, leaning forward, bracing his arms loosely on his knees. "I've been practicing."

"It shows. Maybe you can show me how you did it sometime?"

His head hung between his shoulders, back tense. Shadows stretched on behind him, swathing the sand in darkness. "Get some rest, Eva. We're leaving for Dragon Canyon at first light."

Gutted. This was what it felt like to be completely and utterly gutted.

Feeling a lump forming in her throat, she climbed to her feet. She wouldn't cry. Wouldn't beg. Wouldn't crumble.

Because this wasn't the end.

She'd fought her way to get back to him and she'd be damned if she'd let him get in between them.

Time. He just needed time. A moment to process what they had just faced. So did she. It all still felt like a dream she hadn't woken up from yet.

She limped her way to Arkon's embrace and settled into his awaiting claws. He held her close. Kept her warm. Kept her safe. Made her feel loved when all she felt was hollow inside.

CHAPTER 65
THE FRACTURING

What will hurt more? Grayson wondered numbly as he stared at the flames licking the sky in front of him. *Fire raking my flesh or the fracture in my soul?*

It started when Eva walked—limped—away from him, a crease on her brow, shoulders curling in on herself. The fracture. Unhurried but savage. Its ruin was thorough, its claws inescapable.

And it had been growing in intensity since. It had surpassed the dull ache in his wrist that still clung to his bones long after being fully healed. It passed the acrid burn of failure down his throat.

Would fire be enough to burn it away or would it only fuel the spread?

He shut his eyes, clenching his fists tight beneath his cloak.

Images flashed through his mind. Of Eva standing in front of an altar, the gauntlet in her hands. Bloodied. Battered. Swollen. That fire of defiance in her eyes as she faced Darius without a flicker of fear in her eyes. That gritty determination that said she'd rather die than kneel.

He wasn't sure if he loved her more for it or if he feared it. Feared *her.*

That look forced him to imagine a world where she didn't exist.

Closing his eyes didn't calm his mind. He was hit with one thing after the other.

Eva. Again. Pinned to the altar, with Darius's hand on her throat. Watching her struggle to kick him off her. Flounder with the last of her strength to save herself.

Rage coursed through his veins like a violent tide. Darius had laid his hands on her, and Grayson hadn't been fast enough to stop it. Again.

Always too slow.

Always too late.

Darius wasn't going to be the last one to target her. Because of her power or because of her association with him. More would come. More would try to take what didn't belong to them. More would try to ruin what she had made of her life.

The vestiges, most of all, threatened her very existence.

This gauntlet was only the first of five. The others would be just as protected as this one—just as dangerous. Hargin wanted his squad to go after them all. Prevent them from getting into the wrong hands.

How many times would Grayson be too late?

How many times would he fail Eva?

How many scars must she endure because he couldn't keep her safe?

He'd been the one to peel the dressings from Eva's back once they had found a safe place to recoup. He had been the one who had to listen to the painful whimpers leaving her lips, even when she was unconscious, as each laceration was opened up to the cool desert night.

Her lips were thin and peeling from dehydration, cheekbones jutting as the life was starved out of her, skin stained black and blue, beaten. Seeing the raw, angry markings raking the entire length of her back killed a part of him. And with each agonising minute that passed since, he felt himself slipping away.

Eighteen fucking lashings.

A present for him. Condemning him to see Darius's brand on her skin every time she stripped for him.

Eran had tried to heal them, scars included, but they were too deep, left to close and reopen too many times for him to mend them fully. It would take days and many treatments for the wounds to fully close. But the scars would remain.

If it weren't for Grayson, Darius wouldn't have marked her, made her feel the sting of failure and disappointment. He wouldn't have made her one of *them.*

Bile rose up his throat knowing that she would have to bear that brand for the rest of her life.

That wasn't what he wanted for her.

She shouldn't have to look over her shoulder at every turn in her life. She shouldn't have to scan the crowd and look for an assassin. She shouldn't have to fight for her life—for the right to *breathe.*

She deserved a life of freedom and love and hope. She deserved someone who could give her that life.

"*That is not your decision to make,*" Eran interjected. Grayson had been trying to shut him out of his mind, but since he woke up in the temple, the dragon had thoroughly rooted himself in his mind with no sign of leaving. "*Her life will always be perilous, regardless if you are in it or not. Why not fight at her side?*"

Fight at her side? There was no higher honour. When they faced Darius, they did so as a single unit. He'd never fought like that with anyone. There was no thought, no second-guessing, no unpredictability. He reacted and she followed. He needed support and she gave it to him without hesitation.

She was utterly enchanting, a blade come to life—sharp, fast, beautiful.

But the entire time he was *terrified* of losing her. Of watching a blade sink into her gut. Of the gauntlet pulverising her face beyond recognition. Darius crushing the life out of her. Wondering which glance would be their final.

"*I'm not deciding for her,*" Grayson shot back. "*I'm giving her the chance to choose something better. Someone who can give her a life I never can.*"

"*Your dream—*"

"*That's all it was—a dream.*"

"*Don't shut her out,*" Eran implored. "*She brings out the best in you.*"

Grayson gritted his teeth. "*And what about her? What do I bring out in her? Hm?*" He pressed the silence in the Bond. "*Death,*" he spat, because Eran refused to say it. He loved Eva as much as Grayson did, but his loyalty would always be to his rider first. And yes, Eva revived a part of himself he thought long dead. She showed him how to love, to hope, to be *himself.* Showed him that he wasn't done yet. He had so much more to learn with his magic—with life. He'd never been more lucky than to receive that gift from her.

But the cost of it was her soul.

"*Did you see her eyes?*" Grayson pushed, relentless. He had to see it. Acknowledge what he had done to her. See why he was no good for her.

A long pause.

Eran shifted, sinking deeper into the sand. His emerald eyes slid to Eva as she curled into the safety of Arkon's claws. Her dragon coiled himself tight around her, allowing a sliver of her starlight hair to shine through the cracks. He cradled her with the care and attention of a newly hatched dragonling.

Grayson's heart twisted, knowing he'd never be that close to her again. To feel her feathery soft hair between his fingers. Her full lips on his flesh. Hear her heart beat against his.

Eran dipped his head in defeat. "*I did.*"

The light Grayson cherished in her eyes was gone. Darkness had touched her heart and she'd never be able to get it back.

He couldn't help but think that he had a hand in it. He might not have held the whip or raised a hand or starved her. But he betrayed the man who did. Darius would never have branded her if he didn't hate Grayson so much. Wouldn't have tortured her. Might not have snuffed out the light in her eyes so quickly.

Grayson couldn't undo what had been done to her, but he could make sure it never happened again. He'd find the other vestiges. He alone would endure their trials and face their monsters. Then he'd hunt Eva's enemies—kings, assassins, mercenaries—to the very edges of the world and destroy them with the power of the gods. Never again would she be hunted. Never again would she fear the shadows. Never again would anyone be allowed to *come close* to taking her will away.

"*I am going to miss our Precious One*," Eran murmured into his mind, soft with empathy, tight with remorse. His anguish tore through their Bond and added on to Grayson's.

"*Me too*."

If she hated him for it, so be it.

At least she'd be alive to hate him.

CHAPTER 66
NEVER ENOUGH

Eva stared in the mirror in the comfort of her own room, shears in one hand, a clump of hair in the other. Dravyn had done a decent job of tidying her hair and making it even throughout. But this morning when she woke up in her own bed for the first time in months, she noticed a strand he'd missed.

She stared at herself, taking inventory of every bruise, every cut, the way her left eyelid swelled. A gash bisected her eyebrow. A chunk was missing from her bottom lip, where she had bitten it at some point.

Her body hurt.

Gods. It hurt.

The healers had given her salves and potions to get her through the night. They'd tried to convince her to stay in the Infirmary after her initial examination. They had questions—so many godsdamned questions—and wanted to run more tests, but she refused. It was too open. Too exposed. With only a gauzy curtain standing between her and whoever was on the other side. She'd promised them they'd find all of their answers in her report--if they let her sit down and write it.

Here, in her apartment, she thought she'd feel safe enough to recount the events in the Desert Lands. She thought she'd have a good night's sleep in her bed.

She was wrong.

Her report was a glossed-over recounting, with only absolutely necessary details. She hadn't slept a wink. She sat in her bed, knife balancing on her knee and stared at the door, traced shadows moving with the moon.

Anna didn't return from her examination, but Eva suspected she spent the night with Jacob. After everything they went through, sleeping in the arms of the man she loved sounded like the perfect remedy to chase the nightmares away.

But the man Eva loved was cold, distant. He spared her a single glance when they arrived in Dragon Canyon yesterday. She'd slid off Arkon's back and fell onto her hands and knees. The moment had been embarrassing enough—collasping in the Stables in front of at least a dozen Knights—but it hurt more that it was Jacob who helped her to her feet. Who carried her to the Infirmary. Who sat by her side and held her hand while the healers performed their tests.

He just needs time, she reminded herself. They'd both gone through their own hell, and while Eva needed love and comfort to heal, he needed space.

And she would respect that.

A tear burned down her cheeks. It was the first time she'd allowed herself to cry since they got back. To embrace the aching hollowness shovelling out her heart.

It's only temporary.

The door handle jiggled. Eva swiped her knife from her dresser and faced the door, bracing.

Anna slipped through the door, ducking her head sheepishly when she spotted Eva. "Hey," she said softly.

Eva put the knife away, turned her back to her, and wiped the tears away before she noticed them. "Hey."

Anna came up behind her, close enough for her to feel her warmth and smell the sweet jasmine scent, but didn't touch her. She knew better.

"I didn't expect to see you here," Anna said, keeping her tone soft. "I thought Grayson would be glued to your side."

Eva flinched, because she had thought the same. Had been banking on it. "I haven't seen him since we left the Stables. I'm going to see Eran in a few minutes. I'll ask him about Grayson, see where his head is at."

The last thing she wanted to do was push him, but she needed him. She needed to feel safe and loved and know that she was *enough*.

Anna nodded. "I think that's a good idea. Do you want me to walk you down?"

Eva peered at her. Most of her injuries were gone, with only a few patches of green and yellow to ever tell the world what she had endured. "No. I'll be okay."

After Eran had healed her, she would feel better. The sharp pains and deep aches will go away. The fear and anxiety will disappear. The feeling that she was being watched will fade away like a distant memory.

She wouldn't be weak and feeble for long.

Anna shifted behind her. "If there's anything you want to talk about, you'll come to me, right?"

An image crossed her mind—Darius slamming a rock into the side of Anna's face, while Eva was held back and helpless to save her.

"Of course," she said quickly. Anna didn't have to worry. Eva would get stronger so she could protect her. So she wouldn't have to *endure* for her again.

Eva slipped past her. "I'll be back in a couple hours then we can go for a run if you're up to it."

Anna watched her, eyes searching her face for something. Eva didn't know what. "Actually, I was thinking we could pick up our training next week. We should rest. We've earned it."

Eva paused in the doorway. *Oh. That's what she's looking for.*

The breaking point. She was waiting for Eva to crumble. Waiting for the pain and memories to be too much.

I'm not weak.

Without a word, she started down the hallway and made her way to the healing pools.

All the way down the stairs.

Every step lanced at her side, every breath caught in her lungs. Her joints protested, stiff and rusty. She had to pause three quarters of the way to catch her breath.

"*Don't push yourself, Little One,*" Arkon implored. "*Your body is still healing from the Mithbane... among other things.*"

"*I'm fine.*"

"*You are* not *fine!*" His voice boomed in her mind and gave her a headache. "*You cannot lie to me, Eva. You can barely hold on to the railing.*"

She clenched the very hand he spoke of and gritted her teeth when she couldn't even make her knuckles go white. "*I want to be alone.*"

She threw up her walls and locked them tight in case he had any ideas of creeping back in.

When she reached the bottom, sweat beaded down the side of her face. Trickled down her back, running over every ridge of her new scars. Her muscles trembled, stopping her from taking another step for too long a time.

She stood outside of the pool room for a moment to collect herself. Eran was already inside, waiting for her, and relief flooded through her at the sight of him. Both because her message reached him, and because he was familiar, warm in the way he regarded her.

He stood, wings fluttering against his back as she approached. "Good morning, Eva." His eyes flicked to the door behind her, as if expecting someone else to be accompanying her. "Did you go down the stairs by yourself?"

"Yes." She rolled her shoulders back, ignoring the ache as she did.

A growl rumbled through his body, and the tip of his tail flickered like an angry cat. "You shouldn't have. What if you fell?"

"I didn't fall. I *won't* fall. I feel better than I look." If she had a tail, it would be flicking all over the damned cave.

"I will be the judge of that." He nodded towards the pool in front of him, which was already bubbling and glowing with his magic. "In the pool you go."

She bit back a wince as she lowered herself into the water, each step burning. But the moment the warm water closed over her shoulders, a shaky breath left her lungs—like something inside had finally released. She waded over to the bench in front of the azure dragon and relaxed into the stone.

"Thank you for doing this, Eran," she murmured, eyes closed. The weight of her sleepless night was catching up with her, and his gentle magic was just the touch she needed to let go.

"Of course," he said softly, lowering his head so that his snout brushed against her head. "Anything for you, Precious One."

"Anything?"

A beat passed between them.

"What do you need?"

She twisted on the bench, sitting cross-legged, and reached out for his snout. Eagerly, he pressed his muzzle into her palm and shut his eyes, steam billowed out of his nostrils, encasing her in his warmth.

"How is he?" she asked, throat tight. She had to bite her lip to stop the tears that welled up in her eyes.

Eran opened his eyes, something old and soul-deep stirring within those emerald orbs. "You're asking about Grayson." A statement, not a question, and one that seemingly upset him. His wings flattened against his back and the magic in the water faltered for a beat. "You need not concern yourself with him right now. Focus on yourself. My magic can mend your bones and close your wounds, but it can't return your strength or fix ailments of the mind."

Anger flared inside of her.

"Rest, Eva."

"Eat some more, Eva."

"You shouldn't be doing that right now, Eva."

Everywhere she went, she was treated like a fragile doll, one breath away from disintegrating and being carried away by the wind. They stood at a distance, watching, waiting for her to break.

But she wouldn't. She was better than that. Stronger than that. If Darius Fortys couldn't break her beneath the desert or in the heart of an ancient temple—then she wouldn't let him break her when he wasn't even around to touch her.

She wasn't his. She wasn't a puppet. She was not *weak*.

And he was dead.

She slammed her fists into the water. "I don't need to focus on myself," she ground out. "There's nothing to work on. I'm *fine*. I'm ready to train. Ready to fight. But no one will let me. Don't be like the others, Eran. Don't hold back on me now." Not when she needed him—needed Grayson—more than ever. If they started to pull away from her...

His emerald eyes twisted with remorse—and regret. A deep regret she didn't understand.

He pressed his snout into her chest with so much pressure she nearly fell off the bench. "You are strong, Precious One, of that I have no doubt. You are capable, far more than people give you credit for. You will do remarkable things. You don't need him to achieve greatness."

She flinched out of his grasp, a tear slipping down her cheeks with emotion that hadn't quite caught up with her yet. She stared up at him, brow furrowed. "Wha—" Her voice wavered, though she didn't know why. "What are you talking about?"

Were they still talking about Grayson? She felt like she was missing something.

Footsteps sounded behind her.

On instinct, she reached for her dagger. She whirled, fighting against the weight of water to face the newcomer.

But then all of the tension in her body ebbed away when a familiar form clad in black—cloak, under armour, pants, and boots—approached them. He was cleanly shaven, the bruises and cuts he bore last time she saw him, gone. His hair held a shimmer to it under the lightstones, trimmed just above his ears.

Grayson.

Her heart swelled at the sight of him. She'd been worried he was avoiding her, but it had all been in her head. He'd just needed time to process.

He stood a few feet away from the pool's edge, thumbs tucked into his pockets. Those dark eyes swept over the cavern, soaking in every shadow and pool with the cool precision of a predator.

When his gaze lastly landed on her, her stomach twisted. The light that usually filled those storm cloud eyes when he looked at her was gone. She stared at darkness and it stared back, cold, unrecognisable.

She moistened her lips, shifting in the pool. The water around her suddenly felt thicker, heavier, as if she was in a pool of honey.

"H—hey." She hated how hesitant she sounded, how frail and vulnerable she felt half-submerged while he looked down on her.

Something was off, different from the out of place feeling she'd felt since she returned. This one ran deeper, tied only between them.

Ever since she'd been back, there was this... disconnect between them. She hated it, and desperately wanted to make things right. For them to go back to how they were before he had to save her.

His gaze flickered down to the knife she held in an almost white-knuckled grip. She immediately tucked it back into its sheath, but he missed it, already looking at Eran. "Are you done?" His tone was flat, painfully distant.

A rumble ran through Eran's body, eliciting a shudder along his scales. "I am."

"Good." His eyes snapped down to her, noting that they were now empty, then they jumped up to her face, scanning it for anything out of place. He wouldn't find anything. The throb she'd felt before Eran healed her was gone, her lip no longer split when she ran her tongue over it. All that remained were the scars on her back that were too deep to completely erase and the ache in her heart that he couldn't reach. "You all right?"

She nodded, suddenly nervous, like she was meeting him for the very first time, hit by that aura of raw power and invincibility, and having no idea if she should run from it or cling to it.

Only, this prickling anxiety had nothing to do with him, but what he might see beyond the mask she had carefully constructed. She didn't want him to see the truth, only the strength, her resolve to be better.

His eyes narrowed a fraction, almost indiscernible. Anyone else would have missed it. But she didn't, and his doubt filled her gut with dread. She'd seen that look at least a dozen times since she returned to Dragon Canyon. She'd seen it on the healers' faces, on Jacob's, on Anna's—she hadn't thought she'd ever see it on his.

With a heavy huff, Eran released the tension she hadn't noticed increasing between them, wrung tight by silence and too much unsaid. He pressed his snout into her chest, coiling his tail around and around her waist, almost too tight to breathe. "Goodbye, Precious One."

She rested her cheek between his nostrils, suddenly in need of the kind of comfort only a dragon could provide. There was just something incredibly soothing about being held by a colossal, ancient and powerful creature, knowing that, even with all of their wisdom earned over the years, they still respected and cherished her.

"Thank you for everything, Eran. I'll see you later."

Silently, slowly, as if the cold air was freezing his blood, he peeled himself away. He cast a final unreadable look to Grayson then leapt out of the gaping maw opening into the canyon.

Eva climbed out of the pool—then realised that she hadn't removed her clothes or thought to bring a spare set. They were heavy and dripping all over the floor, water clumsily pooling at her feet.

She looked like a mess.

Grayson wordlessly crossed the room, snagging a towel rolled up on a shelf, then handed it out to her. His fingers slipped from the fabric the moment her hand closed around it.

"Thanks," she murmured, lamely wringing out her shirt before using the towel to dry her hair. Instinctively, she leaned to the side to rub the sopping tresses between the folds in the fabric—but when she tipped forward there was no hair to dry. It barely shifted from her face when she moved. Pretending it was all part of her plan, that she was definitely adjusting like a normal person, she dumped the towel on her head and massaged it into her scalp.

Grayson cleared his throat, having watched her silently, waiting patiently. "Can we talk?"

"Of course," she answered hoarsely, as if she'd been screaming for hours—or swallowed a mouthful of gravel. She licked her lips, thinking it might help. "I think we need to."

Seeing there was no point in trying to dry her clothes, she tossed the towel into the dirty bin and faced him, bracing herself to say the things she needed to say to him. For his sake as much as her own.

"I don't blame you for what he did—" she started, but then he went and talked over her.

"Our time apart has given me a lot to think about." He inhaled sharply, knuckles white at his sides, like his own words had cut into him.

She blinked at him, at the hard edge in his eyes, the cold, clipped nature of his voice. It sounded forced yet restrained at the same time. Clearly he had things he needed to say too, but she had a sinking feeling that she didn't want to hear what he had to say.

He continued, the words coming out rough, choppy, "Moving forward, we should keep our relationship strictly professional."

She stared at him, took in the strained muscles against his throat, the tight set of his jaw, the impossible to read mask on his face. Her stomach dropped, but her heart refused to believe it. Refused to think that distance had torn them apart, not made them yearn for each other more. She remembered every letter he sent. Every carefully crafted word, both in structure and in prose to protect their missions and their relationship. She refused to believe that a man who threatened to ruin anyone who laid a hand on her would just *give up* on her. On them.

She clenched her fists, unsure what else to do with them. What she really wanted to do was reach out to him, to take his hand and pull him close—but he was already closed off and distant. She didn't want to push too hard and give him more reasons to stay away.

"We can take things slow," she offered, not begging—she'd never beg—but as a compromise. "We don't have to make anything official. Everyone else can see us as just that—professionals—but I don't want to give up on us before we've even given it a chance... And I don't think you want to either."

Shaking his head, he backed up a step, then another, as if she was cornering him, but she stood right where she was, even when it killed her that he was putting more distance between them. It made her question everything between them all over again. Maybe she hadn't known him as well as she thought she did. Maybe she'd misread all of the signs. Maybe she had been a fool to think the Slayer of Souls could love.

"You're wrong," he said, tone stern. Final. "Getting involved with you was a mistake."

The words hit her like a gut punch. This time, she did move, but not towards him. She staggered back, as if he had hit her. Her stomach roiled as violently as if his fist had hit her as hard as Darius had.

A mistake.

She was a mistake. A failure. Weak. Too weak to save herself. Too weak to stand by his side.

"*You're in my way*," he'd said. Then, she thought he was trying to protect her, sacrifice himself so she didn't have to.

But she saw it for what it really was now and the truth speared her heart. Shattered her core.

She would never be good enough. Not to protect her family and Brar, not for Sasha and Syran, not for Anna...

Not even for the man she loved.

And that made her furious. Over and over again she fought to prove anyone who told her she wasn't worth their time or energy that they were wrong. She clawed her way into Arkon's lair with her dying breath. She trained her body raw, bleeding to the bone. She learned to refine her behaviour to master King Renkon's court. She fought Sandhounds and Sandworms. Unlocked Soul Magic. Had *finally* thought that she'd found her place in this world. Had *earned* it.

But it wasn't enough.

She never would be.

"I see how it is," she spat, vitriol spewing from her mouth. "I make one slip up and I'm suddenly not good enough for you. Is that it? Grayson Smith expects perfection, and when he doesn't get it, you get discarded like trash."

Darkness loomed over him. He advanced on her, pointing a finger in her face. "A slip up? He *beat you to a fucking pulp*, Eva. He broke your bones and flayed your skin. You didn't slip up—you got outplayed and outmatched. Every time I close my eyes, all I see is your battered and bruised body. You pinned underneath him, helpless-"

"I'm not helpless!"

He exploded. "Yes, you are!" The moment the words came out, he sucked in a deep breath, eyes shuttering. "He won't be the last. More will come. More will hurt you to hurt me. I'm not going to wait for them to trickle in one by one. I'm not going to watch your life be thrown deeper and deeper into shadow."

"Then we fight them *together*." Out of instinct, desperation, she tried to reach for his hand, but he pulled back. "We're stronger together."

"No." He shook his head. "We're not. I can't be who I need to be when I'm with you."

"You think you're protecting me? You're not. You're abandoning me, Grayson. And that's the one thing I didn't think you'd ever do."

"You'll be better off without me."

"You should have figured that out *before* you vowed to make things right. *Before* you showed me the man you really are. *Before* I fell in love with you..." Her body shook, not due to weakness this time, but because she was so angry—at him and at herself—she couldn't contain it. "I wish you had never bothered to begin with."

He looked down, a sharp edge in his eyes. "At least we can agree on that. We're done."

He spun on his heel and marched out of the room, but something stopped him in the doorway. His fingers dug into the frame, as if standing there took strenuous effort. "Goodbye, Eva."

Then, just like that... he was gone.

And so was her mask. It cracked all around, crumbling at the edges.

No. No. No. No!

She fell back on her rump and curled in on herself. Big, globbing tears streaked down her face and she *cried*. The scars on her back stretched as she held herself tight.

It wasn't supposed to be like this. She was supposed to return here and get better. The ache was supposed to go away. The fear was supposed to stop. She was supposed to curl into Grayson's side and forget about the world. To breathe him in, to absorb his strength, to feel loved and *wanted*.

He wasn't supposed to leave.

She wasn't supposed to break.

She sensed Arkon's presence in the cave before his claws came around her gently and pulled her into his embrace. He coiled his tail around her, tucking his head into her side, and draped his wing over them to give her privacy and the safety of his body.

A sob tore through her throat as she clutched his scales, not caring if the tips broke through skin. She didn't feel it, didn't feel his warmth or breath—only the searing agony of failure and humiliation raking its vicious claws over her heart. It burned hot and fast through her chest, slicing through her veins and squeezing her lungs, rendering her utterly powerless in its clutches. It didn't matter how hard she held onto him, how deeply he wove his soul into hers, it was all consuming.

I am not weak. I am not weak. I am not weak.

But she was.

She told herself over and over and over again that she would not break. She was better, stronger, than that. She wouldn't let Darius win.

But he did win. He was right: she was pathetic, a disappointment to everyone around her. She'd failed her family, Sasha and Syran. Anna. Grayson. *Arkon.*

Her dragon most of all.

"I'm sorry," she murmured into his scales. "I'm so sorry."

He held her tighter, light vibrations running through each individual scale. "Do not apologise, Little One. There is nothing to apologise for."

Her head shook as she clutched onto the horns on his snout. "You gave me a piece of yourself because you thought I was worthy of it... but I'm not. I've let you down and now you're stuck with me."

"Oh, Eva," he murmured against her, "I am not *stuck* with you. You have not let me down. You are as worthy today as you were the night I shed a tear for you."

She peeled back enough so she could look into one of his blue eyes to see if he really meant it—despite their souls being so interwoven in that moment she couldn't tell where she ended he began. Despite feeling his soul sing nothing but pride and love for her. He held the utmost respect for her and loved her as much as one of his brood. No one could ever admire her as much as he did, even when she was a jagged pile of tears and misery.

His unconditional love was irrefutable, yet she still doubted it. "But you're the last of your kind because of me."

His remorse rippled through their Bond, but it didn't change how he regarded her. In fact, it only made him treasure her more, because now they were all what they had. "I do not blame you for Syran's demise. Both he and Sasha knew the risks of willingly walking in an ambush. Our plan was solid—but we were blindsided. It happens to the best of warriors. There was nothing you could have done to save them."

"I should have helped her. I should have moved faster. If I was better-"

"Stop," he growled, lifting his head to look at her head on. "You followed mine and Sasha's orders. You. Are. Not. To. Blame."

"But he said I was weak." She flinched, her body instinctively remembering every fist, every blade, every lashing she earned for showing weakness. "I could have saved her, saved Syran."

"Of course he did," Arkon snorted. "Men often degrade and punish those they cannot control. Those they fear."

She wanted to believe him, to hold on to his words, his scales, his strength. But there was still that voice in her head that whispered all of the things she could have done differently, reminding her that she would always be the scared girl who watched Brar burn to the ground and did nothing to stop it.

Arkon squeezed then released her, uncoiling his tail and opening up his wing. Fresh air swathed her in a balmy cloak that eased the ache in her chest. Even for just a moment. "Give it time, Little One. I will always be here to remind you that you are worthy, of me, of love, of the power simmering in your soul. And I will keep telling you until you believe it."

She managed a smile for him; it was crooked and awkward, falling apart at the edges, but it was an attempt. A start.

"Thank you."

He bumped her chest. "I am here for you, always and forever, Little One."

Her gaze turned towards the spot Grayson had been standing when he ended things between them.

"*We're done.*" The words echoed in her mind over and over again, striking harder than the last.

She wasn't sure what she wanted to do more: scream, cry, or hit something. Instead, she chose to do none of those things, and entirely ignored the urges as well as the bubbling emotions swimming to the surface. She tucked them close to her chest, safely behind dragon scale armour and the sheer will to keep standing. No matter what the gods threw at her, she wouldn't bend. No matter how brittle she felt on the inside, she wouldn't warp under the pressure.

With Arkon's help, she'd pick up the pieces of her heart and soul, and stitch them back together again. Until then, she had to wear a mask. Had to pretend that she was holding everything together.

Show no weakness.

"Private Greene?"

Her eyes jerked upward, to the doorway where a young man with a satchel greeted her. He inclined his head then approached. If he noticed that she'd been crying a few minutes ago, he made no indication of it.

Arkon hissed at him as he approached, causing his step to falter. Eva closed the gap between them, sending a soothing touch down the Bond, grazing the inner walls of his mind.

"*You can hiss at Grayson next time you see him,*" she mildly scolded her protective dragon, "*but this man has done nothing.*"

"*I'll hiss at anyone who disturbs my Soul Bound.*"

Eyes hovering on Arkon and his bristling scales, the messenger reached into his satchel and held out a letter with a trembling hand. Clearly, he wasn't used to being around dragons—especially possessive ones. "This missive came in for you," he said, a tremor in his voice. "It has the royal seal."

Frowning, she took the letter. "Thank you."

The man inclined his head again then scampered out of the cave as fast as his legs could carry him.

Curiously, she broke the green wax seal and freed the thick parchment from the envelope.

Private Evangeline Greene,

I need you here. Now. Yesterday. As soon as you read this.

Yours truly,

Prince Leonidas Kain

Dread trickled down her spine like a familiar friend. There was no flare to his letter, no teasing extravagance. This was a command from her prince, not a request from her friend.

He needed his storm dragon rider.

"I don't have a saddle," Arkon reminded her as he lowered his belly to the ground.

"We don't have time to saddle up—or change," she added, realising she was *still* in her sopping wet clothes. Gods, she really was a mess. "He needs me."

"Then let us make haste. Brace your heels on the joints of my wings and hold on to the biggest scale at the base of my neck. You will find the best leverage against the wind."

Without hesitation, she bounced off his foreleg, reached for the scale he spoke of and hauled herself into the dip just below his withers. As soon as her feet touched his wing joints, he launched out of the cave and set course for Kain Castle.

CHAPTER 67
THE SHATTERING

Grayson could only hold himself together long enough to step into the hallway and close the door behind him. He collapsed back against the raw stone wall outside of the healing pools. The jagged wall dug into his back, snagged at his hair as he tipped his head back. Its frigid clutches burrowed deep into his spine.

He didn't care. Didn't feel it. Didn't feel anything other than the tearing in his chest as if something was prying his ribs apart. And when he heard the first muffled sob on the other side of the door? His knees gave out on him and he was left clawing on the ground, nails biting into stone, flesh peeling away from bone—and still the pain didn't surmount to the pain in his chest.

I'm dying. I'm fucking dying and there isn't a single weapon in sight.

He'd cut off Eva's ties to him—not his ties to her. No. Those could never break. He was irrevocably hers. Nothing could erase her from his mind, every fibre in his being, the very essence of his soul.

But it had to be done.

She needed to hate him. Maybe then she could see that he was no good for her. He'd only bring her more danger, more death.

"*I wish you had never bothered to begin with.*" Her words kept playing over and over in his head, no matter how hard he tried to shut them out. She always had a way of embedding herself deep inside of him, and, when her words are laced with vitriol and hate, there was no forgetting them.

In another life, they might have had a future together. In another life where he wasn't once Deximus Fortys and Eva wasn't the storm dragon rider.

But they weren't in another life. *This* was their life, and in this life, he was about to go where she couldn't follow. She had to stay here, safe, hating him, away from the vestiges, away from anyone else who wanted to claim their power.

Eran's presence wove into his thoughts, gentle and tentative. Grayson didn't know it was possible for the dragon to be so compassionate. "*I am ready whenever you are, Gray.*"

"*Don't. Don't pity me.*" Yet, despite how much he loathed the idea, the calming presence of his dragon eased the ache in his chest. Just enough for him to be able to stand and breathe a little easier.

An indignant scoff echoed down their Bond. "*I do not pity you. You had something precious and powerful—and you shredded it to pieces.*"

"*Then what's with this bullshit coddling? You were furious earlier.*" He'd tried to talk Grayson out of this the moment he'd decided this was the only way to protect Eva.

"*Because it's been done and while I don't agree with your methods...*" Eran huffed, and Grayson swore he could feel his breath spill over his skin, even though the dragon was in the Stables waiting for him. "*The idea of hunting and killing sates an itch I am in dire need of scratching.*"

Grayson could feel it deep in his dragon's core—the anger. He hid it well, far better than Grayson, but it was there, roiling like magma bubbles, ready to burst.

"*Feeling a little bloodthirsty, are we?*" As much as Eran influenced him, it went the other way, too. Grayson's anger was his dragon's—and the world would quake in terror at their feet.

"*I want to protect our Precious One,*" Eran declared fiercely, as if the words had come from Grayson's own heart. "*I want to avenge the life stolen from you. I will sink my teeth into Sylus's flesh and relish the taste of his blood.*"

Grayson smiled darkly at that. "*Sylus is first on the list.*"

Now that Darius was dead, the next threat to Eva was the man who wanted her gone. He feared a prophecy being his undoing? He should fear the monster he created.

He was robbed of giving Darius the slow, painful death he deserved, but what he missed out with his brother, he would take it out on the gods, on Sylus and his army, on anyone who got in his way.

His blood burned hot in his veins.

Good.

He needed that.

The rage.

Rage was much better than the debilitating ache in his chest. His fury fueled him, drove him forward—gave him purpose. Nodding even though his dragon couldn't see it, he stole a deep breath and quietened his mind. He shoved the hurt, the loss, the impossibly deep cavern building inside him aside. Anything that would hold him back was purged from his mind, buried beneath rubble, steel, and mithril.

The hallway stretched before him, dimly lit by the tiny lightstones embedded into the rock. The chill gnawed at his bones, biting through the fabric of his tunic, but he didn't care. The cold sharpened him, made each step feel deliberate, each breath measured. His boots echoed against the stone, a hollow rhythm that matched the pulse in his veins.

Grayson strode to his room, heart steady, muscles loose but ready. His bag sat neatly on the bed, packed and waiting. Two envelopes lay stacked atop one another—one thick, one thin. He plucked the thinner one, laying it carefully on Jacob's pillow, mindful even of the soft crease of the sheets. He wouldn't be back until later tonight—if Anna even allowed him that—but the thought barely grazed him. It was for the better that he didn't see his friends before he left.

Every second he lingered increased the risk of being tracked. By the time Jacob read the letter, he'd be too far away to follow, even with Anna's special tracking magic.

Yet he couldn't stop himself from standing at the end of Jacob's bed, staring at the measly piece of paper Grayson had tried and failed at summing up the entirety of their relationship and what Jacob's friendship meant to him. He'd settled with the basics. It wasn't fair, he knew, nor was it even a slither of the truth of what Jacob meant to him.

But Grayson didn't know how to say it. Eva made it easy to spill his guts out to her—but Jacob? Grayson had wasted six sheets of parchment before giving up and only telling him enough so he wouldn't panic or come after him.

Grayson waited for the guilt to creep in, for shame to sink in his stomach. But they never came. He felt nothing for leaving his friends behind.

He was doing this for them, after all. He would endure the weight of the world so they didn't have to.

Feeling as though his limbs weighed a thousand pounds, he swung his bag over his shoulder. He'd stashed his weapons on Eran's saddle earlier, leaving him with his clothes, rations, and the compass on his person.

He left the room without looking back.

His last stop was outside of Hargin's office. He slipped the other letter into her file folder in the hall. He felt like a coward for not handing in his resignation in person, but he knew she'd try to stop him if she had any warning of his intentions.

He'd done things her way long enough. If he had continued to do things her way, he didn't want to think about where Eva would be right now.

She wouldn't be here, of that he was certain. Not when she could barely stand when he found her. Not when it took all of her strength to breathe. Eva held up a strong front, but he knew what Darius had done to her. Knew that nobody, no matter how strong and stubborn they were, could withstand that kind of punishment. He knew because he'd seen it. He'd watched men and women of all different shapes, sizes, backgrounds slowly get whittled down by Darius's cruelty.

He'd seen it—and he could see it in his mind's eye what he did to Eva. Every bruise, every cut, he could envision how Darius did it, and the dark smile he wore as he did it.

Grayson's blood simmered through his body, sending a prickling sensation over his flesh.

Never again.

I'll kill them all, Starling. You'll never feel fear again. Not the helpless kind of fear. She was a Dragon Knight and would face many monsters—but that was all they were: hungry, mindless beasts. They would crave her blood, not her power, and she would bring them to their end. It was the monsters that wanted to trap her, claim her power for their own, that he was going after.

"*Come,*" Eran said. "*If we linger any longer, someone will get wind of our departure.*"

Grayson cast one last glance at the letter. This was it: the point of no return. Once he walked away from that letter there was no coming back. Not to Dragon Canyon. Not to Aboria.

A humorousless laugh escaped his lips. Here he was, leaving his home, his people. Again. At least it was on better terms this time.

Sort of.

No villages had burned this time. No one had died. No armies decimated in his wake.

Just a shattered heart and a wilted soul, which felt worse.

He'd left Hargin a detailed rundown of his plan. It should be enough to stop her from calling him a traitor—he was doing this for Aboria's benefit, after all—but he also wasn't going to fool himself into believing she'd welcome him back. He was going rogue, and the Dragon Knights had no place for renegades.

Steeling himself, he marched down to the Stables. Each step felt heavier than the last, dragged down by memories. Hearty meals with Jacob and Anna, practicing aerials in the canyon, the first time he godsdamned *laughed.*

He might not have been born in Aboria or went through the Trials with the other Knights or was even beloved by the officers—but Dragon Canyon had felt more like a home than Estrus ever did. And that home turned into a future when Eva arrived. Being a Dragon Knight became so much more than a way to atone for his sins when he met her. She gave him a reason to care. Showed him how to look past his past.

He was leaving little pieces of himself around the base, in the walls; his name was marked on Big Bertha when he broke the record. But a chunk of his heart, his fucking soul, was ripped out of him when he walked away from Eva in the healing pools. That part was hers, forever, whether she wanted it or not. It would follow her wherever her life without him took her.

Eran lowered his colossal head down to him, emerald eyes molten with grief and sorrow—pain Grayson had caused. They were both leaving something behind. "We may not be with her, but we will ensure she has a life to live."

Grayson dragged his fingers over the small round scales surrounding his nostrils, focusing on the heat of his breath, not on the searing pain in his heart.

It was just the two of them now.

They might not be whole ever again, but at least they had each other.

Always.

Others may come and go in their life, but their Bond was unshakable. Unbreakable.

That might have been the one good thing he did for Eva: stopped her from shattering her Bond with Arkon.

His hand began to shake. He yanked it to his side then climbed up Eran's side into the saddle. Once he settled into the familiar, worn-down leather, he freed the compass from his pocket and held it in his palm.

It flared to life, glowing a golden hue that warmed the chill in Grayson's bones. Its magic pulsed to the rhythm of his heart, attuned to him and only him.

Why the gods chose him to seek out the vestiges was a mystery to him. If they thought good would come from him then they were sorely mistaken. His soul only bled black. His life was shrouded in shadow and darkness and death.

No good ever came from a Fortys. Try as hard as he did to resist it, he couldn't deny whose blood beat through his veins. This blood was a curse. He couldn't rid himself of it, but at the very least he could drag his enemies down with him.

The compass whirled, awaiting a command. His eyes shuttered, closing out the world around him.

The compass sought what his heart truly desired. It had been Eva, but he only brought her pain, so now he needed a new desire. A purpose.

When he shut his eyes, it wasn't riches or peace that he saw. It wasn't even Eva's face, naked flesh flushed beneath him, smile beaming like a new dawn.

No. He saw Darius dead at his feet. Sylus hanging from a pike. Bodies, countless bodies, strewn across a field—all of them had some agenda to use Eva, abuse her, hurt her. And on his person were the vestiges the gods left behind. A shield braced on his arm, a cape billowing behind him in the wind, a chest piece sitting solid on his chest, a red gauntlet glowing on his left hand, and a halberd with sparks dancing around the tip in his right.

"Which one do we want first?" Eran asked, swinging his head around at an awkward angle to eye him.

He'd told Hargin he would be going after the shield first. The gauntlet had been formidable—and would be again if someone unearthed it from the rubble in the Desert Lands before he could find it again. They were going to need all of the defences they could get.

"The shield," Grayson commanded. "You've said your goodbyes?"

Eran bowed his head. "To everyone but Arkon. I couldn't find him."

Grayson ignored the twinge in his heart. If he got worked up every time Eva came up, he'd never find the strength to do what he needed to. "I'm sorry, my friend."

Eran shook his head, which then rippled down his body to the tip of his tail. "Never mind it now. Where is the shield?"

"East. We're going East."

"Then let us make haste."

CHAPTER 68

THE IMPOSSIBLE. THE IMPROBABLE.

Kain Castle fell into Eva's sights just as the sun began to dip behind the mountains in the distance. They arrived in time to witness the stained-glass windows bathed in the vibrant orange and red of the sunset. Its light reflected off the windows and cast their beautiful rays over the gardens surrounding the castle.

Truly stunning. A breath of fresh air after sand, caves, and decrepit temples worshiping the god of war.

But she didn't trust it. Leo wouldn't have summoned her with such urgency if it wasn't important. She needed to keep her guard up, eyes vigilant for anything out of place.

But as they circled over spires and gates, her now-dry under armour and riding pants undulating in the breeze, they couldn't find anything amiss.

No fires. No screams.

No sign of any confrontation.

By the time Arkon alighted on the gravel landing pad, she was shivering. Perhaps she should have made time to change, because without her dragon scale jacket and gloves to protect her from the bitter winter winds, her fingers had gone numb, lips blue, and her legs were chaffed terribly from the lack of a saddle to protect her thighs.

Captain Nestor Quade and a handful of guards were standing at the edge of the landing pad to greet them. She slid off Arkon's back, joints stiff from the brutal flight.

The Captain inclined his head respectfully, choosing to ignore her dishevelled state, of which she was grateful for. "We've been expecting you, Private Greene. Right this way."

Quade led the way, the guards falling into a tight formation behind them. She scanned the castle grounds, noting the extra security patrolling through the gardens and stationed outside every exit. The barracks was lively, brimming with activity, but no laughter, no jokes. The air was tense, like a taut bowstring.

Her fingers brushed over her daggers, grateful she at least had those with her. "What's going on? Is Leo—I mean, Prince Leonidas all right?"

His face pinched, brow furrowing, mouth tight. "He insisted that he be the one to inform you of the situation—but I can assure you he is safe and unharmed."

That was all she could ask for. Her stomach knotted tighter with every step, but knowing that Leo was okay took the edge off. A smidge.

They entered the foyer, met by a grand staircase. The way up would take her to his chambers, but Quade led her down the hallway for the west wing. In all of her visits to the castle, she'd never been to this part.

Her heart pounded to the rhythm of her boots on the marble floor. *Where are they taking me? Where's Leo?*

They halted in front of a double entry door, too extravagant to be an ordinary room. The wood adorned metal golden vines that wove together to form a tree on each panel.

Is this the throne room??

"This is where I leave you," Quade said. "If you are in need of us, Private, do not hesitate to call for us."

With a sharp, but by no means discourteous bow, he went back down the hall they had come from, his cluster of soldiers following right behind him.

Eva blinked at the door, questions flooding every corner of her mind. This was her most bizarre visit to the castle yet. While the servants were always courteous to her, sometimes even excited to meet a Dragon Knight, the guards were usually unmoved by her presence. Something had changed, and she wasn't sure if she liked it.

Breathing in a breath of courage, she pushed one panel inwards and peeked inside.

Leo was pacing the length of the polished marble floors with his hands tucked behind his back. A velvety green cape with golden whirls that matched the design on the door billowed in his wake, moving as if it had a mind of its own. His expression was a mask of steel and something much deeper and troublesome for Eva to name. His lapis-blue eyes bore into the marble column—until he spun on his heel and strode to its twin across the room.

When he heard the door open, he snapped his attention to her immediately.

She flinched at the abruptness of the movement.

His lips parted, eyes widening, as if he couldn't believe she was really standing in the same room as him. "You're here," he breathed, voice laden with far more emotion she expected to hear.

"You called," she answered simply.

They stood on opposite ends of the room, frozen in place as they stared at each other. Eva couldn't take another step. There was something about being here, in this castle, in a room she'd never set foot in—and seeing *him* again, the light in his otherwise dark eyes. The first gleam of light she'd seen since she'd been dragged away from Sasha's ruined corpse and into the bowels of the Five Hells.

His hair was groomed perfectly, despite the day being almost done, his buttoned up, long sleeve shirt crisp, wrinkle free. His shoes, the leather and golden buckles, were shinier than the marble floor.

He was perfect. Handsome and achingly perfect.

Seeing him made her realise just how deep her hurt ran. Between the grief, the fear, and the infuriating heartache... she was not okay.

And he was looking at her like she might slip away if he looked away. There was nothing sensual about it. No twinkle of mischief. No breath of reprieve.

Eyes welled with emotion, he closed the gap between them rapidly, absorbing in every detail he could catch. Slowly, he lifted a hand to her face, thumb brushing over her eyebrow then her cheek then her lip. His touch was more clinical than affectionate, just another examination—then she realised that each spot he touched was a place she had been injured.

He'd read the report from her healers.

“You're cold,” he said. Voice grated, as if he had swallowed broken glass. Snapping out of his spell, he looked over the rest of her and scowled. “Where's your armour?”

“I—I—” The words caught in her throat when he unclipped his cape then swung it over her shoulders, clasping the broach at the hollow of her throat. The fur lining was soft and warm. Her body finally relaxed, the shivering ceasing. “Your letter sounded urgent, so I dropped everything and came.”

His features melted into something soft and tender and so full of warmth her heart swelled. “It is urgent. The utmost of importance.”

His fingers curled into her hair. He noticed the length, but said nothing, treated her as if it had been that length all along.

Those lapis eyes trailed down to her lips. “But I have one request before I ask for your help.”

“What is it?”

“Tell me you're all right. I read your report. Read your healers' examination. Memorised every injury they accounted for.” His lips pressed together in a tight line, eyes skewed in agony. “If I had known Darius had you...”

She laid a hand on his chest, stopping him gently. “It's all right, Leo.”

She barely finished her sentence before his mouth was on hers. It was a gentle stroke, a tender touch, then he was pulling back, just enough to press his forehead against hers. “I'm sorry. I know you're loyal to him—but I just...” He sighed, breath spilling over her lips and curling against something deep and vulnerable in her belly. “I'm so grateful that you've returned, that you're no longer hurting. I know you're with him and taken care of, but if you need anything, Eva, *anything*, just say the word and it's yours." With one last exhale, he stepped back, his warmth vanishing.

She stood stock still and stared, too shocked for anything else. He spoke so fervently, with tides churning in his gaze as he beheld her with fierce love.

Suddenly, words she'd spoken months ago popped into her head: *"You want to send him a message? Show him how different you are now. Show him the man I love."* She'd said them, believing she knew everything about Grayson, that he could do no wrong and would fight by her side forever. She'd been a fool then. Grayson's fierce possessiveness wasn't love. His devotion to her wasn't a quiet declaration of loyalty.

This was.

Leo standing before her, offering her everything—including his heart—despite thinking she'd chosen another. Still fighting for her when all hope appeared lost.

That was love.

And she so desperately wanted to be loved. Held. Touched.

She needed to be enough for just *one* person. And that one person might be Leo.

She grabbed his shirt and pulled him back, tipping her head back to meet his lips. "I hold no loyalty to him."

Then she slanted her mouth over his and sank into his embrace. He opened up to her instinctively, tongue darting over the seam of her lips. She invited him in, tangling her fingers into his hair, breathing him in, taking in his perfection as if he could absolve the stains on her heart.

Moaning, his hands slid down her sides, his grip firm but careful, as if he knew of the scars beneath her skin. It only made her want him more, made the heat rising inside of her coil tighter, demanding more.

He tugged her hips against his, a hand slipping to her rear and pressing her tight against his desire.

Her insides tightened with need, with a longing to be filled. Her heart so desperately wanted to beat next to his, to know what it felt like to be loved. Cherished.

His mouth slipped from her, dipping for her throat, biting and sucking as he went. "I want you in my lap. On my throne. I need to be inside you, my love."

Her heart cracked just a bit at that. *His love.*

"Then take me to your throne."

Chuckling, he squeezed her ass and nipped at the base of her neck before pulling away. "Trust me, I will. But not right now."

It took her mind a minute to clear the lustful fog and remember why she was here. He'd summoned her, and she had a feeling it wasn't to check in on her. Though, she was very much enjoying the distraction.

Clamping down on her desire, she stepped out of his embrace. It was near impossible to think with him so close. He seemed to understand that and took a step back himself, smoothing out a wrinkle she'd put in his shirt and straightening out his hair.

"Why did you ask for me?"

He loosed a strained breath, slowly gathering his composure. "It'll be better if I just show you... But brace yourself, love. This won't be easy for you."

Her heart seized, panic skittering down her spine like a dozen spiders.

"What do you mean?"

He held his hand out to her, utterly solemn, entirely patient. He'd stand there, hand outstretched, all night if that's how long it took for her to gain the courage to go with him.

"*Arkon, do you sense anything amiss?*"

A sense of unease trickled down the Bond. "*I sense magic here. It's powerful, but not ominous. I'm looking for the source. Go with him. Be vigilant. Be brave.*"

Afraid, she slid her hand into Leo's. He squeezed it tight but comforting. "I will not leave your side," he vowed, meant to instill confidence in her bones, but instead it only made her more nervous.

She took a deep breath, to calm her racing heart and to steady herself. Was she ready for more surprises? No. Probably not. Did she have much of a choice? No.

But her duty came first.

He needed his storm dragon rider, and she wouldn't let him down.

Heart pounding in her ears, they left the throne room, hand in hand, and walked to a familiar hallway. Last time she had been down here, she was wearing a gown, rather than under armour and riding pants. It had been dark, then too. Chaotic. The only thing on her mind was getting to the dungeon as fast as possible.

And to the dungeon they went.

The stairs transformed from a luxurious, polished hardwood to a dark, dank stone. The walls were lit up by flamed sconces instead of lightstones. The air grew colder, harsher with every step they took, warning her to stay away.

Last time she'd been down here, she had her ass handed to her and been brutally marked by the man of her nightmares. Yet another scar she bore because of Darius Fortys.

The scars on her back heated and tightened against her flesh. Copper trickled over her tongue before she realised she'd bitten into her bottom lip.

The dungeon was suddenly too small. Flames flickered shadows along the walls, making her flinch at the sharp movement. Prisoners scraped against their stone enclosures, and a shiver chased down her spine that had nothing to do with the cold. Leo's cape did wonders to keep her warm, but it couldn't protect her from her imagination. Not as each noise reminded her of that awful creature that had chased her, forced her to run because she was too weak to fight back.

Her chest tightened as more images flashed through her mind, each one more visceral than the last—

As if sensing her distress, Leo squeezed her hand then brought her knuckles up to his lips. The softness of his mouth on her skin, the gentleness of the gesture, was enough to bring her back to the present. To him.

They strode past another door, going deeper still into the dungeon. Walking down, down, down the very same hallway she'd run through to stop Darius from escaping.

"What are we doing here?" she asked, keeping her voice low.

"We're almost there," he said instead of answering her.

Her stomach twisted violently. Having skipped lunch and dinner didn't help her stomach either. Only acid was left to roil inside her and it burned in her throat.

It didn't help when they stopped right in front of Darius's old cell. Or when the person in the cell had the same black hair and pale skin. He was shirtless, leaving the marid of scars on full display. His head was tipped downward, chin tucked against his chest, but she didn't have to see his face to know who it was.

Eva's entire body froze over. Blood drained from her face, leaving her dizzy and nauseated. She would have fallen over if Leo hadn't wrapped an arm around her waist.

No... No. He couldn't be here.

"Why the fuck did you bring me down here? Why isn't he dead??"

He should have been killed immediately on sight.

Except, his head flicked up, and glacial eyes locked onto her.

A gasp lodged in her throat.

It wasn't Darius locked in this cell... it was *Dravyn.*

Her eyes widened, heart beating against her ribs like a restless beast rearing to be free of its cage.

"Wh—what are you doing here?" She looked to Leo. "What's going on?"

Dravyn snorted, very comfortable for someone sitting in a dungeon. "You didn't tell her?"

Leo shot him a glare then turned to her with an apology in his eyes. “I thought it would be easier to explain if I brought you down to him. He—” Leo thrust an accusatory finger Dravyn's way “—wants asylum and he seems to think that *you* will vouch for his character.”

Her head snapped back to Dravyn, the derisive grin on his face, then back to Leo. “You're kidding me, right?”

“Precious.”

It wasn't his tone that brought her back to him, but the *name*. The same name Eran had used. The name she thought she'd never hear again, because... because... Grayson abandoned her. Didn't want anything to do with the weak storm dragon rider.

Tears burned in her eyes, heart twisting beyond recognition.

Dravyn's gaze was unwavering. “Beat me, kill me, free me—I don't give a fuck. But my life isn't only my life anymore.”

“What do you mean? What happened?”

He rose out of his cot in one smooth motion and approached the bars slowly, taking every step with care, hands held up, visible. Non-threatening.

His fingers curled around the bars.

And that's when she saw it.

The scar.

White, blue-tipped scales raked the length of his sternum, dead centre on his chest. Blood dried and peeled on his skin, flaking down his abs, leading a trail to the blood stain on his pants. The wound that had caused the staining was long since gone, the scar had ensured that. The *dragon* who had shed its tear to save him had ensured it.

“Guess this means I'm one of you now.”

Eva just stared, unblinking, not breathing. Her whole world narrowed down to that mark on his chest. The impossible. The improbable. A mark of the beginning of something extraordinary—or the end of everything she knew.

Asturias guide us. Another Fortys has become Soul Bound.

EPILOGUE

King Sylus Fortys strode through his city's streets, boots crunching beneath snow and ice. Stone carried his buildings high, casting shadows from the afternoon sun over the main square, dusted with white powder. Icicles hung from rooftops, glistening in the frozen landscape Solvarra had become overnight. Several men shoveled at pathways, scraping and grunting. Their breath mingled with the gentle drifts of snow falling from overhead. Wind from the fractures whistled between buildings and people.

Fractures that were now full of packed snow and impenetrable ice.

His people bowed as he passed by, silence hanging in his wake like a thick morning fog. Mothers pinned their children to their sides. Vendors shrank back into their booths.

If these people mined as hard as they avoided him, they wouldn't be behind schedule—and they would have beaten the snowstorm before it hit.

But now they would have to wait until the mines had thawed. Weeks without new inventory. Weeks without shipments leaving his harbours.

These mines were what kept these people fed during the winter. Yet they slacked. Yet they revolted against him.

The air shifted behind him. Sylus glanced back as Salik slinked out of the shadows and trailed one step behind him. There were no guards to stop him. Sylus walked his streets alone.

"Speak."

Sylus knew that the news he carried couldn't be good if he was here instead of watching Darius.

He readied for the worst case and reminded himself that he was in public. While it was necessary for his people to remember his wrath, it wouldn't do him any good to lose his composure in front of them. Even the smallest crack in his armour would give the Wayward Starlings fuel to build their uprising.

Salik dipped his head. "The temple fell. The collapse buried everything inside."

Sylus didn't stop walking. "I see. The gauntlet?"

"Buried beneath the rubble."

That was... inconvenient, but nothing a handful of workers couldn't fix.

"Darius?"

Salik's head shook, a sadness in his eyes that had no place in being there. "Dead, along with Dravyn."

"Can you confirm that?"

A beat of silence.

"No," Salik gave in. "I couldn't find either of their bodies."

"Then we cannot assume they're dead."

Sylus had made that mistake once before and lost his son to the Aborians. He would not make it again.

Salik fell silent, but the air around him was charged, not submissive.

"You have more to say," Sylus pushed.

"Yes." Salik's eyes scanned the street, watching people closely as they fled the road to make room for their king. "Darius and Dravyn didn't enter the temple alone. He found the storm dragon rider and held her captive. I also found out that he hired an apothecary while he was here. He commissioned them to make a new poison—Mithbane. It nullifies magic in magic wielders."

An interesting, but not entirely unexpected development. Darius was a tenacious beast. Once he had his eyes set on something, very little could pull him away. Not even the death of his most loyal pawn.

"This alchemist—bring them in. I want them to make Mithbane for the army."

Salik shook his head. "Darius killed him and took the recipe."

This news gave him pause. It was one thing for Darius to work on a secret poison. It wasn't the first time he'd invented a new perverse way to torment his toys. But it was an entirely different matter to withhold this information and cover his tracks afterward. That reeked of betrayal.

The thought sliced through his chest, burned his lungs, filled his throat with acid.

He knew this day would come. He trusted Darius for his obedience. But obedience without loyalty was just delayed betrayal. Dex never needed obedience. He needed purpose.

The gauntlet was his final test—and like all the others, he failed. Salik was supposed to kill him and take the gauntlet from his cold, dead hands if he showed any signs of betraying them. But he couldn't have followed them into the temple undetected.

This complicated things.

Darius was never supposed to learn about the power of the gauntlet. He was supposed to find it and retrieve it for Sylus to use.

He needed to be dealt with.

Which meant that he had no one to hand down the crown to.

Dravyn was out of the question. He would make a fine Shadow, but a king? That title was only befitting of a greater man. He hadn't built Estrus into its glory for it to crumble beneath the hands of a delinquent.

"Dex was in the Desert Lands," Salik spoke softly, as to not draw attention from others. "Something has changed in him. He's not quite the man we last saw, but not the Dragon Knight my scouts informed me of. Perhaps... he could handle Darius. He has magic and our training—nothing could stop him. Not even Darius with the gauntlet."

Sylus's eyes narrowed, finding a flaw in his logic. "Then why didn't he end him in the Desert Lands?"

It would have saved them the trouble if he had.

"It appears he cares deeply for the storm dragon rider. He protects her like a wyvern protects its brood. His heart wasn't in the kill."

A scoff worked it's way up his throat. Affection? He thought he'd trained his sons better than that. There was no place for love in the Fortys bloodline. Love made them blind. Love made a fool of them. Love made them *weak*.

That much was proven when Katerina stumbled into his life on that long, stormy night.

Eva Greene. The storm dragon rider. Dex's weakness. Darius's obsession.

Everything always came back to her.

"*She will be your undoing*," the old crone had whispered thirty-two years ago. He'd laughed at the time.

He wasn't laughing now.

He'd gone through every measure to ensure the prophecy never came to pass. But, in doing so, he failed to consider that this woman, the one with hair the colour of ash, who rode a black dragon, wouldn't be the one to *slay* him.

But to turn his sons against him.

"Find Dex," Sylus commanded. "If he wants to protect his storm dragon rider, inform him that his brother is still alive and hell-bent on claiming her."

Salik nodded, dutiful as always. "And what if I find the girl?"

"Leave her for now." He would not have another one of his clan fall prey to the storm dragon rider. Once he had the artifacts, she'd not longer be a threat. "It's time you gather your team. I need someone *dependable* to retrieve the artifacts."

Salik grimaced, shifting his weight to adjust the broadsword strapped to his back, as if the mere thought of them unsettled him. As they should, even his own Shadow. "You're sending them on a retrieval mission? They won't be happy."

"Tell them they can whet their swords along the way as long as they bring me the artifacts."

Salik's eyes hardened with resolve. "I'll send word. Which one do you want them to start with?"

"The chest piece."

If Darius had the gauntlet, he was too dangerous to approach. The chest piece would protect him until he could gather more.

"Consider it done, Your Grace."

"Good. Now hand me your whip. It seems the people need to be reminded who rules over these lands."

If You Enjoyed This Read...

Please Consider...

Please consider leaving a review. Reviews help indie authors spread their art with a wider audience.

ACKNOWLEDGEMENTS

Thank you to you, my lovely readers. This series has followed me through some of the hardest times in my life. There were some days where I just needed to *write*, to escape the world when it was too hard to be in it. Soul Bound and Blood Bound helped me process grief, trauma, depression, and anxiety, and I honestly don't know where I would be today if I couldn't write my heart out.

Thank you, Hudson. My best friend, my husband, my inspiration. Grayson, Jacob, and Darius would be completely flat characters if it weren't for everything we've been through, and I wasn't able to watch you grow into the man I'm so damned proud to call my husband this year. Thank you so, so much for supporting my writing and listening to me when I needed to talk out my scenes (especially the battle at Last Drop). Don't worry about the maniacal laughter. Your wifu isn't crazy, I promise—just plotting some diabolical arcs for my beloved characters.

Thank you to my fur babies, Ninja and Baron. Thank you for letting me finish my sentences/paragraphs/chapters before giving you the attention you so dearly crave as soon as I pick up my laptop. Thank you for being so empathetic, and snuggling with me before I knew I needed it. You're the real dragons in my life.

Thank you to my mum, my number one fan. Thank you for selling my books at your farmer's market and making cool dragon art to pair with my books. Thank you for teaching me the ropes; I'm excited that I now get to set up my own table and connect with fans.

Thank you to my friends and family. Thank you for listening to me rant about the complexities of character development and encouraging me to create these fantastical worlds. Especially, you Corrie, Koko, and Steff! You have had my back from day one, helping me grow as a person and an author. My books are in stores because of you. I love hearing you fangirl over my books... and I'm sure you'll have some things about Blood Bound's ending. Sorry not sorry. I'll make it up to you in the next book <3.

A very special and heartfelt thank you to my followers. You gave me the courage to publish. You raved about my books from the very first page. I wouldn't have bothered if you all hadn't been so encouraging and supportive. Truly, thank you from the very bottom of my heart. This has only been possible because of you.

www.ingramcontent.com/pod-product-compliance
Lightning Source LLC
LaVergne TN
LVHW041051080826
845145LV00007B/1531